R.D. Blackmore

Springhaven

R.D. Blackmore

Springhaven

1st Edition | ISBN: 978-3-73409-025-7

Place of Publication: Frankfurt am Main, Germany

Year of Publication: 2019

Outlook Verlag GmbH, Germany.

SPRINGHAVEN:

A Tale of the Great War

By R. D. Blackmore

1887

CHAPTER I

WHEN THE SHIP COMES HOME

In the days when England trusted mainly to the vigor and valor of one man, against a world of enemies, no part of her coast was in greater peril than the fair vale of Springhaven. But lying to the west of the narrow seas, and the shouts both of menace and vigilance, the quiet little village in the tranquil valley forbore to be uneasy.

For the nature of the place and race, since time has outlived memory, continually has been, and must be, to let the world pass easily. Little to talk of, and nothing to do, is the healthy condition of mankind just there. To all who love repose and shelter, freedom from the cares of money and the cark of fashion, and (in lieu of these) refreshing air, bright water, and green country, there is scarcely any valley left to compare with that of Springhaven. This valley does not interrupt the land, but comes in as a pleasant relief to it. No glaring chalk, no grim sandstone, no rugged flint, outface it; but deep rich meadows, and foliage thick, and cool arcades of ancient trees, defy the noise that men make. And above the trees, in shelving distance, rise the crests of upland, a soft gray lias, where orchards thrive, and greensward strokes down the rigor of the rocks, and quick rills lace the bosom of the slope with tags of twisted silver.

In the murmur of the valley twenty little waters meet, and discoursing their way to the sea, give name to the bay that receives them and the anchorage they make. And here no muddy harbor reeks, no foul mouth of rat-haunted drains, no slimy and scraggy wall runs out, to mar the meeting of sweet and salt. With one or two mooring posts to watch it, and a course of stepping-stones, the brook slides into the peaceful bay, and is lost in larger waters. Even so, however, it is kindly still, for it forms a tranquil haven.

Because, where the ruffle of the land stream merges into the heavier disquietude of sea, slopes of shell sand and white gravel give welcome pillow to the weary keel. No southerly tempest smites the bark, no long groundswell upheaves her; for a bold point, known as the "Haven-head," baffles the storm in the offing, while the bulky rollers of a strong spring-tide, that need no wind to urge them, are broken by the shifting of the shore into a tier of white-frilled steps. So the deep-waisted smacks that fish for many generations, and even the famous "London trader" (a schooner of five-and-forty tons), have rest from their labors, whenever they wish or whenever they can afford it, in the arms of the land, and the mouth of the water, and under the eyes of

Springhaven.

At the corner of the wall, where the brook comes down, and pebble turns into shingle, there has always been a good white gate, respected (as a white gate always is) from its strong declaration of purpose. Outside of it, things may belong to the Crown, the Admiralty, Manor, or Trinity Brethren, or perhaps the sea itself—according to the latest ebb or flow of the fickle tide of Law Courts—but inside that gate everything belongs to the fine old family of Darling.

Concerning the origin of these Darlings divers tales are told, according to the good-will or otherwise of the diver. The Darlings themselves contend and prove that stock and name are Saxon, and the true form of the name is "Deerlung," as witness the family bearings. But the foes of the race, and especially the Carnes, of ancient Sussex lineage, declare that the name describes itself. Forsooth, these Darlings are nothing more, to their contemptuous certainty, than the offset of some court favorite, too low to have won nobility, in the reign of some light-affectioned king.

If ever there was any truth in that, it has been worn out long ago by friction of its own antiquity. Admiral Darling owns that gate, and all the land inside it, as far as a Preventive man can see with his spy-glass upon the top bar of it. And this includes nearly all the village of Springhaven, and the Hall, and the valley, and the hills that make it. And how much more does all this redound to the credit of the family when the gazer reflects that this is nothing but their younger tenement! For this is only Springhaven Hall, while Darling Holt, the headquarters of the race, stands far inland, and belongs to Sir Francis, the Admiral's elder brother.

When the tides were at their spring, and the year 1802 of our era in the same condition, Horatia Dorothy Darling, younger daughter of the aforesaid Admiral, choosing a very quiet path among thick shrubs and under-wood, came all alone to a wooden building, which her father called his Round-house. In the war, which had been patched over now, but would very soon break out again, that veteran officer held command of the coast defense (westward of Nelson's charge) from Beachy Head to Selsey Bill. No real danger had existed then, and no solid intent of invasion, but many sharp outlooks had been set up, and among them was this at Springhaven.

Here was established under thatch, and with sliding lights before it, the Admiral's favorite Munich glass, mounted by an old ship's carpenter (who had followed the fortunes of his captain) on a stand which would have puzzled anybody but the maker, with the added security of a lanyard from the roof. The gear, though rough, was very strong and solid, and afforded more range and firmer rest to the seven-feet tube and adjustments than a costly mounting by a London optician would have been likely to supply. It was a pleasure to look through such a glass, so clear, and full of light, and firm; and one who could have borne to be looked at through it, or examined even by a microscope, came now to enjoy that pleasure.

Miss Dolly Darling could not be happy—though her chief point was to be so—without a little bit of excitement, though it were of her own construction. Her imagination, being bright and tender and lively, rather than powerful, was compelled to make its own material, out of very little stuff sometimes. She was always longing for something sweet and thrilling and romantic, and what chance of finding it in this dull place, even with the longest telescope? For the war, with all its stirring rumors and perpetual motion on shore and sea, and access of gallant visitors, was gone for the moment, and dull peace was signed.

This evening, as yet, there seemed little chance of anything to enliven her. The village, in the valley and up the stream, was hidden by turns of the land and trees; her father's house beneath the hill crest was out of sight and hearing; not even a child was on the beach; and the only movement was of wavelets leisurely advancing toward the sea-wall fringed with tamarisk. The only thing she could hope to see was the happy return of the fishing-smacks, and perhaps the "London trader," inasmuch as the fishermen (now released from fencible duty and from French alarm) did their best to return on Saturday night to their moorings, their homes, the disposal of fish, and then the deep slumber of Sunday. If the breeze should enable them to round the Head, and the tide avail for landing, the lane to the village, the beach, and even the sea itself would swarm with life and bustle and flurry and incident. But Dolly's desire was for scenes more warlike and actors more august than these.

Beauty, however, has an eye for beauty beyond its own looking-glass. Deeply as Dolly began to feel the joy of her own loveliness, she had managed to learn, and to feel as well, that so far as the strength and vigor of beauty may compare with its grace and refinement, she had her own match at Springhaven. Quite a hardworking youth, of no social position and no needless education, had such a fine countenance and such bright eyes that she neither could bear to look at him nor forbear to think of him. And she knew that if the fleet came home she would see him on board of the Rosalie.

Flinging on a shelf the small white hat which had scarcely covered her dark brown curls, she lifted and shored with a wooden prop the southern casement of leaded glass. This being up, free range was given to the swinging telescope along the beach to the right and left, and over the open sea for miles, and into the measureless haze of air. She could manage this glass to the best advantage, through her father's teaching, and could take out the slide and clean the lenses, and even part the object-glass, and refix it as well as possible. She belonged to the order of the clever virgins, but scarcely to that of the wise ones.

CHAPTER II

WITH HER CREW AND CARGO

Long after the time of those who write and those who read this history, the name of Zebedee Tugwell will be flourishing at Springhaven.

To achieve unmerited honor is the special gift of thousands, but to deserve and win befalls some few in every century, and one of these few was Zebedee. To be the head-man of any other village, and the captain of its fishing fleet, might prove no lofty eminence; but to be the leader of Springhaven was true and arduous greatness. From Selsey Bill to Orfordness, taking in all the Cinque Ports and all the port of London, there was not a place that insisted on, and therefore possessed, all its own rights so firmly as this village did. Not less than seven stout fishing-smacks—six of them sloops, and the seventh a dandy—formed the marine power of this place, and behaved as one multiplied by seven. All the bold fishermen held their line from long-established ancestry, and stuck to the stock of their grandfathers, and their wisdom and freedom from prejudice. Strength was condensed into clear law with them—as sinew boils down into jelly—and character carried out its force as the stamp of solid impress. What the father had been, the son became, as the generation squared itself, and the slates for the children to do their copies were the tombstones of their granddads. Thus brave Etruria grew, and thus the Rome which was not built in a day became the flower of the world, and girt in unity of self seven citadels.

There was Roman blood—of the Tenth Legion, perhaps—in the general vein of Springhaven. There was scarcely a man who pretended to know much outside of his own business, and there was not a woman unable to wait (when her breath was quite gone) for sound reason. Solidity, self-respect, pure absence of frivolous humor, ennobled the race and enabled them to hold together, so that everybody not born in Springhaven might lament, but never repair, his loss.

This people had many ancient rules befitting a fine corporation, and among them were the following: "Never do a job for a stranger; sleep in your own bed when you can; be at home in good time on a Saturday; never work harder than you need; throw your fish away rather than undersell it; answer no question, but ask another; spend all your money among your friends; and above all, never let any stranger come a-nigh your proper fishing ground, nor land any fish at Springhaven."

7

These were golden laws, and made a snug and plump community. From the Foreland to the Isle of Wight their nets and lines were sacred, and no other village could be found so thriving, orderly, well-conducted, and almost well-contented. For the men were not of rash enterprise, hot labor, or fervid ambition; and although they counted things by money, they did not count one another so. They never encouraged a friend to work so hard as to grow too wealthy, and if he did so, they expected him to grow more generous than he liked to be. And as soon as he failed upon that point, instead of adoring, they growled at him, because every one of them might have had as full a worsted stocking if his mind had been small enough to forget the difference betwixt the land and sea, the tide of labor and the time of leisure.

To these local and tribal distinctions they added the lofty expansion of sons of the sea. The habit of rising on the surge and falling into the trough behind it enables a biped, as soon as he lands, to take things that are flat with indifference. His head and legs have got into a state of firm confidence in one another, and all these declare—with the rest of the body performing as chorus gratis—that now they are come to a smaller affair, upon which they intend to enjoy themselves. So that, while strenuous and quick of movement—whenever they could not help it—and sometimes even brisk of mind (if anybody strove to cheat them), these men generally made no griefs beyond what they were born to.

Zebedee Tugwell was now their chief, and well deserved to be so. Every community of common-sense demands to have somebody over it, and nobody could have felt ashamed to be under Captain Tugwell. He had built with his own hands, and bought—for no man's work is his own until he has paid for as well as made it—the biggest and smartest of all the fleet, that dandy-rigged smack, the Rosalie. He was proud of her, as he well might be, and spent most of his time in thinking of her; but even she was scarcely up to the size of his ideas. "Stiff in the joints," he now said daily—"stiff in the joints is my complaint, and I never would have believed it. But for all that, you shall see, my son, if the Lord should spare you long enough, whether I don't beat her out and out with the craft as have been in my mind this ten year."

But what man could be built to beat Zebedee himself, in an age like this, when yachts and men take the prize by profundity of false keel? Tugwell yearned for no hot speed in his friends, or his house, or his wife, or his walk, or even his way of thinking. He had seen more harm come from one hour's hurry than a hundred years of care could cure, and the longer he lived the more loath he grew to disturb the air around him.

"Admirable Nelson," he used to say—for his education had not been so large as the parts allotted to receive it; "to my mind he is a brave young man, with great understanding of his dooties. But he goeth too fast, without clearing of his way. With a man like me 'longside of 'un, he'd have brought they boats out of Bulong. See how I brings my boats in, most particular of a Saturday!"

It was Saturday now, when Miss Dolly was waiting to see this great performance, of which she considered herself, as the daughter of an admiral, no mean critic. And sure enough, as punctual as in a well-conducted scheme of war, and with nice forecast of wind and tide, and science of the supper-time, around the westward headland came the bold fleet of Springhaven!

Seven ships of the line—the fishing line—arranged in perfect order, with the Rosalie as the flag-ship leading, and three upon either quarter, in the comfort and leisure of the new-born peace, they spread their sails with sunshine. Even the warlike Dolly could not help some thoughts of peacefulness, and a gentle tide of large good-will submerged the rocks of glory.

"Why should those poor men all be killed?" she asked herself, as a new thing, while she made out, by their faces, hats, fling of knee or elbow, patch upon breeches, or sprawl of walking toward the attentive telescope, pretty nearly who everybody of them was, and whatever else there was about him. "After all, it is very hard," she said, "that they should have to lose their lives because the countries fight so."

But these jolly fellows had no idea of losing their lives, or a hair of their heads, or anything more than their appetites, after waging hot war upon victuals. Peace was proclaimed, and peace was reigning; and the proper British feeling of contempt for snivelly Frenchmen, which produces the entente cordiale, had replaced the wholesome dread of them. Not that Springhaven had ever known fear, but still it was glad to leave off terrifying the enemy. Lightness of heart and good-will prevailed, and every man's sixpence was going to be a shilling.

In the tranquil afternoon the sun was making it clear to the coast of Albion that he had crossed the line once more, and rediscovered a charming island. After a chilly and foggy season, worse than a brave cold winter, there was joy in the greeting the land held out, and in the more versatile expression of the sea. And not beneath the contempt of one who strives to get into everything, were the creases and patches of the sails of smacks, and the pattern of the resin-wood they called their masts, and even the little striped things (like frogs with hats on, in the distance) which had grown to believe themselves the only object the sun was made to shine upon.

But he shone upon the wide sea far behind, and the broad stretch of land before them, and among their slowly gliding canvas scattered soft touches of wandering light. Especially on the spritsail of the Rosalie, whereunder was sitting, with the tiller in his hand and a very long pipe in his mouth, Captain Zebedee Tugwell. His mighty legs were spread at ease, his shoulders solid against a cask, his breast (like an elephant's back in width, and bearing a bright blue crown tattooed) shone out of the scarlet woolsey, whose plaits were filled with the golden shower of a curly beard, untouched with gray. And his face was quite as worthy as the substance leading up to it, being large and strengthful and slow to move, though quick to make others do so. The forehead was heavy, and the nose thickset, the lower jaw backed up the resolution of the other, and the wide apart eyes, of a bright steel blue, were as steady as a brace of pole-stars.

"What a wonderful man!" fair Dolly thought, as the great figure, looking even grander in the glass, came rising upon a long slow wave—"what a wonderful man that Tugwell is! So firmly resolved to have his own way, so thoroughly dauntless, and such a grand beard! Ten times more like an admiral than old Flapfin or my father is, if he only knew how to hold his pipe. There is something about him so dignified, so calm, and so majestic; but, for all that, I like the young man better. I have a great mind to take half a peep at him; somebody might ask whether he was there or not."

Being a young and bashful maid, as well as by birth a lady, she had felt that it might be a very nice thing to contemplate sailors in the distance, abstract sailors, old men who pulled ropes, or lounged on the deck, if there was one. But to steal an unsuspected view at a young man very well known to her, and acknowledged (not only by his mother and himself, but also by every girl in the parish) as the Adonis of Springhaven—this was a very different thing, and difficult to justify even to one's self. The proper plan, therefore, was to do it, instead of waiting to consider it.

"How very hard upon him it does seem," she whispered to herself, after a good gaze at him, "that he must not even dream of having any hope of me, because he has not happened to be born a gentleman! But he looks a thousand times more like one than nine out of ten of the great gentlemen I know—or at any rate he would if his mother didn't make his clothes."

For Zebedee Tugwell had a son called "Dan," as like him as a tender pea can be like a tough one; promising also to be tough, in course of time, by chafing of the world and weather. But at present Dan Tugwell was as tender to the core as a marrowfat dallying till its young duck should be ready; because Dan was podding into his first love. To the sympathetic telescope his heart was low, and his mind gone beyond astronomical range, and his hands (instead of briskly pairing soles) hung asunder, and sprawled like a star-fish.

"Indeed he does look sad," said Miss Dolly, "he is thinking of me, as he always does; but I don't see how anybody can blame me. But here comes daddy, with dear old Flapfin! I am not a bit afraid of either of them; but perhaps I had better run away."

CHAPTER III

AND HER TRUE COMMANDER

The nature of "Flapfin"—as Miss Dolly Darling and other young people were pleased to call him—was to make his enemies run away, but his friends keep very near to him. He was one of the simplest-minded men that ever trod the British oak. Whatever he thought he generally said; and whatever he said he meant and did. Yet of tricks and frauds he had quick perception, whenever they were tried against him, as well as a marvellous power of seeing the shortest way to everything. He enjoyed a little gentle piece of vanity, not vainglory, and he never could sec any justice in losing the credit of any of his exploits. Moreover, he was gifted with the highest faith in the hand of the Almighty over him (to help him in all his righteous deeds), and over his enemies, to destroy them. Though he never insisted on any deep piety in his own behavior, he had a good deal in his heart when time allowed, and the linstocks were waiting the signal. His trust was supreme in the Lord and himself; and he loved to be called "My Lord Admiral."

And a man of this noble type deserved to be met with his own nobility. But the English government, according to its lights—which appear to be everlasting—regarded him as the right man, when wanted, but at other times the wrong one. They liked him to do them a very good turn, but would not let him do himself one; and whenever he looked for some fair chance of a little snug prize-money, they took him away from the likely places, and set him to hard work and hard knocks. But his sense of duty and love of country enabled him to bear it, with grumbling.

"I don't care a rope's end," he was saying, with a truthfulness simple and solid as beefsteak is, "whether we have peace or war; but let us have one or the other of them. I love peace—it is a very fine thing—and I hate to see poor fellows killed. All I want is to spend the rest of my life ashore, and lay out the garden. You must come and see what a bridge I have made to throw across the fish-pond. I can do well enough with what I have got, as soon as my farm begins to pay, and I hope I may never hear another shotted cannon; but, my dear Lingo, you know as well as I do how much chance there is of that."

"Laudo manentem. Let us praise her while we have got her. Parson Twemlow keeps up my Latin, but you have forgotten all yours, my friend. I brought you down here to see the fish come in, and to choose what you like best for dinner. In the days when you were my smallest youngster, and as proud as Punch to dine with me, your taste was the finest in the ship, because your stomach was the weakest. How often I thought that the fish would eat you! and but for your wonderful spirit, my friend, that must have happened long ago. But your nature was to fight, and you fought through, as you always do. A drumstick for your praise of peace!"

Admiral Darling, a tall, stout man in the sixty-fifth year of his age, looked down at his welcome and famous guest as if he knew a great deal more of his nature than the owner did. And this made that owner, who thought very highly of his own perception, look up and laugh.

"Here comes the fish!" he cried. "Come along, Darling. Never lose a moment—that's my rule. You can't get along as fast as I can. I'll go and settle all the business for you."

"Why should you be in such a hurry always? You will never come to my age if you carry on so. You ought to tow a spar astern. Thank God, they don't know who he is, and I'll take good care not to let them know. If this is what comes of quick promotion, I am glad that I got on slowly. Well, he may do as he likes for me. He always does—that's one thing."

Stoutly grumbling thus, the elder and far heavier Admiral descended the hill to the white gate slowly, as behooved the owner. And, by the time he halted there, the other had been upon the beach five minutes, and taken command of the fishing fleet.

"Starboard there! Brail up your gaff! Is that the way to take the ground? Ease helm, Rosalie. Smartly, smartly. Have a care, you lubber there. Fenders out! So, so. Now stand by, all! There are two smart lads among you, and no more. All the rest are no better than a pack of Crappos. You want six months in a man-of-war's launch. This is what comes of peace already!"

The fishermen stared at this extraordinary man, who had taken all the business out of Master Tugwell's hands; but without thinking twice about it, all obeyed him with a speed that must have robbed them of a quantity of rust. For although he was not in uniform, and bore no sword, his dress was conspicuous, as he liked to have it, and his looks and deeds kept suit with it. For he wore a blue coat (very badly made, with gilt buttons and lappets too big for him), a waistcoat of dove-colored silk, very long, coming over the place where his stomach should have been, and white plush breeches, made while he was blockading Boulogne in 1801, and therefore had scarcely any flesh upon his bones. Peace having fattened him a little, these breeches had tightened upon him (as their way is with a boy having six weeks' holiday); but still they could not make his legs look big, though they showed them sharp and muscular. Below them were brisk little sinewy calves in white silk hose, with a taper descent to ankles as fine as a lady's, and insteps bright with large silver buckles. Yet that which surpassed all the beauty of the clothes was the vigor of the man inside them, who seemed to quicken and invigorate the whole, even to the right sleeve, doubled up from the want of any arm inside it. But the loss of the right arm, and the right eye also, seemed to be of no account to the former owner, so hard did he work with the residue of his body, and so much did he express with it.

His noble cocked hat was in its leathern box yet, for he was only just come from Merton; but the broad felt he wore was looped up in front, and displayed all the power of his countenance, or rather the vigor; for power is heavy, and his face was light and quickness. Softness also, and a melancholy gift of dreaminess and reflection, enlarged and impressed the effect of a gaze and a smile which have conquered history.

"Why don't 'ee speak up to 'un, Cap'en Zeb?" cried young Harry Shanks, of the Peggy, the smartest smack next to the Rosalie. "Whoever can 'a be, to make thee so dumb? Doth 'a know our own business afore our own selves? If 'ee don't speak up to 'un, Cap'en Zeb, I'll never take no more commands from thee."

"Harry Shanks, you was always a fool, and you always will be," Master Tugwell replied, with his deep chest voice, which no gale of wind could blow away. "Whether he be wrong or right—and I won't say but what I might have done it better—none but a fool like you would dare to set his squeak up against Admirable Lord Nelson."

CHAPTER IV

AND HER FAITHFUL CHAPLAIN

"I am not a man of the world, but a man of the Word," said Parson Twemlow, the Rector of Springhaven; "and I shall not feel that I have done my duty unless I stir him up to-morrow. His valor and glory are nothing to me, nor even his value to the country. He does his duty, and I shall do mine. It is useless to talk to me, Maria; I never shall have such a chance again."

"Well, dear, you know best," replied Mrs. Twemlow; "and duty is always the highest and best and most sacred consideration. But you surely should remember, for Eliza's sake, that we never shall dine at the Hall again."

"I don't care a snap for their dinners, or the chance of Eliza catching some young officer; and very few come while this peace goes on. I won't shirk my duty for any of that."

"Nothing would ever make you shirk your duty, Joshua. And I hope that you know me too well to suppose that I ever would dream of suggesting it. But I do want to see you a Canon, and I know that he begins to have influence in the Church, and therefore the Church is not at all the place to allude to his private affairs in. And, after all, what do we know about them? It does seem so low to be led away by gossip."

"Maria," said the Rector, severely sorry, "I must beg you to leave me to my conscience. I shall not refer to his private affairs. I shall put leading truths in a general way, and let him make the home application."

"Put the cap on if it fits. Very well: you will injure yourself, and do no one any good. Lord Nelson won't know it; he is too simple-minded. But Admiral Darling will never forgive us for insulting him while he is staying at the Hall."

"Maria! Well, I have long given up all attempts at reasoning with you. If I see a man walking into a furnace, do I insult him by saying beware?"

"As I am beyond all reason, Joshua, it is far above me to understand that. But if you escape insulting him, what you do is far worse, and quite unlike a gentleman. You heap a whole pile of insults upon your own brother clergymen."

"I do not at all understand you, Maria: you fly off in such a way from one thing to another!"

"Not at all. Anybody who is not above paying attention must understand me. When he is at Merton he goes to church, and his Rector is bound to look after him. When he is at sea, he has his Chaplain, who preaches whenever the weather permits, and dare not neglect his duties. But the strongest point of all is this—his very own father and brother are clergymen, and bound to do their best for him. All these you insult, and in so many words condemn for neglecting their duty, because you are unable to resist the pleasure of a stray shot at a celebrated man when he comes down here for hospitality."

"My dear, you have put the matter in a new light," said the Rev. Joshua Twemlow; "I would be the last man in the world to cast a slur upon any brother clergyman. But it is a sad denial to me, because I had put it so neatly, and a line of Latin at the end of it."

"Never mind, dear. That will do for some one else who deserves it, and has got no influence. And if you could only put instead of it one of your beautifully turned expressions about our debt of gratitude to the noble defender of our country—"

"No, no, Maria!" said her husband, with a smile; "be content without pushing your victory further than Nelson himself would push it. It may be my duty to spare him, but I will not fall down and worship him."

Joshua Twemlow, Bachelor of Divinity, was not very likely to worship anybody, nor even to admire, without due cause shown. He did not pretend to be a learned man, any more than he made any other pretense which he could not justify. But he loved a bit of Latin, whenever he could find anybody to share it with him, and even in lack of intelligent partners he indulged sometimes in that utterance. This was a grievance to the Squire of the parish, because he was expected to enjoy at ear-shot that which had passed out of the other ear in boyhood, with a painful echo behind it. But the Admiral had his revenge by passing the Rector's bits of Latin on—when he could remember them—to some one entitled to an explanation, which he, with a pleasant smile, vouchsafed. This is one of the many benefits of a classical education.

But what are such little tags, compared with the pith and marrow of the man himself? Parson Twemlow was no prig, no pedant, and no popinjay, but a sensible, upright, honorable man, whose chief defect was a quick temper. In parish affairs he loved to show his independence of the Hall, and having a stronger will than Admiral Darling, he mostly conquered him. But he knew very well how far to go, and never pressed the supremacy of the Church beyond endurance.

His wife, who was one of the Carnes of Carne Castle, some few miles to the westward, encouraged him strongly in holding his own when the Admiral strove to override him. That was her manner of putting the case; while Admiral Darling would rather have a score of nightmares than override any one. But the Carnes were a falling as much as the Darlings were a rising family, and offense comes down the hill like stones dislodged by the upward traveller. Mrs. Twemlow knew nothing she disliked so much as any form of haughtiness; it was so small, so petty, so opposed to all true Christianity. And this made her think that the Darlings were always endeavoring to patronize her—a thing she would much rather die than put up with.

This excellent couple had allowed, however, their only son Erle, a very fine young man, to give his heart entirely to Faith Darling, the Admiral's eldest daughter, and to win hers to an equal extent; and instead of displaying any haughtiness, her father had simply said: "Let them wait two years; they are both very young, and may change their minds. If they keep of the same mind for two years, they are welcome to one another."

For a kinder-hearted man than Admiral Darling never saw the sun. There was nothing about him wonderful in the way of genius, heroism, large-mindedness, or unselfishness. But people liked him much better than if he combined all those vast rarities; because he was lively, genial, simple, easily moved to wrath or grief, free-handed, a little fond, perhaps, of quiet and confidential brag, and very fond of gossip.

"I tell you," he said to Lord Nelson now, as they walked down the hill to the church together that lovely Sunday morning, "you will not have seen a finer sight than our fishermen in church—I dare say never. Of course they don't all go. Nobody could expect it. But as many as a reasonable man could desire come there, because they know I like it. Twemlow thinks that they come to please him; but he finds a mighty difference in his congregation when I and my daughters are out of the parish. But if he goes away, there they are all the same, or perhaps even more, to get a change from him. That will show which of us they care about pleasing."

"And they are quite right. I hate the levelling system," the hero of the Nile replied. "A man should go to church to please his landlord, not to please the parson. Is the Chaplain to settle how many come to prayers?"

"That is the right way to look at the thing," said the larger-bodied Admiral; "and I only wish Twemlow could have heard you. I asked him to dine with us yesterday, as you know, because you would have done him so much good; but he sent some trumpery excuse, although his wife was asked to come with him. She stopped him, no doubt; to look big, I dare say; as if they could dine with a Lord Nelson every day!"

"They can do that every day, when they dine with a man who has done his duty. But where is my pretty godchild Dolly? Horatia seems too long for you. What a long name they gave me! It may have done very well for my granduncle. But, my dear Lingo, look sharp for your Dolly. She has no mother, nor even a duenna—she has turned her off, she said yesterday. Your daughter Faith is an angel, but Dolly—"

"My Dolly is a little devil, I suppose! You always found out everything. What have you found my Dolly at? Perhaps she got it at her baptism." A word against his pet child was steel upon flint to Admiral Darling.

"I am not concerned with your opinion," Lord Nelson answered, loftily. "But Horatia Dorothy Darling is my godchild by baptism, and you will find her down in my will for a thousand pounds, if she behaves well, and if it should please the Lord to send me some of the prize-money I deserve."

This was announced in such a manner, with the future testator's useful eye bearing brightly on his comrade, and his cocked hat lifted as he spoke of the great Awarder of prizes, that no one able to smile could help a friendly and simple smile at him. So Admiral Darling forgot his wrath, which never had long memory, and scorning even to look round for Dolly, in whom he felt such confidence, took the mighty warrior by the good arm and led him toward the peaceful bells.

"Hurry; we shall be late," he said. "You remember when we called you 'Hurry,' because of being always foremost? But they know better than to stop the bells till they see me in the church porch. Twemlow wanted to upset that, for the parsons want to upset everything. And I said: 'Very well; then I shall square it by locking the gate from your shrubbery. That will give me five minutes to come down the hill.' For my grandfather put up that gate, you must know, and of course the key belongs to me. It saves Twemlow a cable's-length every time, and the parsons go to church so often now, he would have to make at least another knot a month. So the bells go on as they used to do. How many bells do you make it, Mr. Nelson?"

"Eight bells, sir," Lord Nelson replied, saluting like the middy in charge of the watch. And at this little turn they both laughed, and went on, with memory of ancient days, to church.

CHAPTER V

OPINION, MALE AND FEMALE

The fine young parsons of the present generation are too fond of asking us why we come to church, and assigning fifty reasons out of their own heads, not one of which is to our credit or theirs; whereas their proper business is to cure the fish they have caught, instead of asking how they caught them. Mr. Twemlow had sense enough for this, and treated the largest congregation he had ever preached to as if they were come for the good of their souls, and should have it, in spite of Lord Nelson. But, alas! their bodies fared not so well, and scarcely a man got his Sunday dinner according to his liking. Never a woman would stay by the fire for the sake of a ten-pound leg of mutton, and the baker put his shutters up at half past ten against every veal pie and every loin of pork. Because in the church there would be seen this day (as the servants at the Hall told every one) the man whom no Englishman could behold without pride, and no Frenchman with it—the victor of the Nile, and of Copenhagen, and countless other conflicts. Knowing that he would be stared at well, he was equal to the occasion, and the people who saw him were so proud of the sight that they would talk of it now if they were alive.

But those who were not there would exhibit more confidence than conscience by describing every item of his raiment, which verily even of those who beheld it none could do well, except a tailor or a woman. Enough that he shone in the light of the sun (which came through a windowful of bull's-eyes upon him, and was surprised to see stars by daylight), but the glint of his jewels and glow of his gold diverted no eye from the calm, sad face which in the day of battle could outflash them all. That sensitive, mild, complaisant face (humble, and even homely now, with scathe and scald and the lines of middle age) presented itself as a great surprise to the many who came to gaze at it. With its child-like simplicity and latent fire, it was rather the face of a dreamer and poet than of a warrior and hero.

Mrs. Cheeseman, the wife of Mr. Cheeseman, who kept the main shop in the village, put this conclusion into better English, when Mrs. Shanks (Harry's mother) came on Monday to buy a rasher and compare opinions.

"If I could have fetched it to my mind," she said, "that Squire Darling were a tarradiddle, and all his wenches liars—which some of them be, and no mistake—and if I could refuse my own eyes about gold-lace, and crown jewels, and arms off, happier would I sleep in my bed, ma'am, every night the Lord seeth good for it. I would sooner have found hoppers in the best ham in the shop than have gone to church so to delude myself. But there! that Cheeseman would make me do it. I did believe as we had somebody fit to do battle for us against Boney, and I laughed about all they invasion and scares. But now—why, 'a can't say bo to a goose! If 'a was to come and stand this moment where you be a-standing, and say, 'Mrs. Cheeseman, I want a fine rasher,' not a bit of gristle would I trim out, nor put it up in paper for him, as I do for you, ma'am."

And Widow Shanks quite agreed with her.

"Never can I tell you what my feelings was, when I seed him a-standing by the monument, ma'am. But I said to myself—'why, my poor John, as is now in heaven, poor fellow, would 'a took you up with one hand, my lord, stars and garters and crowns and all, and put you into his sow-west pocket.' And so he could have done, Mrs. Cheeseman."

But the opinion of the men was different, because they knew a bee from a bull's foot.

"He may not be so very big," they said, "nor so outrageous thunderin', as the missus looked out for from what she have read. They always goes by their own opinions, and wrong a score of times out of twenty. But any one with a fork to his leg can see the sort of stuff he is made of. He 'tended his duty in the house of the Lord, and he wouldn't look after the women; but he kept his live eye upon every young chap as were fit for a man-of-war's-man—Dan Tugwell especial, and young Harry Shanks. You see if he don't have both of they afore ever the war comes on again!"

Conscious of filling the public eye, with the privilege of being upon private view, Lord Nelson had faced the position without flinching, and drawn all the fire of the enemy. After that he began to make reprisals, according to his manner, taking no trouble to regard the women—which debarred them from thinking much of him—but settling with a steady gaze at each sea-faring man, whether he was made of good stuff or of pie-crust. And to the credit of the place it must be said that he found very little of that soft material, but plenty of good stuff, slow, perhaps, and heavy, but needing only such a soul as his to rouse it.

"What a fine set of fellows you have in your village!" he said to Miss Darling after dinner, as she sat at the head of her father's table, for the Admiral had long been a widower. "The finest I have seen on the south coast anywhere. And they look as if they had been under some training. I suppose your father had most of them in the Fencibles, last summer?"

"Not one of them," Faith answered, with a sweet smile of pride. "They have their own opinions, and nothing will disturb them. Nobody could get them to believe for a moment that there was any danger of invasion. And they carried on all their fishing business almost as calmly as they do now. For that, of course, they may thank you, Lord Nelson; but they have not the smallest sense of the obligation."

"I am used to that, as your father knows; but more among the noble than the simple. For the best thing I ever did I got no praise, or at any rate very little. As to the Boulogne affair, Springhaven was quite right. There was never much danger of invasion. I only wish the villains would have tried it. Horatia, would you like to see your godfather at work? I hope not. Young ladies should be peaceful."

"Then I am not peaceful at all," cried Dolly, who was sitting by the maimed side of her "Flapfin," as her young brother Johnny had nicknamed him. "Why, if there was always peace, what on earth would any but very low people find to do? There could scarcely be an admiral, or a general, or even a captain, or —well, a boy to beat the drums."

"But no drum would want to be beaten, Horatia," her elder sister Faith replied, with the superior mind of twenty-one; "and the admirals and the generals would have to be—"

"Doctors, or clergymen, or something of that sort, or perhaps even worse— nasty lawyers." Then Dolly (whose name was "Horatia" only in presence of her great godfather) blushed, as befitted the age of seventeen, at her daring, and looked at her father.

"That last cut was meant for me," Frank Darling, the eldest of the family, explained from the opposite side of the table. "Your lordship, though so well known to us, can hardly be expected to know or remember all the little particulars of our race. We are four, as you know; and the elder two are peaceful, while the younger pair are warlike. And I am to be the 'nasty lawyer,' called to the bar in the fullness of time—which means after dining sufficiently—to the great disgust of your little godchild, whose desire from her babyhood has been to get me shot."

"LITTLE, indeed! What a word to use about me! You told a great story. But now you'll make it true."

"To wit—as we say at Lincoln's Inn—she has not longed always for my death in battle, but henceforth will do so; but I never shall afford her that gratification. I shall keep out of danger as zealously as your lordship rushes into it."

"Franky going on, I suppose, with some of his usual nonsense," Admiral Darling, who was rather deaf, called out from the bottom of the table.

"Nobody pays much attention to him, because he does not mean a word of it. He belongs to the peace—peace—peace-at-any-price lot. But when a man wanted to rob him last winter, he knocked him down, and took him by the throat, and very nearly killed him."

"That's the only game to play," exclaimed Lord Nelson, who had been looking at Frank Darling with undisguised disgust. "My young friend, you are not such a fool after all. And why should you try to be one?"

"My brother," said the sweet-tempered Faith, "never tries to be a fool, Lord Nelson; he only tries to be a poet."

This made people laugh; and Nelson, feeling that he had been rude to a youth who could not fairly answer him, jumped from his chair with the lightness of a boy, and went round to Frank Darling, with his thin figure leaning forward, and his gray unpowdered hair tossed about, and upon his wrinkled face that smile which none could ever resist, because it was so warm and yet so sad.

"Shake hands, my dear young friend," he cried, "though I can not offer the right one. I was wrong to call you a fool because you don't look at things as I do. Poets are almost as good as sailors, and a great deal better than soldiers. I have felt a gift that way myself, and turned out some very tidy lines. But I believe they were mainly about myself, and I never had time to go on with them."

Such little touches of simplicity and kindness, from a man who never knew the fear of men, helped largely to produce that love of Nelson which England felt, and will always feel.

"My lord," replied the young man, bending low—for he was half a cubit higher than the mighty captain—"it is good for the world that you have no right arm, when you disarm it so with your left one."

25

CHAPTER VI

AS OTHERS SEE US

Admiral Darling was very particular in trying to keep his grounds and garden tolerably tidy always. But he never succeeded, for the simple reason that he listened to every one's excuses; and not understanding a walk or a lawn half so well as the deck of a battle-ship, he was always defeated in argument.

"Here's a state of things!" he used to say in summer-time; "thistles full of seed within a biscuit-heave of my front door, and other things—I forget their names—with heads like the head of a capstan bursting, all as full of seeds as a purser is of lies!"

"Your lordship do not understand them subjects," Mr. Swipes, the head gardener, was in the habit of replying; "and small blame to you, in my opinion, after so many years upon the briny wave. Ah! they can't grow them things there."

"Swipes, that is true, but to my mind not at all a satisfactory reason for growing them here, just in front of the house and the windows. I don't mind a few in the kitchen-garden, but you know as well as I do, Swipes, that they can have no proper business here."

"I did hear tell down to the Club, last night," Mr. Swipes would reply, after wiping his forehead, as if his whole mind were perspired away, "though I don't pretend to say how far true it may be, that all the land of England is to be cultivated for the public good, same as on the continent, without no propriety or privacy, my lord. But I don't altogether see how they be to do it. So I thought I'd better ask your lordship."

"For the public good! The public-house good, you mean." The Admiral answered nine times out of ten, being easily led from the track of his wrath, and tired of telling Swipes that he was not a lord. "How many times more must I tell you, Swipes, that I hate that Jacobin association? Can you tell me of one seaman belonging to it? A set of fish-jobbers, and men with barrows, and cheap-jacks from up the country. Not one of my tenants would be such a fool as to go there, even if I allowed him. I make great allowances for you, Swipes, because of your obstinate nature. But don't let me hear of that Club any more, or YOU may go and cultivate for the public good."

"Your lordship knows that I goes there for nothing except to keep up my burial. And with all the work there is upon this place, the Lord only knows when I may be requiring of it. Ah! I never see the like; I never did. And a blade of grass the wrong way comes down on poor old Swipes!"

Hereupon the master, having done his duty, was relieved from overdoing it, and went on other business with a peaceful mind. The feelings, however, of Mr. Swipes were not to be appeased so lightly, but demanded the immediate satisfaction of a pint of beer. And so large was his charity that if his master fell short of duty upon that point, he accredited him with the good intention, and enabled him to discharge it.

"My dear soul," he said, with symptoms of exhaustion, to good Mrs. Cloam, the housekeeper, who had all the keys at her girdle, about ten o'clock on the Monday morning, "what a day we did have yesterday!"

"A mercy upon me, Mr. Swipes," cried Mrs. Cloam, who was also short of breath, "how you did exaggerate my poor narves, a-rushing up so soft, with the cold steel in both your hands!"

"Ah! ma'am, it have right to be a good deal wuss than that," the chivalrous Swipes made answer, with the scythe beside his ear. "It don't consarn what the masters say, though enough to take one's legs off. But the ladies, Mrs. Cloam, the ladies—it's them as takes our heads off."

"Go 'long with you, Mr. Swipes! You are so disastrous at turning things. And how much did he say you was to have this time? Here's Jenny Shanks coming up the passage."

"Well, he left it to myself; he have that confidence in me. And little it is I should ever care to take, with the power of my own will, ma'am. Why, the little brown jug, ma'am, is as much as I can manage even of our small beer now. Ah! I know the time when I would no more have thought of rounding of my mouth for such small stuff than of your growing up, ma'am, to be a young woman with the sponsorship of this big place upon you. Wonderful! wonderful! And only yesterday, as a man with a gardening mind looks at it, you was the prettiest young maiden on the green, and the same—barring marriage—if you was to encounter with the young men now."

"Oh," said Mrs. Cloam, who was fifty, if a day, "how you do make me think of sad troubles, Mr. Swipes! Jenny, take the yellow jug with the three beef-eaters on it, and go to the third cask from the door—the key turns upside down, mind—and let me hear you whistle till you bring me back the key. Don't tell me nonsense about your lips being dry. You can whistle like a blackbird when you choose."

"Here's to your excellent health, Mrs. Cloam, and as blooming as it finds you now, ma'am! As pretty a tap as I taste since Christmas, and another dash of malt would 'a made it worthy a'most to speak your health in. Well, ma'am, a leetle drop in crystal for yourself, and then for my business, which is to inquire after your poor dear health to-day. Blooming as you are, ma'am, you must bear in mind that beauty is only skin-deep, Mrs. Cloam; and the purtier a flower is, the more delicate it grows. I've a-been a-thinking of you every night, ma'am, knowing how you must 'a been put about and driven. The Admiral have gone down to the village, and Miss Dolly to stare at the boats going out."

"Then I may speak a word for once at ease, Mr. Swipes, though the Lord alone knows what a load is on my tongue. It requires a fine gardener, being used to delicacy, to enter into half the worry we have to put up with. Heroes of the Nile, indeed, and bucklers of the country! Why, he could not buckle his own shoe, and Jenny Shanks had to do it for him. Not that I blame him for having one arm, and a brave man he is to have lost it, but that he might have said something about the things I got up at a quarter to five every morning to make up for him. For cook is no more than a smoke-jack, Mr. Swipes; if she keeps the joint turning, that's as much as she can do."

"And a little too fond of good beer, I'm afeard," replied Mr. Swipes, having emptied his pot. "Men's heads was made for it, but not women's, till they come to superior stations in life. But, oh, Mrs. Cloam, what a life we lead with the crotchets of they gentry!"

"It isn't that so much, Mr. Swipes, if only there was any way of giving satisfaction. I wish everybody who is born to it to have the very best of everything, likewise all who have fought up to it. But to make all the things and have nothing made of them, whether indigestion or want of appetite, turns one quite into the Negroes almost, that two or three people go on with."

"I don't look at what he hath aten or left," Mr. Swipes made answer, loftily; "that lieth between him and his own stommick. But what hath a' left for me, ma'am? He hath looked out over the garden when he pleased, and this time of year no weeds is up, and he don't know enough of things to think nothing of them. When his chaise come down I was out by the gate with a broom in my hand, and I pulled off my hat, but his eye never seemed to lay hold of me."

"His eye lays hold of everything, whether he makes 'em feel or no. One thing I'm sure of—he was quite up to Miss Dolly, and the way she carries on with you know who, every blessed Sunday. If that is what they go to church for—"

"But, my dear soul," said the genial Swipes, whose heart was enlarged with the power of good beer, "when you and I was young folk, what did we go to church for? I can't speak for you, ma'am, being ever so much younger, and a baby in the gallery in long clothes, if born by that time; but so far as myself goes, it was the girls I went to look at, and most of 'em come as well to have it done to them."

"That never was my style, Mr. Swipes, though I know there were some not above it. And amongst equals I won't say that there need be much harm in it. But for a young man in the gallery, with a long stick of the vile-base in his hand, and the only clean shirt of the week on his back, and nothing but a plank of pitch to keep him, however good-looking he may be, to be looking at the daughter, and the prettiest one too, though not the best, some people think, of the gentleman that owns all the houses and the haven—presumption is the smallest word that I can find to use for it; and for her to allow it, fat—fat something in the nation."

"Well, ma'am," said Mr. Swipes, whose views were loose and liberal, "it seems a little shock at first to those on trust in families. But Dannel is a brave boy, and might fight his way to glory, and then they has the pick of the femmels up to a thousand pound a year. You know what happened the miller's son, no further off than Upton. And if it hadn't been for Dannel, when she was a little chit, where would proud Miss Dolly be, with her feathers and her furbelows? Natur' is the thing I holds by, and I sees a deal of it. And betwixt you and me and the bedpost, ma'am, whoever hath Miss Dolly will have to ride to London on this here scythe. Miss Faith is the lass for a good quiet man, without no airs and graces, and to my judgment every bit as comely, and more of her to hold on by. But the Lord 'a mercy upon us. Mrs. Cloam, you've a-been married like my poor self; and you knows what we be, and we knows what you be. Looks 'ain't much to do with it after the first week or two. It's the cooking, and the natur', and the not going contrairy. B'lieve Miss Dolly would go contrairy to a hangel, if her was j'ined to him three days."

"Prejudice! prejudice!" the housekeeper replied, while shaking her finger severely at him. "You ought to be above such opinions, Mr. Swipes, a superior man, such as you are. If Miss Faith came into your garden reading books, and finding fault here and there, and sniffing at the flowers, a quarter so often as pretty Dolly does, perhaps you wouldn't make such a perfect angel of her, and run down her sister in comparison. But your wonderful Miss Faith comes peeping here and poking there into pots and pans, and asking the maids how their mothers are, as if her father kept no housekeeper. She provoked me so in the simple-room last week, as if I was hiding thieves there, that I asked her at last whether she expected to find Mr. Erle there. And you should have seen how she burst out crying; for something had turned on her mind before."

"Well, I couldn't have said that to her," quoth the tender-hearted Swipes

—"not if she had come and routed out every key and every box, pot, pan, and pannier in the tool-house and stoke-hole and vinery! The pretty dear! the pretty dear! And such a lady as she is! Ah, you women are hard-hearted to one another, when your minds are up! But take my word for it, Mrs. Cloam, no one will ever have the chance of making your beautiful Miss Dolly cry by asking her where her sweetheart is."

CHAPTER VII

A SQUADRON IN THE DOWNS

"My dear girls, all your courage is gone," said Admiral Darling to his daughters at luncheon, that same Monday; "departed perhaps with Lord Nelson and Frank. I hate the new style of such come-and-go visits, as if there was no time for anything. Directly a man knows the ways of the house, and you can take him easily, off he goes. Just like Hurry, he never can stop quiet. He talks as if peace was the joy of his life, and a quiet farm his paradise, and very likely he believes it. But my belief is that a year of peace would kill him, now that he has made himself so famous. When that sort of thing begins, it seems as if it must go on."

"But, father dear," exclaimed the elder daughter, "you could have done every single thing that Lord Nelson has ever contrived to do, if you had only happened to be there, and equally eager for destruction. I have heard you say many times, though not of course before him, that you could have managed the battle of the Nile considerably better than he did. And instead of allowing the great vessel to blow up, you would have brought her safe to Spithead."

"My dear, you must have quite misunderstood me. Be sure that you never express such opinions, which are entirely your own, in the presence of naval officers. Though I will not say that they are quite without foundation."

"Why, papa," cried Miss Dolly, who was very truthful, when her own interests were not involved, "you have often said twice as much as that. How well I remember having heard you say—"

"You young people always back up one another, and you don't care what you make your poor father say. I wonder you don't vow that I declared I could jump over the moon with my uniform on. But I'll tell you what we'll do, to bring back your senses—we will go for a long ride this fine afternoon. I've a great mind to go as far as Stonnington."

"Now how many times have you told us that? I won't believe it till we get there," young Dolly answered, with her bright eyes full of joy. "You must be ashamed of yourself, papa, for neglecting your old friend's son so long."

"Well, to tell you the truth, I am, my dear," confessed the good-natured Admiral; "but no one but myself has the least idea of the quantity of things I have to do."

"Exactly what old Swipes said this very morning, only much more impressively. And I really did believe him, till I saw a yellow jug, and a horn that holds a pint, in the summer-house. He threw his coat over them, but it was too late."

"Dolly, I shall have to put you in the blackhole. You belong too much to the rising generation, or the upstart generation is the proper word. What would Lord Nelson say? I must have him back again. He is the man for strict discipline."

"Oh, I want to ask one thing about my great godfather. You know he only came down with one portmanteau, and his cocked-hat box, and two hampers. But when I went into his bedroom to see, as a goddaughter should, that his pillow was smooth, there he had got tacked up at the head of his bed a picture of some very beautiful lady, and another at the side, and another at the foot! And Jenny Shanks, who couldn't help peeping in, to see how a great hero goes to sleep, wishes that she may be an old maid forever if she did not see him say his prayers to them. Now the same fate befall me if I don't find out who it is. You must know, papa, so you had better tell at once."

"That hussy shall leave the house tomorrow. I never heard of anything so shameless. Mrs. Cloam seems to have no authority whatever. And you too, Dolly, had no business there. If any one went to see the room comfortable, it should have been Faith, as the lady of the house. Ever since you persuaded me that you were too old for a governess, you seem to be under no discipline at all."

"Now you know that you don't mean that, papa. You say those cruel things just to make me kiss you," cried Dolly, with the action suited to the word, and with her bright hair falling upon his snowy beard the father could not help returning the salute; "but I must know who that lady is. And what can he want with three pictures of her?"

"How should I know, Dolly? Perhaps it is his mother, or perhaps it is the Queen of Naples, who made a Duke of him for what he did out there. Now be quick, both of you, or no ride to-day. It is fifteen long miles to Stonnington, I am sure, and I am not going to break my neck. As it is, we must put dinner off till half past six, and we shall all be starved by that time. Quick, girls, quick! I can only give you twenty minutes."

The Admiral, riding with all the vigor of an ancient mariner, looked well between his two fair daughters, as they turned their horses' heads inland, and made over the downs for Stonnington. Here was beautiful cantering ground, without much furze or many rabbit-holes, and lovely air flowing over green waves of land, to greet and to deepen the rose upon young cheeks. Behind them was the broad sea, looking steadfast, and spread with slowly travelling tints; before them and around lay the beauty of the earth, with the goodness of the sky thrown over it. The bright world quivered with the breath of spring, and her smile was shed on everything.

"What a lovely country we have been through! I should like to come here every day," said Faith, as they struck into the London road again. "If Stonnington is as nice as this, Mr. Scudamore must be happy there."

"Well, we shall see," her father answered. "My business has been upon the coast so much, that I know very little about Stonnington. But Scudamore has such a happy nature that nothing would come much amiss to him. You know why he is here, of course?"

"No, I don't, papa. You are getting so mysterious that you never tell us anything now," replied Dolly. "I only know that he was in the navy, and now he is in a grammar school. The last time I saw him he was about a yard high."

"He is a good bit short of two yards now," said the Admiral, smiling as he thought of him, "but quite tall enough for a sailor, Dolly, and the most active young man I ever saw in my life, every inch of him sound and quick and true. I shall think very little of your judgment unless you like him heartily; not at first, perhaps, because he is so shy, but as soon as you begin to know him. I mean to ask him to come down as soon as he can get a holiday. His captain told me, when he served in the Diomede, that there was not a man in the ship to come near him for nimbleness and quiet fearlessness."

"Then what made him take to his books again? Oh, how terribly dull he must find them! Why, that must be Stonnington church, on the hill!"

"Yes, and the old grammar school close by. I was very near going there once myself, but they sent me to Winchester instead. It was partly through me that he got his berth here, though not much to thank me for, I am afraid. Sixty pounds a year and his rations isn't much for a man who has been at Cambridge. But even that he could not get in the navy when the slack time came last year. He held no commission, like many other fine young fellows, but had entered as a first-class volunteer. And so he had no rating when this vile peace was patched up—excuse me, my dear, what I meant to say was, when the blessings of tranquillity were restored. And before that his father, my dear old friend, died very suddenly, as you have heard me say, without leaving more than would bury him. Don't talk any more of it. It makes me sad to think of it."

"But," persisted Dolly, "I could never understand why a famous man like Sir Edmond Scudamore—a physician in large practice, and head doctor to the King, as you have often told us—could possibly have died in that sort of way, without leaving any money, or at least a quantity of valuable furniture and jewels. And he had not a number of children, papa, to spend all his money, as I do yours, whenever I get the chance; though you are growing so dreadfully stingy now that I never can look even decent."

"My dear, it is a very long sad story. Not about my stinginess, I mean—though that is a sad story, in another sense, but will not move my compassion. As to Sir Edmond, I can only tell you now that, while he was a man of great scientific knowledge, he knew very little indeed of money matters, and was not only far too generous, but what is a thousand times worse, too trustful. Being of an honorable race himself, and an honorable sample of it, he supposed that a man of good family must be a gentleman; which is not always the case. He advanced large sums of money, and signed bonds for a gentleman, or rather a man of that rank, whose name does not concern you; and by that man he was vilely betrayed; and I would rather not tell you the rest of it. Poor Blyth had to leave Cambridge first, where he was sure to have done very well indeed, and at his wish he was sent afloat, where he would have done even better; and then, as his father's troubles deepened, and ended in his death of heart complaint, the poor boy was left to keep his broken-hearted mother upon nothing but a Latin Grammar. And I fear it is like a purser's dip. But here we are at Stonnington—a long steep pitch. Let us slacken sail, my dears, as we have brought no cockswain. Neither of you need land, you know, but I shall go into the schoolroom."

"One thing I want to know," said the active-minded Dolly, as the horses came blowing their breath up the hill: "if his father was Sir Edmond, and he is the only child, according to all the laws of nature, he ought to be Sir Blyth Scudamore."

"It shows how little you have been out—as good Mrs. Twemlow expresses it—that you do not even understand the laws of nature as between a baronet and a knight."

"Oh, to be sure; I recollect! How very stupid of me! The one goes on, and the other doesn't, after the individual stops. But whose fault is it that I go out so little? So you see you are caught in your own trap, papa."

CHAPTER VIII

A LESSON IN THE AENEID

In those days Stonnington was a very pretty village, and such it continued to be until it was ravaged by a railway. With the railway came all that is hideous and foul, and from it fled all that is comely. The cattle-shed, called by rail-highwaymen "the Station," with its roof of iron Pan-pipes and red bull's-eyes stuck on stack-poles, whistles and stares where the grand trees stood and the village green lay sleeping. On the site of the gray-stone grammar school is an "Operative Institute," whose front (not so thick as the skin of a young ass) is gayly tattooed with a ringworm of wind-bricks. And the old manor-house, where great authors used to dine, and look out with long pipes through the ivy, has been stripped of every shred of leaf, and painted red and yellow, and barge-boarded into "the Temperance Tap."

Ere ever these heathen so furiously raged, there was peace and content, and the pleasure of the eyes, and of neighborly feeling abundance. The men never burst with that bubble of hurry which every man now is inflated with; and the women had time enough to mind one another's affairs, without which they grow scandalous. And the trees, that kept company with the houses, found matter for reflection in their calm blue smoke, and the green crop that promised a little grove upon the roof. So that as the road went up the hill, the traveller was content to leave his legs to nature, while his eyes took their leisure of pleasant views, and of just enough people to dwell upon.

At the top of the hill rose the fine old church, and next to it, facing on the road itself, without any kind of fence before it, stood the grammar school of many generations. This was a long low building, ridged with mossy slabs, and ribbed with green, where the drip oozed down the buttresses. But the long reach of the front was divided by a gable projecting a little into the broad high-road. And here was the way, beneath a low stone arch, into a porch with oak beams bulging and a bell-rope dangling, and thence with an oaken door flung back into the dark arcade of learning.

This was the place to learn things in, with some possibility of keeping them, and herein lay the wisdom of our ancestors. Could they ever have known half as much as they did, and ten times as much as we know, if they had let the sun come in to dry it all up, as we do? Will even the fourteen-coated onion root, with its bottom exposed to the sun, or will a clever puppy grow long ears, in the power of strong daylight?

The nature and nurture of solid learning were better understood when schools were built from which came Shakespeare and Bacon and Raleigh; and the glare of the sun was not let in to baffle the light of the eyes upon the mind. And another consideration is that wherever there is light, boys make a noise, which conduces but little to doctrine; whereas in soft shadow their muscles relax, and their minds become apprehensive. Thus had this ancient grammar school of Stonnington fostered many scholars, some of whom had written grammars for themselves and their posterity.

The year being only at the end of March, and the day going on for five o'clock, the light was just right, in the long low room, for correction of manners and for discipline. Two boys had been horsed and brushed up well, which had strengthened the conscience of all the rest, while sobs and rubs of the part affected diffused a tender silence. Dr. Swinks, the head-master, was leaning back in his canopied oaken chair, with the pride inspired by noble actions.

"What wonderfully good boys!" Dolly whispered, as she peeped in through the dark porch with Faith, while her father was giving the horses in charge to the hostler from the inn across the way; "I declare that I shall be frightened even to look at Mr. Scudamore, if this is a specimen of what he does. There is scarcely a boy looking off his book. But how old he does look! I suppose it must be the effect of so much hard teaching."

"You silly thing," her sister answered; "you are looking at the great head-master. Mr. Scudamore is here at the bottom of the school. Between these big hinges you can see him; and he looks as young as you do."

Miss Dolly, who dearly loved any sly peep, kept her light figure back and the long skirt pulled in, as she brought her bright eyes to the slit between the heavy black door and the stone-work. And she speedily gave her opinion.

"He is nothing but a regular frump. I declare I am dreadfully disappointed. No wonder the title did not come on! He is nothing but a very soft-natured stupe. Why, the boys can do what they like with him!"

Certainly the scholars of the Virgil class, which Blyth Scudamore was dealing with, had recovered from the querimonies of those two sons of Ovid, on the further side of Ister, and were having a good laugh at the face of "Captain Scuddy," as they called their beloved preceptor. For he, being gifted with a gentle sense of humor, together with a patient love of the origin of things, was questing in his quiet mind what had led a boy to render a well-known line as follows: "Such a quantity of salt there was, to season the Roman nation." Presently he hit upon the clue to this great mystery. "Mola, the salted cake," he said; "and the next a little error of conjugation. You have looked out your words, Smith, but chanced upon the wrong ones."

"Oh, Captain Scuddy," cried the head boy, grinning wisely, though he might have made just the same blunder himself; "after that, do tell us one of your sea-stories. It will strike five in about five minutes. Something about Nelson, and killing ten great Frenchmen."

"Oh, do," cried the other little fellows, crowding round him. "It is ever so much better than Virgil, Captain Scuddy!"

"I am not Captain Scuddy, as I tell you every day. I'm afraid I am a great deal too good-natured with you. I shall have to send a dozen of you up to be caned."

"No, you couldn't do that if you tried, Captain Scuddy. But what are you thinking of, all this time? There are two pretty ladies in riding-habits peeping at you from the bell porch. Why, you have got sweethearts, Captain Scuddy! What a shame of you never to have told us!"

The youngest and fairest of all the boys there could scarcely have blushed more deeply than their classical tutor did, as he stooped for his hat, and shyly went between the old desks to the door in the porch. All the boys looked after him with the deepest interest, and made up their minds to see everything he did. This was not at all what he desired, and the sense of it increased his hesitation and confusion. Of the Admiral's lovely daughters he had heard while in the navy, and now he was frightened to think that perhaps they were come here to reconnoitre him. But luckily the Admiral was by this time to the fore, and he marched into the school-room and saluted the head-master.

"Dr. Swinks," he said, "I am your very humble servant, Vice-Admiral of the Blue, Charles Darling, and beg a thousand pardons for intrusion on deep learning. But they tell me that your watch is over in some half a minute. Allow me to ask for the son of an old friend, Blyth Scudamore, late of the Diomede frigate, but now of this ancient and learned grammar school. When his labors are over, I would gladly speak with him."

"Boys may go," the head-master pronounced, as the old clock wheezed instead of striking. "Sir, my valued young coadjutor is advancing from the fourth form toward you."

The Doctor was nice in his choice of words, and prided himself on Johnsonian precision, but his young coadjutor's advance was hardly to be distinguished from a fine retreat. Like leaves before the wind, the boys rushed out by a back door into the play-ground, while the master solemnly passed to his house, with a deep slow bow to the ladies; and there was poor Scudamore —most diffident of men whenever it came to lady-work—left to face the visitors with a pleasing knowledge that his neckcloth was dishevelled, and his hair sheafed up, the furrows of his coat broadcast with pounce, and one of his hands gone to sleep from holding a heavy Delphin for three-quarters of an hour.

As he came out thus into the evening light, which dazed his blue eyes for a moment, Miss Dolly turned away to hide a smile, but Faith, upon her father's introduction, took his hand and looked at him tenderly. For she was a very soft-hearted young woman, and the tale of his troubles and goodness to his mother had moved her affection toward him, while as one who was forever pledged—according to her own ideas—to a hero beyond comparison, she was able to regard young men with mercy, and with pity, if they had none to love. "How hard you have been at work!" she said; "it makes us seem so lazy! But we never can find any good thing to do."

"That's a cut at me," cried the Admiral. "Scudamore, when you come to my age, be wiser than to have any daughters. Sure enough, they find no good to do; and they not only put all the fault of that on me, but they make me the victim of all the mischief they invent. Dolly, my darling, wear that cap if it fits. But you have not shaken hands with Mr. Scudamore yet. I hope you will do so, some hundreds of times."

"Not all at once, papa; or how thankful he would be! But stop, I have not got half my glove off; this fur makes them stick so."

Miss Dolly was proud of her hands, and lost few chances of getting them looked at. Then with a little smile, partly at herself for petulance, partly to him for forgiveness, she offered her soft warm rich white hand, and looked at him beautifully as he took it. Alack and alas for poor "Captain Scuddy"!

His eyes, with a quick shy glance, met hers; and hers with soft inquiry answered, "I wonder what you think of me?" Whenever she met a new face, this was her manner of considering it.

"Scudamore, I shall not allow you any time to think about it," Admiral Darling broke in suddenly, so that the young man almost jumped. "Although you have cut the service for a while, because of our stingy peacefulness, you are sure to come back to us again when England wants English, not Latin and Greek. I am your commanding officer, and my orders are that you come to us from Saturday till Monday. I shall send a boat—or at least I mean a buggy—to fetch you, as soon as you are off duty, and return you the same way on Monday. Come, girls, 'twill be dark before we are home; and since the patrols were withdrawn, I hear there's a highwayman down this road again. That is one of the blessings of peace, Scudamore; even as Latin and Greek are. 'Apertis otia portis'—Open the gates for laziness. Ah, I should have done well at old Winton, they tell me, if I had not happened to run away to sea."

CHAPTER IX

THE MAROON

If yet there remained upon our southern coast a home for the rarer virtues, such as gratitude, content, liberality (not of other people's goods alone), faith in a gracious Providence, and strict abstinence from rash labor, that home and stronghold was Springhaven. To most men good success brings neither comfort, nor tranquillity, nor so much as a stool to sit upon, but comes as a tread-mill which must be trodden without any getting to the top of it. Not so did these wise men take their luck. If ever they came from the fickle wave-bosom to the firm breast of land on a Saturday, with a fine catch of fish, and sold it well—and such was their sagacity that sooner would they keep it for cannibal temptation than sell it badly—did they rush into the waves again, before they had dried their breeches? Not they; nor did their wives, who were nearly all good women, stir them up to be off again. Especially at this time of year, with the days pulling out, and the season quickening, and the fish coming back to wag their tails upon the shallows, a pleasant race of men should take their pleasure, and leave flints to be skinned by the sons of flint.

This was the reason why Miss Dolly Darling had watched in vain at the Monday morning tide for the bold issue of the fishing fleet. The weariless tide came up and lifted the bedded keel and the plunged forefoot, and gurgled with a quiet wash among the straky bends, then lurched the boats to this side and to that, to get their heft correctly, and dandled them at last with their bowsprits dipped and their little mast-heads nodding. Every brave smack then was mounted, and riding, and ready for a canter upon the broad sea: but not a blessed man came to set her free. Tethered by head and by heel, she could only enjoy the poised pace of the rocking-horse, instead of the racer's delight in careering across the free sweep of the distance.

Springhaven had done so well last week, that this week it meant to do still better, by stopping at home till the money was gone, and making short work afterward. Every man thoroughly enjoyed himself, keeping sober whenever good manners allowed, foregoing all business, and sauntering about to see the folk hard at work who had got no money. On Wednesday, however, an order was issued by Captain Zebedee Tugwell that all must be ready for a three days' trip when the tide should serve, which would be at the first of the ebb, about ten in the morning. The tides were slackening now, and the smacks had required some change of berth, but still they were not very far from the Admiral's white gate.

"I shall go down to see them, papa, if you please," Dolly said to her father at breakfast-time. "They should have gone on Monday; but they were too rich; and I think it very shameful of them. I dare say they have not got a halfpenny left, and that makes them look so lively. Of course they've been stuffing, and they won't move fast, and they can't expect any more dinner till they catch it. But they have got so much bacon that they don't care."

"What could they have better, I should like to know?" asked the Admiral, who had seen hard times. "Why, I gave seven men three dozen apiece for turning their noses up at salt horse, just because he whisked his tail in the copper. Lord bless my soul! what is the nation coming to, when a man can't dine upon cold bacon?"

"No, it is not that, papa. They are very good in that way, as their wives will tell you. Jenny Shanks tells me the very same thing, and of course she knows all about them. She knew they would never think of going out on Monday, and if I had asked her I might have known it too. But she says that they are sure to catch this tide."

"Very well, Dolly. Go you and catch them. You are never content without seeing something. Though what there is to see in a lot of lubberly craft pushing off with punt-poles—"

"Hush, papa, hush! Don't be so contemptuous. What did my godfather say the other day? And I suppose he understands things."

"Don't quote your godfather against your father. It was never intended in the Catechism. And if it was, I would never put up with it."

Dolly made off; for she knew that her father, while proud of his great impartiality, candor, and scorn of all trumpery feeling, was sometimes unable to make out the reason why a queer little middy of his own should now stand upon the giddy truck of fame, while himself, still ahead of him in the Navy List, might pace his quarter-deck and have hats touched to him, but never a heart beat one pulse quicker. Jealous he was not; but still, at least in his own family—

Leaving her dear father to his meditations, which Faith ran up to kiss away, fair Dolly put on a plain hat and scarf, quite good enough for the fishermen, and set off in haste for the Round-house, to see the expedition start. By the time she was there, and had lifted the sashes, and got the spy-glass ready, the flow of the tide was almost spent, and the brimming moment of the slack was nigh. For this all the folk of the village waited, according to the tradition of the place; the manhood and boyhood, to launch forth; old age, womanhood, and childhood, to contribute the comfort of kind looks and good-by. The tides, though not to be compared to the winds in fickleness, are capricious here, having sallies of irregularity when there has been a long period of northeast winds, bringing a counter-flow to the Atlantic influx. And a man must be thoroughly acquainted with the coast, as well as the moon and the weather, to foretell how the water will rise and fall there. For the present, however, there was no such puzzle. The last lift of the quiet tide shone along the beach in three straight waves, shallow steps that arose inshore, and spent themselves without breaking.

"Toorn o' the tide!" the Captain shouted; "all aboord, aboord, my lads! The more 'ee bide ashore, the wuss 'ee be. See to Master Cheeseman's craft! Got a good hour afront of us. Dannel, what be mooning at? Fetch 'un a clout on his head, Harry Shanks; or Tim, you run up and do it. Doubt the young hosebird were struck last moon, and his brains put to salt in a herring-tub. Home with you, wife! And take Dan, if you will. He'd do more good at the chipping job, with the full moon in his head so."

"Then home I will take my son, Master Tugwell," his wife answered, with much dignity, for all the good wives of Springhaven heard him, and what would they think of her if she said nothing? "Home I will take my son and yours, and the wisest place for him to abide in, with his father set agin him so. Dannel, you come along of me. I won't have my eldest boy gainsaid so."

Zebedee Tugwell closed his lips, and went on with his proper business. All the women would side with him if he left them the use of their own minds, and the sound of his wife's voice last; while all the men in their hearts felt wisdom. But the young man, loath to be left behind, came doubtfully down to the stern of the boat, which was pushed off for the Rosalie. And he looked at the place where he generally sat, and then at his father and the rest of them.

"No gappermouths here!" cried his father, sternly. "Get theezell home with the vemmelvolk. Shove off without him, Tim! How many more tides would 'ee lose?"

Young Dan, whose stout legs were in the swirling water, snatched up his striped woolsey from under the tiller, threw it on his shoulder, and walked off, without a farewell to any one. The whole of Springhaven that could see saw it, and they never had seen such a thing before. Captain Zeb stood up and stared, with his big forehead coming out under his hat, and his golden beard shining in the morning sun; but the only satisfaction for his eyes was the back of his son growing smaller and smaller.

"Chip of the old block!" "Sarve 'ee right, Cap'en!" "Starve 'un back to his manners again!" the inferior chieftains of the expedition cried, according to their several views of life. But Zebedee Tugwell paid no heed to thoughts outside of his own hat and coat. "Spake when I ax you," he said, urbanely, but with a glance which conveyed to any too urgent sympathizer that he would be knocked down, when accessible.

But, alas! the less-disciplined women rejoiced, with a wink at their departing lords, as Mrs. Zebedee set off in chase of her long-striding Daniel. The mother, enriched by home affections and course of duties well performed, was of a rounded and ample figure, while the son was tall, and thin as might be one of strong and well-knit frame. And the sense of wrong would not permit him to turn his neck, or take a glance at the enterprise which had rejected him.

"How grand he does look! what a noble profile!" thought Dolly, who had seen everything without the glass, but now brought it to bear upon his countenance. "He is like the centurion in the painted window, or a Roman medallion with a hat on. But that old woman will never catch him. She might just as well go home again. He is walking about ten miles an hour, and how beautifully straight his legs are! What a shame that he should not be a gentleman! He is ten times more like one than most of the officers that used to come bothering me so. I wonder how far he means to go? I do hope he won't make away with himself. It is almost enough to make him do it, to be so insulted by his own father, and disgraced before all the village, simply because he can't help having his poor head so full of me! Nobody shall ever say that I did anything to give him the faintest encouragement, because it would be so very wicked and so cruel, considering all he has done for me. But if he comes back, when his father is out of sight, and he has walked off his righteous indignation, and all these people are gone to dinner, it might give a turn to his thoughts if I were to put on my shell-colored frock and the pale blue sash, and just go and see, on the other side of the stepping-stones, how much longer they mean to be with that boat they began so long ago."

CHAPTER X

ACROSS THE STEPPING-STONES

Very good boats were built at this time in the south of England, stout, that is to say, and strong, and fit to ride over a heavy sea, and plunge gallantly into the trough of it. But as the strongest men are seldom swift of foot or light of turn, so these robust and sturdy boats must have their own time and swing allowed them, ere ever they would come round or step out. Having met a good deal of the sea, they knew, like a man who has felt a good deal of the world, that heavy endurance and patient bluffness are safer to get through the waves somehow than sensitive fibre and elegant frame.

But the sea-going folk of Springhaven had learned, by lore of generations, to build a boat with an especial sheer forward, beam far back, and deep run of stern, so that she was lively in the heaviest of weather, and strong enough to take a good thump smiling, when unable to dance over it. Yet as a little thing often makes all the difference in great things, it was very difficult for anybody to find out exactly the difference between a boat built here and a boat built ten or twenty miles off, in imitation of her. The sea, however, knew the difference in a moment between the true thing and the counterfeit, and encouraged the one to go merrily on, while it sent back the other staggering. The secret lay chiefly in a hollow curve forward of nine or ten planks upon either side, which could only be compassed by skilful use of adze and chisel, frame-saw and small tools, after choice of the very best timber, free from knots, tough, and flexible. And the best judge of these points was Zebedee Tugwell.

Not having cash enough just at present (by reason of family expenses, and the high price of bread and of everything else) to set upon the stocks the great smack of the future, which should sail round the Rosalie, Captain Tugwell was easing his mind by building a boat for stormy weather, such as they very seldom have inshore, but are likely to meet with outside the Head. As yet there were not many rowing boats here fit to go far in tumbling water, though the few that could do it did it well, and Tugwell's intention was to beat them all, in power, and spring, and buoyancy. The fame of his meaning was spread for as much as twenty leagues along the coast; and jealous people laughed, instead of waiting for him to finish it.

Young Daniel had been well brought up in the mysteries of his father's craft, and having a vigorous turn of wrist, as well as a true eye and quick brain, he was even outgrowing the paternal skill, with experiments against experience. He had beautiful theories of his own, and felt certain that he could prove them, if any one with cash could be brought to see their beauty. His father admitted that he had good ideas, and might try them, if any fool would find the money.

Wroth as he had been at the sharp rebuff and contumely of his father, young Daniel, after a long strong walk, began to look at things more peaceably. The power of the land and the greatness of the sea and the goodness of the sky unangered him, and the air that came from some oyster beds, as the tide was falling, hungered him. Home he went, in good time for dinner, as the duty of a young man is; and instead of laughing when he came by, the maids of Springhaven smiled at him. This quite righted him in his own opinion, yet leaving him the benefit of the doubt which comes from a shake in that cradle lately. He made a good dinner, and shouldered his adze, with a frail of tools hanging on the neck of it, and troubled with nothing but love—which is a woe of self-infliction—whistled his way to the beach, to let all the women understand that he was not a bit ashamed. And they felt for him all the more, because he stood up for himself a little.

Doubtful rights go cheap; and so the foreshore westward of the brook being claimed by divers authorities, a tidy little cantle of it had been leased by Admiral Darling, lord of the manor, to Zebedee Tugwell, boat-builder, for the yearly provent of two and sixpence sterling. The Admiral's man of law, Mr. Furkettle, had strongly advised, and well prepared the necessary instrument, which would grow into value by-and-by, as evidence of title. And who could serve summary process of ejectment upon an interloper in a manner so valid as Zebedee's would be? Possession was certain as long as he lived; ousters and filibusters, in the form of railway companies and communists, were a bubble as yet in the womb of ages.

This piece of land, or sand, or rush, seemed very unlikely to be worth dispute. If seisin corporeal, user immemorial, and prescription for levance and couchance conferred any title indefeasible, then were the rabbits the owners in fee-simple, absolute, paramount, and source of pedigree. But they, while thoroughly aware of this, took very little heed to go into it, nor troubled their gentle natures much about a few yards of sand or grass, as the two-legged creatures near them did. Inasmuch as they had soft banks of herb and vivid moss to sit upon, sweet crisp grass and juicy clover for unlabored victuals—as well as a thousand other nibbles which we are too gross to understand—and for beverage not only all the abundance of the brook (whose brilliance might taste of men), but also a little spring of their own which came out of its hole like a rabbit; and then for scenery all the sea, with strange things running over it, as well as a great park of their own having countless avenues of rush, ragwort, and thistle-stump—where would they have deserved to be, if they had not been contented? Content they were, and even joyful at the proper time of day. Joyful in the morning, because the sun was come again; joyful in the middle day to see how well the world went; and in the evening merry with the tricks of their own shadows.

Quite fifteen stepping-stones stepped up—if you counted three that were made of wood—to soothe the dignity of the brook in its last fresh-water moments, rather than to gratify the dry-skin'd soles of gentlefolk. For any one, with a five-shilling pair of boots to terminate in, might skip dry-footed across the sandy purlings of the rivulet. And only when a flood came down, or the head of some springtide came up, did any but playful children tread the lichened cracks of the stepping-stones. And nobody knew this better than Horatia Dorothy Darling.

The bunnies who lived to the west of the brook had reconciled their minds entirely now to the rising of that boat among them. At first it made a noise, and scratched the sand, and creaking things came down to it; and when the moon came through its ribs in the evening, tail was the quarter to show to it. But as it went on naturally growing, seldom appearing to make much noise, unless there was a man very near it, and even then keeping him from doing any harm—outside the disturbance that he lives in—without so much as a council called, they tolerated this encroachment. Some of the bolder fathers came and sat inside to consider it, and left their compliments all round to the masters of the enterprise. And even when Daniel came to work, as he happened to do this afternoon, they carried on their own work in its highest form—that of play—upon the premises they lent him.

Though not very large, it was a lively, punctual, well-conducted, and pleasant rabbit-warren. Sudden death was avoidable on the part of most of its members, nets, ferrets, gins, and wires being alike forbidden, foxes scarcely ever seen, and even guns a rare and very memorable visitation. The headland staves the southern storm, sand-hills shevelled with long rush disarm the western fury, while inland gales from north and east leap into the clouds from the uplands. Well aware of all their bliss, and feeling worthy of it, the blameless citizens pour forth, upon a mild spring evening, to give one another the time of day, to gaze at the labors of men upon the sea, and to take the sweet leisure, the breeze, and the browse. The gray old conies of curule rank, prime senators of the sandy beach, and father of the father-land, hold a just session upon the head borough, and look like brown loaves in the distance. But these are conies of great mark and special character, full of light and leading, because they have been shot at, and understand how to avoid it henceforth. They are satisfied to chew very little bits of stuff, and particular to have no sand in it, and they hunch their round backs almost into one another, and double up their legs to keep them warm, and reflect on their friends' gray whiskers. And one of their truest pleasures is, sitting snug at their own doors, to watch their children's gambols.

For this is the time, with the light upon the slope, and the freshness of salt flowing in from the sea, when the spirit of youth must be free of the air, and the quickness of life is abounding. Without any heed of the cares that are coming, or the prick-eared fears of the elders, a fine lot of young bunnies with tails on the frisk scour everywhere over the warren. Up and down the grassy dips and yellow piles of wind-drift, and in and out of the ferny coves and tussocks of rush and ragwort, they scamper, and caper, and chase one another, in joy that the winter is banished at last, and the glorious sun come back again.

Suddenly, as at the wave of a wand, they all stop short and listen. The sun is behind them, low and calm, there is not a breath of wind to stir their flax, not even the feather of a last year's bloom has moved, unless they moved it. Yet signal of peril has passed among them; they curve their soft ears for the sound of it, and open their sensitive nostrils, and pat upon the ground with one little foot to encourage themselves against the panting of their hearts and the traitorous length of their shadows.

Ha! Not for nothing was their fear this day. An active and dangerous specimen of the human race was coming, lightly and gracefully skimming the moss, above salt-water reach, of the stepping-stones. The steps are said to be a thousand years old, and probably are of half that age, belonging to a time when sound work was, and a monastery flourished in the valley. Even though they come down from great Hercules himself, never have they been crossed by a prettier foot or a fairer form than now came gayly over them. But the rabbits made no account of that. To the young man with the adze they were quite accustomed, and they liked him, because he minded his own business, and cared nothing about theirs; but of this wandering maiden they had no safe knowledge, and judged the worst, and all rushed away, some tenscore strong, giving notice to him as they passed the boat that he also had better be cautious.

Daniel was in a sweet temper now, by virtue of hard labor and gratified wit. By skill and persistence and bodily strength he had compassed a curve his father had declared impossible without a dock-yard. Three planks being fixed, he was sure of the rest, and could well afford to stop, to admire the effect, and feel proud of his work, and of himself the worker. Then the panic of the conies made him turn his head, and the quick beat of his heart was quickened by worse than bodily labor.

Miss Dolly Darling was sauntering sweetly, as if there were only one sex in the world, and that an entirely divine one. The gleam of spring sunset was bright in her hair, and in the soft garnish of health on her cheeks, and the vigorous play of young life in her eyes; while the silvery glance of the sloping shore, and breezy ruffle of the darkening sea, did nothing but offer a foil for the form of the shell-colored frock and the sky-blue sash.

Young Daniel fell back upon his half-shaped work, and despised it, and himself, and everything, except what he was afraid to look at. In the hollow among the sand-hills where the cradle of the boat was, fine rushes grew, and tufts of ragwort, and stalks of last year's thistles, and sea-osiers where the spring oozed down. Through these the white ribs of the rising boat shone forth like an elephant's skeleton; but the builder entertained some hope, as well as some fear, of being unperceived.

But a far greater power than his own was here. Curved and hollow ships are female in almost all languages, not only because of their curves and hollows, but also because they are craft—so to speak.

"Oh, Captain Tugwell, are you at work still? Why, you really ought to have gone with the smacks. But perhaps you sent your son instead. I am so glad to see you! It is such nice company to hear you! I did not expect to be left alone, like this."

"If you please, miss, it isn't father at all. Father is gone with the fishing long ago. It is only me, Daniel, if you please, miss."

"No, Daniel, I am not pleased at all. I am quite surprised that you should work so late. It scarcely seems respectable."

At this the young man was so much amazed that he could only stare while she walked off, until the clear duty of righting himself in her good opinion struck him. Then he threw on his coat and ran after her.

"If you please, Miss Dolly—will you please, Miss Dolly?" he called, as she made off for the stepping-stones; but she did not turn round, though her name was "Miss Dolly" all over Springhaven, and she liked it. "You are bound to stop, miss," he said, sternly; and she stopped, and cried, "What do you mean by such words to me?"

"Not any sort of harm, miss," he answered, humbly, inasmuch as she had obeyed him; "and I ask your pardon for speaking so. But if you think twice you are bound to explain what you said concerning me, now just."

"Oh, about your working so late, you mean. I offered good advice to you. I think it is wrong that you should go on, when everybody else has left off long ago. But perhaps your father makes you."

"Father is a just man," said young Tugwell, drawing up his own integrity; "now and then he may take a crooked twist, or such like; but he never goeth out of fair play to his knowledge. He hath a-been hard upon me this day; but the main of it was to check mother of her ways. You understand, miss, how the women-folk go on in a house, till the other women hear of it. And then out-of-doors they are the same as lambs."

"It is most ungrateful and traitorous of you to your own mother to talk so. Your mother spoils you, and this is all the thanks she gets! Wait till you have a wife of your own, Master Daniel!"

"Wait till I am dead then I may, Miss Dolly," he answered, with a depth of voice which frightened her for a moment; and then he smiled and said, "I beg your pardon," as gracefully as any gentleman could say it; "but let me see you safe to your own gate; there are very rough people about here now, and the times are not quite as they used to be, when we were a-fighting daily."

He followed her at a respectful distance, and then ran forward and opened the white gate. "Good-night, Daniel," the young lady said, as he lifted his working cap to her, showing his bright curls against the darkening sea; "I am very much obliged to you, and I do hope I have not said anything to vex you. I have never forgotten all you did for me, and you must not mind the way I have of saying things."

"What a shame it does appear—what a fearful shame it is," she whispered to herself as she hurried through the trees—"that he should be nothing but a fisherman! He is a gentleman in everything but birth and education; and so strong, and so brave, and so good-looking!"

CHAPTER XI

NO PROMOTION

"Do it again now, Captain Scuddy; do it again; you know you must."

"You touched the rim with your shoe, last time. You are bound to do it clean, once more."

"No, he didn't. You are a liar; it was only the ribbon of his shoe."

"I'll punch your head if you say that again. It was his heel, and here's the mark."

"Oh, Scuddy dear, don't notice them. You can do it fifty times running, if you like. Nobody can run or jump like you. Do it just once more to please me."

Kitty Fanshawe, a boy with large blue eyes and a purely gentle face, looked up at Blyth Scudamore so faithfully that to resist him was impossible.

"Very well, then; once more for Kitty," said the sweetest-tempered of mankind, as he vaulted back into the tub. "But you know that I always leave off at a dozen. Thirteen—thirteen I could never stop at. I shall have to do fourteen at least; and it is too bad, just after dinner. Now all of you watch whether I touch it anywhere."

A barrel almost five feet in height, and less than a yard in breadth, stood under a clump of trees in the play-ground; and Blyth Scudamore had made a clean leap one day, for his own satisfaction, out of it. Sharp eyes saw him, and sharp wits were pleased, and a strong demand had arisen that he should perform this feat perpetually. Good nerve, as well as strong spring, and compactness of power are needed for it; and even in this athletic age there are few who find it easy.

"Come, now," he said, as he landed lightly, with both heels together; "one of you big fellows come and do it. You are three inches taller than I am. And you have only got to make up your minds."

But all the big fellows hung back, or began to stimulate one another, and to prove to each other how easy it was, by every proof but practice. "Well, then, I must do it once more," said Blyth, "for I dare not leave off at thirteen, for fear of some great calamity, such as I never could jump out of."

But before he could get into the tub again, to prepare for the clear spring out of it, he beheld a man with silver buttons coming across the playing-field.

His heart fell into his heels, and no more agility remained in him. He had made up his mind that Admiral Darling would forget all about him by Saturday; and though the fair image of Dolly would abide in that quiet mind for a long while, the balance of his wishes (cast by shyness) was heavily against this visit. And the boys, who understood his nature, with a poignant love—like that of our friends in this world—began to probe his tender places.

"One more jump, Captain Scuddy! You must; to show the flunky what you can do."

"Oh, don't I wish I was going? He'll have turtle soup, and venison, and two men behind his chair."

"And the beautiful young ladies looking at him every time he takes a mouthful."

"But he dare not go courting after thirteen jumps. And he has vowed that he will have another. Come, Captain Scuddy, no time to lose."

But Scudamore set off to face his doom, with his old hat hanging on the back of his head—as it generally did—and his ruddy face and mild blue eyes full of humorous diffidence and perplexity.

"If you please, sir, his honour the Hadmiral have sent me to fetch 'e and your things; and hoss be baiting along of the Blue Dragon."

"I am sorry to say that I forgot all about it, or, at least, I thought that he would. How long before we ought to start?"

"My name is Gregory, sir—Coachman Gregory—accustomed always to a pair, but doesn't mind a single hoss, to oblige the Hadmiral, once in a way. About half an hour, sir, will suit me, unless they comes down to the skittle-alley, as ought to be always on a Saturday afternoon; but not a soul there when I looked in."

Any man in Scudamore's position, except himself, would have grieved and groaned. For the evening dress of that time, though less gorgeous than of the age before, was still an expensive and elaborate affair; and the young man, in this ebb of fortune, was poorly stocked with raiment. But he passed this trouble with his usual calmness and disregard of trifles. "If I wear the best I have got," he thought, "I cannot be charged with disrespect. The Admiral knows what a sailor is; and, after all, who will look at me?" Accordingly he went just as he was, for he never wore an overcoat, but taking a little canvas kit, with pumps and silk stockings for evening wear, and all the best that he could muster of his Volunteer equipment.

The Admiral came to the door of the Hall, and met him with such hearty warmth, and a glance of such kind approval at his open throat and glowing cheeks, that the young man felt a bound of love and tender veneration towards him, which endured for lifetime.

"Your father was my dearest friend, and the very best man I ever knew. I must call you 'Blyth,'" said the Admiral, "for if I call you 'Scudamore,' I shall think perpetually of my loss."

At dinner that day there was no other guest, and nothing to disturb the present one, except a young lady's quick glances, of which he endeavored to have no knowledge. Faith Darling, a gentle and beautiful young woman, had taken a natural liking to him, because of his troubles, and simplicity, and devotion to his widowed mother. But to the younger, Dolly Darling, he was only a visitor, dull and stupid, requiring, without at all repaying, the trouble of some attention. He was not tall, nor handsome, nor of striking appearance in any way; and although he was clearly a gentleman, to her judgment he was not an accomplished, or even a clever one. His inborn modesty and shyness placed him at great disadvantage, until well known; and the simple truth of his nature forbade any of the large talk and bold utterance which pleased her as yet among young officers.

"What a plague he will be all day tomorrow!" she said to her sister in the drawing-room. "Father was obliged, I suppose, to invite him; but what can we do with him all the day? Sundays are dull enough, I am sure, already, without our having to amuse a gentleman who has scarcely got two ideas of his own, and is afraid to say 'bo' to a goose, I do believe. Did you hear what he said when I asked him whether he was fond of riding?"

"Yes; and I thought it so good of him, to answer so straightforwardly. He said that he used to be very fond of it, but was afraid that he should fall off now."

"I should like to see him. I tell you what we'll do. We will make him ride back on Monday morning, and put him on 'Blue Bangles,' who won't have seen daylight since Friday. Won't he jump about a bit! What a shame it is, not to let us ride on Sundays!"

Ignorant of these kind intentions, Scudamore was enjoying himself in his quiet, observant way. Mr. Twemlow, the rector of the parish, had chanced—as he often chanced on a Saturday, after buckling up a brace of sermons—to issue his mind (with his body outside it) for a little relief of neighbourhood. And these little airings of his chastening love—for he loved everybody, when he had done his sermon—came, whenever there was a fair chance of it, to a glass of the fine old port which is the true haven for an ancient Admiral.

"Just in time, Rector," cried Admiral Darling, who had added by many a hardship to his inborn hospitality. "This is my young friend Blyth Scudamore, the son of one of my oldest friends. You have heard of Sir Edmond Scudamore?"

"And seen him and felt him. And to him I owe, under a merciful Providence, the power of drinking in this fine port the health of his son, which I do with deep pleasure, for the excellence both of end and means."

The old man bowed at the praise of his wine, and the young one at that of his father. Then, after the usual pinch of snuff from the Rector's long gold box, the host returned to the subject he had been full of before this interruption.

"The question we have in hand is this. What is to be done with our friend Blyth? He was getting on famously, till this vile peace came. Twemlow, you called it that yourself, so that argument about words is useless. Blyth's lieutenancy was on the books, and the way they carry things on now, and shoot poor fellows' heads off, he might have been a post-captain in a twelvemonth. And now there seems nothing on earth before him better than Holy-Orders."

"Admiral Darling is kind enough to think," said Scudamore, in his mild, hesitative way, blushing outwardly, but smiling inwardly, "that I am too good to be a clergyman."

"And so you are, and Heaven knows it, Blyth, unless there was a chance of getting on by goodness, which there is in the Navy, but not in the Church. Twemlow, what is your opinion?"

"It would not be modest in me," said the Rector, "to stand up too much for my own order. We do our duty, and we don't get on."

"Exactly. You could not have put it better. You get no vacancies by shot and shell, and being fit for another world, you keep out of it. Have you ever heard me tell the story about Gunner MacCrab, of the Bellerophon?"

"Fifty times, and more than that," replied the sturdy parson, who liked to make a little cut at the Church sometimes, but would not allow any other hand to do it. "But now about our young friend here. Surely, with all that we know by this time of the character of that Bony, we can see that this peace is a mere trick of his to bamboozle us while he gets ready. In six months we shall be at war again, hammer and tongs, as sure as my name is Twemlow."

"So be it!" cried the Admiral, with a stamp on his oak floor, while Scudamore's gentle eyes flashed and fell; "if it is the will of God, so be it. But if it once begins again, God alone knows where France will be before you and I are in our graves. They have drained all our patience, and our pockets very nearly; but they have scarcely put a tap into our energy and endurance. But what are they? A gang of slaves, rammed into the cannon by a Despot."

"They seem to like it, and the question is for them. But the struggle will be desperate, mountains of carnage, oceans of blood, universal mourning, lamentation, and woe. And I have had enough trouble with my tithes already."

"Tithes are dependent on the will of the Almighty," said the Admiral, who paid more than he altogether liked; "but a war goes by reason and good management. It encourages the best men of the day, and it brings out the difference between right and wrong, which are quite smothered up in peace time. It keeps out a quantity of foreign rubbish and stuff only made to be looked at, and it makes people trust one another, and know what country they belong to, and feel how much they have left to be thankful for. And what is the use of a noble fleet, unless it can get some fighting? Blyth, what say you? You know something about that."

"No, sir, I have never been at close quarters yet. And I doubt—or at least I am certain that I should not like it. I am afraid that I should want to run down below."

Mr. Twemlow, having never smelled hostile powder, gazed at him rather loftily, while the young man blushed at his own truth, yet looked up bravely to confirm it.

"Of all I have ever known or met," said Admiral Darling, quietly, "there are but three—Nelson and two others, and one of those two was half-witted—who could fetch up muzzle to muzzle without a feeling of that sort. The true courage lies in resisting the impulse, more than being free from it. I know that I was in a precious fright the first time I was shot at, even at a decent distance; and I don't pretend to like it even now. But I am pretty safe now from any further chance, I fear. When we cut our wisdom-teeth, they shelf us. Twemlow, how much wiser you are in the Church! The older a man gets, the higher they promote him."

"Then let them begin with me," the Rector answered, smiling; "I am old enough now for almost anything, and the only promotion I get is stiff joints, and teeth that crave peace from an olive. Placitam paci, Mr. Scudamore knows the rest, being fresh from the learned Stonnington. But, Squire, you know that I am content. I love Springhaven, Springhaven loves me, and we chasten one another."

"A man who knows all the Latin you know, Rector—for I own that you beat me to the spelling-book—should be at least an Archdeacon in the Church, which is equal to the rank of Rear-Admiral. But you never have pushed as you should do; and you let it all off in quotations. Those are very comforting to the mind, but I never knew a man do good with them, unless they come out of the Bible. When Gunner Matthew of the Erigdoupos was waiting to have his leg off, with no prospect before him—except a better world—you know what our Chaplain said to him; and the effect upon his mind was such, that I have got him to this day upon my land."

"Of course you have—the biggest old poacher in the county. He shoots half your pheasants with his wooden leg by moonlight. What your Chaplain said to him was entirely profane in the turn of a text of Holy-Writ; and it shows how our cloth is spoiled by contact with yours"—for the Admiral was laughing to himself at this old tale, which he would not produce before young Scudamore, but loved to have out with the Rector—"and I hope it will be a good warning to you, Squire, to settle no more old gunners on your property. You must understand, Mr. Scudamore, that the Admiral makes a sort of Naval Hospital, for all his old salts, on his own Estates."

"I am sure it is wonderfully kind in him," the young man answered, bravely, "for the poor old fellows are thrown to the dogs by the country, when it has disabled them. I have not seen much of the service, but quite enough to know that, Mr. Twemlow."

"I have seen a great deal, and I say that it is so. And my good friend knows it as well as I do, and is one of the first to lend a helping hand. In all such cases he does more than I do, whenever they come within his knowledge. But let us return to the matter in hand. Here is a young man, a first-rate sailor, who would have been under my guardianship, I know, but for—but for sad circumstances. Is he to be grinding at Virgil and Ovid till all his spirit goes out of him, because we have patched up a very shabby peace? It can never last long. Every Englishman hates it, although it may seem to save his pocket. Twemlow, I am no politician. You read the papers more than I do. How much longer will this wretched compact hold? You have predicted the course of things before."

"And so I will again," replied the Rector. "Atheism, mockery, cynicism, blasphemy, lust, and blood-thirstyness cannot rage and raven within a few leagues of a godly and just nation without stinking in their nostrils. Sir, it is our mission from the Lord to quench Bony, and to conquer the bullies of Europe. We don't look like doing it now, I confess. But do it we shall, in the end, as sure as the name of our country is England."

"I have no doubt of it," said the Admiral, simply; "but there will be a deal of fighting betwixt this and then. Blyth, will you leave me to see what I can do, whenever we get to work again?"

"I should think that I would, sir, and never forget it. I am not fond of fighting; but how I have longed to feel myself afloat again!"

CHAPTER XII

AT THE YEW-TREE

All the common-sense of England, more abundant in those days than now, felt that the war had not been fought out, and the way to the lap of peace could only be won by vigorous use of the arms. Some few there were even then, as now there is a cackling multitude, besotted enough to believe that facts can be undone by blinking them. But our forefathers on the whole were wise, and knew that nothing is trampled more basely than right that will not right itself.

Therefore they set their faces hard, and toughened their hearts like knotted oak, against all that man could do to them. There were no magnificent proclamations, no big vaunts of victory at the buckling on of armour, but the quiet strength of steadfast wills, and the stern resolve to strike when stricken, and try to last the longest. And so their mother-land became the mother of men and freedom.

In November, 1802, the speech from the throne apprised the world that England was preparing. The widest, longest, and deadliest war, since the date of gunpowder, was lowering; and the hearts of all who loved their kin were heavy, but found no help for it.

The sermon which Mr. Twemlow preached in Springhaven church was magnificent. Some parishioners, keeping memory more alert than conscience, declared that they had received it all nine, or it might be ten, years since, when the fighting first was called for. If so, that proved it none the worse, but themselves, for again requiring it. Their Rector told them that they thought too much of their own flesh-pots and fish-kettles, and their country might go to the bottom of the sea, if it left them their own fishing-grounds. And he said that they would wake up some day and find themselves turned into Frenchmen, for all things were possible with the Lord; and then they might smite their breasts, but must confess that they had deserved it. Neither would years of prayer and fasting fetch them back into decent Englishmen; the abomination of desolation would be set up over their doorways, and the scarlet woman of Babylon would revel in their sanctuaries.

"Now don't let none of us be in no hurry," Captain Tugwell said, after dwelling and sleeping upon this form of doctrine; "a man knoweth his own trade the best, the very same way as the parson doth. And I never knew no good to come of any hurry. Our lives are given us by the Lord. And He never would 'a made 'em threescore and ten, or for men of any strength fourscore, if His will had been to jerk us over them. Never did I see no Frenchman as could be turned to an Englishman, not if he was to fast and pray all day, and cut himself with knives at the going down of the sun. My opinion is that Parson Twemlow were touched up by his own conscience for having a nephew more French than English; and 'Caryl Carne' is the name thereof, with more French than English sound to it."

"Why, he have been gone for years and years," said the landlord of the Darling Arms, where the village was holding council; "he have never been seen in these parts since the death of the last Squire Carne, to my knowledge."

"And what did the old Squire die of, John Prater? Not that he were to be called old—younger, I dare say, than I be now. What did he die of, but marrying with a long outlandish 'ooman? A femmel as couldn't speak a word of English, to be anyhow sure of her meaning! Ah, them was bad times at Carne Castle; and as nice a place as need be then, until they dipped the property. Six grey horses they were used to go with to London Parliament every year, before the last Squire come of age, as I have heered my father say scores of times, and no lie ever come from his mouth, no more than it could from mine, almost. Then they dropped to four, and then to two, and pretended that the roads were easier."

"When I was down the coast, last week, so far as Littlehampton," said a stout young man in the corner, "a very coorous thing happened me, leastways by my own opinion, and glad shall I be to have the judgment of Cappen Zeb consarning it. There come in there a queer-rigged craft of some sixty ton from Halvers, desiring to set up trade again, or to do some smoogling, or spying perhaps. Her name was the Doctor Humm, which seem a great favorite with they Crappos, and her skipper had a queer name too, as if he was two men in one, for he called himself 'Jacks'; a fellow about forty year old, as I hauled out of the sea with a boat-hook one night on the Varners. Well, he seemed to think a good deal of that, though contrary to their nature, and nothing would do but I must go to be fated with him everywhere, if the folk would change his money. He had picked up a decent bit of talk from shipping in the oyster line before the war; and I put his lingo into order for him, for which he was very thankful."

"And so he was bound to be. But you had no call to do it, Charley Bowles." Captain Tugwell spoke severely, and the young man felt that he was wrong, for the elders shook their heads at him, as a traitor to the English language.

"Well, main likely, I went amiss. But he seemed to take it so uncommon kind of me hitching him with a boat-hook, that we got on together wonderful, and he called me 'Friar Sharley,' and he tried to take up with our manners and customs; but his head was outlandish for English grog. One night he was three sheets in the wind, at a snug little crib by the river, and he took to the brag as is born with them. 'All dis contray in one year now,' says he, nodding over his glass at me, 'shall be of the grand nashong, and I will make a great man of you, Friar Sharley. Do you know what prawns are, my good friend?' Well, I said I had caught a good many in my time; but he laughed and said, 'Prawns will catch you this time. One tousand prawns, all with two hondred men inside him, and the leetle prawns will come to land at your house, Sharley. Bootiful place, quiet sea, no bad rocks. You look out in the morning, and the white coast is made black with them.' Now what do you say to that, Cappen Tugwell?"

"I've a-heered that style of talk many times afore," Master Tugwell answered, solidly; "and all I can say is that I should have punched his head. And you deserve the same thing, Charley Bowles, unless you've got more than that to tell us."

"So I might, Cappen, and I won't deny you there. But the discourse were consarning Squire Carne now just, and the troubles he fell into, before I was come to my judgment yet. Why, an uncle of mine served footman there— Jeremiah Bowles, known to every one, until he was no more heard of."

Nods of assent to the fame of Jeremiah encouraged the stout young man in his tale, and a wedge of tobacco rekindled him.

"Yes, it were a coorous thing indeed, and coorous for me to hear of it, out of all mast-head of Springhaven. Says Moosoo Jacks to me, that night when I boused him up unpretending: 'You keep your feather eye open, my tear,' for such was his way of pronouncing it, 'and you shall arrive to laglore, laglore— and what is still nobler, de monnay. In one two tree month, you shall see a young captain returned to his contray dominion, and then you will go to his side and say Jacks, and he will make present to you a sack of silver.' Well, I hailed the chance of this pretty smart, you may suppose, and I asked him what the sailor's name would be, and surprised I was when he answered Carne, or Carny, for he gave it in two syllables. Next morning's tide, the Doctor Humm cleared out, and I had no other chance of discourse with Moosoo Jacks. But I want to know what you think, Cappen Zeb."

"So you shall," said the captain of Springhaven, sternly. "I think you had better call your Moosoo Jacks 'Master Jackass,' or 'Master Jackanapes,' and put your own name on the back of him. You been with a Frenchman hob and nobbing, and you don't even know how they pronounce themselves, unchristian as it is to do so. 'Jarks' were his name, the very same as Navy beef, and a common one in that country. But to speak of any Carne coming nigh us with French plottings, and of prawns landing here at Springhaven

—'tis as likely as I should drop French money into the till of this baccy-box. And you can see that I be not going to play such a trick as that, John Prater."

"Why to my mind there never was bigger stuff talked," the landlord spoke out, without fear of offence, for there was no other sign-board within three miles, "than to carry on in that way, Charley. What they may do at Littlehampton is beyond my knowledge, never having kept a snug crib there, as you was pleased to call it. But at Springhaven 'twould be the wrong place for hatching of French treacheries. We all know one another a deal too well for that, I hope."

"Prater, you are right," exclaimed Mr. Cheeseman, owner of the main shop in the village, and universally respected. "Bowles, you must have an imagination the same as your uncle Jerry had. And to speak of the Carnes in a light way of talking, after all their misfortunes, is terrible. Why, I passed the old castle one night last week, with the moon to one side of it, and only me in my one-horse shay to the other, and none but a man with a first-rate conscience would have had the stomach to do so. However, I seed no ghosts that time, though I did hear some noises as made me use the whip; and the swing of the ivy was black as a hearse. A little drop more of my own rum, John: it gives me quite a chill to think of it."

"I don't take much account of what people say," Harry Shanks, who had a deep clear voice, observed, "without it is in my own family. But my own cousin Bob was coming home one night from a bit of sweethearting at Pebbleridge, when, to save the risk of rabbit-holes in the dark, for he put out his knee-cap one time, what does he do but take the path inland through the wood below Carne Castle—the opposite side to where you was, Master Cheeseman, and the same side as the moon would be, only she wasn't up that night. Well, he had some misgivings, as anybody must; still he pushed along, whistling and swinging his stick, and saying to himself that there was no such thing as cowardice in our family; till just at the corner where the big yew-tree is, that we sometimes starboard helm by when the tide is making with a nor'west wind; there Bob seed a sight as made his hair crawl. But I won't say another word about it now, and have to go home in the dark by myself arter'ards."

"Come, now, Harry!" "Oh, we can't stand that!" "We'll see you to your door, lad, if you out with it, fair and forcible."

Of these and other exhortations Harry took no notice, but folded his arms across his breast, and gazed at something which his mind presented.

"Harry Shanks, you will have the manners"—Captain Tugwell spoke impressively, not for his own sake, for he knew the tale, and had been consulted about it, but from sense of public dignity—"to finish the story which you began. To begin a yarn of your own accord, and then drop it all of a heap, is not respectful to present company. Springhaven never did allow such tricks, and will not put up with them from any young fellow. If your meaning was to drop it, you should never have begun."

Glasses and even pipes rang sharply upon the old oak table in applause of this British sentiment, and the young man, with a sheepish look, submitted to the voice of the public.

"Well, then, all of you know where the big yew-tree stands, at the break of the hill about half a mile inland, and how black it looms among the other stuff. But Bob, with his sweetheart in his head, no doubt, was that full of courage that he forgot all about the old tree, and the murder done inside it a hundred and twenty years ago, they say, until there it was, over his head a'most, with the gaps in it staring like ribs at him. 'Bout ship was the word, pretty sharp, you may be sure, when he come to his wits consarning it, and the purse of his lips, as was whistling a jig, went as dry as a bag with the bottom out. Through the grey of the night there was sounds coming to him, such as had no right to be in the air, and a sort of a shiver laid hold of his heart, like a cold hand flung over his shoulder. As hard as he could lay foot to the ground, away he went down hill, forgetting of his kneecap, for such was the condition of his mind and body.

"You must understand, mates, that he hadn't seen nothing to skeer him, but only heard sounds, which come into his ears to make his hair rise; and his mind might have put into them more than there was, for the want of intarpreting. Perhaps this come across him, as soon as he felt at a better distance with his wind short; anyhow, he brought up again' a piece of rock-stuff in a hollow of the ground, and begun to look skeerily backward. For a bit of a while there was nothing to distemper him, only the dark of the hill and the trees, and the grey light a-coming from the sea in front. But just as he were beginning for to call himself a fool, and to pick himself onto his legs for trudging home, he seed a thing as skeered him worse than ever, and fetched him flat upon his lower end.

"From the black of the yew-tree there burst a big light, brighter than a lighthouse or a blue thunder-bolt, and flying with a long streak down the hollow, just as if all the world was a-blazing. Three times it come, with three different colours, first blue, and then white, and then red as new blood; and poor Bob was in a condition of mind must be seen before saying more of it. If he had been brought up to follow the sea, instead of the shoemaking, maybe his wits would have been more about him, and the narves of his symptom more ship-shape. But it never was borne into his mind whatever, to keep a lookout upon the offing, nor even to lie snug in the ferns and watch the yew-tree. All he was up for was to make all sail, the moment his sticks would carry it; and he feared to go nigh his sweetheart any more, till she took up with another fellow."

"And sarve him quite right," was the judgment of the room, in high fettle with hot rum and water; "to be skeered of his life by a smuggler's signal! Eh, Cappen Zebedee, you know that were it?"

But the captain of Springhaven shook his head.

CHAPTER XIII

WHENCE, AND WHEREFORE?

At the rectory, too, ere the end of that week, there was no little shaking of heads almost as wise as Zebedee Tugwell's. Mrs. Twemlow, though nearly sixty years of age, and acquainted with many a sorrow, was as lively and busy and notable as ever, and even more determined to be the mistress of the house. For by this time her daughter Eliza, beginning to be twenty-five years old—a job which takes some years in finishing—began at the same time to approve her birth by a vigorous aim at the mastery. For, as everybody said, Miss Eliza was a Carne in blood and breed and fibre. There was little of the Twemlow stock about her—for the Twemlows were mild and humorous—but plenty of the strength and dash and wildness and contemptuous spirit of the ancient Carnes.

Carne a carne, as Mr. Twemlow said, when his wife was inclined to be masterful—a derivation confirmed by the family motto, "Carne non caret carne." In the case, however, of Mrs. Twemlow, age, affliction, experience, affection, and perhaps above all her good husband's larger benevolence and placidity, had wrought a great change for the better, and made a nice old lady of her. She was tall and straight and slender still; and knew how to make the most, by grave attire and graceful attitude, of the bodily excellence entailed for ages on the lineage of Carne. Of moral goodness there had not been an equally strict settlement, at least in male heredity. So that Mrs. Twemlow's thoughts about her kith and kindred were rather sad than proud, unless some ignorance was shown about them.

"Poor as I am," said Mr. Twemlow, now consulting with her, "and poor as every beneficed clergyman must be, if this war returns, I would rather have lost a hundred pounds than have heard what you tell me, Maria."

"My dear, I cannot quite see that," his wife made thoughtful answer; "if he only had money to keep up the place, and clear off those nasty incumbrances, I should rejoice at his coming back to live where we have been for centuries."

"My dear, you are too poetical, though the feeling is a fine one. Within the old walls there can scarcely be a room that has a sound floor to it. And as for the roof, when that thunder-storm was, and I took shelter with my pony— well, you know the state I came home in, and all my best clothes on for the Visitation. Luckily there seems to be no rheumatism in your family, Maria; and perhaps he is too young as yet to pay out for it till he gets older. But if he comes for business, and to see to the relics of his property, surely he might have a bedroom here, and come and go at his liking. After all his foreign fanglements, a course of quiet English life and the tone of English principles might be of the greatest use to him. He would never wish to see the Continent again."

"It is not to be thought of," said Mrs. Twemlow. "I would not have him to live in this house for fifty thousand pounds a year. You are a great deal wiser than I am, Joshua; but of his nature you know nothing, whereas I know it from his childhood. And Eliza is so strong-willed and stubborn—you dislike, of course, to hear me say it, but it is the fact—it is, my dear. And I would rather stand by our daughter's grave than see her fall in love with Caryl Carne. You know what a handsome young man he must be now, and full of French style and frippery. I am sure it is most kind of you to desire to help my poor family; but you would rue the day, my dear, that brought him beneath our quiet roof. I have lost my only son, as it seems, by the will of the Lord, who afflicts us. But I will not lose my only daughter, by any such folly of my own."

Tears rolled down Mrs. Twemlow's cheeks as she spoke of her mysterious affliction; and her husband, who knew that she was not weak-minded, consoled her by sharing her sorrow.

"It shall be exactly as you like," he said, after a quiet interval. "You say that no answer is needed; and there is no address to send one to. We shall hear of it, of course, when he takes possession, if, indeed, he is allowed to do so."

"Who is to prevent him from coming, if he chooses, to live in the home of his ancestors? The estates are all mortgaged, and the park is gone, turned into a pound for Scotch cattle-breeding. But the poor old castle belongs to us still, because no one would take the expense of it."

"And because of the stories concerning it, Maria. Your nephew Caryl is a brave young fellow if he means to live there all alone, and I fear he can afford himself no company. You understand him so much better: what do you suppose his motive is?"

"I make no pretence to understand him, dear, any more than his poor father could. My dear brother was of headstrong order, and it did him no good to contradict him, and indeed it was dangerous to do so; but his nature was as simple as a child's almost, to any one accustomed to him. If he had not married that grand French lady, who revelled in every extravagance, though she knew how we all were impoverished, he might have been living and in high position now, though a good many years my senior. And the worst of it was that he did it at a time when he ought to have known so much better.

However, he paid for it bitterly enough, and his only child was set against him."

"A very sad case altogether," said the rector. "I remember, as if it were yesterday, how angry poor Montagu was with me. You remember what words he used, and his threat of attacking me with his horsewhip. But he begged my pardon, most humbly, as soon as he saw how thoroughly right I was. You are like him in some things, as I often notice, but not quite so generous in confessing you were wrong."

"Because I don't do it as he did, Joshua. You would never understand me if I did. But of course for a man you can make allowance. My rule is to do it both for men and women, quite as fairly as if one was the other."

"Certainly, Maria—certainly. And therefore you can do it, and have always done it, even for poor Josephine. No doubt there is much to be pleaded, by a candid and gentle mind, on her behalf."

"What! that dreadful creature who ruined my poor brother, and called herself the Countess de Lune, or some such nonsense! No, Joshua, no! I have not so entirely lost all English principle as to quite do that. Instead of being largeness, that would be mere looseness."

"There are many things, however, that we never understood, and perhaps never shall in this world," Mr. Twemlow continued, as if talking to himself, for reason on that subject would be misaddressed to her; "and nothing is more natural than that young Caryl should side with his mother, who so petted him, against his poor father, who was violent and harsh, especially when he had to pay such bills. But perhaps our good nephew has amassed some cash, though there seems to be but little on the Continent, after all this devastation. Is there anything, Maria, in his letter to enable us to hope that he is coming home with money?"

"Not a word, I am afraid," Mrs. Twemlow answered, sadly. "But take it, my dear, and read it to me slowly. You make things so plain, because of practice every Sunday. Oh, Joshua, I never can be sure which you are greatest in—the Lessons or the Sermon. But before you begin I will shoot the bolt a little, as if it had caught by accident. Eliza does rush in upon us sometimes in the most unbecoming, unladylike way. And I never can get you to reprove her."

"It would be as much as my place is worth, as the maids say when imagined to have stolen sugar. And I must not read this letter so loud as the Lessons, unless you wish Lizzie to hear every word, for she has all her mother's quick senses. There is not much of it, and the scrawl seems hasty. We might have had more for three and fourpence. But I am not the one to grumble about bad measure—as the boy said about old Busby. Now, Maria, listen, but say nothing; if feminine capacity may compass it. Why, bless my heart, every word of it is French!" The rector threw down his spectacles, and gazed at his wife reproachfully. But she smiled with superior innocence.

"What else could you expect, after all his years abroad? I cannot make out the whole of it, for certain. But surely it is not beyond the compass of masculine capacity."

"Yes, it is, Maria; and you know it well enough. No honest Englishman can endure a word of French. Latin, or Greek, or even Hebrew—though I took to that rather late in life. But French is only fit for women, and very few of them can manage it. Let us hear what this Frenchman says."

"He is not a Frenchman, Joshua. He is an Englishman, and probably a very fine one. I won't be sure about all of his letter, because it is so long since I was at school; and French books are generally unfit to read. But the general meaning is something like this:

'MY BELOVED AND HIGHLY VALUED AUNT,—Since I heard from you there are many years now, but I hope you have held me in memory. I have the intention of returning to the country of England, even in this bad time of winter, when the climate is most funereal. I shall do my best to call back, if possible, the scattered ruins of the property, and to institute again the name which my father made displeasing. In this good work you will, I have faith, afford me your best assistance, and the influence of your high connection in the neighbourhood. Accept, dear aunt, the assurance of my highest consideration, of the most sincere and the most devoted, and allow me the honour of writing myself your most loving and respectful nephew,

'CARYL CARNE.'

Now, Joshua, what do you think of that?"

"Fine words and no substance; like all French stuff. And he never even mentions me, who gave him a top, when he should have had the whip. I will not pretend to understand him, for he always was beyond me. Dark and excitable, moody and capricious, haughty and sarcastic, and devoid of love for animals. You remember his pony, and what he did to it, and the little dog that crawled upon her stomach towards him. For your sake I would have put up with him, my dear, and striven to improve his nature, which is sure to be much worse at six-and-twenty, after so many years abroad. But I confess it is a great relief to me that you wisely prefer not to have him in this house, any more at least than we can help it. But who comes here? What a hurry we are in! Lizzie, my darling, be patient."

"Here's this plague of a door barred and bolted again! Am I not to have an atom of breakfast, because I just happened to oversleep myself? The mornings get darker and darker; it is almost impossible to see to dress oneself."

"There is plenty of tinder in the house, Eliza, and plenty of good tallow candles," Mrs. Twemlow replied, having put away the letter, while her husband let the complainant in. "For the third time this week we have had prayers without you, and the example is shocking for the servants. We shall have to establish the rule you suggest—too late to pray for food, too late to get it. But I have kept your help of bacon hot, quite hot, by the fire. And the teapot is under the cozy."

"Thank you, dear mother," the young lady answered, careless of words, if deeds were in her favour, and too clever to argue the question. "I suppose there is no kind of news this morning to reward one for getting up so early."

"Nothing whatever for you, Miss Lizzie," said her father, as soon as he had kissed her. "But the paper is full of the prospects of war, and the extent of the preparations. If we are driven to fight again, we shall do it in earnest, and not spare ourselves."

"Nor our enemies either, I do hope with all my heart. How long are we to be afraid of them? We have always invaded the French till now. And for them to talk of invading us! There is not a bit of spirit left in this island, except in the heart of Lord Nelson."

"What a hot little patriot this child is!" said the father, with a quiet smile at her. "What would she say to an Englishman, who was more French than English, and would only write French letters? And yet it might be possible to find such people."

"If such a wretch existed," cried Miss Twemlow, "I should like to crunch him as I crunch this toast. For a Frenchman I can make all fair allowance, because he cannot help his birth. But for an Englishman to turn Frenchman —"

"However reluctant we may be to allow it," the candid rector argued, "they are the foremost nation in the world, just now, for energy, valour, decision, discipline, and I fear I must add patriotism. The most wonderful man who has appeared in the world for centuries is their leader, and by land his success has been almost unbroken. If we must have war again, as I fear we must, and very speedily, our chief hope must be that the Lord will support His cause against the scoffer and the infidel, the libertine and the assassin."

"You see how beautifully your father puts it, Eliza; but he never abuses people. That is a habit in which, I am sorry to say, you indulge too freely. You show no good feeling to anybody who differs from you in opinion, and you talk as if Frenchmen had no religion, no principles, and no humanity. And what do you know about them, pray? Have you ever spoken to a Frenchman? Have you ever even seen one? Would you know one if you even set eyes upon him?"

"Well, I am not at all sure that I should," the young lady replied, being thoroughly truthful; "and I have no wish for the opportunity. But I have seen a French woman, mother; and that is quite enough for me. If they are so, what must the men be?"

"There is a name for this process of feminine reasoning, this cumulative and syncopetic process of the mind, entirely feminine (but regarded by itself as rational), a name which I used to know well in the days when I had the ten Fallacies at my fingers' ends, more tenaciously perhaps than the Decalogue. Strange to say, the name is gone from my memory; but—but—"

"But then you had better go after it, my dear," his wife suggested with authority. "If your only impulse when you hear reason is to search after hard names for it, you are safer outside of its sphere altogether."

"I am struck with the truth of that remark," observed the rector; "and the more so because I descry a male member of our race approaching, with a hat —at once the emblem and the crown of sound reason. Away with all fallacies; it is Church-warden Cheeseman!"

CHAPTER XIV

A HORRIBLE SUGGESTION

"Can you guess what has brought me down here in this hurry?" Lord Nelson asked Admiral Darling, having jumped like a boy from his yellow post-chaise, and shaken his old friend's broad right hand with his slender but strenuous left one, even as a big bell is swung by a thin rope. "I have no time to spare—not a day, not an hour; but I made up my mind to see you before I start. I cannot expect to come home alive, and, except for one reason, I should not wish it."

"Nonsense!" said the Admiral, who was sauntering near his upper gate, and enjoying the world this fine spring morning; "you are always in such a confounded hurry! When you come to my time of life, you will know better. What is it this time? The Channel fleet again?"

"No, no; Billy Blue keeps that, thank God! I hate looking after a school of herring-boats. The Mediterranean for me, my friend. I received the order yesterday, and shall be at sea by the twentieth."

"I am very glad to hear it, for your sake. If ever there was a restless fellow —in the good old times we were not like that. Come up to the house and talk about it; at least they must take the horses out. They are not like you; they can't work forever."

"And they don't get knocked about like me; though one of them has lost his starboard eye, and he sails and steers all the better for it. Let them go up to the stable, Darling, while you come down to the beach with me. I want to show you something."

"What crotchet is in his too active brain now?" the elder and stronger man asked himself, as he found himself hooked by the right arm, and led down a track through the trees scarcely known to himself, and quite out of sight from the village. "Why, this is not the way to the beach! However, it is never any good to oppose him. He gets his own way so because of his fame. Or perhaps that's the way he got his fame. But to show me about over my own land! But let him go on, let him go on."

"You are wondering, I dare say, what I am about," cried Nelson, stopping suddenly, and fixing his sound eye—which was wonderfully keen, though he was always in a fright about it—upon the large and peaceful blinkers of his ancient commander; "but now I shall be able to convince you, though I am not a land-surveyor, nor even a general of land-forces. If God Almighty prolongs my life—which is not very likely—it will be that I may meet that scoundrel, Napoleon Bonaparte, on dry land. I hear that he is eager to encounter me on the waves, himself commanding a line-of-battle ship. I should send him to the devil in a quarter of an hour. And ashore I could astonish him, I think, a little, if I had a good army to back me up. Remember what I did at Bastia, in the land that produced this monster, and where I was called the Brigadier; and again, upon the coast of Italy, I showed that I understood all their dry-ground business. Tush! I can beat him, ashore and afloat; and I shall, if I live long enough. But this time the villain is in earnest, I believe, with his trumpery invasion; and as soon as he hears that I am gone, he will make sure of having his own way. We know, of course, there are fifty men as good as myself to stop him, including you, my dear Darling; but everything goes by reputation—the noise of the people—praise-puff. That's all I get; while the luckier fellows, like Cathcart, get the prize-money. But I don't want to grumble. Now what do you see?"

"Well, I see you, for one thing," the Admiral answered, at his leisure, being quite inured to his friend's quick fire, "and wearing a coat that would be a disgrace to any other man in the navy. And further on I see some land that I never shall get my rent for; and beyond that nothing but the sea, with a few fishing-craft inshore, and in the offing a sail, an outward-bound East Indiaman—some fool who wouldn't wait for convoy, with war as good as proclaimed again."

"Nothing but the sea, indeed? The sweep of the land, and the shelter of the bay, the shoaling of the shore without a rock to break it, the headland that shuts out both wind and waves; and outside the headland, off Pebbleridge, deep water for a fleet of line-of-battle ships to anchor and command the land approaches—moreover, a stream of the purest water from deep and never-failing springs—Darling, the place of all places in England for the French to land is opposite to your front door."

"I am truly obliged to you for predicting, and to them for doing it, if ever they attempt such impudence. If they find out that you are away, they can also find out that I am here, as commander of the sea defences, from Dungeness to Selsey-Bill."

"That will make it all the more delightful to land at your front door, my friend; and all the easier to do it. My own plan is to strike with all force at the head-quarters of the enemy, because the most likely to be unprepared. About a year ago, when I was down here, a little before my dear father's death, without your commission I took command of your fishing-craft coming home for their Sunday, and showed them how to take the beach, partly to confirm my own suspicions. There is no other landing on all the south coast, this side of Hayling Island, fit to be compared with it for the use of flat-bottomed craft, such as most of Boney's are. And remember the set of the tide, which makes the fortunes of your fishermen. To be sure, he knows nothing of that himself; but he has sharp rogues about him. If they once made good their landing here, it would be difficult to dislodge them. It must all be done from the land side then, for even a 42-gun frigate could scarcely come near enough to pepper them. They love shoal water, the skulks—and that has enabled them to baffle me so often. Not that they would conquer the country—all brag—but still it would be a nasty predicament, and scare the poor cockneys like the very devil."

"But remember the distance from Boulogne, Hurry. If they cannot cross twenty-five miles of channel in the teeth of our ships, what chance would they have when the distance is nearer eighty?"

"A much better chance, if they knew how to do it. All our cruisers would be to the eastward. One afternoon perhaps, when a haze is on, they make a feint with light craft toward the Scheldt—every British ship crowds sail after them. Then, at dusk, the main body of the expedition slips with the first of the ebb to the westward; they meet the flood tide in mid-channel, and using their long sweeps are in Springhaven, or at any rate the lightest of them, by the top of that tide, just when you are shaving. You laugh at such a thought of mine. I tell you, my dear friend, that with skill and good luck it is easy; and do it they should, if they were under my command."

If anybody else had even talked of such a plan as within the bounds of likelihood, Admiral Darling would have been almost enraged. But now he looked doubtfully, first at the sea (as if it might be thick with prames already), and then at the land—which was his own—as if the rent might go into a Frenchman's pocket, and then at his old and admired friend, who had ruined his sleep for the summer.

"Happily they are not under your command, and they have no man to compare with you;" he spoke rather nervously; while Nelson smiled, for he loved the praise which he had so well earned; "and if it were possible for you to talk nonsense, I should say that you had done it now. But two things surely you have overlooked. In the first place, the French can have no idea of the special opportunities this place affords. And again, if they had, they could do nothing, without a pilot well acquainted with the spot. Though the landing is so easy, there are shoals outside, very intricate and dangerous, and known to none except the natives of the place, who are jealous to the last degree about their knowledge."

"That is true enough; and even I should want a pilot here, though I know every spit of sand eastward. But away fly both your difficulties if there should happen to be a local traitor."

"A traitor at Springhaven! Such a thing is quite impossible. You would laugh at yourself, if you only knew the character of our people. There never has been, and there never will be, a Springhaven man capable of treachery."

"That is good news, ay, and strange news too," the visitor answered, with his left hand on his sword, for he was now in full though rather shabby uniform. "There are not many traitors in England, I believe; but they are as likely to be found in one place as another, according to my experience. Well, well, I am very glad you have no such scoundrels here. I won't say a single word against your people, who are as fine a lot as any in the south of England, and as obstinate as any I could wish to see. Of an obstinate man I can always make good; with a limp one I can do nothing. But bear in mind every word you have heard me say, because I came down on purpose about it; and I generally penetrate the devices of the enemy, though they lead me on a wild-goose-chase sometimes, but only when our own folk back them up, either by lies or stupidity. Now look once more, for you are slower as well as a great deal wiser than I am. You see how this land-locked bight of Springhaven seems made by the Almighty for flat-bottomed craft, if once they can find their way into it; while the trend of the coast towards Pebbleridge is equally suited for the covering fleet, unless a gale from southwest comes on, in which case they must run for it. And you see that the landed force, by crowning the hill above your house and across the valley, might defy our noble Volunteers, and all that could be brought against them, till a hundred thousand cutthroats were established here. And Boney would make his head-quarters at the Hall, with a French cook in your kitchen, and a German butler in your cellar, and my pretty godchild to wait upon him, for the rogue loves pretty maidens."

"That will do. That is quite enough. No wonder you have written poems, Nelson, as you told us the last time you were here. If my son had only got your imagination—but perhaps you know something more than you have told me. Perhaps you have been told—"

"Never mind about that," the great sea-captain answered, turning away as if on springs; "it is high time for me to be off again, and my chaise has springs on her cables."

"Not she. I have ordered her to be docked. Dine with us you shall this day, if we have to dine two hours earlier, and though Mother Cloam rage furiously. How much longer do you suppose you can carry on at this pace? Look at me. I have double your bodily substance; but if I went on as you do—you remember the twenty-four-pounder old Hotcoppers put into the launch, and fired it, in spite of all I could say to him? Well, you are just the same. You have not got the scantling for the metal you carry and are always working. You will either blow up, or else scuttle yourself. Look here, how your seams are opening!" Here Admiral Darling thrust his thumb through the ravelled seam of his old friend's coat, which made him jump back, for he loved his old coat. "Yes, and you will go in the very same way. I wonder how any coat lasts so much as a month, with you inside it."

"This coat," said Nelson, who was most sweet-tempered with any one he loved, though hot as pepper when stirred up by strangers—"this coat is the one I wore at Copenhagen, and a sounder and kinder coat never came on a man's back. Charles Darling, you have made a bad hit this time. If I am no more worn out than this coat is, I am fit to go to sea for a number of years yet. And I hope to show it to a good many Frenchmen, and take as many ships, every time they show fight, as there are buttons on it."

"Then you will double all your captures at the Nile;" such a series of buttons had this coat, though mostly loose upon their moorings, for his guardian angel was not "domestic"; "but you may be trusted not to let them drift so. You have given me a lesson in coast-defence, and now you shall be boarded by the ladies. You possess some gifts of the tongue, my friend, as well as great gifts of hand and eye; but I will back my daughters to beat you there. Come up to the house. No turning of tail."

"I spoke very well in the House of Lords," said Nelson, in his simple way, "in reply to the speech of his Majesty, and again about the Commissioner's Bill; or at least everybody tells me so. But in the House of Ladies I hold my tongue, because there is abundance without it."

This, however, he failed to do when the matter came to the issue; for his godchild Horatia, more commonly called Dolly, happened to be in the mood for taking outrageous liberties with him. She possessed very little of that gift —most precious among women—the sense of veneration; and to her a hero was only a man heroic in acts of utility. "He shall do it," she said to Faith, when she heard that he was come again; "if I have to kiss him, he shall do it; and I don't like kissing those old men."

"Hush!" said her elder sister. "Dolly, you do say things so recklessly. One would think that you liked to kiss younger men! But I am sure that is not your meaning. I would rather kiss Lord Nelson than all the young men in the kingdom."

"Well done, Faith! All the young men in the kingdom! How recklessly you do say things! And you can't kiss him—he is MY godfather. But just see how I get round him, if you have wits enough to understand it."

So these two joined in their kind endeavour to make the visitor useful, the object being so good that doubtful means might be excused for it. In different ways and for divers reasons, each of these young ladies now had taken to like Blyth Scudamore. Faith, by power of pity first, and of grief for her own misfortunes, and of admiration for his goodness to his widowed mother—which made his best breeches shine hard at the knees; and Dolly, because of his shy adoration, and dauntless defence of her against a cow (whose calf was on the road to terminate in veal), as well as his special skill with his pocket-knife in cutting out figures that could dance, and almost sing; also his great gifts, when the tide was out, of making rare creatures run after him. What avails to explore female reason precisely?—their minds were made up that he must be a captain, if Nelson had to build the ship with his one hand for him.

"After that, there is nothing more to be said," confessed the vanquished warrior; "but the daughters of an Admiral should know that no man can be posted until he has served his time as lieutenant; and this young hero of yours has never even held the King's commission yet. But as he has seen some service, and is beyond the age of a middy, in the present rush he might get appointed as junior lieutenant, if he had any stout seconders. Your father is the man, he is always at hand, and can watch his opportunity. He knows more big-wigs than I do, and he has not given offence where I have. Get your father, my dears, to attend to it."

But the ladies were not to be so put off, for they understood the difference of character. Lord Nelson was as sure to do a thing as Admiral Darling was to drop it if it grew too heavy. Hence it came to pass that Blyth Scudamore, though failing of the Victory and Amphion—which he would have chosen, if the choice were his—received with that cheerful philosophy (which had made him so dear to the school-boys, and was largely required among them) his appointment as junior lieutenant to the 38-gun frigate Leda, attached to the Channel fleet under Cornwallis, whose business it was to deal with the French flotilla of invasion.

CHAPTER XV

ORDEAL OF AUDIT

England saw the growing danger, and prepared, with an even mind and well-girt body, to confront it. As yet stood up no other country to help or even comfort her, so cowed was all the Continent by the lash, and spur of an upstart. Alone, encumbered with the pack of Ireland, pinched with hunger and dearth of victuals, and cramped with the colic of Whiggery, she set her strong shoulder to the wheel of fortune, and so kept it till the hill was behind her. Some nations (which owe their existence to her) have forgotten these things conveniently; an Englishman hates to speak of them, through his unjust abhorrence of self-praise; and so does a Frenchman, by virtue of motives equally respectable.

But now the especial danger lay in the special strength of England. Scarcely any man along the coast, who had ever come across a Frenchman, could be led (by quotations from history or even from newspapers) to believe that there was any sense in this menace of his to come and conquer us. Even if he landed, which was not likely—for none of them could box the compass— the only thing he took would be a jolly good thrashing, and a few pills of lead for his garlic. This lofty contempt on the part of the seafaring men had been enhanced by Nelson, and throve with stoutest vigour in the enlightened breasts of Springhaven.

Yet military men thought otherwise, and so did the owners of crops and ricks, and so did the dealers in bacon and eggs and crockery, and even hardware. Mr. Cheeseman, for instance, who left nothing unsold that he could turn a penny by, was anything but easy in his mind, and dreamed such dreams as he could not impart to his wife—on account of her tendency to hysterics— but told with much power to his daughter Polly, now the recognised belle of Springhaven. This vigilant grocer and butterman, tea, coffee, tobacco, and snuffman, hosier also, and general provider for the outer as well as the inner man, had much of that enterprise in his nature which the country believes to come from London. His possession of this was ascribed by all persons of a thoughtful turn to his ownership of that well-built schooner the London Trader. Sailing as she did, when the weather was fine, nearly every other week, for London, and returning with equal frequency, to the women who had never been ten miles from home she was a mystery and a watchword. Not one of them would allow lad of hers to join this romantic galleon, and tempt the black cloud of the distance; neither did Mr. Cheeseman yearn (for reasons of his own about city prices) to navigate this good ship with natives. Moreover, it was absurd, as he said, with a keen sense of his own cheapness, to suppose that he could find the funds to buy and ply such a ship as that!

Truth is a fugitive creature, even when she deigns to be visible, or even to exist. The truth of Mr. Cheeseman's statement had existed, but was long since flown. Such was his worth that he could now afford to buy the London Trader three times over, and pay ready money every time. But when he first invested hard cash in her—against the solid tears of his prudent wife—true enough it was that he could only scrape together one quarter of the sum required. Mrs. Cheeseman, who was then in a condition of absorbing interest with Polly, made it her last request in this world—for she never expected to get over it—that Jemmy should not run in debt on a goose-chase, and fetch her poor spirit from its grave again. James Cheeseman was compelled—as the noblest man may be—to dissemble and even deny his intentions until the blessed period of caudle-cup, when, the weather being pleasant and the wind along the shore, he found himself encouraged to put up the window gently. The tide was coming in with a long seesaw, and upon it, like the baby in the cradle full of sleep, lay rocking another little stranger, or rather a very big one, to the lady's conception.

Let bygones be bygones. There were some reproaches; but the weaker vessel, Mrs. Cheeseman, at last struck flag, without sinking, as she threatened to do. And when little Polly went for her first airing, the London Trader had accomplished her first voyage, and was sailing in triumphantly with a box of "tops and bottoms" from the ancient firm in Threadneedle Street, which has saved so many infants from the power that cuts the thread. After that, everything went as it should go, including this addition to the commercial strength of Britain, which the lady was enabled soon to talk of as "our ship," and to cite when any question rose of the latest London fashion. But even now, when a score of years, save one, had made their score and gone, Mrs. Cheeseman only guessed and doubted as to the purchase of her ship. James Cheeseman knew the value of his own counsel, and so kept it; and was patted on both shoulders by the world, while he patted his own butter.

He wore an apron of the purest white, with shoulder-straps of linen tape, and upon his counter he had a desk, with a carved oak rail in front of it and returned at either end. The joy of his life was here to stand, with goodly shirt sleeves shining, his bright cheeks also shining in the sun, unless it were hot enough to hurt his goods. He was not a great man, but a good one—in the opinion of all who owed him nothing, and even in his own estimate, though he owed so much to himself. It was enough to make any one who possessed a shilling hungry to see him so clean, so ready, and ruddy among the many good things which his looks and manner, as well as his words, commended. And as soon as he began to smack his rosy lips, which nature had fitted up on purpose, over a rasher, or a cut of gammon, or a keg of best Aylesbury, or a fine red herring, no customer having a penny in his pocket might struggle hard enough to keep it there. For the half-hearted policy of fingering one's money, and asking a price theoretically, would recoil upon the constitution of the strongest man, unless he could detach from all cooperation the congenial researches of his eyes and nose. When the weather was cool and the air full of appetite, and a fine smack of salt from the sea was sparkling on the margin of the plate of expectation, there was Mr. Cheeseman, with a knife and fork, amid a presence of hungrifying goods that beat the weak efforts of imagination. Hams of the first rank and highest education, springs of pork sweeter than the purest spring of poetry, pats of butter fragrant as the most delicious flattery, chicks with breast too ample to require to be broken, and sometimes prawns from round the headland, fresh enough to saw one another's heads off, but for being boiled already.

Memory fails to record one-tenth of all the good things gathered there. And why? Because hope was the power aroused, and how seldom can memory endorse it! Even in the case of Mr. Cheeseman's wares there were people who said, after making short work with them, that short weight had enabled them to do so. And every one living in the village was surprised to find his own scales require balancing again every time he sent his little girl to Cheeseman's.

This upright tradesman was attending to his business one cold day in May, 1803, soon after Nelson sailed from Portsmouth, and he stood with his beloved pounds of farm-house butter, bladders of lard, and new-laid eggs, and squares of cream-cheese behind him, with a broad butter-spathe of white wood in his hand, a long goose-pen tucked over his left ear, and the great copper scales hanging handy. So strict was his style, though he was not above a joke, that only his own hands might serve forth an ounce of best butter to the public. And whenever this was weighed, and the beam adjusted handsomely to the satisfaction of the purchaser, down went the butter to be packed upon a shelf uninvaded by the public eye. Persons too scantily endowed with the greatest of all Christian virtues had the hardihood to say that Mr. Cheeseman here indulged in a process of high art discovered by himself. Discoursing of the weather, or the crops, or perhaps the war, and mourning the dishonesty of statesmen nowadays, by dexterous undersweep of keen steel blade, from the bottom of the round, or pat, or roll, he would have away a thin slice, and with that motion jerk it into the barrel which he kept beneath his desk.

"Is this, then, the establishment of the illustrious Mr. Cheeseman?" The time was yet early, and the gentleman who put this question was in riding dress. The worthy tradesman looked at him, and the rosy hue upon his cheeks was marbled with a paler tint.

"This is the shop of the 'umble James Cheeseman," he answered, but not with the alacrity of business. "All things good that are in season, and nothing kept unseasonable. With what can I have the honor of serving you, sir?"

"With a little talk." The stranger's manner was not unpleasantly contemptuous, but lofty, and such as the English shopman loves, and calls "aristocratic."

"To talk with a gentleman is a pleasure as well as an honour," said Cheeseman.

"But not in this public establishment." The visitor waved both hands as he spoke, in a style not then common with Englishmen—though they are learning eloquent gesticulation now. "It is fine, Mr. Cheeseman; but it is not—bah, I forget your English words."

"It is fine, sir, as you are good enough to observe"—the humble James Cheeseman was proud of his shop—"but not, as you remarked, altogether private. That can hardly be expected, where business is conducted to suit universal requirements. Polly, my dear, if your mother can spare you, come and take my place at the desk a few minutes. I have business inside with this gentleman. You may sell almost anything, except butter. If any one wants that, they must wait till I come back."

A very pretty damsel, with a cap of foreign lace both adorning and adorned by her beautiful bright hair, came shyly from a little door behind the counter, receiving with a quick blush the stranger's earnest gaze, and returning with a curtsey the courteous flourish of his looped-up riding-hat. "What a handsome gentleman!" said Polly to herself; "but there is something very sad and very wild in his appearance." Her father's conclusion was the same, and his heart misgave him as he led in this unexpected guest.

"There is no cause for apologies. This place is a very good one," the stranger replied, laying down his heavy whip on the table of a stone-floored room, to which he had been shown. "You are a man of business, and I am come upon dry business. You can conjecture—is it not so?—who I am by this time, although I am told that I do not bear any strong resemblance to my father."

He took off his hat as he spoke, shook back his long black hair, and fixed his jet-black eyes upon Cheeseman. That upright dealer had not recovered his usual self-possession yet, but managed to look up—for he was shorter by a head than his visitor—with a doubtful and enquiring smile.

"I am Caryl Carne, of Carne Castle, as you are pleased to call it. I have not been in England these many years; from the death of my father I have been afar; and now, for causes of my own, I am returned, with hope of collecting the fragments of the property of my ancestors. It appears to have been their custom to scatter, but not gather up again. My intention is to make a sheaf of the relics spread by squanderers, and snapped up by scoundrels."

"To be sure, to be sure," cried the general dealer; "this is vastly to your credit, sir, and I wish you all success, sir, and so will all who have so long respected your ancient and honourable family, sir. Take a chair, sir—please to take a chair."

"I find very little to my credit," Mr. Carne said, dryly, as he took the offered chair, but kept his eyes still upon Cheeseman's; "but among that little is a bond from you, given nearly twenty years agone, and of which you will retain, no doubt, a vivid recollection."

"A bond, sir—a bond!" exclaimed the other, with his bright eyes twinkling, as in some business enterprise. "I never signed a bond in all my life, sir. Why, a bond requires sureties, and nobody ever went surety for me."

"Bond may not be the proper legal term. It is possible. I know nothing of the English law. But a document it is, under hand and seal, and your signature is witnessed, Mr. Cheeseman."

"Ah well! Let me consider. I begin to remember something. But my memory is not as it used to be, and twenty years makes a great hole in it. Will you kindly allow me to see this paper, if you have it with you, sir?"

"It is not a paper; it is written upon parchment, and I have not brought it with me. But I have written down the intention of it, and it is as follows:

"'This indenture made between James Cheeseman (with a long description), of the one part, and Montagu Carne (treated likewise), of the other part, after a long account of some arrangement made between them, witnesseth that in consideration of the sum of 300 pounds well and truly paid by the said Montagu Carne to Cheeseman, he, the said Cheeseman, doth assign, transfer, set over, and so on, to the said Carne, etc., one equal undivided moiety and one half part of the other moiety of and in a certain vessel, ship, trading-craft, and so forth, known or thenceforth to be known as the London Trader, of Springhaven, in the county of Sussex, by way of security for the interest at the rate of five per cent. per annum, payable half-yearly, as well as for the principal sum of 300 pounds, so advanced as aforesaid.'"

"If it should prove, sir, that money is owing," Mr. Cheeseman said, with that exalted candour which made a weak customer condemn his own eyes and nose, "no effort on my part shall be wanting, bad as the times are, to procure it and discharge it. In every commercial transaction I have found, and my experience is now considerable, that confidence, as between man and man, is the only true footing to go upon. And how can true confidence exist, unless —"

"Unless a man shows some honesty. And a man who keeps books such as these," pursued the visitor, suggesting a small kick to a pile of ledgers, "can hardly help knowing whether he owes a large sum or whether he has paid it. But that is not the only question now. In continuation of that document I find a condition, a clause provisional, that it shall be at the option of the aforesaid Montagu Carne, and his representatives, either to receive the interest at the rate before mentioned and thereby secured, or, if he or they should so prefer, to take for their own benefit absolutely three-fourths of the net profits, proceeds, or other increment realised by the trading ventures, or other employment from time to time, of the said London Trader. Also there is a covenant for the insurance of the said vessel, and a power of sale, and some other provisions about access to trading books, etc., with which you have, no doubt, a good acquaintance, Mr. Cheeseman."

That enterprising merchant, importer of commodities, and wholesale and retail dealer was fond of assuring his numerous friends that "nothing ever came amiss to him." But some of them now would have doubted about this if they had watched his face as carefully as Caryl Carne was watching it. Mr. Cheeseman could look a hundred people in the face, and with great vigour too, when a small account was running. But the sad, contemptuous, and piercing gaze—as if he were hardly worth penetrating—and the twirl of the black tuft above the lip, and the firm conviction on the broad white forehead that it was confronting a rogue too common and shallow to be worth frowning at—all these, and the facts that were under them, came amiss to the true James Cheeseman.

"I scarcely see how to take this," he said, being clever enough to suppose that a dash of candour might sweeten the embroilment. "I will not deny that I was under obligation to your highly respected father, who was greatly beloved for his good-will to his neighbours. 'Cheeseman,' he used to say, 'I will stand by you. You are the only man of enterprise in these here parts. Whatever you do is for the good of Springhaven, which belonged to my family for centuries before those new-fangled Darlings came. And, Cheeseman, you may trust to the honour of the Carnes not to grind down a poor man who has his way to make.' Them were his words, sir; how well I recollect them!"

"Too well almost," replied the young man, coldly, "considering how scanty was your memory just now. But it may save time, and painful efforts of your memory, if I tell you at once that I am not concerned in any way with the sentiments of my father. I owe him very little, as you must be well aware; and the matter betwixt you and me is strictly one of business. The position in which I am left is such that I must press every legal claim to the extremest. And having the option under this good document, I have determined to insist upon three-quarters of the clear proceeds of this trading-ship, from the date of the purchase until the present day, as well as the capital sum invested on this security."

"Very well, sir, if you do, there is only one course left me—to go into the Court of Bankruptcy, see all my little stock in trade sold up, and start in life again at the age of fifty-seven, with a curse upon all old families."

"Your curse, my good friend, will not add sixpence to your credit. And the heat you exhibit is not well adapted for calculations commercial. There is one other course which I am able to propose, though I will not give a promise yet to do so—a course which would relieve me from taking possession of this noble ship which has made your fortune, and perhaps from enforcing the strict examination of your trading-books, to which I am entitled. But before I propose any such concession, which will be a grand abdication of rights, one or two things become necessary. For example, I must have some acquaintance with your character, some certitude that you can keep your own counsel, and not divulge everything that arrives within your knowledge; also that you have some courage, some freedom of mind from small insular sentiments, some desire to promote the true interests of mankind, and the destruction of national prejudices."

"Certainly, sir; all of those I can approve of. They are very glorious things," cried Cheeseman—a man of fine liberal vein, whenever two half-crowns were as good as a crown. "We are cramped and trampled and down-trodden by the airs big people give themselves, and the longing of such of us as thinks is to speak our minds about it. Upon that point of freedom, sir, I can heartily go with you, and every stick upon my premises is well insured."

"Including, I hope, the London Trader, according to your covenant. And that reminds me of another question—is it well-found, well-manned, and a good rapid ship to make the voyage? No falsehood, if you please, about this matter."

"She is the fastest sailer on the English coast, built at Dunkirk, and as sound as a bell. She could show her taffrail, in light weather, to any British cruiser in the Channel. She could run a fine cargo of French cognac and foreign laces any day."

"It is not my desire," Caryl Carne replied, "to cheat the British Revenue. For that purpose exist already plenty of British tradesmen. For the present I impress upon you one thing only, that you shall observe silence, a sacred silence, regarding this conversation. For your own sake you will be inclined to do so, and that is the only sake a man pays much attention to. But how much for your own sake you are obliged to keep your counsel, you will very soon find out if you betray it."

CHAPTER XVI

FOX-HILL

When it was known in this fine old village that young Squire Carne from foreign parts was come back to live in the ancient castle, there was much larger outlay (both of words and thoughts) about that than about any French invasion. "Let them land if they can," said the able-bodied men, in discussion of the latter question; "they won't find it so easy to get away again as they seem to put into their reckoning. But the plague of it all is the damage to the fishing."

Not that the squadron of Captain Tugwell was shorn as yet of its number, though all the young men were under notice to hold themselves ready as "Sea-Fencibles." The injury to their trade lay rather in the difficulty of getting to their fishing-grounds, and in the disturbance of these by cruisers, with little respect for their nets and lines. Again, as the tidings of French preparation waxed more and more outrageous, Zebedee had as much as he could do to keep all his young hands loyal. All their solid interest lay (as he told them every morning) in sticking to the Springhaven flag—a pair of soles couchant, herring salient, and mackerel regardant, all upon a bright sea-green—rather than in hankering after roll of drum and Union-Jack. What could come of these but hardship, want of victuals, wounds, and death; or else to stump about on one leg, and hold out a hat for a penny with one arm? They felt that it was true; they had seen enough of that; it had happened in all their own families.

Yet such is the love of the native land and the yearning to stand in front of it, and such is the hate of being triumphed over by fellows who kiss one another and weep, and such is the tingling of the knuckles for a blow when the body has been kicked in sore places, that the heart will at last get the better of the head—or at least it used to be so in England. Wherefore Charley Bowles was in arms already against his country's enemies; and Harry Shanks waited for little except a clear proclamation of prize-money; and even young Daniel was tearing at his kedge like a lively craft riding in a brisk sea-way. He had seen Lord Nelson, and had spoken to Lord Nelson, and that great man would have patted him on the head—so patriotic were his sentiments—if the great man had been a little taller.

But the one thing that kept Dan Tugwell firm to his moorings at Springhaven was the deep hold of his steadfast heart in a love which it knew to be hopeless. To die for his country might become a stern duty, about which he would rather not be hurried; but to die for Miss Dolly would be a wild delight; and how could he do it unless he were at hand? And now there were so many young officers again, landing in boats, coming in post-chaises, or charging down the road on horseback, that Daniel, while touching up the finish of his boat with paint and varnish and Venetian Red, was not so happy as an artist should be who knows how to place the whole. Sometimes, with the paint stirred up and creaming, and the ooze of the brush trimmed warily, through the rushes and ragwort and sea-willow his keen, unconquerable eyes would spy the only figure that quelled them, faraway, shown against the shining water, or shadowed upon the flat mirror of the sand. But, alas! there was always another figure near it, bigger, bulkier, framed with ugly angles, jerking about with the elbow sticking out, instead of gliding gracefully. Likely enough the lovely form, brought nearer to the eyes and heart by love, would flit about beautifully for two sweet moments, filling with rapture all the flashes of the sea and calm of the evening sky beyond; and then the third moment would be hideous. For the figure of the ungainly foe would stride across the delicious vision, huge against the waves like Cyclops, and like him gesticulant, but unhappily not so single-eyed that the slippery fair might despise him. Then away would fly all sense of art and joy in the touch of perfection, and a very nasty feeling would ensue, as if nothing were worth living for, and nobody could be believed in.

That plaguesome Polypheme was Captain Stubbard, begirt with a wife, and endowed with a family almost in excess of benediction, and dancing attendance upon Miss Dolly, too stoutly for his own comfort, in the hope of procuring for his own Penates something to eat and to sit upon. Some evil genius had whispered, or rather trumpeted, into his ear—for he had but one left, and that worked very seldom, through alarm about the bullet which had carried off its fellow—that if he desired, as he did with heart and stomach, to get a clear widening by 200 pounds of his strait ways and restricted means, through Admiral Darling it might be done, and Miss Dolly was the proper one to make him do it. For the Inspectorship of Sea-Fencibles from Selsea-Bill to Dungeness was worth all that money in hard cash yearly; and the late Inspector having quitted this life—through pork boiled in a copper kettle—the situation was naturally vacant; and the Admiral being the man for whose check the Inspectorship was appointed, it is needless to say that (in the spirit of fair play) the appointment was vested in the Admiral.

The opinion of all who knew him was that Captain Stubbard was fairly entitled to look for something higher. And he shared that opinion, taking loftier aim than figures could be made to square with, till the latter prevailed, as they generally do, because they can work without victuals. For although the brave Captain had lost three ribs—or at any rate more than he could spare of them (not being a pig)—in the service of his country, he required as much as ever to put inside them; and his children, not having inherited that loss as scientifically as they should have done, were hard to bring up upon the 15 pounds yearly allowed by Great Britain for each of the gone bones. From the ear that was gone he derived no income, having rashly compounded for 25 pounds.

In the nature of things, which the names have followed, the father is the feeder; and the world is full of remarks unless he becomes a good clothier also. But everything went against this father, with nine little Stubbards running after him, and no ninepence in any of his pockets, because he was shelfed upon half-pay, on account of the depression of the times and of his ribs. But Miss Dolly Darling was resolved to see him righted, for she hated all national meanness.

"What is the use of having any influence," she asked her good father, "unless you employ it for your own friends? I should be quite ashamed to have it said of me, or thought, that I could get a good thing for any one I was fond of, and was mean enough not to do it, for fear of paltry jealousy. Mean is much too weak a word; it is downright dishonest, and what is much worse, cowardly. What is the government meant for, unless it is to do good to people?"

"Certainly, my dear child, certainly. To the people at large, that is to say, and the higher interests of the country."

"Can there be any people more at large than Captain Stubbard and his wife and children? Their elbows are coming out of their clothes, and they have scarcely got a bed to sleep upon. My income is not enough to stop to count, even when I get it paid punctually. But every farthing I receive shall go—that is to say, if it ever does come—into the lap of Mrs. Stubbard, anonymously and respectfully."

"Pay your bills, first," said the Admiral, taking the weather-gage of the discussion: "a little bird tells me that you owe a good trifle, even in Springhaven."

"Then the little bird has got a false bill," replied Dolly, who was not very easy to fluster. "Who is there to spend sixpence with in a little hole of this kind? I am not a customer for tea, coffee, tobacco, snuff, or pepper, nor even for whiting, soles, or conger. Old Cheeseman imports all the fashions, as he says; but I go by my own judgment. And trumpery as my income is, very little of it goes into his till. But I should like to know who told you such a wicked story, father?"

"Things are mentioned in confidence, and I put them together," said the

Admiral. "Don't say another word, or look as if you would be happier if you had something to cry about. Your dear mother used to do it; and it beats me always. I have long had my eye upon Captain Stubbard, and I remember well that gallant action when his three ribs flew away. We called him Adam, because of his wife coming just when his middle rib went, and his name was Adam Stubbard, sure enough. Such men, in the prime of their life, should be promoted, instead of being disabled, for a scratch like that. Why, he walks every bit as well as I do, and his watch-ribbon covers it. And nine children! Lord bless my heart! I scarcely know which way to turn, with only four!"

Within a short fortnight Captain Stubbard was appointed, with an office established at the house of Widow Shanks—though his real office naturally was at the public-house—and Royal Proclamations aroused the valour of nearly everybody who could read them. Nine little Stubbards soon were rigged too smart to know themselves, as the style is of all dandies; and even Mrs. Stubbard had a new belt made to go round her, when the weather was elastic.

"These are the things that prove the eye of an All-wise Providence over us," said the Captain to the Admiral, pointing out six pairs of short legs, galligaskined from one roll of cloth; "these are the things that make one feel the force of the words of David."

"Certainly, yes, to be sure!" replied the gallant senior officer, all at sea as to the passage suggested. "Good legs they have got, and no mistake; like the polished corners of the temple. Let them go and dip them in the sea, while you give the benefit of your opinion here. Not here, I mean, but upon Fox-hill yonder; if Mrs. Stubbard will spare you for a couple of hours, most kindly."

Of the heights that look down with a breezy air upon the snug nest of Springhaven, the fairest to see from a distance, and to tread with brisk foot, is Fox-hill. For the downs, which are channelled with the springs that form the brook, keep this for their own last spring into the air, before bathing in the vigorous composure of the sea. All the other hills fall back a little, to let Fox-hill have the first choice of aspect—or bear the first brunt, as itself would state the matter. And to anybody coming up, and ten times to a stranger, this resolute foreland offers more invitation to go home again, than to come visiting. For the bulge of the breast is steep, and ribbed with hoops coming up in denial, concrete with chalk, muricated with flint, and thornily crested with good stout furze. And the forefront of the head, when gained, is stiff with brambles, and stubbed with sloes, and mitred with a choice band of stanch sting-nettles.

"It would take a better Frenchman," said the Admiral, with that brevity which is the happy result of stoutness up steep hill, "than any of 'they flat-bottoms,' as Swipes, my gardener, calls them, to get through these prickles, Stubbard, without Sark-blewing. Such a wonderfully thin-skinned lot they are! Did I ever tell you the story of our boatswain's mate? But that takes a better sailing breeze than I've got now. You see where we are, don't you?"

"Certainly, Admiral," replied Captain Stubbard, disdaining to lay hand to his injured side, painfully as it yearned for pressure; "we have had a long pull, and we get a fine outlook over the country for leagues, and the Channel. How close at hand everything looks! I suppose we shall have rain, and we want it. I could thump that old castle among the trees into smash, and your church looks as if I could put a shot with a rifle-gun into the bell-chamber."

"And so you could. What I want to show you is that very point, and the importance of it. With a battery of long twenty-fours up here, the landing, the bay, and all the roads are at our mercy. My dear old friend Nelson drew my attention to it."

"It is plain as a pikestaff to Tom, Dick, or Harry:" Captain Stubbard was a frank, straightforward man, and much as he owed to the Admiral's aid, not a farthing would he pay in flattery. "But why should we want to command this spot? There is nothing to protect but a few common houses, and some half-score of fishing-craft, and a schooner that trades to London, and yonder old church, and—oh yes, to be sure, your own house and property, Admiral."

"Those must take their chance, like others. I hope I know better than to think of them in comparison with the good of the country. But if we fail to occupy this important post, the enemy might take us by surprise, and do so."

"Possible, but most improbable. This little place lies, by the trend of the coast, quite out of their course from Boulogne to London; and what is there here to tempt them? No rich town to sack, no great commerce to rob, no valuable shipping to lay hands on."

"No; but there's my house and my two girls; and I don't want my old roof burned, and my daughters put to wait on Boney. But to think of self-interest is below contempt, with our country going through such trials. Neither should we add any needless expense to a treasury already overburdened."

"Certainly not. It would be absolutely wicked. We have a long and costly war before us, and not a shilling should be spent except in case of clear necessity."

"I am very glad indeed to find your opinion so decided, so untainted with petty self-interest." As Admiral Darling spoke he closed a little silver telescope, with which he had been gazing through the wooded coronet of the hill. "I thought it my duty to consult you, Stubbard, before despatching this letter, which, being backed by Nelson's opinion, would probably have received attention. If a strong battery were thrown up here, as it would be in a fortnight from the receipt of this bit of foolscap, the appointment of commandant would rest with me, and I could appoint nobody but your good self, because of your well-known experience in earthworks. The appointment would have doubled your present pay, which, though better than nothing, is far below your merits. But your opinion settles the question otherwise, and I must burn my letter. Let us lose no more time. Mrs. Stubbard will call me a savage, for keeping you away so long."

"Important business," replied the Captain, "will not wait even for ladies, or, rather, they must try to wait for it, and give way to more reasonable urgency. Some time is required for considering this matter, and deciding what is most for the interest of the nation. Oblige me with your spy-glass, Admiral. There is one side on which I have neglected to look out, and that may of all be the most important. A conclusion arrived at by yourself and Nelson is not to be hastily set aside. Your knowledge of the country is so far beyond mine, though I may have had more to do with land-works. We ought to think twice, sir, if the government will pay for it, about a valuable job of this kind."

With these words Captain Stubbard began to use the telescope carefully, forming his opinion through it, and wisely shaking his head, now and then, with a longer and longer focus. Then he closed the glass, and his own lips firmly—whereby a man announces that no other should open his against them —and sternly striding the yard exact, took measurement for the battery. The hill was crowned with a ring of Scotch firs, casting a quiet shade upon the warlike haste of the Captain. If Admiral Darling smiled, it was to the landscape and the offing, for he knew that Stubbard was of rather touchy fibre, and relished no jokes unless of home production. His slow, solid face was enough to show this, and the squareness of his outline, and the forward thrust of his knees as he walked, and the larkspur impress of his lingering heels. And he seldom said much, without something to say.

"Well," cried the Admiral, growing tired of sitting so long upon a fallen trunk, "what conclusion do you feel inclined to come to? 'Tis a fine breezy place to clear the brain, and a briny air to sharpen the judgment."

"Only one tree need come down—this crooked one at the southeast corner." Captain Stubbard began to swing his arms about, like a windmill uncertain of the wind. "All gentlemen hate to have a tree cut down, all blackguards delight in the process. Admiral, we will not hurt your trees. They will add to our strength, by masking it. Six long twenty-fours of the new make, here in front, and two eighteens upon either flank, and I should like to see the whole of the Boulogne flotilla try to take yonder shore by daylight.

That is to say, of course, if I commanded, with good old salts to second me. With your common artillery officers, landlubbers, smell-the-wicks, cross-the-braces sons of guns, there had better not be anything at all put up. They can't make a fortification; and when they have made it, they can't work it. Admiral Darling, you know that, though you have not had the bad luck to deal with them as I have. I may thank one of them for being up here on the shelf."

"Of one thing you may be quite certain," replied the commander of the sea defence; "if we have any battery on this Fox-hill, it shall be constructed and manned by blue-jackets. I have a large draft of them now at discretion. Every man in Springhaven will lend a hand, if paid for it. It would take at least a twelvemonth to get it done from Woolwich. A seaman does a thing before a landsman thinks about it."

CHAPTER XVII

SEA-SIDE LODGINGS

To set a dog barking is easier than to stop him by the soundest reasoning. Even if the roof above his honest head, growing loose on its nails, is being mended, he comes out to ask about the matter, and in strong terms proclaims his opinion to the distance.

After this kind behaved the people about to be protected by this battery. They had dreamed of no danger till they saw their houses beginning to be protected, and for this—though it added to their importance—they were not truly thankful. They took it in various ways, according to their rich variety of reflection; but the way in which nobody took it was that of gratitude and humility.

"Everything upside down," they said, "everything gone clean topsy-turvy! And the deep meaning of it is to rob our fishing, under pretence of the Nationals. It may bring a good bit of money to the place, for the lining of one or two pockets, such as John Prater's and Cheeseman's; but I never did hold so much with money, when shattery ways comes along of it. No daughter of mine stirs out-of-doors after sundown, I can tell them."

Thus were the minds of the men disturbed, or at any rate those of the elder ones; while the women, on the whole, were pleased, although they pretended to be contemptuous. "I'll tell you what I think, ma'am," Mrs. Cheeseman said to Widow Shanks quite early, "if you take a farthing less than half a guinea a week for your dimity-parlour, with the window up the hill, and the little door under the big sweet-briar, I shall think that you are not as you used to be."

"And right you would be, ma'am, and too right there;" Mrs. Shanks sighed deeply as she thought of it. "There is nobody but you can understand it, and I don't mind saying it on that account to you. Whenever I have wanted for a little bit of money, as the nature of lone widows generally does, it has always been out of your power, Mrs. Cheeseman, to oblige me, and quite right of you. But I have a good son, thank the Lord, by the name of Harry, to provide for me; and a guinea a week is the agreement now for the dimity-parlour, and the three leg'd bed, and cold dinner to be paid for extra, such as I might send for to your good shop, with the money ready in the hand of my little girl, and jug below her apron for refreshment from the Darling."

"Well, I never! My dear soul, you have taken all my breath away. Why, it must be the captain of all the gunners. How gunpowder do pay, to be sure!"

"Lor, ma'am, why, don't you know," replied Mrs. Shanks, with some contempt, "that the man with three ribs is the captain of the gunners—the man in my back sitting-room? No dimity-parlour for him with his family, not for a guinea and a half a week. But if I was to tell you who the gentleman is, and one of the highest all round these parts, truthful as you know me, Mrs. Cheeseman, you would say to yourself, what a liar she is!"

"Mrs. Shanks, I never use coarse expressions, even to myself in private. And perhaps I could tell you a thing or two would astonish you more than me, ma'am. Suppose I should tell you, to begin with, who your guinea lodger is?"

"That you could never do, Mrs. Cheeseman, with all your time a-counting changes. He is not of the rank for a twopenny rasher, or a wedge of cheese packed in old petticoat."

These two ladies now looked at one another. They had not had a quarrel for almost three months, and a large arrear of little pricks on either side was pending. Sooner or later it would have to be fought out (like a feud between two nations), with a houseful of loss and woe to either side, but a thimbleful of pride and glory. Yet so much wiser were these women than the most sagacious nations that they put off to a cheaper time their grudge against each other.

"His rank may be royal," said the wife of Mr. Cheeseman, "though a going-downhill kind of royalty, perhaps, and yet he might be glad, Mrs. Shanks, to come where the butter has the milk spots, and none is in the cheese, ma'am."

"If such should be his wish, ma'am, for supper or for breakfast, or even for dinner on a Sunday when the rain comes through the Castle, you may trust me to know where to send him, but not to guarantee him at all of his money."

"They high ones is very apt to slip in that," Mrs. Cheeseman answered, thoughtfully; "they seem to be less particular in paying for a thing than they was to have it good. But a burnt child dreads the fire, as they say; and a young man with a castleful of owls and rats, by reason of going for these hundred years on credit, will have it brought home to him to pay ready money. But the Lord be over us! if I don't see him a-going your way already! Good-by, my dear soul—good-by, and preserve you; and if at any time short of table or bed linen, a loan from an old friend, and coming back well washed, and it sha'n't be, as the children sing, 'A friend with a loan has the pick of your bone, and he won't let you very long alone.'"

"Many thanks to you for friendly meaning, ma'am," said the widow, as she took up her basket to go home, "and glad I may be to profit by it, with the time commanding. But as yet I have had neither sleepers or feeders in my little house, but the children. Though both of them reserves the right to do it, if nature should so compel them—the three-ribbed gentleman with one ear, at five shillings a week, in the sitting-room, and the young man up over him. Their meaning is for business, and studying, and keeping of accounts, and having of a quiet place in bad weather, though feed they must, sooner or later, I depend; and then who is there but Mr. Cheeseman?"

"How grand he do look upon that black horse, quite as solid as if he was glued to it!" the lady of the shop replied, as she put away the money; "and to do that without victuals is beyond a young man's power. He looks like what they used to call a knight upon an errand, in the picture-books, when I was romantic, only for the hair that comes under his nose. Ah! his errand will be to break the hearts of the young ladies that goes down upon the sands in their blue gowns, I'm afraid, if they can only manage with the hair below his nose."

"And do them good, some of them, and be a judgment from the Lord, for the French style in their skirts is a shocking thing to see. What should we have said when you and I were young, my dear? But quick step is the word for me, for I expect my Jenny home on her day out from the Admiral, and no Harry in the house to look after her. Ah! dimity-parlours is a thing as may happen to cut both ways, Mrs. Cheeseman."

Widow Shanks had good cause to be proud of her cottage, which was the prettiest in Springhaven, and one of the most commodious. She had fought a hard fight, when her widowhood began, and the children were too young to help her, rather than give up the home of her love-time, and the cradle of her little ones. Some of her neighbours (who wanted the house) were sadly pained at her stubbornness, and even dishonesty, as they put it, when she knew that she never could pay her rent. But "never is a long time," according to the proverb; and with the forbearance of the Admiral, the kindness of his daughters, and the growth of her own children, she stood clear of all debt now, except the sweet one of gratitude.

And now she could listen to the moaning of the sea (which used to make her weep all night) with a milder sense of the cruel woe that it had drowned her husband, and a lull of sorrow that was almost hope; until the dark visions of wrecks and corpses melted into sweet dreams of her son upon the waters, finishing his supper, and getting ready for his pipe. For Harry was making his own track well in the wake of his dear father.

Now if she had gone inland to dwell, from the stroke of her great calamity —as most people told her to make haste and do—not only the sympathy of the sea, but many of the little cares, which are the ants that bury heavy grief, would have been wholly lost to her. And amongst these cares the foremost always, and the most distracting, was that of keeping her husband's cottage—

as she still would call it—tidy, comfortable, bright, and snug, as if he were coming on Saturday.

Where the brook runs into the first hearing of the sea, to defer its own extinction it takes a lively turn inland, leaving a pleasant breadth of green between itself and its destiny. At the breath of salt the larger trees hang back, and turn their boughs up; but plenty of pretty shrubs come forth, and shade the cottage garden. Neither have the cottage walls any lack of leafy mantle, where the summer sun works his own defeat by fostering cool obstruction. For here are the tamarisk, and jasmin, and the old-fashioned corchorus flowering all the summer through, as well as the myrtle that loves the shore, with a thicket of stiff young sprigs arising, slow of growth, but hiding yearly the havoc made in its head and body by the frost of 1795, when the mark of every wave upon the sands was ice. And a vine, that seems to have been evolved from a miller, or to have prejected him, clambers with grey silver pointrels through the more glossy and darker green. And over these you behold the thatch, thick and long and parti-coloured, eaved with little windows, where a bird may nest for ever.

But it was not for this outward beauty that Widow Shanks, stuck to her house, and paid the rent at intervals. To her steadfast and well-managed mind, the number of rooms, and the separate staircase which a solvent lodger might enjoy, were the choicest grant of the household gods. The times were bad—as they always are when conscientious people think of them—and poor Mrs. Shanks was desirous of paying her rent, by the payment of somebody. Every now and then some well-fed family, hungering (after long carnage) for fish, would come from village pastures or town shambles, to gaze at the sea, and to taste its contents. For in those days fish were still in their duty, to fry well, to boil well, and to go into the mouth well, instead of being dissolute—as nowadays the best is—with dirty ice, and flabby with arrested fermentation. In the pleasant dimity-parlour then, commanding a fair view of the lively sea and the stream that sparkled into it, were noble dinners of sole, and mackerel, and smelt that smelled of cucumber, and dainty dory, and pearl-buttoned turbot, and sometimes even the crisp sand-lance, happily for himself, unhappily for whitebait, still unknown in London. Then, after long rovings ashore or afloat, these diners came back with a new light shed upon them— that of the moon outside the house, of the supper candles inside. There was sure to be a crab or lobster ready, and a dish of prawns sprigged with parsley; if the sea were beginning to get cool again, a keg of philanthropic oysters; or if these were not hospitably on their hinges yet, certainly there would be choice-bodied creatures, dried with a dash of salt upon the sunny shingle, and lacking of perfection nothing more than to be warmed through upon a toasting-fork.

By none, however, of these delights was the newly won lodger tempted. All that he wanted was peace and quiet, time to go through a great trunk full of papers and parchments, which he brought with him, and a breath of fresh air from the downs on the north, and the sea to the south, to enliven him. And in good truth he wanted to be enlivened, as Widow Shanks said to her daughter Jenny; for his eyes were gloomy, and his face was stern, and he seldom said anything good-natured. He seemed to avoid all company, and to be wrapped up wholly in his own concerns, and to take little pleasure in anything. As yet he had not used the bed at his lodgings, nor broken his fast there to her knowledge, though he rode down early every morning and put up his horse at Cheeseman's, and never rode away again until the dark had fallen. Neither had he cared to make the acquaintance of Captain Stubbarb, who occupied the room beneath his for a Royal Office—as the landlady proudly entitled it; nor had he received, to the best of her knowledge, so much as a single visitor, though such might come by his private entrance among the shrubs unnoticed. All these things stirred with deep interest and wonder the enquiring mind of the widow.

"And what do they say of him up at the Hall?" she asked her daughter Jenny, who was come to spend holiday at home. "What do they say of my new gentleman, young Squire Carne from the Castle? The Carnes and the Darlings was never great friends, as every one knows in Springhaven. Still, it do seem hard and unchristianlike to keep up them old enmities; most of all, when the one side is down in the world, with the owls and the bats and the coneys."

"No, mother, no. They are not a bit like that," replied Jenny—a maid of good loyalty; "it is only that he has not called upon them. All gentlefolks have their proper rules of behaviour. You can't be expected to understand them, mother."

"But why should he go to them more than they should come to him, particular with young ladies there? And him with only one horse to their seven or eight. I am right, you may depend upon it, Jenny; and my mother, your grandmother, was a lady's-maid in a higher family than Darling—it depends upon them to come and look him up first, and he have no call to knock at their door without it. Why, it stands to reason, poor young man! And not a bit hath he eaten from Monday."

"Well, I believe I am right, but I'll ask Miss Dolly. She is that sharp, she knows everything, and I don't mind what I say to her, when she thinks that she looks handsome. And it takes a very bad dress, I can tell you, to put her out of that opinion."

"She is right enough there:" Mrs. Shanks shook her head at her daughter for speaking in this way. "The ugliest frock as ever came from France couldn't make her any but a booty. And the Lord knows the quality have come to queer shapes now. Undecent would be the name for it in our ranks of women. Why, the last of her frocks she gave you, Jenny, how much did I put on, at top and bottom, and you three inches shorter than she is! And the slips they ties round them—oh dear! oh dear! as if that was to hold them up and buckle them together! Won't they have the groanings by the time they come to my age?"

CHAPTER XVIII

FRENCH AND ENGLISH

Admiral Darling was now so busy, and so continually called from home by the duties of his commandership, that he could not fairly be expected to call upon Mr. Caryl Carne. Yet that gentleman, being rather sensitive—which sometimes means very spiteful—resented as a personal slight this failure; although, if the overture had been made, he would have ascribed it to intrusive curiosity, and a low desire to behold him in his ruins. But truly in the old man's kindly heart there was no sour corner for ill blood to lurk in, and no dull fibre for ill-will to feed on. He kept on meaning to go and call on Caryl Carne, and he had quite made up his mind to do it, but something always happened to prevent him.

Neither did he care a groat for his old friend Twemlow's advice upon that subject. "Don't go near him," said the Rector, taking care that his wife was quite safe out of hearing; "it would ill become me to say a word against my dear wife's own nephew, and the representative of her family. And, to the utmost of my knowledge, there is nothing to be said against him. But I can't get on with him at all. I don't know why. He has only honored us with a visit twice, and he would not even come to dinner. Nice manners they learn on the Continent! But none of us wept when he declined; not even his good aunt, my wife. Though he must have got a good deal to tell us, and an extraordinary knowledge of foreign ways. But instead of doing that, he seems to sneer at us. I can look at a question from every point of view, and I defy anybody to call me narrow-minded. But still, one must draw the line somewhere, or throw overboard all principles; and I draw it, my dear Admiral, against infidels and against Frenchmen."

"No rational person can do otherwise"—the Admiral's opinion was decisive—"but this young man is of good English birth, and one can't help feeling sorry for his circumstances. And I assure you, Twemlow, that I feel respect as well for the courage that he shows, and the perseverance, in coming home and facing those vile usurers. And your own wife's nephew! Why, you ought to take his part through thick and thin, whatever you may think of him. From all I hear he must be a young man of exceedingly high principle; and I shall make a point of calling upon him the first half-hour I get to spare. To-morrow, if possible; or if not, the day after, at the very latest."

But the needful half-hour had not yet been found; and Carne, who was wont to think the worst of everybody, concluded that the Darling race still cherished the old grudge, which had always been on his own side. For this he cared little, and perhaps was rather glad of it. For the old dwelling-place of his family (the Carne Castle besieged by the Roundheads a hundred and sixty years agone) now threatened to tumble about the ears of any one knocking at the gate too hard. Or rather the remnants of its walls did so; the greater part, having already fallen, lay harmless, and produced fine blackberries.

As a castle, it had been well respected in its day, though not of mighty bulwarks or impregnable position. Standing on a knoll, between the ramp of high land and the slope of shore, it would still have been conspicuous to traveller and to voyager but for the tall trees around it. These hid the moat, and the relics of the drawbridge, the groined archway, and cloven tower of the keep—which had twice been struck by lightning—as well as the windows of the armoury, and the chapel hushed with ivy. The banqueting hall was in better repair, for the Carnes had been hospitable to the last; but the windows kept no wind off, neither did the roof repulse the rain. In short, all the front was in a pretty state of ruin, very nice to look at, very nasty to live in, except for toads, and bats, and owls, and rats, and efts, and brindled slugs with yellow stripes; or on a summer eve the cockroach and the carrion-beetle.

At the back, however, and above the road which Cheeseman travelled in his pony-chaise, was a range of rooms still fit to dwell in, though poorly furnished, and floored with stone. In better times these had been the domain of the house-keeper and the butler, the cook and the other upper servants, who had minded their duty and heeded their comfort more truly than the master and mistress did. For the downfall of this family, as of very many others, had been chiefly caused by unwise marriage. Instead of choosing sensible and active wives to look after their home affairs and regulate the household, the Carnes for several generations now had wedded flighty ladies of good birth and pretty manners, none of whom brought them a pipkinful of money, while all helped to spend a potful. Therefore their descendant was now living in the kitchens, and had no idea how to make use of them, in spite of his French education; of comfort also he had not much idea, which was all the better for him; and he scarcely knew what it was to earn and enjoy soft quietude.

One night, when the summer was in full prime, and the weather almost blameless, this young Squire Carne rode slowly back from Springhaven to his worn-out castle. The beauty of the night had kept him back, for he hated to meet people on the road. The lingering gossips, the tired fagot-bearers, the youths going home from the hay-rick, the man with a gun who knows where the hares play, and beyond them all the truant sweethearts, who cannot have enough of one another, and wish "good-night" at every corner of the lane, till they tumble over one another's cottage steps—all these to Caryl Carne were a smell to be avoided, an eyesore to shut the eyes at. He let them get home and pull their boots off, and set the frying-pan a-bubbling—for they ended the day with a bit of bacon, whenever they could cash or credit it—and then he set forth upon his lonely ride, striking fear into the heart of any bad child that lay awake.

"Almost as good as France is this," he muttered in French, though for once enjoying the pleasure of good English air; "and better than France would it be, if only it were not cut short so suddenly. There will come a cold wind by-and-by, or a chilly black cloud from the east, and then all is shivers and rawness. But if it only remained like this, I could forgive it for producing me. After all, it is my native land; and I saw the loveliest girl to-day that ever I set eyes on. None of their made-up and highly finished demoiselles is fit to look at her—such simple beauty, such charms of nature, such enchanting innocence! Ah, that is where those French girls fail—they are always studying how they look, instead of leaving us to think of it. Bah! What odds to me? I have higher stakes to play for. But according to old Twemlow's description, she must be the daughter of that old bear Darling, with whom I shall have to pick a bone some day. Ha! How amusing is that battery to me! How little John Bull knows the nature of French troops! To-morrow we are to have a grand practice-day; and I hope they won't shoot me in my new lodgings. Nothing is impossible to such an idiot as Stubbard. What a set of imbeciles I have found to do with! They have scarcely wit enough to amuse oneself with. Pest of my soul! Is that you, Charron? Again you have broken my orders."

"Names should be avoided in the open air," answered the man, who was swinging on a gate with the simple delight of a Picard. "The climate is of France so much to-night that I found it my duty to encourage it. For what reason shall not I do that? It is not so often that I have occasion. My dear friend, scold not, but accept the compliment very seldom truthful to your native land. There are none of your clod-pates about to-night."

"Come in at once. The mere sound of your breath is enough to set the neighbourhood wondering. Could I ever have been burdened with a more French Frenchman, though you speak as good English as I do?"

"It was all of that miserable Cheray," the French gentleman said, when they sat in the kitchen, and Jerry Bowles was feeding the fine black horse. "Fruit is a thing that my mouth prepares for, directly there is any warmth in the sun. It puts itself up, it is elevated, it will not have meat, or any substance coarse. Wine of the softest and fruit of the finest is what it must then have, or unmouth itself. That miserable Cheray, his maledictioned name put me forth to be on fire for the good thing he designs. Cherays you call them, and for cherays I despatched him, suspended between the leaves in the good sun. Bah! there is nothing ever fit to eat in England. The cherays look very fine, very fine indeed; and so many did I consume that to travel on a gate was the only palliation. Would you have me stay all day in this long cellar? No diversion, no solace, no change, no conversation! Old Cheray may sit with his hands upon his knees, but to Renaud Charron that is not sufficient. How much longer before I sally forth to do the things, to fight, to conquer the nations? Where is even my little ship of despatch?"

"Captain," answered Caryl Carne, preparing calmly for his frugal supper, "you are placed under my command, and another such speech will despatch you to Dunkirk, bound hand and foot, in the hold of the Little Corporal, with which I am now in communication. Unless by the time I have severed this bone you hand me your sword in submission, my supper will have to be postponed, while I march you to the yew-tree, signal for a boat, and lay you strapped beneath the oarsmen."

Captain Charron, who had held the command of a French corvette, stared furiously at this man, younger than himself, so strongly established over him. Carne was not concerned to look at him; all he cared about was to divide the joint of a wing-rib of cold roast beef, where some good pickings lurked in the hollow. Then the French man, whose chance would have been very small in a personal encounter with his chief, arose and took a naval sword, short but rather heavy, from a hook which in better days had held a big dish-cover, and making a salute rather graceful than gracious, presented the fringed handle to the carver.

"This behaviour is sensible, my friend, and worthy of your distinguished abilities." Carne's resolute face seldom yielded to a smile, but the smile when it came was a sweet one. "Pardon me for speaking strongly, but my instructions must be the law to you. If you were my commander (as, but for local knowledge, and questions of position here, you would be), do you think then that you would allow me to rebel, to grumble, to wander, to demand my own pleasure, when you knew that it would ruin things?"

"Bravo! It is well spoken. My captain, I embrace you. In you lives the spirit of the Grand Army, which we of the sea and of the ships admire always, and always desire to emulate. Ah, if England possessed many Englishmen like you, she would be hard to conquer."

The owner of this old English castle shot a glance at the Frenchman for any sign of irony in his words. Seeing none, he continued, in the friendly vein:

"Our business here demands the greatest caution, skill, reserve, and self-denial. We are fortunate in having no man of any keen penetration in the neighbourhood, at least of those in authority and concerned with public matters. As one of an ancient family, possessing the land for centuries, I have every right to be here, and to pursue my private business in privacy. But if it once gets talked about that a French officer is with me, these stupid people will awake their suspicions more strongly by their own stupidity. In this queer island you may do what you like till the neighbourhood turns against you; and then, if you revolve upon a pin, you cannot suit them. You understand? You have heard me before. It is this that I never can knock into you."

Renaud Charron, who considered himself—as all Frenchmen did then, and perhaps do now—far swifter of intellect than any Englishman, found himself not well pleased at this, and desired to know more about it.

"Nothing can be simpler," the Englishman replied; "and therefore nothing surer. You know the old proverb—'Everything in turn, except scandal, whose turn is always.' And again another saying of our own land—'The second side of the bread takes less time to toast.' We must not let the first side of ours be toasted; we will shun all the fire of suspicion. And to do this, you must not be seen, my dear friend. I may go abroad freely; you must hide your gallant head until matters are ripe for action. You know that you may trust me not to keep you in the dark a day longer than is needful. I have got the old shopkeeper under my thumb, and can do what I please with his trading-ship. But before I place you in command I must change some more of the crew, and do it warily. There is an obstinate Cornishman to get rid of, who sticks to the planks like a limpet. If we throw him overboard, we shall alarm the others; if we discharge him without showing cause, he will go to the old Admiral and tell all his suspicions. He must be got rid of in London with skill, and then we ship three or four Americans, first-rate seamen, afraid of nothing, who will pass here as fellows from Lancashire. After that we may run among the cruisers as we like, with the boldness and skill of a certain Captain Charron, who must be ill in his cabin when his ship is boarded."

"It is famous, it is very good, my friend. The patience I will have, and the obedience, and the courage; and so much the more readily because my pay is good, and keeps itself going on dry land as well as sea."

CHAPTER XIX

IN THE LINE OF FIRE

No wonder there had been a great deal of talking in the village all that evening, for the following notice had appeared in a dozen conspicuous places, beginning with the gate of the church-yard, and ending with two of the biggest mooring-posts, and not even sparing the Admiral's white gate, where it flapped between the two upper rails. It was not printed, but written in round hand, with a liberal supply of capitals, on a stiff sheet of official paper, stamped with the Royal Arms at the top. And those who were in the secret knew that Master Bob Stubbard, the Captain's eldest son, had accomplished this great literary feat at a guerdon of one shilling from the public service funds every time he sucked his pen at the end of it.

"By order of His Majesty King George III. To-morrow being Wednesday, and the fishing-boats at sea, Artillery practice from Fox-hill fort will be carried on from twelve at noon until three P.M. at a mark-boat moored half a mile from the shore. Therefore His Majesty's loyal subjects are warned to avoid the beach westward of the brook between the white flagstaffs, as well as the sea in front of it, and not to cross the line of fire below the village but at their own risk and peril.

"(Signed) ADAM JACKSON STUBBARD, R.N., commanding Fox-hill Battery."

Some indignation was aroused by this; for Mrs. Caper junior (who was Mrs. Prater's cousin) had been confined, out of proper calculation, and for the very first time, the moment the boats were gone on Monday; and her house, being nearest to the fort, and in a hollow where the noise would be certain to keep going round and round, the effect upon her head, not to mention the dear baby's, was more than any one dared to think of, with the poor father so far away. And if Squire Darling had only been at home, not a woman who could walk would have thought twice about it, but gone all together to insist upon it that he should stop this wicked bombardment. And this was most unselfish of all of them, they were sure, because they had so long looked forward to putting cotton-wool in their ears, and seeing how all the enemies of England would be demolished. But Mrs. Caper junior, and Caper, natu minimus, fell fast asleep together, as things turned out, and heard not a single bang of it.

And so it turned out, in another line of life, with things against all calculation, resenting to be reckoned as they always do, like the countless children of Israel. For Admiral Darling was gone far away inspecting, leaving his daughters to inspect themselves.

"You may just say exactly what you consider right, dear," said Miss Dolly Darling to her sister Faith; "and I dare say it makes you more comfortable. But you know as well as I do, that there is no reason in it. Father is a darling; but he must be wrong sometimes. And how can he tell whether he is wrong or right, when he goes away fifty miles to attend to other people? Of course I would never disobey his orders, anymore than you would. But facts change according to circumstances, and I feel convinced that if he were here he would say, 'Go down and see it, Dolly.'"

"We have no right to speculate as to what he might say," replied Faith, who was very clear-headed. "His orders were definite: 'Keep within the grounds, when notice is given of artillery practice.' And those orders I mean to obey."

"And so do I; but not to misunderstand them. The beach is a part of our grounds, as I have heard him say fifty times in argument, when people tried to come encroaching. And I mean to go on that part of his grounds, because I can't see well from the other part. That is clearly what he meant; and he would laugh at us, if we could tell him nothing when he comes home. Why, he promised to take us as far as Portsmouth to see some artillery practice."

"That is a different thing altogether, because we should be under his control. If you disobey him, it is at your own risk, and I shall not let one of the servants go with you, for I am mistress of the household, if not of you."

"What trumpery airs you do give yourself! One would think you were fifty years old at least. Stay at home, if you are such a coward! I am sure dear daddy would be quite ashamed of you. They are popping already, and I mean to watch them."

"You won't go so very far, I am quite sure of that," answered Faith, who understood her sister. "You know your own value, darling Dolly, and you would not go at all, if you had not been forbidden."

"When people talk like that, it goads me up to almost anything. I intend to go, and stand, as near as can be, in the middle of the space that is marked off 'dangerous.'"

"Do, that's a dear. I will lend you my shell-silk that measures twenty yards, that you may be sure of being hit, dear."

"Inhuman, selfish, wicked creature!" cried Dolly, and it was almost crying; "you shall see what comes of your cold-bloodedness! I shall pace to and fro in the direct line of fire, and hang on my back the king's proclamation, inside out, and written on it in large letters—'By order of my sister I do this.' Then what will be said of you, if they only kill me? My feelings might be very sad, but I should not envy yours, Faith."

"Kiss me, at any rate, before you perish, in token of forgiveness;" and Dolly (who dearly loved her sister at the keenest height of rebellion) ran up and kissed Faith, with a smile for her, and a tear for her own self-sacrifice. "I shall put on my shell-pink," she said, "and they won't have the heart to fire shells at it."

The dress of the ladies of the present passing period had been largely affected by the recent peace, which allowed the "French babies"—as the milliners' dolls were called—to come in as quickly as they were conceived. In war time scores of these "doxy-dummies"—as the rough tars called them— were tossed overboard from captured vessels or set up as a mark for tobacco-juice, while sweet eyes in London wept for want of them. And even Mr. Cheeseman had failed to bring any type genuinely French from the wholesale house in St. Mary's Axe, which was famed for canonical issue. But blessed are the patient, if their patience lasts long enough. The ladies of England were now in full enjoyment of all the new French discoveries, which proved to be the right name, inasmuch as they banished all reputable forms of covering. At least, so Mrs. Twemlow said; and the Rector went further than she did, obtaining for his sympathy a recommendation to attend to his own business. But when he showed the Admiral his wife's last book of patterns—from a drawer which he had no right to go to—great laughter was held between the twain, with some glancing over shoulders, and much dread of bad example. "Whatever you do, don't let my girls see it; I'll be bound you won't let your Eliza," said the Admiral, after a pinch of snuff to restore the true balance of his principles; "Faith would pitch it straight into the fire; but I am not quite so sure that my Dolly would. She loves a bit of finery, and she looks well in it."

"Tonnish females," as the magazine of fashion called the higher class of popinjays, would have stared with contempt at both Faith and Dolly Darling in their simple walking-dress that day. Dowdies would have been the name for them, or frumps, or frights, or country gawks, because their attire was not statuesque or classic, as it should have been, which means that they were not half naked.

Faith, the eldest sister, had meant to let young Dolly take the course of her own stubbornness; but no sooner did she see her go forth alone than she threw on cloak and hat, and followed. The day was unsuited for classic apparel, as English days are apt to be, and a lady of fashion would have looked more foolish, and even more indecent, than usual. A brisk and rather crisp east wind had arisen, which had no respect for persons, and even Faith and Dolly in their high-necked country dresses had to handle their tackle warily.

Dolly had a good start, and growing much excited with the petulance of the wind and with her own audacity, crossed the mouth of the brook at a very fine pace, with the easterly gusts to second her. She could see the little mark-boat well out in the offing, with a red flag flaring merrily, defying all the efforts of the gunners on the hill to plunge it into the bright dance of the waves. And now and then she heard what she knew to be the rush of a round shot far above her head, and following the sound saw a little silver fountain leap up into the sunshine and skim before the breeze; then glancing up the hill she saw the gray puff drifting, and presently felt the dull rumble of the air. At the root of the smoke-puffs, once or twice, she descried a stocky figure moving leisurely, and in spite of the distance and huddle of vapour could declare that it was Captain Stubbard. Then a dense mass of smoke was brought down by an eddy of wind, and set her coughing.

"Come away, come away this very moment, Dolly," cried Faith, who had hurried up and seized her hand; "you are past the danger-post, and I met a man back there who says they are going to fire shells, and they have got two short guns on purpose. He says it will be very dangerous till they get the range, and he begged me most earnestly not to come on here. If I were anybody else, he said, he would lay hands on me and hold me back."

"Some old fisherman, no doubt. What do they know about gun practice? I can see Captain Stubbard up there; he would rather shoot himself than me, he said yesterday."

While Dolly was repeating this assurance, the following words were being exchanged upon the smoky parapet: "If you please, sir, I can see two women on the beach, half-way between the posts a'most." "Can't help it—wouldn't stop for all the petticoats in the kingdom. If they choose to go there, they must take their chance. A bit more up, and to you, my good man. Are you sure you put in twenty-three? Steady! so, so—that's beautiful."

"What a noisy thing! What does it come here for? I never saw it fall. There must be some mistake. I hope there's nothing nasty inside it. Run for your life, Faith; it means to burst, I do believe."

"Down on your faces!" cried a loud, stern voice; and Dolly obeyed in an instant. But Faith stood calmly, and said to the man who rushed past her, "I trust in the Lord, sir."

There was no time to answer. The shell had left off rolling, and sputtered more fiercely as the fuse thickened. The man laid hold of this, and tried to pull it out, but could not, and jumped with both feet on it; while Faith, who quite expected to be blown to pieces, said to herself, "What pretty boots he has!"

"A fine bit of gunnery!" said the young man, stooping over it, after treading the last spark into the springy sand. "The little artillery man is wanted here. Ladies, you may safely stay here now. They will not make two hits in proximity to each other."

"You shall not go," said Faith, as he was hurrying away, "until we know who has been so reckless of his life, to save the lives of others. Both your hands are burned—very seriously, I fear."

"And your clothes, sir," cried Dolly, running up in hot terror, as soon as the danger was over; "your clothes are spoiled sadly. Oh, how good it was of you! And the whole fault was mine—or at least Captain Stubbard's. He will never dare to face me again, I should hope."

"Young ladies, if I have been of any service to you," said the stranger, with a smile at their excitement, "I beg you to be silent to the Captain Stubbard concerning my share in this occasion. He would not be gratified by the interest I feel in his beautiful little bombardments, especially that of fair ladies. Ha, there goes another shell! They will make better aim now; but you must not delay. I beseech you to hasten home, if you would do me kindness."

The fair daughters of the Admiral had enjoyed enough of warfare to last them till the end of their honeymoon, and they could not reject the entreaty of a man who had risked his life to save them. Trembling and bewildered, they made off at the quickest step permitted by maiden dignity, with one or two kindly turns of neck, to show that he was meant to follow them. But another sulphurous cloud rushed down from the indefatigable Stubbard, and when it had passed them, they looked back vainly for the gentleman who had spoiled his boots.

CHAPTER XX

AMONG THE LADIES

It would have surprised the stout Captain Stubbard, who thought no small beer of his gunnery, to hear that it was held in very light esteem by the "Frenchified young man overhead," as he called Caryl Carne, to his landlady. And it would have amazed him to learn that this young man was a captain of artillery, in the grand army mustering across the sea, and one of the most able among plenty of ability, and favoured by the great First Consul.

In the gully where the Tugwell boats were built, behind a fringe of rough longshore growth, young Carne had been sitting with a good field-glass, observing the practice of the battery. He had also been able to observe unseen the disobedient practices of young ladies, when their father is widely out of sight. Upon Faith, however, no blame could fall, for she went against her wish, and only to retrieve the rebellious Dolly.

Secure from the danger, these two held council in the comfort of the Admiral's Round-house. There Miss Dolly, who considered it her domain, kept sundry snug appliances congenial to young ladies, for removing all traces of sudden excitement, and making them fit to be seen again. Simple and unfashionable as they were in dress, they were sure to have something to do to themselves after the late derangement, ere ever they could run the risk of meeting any of the brave young officers, who were so mysteriously fond of coming for orders to Springhaven Hall.

"You look well enough, dear," said Faith at last, "and much better than you deserve to look, after leading me such a dance by your self-will. But one thing must be settled before we go back—are we to speak of this matter, or not?"

"How can you ask such a question, Faith?" Miss Dolly loved a bit of secrecy. "Of course we must rather bite our tongues out, than break the solemn pledges which we have given." She had cried a good deal, and she began to cry again.

"Don't cry, that's a darling," said the simple-hearted sister. "You make the whole world seem so cruel when you cry, because you look so innocent. It shall be as you please, if I can only think it right. But I cannot see how we gave a pledge of any sort, considering that we ran away without speaking. The question is—have we any right to conceal it, when father has a right to know everything?"

"He would be in such a sad passion," pleaded Dolly, with a stock of fresh tears only waiting, "and he never would look again at poor Captain Stubbard, and what would become of all his family?"

"Father is a just and conscientious man," replied the daughter who inherited those qualities; "he would not blame Captain Stubbard; he would blame us, and no others."

"Oh, I could not bear to hear you blamed, Faith. I should have to say that it was all my fault. And then how I should catch it, and be punished for a month! Confined to the grounds for a month at least, and never have a bit of appetite. But I am not thinking of myself, I am quite sure of that. You know that I never do that much. I am thinking of that heroic gentleman, who stamped out the sparks so cleverly. All the time I lay on the sand I watched him, though I expected to be blown to pieces every single moment. Oh! what a nasty sensation it was! I expected to find all my hair turned grey. But, thank Heaven, I don't see a streak in it!" To make sure of that, she went to the glass again.

"If all mine had turned grey, 'twould be no odds to nobody—as Captain Zeb says about his income—because I am intended for an old maid." Miss Darling, whose beauty still lacked many years of its prime, turned away for a moment, because her eyes were glistening, and her sister was tired of the subject. "But for yours there are fifty to weep, Dolly. Especially perhaps this young gentleman, towards whom you feel so much gratitude."

"How unkind you are, Faith! All the gratitude I owe him is for saving your life. As for myself, I was flat upon the sand, with a heap of sea-weed between me and the thing. If it had gone off, it would have gone over me; but you chose to stand up, like a stupid. Your life was saved, beyond all doubt, by him; and the way you acknowledge it is to go and tell his chief enemy that he was there observing him!"

"Well, I never!" Faith exclaimed, with more vigour than grace of language. "A minute ago you knew nothing of him, and even wondered who he was, and now you know all about his enemies! I am afraid that you stick at nothing."

"I don't stick thinking, as you do, Miss," Dolly answered, without abashment, and knowing that the elder hated to be so addressed; "but things come to me by the light of nature, without a twelvemonth of brown-study. When I said what you remind me of, in such a hurry, it was perfectly true—so true that you need have no trouble about it, with all your truth. But since that, a sudden idea flashed across me, the sort of idea that proves itself. Your hero you are in such a hurry to betray can be nobody but the mysterious lodger in

Widow Shanks' dimity-parlour, as she calls it; and Jenny has told me all she knows about him, which is a great deal less than she ought to know. I meant to have told you, but you are so grand in your lofty contempt of what you call gossip, but which I call good neighbourly intercourse! You know that he is Mr. Caryl Carne, of course. Everybody knows that, and there the knowledge seems to terminate. Even the Twemlows, his own aunt and uncle, are scarcely ever favoured with his company; and I, who am always on the beach, or in the village, have never had the honour of beholding him, until—until it came to this"—here she imitated with her lips the spluttering of the fuse so well that her sister could not keep from laughing. "He never goes out, and he never asks questions, any more than he answers them, and he never cares to hear what fish they have caught, or anything else, about anybody. He never eats or drinks, and he never says a word about the flowers they put upon his table; and what he does all day long nobody knows, except that he has a lot of books with him. Widow Shanks, who has the best right to know all about him, has made up her mind that his head has been turned by the troubles of his family, except for his going without dinner, which no lunatic ever does, according to her knowledge. And he seems to have got 'Butter Cheeseman,' as they call him, entirely at his beck and call. He leaves his black horse there every morning, and rides home at night to his ancestral ruins. There, now, you know as much as I do."

"There is mischief at the bottom of all this," said Faith; "in these dangerous times, it must not be neglected. We are bound, as you say, to consider his wishes, after all that he has done for us. But the tale about us will be over the place in a few hours, at the latest. The gunners will have known where their bad shot fell, and perhaps they will have seen us with their glasses. How will it be possible to keep this affair from gossip?"

"They may have seen us, without seeing him at all, on account of the smoke that came afterwards. At any rate, let us say nothing about it until we hear what other people say. The shell will be washed away or buried in the sand, for it fell upon the shingle, and then rolled towards the sea; and there need be no fuss unless we choose to make it, and so perhaps ruin Captain Stubbard and his family. And his wife has made such pretty things for us. If he knew what he had done, he would go and shoot himself. He is so excessively humane and kind."

"We will not urge his humanity to that extreme. I hate all mystery, as you know well. But about this affair I will say nothing, unless there is cause to do so, at least until father comes back; and then I shall tell him if it seems to be my duty."

"It won't be your duty, it can't be your duty, to get good people into trouble, Faith. I find it my duty to keep out of trouble, and I like to treat others the same as myself."

"You are such a lover of duty, dear Dolly, because everything you like becomes your duty. And now your next duty is to your dinner. Mrs. Twemlow is coming—I forgot to tell you—as well as Eliza, and Mrs. Stubbard. And if Johnny comes home in time from Harrow, to be Jack among the ladies, we shall hear some wonders, you may be quite sure."

"Oh, I vow, I forgot all about that wicked Johnny. What a blessing that he was not here just now! It is my black Monday when his holidays begin. Instead of getting steadier, he grows more plaguesome. And the wonder of it is that he would tie your kid shoes; while he pulls out my jaconet, and sits on my French hat. How I wish he was old enough for his commission! To-morrow he will be dancing in and out of every cottage, boat, or gun, or rabbit-hole, and nothing shall be hidden from his eyes and ears. Let him come. 'I am accustomed to have all things go awry,' as somebody says in some tragedy. The only chance is to make him fall in love, deeply in love, with Miss Stubbard. He did it with somebody for his Easter week, and became as harmless as a sucking dove, till he found his nymph eating onions raw with a pocketful of boiled limpets. Maggie Stubbard is too perfect in her style for that. She is twelve years old, and has lots of hair, and eyes as large as oysters. I shall introduce Johnny to-morrow, and hope to keep him melancholy all his holidays."

"Perhaps it will be for his good," said Faith, "because, without some high ideas, he gets into such dreadful scrapes; and certainly it will be for our good."

After making light of young love thus, these girls deserved the shafts of Cupid, in addition to Captain Stubbard's shells. And it would have been hard to find fairer marks when they came down dressed for dinner. Mrs. Twemlow arrived with her daughter Eliza, but without her husband, who was to fetch her in the evening; and Mrs. Stubbard came quite alone, for her walkable children—as she called them—were all up at the battery. "Can't smell powder too young in such days as these," was the Captain's utterance; and, sure enough, they took to it, like sons of guns.

"I should be so frightened," Mrs. Twemlow said, when Johnny (who sat at the foot of the table representing his father most gallantly) had said grace in Latin, to astonish their weak minds, "so nervous all the time, so excessively anxious, the whole time that dreadful din was proceeding! It is over now, thank goodness! But how can you have endured it, how can you have gone about your household duties calmly, with seven of your children—I think you said—going about in that fiery furnace?"

"Because, ma'am," replied Mrs. Stubbard, who was dry of speech, and fit mother of heroes, "the cannons are so made, if you can understand, that they do not shoot out of their back ends."

"We are quite aware of that"—Miss Twemlow came to her mother's relief very sharply—"but still they are apt to burst, or to be overloaded, or badly directed, or even to fly back suddenly, as I have heard on good authority."

"Very likely, miss, when they are commanded by young women."

Eliza Twemlow coloured, for she was rather quick of temper; but she did not condescend to pay rudeness in kind.

"It would hardly be a lady-like position, I suppose," she answered, with a curve of her graceful neck—the Carnes had been celebrated for their necks, which were longer than those of the Darlings; "but even under the command of a most skilful man, for instance Captain Stubbard, little accidents will happen, like the fall of a shell upon the beach this afternoon. Some people were close to it, according to the rumour; but luckily it did not explode."

"How providential!" cried Mrs. Twemlow; "but the stupid people would have gone without much pity, whatever had befallen them, unless they were blind, or too ignorant to read. Don't you think so, Faith, my dear?"

"I don't believe a single word of that story," Mrs. Stubbard cut short the question; "for the simple reason that it never could have happened. My husband was to direct every gun himself. Is it likely he would have shelled the beach?"

"Well, the beach is the proper place for shells; but if I had only known it, wouldn't I have come a few hours earlier?" said Johnny. "Even now there must be something left to see; and I am bound to understand that sort of thing. Ladies, I entreat you not to think me rude, if I go as soon as ever you can do without me. I think I have got you nearly everything you want; and perhaps you would rather be without me."

With many thanks and compliments—such a pretty boy he was—the ladies released him gladly; and then Mrs. Twemlow, having reasons of her own, drew nigh to Mrs. Stubbard with lively interest in her children. At first, she received short answers only; for the Captain's wife had drawn more sour juices than sweet uses from adversity. But the wife of the man of peace outflanked the better half of the man of war, drove in her outposts, and secured the key of all her communications.

"I can scarcely believe that you are so kind. My dear Mrs. Twemlow, how good you are! My Bob is a nice boy, so manly and clever, so gentle and well-behaved, even when he knows that I am not likely to find him out. But that you should have noticed it, is what surprises me—so few people now know the difference! But in the House of God—as you so well observe—you can very soon see what a boy is. When I tell him that he may ride your grey pony, I wish you could be there to watch the fine expression of his face. How he does love dumb animals! It was only last Saturday, he knocked down a boy nearly three times his own size for poking a pin into a poor donkey with the fish. And Maggie to have a flower-bed on your front lawn! They won't let her touch a plant, at our cottage, though she understands gardening so thoroughly. She won't sleep a wink to-night, if I tell her, and I had better keep that for the morning. Poor children! They have had a hard time of it; but they have come out like pure gold from the fire—I mean as many of them as can use their legs. But to be on horseback—what will Bob say?"

"You must have met with very little kindness, Mrs. Stubbard, to attach any importance to such mere trifles. It makes me blush to think that there can be a spot in England where such children as yours could pass unnoticed. It is not a question of religious feeling only. Far from it; in fact, quite the opposite; though my husband, of course, is quite right in insisting that all our opinions and actions must be referred to that one standard. But I look at things also from a motherly point of view, because I have suffered such sad trials. Three dear ones in the churchyard, and the dearest of all—the Almighty only knows where he is. Sometimes it is more than I can bear, to live on in this dark and most dreadful uncertainty. My medical man has forbidden me to speak of it. But how can he know what it is to be a mother? But hush! Or darling Faith may hear me. Sometimes I lose all self-command."

Mrs. Twemlow's eyes were in need of wiping, and stout Mrs. Stubbard's in the same condition. "How I wish I could help you," said the latter, softly: "is there anything in the world that I can do?"

"No, my dear friend; I wish there was, for I'm sure that it would be a pleasure to you. But another anxiety, though far less painful, is worrying me as well just now. My poor brother's son is behaving most strangely. He hardly ever comes near us, and he seems to dislike my dear husband. He has taken rooms over your brave husband's Office, and he comes and goes very mysteriously. It is my duty to know something about this; but I dare not ask Captain Stubbard."

"My dear Mrs. Twemlow, it has puzzled me too. But thinking that you knew all about it, I concluded that everything must be quite right. What you tell me has surprised me more than I can tell. I shall go to work quietly to find out all about it. Mystery and secrecy are such hateful things; and a woman is always the best hand at either."

CHAPTER XXI

A GRACIOUS MERCY

As a matter of course, every gunner at the fort was ready to make oath by every colour of the rainbow, that never shot, shell, wad, sponge, or even powder-flake could by any possibility have fallen on the beach. And before they had time to grow much more than doubly positive—that is to say, within three days' time—the sound of guns fired in earnest drowned all questions of bad practice.

For the following Sunday beheld Springhaven in a state of excitement beyond the memory of the very oldest inhabitant, or the imagination of the youngest. Excitement is a crop that, to be large, must grow—though it thrives all the better without much root—and in this particular field it began to grow before noon of Saturday. For the men who were too old to go to sea, and the boys who were too young, and the women who were never of the proper age, all these kept looking from the best lookouts, but nothing could they see to enable them to say when the kettle, or the frying-pan, or gridiron, would be wanted. They rubbed their eyes grievously, and spun round three times, if time had brought or left them the power so to spin; and they pulled an Irish halfpenny, with the harp on, from their pockets, and moistened it with saliva —which in English means spat on it—and then threw it into the pocket on the other side of body. But none of these accredited appeals to heaven put a speck upon the sea where the boats ought to have been, or cast upon the clouds a shade of any sail approaching. Uneasily wondering, the grannies, wives, and little ones went home, when the nightfall quenched all eyesight, and told one another ancient tales of woe.

Yet there is a salve for every sore, a bung for every bunghole. Upon the Sunday morning, when the tide was coming in, and a golden haze hung upon the peaceful sea, and the seven bells of the old grey church were speaking of the service cheerfully, suddenly a deep boom moved the bosom of distance, and palpitated all along the shore. Six or seven hale old gaffers (not too stiff to walk, with the help of a staff, a little further than the rest) were coming to hear parson by the path below the warren, where a smack of salt would season them for doctrine. They knew from long experience, the grandmother of science, that the mist of the sea, coming on at breakfast-time, in the month of August (with the wind where it was and the tides as they were), would be sure to hold fast until dinner-time. Else, good as they were, and preparing punctually once a week for a better world, the hind buttons of their Sunday coats would have been towards the church, and the front ones to the headland. For the bodies of their sons were dearer to them, substantially dearer, than their own old souls.

They were all beginning to be deaf, or rather going on with it very agreeably, losing thereby a great deal of disturbance, and gaining great room for reflection. And now when the sound of a gun from the sea hung shaking in the web of vapour, each of these wise men gazed steadfastly at the rest, to see his own conclusion reflected, or concluded. A gun it was indeed—a big well-shotted gun, and no deafness could throw any doubt on it. There might not be anything to see, but still there would be plenty to hear at the headland—a sound more arousing than the parson's voice, a roar beyond that of all the gallery. "'Tis a battle!" said one, and his neighbour cried, "A rare one!" They turned to the parish church the quarters of farewell, and those of salutation to the battle out at sea.

It was all over the village, in the time it takes to put a hat on, that the British and the French fleets were hammer and tongs at it, within the distance you may throw an apple off Springhaven headland.

Even the young women knew that this was quite impossible, because there was no water there for a collier-brig to anchor; nevertheless, in the hurry and scare, the thoughts of that new battery and Lord Nelson, and above all in the fog, they believed it. So that there was scarcely any room to stand, at the Watch-point, inside the Shag-rock; while in church there was no one who could help being there, by force of holy office, or example.

These latter were not in a devout frame of mind, and (but for the look of it) would have done more good by joining the other congregation. For the sound of cannon-shot came into their ears, like balls of unadulterated pepper, and every report made them look at one another, and whisper—"Ah! there goes some poor fellow's head." For the sacred building was constructed so that the sounds outside of it had more power than the good things offered in the inside.

However, as many, or as few, as did their duty, by joining the good company of the minister, found themselves all the better for it, and more fresh for a start than the runagates. Inasmuch as these latter had nearly got enough of listening without seeing anything, while the steady church-goers had refreshed the entire system by looking about without listening. And to show the truant people where their duty should have bound them, the haze had been thickening all over the sea, while the sun kept the time on the old church dial. This was spoken of for many years, throughout the village, as a Scriptural token of the proper thing to do.

"Well, and what have 'e seen?" asked the senior church-warden—not Cheeseman, who was only the junior, and had neither been at church nor on the headland—but Farmer Graves, the tenant of the Glebe and of Up-farm, the Admiral's best holding; "what have 'e seen, good people all, to leave parson to prache to hisself a'most a sarmon as he's hathn't prached for five year, to my knowledge? Have 'e seen fat bulls of Basan?"

"Naw; but us have heer'd un roar," replied one who was sure to say something. "Wust of it is, there be no making out what language un do roar in."

"One Englishman, I tell 'e, and two Frenchmen," said an ancient tar who had served under Keppel; "by the ring of the guns I could swear to that much. And they loads them so different, that they do."

Before the others had well finished laughing at him, it became his turn to laugh at them. The wind was in the east, and the weather set fair, and but for the sea-mist the power of the sun would have been enough to dazzle all beholders. Already this vapour was beginning to clear off, coiling up in fleecy wisps above the glistening water, but clinging still to any bluff or cliff it could lay hold on.

"Halloa, Jem! Where be going of now?" shouted one or two voices from the Oar-stone point, the furthest outlook of the Havenhead hill.

"To see them Frenchy hoppers get a jolly hiding," Jem Prater replied, without easing his sculls. He was John Prater's nephew, of the "Darling Arms," and had stopped behind the fishing to see his uncle's monthly beer in. "You can't see up there, I reckon, the same as I do here. One English ship have got a job to tackle two Crappos. But, by George! she'll do it, mates. Good bye, and the Lord defend you!"

He had nobody but his little brother Sam, who was holding the tiller, to help him, and his uncle's boat (which he had taken without leave) was neither stout nor handy. But the stir of the battle had fetched him forth, and he meant to see the whole of it without taking harm. Every Englishman had a full right to do this, in a case of such French audacity, and the English sea and air began to give him fair occasion. For now the sun had swept the mist with a besom of gold wire, widening every sweep, and throwing brilliant prospect down it. The gentle heave of the sea flashed forth with the white birds hovering over it, and the curdles of fugitive vapour glowed like pillars of fire as they floated off. Then out of the drift appeared three ships, partly shrouded in their own fog.

The wind was too light for manoeuvring much, and the combatants swung to their broadsides, having taken the breath of the air away by the fury of their fire. All three were standing to the north-north-west, under easy sail, and on the starboard tack, but scarcely holding steerage-way, and taking little heed of it. Close quarters, closer and closer still, muzzle to muzzle, and beard to beard, clinched teeth, and hard pounding, were the order of the day, with the crash of shattered timber and the cries of dying men. And still the ships came onward, forgetting where they were, heaving too much iron to have thought of heaving lead, ready to be shipwrecks, if they could but wreck the enemy.

Between the bulky curls of smoke could be seen the scars of furious battle, splintered masts and shivered yards, tattered sails and yawning bulwarks, and great gaps even of the solid side; and above the ruck of smoke appeared the tricolor flag upon the right hand and the left, and the Union-jack in the middle.

"She've a'got more than she can do, I reckon," said an old man famous in the lobster line; "other a one of they is as big as she be, and two to one seemeth onfair odds. Wish her well out of it—that's all as can be done."

"Kelks, you're a fool," replied the ancient navyman, steadying his spy-glass upon a ledge of rock. "In my time we made very little of that; and the breed may be slacked off a little, but not quite so bad as that would be. Ah! you should a' heard what old Keppel—on the twenty-seventh day of July it was, in the year of our Lord 1778. Talk about Nelson! to my mind old Keppel could have boxed his compass backward. Not but what these men know how to fight quite as well as need be nowadays. Why, if I was aboard of that there frigate, I couldn't do much more than she have done. She'll have one of them, you see if she don't, though she look to have the worst of it, till you comes to understand. The Leader her name is, of thirty-eight guns, and she'll lead one of they into Portsmouth, to refit."

It was hard to understand the matter, in its present aspect, at all as the ancient sailor did; for the fire of the Leda ceased suddenly, and she fell behind the others, as if hampered with her canvas. A thrill of pain ran through all the gazing Britons.

"How now, old Navy-Mike?" cried the lobster man. "Strike is the word, and no mistake. And small blame to her either. She hathn't got a sound thread to draw, I do believe. Who is the fool now, Mike? Though vexed I be to ask it."

"Wait a bit, old lobster-pot. Ah, there now, she breezes! Whistle for a wind, lads, whistle, whistle. Sure as I'm a sinner, yes! She's laying her course to board the Frenchman on the weather quarter. With a slant of wind she'll do it, too, if it only holds two minutes. Whistle on your nails, my boys, for the glory of old England."

In reply to their shrill appeal—for even the women tried to whistle—or perhaps in compulsory sequence of the sun, the wind freshened briskly from the sunny side of east. The tattered sails of the brave ship filled, with the light falling through them upon one another, the head swung round at the command of helm, the pennons flew gaily and the ensign flapped, and she bore down smoothly on the outer and therefore unwounded side of the enemy.

"That's what I call judgmatical," old Mike shouted, with a voice that rivalled cannon; "whoever thought of that deserves three epulets, one on each shoulder and one upon his head. Doubt if old Keppel would have thought of that, now. You see, mates, the other Crappo can't fire at her without first hitting of her own consort. And better than that—ever so much better—the tilt of the charge will throw her over on her wounds. Master Muncher hath two great holes 'twixt wind and water on his larboard side, and won't they suck the briny, with the weight of our bows upon the starboard beam? 'Twill take fifty hands to stop leaks, instead of stopping boarders."

The smoke was drifting off, and the sun shone bravely. The battle had been gliding toward the feet of the spectators; and now from the height of the cliff they could descry the decks, the guns, the coils of rope, the turmoil, and dark rush of men to their fate. Small fights, man to man, demanded still the power of a telescope, and distance made the trenchant arms of heroes, working right and left, appear like the nippers of an earwig. The only thing certain was that men were being killed, and glory was being manufactured largely.

"She've a doed it, she've a doed it rarely. There's not a d——d froggy left to go to heaven; or if there be so he's a' battened down below," old Mike shouted, flourishing his spy-glass, which rattled in its joints as much as he did; "down comes the blood, froth, and blue blazes, as they call the Republican emrods, and up goes the Union-jack, my hearties. Three cheers! three cheers! Again! again! again!"

From the sea far below, and far away, came also the volume of a noble English shout, as the flag began to flutter in the quickening breeze, and the sea arose and danced with sunshine. No one, who had got all his blood left in him, could think of anything but glory.

"My certy, they had better mind their soundings, though!" said the old navy-man, with a stitch in his side and a lump in his throat, from loud utterance; "five fathoms is every inch of it where they be now, and the tide making strong, and precious little wind to claw off with. Jem Prater! Jem Prater! Oar up, and give signal. Ah, he's too far off to do any good. In five minutes more they'll be on the White Pig, where no ship ever got off again. Oh, thank the Lord, mates, thank the Lord, for his mercy endureth forever! The other froggy is stuck hard and fast, and our lads will just fetch out in time."

Old Navy-Mike had made no mistake. The consort of the captured frigate, a corvette of twenty-four guns, had boldly stood on with the intention of rounding to the wind, crossing the bows of the other twain, and retrieving the fortunes of the day perhaps, by a broadside into the shattered upper works of the terribly hampered British ship. The idea was clever and spirited, and had a very fair chance of success; but the land below the sea forefended it. Full of fine ardour and the noble thirst for fame, speeding on for the palm of high enterprise and the glory of the native land, alas, they stuck fast in a soft bit of English sand! It was in their power now to swear by all they disbelieved in, and in everything visible and too tangible; but their power was limited strictly to that; and the faster they swore, the faster they were bound to stick.

Springhaven dined well, with its enemy so placed, and a message from the Leda by Jem Prater, that the fishing fleet was rescued, and would be home to early supper, and so much to be talked about all dinner-time, that for once in his life nearly everybody found it more expedient to eat with his fork than his knife. Then all who could be spared from washing up, and getting ready for further cookery, went duly to church in the afternoon, to hear the good rector return humble thanks for a Gracious Mercy to the British arms, and to see a young man, who had landed with despatches, put a face full of gunpowder in at window, to learn whether Admiral Darling was there.

CHAPTER XXII

A SPECIAL URGENCY

Admiral Darling was not in church. His duty to his country kept him up the hill, and in close consultation with Captain Stubbard, who was burning to fire his battery.

"I never knew such bad luck in all my life. The devil has been appointed First Lord of the weather ever since I came to Springhaven." As Stubbard declared these great truths he strode about in his little fortress, delivering a kick at the heels of things which had no right to be lumbering there. "To think that I should never have seen those beggars, when but for the fog I could have smashed them right and left. Admiral, these things make a Christian an infidel."

"Nonsense, sir!" said the Admiral, sternly, for a man of his kind nature; "you forget that without the fog, or rather the mist—for it was only that— those fellows would never have come within range. We have very great blessings to be thankful for, though the credit falls not to our battery. The Frenchmen fought wonderfully well, as well as the best Englishman could have done, and to capture them both is a miracle of luck, if indeed we can manage to secure them. My friend, young Honyman, of the Leda, has proved himself just what I said he would be; and has performed a very gallant exploit, though I fear he is severely wounded. But we shall know more now, for I see a young fellow jumping up the hill, like a kangaroo, and probably he comes for orders. One thing we have learned, Stubbard, and must take the hint to-morrow—put a hut on the Haven head, and keep a watchman there. Why, bless my heart, it is Blyth Scudamore that's coming! There is nobody else that can skip like that."

The young lieutenant entered between two guns—the gunners were dismissed in great disgust to dinner—with his pleasant face still a little grimed with gunpowder, and flushed by his hurry up the steep hill-side.

"This for you, sir," he said, saluting the Admiral, presenting his letter, and then drawing back; "and I am to wait your convenience for reply."

"What next will the service come to," asked the Admiral of Captain Stubbard, "when a young man just commissioned gives himself such mighty airs? Shake hands, Blyth, and promise you will come and dine with us, unless you are ordered to return on board at once. How is your good captain? I knew him when he wore Nankins. Jem Prater brought word that he was wounded. I hope it is not serious."

"No, sir; not much to speak of. He has only lost three fingers. That was why I wrote this letter—or report, I ought to call it, if anybody else had written it. Oh, sir! I cannot bear to think of it! I was fifth luff when the fight began, and now there is only one left above me, and he is in command of our biggest prize, the Ville d'Anvers. But, Admiral, here you will find it all, as I wrote it, from the lips, when they tied up the fingers, of Captain Honyman."

"How could you tie them up when they were gone?" Captain Stubbard enquired, with a sneer at such a youth. He had got on very slowly in his early days, and could not bear to see a young man with such vacancies before him. "Why, you are the luckiest lad I ever saw! Sure to go up at least three steps. How well you must have kept out of it! And how happy you must feel, Lieutenant Scudamore!"

"I am not at all happy at losing dear friends," the young man answered, gently, as he turned away and patted the breech of a gun, upon which there was a little rust next day; "that feeling comes later in life, I suppose."

The Admiral was not attending to them now, but absorbed in the brief account of the conflict, begun by Captain Honyman in his own handwriting, and finished by his voice, but not his pen. Any one desirous to read this may do so in the proper place. For the present purpose it is enough to say that the modesty of the language was scarcely surpassed by the brilliancy of the exploit. And if anything were needed to commend the writer to the deepest good will of the reader, it was found in the fact that this enterprise sprang from warm zeal for the commerce of Springhaven. The Leda had been ordered on Friday last to protect the peaceful little fishing fleet from a crafty design for their capture, and this she had done with good effect, having justice on her side, and fortune. The particulars of the combat were not so clear, after the captain's three fingers were gone; but if one made proper allowance for that, there was not very much to complain of. The Admiral considered it a very good report; and then put on his spectacles, and thought it still better.

"Why! why! why!" he said—for without affectation many officers had caught the style of His then Gracious Majesty—"What's this? what's this? Something on the other side, in a different man's handwriting, and mighty difficult to read, in my opinion. Stubbard, did you ever see such a scrawl? Make it out for me. You have good eyes, like a hawk, or the man who saw through a milestone. Scudamore, what was his name? You know."

"Three fingers at five pounds apiece per annum as long as he lives!" Captain Stubbard computed on his own: "fifteen pounds a year perhaps for forty years, as you seem to say how young he is; that comes to just 600 pounds, and his hand as good as ever"—("I'll be hanged if it is, if he wrote this!" the Admiral interjected)—"and better, I must say, from a selfish point of view, because of only two nails left to clean, and his other hand increased in value; why, the scale is disgraceful, iniquitous, boobyish, and made without any knowledge of the human frame, and the comparative value of its members. Lieutenant Scudamore, look at me. Here you see me without an ear, damaged in the fore-hatch, and with the larboard bow stove in—and how much do I get, though so much older?"

"Well, if you won't help me, Stubbard," said the Admiral, who knew how long his friend would carry on upon that tack, "I must even get Scudamore to read it, though it seems to have been written on purpose to elude him. Blyth, my dear boy, can you explain it?"

"It was—it was only something, sir"—the lieutenant blushed, and hesitated, and looked away unmanfully—"which I asked Captain Honyman to leave out, because—because it had nothing to do with it. I mean, because it was of no importance, even if he happened to have that opinion. His hand was tied up so, that I did not like to say too much, and I thought that he would go to sleep, because the doctor had made him drink a poppy head boiled down with pigtail. But it seems as if he had got up after that—for he always will have his own way—while I was gone to put this coat on; and perhaps he wrote that with his left hand, sir. But it is no part of the business."

"Then we will leave it," said Admiral Darling, "for younger eyes than mine to read. Nelson wrote better with his left hand than ever he did with his right, to my thinking, the very first time that he tried it. But we can't expect everybody to do that. There is no sign of any change of weather, is there, Stubbard? My orders will depend very much upon that. I must go home and look at the quicksilver before I know what is best to do. You had better come with me, Scudamore."

Admiral Darling was quite right in this. Everything depended upon the weather; and although the rough autumn was not come yet, the prime of the hopeful year was past. The summer had not been a grand one, such as we get about once in a decade, but of loose and uncertain character, such as an Englishman has to make the best of. It might be taking up for a golden autumn, ripening corn, and fruit, and tree, or it might break up into shower and tempest, sodden earth, and weltering sky.

"Your captain refers to me for orders," said Admiral Darling to Scudamore, while they were hastening to the Hall, "as Commander of the Coast Defence, because he has been brought too far inshore, and one of the Frenchmen is stranded. The frigate you boarded and carried is the Ville d'Anvers, of forty guns. The corvette that took the ground, so luckily for you, when half of your hands were aboard the prize, is the Blonde, teak-built, and only launched last year. We must try to have her, whatever happens. She won't hurt where she is, unless it comes on to blow. Our sands hold fast without nipping, as you know, like a well-bred sheep-dog, and the White Pig is the toughest of all of them. She may stay there till the equinox, without much mischief, if the present light airs continue. But the worst job will be with the prisoners; they are the plague of all these affairs, and we can't imitate Boney by poisoning them. On the whole, it had better not have happened, perhaps. Though you must not tell Honyman that I said so. It was a very gallant action, very skilful, very beautiful; and I hope he will get a fine lift for it; and you too, my dear Blyth, for you must have fought well."

"But, Admiral, surely you would have been grieved if so many of your tenants, and their boats as well, had been swept away into a French harbour. What would Springhaven be without its Captain Zebedee?"

"You are right, Blyth; I forgot that for the moment. There would have been weeping and wailing indeed, even in our own household. But they could not have kept them long, though the loss of their boats would have been most terrible. But I cannot make out why the French should have wanted to catch a few harmless fishing-smacks. Aquila non captat muscas, as you taught the boys at Stonnington. And two ships despatched upon a paltry job of that sort! Either Captain Honyman was strangely misinformed, or there is something in the background, entirely beyond our knowledge. Pay attention to this matter, and let me know what you hear of it—as a friend, Blyth, as a friend, I mean. But here we are! You must want feeding. Mrs. Cloam will take care of you, and find all that is needful for a warrior's cleanup. I must look at the barometer, and consider my despatches. Let us have dinner, Mrs. Cloam, in twenty minutes, if possible. For we stand in real need of it."

Concerning that there could be no doubt. Glory, as all English officers know, is no durable stay for the stomach. The urgency of mankind for victuals may roughly be gauged by the length of the jaw. Captain Stubbard had jaws of tremendous length, and always carried a bag of captain's biscuits, to which he was obliged to have recourse in the height of the hottest engagement. Scudamore had short jaws, well set up, and powerful, without rapacity. But even these, after twelve hours of fasting, demanded something better than gunpowder. He could not help thinking that his host was regarding the condition of affairs very calmly, until he remembered that the day was Sunday, when no Briton has any call to be disturbed by any but sacred insistency. At any rate, he was under orders now, and those orders were entirely to his liking. So he freshened up his cheerful and simple-minded face, put his sailor-knot neckcloth askew, as usual, and with some trepidation went down to dinner.

The young ladies would not have been young women if they had not received him warmly. Kind Faith, who loved him as a sister might—for she had long discovered his good qualities—had tears in her beautiful eyes, as she gave him both hands, and smiled sweetly at his bashfulness. And even the critical Dolly, who looked so sharply at the outside of everything, allowed her fair hand to stay well in his, and said something which was melody to him. Then Johnny, who was of a warlike cast, and hoped soon to destroy the French nation, shook hands with this public benefactor already employed in that great work.

"I shall scarcely have time for a bit of dinner," said Admiral Darling, as they sat down. "I have sent word to have the Protector launched, and to give little Billy a feed of corn. All you young people may take your leisure. Youth is the time that commands time and space. But for my part, if I can only manage this plate of soup, and a slice of that fish, and then one help of mutton, and just an apple-fritter, or some trifle of that sort, I shall be quite as lucky as I can hope to be. Duty perpetually spoils my dinner, and I must get some clever fellow to invent a plate that will keep as hot as duty is in these volcanic times. But I never complain; I am so used to it. Eat your dinners, children, and don't think of mine."

Having scarcely afforded himself an hour, the Admiral, in full uniform, embarked upon little Billy, a gentle-minded pony from the west country, who conducted his own digestion while he consulted that of his rider. At the haven they found the Protector ready, a ten-oared galley manned by Captain Stubbard's men, good samples of Sea-Fencibles. And the Captain himself was there, to take the tiller, and do any fighting if the chance should arise, for he had been disappointed all the morning. The boat which brought Scudamore had been recalled by signal from the Leda, and that active young officer having sought her vainly, and thereby missed the Protector, followed steadily in Mr. Prater's boat, with the nephew, Jem, pulling the other oar, and Johnny Darling, who raged at the thought of being left behind, steering vaguely. And just as they rounded the harbour-head, the long glassy sweep of the palpitating sea bore inward and homeward the peaceful squadron, so wistfully watched for and so dearly welcome.

CHAPTER XXIII

YOH-HEAVE-OH!

"Her condition was very bad, as bad as could be, without going straight to the bottom," the Admiral said to the Rector that night, as they smoked a pipe together; "and to the bottom she must have gone, if the sea had got up, before we thrummed her. Honyman wanted to have her brought inside the Head; but even if we could have got there, she would ground at low water and fill with the tide. And what could we do with all those prisoners? With our fresh hands at the pumps, we very soon fetched the water out of her, and made her as tight as we could; and I think they will manage to take her to Portsmouth. She has beautiful lines. I never saw a smarter ship. How she came to the wind, with all that water in her! The wind is all right for Portsmouth, and she will be a fine addition to the Navy."

"But what is become of the other vessel, craft, corvette, or whatever you call her? You say that she is scarcely hurt at all. And if she gets off the White Pig's back in the night, she may come up and bombard us. Not that I am afraid; but my wife is nervous, and the Rectory faces the sea so much. If you have ordered away the Leda, which seems to have conquered both of them, the least you can do is to keep Captain Stubbard under arms all night in his battery."

"I have a great mind to do so; it would be a good idea, for he was very much inclined to cut up rough to-day. But he never would forgive me, he is such a hog at hammock—as we used to say, until we grew too elegant. And he knows that the Blonde has hauled down her colours, and Scudamore is now prize-captain. I have sent away most of her crew in the Leda, and I am not at all sure that we ought not to blow her up. In the end, we shall have to do so, no doubt; for nothing larger than a smack has ever got off that sand, and floated. But let our young friend try; let him have a fair trial. He has the stuff of a very fine seaman in him. And if he should succeed, it would be scored with a long leg for him. Halloa! Why, I thought the girls were fast asleep long ago!"

"As if we could sleep, papa, with this upon our minds!" Dolly waved an open letter in the air, and then presented it. "Perhaps Faith might, but I am sure I never could. You defied us to make out this, which is on the other leaf; and then, without giving us fair play, you took it to the desk in your Oak-room, and there you left it. Well, I took the liberty of going there for it, for there can't be any secret about a thing that will be printed; and how are they to print it, if they can't contrive to read it? How much will you pay me for interpreting, papa? Mr. Twemlow, I think I ought to have a guinea. Can you read it, now, with all your learning, and knowledge of dead languages?"

"My dear, it is not my duty to read it, and not at all my business. It seems to be written with the end of a stick, by a boy who was learning his letters. If you can interpret it, you must be almost a Daniel."

"Do you hear that, papa, you who think I am so stupid? Faith gave it up; she has no perseverance, or perhaps no curiosity. And I was very nearly beaten too, till a very fine idea came into my head, and I have made out every word except three, and perhaps even those three, if Captain Honyman is not very particular in his spelling. Can you tell me anything about that, papa?"

"Yes, Dolly, just what you have heard from me before. Honyman is a good officer; a very good one, as he has just proved. No good officer ever spells well, whether in the army or the navy. Look at Nelson's letters. I am inclined to ascribe my own slow promotion to the unnatural accuracy of my spelling, which offended my lords, because it puzzled them."

"Then all is straight sailing, as you say, papa. But I must tell you first how I found it out, or perhaps you won't believe me. I knew that Captain Honyman wrote this postscript, or whatever it is, with his left hand, so I took a pen in my own left hand, and practised all the letters, and the way they join, which is quite different from the other hand. And here is the copy of the words, as my left hand taught my right to put them down, after inking ever so many fingers:

"'We never could have done it without Scudamore. He jumped a most wonderful jump from our jib-boom into her mizzen chains, when our grapples had slipped, and we could get no nearer, and there he made fast, though the enemy came at him with cutlasses, pikes, and muskets. By this means we borded and carried the ship, with a loss as above reported. When I grew faint from a trifling wound, Luff Scudamore led the borders with a cool courage that discomfited the fo.'"

"Robert Honyman all over!" cried the Admiral, with delight. "I could swear that he wrote it, if it was written with his toes. 'Twas an old joke against him, when he was lieutenant, that he never could spell his own title; and he never would put an e after an o in any word. He is far too straightforward a man to spell well; and now the loss of three fingers will cut his words shorter than ever, and be a fine excuse for him. He was faint again, when I boarded the Leda, partly no doubt through strong medical measures; for the doctor, who is an ornament to his profession, had cauterised his stumps with a marlinspike, for fear of inflammation. And I heard that he had singed the other finger off. But I hope that may prove incorrect. At any rate, I could not bear to disturb him, but left written orders with Scudamore; for the senior was on board the prize. Dolly, be off to bed, this moment."

"Well, now," said the Rector, drawing near, and filling another deliberative pipe, "I have no right to ask what your orders were, and perhaps you have no right to tell me. But as to the ship that remains in my parish, or at any rate on its borders, if you can tell me anything, I shall be very grateful, both as a question of parochial duty, and also because of the many questions I am sure to have to answer from my wife and daughter."

"There is no cause for secrecy; I will tell you everything:" the Admiral hated mystery. "Why, the London papers will publish the whole of it, and a great deal more than that, in three days' time. I have sent off the Leda with her prize to Portsmouth. With this easterly breeze and smooth water, they will get there, crippled as they are, in some twenty-four hours. There the wounded will be cared for, and the prisoners drafted off. The Blonde, the corvette which is aground, surrendered, as you know, when she found herself helpless, and within range of our new battery. Stubbard's men longed to have a few shots at her; but of course we stopped any such outrage. Nearly all her officers and most of her crew are on board the Leda, having given their parole to attempt no rising; and Frenchmen are always honourable, unless they have some very wicked leader. But we left in the corvette her captain, an exceedingly fine fellow, and about a score of hands who volunteered to stay to help to work the ship, upon condition that if we can float her, they shall have their freedom. And we put a prize crew from the Leda on board her, only eight-and-twenty hands, which was all that could be spared, and in command of them our friend Blyth Scudamore. I sent him to ask Robert Honyman about it, when he managed to survive the doctor, for a captain is the master of his own luffs; and he answered that it was exactly what he wished. Our gallant frigate lost three lieutenants in this very spirited action, two killed and one heavily wounded. And the first is in charge of the Ville d'Anvers, so there was nobody for this enterprise except the gentle Scuddy, as they call him. He is very young for such a business, and we must do all we can to help him."

"I have confidence in that young man," said Mr. Twemlow, as if it were a question of theology; "he has very sound views, and his principles are high; and he would have taken holy orders, I believe, if his father's assets had permitted it. He perceives all the rapidly growing dangers with which the Church is surrounded, and when I was in doubt about a line of Horace, he showed the finest diffidence, and yet proved that I was right. The 'White Pig,' as the name of a submarine bank, is most clearly of classic origin. We find it in Homer, and in Virgil too; and probably the Romans, who undoubtedly had a naval station in Springhaven, and exterminated the oyster, as they always

144

did—"

"Come, come, Twemlow," said the Admiral, with a smile which smoothed the breach of interruption, "you carry me out of my depth so far that I long to be stranded on my pillow. When your great book comes out, we shall have in perfect form all the pile of your discoveries, which you break up into little bits too liberally. The Blonde on the Pig is like Beauty and the Beast. If gentle Scuddy rescues her, it won't be by Homer, or Horace, or even holy orders, but by hard tugs and stout seamanship."

"With the blessing of the Lord, it shall be done," said the Rector, knocking his pipe out; "and I trust that Providence may see fit to have it done very speedily; for I dread the effect which so many gallant strangers, all working hard and apparently in peril, may produce upon the females of this parish."

But the Admiral laughed, and said, "Pooh, pooh!" for he had faith in the maids of Springhaven.

For these there was a fine time now in store—young men up and down everywhere, people running in and out with some new news, before they could get their hats on, the kettle to boil half a dozen times a day, and almost as much to see as they could talk of. At every high-water that came by daylight—and sometimes there were two of them—every maid in the parish was bound to run to the top of a sand-hill high enough to see over the neck of the Head, and there to be up among the rushes all together, and repulse disdainfully the society of lads. These took the matter in a very different light, and thought it quite a pity and a piece of fickle-mindedness, that they might go the round of crab-pots, or of inshore lug-lines, without anybody to watch them off, or come down with a basket to meet them.

For be it understood that the great fishing fleet had not launched forth upon its labours. Their narrow escape from the two French cruisers would last them a long time to think over, and to say the same thing to each other about it that each other had said to them every time they met. And they knew that they could not do this so well as to make a new credit of it every time, when once they were in the same craft together, and could not go asunder more than ten yards and a half. And better, far better, than all these reasons for staying at home and enjoying themselves, was the great fact that they could make more money by leisure than by labour, in this nobly golden time.

Luck fostered skill in this great affair, which deserves to be recorded for the good of any village gifted with like opportunity. It appears that the British Admiralty had long been eager for the capture of the Blonde, because of her speed and strength and beauty, and the mischief she had done to English trade. To destroy her would be a great comfort, but to employ her aright would be glorious; and her proper employment was to serve as a model for English frigates first, and then to fight against her native land. Therefore, no sooner did their lordships hear what had happened at Springhaven than they sent down a rider express, to say that the ship must be saved at any price. And as nothing could be spared from the blockading force, or the fleet in the Downs, or the cruising squadron, the Commander of the coast-defence was instructed to enrol, impress, or adapt somehow all the men and the matter available. Something was said about free use of money in the service of His Majesty, but not a penny was sent to begin upon. But Admiral Darling carried out his orders, as if he had received them framed in gold. "They are pretty sure to pay me in the end," he said; "and if they don't, it won't break me. I would give 500 pounds on my own account, to carry that corvette to Spithead. And it would be the making of Scudamore, who reminds me of his father more and more, every time I come across him."

The fleet under Captain Tugwell had quite lately fallen off from seven to five, through the fierce patriotism of some younger members, and their sanguine belief in bounty-money. Captain Zeb had presented them with his experience in a long harangue—nearly fifty words long—and they looked as if they were convinced by it. However, in the morning they were gone, having mostly had tiffs with their sweethearts—which are fervent incentives to patriotism—and they chartered themselves, and their boats were numbered for the service of their Country. They had done their work well, because they had none to do, except to draw small wages, and they found themselves qualified now for more money, and came home at the earliest chance of it.

Two guineas a day for each smack and four hands, were the terms offered by the Admiral, whose hard-working conscience was twitched into herring-bones by the strife between native land and native spot. "I have had many tussles with uncertainty before," he told Dolly, going down one evening, "but never such vexation of the mind as now. All our people expect to get more for a day, than a month of fine fishing would bring them; while the Government goes by the worst time they make, and expects them to throw in their boats for nothing. 'The same as our breeches,' Tugwell said to me; 'whenever we works, we throws in they, and we ought to do the very same with our boats.' This makes it very hard for me."

But by doing his best, he got over the hardship, as people generally do. He settled the daily wages as above, with a bonus of double that amount for the day that saw the Blonde upon her legs again. Indignation prevailed, or pretended to do so; but common-sense conquered, and all set to work. Hawsers, and chains, and buoys, and all other needful gear and tackle were provided by the Admiralty from the store-house built not long ago for the

Fencibles. And Zebedee Tugwell, by right of position, and without a word said for it—because who could say a word against it?—became the commander of the Rescue fleet, and drew double pay naturally for himself and family.

"I does it," he said, "if you ask me why I does it, without any intention of bettering myself, for the Lord hath placed me above need of that; but mainly for the sake of discipline, and the respectability of things. Suppose I was under you, sir, and knew you was getting no more than I was, why, my stomach would fly every time that you gave me an order without a 'Please, Zebedee!' But as soon as I feels that you pocket a shilling, in the time I take pocketing twopence, the value of your brain ariseth plain before me; and instead of thinking what you says, I does it."

CHAPTER XXIV

ACCORDING TO CONTRACT

When the Blonde had been on the White Pig for a week, in spite of all the science of Scudamore, ready money of the Admiral, and efforts of the natives, there began to be signs of a change in the weather. The sea was as smooth, and the sky as bright, and the land as brown as ever; but the feel of the air was not the same, and the sounds that came through it were different. "Rain afore Friday," said Captain Zeb, "and a blow from sowwest afore Sunday. 'Twill break up the Blunder, I reckon, my lads."

With various aspects they looked at him, all holding sweet converse at the Darling Arms, after the manifold struggles of the day. The eyes of the younger men were filled with disappointment and anger, as at a sure seer of evil; the elder, to whom cash was more important, gazed with anxiety and dismay; while a pair, old enough to be sires of Zebedee, nodded approval, and looked at one another, expecting to receive, but too discreet to give, a wink. Then a lively discourse arose and throve among the younger; and the elders let them hold it, while they talked of something else.

On the following morning two dialogues were held upon different parts of Springhaven shore, but each of great import to the beautiful captive still fast aground in the offing. The first was between Captain Zebedee Tugwell and Lieutenant Scudamore. The gentle Scuddy, still hoping against hope, had stuck fast to his charge, upon whose fortunes so much of his own depended. If he could only succeed in floating and carrying her into Portsmouth, his mark would be made, his position secured far quicker than by ten gallant actions; and that which he cared for a hundredfold, the comfort of his widowed mother, would be advanced and established. For, upon the valuation of the prizes, a considerable sum would fall to him, and every farthing of it would be sent to her. Bright with youthful hope, and trustful in the rising spring of tide, which had all but released them yesterday, according to his firm belief, he ran from the Hall through the Admiral's grounds, to meet the boat which was waiting for him, while he was having breakfast and council with his chief. Between the Round-house and the old white gate he heard a low whistle from a clump of shrubs, and turning that way, met Tugwell. With that prince of fishermen he shook hands, according to the manner of Springhaven, for he had learned to admire the brave habit of the man, his strong mind, and frank taciturnity. And Tugwell on his part had taken a liking to the simple and cheerful young officer, who received his suggestions, was kind to all hands, and so manfully bore the daily disappointment.

"Nobody in there?" asked Zeb, with one finger pointing to the Round-house; "then sit down on this bit of bank, sir, a minute. Less chance to be shot at by any French ship."

The bit of bank really was a bit of hollow, where no one could see them from the beach, or lane, or even from the Round-house. Scudamore, who understood his man, obeyed; and Tugwell came to his bearings on a clump of fern before him.

"How much will Government pay the chaps as fetches her out of that snug little berth? For division to self and partners, how much? For division to self and family, how much?"

"I have thought about that," the lieutenant answered, with little surprise at the question, but much at the secrecy thrown around it; "and I think it would be very unsafe to count upon getting a penny beyond the Admiral's terms—double pay for the day that we float her."

Captain Zebedee shook his head, and the golden sheaf of his Olympian beard ruffled and crisped, as to an adverse wind.

"Can't a'most believe it," he replied, with his bright eyes steadily settled on Scudamore's; "the English country, as I belongs to, can't quite 'a coom to that yet!"

"I fear that it has indeed," Blyth answered, very gravely; "at least I am sure of this, Master Tugwell, that you must not look forward to any bounty, bonus, or premium, or whatever it is called, from the Authorities who should provide it. But for myself, and the difference it will make to me whether we succeed or fail, I shall be happy, and will give my word, to send you 50 pounds, to be divided at your discretion among the smacks. I mean, of course, as soon as I get paid."

Scudamore was frightened by the size of his own promise; for he had never yet owned 50 pounds in the solid. And then he was scared at the wholesale loss of so large a sum to his mother.

"Never fear, lad," honest Tugwell replied, for the young man's face was fair to read; "we'll not take a farden of thy hard airnings, not a brass farden, so help me Bob! Gentlefolks has so much call for money, as none of us know nothing of. And thou hast helped to save all the lot of us from Frenchies, and been the most forwardest, as I hear tell. But if us could 'a got 50 pounds out of Government, why so much more for us, and none the less for they. But a Englishman must do his duty, in reason, and when 'a don't hurt his self by the same. There's a change in the weather, as forbids more sport. You shall have the Blunder off to-morrow, lad. Wouldn't do to be too sudden like."

"I fear I am very stupid, Master Tugwell. But I don't see how you can manage it so surely, after labouring nine days all in vain."

Zebedee hesitated half a moment, betwixt discretion and the pride of knowledge. Then the latter vanquished and relieved his mind.

"I trust in your honour, sir, of course, to keep me clear. I might have brought 'e off the Pig, first day, or second to the latest, if it were sound business. But with winter time coming, and the week's fishing lost, our duty to our families and this place was to pull 'e on harder, sir, to pull 'e aground firmer; and with the help of the Lord we have a-doed it well. We wasn't a-going to kill the goose as laid the golden eggs. No offence to you, sir; it wasn't you as was the goose."

Master Tugwell rubbed his pockets with a very pleasant smile, and then put his elbows on his great square knees, and complacently studied the lieutenant's smaller mind.

"I can understand how you could do such a thing," said Scudamore, after he had rubbed his eyes, and then looked away for fear of laughing, "but I cannot understand by what power on earth you are enabled to look at me and tell me this. For nine days you have been paid every night, and paid pretty well, as you yourself acknowledge, to haul a ship off a shoal; and all the time you have been hauling her harder upon it!"

"Young man," replied Tugwell, with just indignation, "a hofficer should be above such words. But I forgive 'e, and hope the Lord will do the same, with allowance for youth and ill-convenience. I might 'a knowed no better, at your age and training."

"But what were you paid for, just answer me that, unless it was to pull the Blonde off the sand-bank? And how can you pretend that you have done an honest thing by pulling her further upon the bank?"

"I won't ask 'e, sir, to beg my pardon for saying what never man said to me, without reading the words of the contraction;" Zeb pulled out a paper from his hat, and spread it, and laid a stone at every corner; "this contraction was signed by yourself and Squire Darling, for and on behalf of the kingdom; and the words are for us to give our services, to pull, haul, tow, warp, or otherwise as directed, release, relieve, set free, and rescue the aforesaid ship, or bark, or vessel, craft, or—"

"Please not to read all that," cried Scuddy, "or a gale of wind may come before you are half-way through. It was Admiral Darling's lawyer, Mr. Furkettle, who prepared it, to prevent any chance of misunderstanding."

"Provided always," continued Tugwell, slowly, "and the meaning, condition, purport, object, sense, and intention of this agreement is, that the aforesaid Zebedee Tugwell shall submit in everything to the orders, commands, instructions, counsel, directions, injunctions, authority, or discretion, whether in writing or otherwise, of the aforesaid—"

"I would not interrupt you if I could help it"—Scudamore had a large stock of patience (enhanced by laborious practice at Stonnington), but who might abide, when time was precious, to see Zebedee feeling his way with his fingers along the bottom and to the end of every word, and then stopping to congratulate himself at the conquest of every one over two syllables? "But excuse me for saying that I know all these conditions; and the tide will be lost, if we stop here."

"Very good, sir; then you see how it standeth. Who hath broken them? Not us! We was paid for to haul; and haul we did, according to superior orders. She grounded from the south, with the tide making upp'ard, somewhere about three-quarter flow; and the Squire, and you, and all the rest of 'e, without no knowledge of the Pig whatsomever, fastens all your pulley-haulies by the starn, and says, 'now pull!' And pull we did, to the tune of sixteen guineas a day for the good of Springhaven."

"And you knew all the time that it was wrong! Well, I never came across such people. But surely some one of you would have had the honesty—I beg pardon, I mean the good-will—to tell us. I can scarcely imagine some forty men and boys preserving such a secret for nine whole days, hauling for their lives in the wrong direction, and never even by a wink or smile—"

"Springhaven is like that," said Master Tugwell, proudly; "we does a thing one and all together, even if us reasons consarning it. And over and above that, sir, there is but two men in Springhaven as understands the White Pig, barring my own self. The young 'uns might 'a smelt a rat, but they knew better than to say so. Where the Blunder grounded—and she hath airned her name, for the good of the dwellers in this village—is the chine of the Pig; and he hath a double back, with the outer side higher than the inner one. She came through a narrow nick in his outer back, and then plumped, stem on, upon the inner one. You may haul at her forever by the starn, and there she'll 'bide, or lay up again on the other back. But bring her weight forrard, and tackle her by the head, and off she comes, the very next fair tide; for she hath berthed herself over the biggest of it, and there bain't but a basketful under her forefoot."

"Then, Master Tugwell, let us lose no time, but have at her at once, and be done with it." Scudamore jumped up, to give action to his words; but Tugwell sate aground still, as firmly as the Blonde.

"Begging of your pardon, sir, I would invite of you not to be in no sart of hurry hasting forwardly. Us must come off gradual, after holding on so long there, and better to have Squire Darling round the corner first, sir. Not that he knoweth much about it, but 'a might make believe to do so. And when 'a hath seen us pull wrong ways, a hundred and twenty guineas' worth, a' might grudge us the reward for pulling right ways. I've a-knowed 'un get into that state of mind, although it was his own tenants."

The lieutenant was at length compelled to laugh, though for many reasons loth to do so. But the quiet contempt for the Admiral's skill, and the brief hint about his character, touched his sense of the ludicrous more softly than the explanation of his own mishaps. Then the Captain of Springhaven smiled almost imperceptibly; for he was a serious man, and his smiles were accustomed to be interior.

"I did hear tell," he said, stroking his beard, for fear of having discomposed it, "that the Squire were under compulsion to go a bit westward again to-morrow. And when he cometh back he would be glad to find us had managed the job without him. No fear of the weather breaking up afore Friday, and her can't take no harm for a tide or two. If you thinks well, sir, let us heave at her to-day, as afore, by superior orders. Then it come into your mind to try t'other end a bit, and you shift all the guns and heavy lumber forrard to give weight to the bows and lift the starn, and off her will glide at the first tug to-morrow, so sure as my name is Zebedee. But mind one thing, sir, that you keep her, when you've got her. She hath too many furriner natives aboard of her, to be any way to my liking."

"Oh, there need be no doubt about them," replied Blyth; "we treat them like ourselves, and they are all upon their honour, which no Frenchman ever thinks of breaking. But my men will be tired of waiting for me. I shall leave you to your plans, Tugwell."

"Ah, I know the natur' of they young men," Captain Zebedee mused, as he sate in his hollow, till Scudamore's boat was far away; "they be full of scruples for themselves and faith in other fellows. He'll never tell Squire, nor no one else here, what I laid him under, and the laugh would go again' him, if he did. We shall get to-day's money, I reckon, as well as double pay to-morrow, and airn it. Well, it might 'a been better, and it might be wuss."

About two miles westward of the brook, some rocks marked the end of the fine Springhaven sands and the beginning of a far more rugged beach, the shingles and flint shelves of Pebbleridge. Here the chalk of the Sussex backbone (which has been plumped over and sleeked by the flesh of the valley) juts forth, like the scrags of a skeleton, and crumbles in low but rugged cliffs into the flat domain of sea. Here the landing is bad, and the anchorage worse, for a slippery shale rejects the fluke, and the water is usually kept in a fidget between the orders of the west wind and scurry of the tide.

This very quiet morning, with the wind off shore, and scarcely enough of it to comb the sea, four smart-looking Frenchmen, with red caps on their heads, were barely holding way upon the light gig of the Blonde, while their Captain was keeping an appointment with a stranger, not far from the weed-strewn line of waves. In a deep rocky channel where a land-spring rose (which was still-born except at low water), and laver and dilsk and claw-coral showed that the sea had more dominion there than the sky, two men stood facing each other; and their words, though belonging to the most polite of tongues, were not so courteous as might be. Each man stood with his back to a rock—not touching it, however, because it was too wet—one was as cold and as firm as the rock, the other like the sea, tumultuous. The passionate man was Captain Desportes, and the cold one Caryl Carne.

"Then you wish me to conclude, monsieur," Carne spoke as one offering repentance, "that you will not do your duty to your country, in the subject set before you? I pray you to deliberate, because your position hangs upon it."

"Never! Never! Once more, Captain, with all thanks for your consideration, I refuse. My duty to my own honour has first place. After that my duty to my country. Speak of it no more, sir; it quite is to insult me."

"No, Captain Desportes, it is nothing of that kind, or I should not be here to propose it. Your parole is given only as long as your ship continues upon the sand. The moment she floats, you are liberated. Then is the time for a noble stroke of fortune. Is it not so, my dear friend?"

"No, sir. This affair is impossible. My honour has been pledged, not until the ship is floating, but until I am myself set free in France. I am sorry not to see things as you see them for me; but the question is for my own consideration."

Captain Desportes had resented, as an honest man must do, especially when more advanced in years, the other's calm settlement, without invitation, of matters which concerned his own conscience. And as most mankind—if at all perceptive—like or dislike one another at a glance, Desportes, being very quick and warm of nature, had felt at first sight a strong repulsion from the cold and arrogant man who faced him. His age was at least twice that of Carne, he had seen much service in the better days of France, and had risen slowly by his own skill and valour; he knew that his future in the service depended upon his decision in this matter, and he had a large family to maintain. But his honour was pledged, and he held fast by it.

"There is one consideration," Carne replied, with rancour slowly kindling in his great black eyes, "which precedes all others, even that of honour, in the mind of a trusted officer. It is not that of patriotism—which has not its usual weight with monsieur—but it is that of obedience, discipline, loyalty, faith, towards those who have placed faith in him. Captain Desportes, as commander of a ship, is entrusted with property; and that confidence is the first debt upon his honour."

To Desportes, as to most men of action, the right was plainer than the reason. He knew that this final plea was unsound, but he did not see how to contest it. So he came back to fact, which was easier for him.

"How am I to know, monsieur, what would be the wishes of those who have entrusted me with my position? You are placed in authority by some means here, in your own country, but against it. That much you have proved to me, by papers. But your credentials are general only. They do not apply to this especial case. If the Chief of the State knew my position, he would wish me to act as I mean to act, for the honour and credit of our nation."

"Are you then acquainted with his signature? If so, perhaps you will verify this, even if you are resolved to reject it."

Carne drew a letter from an inner pocket, and carefully unfolded it. There were many words and minute directions upon various subjects, written by the hand of the most minute, and yet most comprehensive, of mankind.

"There is nothing in this that concerns you," he said, after showing the date, only four days old, "except these few words at the end, which perhaps you may like to read, before you make final decision. The signature of the Chief is clear."

Captain Desportes read aloud—"It is of the utmost importance to me, that the Blonde should not be captured by the enemy, as the Ville d'Anvers has been. You tell me that it is ashore near you, and the Captain and crew upon parole, to be liberated if they assist in the extrication of the vessel. This must not be. In the service of the State, I demand that they consider not at all their parole. The well-known speed and light draught of that vessel have rendered her almost indispensable to me. When the vessel is free, they must rise upon the enemy, and make for the nearest of our ports without delay. Upon this I insist, and place confidence in your established courage and management, to accomplish it to my satisfaction."

"Your orders are clear enough," said Caryl Carne. "What reason can you give, as an officer of the Republic, for disobeying them?"

Desportes looked at his ship in the distance, and then at the sea and the sky, with a groan, as if he were bidding farewell to them. Carne felt sure that he had prevailed, and a smile shed light, but not a soft light, on his hard pale countenance.

"Be in no rash haste," said the French sea-captain, and he could not have found words more annoying to the cold proud man before him; "I do not recognise in this mandate the voice of my country, of the honourable France, which would never say, 'Let my sons break their word of honour!' This man speaks, not as Chief of a grand State, not as leader of noble gentlemen, but as Emperor of a society of serfs. France is no empire; she is a grand nation of spirit, of valour, above all, of honour. The English have treated me, as I would treat them, with kindness, with largeness, with confidence. In the name of fair France, I will not do this thing."

Carne was naturally pale, but now he grew white with rage, and his black eyes flashed.

"France will be an empire within six months; and your honour will be put upon prison diet, while your family starve for the sake of it."

"If I ever meet you under other circumstances," replied the brave Frenchman, now equally pale, "I shall demand reparation, sir."

"With great pleasure," replied Carne, contemptuously; "meanwhile monsieur will have enough to do to repair his broken fortunes."

Captain Desportes turned his back, and gave a whistle for his crew, then stepped with much dignity into his boat. "To the Blonde, lads," he cried, "to the unsullied Blonde!" Then he sate, looking at her, and stroked his grizzled beard, into which there came trickling a bitter tear or two, as he thought of his wife and family. He had acted well; but, according to the measure of the present world, unwisely.

CHAPTER XXV

NO CONCERN OF OURS

The very next morning it was known to the faithful of Springhaven that the glory of the place would be trebled that day, and its income increased desirably. That day, the fair stranger (which had so long awakened the admiration of the women, and the jealousy of the men) would by the consummate skill of Captain Zeb—who had triumphed over all the officers of the British Navy—float forth magnificently from her narrow bed, hoist her white sails, and under British ensign salute the new fort, and shape a course for Portsmouth. That she had stuck fast and in danger so long was simply because the cocked hats were too proud to give ear to the wisdom in an old otter-skin. Now Admiral Darling was baffled and gone; and Captain Tugwell would show the world what he could do, and what stuff his men were made of, if they only had their way. From old Daddy Stakes, the bald father of the village, to Mrs. Caper junior's baby—equally bald, but with a crop as sure of coming as mustard and cress beneath his flannel—some in arms, some on legs, some upon brave crutches, all were abroad in the soft air from the west, which had stolen up under the stiff steel skirt of the east wind, exactly as wise Captain Zeb predicted.

"My dear," said Mrs. Twemlow to the solid Mrs. Stubbard, for a very sweet friendship had sprung up between these ladies, and would last until their interests should happen to diverge, "this will be a great day for my dear husband's parish. Perhaps there is no other parish in the kingdom capable of acting as Springhaven has, so obedient, so disciplined, so faithful to their contract! I am told that they even pulled the vessel more aground, in preference to setting up their own opinions. I am told that as soon as the Admiral was gone—for between you and me he is a little overbearing, with the very best intentions in the world, but too confident in his own sagacity—then that clever but exceedingly modest young man, Lieutenant Scudamore, was allowed at last to listen to our great man Tugwell, who has long been the oracle of the neighbourhood about the sea, and the weather, and all questions of that kind. And between you and me, my dear, the poor old Admiral seems a little bit jealous of his reputation. And what do you think he said before he went, which shows his high opinion of his own abilities? Tugwell said something in his rough and ready way, which, I suppose, put his mightiness upon the high ropes, for he shouted out in everybody's hearing, 'I'll tell you what it is, my man, if you can get her off, by any of your'—something I must not repeat—'devices, I'll give you fifty guineas, five-and-twenty for yourself, and the rest to be divided among these other fellows.' Then Zebedee pulled out a Testament from his pocket, for he is a man of deep religious convictions, and can read almost all the easy places, though he thinks most of the hard ones, and he made his son Dan (who is a great scholar, as they say, and a very fine-looking youth as well) put down at the end what the Admiral had said. Now, what do you think of that, dear Mrs. Stubbard?"

"I think," replied that strong-minded lady, "that Tugwell is an arrant old fox; and if he gets the fifty guineas, he will put every farthing into his own pocket."

"Oh, no! He is honest as the day itself. He will take his own twenty-five, and then leave the rest to settle whether he should share in their twenty-five. But we must be quick, or we shall lose the sight. Quite a number of people are come from inland. How wonderfully quickly these things spread! They came the first day, and then made up their minds that nothing could be done, and so they stopped at home. But now, here they are again, as if by magic! If the ship gets off, it will be known halfway to London before nightfall. But I see Captain Stubbard going up the hill to your charming battery. That shows implicit faith in Tugwell, to return the salute of the fair captive! It is indeed a proud day for Springhaven!"

"But it isn't done yet. And perhaps it won't be done. I would rather trust officers of the navy than people who catch crabs and oysters. I would go up to the battery, to laugh at my husband, but for the tricks the children play me. My authority is gone, at the very first puff of smoke. How children do delight in that vile gunpowder!"

"So they ought, in the present state of our country, with five hundred thousand of Frenchmen coming. My dear Mrs. Stubbard, how thankful we should be to have children who love gunpowder!"

"But not when they blow up their mother, ma'am."

"Oh, here comes Eliza!" cried Mrs. Twemlow. "I am so glad, because she knows everything. I thought we had missed her. My dear child, where are Faith and Dolly Darling gone? There are so many strangers about to-day that the better class should keep together."

"Here are three of us at any rate," replied the young lady, who considered her mother old-fashioned: "enough to secure one another's sanctity from the lower orders. Faith has gone on to the headland, with that heroic mannikin, Johnny. Dolly was to follow, with that Shanks maid to protect her, as soon as her hat was trimmed, or some such era. But I'll answer for it that she loses herself in the crowd, or some fib of that sort."

"Eliza!" said her mother, and very severely, because Mrs. Stubbard was present, "I am quite astonished at your talking so. You might do the greatest injury to a very lively and harmless, but not over-prudent girl, if any one heard you who would repeat it. We all know that the Admiral is so wrapped up in Dolly that he lets her do many things which a mother would forbid. But that is no concern of ours; and once for all, if such things must be said, I beg that they may not be said by you."

In the present age, Mrs. Twemlow would have got sharp answer. But her daughter only looked aggrieved, and glanced at Mrs. Stubbard, as if to say, "Well, time will show whether I deserve it." And then they hastened on, among the worse class, to the headland.

Not only all the fishing-smacks, and Captain Stubbard's galley, but every boat half as sound as a hat, might now be seen near the grounded vessel, preparing to labour or look on. And though the White Pig was allowed to be three-quarters of a mile from the nearest point, the mighty voice of Captain Zeb rode over the flickering breadth of sea, and through the soft babble of the waves ashore. The wind was light from southwest, and the warp being nearly in the same direction now, the Blonde began to set her courses, to catch a lift of air, when the tide should come busily working under her. And this would be the best tide since she took the ground, last Sunday week, when the springs were going off. As soon as the hawsers were made fast, and the shouts of Zebedee redoubled with great strength (both of sound and of language), and the long ropes lifted with a flash of splashes, and a creak of heavy wood, and the cry was, "With a will! with a will, my gay lads!" every body having a sound eye in it was gazing intently, and every heart was fluttering, except the loveliest eyes and quickest heart in all Springhaven.

Miss Dolly had made up her mind to go, and would have had warm words ready for any one rash enough to try to prevent her. But a very short note which was put into her hand about 10 A.M. distracted her.

"If you wish to do me a real service, according to your kind words of Saturday, be in the upper shrubbery at half past eleven; but tell no one except the bearer. You will see all that happens better there than on the beach, and I will bring a telescope."

Dolly knew at once who had written this, and admired it all the more because it was followed by no signature. For years she had longed for a bit of romance; and the common-sense of all the world irked her. She knew as well as possible that what she ought to do was to take this letter to her sister Faith, and be guided by her advice about it. Faith was her elder by three years or more, and as steadfast as a rock, yet as tender as young moss. There was no fear that Faith would ride the high horse with her, or lay down the law severely; she was much more likely to be too indulgent, though certain not to play with wrong.

All this the younger sister knew, and therefore resolved to eschew that knowledge. She liked her own way, and she meant to have it, in a harmless sort of way; her own high spirit should be her guide, and she was old enough now to be her own judge. Mr. Carne had saved her sister's life, when she stood up in that senseless way; and if Faith had no gratitude, Dolly must feel, and endeavour to express it for her.

Reasoning thus, and much better than this, she was very particular about her hat, and French pelerine of fluted lawn, and frock of pale violet trimmed on either side with gathered muslin. Her little heart fluttered at being drawn in, when it should have been plumped up to her neck, and very nearly displayed to the public; but her father was stern upon some points, and never would hear of the classic discoveries. She had not even Grecian sandals, nor a "surprise fan" to flutter from her wrist, nor hair oiled into flat Lesbian coils, but freedom of rich young tresses, and of graceful figure, and taper limbs. There was no one who could say her nay, of the lovers of maiden nature.

However, maidens must be discreet, even when most adventurous; and so she took another maid to help her, of respected but not romantic name—Jenny Shanks, who had brought her that letter. Jenny was much prettier than her name, and the ground she trod on was worshipped by many, even when her shoes were down at heel. Especially in this track remained the finer part of Charley Bowles's heart (while the coarser was up against the Frenchmen), as well as a good deal of Mr. Prater's nephew's, and of several other sole-fishers. This enabled Jenny to enter kindly into tender questions. And she fetched her Sunday bonnet down the trap-ladder where she kept it—because the other maids were so nasty—as soon as her letter was delivered.

"Your place, Jenny, is to go behind," Miss Dolly said, with no small dignity, as this zealous attendant kept step for step with her, and swung her red arm against the lady's fair one. "I am come upon important business, Jenny, such as you cannot understand, but may stay at a proper distance."

"Lor, miss, I am sure I begs your pardon. I thought it was a kind of coorting-match, and you might be glad of my experience."

"Such things I never do, and have no idea what you mean. I shall be much obliged to you, Jenny, if you will hold your tongue."

"Oh yes, miss; no fear of my telling anybody. Wild horses would never pull a syllable out of me. The young men is so aggravating that I keep my proper distance from them. But the mind must be made up, at one time or other."

Dolly looked down at her with vast contempt, which she would not lower herself by expressing, even with favour of time and place. Then turning a corner of the grassy walk, between ground-ash and young larches, they came upon an opening planted round with ilex, arbutus, juniper, and laurel, and backed by one of the rocks which form the outworks of the valley. From a niche in this rock, like the port-hole of a ship, a rill of sparkling water poured, and beginning to make a noise already, cut corner's—of its own production—short, in its hurry to be a brook, and then to help the sea. And across its exit from the rock (like a measure of its insignificance) a very comfortable seat was fixed, so that any gentleman—or even a lady with divided skirts—might freely sit with one foot on either bank of this menacing but not yet very formidable stream. So that on the whole this nook of shelter under the coronet of rock was a favourite place for a sage cock-pheasant, or even a woodcock in wintry weather.

Upon that bench (where the Admiral loved to sit, in the afternoon of peace and leisure, observing with a spy-glass the manoeuvres of his tranquil fishing fleet) Caryl Carne was sitting now, with his long and strong legs well spread out, his shoulders comfortably settled back, and his head cast a little on one side, as if he were trying to compute his property. Then, as Dolly came into the opening, he arose, made a bow beyond the compass of any true Briton, and swinging his hat, came to meet her. Dolly made a curtsey in the style impressed upon her by her last governess but one—a French lady of exceedingly high ancestry and manners—and Carne recognised it as a fine thing out of date.

"Jenny, get away!" said Dolly—words not meant for him to hear, but he had grave command of countenance.

"This lays me under one more obligation:" Carne spoke in a low voice, and with a smile of diffidence which reminded her of Scudamore, though the two smiles were as different as night and day. "I have taken a great liberty in asking you to come, and that multiplies my gratitude for your good-will. For my own sake alone I would not have dared to sue this great favour from you, though I put it so, in terror of alarming you. But it is for my own sake also, since anything evil to you would be terrible to me."

"No one can wish to hurt me," she answered, looking up at him bravely, and yet frightened by his gaze, "because I have never harmed any one. And I assure you, sir, that I have many to defend me, even when my father is gone from home."

"It is beyond doubt. Who would not rush to do so? But it is from those who are least suspected that the danger comes the worst. The most modest of all gentlemen, who blushes like a damsel, or the gallant officer devoted to his wife and children, or the simple veteran with his stars, and scars, and downright speech—these are the people that do the wrong, because no one believes it is in them."

"Then which of the three is to carry me off from home, and friends, and family—Lieutenant Scudamore, Captain Stubbard, or my own godfather, Lord Nelson?"

This young man nourished a large contempt for the intellect of women, and was therefore surprised at the quickness and spirit of the girl whom he wished to terrify. A sterner tone must be used with her.

"I never deal in jokes," he said, with a smile of sad sympathy for those who do; "my life is one perpetual peril, and that restrains facetiousness. But I can make allowance for those who like it."

Miss Dolly, the pet child of the house, and all the people round it—except the gardener, Mr. Swipes, who found her too inquisitive—quick as she was, could not realise at once the possibility of being looked down upon.

"I am sorry that you have to be so grave," she said, "because it prevents all enjoyment. But why should you be in such continual danger? You promised to explain it, on Saturday, only you had no time then. We are all in danger from the French, of course, if they ever should succeed in landing. But you mean something more than that; and it seems so hard, after all your losses, that you should not be safe from harm."

With all her many faults—many more than she dreamed of—fair Dolly had a warm and gentle heart, which filled her eyes with tender loveliness, whenever it obtained command of them. Carne, who was watching them steadfastly for his own purpose, forgot that purpose, and dropped his dark eyes, and lost the way to tell a lie.

"If I may ask you," he said, almost stammering, and longing without knowledge for the blessing of her touch, "to—to allow me just to lead you to this seat, I may perhaps be able—I will not take the liberty of sitting at your side—but I may perhaps be able to explain as much of my affairs as you can wish to hear of them, and a great deal more, I fear, a great deal more, Miss Darling."

Dolly blushed at the rich tone in which he pronounced her name, almost as if it were an adjective; but she allowed him to take her hand, and lead her to the bench beneath the rock. Then, regardless of his breeches, although of fine padusoy, and his coat, though of purple velvet, he sate down on the bank of the rill at her feet, and waited for her to say something. The young lady loved mainly to take the lead, but would liefer have followed suit just now.

"You have promised to tell me," she said, very softly, and with an unusual timidity, which added to her face and manner almost the only charm they lacked, "some things which I do not understand, and which I have no right to ask you of, except for your own offer. Why should you, without injuring any one, but only having suffered loss of all your family property, and of all your rights and comforts, and living in that lonely place which used to be full of company—why should you be in danger now, when you have nothing more to be robbed of? I beg your pardon—I mean when all your enemies must have done their worst."

"You are too young yet to understand the world," he answered, with a well-drawn sigh; "and I hope most truly that you may never do so. In your gentle presence I cannot speak with bitterness, even if I could feel it. I will not speak harshly of any one, however I may have been treated. But you will understand that my life alone remains betwixt the plunderers and their prey, and that my errand here prevents them from legally swallowing up the spoil."

Miss Dolly's idea of the law, in common with that of most young ladies, suggested a horrible monster ravening to devour the fallen. And the fall of the Carnes had long been a subject of romantic interest to her.

"Oh, I see!" she exclaimed, with a look of deep wisdom. "I can quite understand a thing like that, from what I have heard about witnesses. I hope you will be very careful. My sister owes so much to you, and so do I."

"You must never speak of that again, unless you wish to grieve me. I know that I have said too much about myself; but you alone care to know anything about me; and that beguiles one out—out of one's wits. If I speak bad English, you will forgive me. I have passed so many years on the Continent, and am picking up the language of my childhood very slowly. You will pardon me, when I am misled by—by my own signification."

"Well done!" cried the innocent Dolly. "Now that is the very first piece of bad English you have used, to the best of my belief, and I am rather quick in that. But you have not yet explained to me my own danger, though you asked me to come here for that purpose, I believe."

"But you shall not be so; you shall not be in danger. My life shall be given for your defence. What imports my peril compared with yours? I am not of cold blood. I will sacrifice all. Have faith in me purely, and all shall be done."

"All what?" Dolly asked, with a turn of common-sense, which is the most provoking of all things sometimes; and she looked at him steadily, to follow up her question.

"You cannot be persuaded that you are in any danger. It is possible that I have been too anxious. Do you speak the French language easily? Do you comprehend it, when spoken quickly?"

"Not a word of it. I have had to learn, of course, and can pronounce very well, my last mistress said; but I cannot make it out at all in the way the French people pronounce it, when one comes to talk with them."

"It is very wrong of them, and the loss is theirs. They expect us to copy them even in their language, because we do it in everything else. Pardon me —one moment. May I look at the great enterprise which is to glorify Springhaven? It is more than kind of you to be here instead of there. But this, as I ventured to say, is a far better place to observe the operation. Your words reminded me of Captain Desportes, who has been, I think, your father's guest. A very gallant sailor, and famed for the most unexpected exploits. Without doubt, he would have captured all three ships, if he had not contrived to run his own aground."

"How could he capture his own ship? I thought that you never dealt in jokes. But if you dislike them, you seem to be fond of a little mystery. I like the French captain very much, and he took the trouble to speak slowly for me. My father says that he bears his misfortune nobly, and like a perfect gentleman. Mr. Scudamore admires him, and they are great friends. And yet, sir, you seem inclined to hint that I am in danger from Captain Desportes!"

"Ha! she is afloat! They have succeeded. I thought that they had so arranged it. The brave ship spreads her pinions. How clever the people of Springhaven are! If you will condescend to look through this glass, you will see much embracing of the Saxon and the Gaul, or rather, I should say, of the Saxon by the Gaul. Old Tugwell is not fond to be embraced."

"Oh, let me see that! I must see that!" cried Dolly, with all reserve and caution flown; "to see Capp'en Zeb in the arms of a Frenchman—yes, I declare, two have got him, if not three, and he puts his great back against the mast to disentangle it. Oh, what will he do next? He has knocked down two, in reply to excessive cordiality. What wonderful creatures Frenchmen are! How kind it is of you to show me this! But excuse me, Mr. Carne; there will be twenty people coming to the house before I can get back almost. And the ship will salute the battery, and the battery will return it. Look! there goes a great puff of smoke already. They can see me up here, when they get to that corner."

"But this spot is not private? I trust that I have not intruded. Your father allows a sort of foot-path through this upper end of his grounds?"

"Yes, to all the villagers, and you are almost one of them; there is no right of way at all; and they very seldom come this way, because it leads to nowhere. Faith is fond of sitting here, to watch the sea, and think of things. And so am I—sometimes, I mean."

CHAPTER XXVI

LONG-PIPE TIMES

Daily now the roar and clank of war grew loud and louder, across the narrow seas, and up the rivers, and around the quiet homes of England. If any unusual cloud of dust, any moving shade, appeared afar, if the tramp of horses in the lane were heard, or neigh of a colt from the four-cross roads, people at dinner would start up and cry, "The French, the French have landed!" while the men in the fields would get nearer the hedge to peep through it, and then run away down the ditch.

But the nation at large, and the governing powers, certainly were not in any great fright. Nay, rather they erred, if at all, on the side of tranquillity and self-confidence; as one who has been fired at with blank-cartridge forgets that the click of the trigger will not tell him when the bullet has been dropped in. The bullet was there this time; and it missed the heart of Britannia, only through the failure of the powder to explode all at once.

It was some years before all this was known; even Nelson had no perception of it; and although much alarm was indulged in on the sly, the few who gave voice to it were condemned as faint-hearted fellows and "alarmists." How then could Springhaven, which never had feared any enemies, or even neighbours, depart from its habits, while still an eye-witness of what had befallen the Frenchman? And in this state of mind, having plenty to talk of, it did not (as otherwise must have been done) attach any deep importance to the strange vagaries of the London Trader.

That great Institution, and Royal Exchange, as well as central embassy of Fashion, had lately become most uncertain in its dates, which for years had announced to loose-reckoning housewives the day of the week and the hour to buy candles. Instead of coming home on a Saturday eve, in the van of all the fishing fleet, returning their cheers and those of customers on the beach, the London Trader arrived anywhere, as often in the dark as daylight, never took the ground at all, and gave a very wide berth to Captain Zeb Tugwell, his craft, and his crews. At times she landed packages big and bulky, which would have been searched (in spite of London bills of lading) if there had been any Custom-house here, or any keen Officer of Customs. But these were delivered by daylight always, and carted by Mr. Cheeseman's horse direct to his master's cellars; and Cheeseman had told everybody that his wife, having come into a little legacy, was resolved in spite of his advice to try a bit of speculation in hardware, through her sister miles away at Uckfield. Most of the neighbours liked Mrs. Cheeseman, because she gave good weight (scarcely half an ounce short, with her conscience to her family thrown in against it), as well as the soundest piece of gossip to be had for the money in Springhaven. And therefore they wished her well, and boxed their children's ears if they found them poking nose into her packages. Mrs. Cheeseman shook her head when enquired of on the subject, and said with grave truth that the Lord alone can tell how any of poor people's doings may turn out.

Some other things puzzled the village, and would in more sensible times have produced a sensation. Why did Mr. Cheeseman now think nothing of as much as three spots on his white linen apron, even in the first half of the week? Why was he seldom at John Prater's now, and silent in a corner even when he did appear? What was become of the ruddy polish, like that of a Winter Redstrake, on his cheeks, which made a man long for a slice of his ham? Why, the only joke he had made for the last three months was a terrible one at his own expense. He had rushed down the street about ten o'clock one morning, at a pace quite insane for a middle-aged man, with no hat on his head and no coat on his back, but the strings of his apron dashed wild on the breeze, and his biggest ham-carver making flashes in his hand. It was thought that some boy must have run off with a penny, or some visitor changed a bad shilling; but no, there was no such good reason to give for it.

The yearning of all ages, especially dotage, is for a relapse to the infantile state when all playthings were held in common. And this wisest of all places (in its own opinion) had a certain eccentric inclination towards the poetic perfection when it will be impossible to steal, because there will be nothing left worth stealing. Still everybody here stuck to his own rights, and would knock down anybody across them, though finding it very nice to talk as if others could have no such standing-point. Moreover, they had sufficient common-sense to begin with the right end foremost, and to take a tender interest in one another's goods, moveable, handy, and divisible; instead of hungering after hungry land, which feeds nobody, until itself well fed and tended, and is as useless without a master as a donkey or a man is. The knowledge of these rudiments of civilization was not yet lost at Springhaven; and while everybody felt and even proved his desire to share a neighbour's trouble, nobody meddled with any right of his, save his right to be assisted.

Among them throve the old English feeling of respect for ancient families, which is nowadays called "toadyism" by those whom it baulks of robbery. To trade upon this good-will is almost as low a thing as any man can do, even when he does it for good uses. But to trade upon it, for the harm of those who feel it, and the ruin of his country, is without exception the very lowest—and this was what Caryl Carne was at.

He looked at the matter in a wholly different light, and would have stabbed any man who put it as above; for his sense of honour was as quick and hot as it was crooked and misguided. His father had been a true Carne, of the old stamp—hot-blooded, headstrong, stubborn, wayward, narrow-minded, and often arrogant; but—to balance these faults and many others—truthful, generous, kind-hearted, affectionate, staunch to his friends, to his inferiors genial, loyal to his country, and respectful to religion. And he might have done well, but for two sad evils—he took a burdened property, and he plunged into a bad marriage.

His wife, on the other hand, might have done well, if she had married almost anybody else. But her nature was too like his own, with feminine vanity and caprice, French conceit, and the pride of noble birth—in the proudest age of nobility—hardening all her faults, and hammering the rivets of her strong self-will. To these little difficulties must be added the difference of religion; and though neither of them cared two pins for that, it was a matter for crossed daggers. A pound of feathers weighs as much as (and in some poise more than) a pound of lead, and the leaden-headed Squire and the feather-headed Madame swung always at opposite ends of the beam, until it broke between them. Tales of rough conflict, imprisonment, starvation, and even vile blows, were told about them for several years; and then "Madame la Comtesse" (as her husband disdainfully called her) disappeared, carrying off her one child, Caryl. She was still of very comely face and form; and the Squire made known to all whom it concerned, and many whom it did not concern, that his French wife had run away with a young Frenchman, according to the habit of her race and kind. In support of this charge he had nothing whatever to show, and his friends disbelieved it, knowing him to be the last man in the world to leave such a wrong unresented.

During the last three generations the fortunes of the Carnes had been declining, slowly at first, and then faster and faster; and now they fell with the final crash. The lady of high birth and great beauty had brought nothing else into the family, but rather had impoverished it by her settlement, and wild extravagance afterwards. Her husband Montagu Carne staved off the evil day just for the present, by raising a large sum upon second mortgage and the security of a trustful friend. But this sum was dissipated, like the rest; for the Squire, being deeply wounded by his wife's desertion, proved to the world his indifference about it by plunging into still more reckless ways. He had none to succeed him; for he vowed that the son of the adulteress—as he called her—should never have Carne Castle; and his last mad act was to buy five-and-twenty barrels of powder, wherewith to blow up his ancestral home. But ere he could accomplish that stroke of business he stumbled and fell down the old chapel steps, and was found the next morning by faithful Jeremiah, as cold as the ivy which had caught his feet, and as dead as the stones he would have sent to heaven.

No marvel that his son had no love for his memory, and little for the land that gave him birth. In very early days this boy had shown that his French blood was predominant. He would bite, and kick, and scratch, instead of striking, as an English child does, and he never cared for dogs or horses, neither worshipped he the gamekeeper. France was the proper land for him, as his mother always said with a sweet proud smile, and his father with a sneer, or a brief word now condemned. And France was the land for him (as facts ordained) to be nourished, and taught, and grown into tall manhood, and formed into the principles and habitude and character which every nation stamps upon the nature of its members.

However, our strong point—like that of all others—is absolute freedom from prejudice; and the few English people who met Caryl Carne were well pleased with his difference from themselves. Even the enlightened fishermen, imbued with a due contempt for Crappos, felt a kindly will towards him, and were touched by his return to a ruined home and a lonely life. But the women, romantic as they ought to be, felt a tender interest in a young man so handsome and so unlucky, who lifted his hat to them, and paid his way.

Among the rising spirits of the place, who liked to take a larger view, on the strength of more education, than their fathers had found confirmed by life, Dan Tugwell was perhaps the foremost. In the present days he might have been a hot radical, even a socialist; but things were not come to that pass yet among people brought up to their duty. And Dan's free sentiments had not been worked by those who make a trade of such work now. So that he was pleased and respectful, instead of carping and contradictory, when persons of higher position than his own would discuss the condition of the times with him. Carne had discovered this, although as a rule he said little to his neighbours, and for reasons of his own he was striving to get a good hold upon this young fellow. He knew that it could not be done in a moment, nor by any common corruption; the mind of the youth being keen, clear-sighted, and simple—by reason of soundness. Then Carne accidentally heard of something, which encouraged and helped him in his design upon Dan.

Business was slack upon the sea just now, but unusually active upon land, a tide of gold having flowed into Springhaven, and bubbled up in frying-pans and sparkled in new bonnets. The fishing fleet had captured the finest French frigate—according to feminine history—that ever endeavoured to capture them. After such a prisoner, let the fish go free, till hunger should spring again in the human breast, or the part that stands up under it. The hero of the whole (unlike most heroes) had not succeeded in ruining himself by his services to his country, but was able to go about patting his pocket, with an echo in his heart, every time it tinkled, that a quantity more to come into it was lying locked up in a drawer at home. These are the things that breed present happiness in a noble human nature, all else being either of the future or the past; and this is the reason why gold outweighs everything that can be said against it.

Captain Tugwell, in his pithy style, was wont to divide all human life into two distinctive tenses—the long-pipe time and the short-pipe time. The long-pipe time was of ease and leisure, comfort in the way of hot victuals and cool pots, the stretching of legs without strain of muscle, and that ever-fresh well-spring of delight to the hard worker, the censorial but not censorious contemplation of equally fine fellows, equally lazy, yet pegging hard, because of nothing in their pockets to tap. Such were the golden periods of standing, or, still better, sitting with his back against a tree, and a cool yard of clay between his gently smiling lips, shaving with his girdle-knife a cake of rich tobacco, and then milling it complacently betwixt his horny palms, with his resolute eyes relaxing into a gentle gaze at the labouring sea, and the part (where his supper soon would be) warming into a fine condition for it, by good-will towards all the world. As for the short-pipe times, with a bitter gale dashing the cold spray into his eyes, legs drenched with sleet, and shivering to the fork, and shoulders racked with rheumatism against the groaning mast, and the stump of a pipe keeping chatter with his teeth—away with all thought of such hardship now, except what would serve to fatten present comfort.

But fatherly feeling and sense of right compelled Captain Zeb to check idle enjoyment from going too far—i. e., further than himself. Every other member of his family but himself, however good the times might be, must work away as hard as ever, and earn whatever victuals it should please the Lord to send them. There was always a job to be found, he knew that, if a young man or maid had a mind for it; and "no silver no supper" was the order of his house. His eldest son Dan was the first to be driven—for a good example to the younger ones—and now he was set to work full time and overtime, upon a heavy job at Pebbleridge.

Young Daniel was not at all afraid of work, whenever there was any kind of skill to be shown, or bodily strength to be proved by it. But the present task was hateful to him; for any big-armed yokel, or common wood-hewer, might have done as much as he could do, and perhaps more, at it, and could have taken the same wage over it. Mr. Coggs, of Pebbleridge, the only wheelwright within ten miles of Springhaven, had taken a Government contract to supply within a certain time five hundred spoke-wheels for ammunition tumbrils, and as many block-wheels for small artillery; and to hack out these latter for better men to finish was the daily task of Dan Tugwell.

This job swelled his muscles and enlarged his calves, and fetched away all the fat he had been enabled to form in loftier walks of art; but these outward improvements were made at the expense of his inner and nobler qualities. To hack and hew timber by the cubic foot, without any growing pleasure of proportion or design, to knit the brows hard for a struggle with knots, and smile the stern smile of destruction; and then, after a long and rough walk in the dark—for the equinox now was impending—to be joked at by his father (who had lounged about all day), and have all his money told into the paternal pocket, with narrow enquiries, each Saturday night. But worst of all to know that because he was not born with a silver spoon in his mouth, he had no heart —no heart that he could offer where he laid it; but there it must lie, and be trodden on in silence, while rakish-looking popinjays—But this reflection stopped him, for it was too bitter to be thought out, and fetched down his quivering hand upon his axe. Enough that these things did not tend to a healthy condition of mind, or the proper worship of the British Constitution. However, he was not quite a Radical yet.

CHAPTER XXVII

FAIR IN THEORY

One Saturday evening, when the dusk was just beginning to smoothe the break of billow and to blunt the edge of rock, young Dan Tugwell swung his axe upon his shoulder, with the flag basket hanging from it in which his food had been, and in a rather crusty state of mind set forth upon his long walk home to Springhaven. As Harry Shanks had said, and almost everybody knew, an ancient foot-path, little used, but never yet obstructed, cut off a large bend of the shore, and saved half a mile of plodding over rock and shingle. This path was very lonesome, and infested with dark places, as well as waylaid with a very piteous ghost, who never would keep to the spot where he was murdered, but might appear at any shady stretch or woody corner. Dan Tugwell knew three courageous men who had seen this ghost, and would take good care to avoid any further interview, and his own faith in ghosts was as stanch as in gold; yet such was his mood this evening that he determined to go that way and chance it, not for the saving of distance, but simply because he had been told in the yard that day that the foot-path was stopped by the landowner. "We'll see about that," said Dan; and now he was going to see about it.

For the first field or two there was no impediment, except the usual stile or gate; but when he had crossed a little woodland hollow, where the fence of the castle grounds ran down to the brow of the cliff, he found entrance barred. Three stout oak rails had been nailed across from tree to tree, and on a board above them was roughly painted: "No thoroughfare. Tresspassers will be prosecuted." For a moment the young man hesitated, his dread of the law being virtuously deep, and his mind well assured that his father would not back him up against settled authorities. But the shame of turning back, and the quick sense of wrong, which had long been demanding some outlet, conquered his calmer judgment, and he cast the basket from his back. Then swinging his favourite axe, he rushed at the oaken bars, and with a few strokes sent them rolling down the steep bank-side.

"That for your stoppage of a right of way!" he cried; "and now perhaps you'll want to know who done it."

To gratify this natural curiosity he drew a piece of chalk from his pocket, and wrote on the notice-board in large round hand, "Daniel Tugwell, son of Zebedee Tugwell, of Springhaven." But suddenly his smile of satisfaction fled, and his face turned as white as the chalk in his hand. At the next turn of the path, a few yards before him, in the gray gloom cast by an ivy-mantled tree, stood a tall dark figure, with the right arm raised. The face was indistinct, but (as Dan's conscience told him) hostile and unforgiving; there was nothing to reflect a ray of light, and there seemed to be a rustle of some departure, like the spirit fleeing.

The ghost! What could it be but the ghost? Ghosts ought to be white; but terror scorns all prejudice. Probably this murdered one was buried in his breeches. Dan's heart beat quicker than his axe had struck; and his feet were off to beat the ground still quicker. But no Springhaven lad ever left his baggage. Dan leaped aside first to catch up his basket, and while he stooped for it, he heard a clear strong voice.

"Who are you, that have dared to come and cut my fence down?"

No ghost could speak like that, even if he could put a fence up. The inborn courage of the youth revived, and the shame of his fright made him hardier. He stepped forward again, catching breath as he spoke, and eager to meet any man in the flesh.

"I am Daniel Tugwell, of Springhaven. And no living man shall deny me of my rights. I have a right to pass here, and I mean to do it."

Caryl Carne, looking stately in his suit of black velvet, drew sword and stood behind the shattered barrier. "Are you ready to run against this?" he asked. "Poor peasant, go back; what are your rights worth?"

"I could smash that skewer at a blow," said Daniel, flourishing his axe as if to do it; "but my rights, as you say, are not worth the hazard. What has a poor man to do with rights? Would you stop a man of your own rank, Squire Carne?"

"Ah, that would be a different thing indeed! Justice wears a sword, because she is of gentle birth. Work-people with axes must not prate of rights, or a prison will be their next one. Your right is to be disdained, young man, because you were not born a gentleman; and your duty is to receive scorn with your hat off. You like it, probably, because your father did. But come in, Daniel; I will not deny you of the only right an English peasant has—the right of the foot to plod in his father's footsteps. The right of the hand, and the tongue, and the stomach—even the right of the eye is denied him; but by some freak of law he has some little right of foot, doubtless to enable him to go and serve his master."

Dan was amazed, and his better sense aroused. Why should this gentleman step out of the rank of his birth, to talk in this way? Now and then Dan himself had indulged in such ideas, but always with a doubt that they were wicked, and not long enough to make them seem good in his eyes. He knew that some fellows at "the Club" talked thus; but they were a lot of idle strangers, who came there chiefly to corrupt the natives, and work the fish trade out of their hands. These wholesome reflections made him doubt about accepting Squire Carne's invitation; and it would have been good for him if that doubt had prevailed, though he trudged a thousand miles for it.

"What! Break down a fence, and then be afraid to enter! That is the style of your race, friend Daniel. That is why you never get your rights, even when you dare to talk of them. I thought you were made of different stuff. Go home and boast that you shattered my fence, and then feared to come through it, when I asked you." Carne smiled at his antagonist, and waved his hand.

Dan leaped in a moment through the hanging splinters, and stood before the other, with a frown upon his face. "Then mind one thing, sir," he said, with a look of defiance, while touching his hat from force of habit, "I pass here, not with your permission, but of right."

"Very well. Let us not split words," said Carne, who had now quite recovered his native language. "I am glad to find a man that dares to claim his rights, in the present state of England. I am going towards Springhaven. Give me the pleasure of your company, and the benefit of your opinion upon politics. I have heard the highest praise of your abilities, my friend. Speak to me just as you would to one of your brother fishermen. By the accident of birth I am placed differently from you; and in this country that makes all the difference between a man and a dog, in our value. Though you may be, and probably are, the better man—more truthful, more courageous, more generous, more true-hearted, and certain to be the more humble of the two. I have been brought up where all men are equal, and the things I see here make a new world to me. Very likely these are right, and all the rest of the world quite wrong. Englishmen always are certain of that; and as I belong to the privileged classes, my great desire is to believe it. Only I want to know how the lower orders—the dregs, the scum, the dirt under our feet, the slaves that do all the work and get starved for it—how these trampled wretches regard the question. If they are happy, submissive, contented, delighted to lick the boots of their betters, my conscience will be clear to accept their homage, and their money for any stick of mine they look at. But you have amazed me by a most outrageous act. Because the lower orders have owned a path here for some centuries, you think it wrong that they should lose their right. Explain to me, Daniel, these extraordinary sentiments."

"If you please, sir," said Dan, who was following in the track, though invited to walk by the side, of Caryl Carne, "I can hardly tell you how the lower orders feel, because father and me don't belong to them. Our family have always owned their own boat, and worked for their own hand, this two hundred years, and, for all we know, ever since the Romans was here. We call them the lower orders, as come round to pick up jobs, and have no settlement in our village."

"A sound and very excellent distinction, Dan. But as against those who make the laws, and take good care to enforce them, even you (though of the upper rank here) must be counted of the lower order. For instance, can you look at a pheasant, or a hare, without being put into prison? Can you dine in the same room with Admiral Darling, or ask how his gout is, without being stared at?"

"No, sir. He would think it a great impertinence, even if I dared to do such a thing. But my father might do it, as a tenant and old neighbour. Though he never gets the gout, when he rides about so much."

"What a matter-of-fact youth it is! But to come to things every man has a right to. If you saved the life of one of the Admiral's daughters, and she fell in love with you, as young people will, would you dare even lift your eyes to her? Would you not be kicked out of the house and the parish, if you dared to indulge the right of every honest heart? Would you dare to look upon her as a human being, of the same order of creation as yourself, who might one day be your wife, if you were true and honest, and helped to break down the absurd distinctions built up by vile tyranny between you? In a word, are you a man— as every man is on the Continent—or only an English slave, of the lower classes?"

The hot flush of wrath, and the soft glow of shame, met and deepened each other on the fair cheeks of this "slave"; while his mind would not come to him to make a fit reply. That his passion for Dolly, his hopeless passion, should thus be discovered by a man of her own rank, but not scorned or ridiculed, only pitied, because of his want of manly spirit; that he should be called a "slave" because of honest modesty, and even encouraged in his wild hopes by a gentleman, who had seen all the world, and looked down from a lofty distance on it; that in his true estimate of things there should be nothing but prejudice, low and selfish prejudice, between—Well, he could not think it out; that would take him many hours; let this large-minded man begin again. It was so dark now, that if he turned round on him, unless he was a cat, he would be no wiser.

"You do well to take these things with some doubt," continued Carne, too sagacious to set up argument, which inures even young men in their own opinions; "if I were in your place, I should do the same. Centuries of oppression have stamped out the plain light of truth in those who are not allowed it. To me, as an individual, it is better so. Chance has ordained that I should belong to the order of those who profit by it. It is against my interest to speak as I have done. Am I likely to desire that my fences should be broken, my property invaded, the distinction so pleasing to me set aside, simply because I consider it a false one? No, no, friend Daniel; it is not for me to move. The present state of things is entirely in my favour. And I never give expression to my sense of right and wrong, unless it is surprised from me by circumstances. Your bold and entirely just proceedings have forced me to explain why I feel no resentment, but rather admiration, at a thing which any other land-owner in England would not rest in his bed until he had avenged. He would drag you before a bench of magistrates and fine you. Your father, if I know him, would refuse to pay the fine; and to prison you would go, with the taint of it to lie upon your good name forever. The penalty would be wrong, outrageous, ruinous; no rich man would submit to it, but a poor man must. Is this the truth, Daniel, or is it what it ought to be—a scandalous misdescription of the laws of England?"

"No, sir; it is true enough, and too true, I am afraid. I never thought of consequences, when I used my axe. I only thought of what was right, and fair, and honest, as between a man who has a right, and one who takes it from him."

"That is the natural way to look at things, but never permitted in this country. You are fortunate in having to deal with one who has been brought up in a juster land, where all mankind are equal. But one thing I insist upon; and remember it is the condition of my forbearance. Not a single word to any one about your dashing exploit. No gentleman in the county would ever speak to me again, if I were known to have put up with it."

"I am sure, sir," said Daniel, in a truly contrite tone, "I never should have done such an impudent thing against you, if I had only known what a nice gentleman you are. I took you for nothing but a haughty land-owner, without a word to fling at a poor fisherman. And now you go ever so far beyond what the Club doth, in speaking of the right that every poor man hasn't. I could listen to you by the hour, sir, and learn the difference between us and abroad."

"Tugwell, I could tell you things that would make a real man of you. But why should I? You are better as you are; and so are we who get all the good out of you. And besides, I have no time for politics at present. All my time is occupied with stern business—collecting the ruins of my property."

"But, sir—but you come down here sometimes from the castle in the evening; and if I might cross, without claiming right of way, sometimes I might have the luck to meet you."

"Certainly you may pass, as often as you please, and so may anybody who sets value on his rights. And if I should meet you again, I shall be glad of it. You can open my eyes, doubtless, quite as much as I can yours. Good-night, my friend, and better fortunes to you!"

"It was worth my while to nail up those rails," Carne said to himself, as he went home to his ruins. "I have hooked that clod, as firm as ever he hooked a cod. But, thousand thunders! what does he mean, by going away without touching his hat to me?"

CHAPTER XXVIII

FOUL IN PRACTICE

"I hope, my dear, that your ride has done you good," said the Rector's wife to the Rector, as he came into the hall with a wonderfully red face, one fine afternoon in October. "If colour proves health, you have gained it."

"Maria, I have not been so upset for many years. Unwholesome indignation dyes my cheeks, and that is almost as bad as indigestion. I have had quite a turn—as you women always put it. I am never moved by little things, as you know well, and sometimes to your great disgust; but to-day my troubles have conspired to devour me. I am not so young as I was, Maria. And what will the parish come to, if I give in?"

"Exactly, dear; and therefore you must not give in." Mrs. Twemlow replied with great spirit, but her hands were trembling as she helped him to pull off his new riding-coat. "Remember your own exhortations, Joshua—I am sure they were beautiful—last Sunday. But take something, dear, to restore your circulation. A reaction in the system is so dangerous."

"Not anything at present," Mr. Twemlow answered, firmly; "these mental cares are beyond the reach of bodily refreshments. Let me sit down, and be sure where I am, and then you may give me a glass of treble X. In the first place, the pony nearly kicked me off, when that idiot of a Stubbard began firing from his battery. What have I done, or my peaceful flock, that a noisy set of guns should be set up amidst us? However, I showed Juniper that he had a master, though I shall find it hard to come down-stairs tomorrow. Well, the next thing was that I saw James Cheeseman, Church-warden Cheeseman, Buttery Cheeseman, as the bad boys call him, in the lane, in front of me not more than thirty yards, as plainly as I now have the pleasure of seeing you, Maria; and while I said 'kuck' to the pony, he was gone! I particularly wished to speak to Cheeseman, to ask him some questions about things I have observed, and especially his sad neglect of public worship—a most shameful example on the part of a church-warden—and I was thinking how to put it, affectionately yet firmly, when, to my great surprise, there was no Cheeseman to receive it! I called at his house on my return, about three hours afterwards, having made up my mind to have it out with him, when they positively told me—or at least Polly Cheeseman did—that I must be mistaken about her 'dear papa,' because he was gone in the pony-shay all the way to Uckfield, and would not be back till night."

"The nasty little story-teller!" Mrs. Twemlow cried. "But I am not at all surprised at it, when I saw how she had got her hair done up, last Sunday."

"No; Polly believed it. I am quite sure of that. But what I want to tell you is much stranger and more important, though it cannot have anything at all to do with Cheeseman. You know, I told you I was going for a good long ride; but I did not tell you where, because I knew that you would try to stop me. But the fact was that I had made up my mind to see what Caryl Carne is at, among his owls and ivy. You remember the last time I went to the old place I knocked till I was tired, but could get no answer, and the window was stopped with some rusty old spiked railings, where we used to be able to get in at the side. All the others are out of reach, as you know well; and being of a yielding nature, I came sadly home. And at that time I still had some faith in your friend Mrs. Stubbard, who promised to find out all about him, by means of Widow Shanks and the Dimity-parlour. But nothing has come of that. Poor Mrs. Stubbard is almost as stupid as her husband; and as for Widow Shanks—I am quite sure, Maria, if your nephew were plotting the overthrow of King, Church, and Government, that deluded woman would not listen to a word against him."

"She calls him a model, and a blessed martyr"—Mrs. Twemlow was smiling at the thought of it; "and she says she is a woman of great penetration, and never will listen to anything. But it only shows what I have always said, that our family has a peculiar power, a sort of attraction, a superior gift of knowledge of their own minds, which makes them—But there, you are laughing at me, Joshua!"

"Not I; but smiling at my own good fortune, that ever I get my own way at all. But, Maria, you are right; your family has always been distinguished for having its own way—a masterful race, and a mistressful. And so much the more do the rest of mankind grow eager to know all about them. In an ordinary mind, such as mine, that feeling becomes at last irresistible; and finding no other way to gratify it, I resolved to take the bull by the horns, or rather by the tail, this morning. The poor old castle has been breaking up most grievously, even within the last twenty years, and you, who have played as a child among the ruins of the ramparts, would scarcely know them now. You cannot bear to go there, which is natural enough, after all the sad things that have happened; but if you did, you would be surprised, Maria; and I believe a great part has been knocked down on purpose. But you remember the little way in from the copse, where you and I, five-and-thirty years ago—"

"Of course I do, darling. It seems but yesterday; and I have a flower now which you gathered for me there. It grew at a very giddy height upon the wall, full of cracks and places where the evening-star came through; but up you went, like a rocket or a race-horse; and what a fright I was in, until you came down safe! I think that must have made up my mind to have nobody except my Joshua."

"Well, my dear, you might have done much worse. But I happened to think of that way in, this morning, when you put up your elbow, as you made the tea, exactly as you used to do when I might come up there. And that set me thinking of a quantity of things, and among them this plan which I resolved to carry out. I took the trouble first to be sure that Caryl was down here for the day, under the roof of Widow Shanks; and then I set off by the road up the hill, for the stronghold of all the Carnes. Without further peril than the fight with the pony, and the strange apparition of Cheeseman about half a mile from the back entrance, I came to the copse where the violets used to be, and the sorrel, and the lords and ladies. There I tethered our friend Juniper in a quiet little nook, and crossed the soft ground, without making any noise, to the place we used to call our little postern. It looked so sad, compared with what it used to be, so desolate and brambled up and ruinous, that I scarcely should have known it, except for the gray pedestal of the prostrate dial we used to moralise about. And the ground inside it, that was nice turf once, with the rill running down it that perhaps supplied the moat—all stony now, and overgrown, and tangled, with ugly-looking elder-bushes sprawling through the ivy. To a painter it might have proved very attractive; but to me it seemed so dreary, and so sombre, and oppressive, that, although I am not sentimental, as you know, I actually turned away, to put my little visit off, until I should be in better spirits for it. And that, my dear Maria, would in all probability have been never.

"But before I had time to begin my retreat, a very extraordinary sound, which I cannot describe by any word I know, reached my ears. It was not a roar, nor a clank, nor a boom, nor a clap, nor a crash, nor a thud, but if you have ever heard a noise combining all those elements, with a small percentage of screech to enliven them, that comes as near it as I can contrive to tell. We know from Holy Scripture that there used to be such creatures as dragons, though we have never seen them; but I seemed to be hearing one as I stood there. It was just the sort of groan you might have expected from a dragon, who had swallowed something highly indigestible."

"My dear! And he might have swallowed you, if you had stopped. How could you help running away, my Joshua? I should have insisted immediately upon it. But you are so terribly intrepid!"

"Far from it, Maria. Quite the contrary, I assure you. In fact, I did make off, for a considerable distance; not rapidly as a youth might do, but with self-reproach at my tardiness. But the sound ceased coming; and then I remembered how wholly we are in the hand of the Lord. A sense of the power of right rose within me, backed up by a strong curiosity; and I said to myself that if I went home, with nothing more than that to tell you, I should not have at all an easy time of it. Therefore I resolved to face the question again, and ascertain, if possible, without self-sacrifice, what was going on among the ruins. You know every stick and stone, as they used to be, but not as they are at present; therefore I must tell you. The wall at the bottom of the little Dial-court, where there used to be a sweet-briar hedge to come through, is entirely gone, either tumbled down or knocked down—the latter I believe to be the true reason of it. Also, instead of sweet-briar, there is now a very flourishing crop of sting-nettles. But the wall at the side of the little court stands almost as sound as ever; and what surprised me most was to see, when I got further, proceeding of course very quietly, that the large court beyond (which used to be the servants' yard, and the drying-ground, and general lounging-place) had a timber floor laid down it, with a rope on either side, a long heavy rope on either side; and these ropes were still quivering, as if from a heavy strain just loosened. All this I could see, because the high door with the spikes, that used to part the Dial-court from this place of common business, was fallen forward from its upper hinge, and splayed out so that I could put my fist through.

"By this time I had quite recovered all my self-command, and was as calm as I am now, or even calmer, because I was under that reaction which ensues when a sensible man has made a fool of himself. I perceived, without thinking, that the sound which had so scared me proceeded from this gangway, or timberway, or staging, or whatever may be the right word for it; and I made up my mind to stay where I was, only stooping a little with my body towards the wall, to get some idea of what might be going forward. And then I heard a sort of small hubbub of voices, such as foreigners make when they are ordered to keep quiet, and have to carry on a struggle with their noisy nature.

"This was enough to settle my decision not to budge an inch, until I knew what they were up to. I could not see round the corner, mind—though ladies seem capable of doing that, Maria—and so these fellows, who seemed to be in two lots, some at the top and some at the bottom of the plankway, were entirely out of my sight as yet, though I had a good view of their sliding-plane. But presently the ropes began to strain and creak, drawn taut—as our fishermen express it—either from the upper or the lower end, and I saw three barrels come sliding down—sliding, not rolling (you must understand), and not as a brewer delivers beer into a cellar. These passed by me; and after a little while there came again that strange sepulchral sound, which had made me feel so uneasy.

"Maria, you know that I can hold my own against almost anybody in the world but you; and although this place is far outside my parish boundaries, I felt that as the Uncle of the present owner—so far at least as the lawyers have not snapped him up—and the brother-in-law of the previous proprietor, I possessed an undeniable legal right—quo warranto, or whatever it is called— to look into all proceedings on these premises. Next to Holy Scripture, Horace is my guide and guardian; and I called to mind a well-known passage, which may roughly be rendered thus: 'If the crushed world tumble on him, the ruins shall strike him undismayed.' With this in my head, I went softly down the side-wall of the Dial-court (for there was no getting through the place where I had been peeping) to the bottom, where there used to be an old flint wall, and a hedge of sweet-briar in front of it. You remember the pretty conceit I made —quaint and wholesome as one of Herrick's—when you said something—but I verily believe we were better in those days than we ever have been since. Now don't interrupt me about that, my dear.

"Some of these briars still were there, or perhaps some of their descendants, straggling weakly among the nettles, and mullein, and other wild stuff, but making all together a pretty good screen, through which I could get a safe side-view of the bottom of the timber gangway. So I took off my hat, for some ruffian fellows like foreign sailors were standing below, throwing out their arms, and making noises in their throats, because not allowed to scream as usual. It was plain enough at once to any one who knew the place, that a large hole had been cut in the solid castle wall, or rather, a loophole had been enlarged very freely on either side, and brought down almost to the level of the ground outside. On either side of this great opening stood three heavy muskets at full cock, and it made my blood run cold to think how likely some fatal discharge appeared. If I had been brought up to war, Maria, as all the young people are bound to be now, I might have been more at home with such matters, and able to reconnoitre calmly; but I thought of myself, and of you, and Eliza, and what a shocking thing it would be for all of us—but a merciful Providence was over me.

"Too late I regretted the desire for knowledge, which had led me into this predicament, for I durst not rush off from my very sad position, for my breath would soon fail me, and my lower limbs are thick from the exercise of hospitality. How I longed for the wings of a dove, or at any rate for the legs of Lieutenant Blyth Scudamore! And my dark apprehensions gained double force when a stone was dislodged by my foot (which may have trembled), and rolled with a sharp echo down into the ballium, or whatever it should be called, where these desperadoes stood. In an instant three of them had their long guns pointed at the very thicket which sheltered me, and if I had moved or attempted to make off, there would have been a vacancy in this preferment.

But luckily a rabbit, who had been lying as close as I had, and as much afraid of me perhaps as I was of those ruffians, set off at full speed from the hop of the stone, and they saw him, and took him for the cause of it. This enabled me to draw my breath again, and consider the best way of making my escape, for I cared to see nothing more, except my own house-door.

"Happily the chance was not long in coming. At a shout from below—which seemed to me to be in English, and sounded uncommonly like 'now, then!'—all those fellows turned their backs to me, and began very carefully to lower, one by one, the barrels that had been let down the incline. And other things were standing there, besides barrels: packing-cases, crates, very bulky-looking boxes, and low massive wheels, such as you often see to artillery. You know what a vast extent there is of cellars and vaults below your old castle, most of them nearly as sound as ever, and occupied mainly by empty bottles, and the refuse of past hospitality. Well, they are going to fill these with something—French wines, smuggled brandy, contraband goods of every kind you can think of, so long as high profit can be made of them. That is how your nephew Caryl means to redeem his patrimony. No wonder that he has been so dark and distant! It never would have done to let us get the least suspicion of it, because of my position in the Church, and in the Diocese. By this light a thousand things are clear to me, which exceeded all the powers of the Sphinx till now."

"But how did you get away, my darling Joshua?" Mrs. Twemlow enquired, as behoved her. "So fearless, so devoted, so alive to every call of duty—how could you stand there, and let the wretches shoot at you?"

"By taking good care not to do it," the Rector answered, simply. "No sooner were all their backs towards me, than I said to myself that the human race happily is not spiderine. I girt up my loins, or rather fetched my tails up under my arms very closely, and glided away, with the silence of the serpent, and the craft of the enemy of our fallen race. Great care was needful, and I exercised it; and here you behold me, unshot and unshot-at, and free from all anxiety, except a pressing urgency for a bowl of your admirable soup, Maria, and a cut from the saddle I saw hanging in the cellar."

CHAPTER XXIX

MATERNAL ELOQUENCE

Sufficient for the day is the evil thereof; and more than sufficient with most of us. Mr. Twemlow and his wife resolved discreetly, after a fireside council, to have nothing to say to Carne Castle, or about it, save what might be forced out of them. They perceived most clearly, and very deeply felt, how exceedingly wrong it is for anybody to transgress, or even go aside of, the laws of his country, as by Statute settled. Still, if his ruin had been chiefly legal; if he had been brought up under different laws, and in places where they made those things which he desired to deal in; if it was clear that those things were good, and their benefit might be extended to persons who otherwise could have no taste of them; above all, if it were the first and best desire of all who heard of it to have their own fingers in the pie—then let others stop it, who by duty and interest were so minded; the Rector was not in the Commission of the Peace—though he ought to have been there years ago —and the breach of the law, if it came to that, was outside of his parish boundary. The voice of the neighbourhood would be with him, for not turning against his own nephew, even if it ever should come to be known that he had reason for suspicions.

It is hard to see things in their proper light, if only one eye has a fly in it; but if both are in that sad condition, who shall be blamed for winking? Not only the pastor, but all his flock, were in need of wire spectacles now, to keep their vision clear and their foreheads calm. Thicker than flies around the milk-pail, rumours came flitting daily; and even the night—that fair time of thinking—was busy with buzzing multitude.

"Long time have I lived, and a sight have I seed," said Zebedee Tugwell to his wife, "of things as I couldn't make no head nor tail of; but nothing to my knowledge ever coom nigh the sort of way our folk has taken to go on. Parson Twemlow told us, when the war began again, that the Lord could turn us all into Frenchmen, if we sinned against Him more than He could bear. I were fool enough to laugh about it then, not intaking how it could be on this side of Kingdom Come, where no distinction is of persons. But now, there it is—a thing the Almighty hath in hand; and who shall say Him nay, when He layeth His hand to it?"

"I reckon, 'a hath begun with you too, Zeb," Mrs. Tugwell would answer, undesirably. "To be always going on so about trash trifles, as a woman hath a right to fly up at, but no man! Surely Dan hath a right to his politics and his parables, as much as any lame old chap that sitteth on a bench. He works hard all day, and he airns his money; and any man hath a right to wag his tongue of night-time, when his arms and his legs have been wagging all day."

"Depends upon how he wags 'un." The glance of old Tugwell was stern, as he spoke, and his eyebrows knitted over it. "If for a yarn, to plaise children or maidens, or a bit of argyment about his business, or talk about his neighbours, or aught that consarns him—why, lads must be fools, and I can smoke my pipe and think that at his age I was like him. But when it comes to talking of his betters, and the Government, and the right of everybody to command the ship, and the soup—soup, what was it?"

"Superior position of the working classes, dignity of labour, undefeasible rights of mankind to the soil as they was born in, and soshallistick—something."

"So—shall—I—stick equality," Mr. Tugwell amended, triumphantly; "and so shall I stick him, by the holy poker, afore the end of the week is out. I've a-been fool enough to leave off ropesending of him now for a matter of two years, because 'a was good, and outgrowing of it like, and because you always coom between us. But mind you, mother, I'll have none of that, next time. Business I means, and good measure it shall be."

"Zeb Tugwell," said his wife, longing greatly to defy him, but frightened by the steadfast gaze she met, "you can never mean to say that you would lay your hand on Dan—a grown man, a'most as big as yourself, and a good half-head taller! Suppose he was to hit you back again!"

"If he did, I should just kill him," Zeb answered, calmly. "He would be but a jellyfish in my two hands. But there, I'll not talk about it, mother. No need to trouble you with it. 'Tis none of my seeking—the Lord in heaven knows—but a job as He hath dutified for me to do. I'll go out, and have my pipe, and dwell on it."

"And I may lay a deal of it on myself," Mrs. Tugwell began to moan, as soon as he was gone; "for I have cockered Dan up, and there's no denying it, afore Tim, or Tryphena, or Tabby, or Debby, or even little Solomon. Because he were the first, and so like his dear father, afore he got on in the world so. Oh, it all comes of that, all the troubles comes of that, and of laying up of money, apart from your wife, and forgetting almost of her Christian name! And the very same thing of it—money, money, and the getting on with breeches that requireth no mending, and the looking over Church-books at gay young ladies—all of it leadeth to the same bad end of his betters, and the Government, and the Soshallistick Quality.

"Why, with all these mercies," continued Mrs. Tugwell, though not in a continuous frame of mind, as Daniel came in, with a slow heavy step, and sat down by the fire in silence, "all these mercies, as are bought and paid for, from one and sixpence up to three half-crowns, and gives no more trouble beyond dusting once a week—how any one can lay his eyes on other people's property, without consideration of his own, as will be after his poor mother's time, is to me quite a puzzle and a pin-prick. Not as if they was owing for, or bought at auction, or so much as beaten down by sixpence, but all at full price and own judgment, paid for by airnings of labour and perils of the deep. And as Widow Shanks said, the last time she was here, by spoiling of the enemies of England, who makes us pay tremenjious for 'most everything we lives on. And I know who would understand them crackeries, and dust them when I be gone to dust, and see her own pretty face in them, whenever they has the back-varnish."

Dan knew that the future fair owner and duster designed by his mother was Miss Cheeseman, towards whom he had cherished tender yearnings in the sensible and wholesome days. And if Polly Cheeseman had hung herself on high—which she might have done without a bit of arrogance—perhaps she would still have been to this young man the star of fate and glory, instead of a dip, thirty-two to the pound; the like whereof she sold for a farthing. Distance makes the difference. "He that won't allow heed shall pay dear in his need;" the good mother grew warm, as the son began to whistle; "and to my mind, Master Dan, it won't be long afore you have homer things to think of than politics. 'Politics is fiddle-sticks' was what men of my age used to say; sensible men with a house and freehold, and a pig of their own, and experience. And such a man I might have had, and sensible children by him, children as never would have whistled at their mother, if it hadn't been for your poor father, Dan. Misguided he may be, and too much of his own way, and not well enough in his own mind to take in a woman's—but for all that he hath a right to be honoured by his children, and to lead their minds in matters touching of the King, and Church, and true religion. Why only last night, no, the night afore last, I met Mrs. Prater, and I said to her—"

"You told me all that, mother; and it must have been a week ago; for I have heard it every night this week. What is it you desire that I should do, or say, or think?"

"Holy mercy!" cried Mrs. Tugwell, "what a way to put things, Dan! All I desire is for your good only, and so leading on to the comfort of the rest. For the whole place goes wrong, and the cat sits in the corner, when you go on with politics as your dear father grunts at. No doubt it may all be very fine and just, and worth a man giving his life for, if he don't care about it, nor nobody else—but even if it was to keep the French out, and yourn goeth nearer to letting them in, what difference of a button would it make to us, Dan, compared to our sticking together, and feeding with a knowledge and a yielding to the fancies of each other?"

"I am sure it's no fault of mine," said Daniel, moved from his high ropes by this last appeal; "to me it never matters twopence what I have for dinner, and you saw me give Tim all the brown of the baked potatoes the very last time I had my dinner here. But what comes above all those little bothers is the necessity for insisting upon freedom of opinion. I don't pretend to be so old as my father, nor to know so much as he knows about the world in general. But I have read a great deal more than he has, of course, because he takes a long time to get a book with the right end to him; and I have thought, without knowing it, about what I have read, and I have heard very clever men (who could have no desire to go wrong, but quite the other way) carrying on about these high subjects, beyond me, but full of plain language. And I won't be forced out of a word of it by fear."

"But for love of your mother you might keep it under, and think it all inside you, without bringing of it out, in the presence of your elders. You know what your father is—a man as never yet laid his tongue to a thing without doing of it—right or wrong, right or wrong; and this time he hath right, and the law, and the Lord, and the King himself, to the side of him. And a rope's-end in his pocket, Dan, as I tried to steal away, but he were too wide-awake. Such a big hard one you never did see!"

"A rope's end for me, well turned twenty years of age!" cried Daniel, with a laugh, but not a merry one; "two can play at that game, mother. I'll not be ropes ended by nobody."

"Then you'll be rope-noosed;" the poor mother fell into the settle, away from the fire-light, and put both hands over her eyes, to shut out the spectacle of Dan dangling; "or else your father will be, for you. Ever since the Romans, Dan, there have been Tugwells, and respected ten times more than they was. Oh do 'e, do 'e think; and not bring us all to the grave, and then the gallows! Why I can mind the time, no more agone than last Sunday, when you used to lie here in the hollow of my arm, without a stitch of clothes on, and kind people was tempted to smack you in pleasure, because you did stick out so prettily. For a better-formed baby there never was seen, nor a finer-tempered one, when he had his way. And the many nights I walked the floor with you, Dan, when your first tooth was coming through, the size of a horse-radish, and your father most wonderful to put up with my coo to you, when he had not had a night in bed for nigh three weeks—oh, Dan, do 'e think of things as consarneth your homer life, and things as is above all reason; and let they blessed politics go home to them as trades in them."

192

Mrs. Tugwell's tender recollections had given her a pain in the part where Dan was nursed, and driven her out of true logical course; but she came back to it, before Dan had time to finish the interesting pictures of himself which she had suggested.

"Now can you deny a word of that, Dan? And if not, what is there more to say? You was smacked as a little babe, by many people kindly, when ever so much tenderer than you now can claim to be. And in those days you never could have deserved it yet, not having framed a word beyond 'Mam,' and 'Da,' and both of those made much of, because doubtful. There was nothing about the Constitooshun then, but the colour of the tongue and the condition of the bowels; and if any fool had asked you what politics was, you would have sucked your thumb, and offered them to suck it; for generous you always was, and just came after. And what cry have bigger folk, grown upright and wicked, to make about being smacked, when they deserve it, for meddling with matters outside of their business, by those in authority over them?"

"Well, mother, I daresay you are right, though I don't altogether see the lines of it. But one thing I will promise you—whatever father does to me, I will not lift a hand against him. But I must be off. I am late already."

"Where to, Dan? Where to? I always used to know, even if you was going courting. Go a-courting, Dan, as much as ever you like, only don't make no promises. But whatever you do, keep away from that bad, wicked, Free and Frisky Club, my dear."

"Mother, that's the very place I am just bound to. After all you have said, I would have stayed away to-night, except for being on the list, and pledged in honour to twenty-eight questions, all bearing upon the grand issues of the age."

"I don't know no more than the dead, what that means, Dan. But I know what your father has got in his pocket for you. And he said the next time you went there, you should have it."

CHAPTER XXX

PATERNAL DISCIPLINE

"The Fair, Free, and Frisky"—as they called themselves, were not of a violent order at all, neither treasonable, nor even disloyal. Their Club, if it deserved the name, had not been of political, social, or even convivial intention, but had lapsed unawares into all three uses, and most of all that last mentioned. The harder the times are, the more confidential (and therefore convivial) do Englishmen become; and if Free-trade survives with us for another decade, it will be the death of total abstinence. But now they had bad times, without Free-trade—that Goddess being still in the goose-egg—and when two friends met, without a river between them, they were bound to drink one another's health, and did it, without the unstable and cold-blooded element. The sense of this duty was paramount among the "Free and Frisky," and without it their final cause would have vanished long ago, and therewith their formal one.

None of the old-established folk of the blue blood of Springhaven, such as the Tugwells, the Shankses, the Praters, the Bowleses, the Stickfasts, the Blocks, or the Kedgers, would have anything to do with this Association, which had formed itself among them, like an anti-corn-law league, for the destruction of their rights and properties. Its origin had been commercial, and its principles aggressive, no less an outrage being contemplated than the purchase of fish at low figures on the beach, and the speedy distribution of that slippery ware among the nearest villages and towns. But from time immemorial the trade had been in the hands of a few staunch factors, who paid a price governed by the seasons and the weather, and sent the commodity as far as it would go, with soundness, and the hope of freshness. Springhaven believed that it supplied all London, and was proud and blest in so believing. With these barrowmen, hucksters and pedlars of fish, it would have no manifest dealing; but if the factors who managed the trade chose to sell their refuse or surplus to them, that was their own business. In this way perhaps, and by bargains on the sly, these petty dealers managed to procure enough to carry on their weekly enterprise, and for a certain good reason took a room and court-yard handy to the Darling Arms, to discuss other people's business and their own. The good reason was that they were not allowed to leave the village, with their barrows or trucks or baskets, until the night had fallen, on penalty of being pelted with their own wares. Such was the dignity of this place, and its noble abhorrence of anything low.

The vision of lofty institutions, which one may not participate, inspires in the lower human nature more jealousy than admiration. These higglers may have been very honest fellows, in all but pecuniary questions, and possibly continued to be so in the bosom of their own families. But here in Springhaven, by the force of circumstances they were almost compelled to be radicals: even as the sweetest cow's milk turns sour, when she can just reach red clover with her breath, but not her lips. But still they were not without manners, and reason, and good-will to people who had patience with them. This enabled them to argue lofty questions, without black eyes, or kicking, or even tweak of noses; and a very lofty question was now before them.

To get once into Admiral Darling's employment was to obtain a vested interest; so kind was his nature and so forgiving, especially when he had scolded anybody. Mr. Swipes, the head gardener for so many years, held an estate of freehold in the garden—although he had no head, and would never be a gardener, till the hanging gardens of Babylon should be hung on the top of the tower of Babel—with a vested remainder to his son, and a contingent one to all descendants. Yet this man, although his hands were generally in his pockets, had not enough sense of their linings to feel that continuance, usage, institution, orderly sequence, heredity, and such like, were the buttons of his coat and the texture of his breeches, and the warmth of his body inside them. Therefore he never could hold aloof from the Free and Frisky gatherings, and accepted the chair upon Bumper-nights, when it was a sinecure benefice.

This was a Bumper-night, and in the chair sat Mr. Swipes, discharging gracefully the arduous duties of the office, which consisted mainly in calling upon members for a speech, a sentiment, or a song, and in default of mental satisfaction, bodily amendment by a pint all round. But as soon as Dan Tugwell entered the room, the Free and Friskies with one accord returned to loftier business. Mr. Swipes, the gay Liber of the genial hour, retired from the chair, and his place was taken by a Liberal—though the name was not yet invented—estranged from his own godfather. This was a hard man, who made salt herrings, and longed to cure everything fresh in the world.

Dan, being still a very tender youth, and quite unaccustomed to public speaking, was abashed by these tokens of his own importance, and heartily wished that he had stopped at home. It never occurred to his simple mind that his value was not political, but commercial; not "anthropological," but fishy, the main ambition of the Free and Frisky Club having long been the capture of his father. If once Zeb Tugwell could be brought to treat, a golden era would dawn upon them, and a boundless vision of free-trade, when a man might be paid for refusing to sell fish, as he now is for keeping to himself his screws. Dan knew not these things, and his heart misgave him, and he wished that he had never heard of the twenty-eight questions set down in his name for solution.

However, his disturbance of mind was needless, concerning those great issues. All the members, except the chairman, had forgotten all about them; and the only matter they cared about was to make a new member of Daniel. A little flourish went on about large things (which nobody knew, or cared to know), then the table was hammered with the heel of a pipe, and Dan was made a Free and Frisky. An honorary member, with nothing to pay, and the honour on their side, they told him; and every man rose, with his pot in one hand and his pipe in the other, yet able to stand, and to thump with his heels, being careful. Then the President made entry in a book, and bowed, and Dan was requested to sign it. In the fervour of good-will, and fine feeling, and the pride of popularity, the young man was not old enough to resist, but set his name down firmly. Then all shook hands with him, and the meeting was declared to be festive, in honour of a new and noble member.

It is altogether wrong to say—though many people said it—that young Dan Tugwell was even a quarter of a sheet in the wind, when he steered his way home. His head was as solid as that of his father; which, instead of growing light, increased in specific, generic, and differential gravity, under circumstances which tend otherwise, with an age like ours, that insists upon sobriety, without allowing practice. All Springhaven folk had long practice in the art of keeping sober, and if ever a man walked with his legs outside his influence, it was always from defect of proper average quite lately.

Be that as it may, the young man came home with an enlarged map of the future in his mind, a brisk and elastic rise in his walk, and his head much encouraged to go on with liberal and indescribable feelings. In accordance with these, he expected his mother to be ready to embrace him at the door, while a saucepan simmered on the good-night of the wood-ash, with just as much gentle breath of onion from the cover as a youth may taste dreamily from the lips of love. But oh, instead of this, he met his father, spread out and yet solid across the doorway, with very large arms bare and lumpy in the gleam of a fireplace uncrowned by any pot. Dan's large ideas vanished, like a blaze without a bottom.

"Rather late, Daniel," said the captain of Springhaven, with a nod of his great head, made gigantic on the ceiling. "All the rest are abed, the proper place for honest folk. I suppose you've been airning money, overtime?"

"Not I," said Dan; "I work hard enough all day. I just looked in at the Club, and had a little talk of politics."

"The Club, indeed! The stinking barrow-grinders! Did I tell you, or did I forget to tell you, never to go there no more?"

"You told me fast enough, father; no doubt about that. But I am not aboard your boat, when I happen on dry land, and I am old enough now to have opinions of my own."

"Oh, that's it, is it? And to upset all the State, the King, the House of Lords, and the Parliamentary House, and all as is descended from the Romans? Well, and what did their Wusships say to you? Did they anoint you king of slooshings?"

"Father, they did this—and you have a right to know it;" Dan spoke with a grave debative tone, though his voice became doubtful, as he saw that his father was quietly seeking for something; "almost before I knew what was coming, they had made me a member, and I signed the book. They have no desire to upset the kingdom; I heard no talk of that kind; only that every man should have his own opinions, and be free to show what can be said for them. And you know, father, that the world goes on by reason, and justice, and good-will, and fair play—"

"No, it don't," cried the captain, who had found what he wanted; "if it had to wait for they, it would never go on at all. It goes on by government, and management, and discipline, and the stopping of younkers from their blessed foolery, and by the ten commandments, and the proverbs of King Solomon. You to teach your father how the world goes on! Off with your coat, and I'll teach you."

"Father," said Dan, with his milder nature trembling at the stern resolution in his father's eyes, as the hearth-fire flashing up showed their stronger flash, "you will never do such a thing, at my age and size?"

"Won't I?" answered Zebedee, cracking in the air the three knotted tails of the stout hempen twist. "As for your age, why, it ought to know better; and as for your size, why, the more room for this!"

It never came into Daniel's head that he should either resist or run away. But into his heart came the deadly sense of disgrace at being flogged, even by his own father, at full age to have a wife and even children of his own.

"Father," he said, as he pulled off his coat and red striped shirt, and showed his broad white back, "if you do this thing, you will never set eyes on my face again—so help me God!"

"Don't care if I don't," the captain shouted. "You was never son of mine, to be a runagate, and traitor. How old be you, Master Free and Frisky, to larn me how the world goes on?"

"As if you didn't know, father! The fifteenth of last March I was twenty years of age."

"Then one for each year of your life, my lad, and another to make a man of thee. This little tickler hath three tails; seven threes is twenty-one—comes just right."

When his father had done with him, Dan went softly up the dark staircase of old ship timber, and entering his own little room, struck a light. He saw that his bed was turned down for him, by the loving hand of his mother, and that his favourite brother Solomon, the youngest of the Tugwell race, was sleeping sweetly in the opposite cot. Then he caught a side view of his own poor back in the little black-framed looking-glass, and was quite amazed; for he had not felt much pain, neither flinched, nor winced, nor spoken. In a moment self-pity did more than pain, indignation, outrage, or shame could do; it brought large tears into his softened eyes, and a long sob into his swelling throat.

He had borne himself like a man when flogged; but now he behaved in the manner of a boy. "He shall never hear the last of this job," he muttered, "as long as mother has a tongue in her head." To this end he filled a wet sponge with the red proofs of his scourging, laid it where it must be seen, and beside it a leaf torn from his wage-book, on which he had written with a trembling hand: "He says that I am no son of his, and this looks like it. Signed, Daniel Tugwell, or whatever my name ought to be."

Then he washed and dressed with neat's-foot oil all of his wounds that he could reach, and tied a band of linen over them, and, in spite of increasing smarts and pangs, dressed himself carefully in his Sunday clothes. From time to time he listened for his father's step, inasmuch as there was no bolt to his door, and to burn a light so late was against all law. But nobody came to disturb him; his mother at the end of the passage slept heavily, and his two child-sisters in the room close by, Tabby and Debby, were in the land of dreams, as far gone as little Solly was. Having turned out his tools from their flat flag basket, or at least all but three or four favourites, he filled it with other clothes likely to be needed, and buckled it over his hatchet-head. Then the beating of his heart was like a flail inside a barn, as he stole along silently for one terrible good-bye.

This was to his darling pet of all pets, Debby, who worshipped this brother a great deal more than she worshipped her heavenly Father; because, as she said to her mother, when rebuked—"I can see Dan, mother, but I can't see Him. Can I sit in His lap, mother, and look into His face, and be told pretty stories, and eat apples all the time?" Tabby was of different grain, and her deity was Tim; for she was of the Tomboy kind, and had no imagination. But Debby was enough to make a sound and seasoned heart to ache, as she lay in her little bed, with the flush of sleep deepening the delicate tint of her cheeks, shedding bright innocence fresh from heaven on the tranquil droop of eyelid and the smiling curve of lip. Her hair lay fluttered, as if by play with the angels that protected her; and if she could not see her heavenly Father, it was not because she was out of His sight.

A better tear than was ever shed by self-pity, or any other selfishness, ran down the cheek she had kissed so often, and fell upon her coaxing, nestling neck. Then Dan, with his candle behind the curtain, set a long light kiss upon the forehead of his darling, and with a heart so full, and yet so empty, took one more gaze at her, and then was gone. With the basket in his hand, he dropped softly from his window upon the pile of seaweed at the back of the house—collected to make the walls wholesome—and then, caring little what his course might be, was led perhaps by the force of habit down the foot-path towards the beach. So late at night, it was not likely that any one would disturb him there, and no one in the cottage which he had left would miss him before the morning. The end of October now was near, the nights were long, and he need not hurry. He might even lie down in his favourite boat, the best of her size in Springhaven, the one he had built among the rabbits. There he could say good-bye to all that he had known and loved so long, and be off before dawn, to some place where he might earn his crust and think his thoughts.

CHAPTER XXXI

SORE TEMPTATION

When a man's spirit and heart are low, and the world seems turned against him, he had better stop both ears than hearken to the sound of the sad sea waves at night. Even if he can see their movement, with the moon behind them, drawing paths of rippled light, and boats (with white sails pluming shadow, or thin oars that dive for gems), and perhaps a merry crew with music, coming home not all sea-sick—well, even so, in the summer sparkle, the long low fall of the waves is sad. But how much more on a winter night, when the moon is away below the sea, and weary waters roll unseen from a vast profundity of gloom, fall unreckoned, and are no more than a wistful moan, as man is!

The tide was at quarter-ebb, and a dismal haze lay thick on shore and sea. It was not enough to be called a fog, or even a mist, but quite enough to deaden the gray light, always flowing along the boundary of sky and sea. But over the wet sand and the white frill of the gently gurgling waves more of faint light, or rather perhaps, less of heavy night, prevailed. But Dan had keen eyes, and was well accustomed to the tricks of darkness; and he came to take his leave forever of the fishing squadron, with a certainty of knowing all the five, as if by daylight—for now there were only five again.

As the tide withdrew, the fishing-smacks (which had scarcely earned their name of late) were compelled to make the best of the world until the tide came back again. To judge by creakings, strainings, groanings, and even grindings of timber millstones [if there yet lives in Ireland the good-will for a loan to us], all these little craft were making dreadful hardship of the abandonment which man and nature inflicted on them every thirteenth hour. But all things do make more noise at night, when they get the chance (perhaps in order to assert their own prerogative), and they seem to know that noise goes further, and assumes a higher character, when men have left off making it.

The poor young fisherman's back was getting very sore by this time, and he began to look about for the white side-streak which he had painted along the water-line of that new boat, to distract the meddlesome gaze of rivals from the peculiar curve below, which even Admiral Darling had not noticed, when he passed her on the beach; but Nelson would have spied it out in half a second, and known all about it in the other half. Dan knew that he should find a very fair berth there, with a roll or two of stuff to lay his back on, and a piece of tarpauling to draw over his legs. In the faint light that hovered from the breaking of the wavelets he soon found his boat, and saw a tall man standing by her.

"Daniel," said the tall man, without moving, "my sight is very bad at night, but unless it is worse than usual, you are my admired friend Daniel. A young man in a thousand—one who dares to think."

"Yes, Squire Carne," the admired friend replied, with a touch of hat protesting against any claim to friendship: "Dan Tugwell, at your service. And I have thought too much, and been paid out for it."

"You see me in a melancholy attitude, and among melancholy surroundings." Caryl Carne offered his hand as he spoke, and Dan took it with great reverence. "The truth is, that anger at a gross injustice, which has just come to my knowledge, drove me from my books and sad family papers, in the room beneath the roof of our good Widow Shanks. And I needs must come down here, to think beside the sea, which seems to be the only free thing in England. But I little expected to see you."

"And I little expected to be here, Squire Carne. But if not making too bold to ask—was it anybody that was beaten?"

"Beaten is not the right word for it, Dan; cruelly flogged and lashed, a dear young friend of mine has been, as fine a young fellow as ever lived—and now he has not got a sound place on his back. And why? Because he was poor, and dared to lift his eyes to a rich young lady."

"But he was not flogged by his own father?" asked Dan, deeply interested in this romance, and rubbing his back, as the pain increased with sympathy.

"Not quite so bad as that," replied the other; "such a thing would be impossible, even in England. No; his father took his part, as any father in the world would do; even if the great man, the young lady's father, should happen to be his own landlord."

A very black suspicion crossed the mind of Dan, for Carne possessed the art of suggesting vile suspicions: might Admiral Darling have discovered something, and requested Dan's father to correct him? It was certain that the Admiral, so kind of heart, would never have desired such severity; but he might have told Captain Tugwell, with whom he had a talk almost every time they met, that his eldest son wanted a little discipline; and the Club might have served as a pretext for this, when the true crime must not be declared, by reason of its enormity. Dan closed his teeth, and English air grew bitter in his mouth, as this belief ran through him.

"Good-night, my young friend; I am beginning to recover," Carne continued, briskly, for he knew that a nail snaps in good oak, when the hammer falls too heavily. "What is a little bit of outrage, after all? When I have been in England a few years more, I shall laugh at myself for having loved fair play and self-respect, in this innocent young freshness. We must wag as the world does; and you know the proverb, What makes the world wag, but the weight of the bag?"

"But if you were more in earnest, sir—or at least—I mean, if you were not bound here by property and business, and an ancient family, and things you could not get away from, and if you wanted only to be allowed fair play, and treated as a man by other men, and be able to keep your own money when you earned it, or at least to buy your own victuals with it—what would you try to do, or what part of the country would you think best to go to?"

"Dan, you must belong to a very clever family. It is useless to shake your head—you must; or you never could put such questions, so impossible to answer. In all this blessed island, there is no spot yet discovered, where such absurd visions can be realized. Nay, nay, my romantic friend; be content with more than the average blessings of this land. You are not starved, you are not imprisoned, you are not even beaten; and if you are not allowed to think, what harm of that? If you thought all day, you would never dare to act upon your thoughts, and so you are better without them. Tush! an Englishman was never born for freedom. Good-night."

"But, sir, Squire Carne," cried Dan, pursuing him, "there is one thing which you do not seem to know. I am driven away from this place to-night; and it would have been so kind of you to advise me where to go to."

"Driven away!" exclaimed Carne, with amazement. "The pride of the village driven out of it! You may be driving yourself away, Tugwell, through some scrape, or love affair; but when that blows over you will soon come back. What would Springhaven do without you? And your dear good father would never let you go."

"I am not the pride, but the shame, of the village." Dan forgot all his home-pride at last. "And my dear good father is the man who has done it. He has leathered me worse than the gentleman you spoke of, and without half so much to be said against him. For nothing but going to the Club to-night, where I am sure we drank King George's health, my father has lashed me so, that I am ashamed to tell it. And I am sure that I never meant to tell it, until your kindness, in a way of speaking, almost drove it out of me."

"Daniel Tugwell," Carne answered, with solemnity, "this is beyond belief, even in England. You must have fallen asleep, Dan, in the middle of large thoughts, and dreamed this great impossibility."

"My back knows whether it has been a dream, sir. I never heard of dreams as left one-and-twenty lines behind them. But whether it be one, or whether it be twenty, makes no odds of value. The disgrace it is that drives me out."

"Is there no way of healing this sad breach?" Carne asked, in a tone of deep compassion; "if your father could be brought to beg your pardon, or even to say that he was sorry—"

"He, sir! If such a thing was put before him, his answer would be just to do it again, if I were fool enough to go near him. You are too mild of nature, sir, to understand what father is."

"It is indeed horrible, too horrible to think of"—the voice of this kind gentleman betrayed that he was shuddering. "If a Frenchman did such a thing, he would be torn to pieces. But no French father would ever dream of such atrocity. He would rather flog himself within an inch of his own life."

"Are they so much better, then, and kinder, than us Englishmen?" In spite of all his pain and grief, Dan could not help smiling at the thought of his father ropesending himself. "So superior to us, sir, in every way?"

"In almost every way, I am sorry to confess. I fear, indeed, in every way, except bodily strength, and obstinate, ignorant endurance, miscalled 'courage,' and those rough qualities—whatever they may be—which seem needful for the making of a seaman. But in good manners, justice, the sense of what is due from one man to another, in dignity, equality, temperance, benevolence, largeness of feeling, and quickness of mind, and above all in love of freedom, they are very, very sadly far beyond us. And indeed I have been led to think from some of your finer perceptions, Dan, that you must have a share of French blood in your veins."

"Me, sir!" cried Dan, jumping back, in a style which showed the distance between faith and argument; "no, sir, thank God there was never none of that; but all English, with some of the Romans, who was pretty near equal to us, from what I hear. I suppose, Squire Carne, you thought that low of me because I made a fuss about being larruped, the same as a Frenchman I pulled out of the water did about my doing of it, as if I could have helped it. No Englishman would have said much about that; but they seem to make more fuss than we do. And I dare say it was French-like of me, to go on about my hiding."

"Daniel," answered Caryl Carne, in alarm at this British sentiment; "as a man of self-respect, you have only one course left, if your father refuses to apologise. You must cast off his tyranny; you must prove yourself a man; you must begin life upon your own account. No more of this drudgery, and slavery for others, who allow you no rights in return. But a nobler employment among free people, with a chance of asserting your courage and manhood, and a certainty that no man will think you his bondslave because you were born upon his land, or in his house. My father behaved to me—well, it does not matter. He might have repented of it, if he had lived longer; and I feel ashamed to speak of it, after such a case as yours. But behold, how greatly it has been for my advantage! Without that, I might now have been a true and simple Englishman!"

Carne (who had taken most kindly to the fortune which made him an untrue Englishman) clapped his breast with both hands; not proudly, as a Frenchman does, nor yet with that abashment and contempt of demonstration which make a true Briton very clumsy in such doings; while Daniel Tugwell, being very solid, and by no means "emotional"—as people call it nowadays—was looking at him, to the utmost of his power (which would have been greater by daylight), with gratitude, and wonder, and consideration, and some hesitation about his foreign sentiments.

"Well, sir," said Dan, with the usual impulse of the British workman, "is there any sort of work as you could find for me, to earn my own living, and be able to think afterwards?"

"There is work of a noble kind, such as any man of high nature may be proud to share in, to which it is possible that I might get an entrance for you, if there should be a vacancy; work of high character, such as admits of no higgling and haggling, and splitting of halfpence, but an independent feeling, and a sense of advancing the liberty of mankind, without risking a penny, but putting many guineas into one's own pocket, and so becoming fitted for a loftier line of life."

"Is it smuggling, sir?" Daniel asked, with sore misgivings, for he had been brought up to be very shy of that. "Many folk consider that quite honest; but father calls it roguery—though I never shall hear any more of his opinions now."

"Sigh not, friend Daniel; sigh not so heavily at your own emancipation." Carne never could resist the chance of a little bit of sarcasm, though it often injured his own plots. "Smuggling is a very fine pursuit, no doubt, but petty in comparison with large affairs like ours. No, Dan Tugwell, I am not a smuggler, but a high politician, and a polisher of mankind. How soon do you think of leaving this outrageous hole?"

Despite the stupid outrage upon himself, Dan was too loyal and generous of nature to be pleased with this description of his native place. But Carne, too quick of temper for a really fine intriguer, cut short his expostulations.

"Call it what you please," he said; "only make your mind up quickly. If you wish to remain here, do so: a man of no spirit is useless to me. But if you resolve to push your fortunes among brave and lofty comrades, stirring scenes, and brisk adventures, meet me at six to-morrow evening, at the place where you chopped down my rails. All you want will be provided, and your course of promotion begins at once. But remember, all must be honour bright. No shilly-shallying, no lukewarmness, no indifference to a noble cause. Faint heart never won fair lady."

The waning moon had risen, and now shone upon Carne's face, lighting up all its gloomy beauty, and strange power of sadness. Dan seemed to lose his clear keen sight beneath the dark influence of the other's gaze; and his will, though not a weak one, dropped before a larger and stronger. "He knows all about me and Miss Dolly," said the poor young fisherman to himself; "I thought so before, and I am certain of it now. And, for some reason beyond my knowledge, he wishes to encourage it. Oh, perhaps because the Carnes have always been against the Darlings! I never thought of that before."

This was a bitter reflection to him, and might have inclined him the right way, if time had allowed him to work it out. But no such time was afforded; and in the confusion and gratitude of the moment, he answered, "Sir, I shall be always at your service, and do my very best in every way to please you." Caryl Carne smiled; and the church clock of Springhaven solemnly struck midnight.

CHAPTER XXXII

THE TRIALS OF FAITH

He following day, the 27th of October, was a dark one in the calendar of a fair and good young lady. Two years would then have passed since Faith Darling, at the age of twenty, had received sad tidings, which would make the rest of her life flow on in shadow. So at least she thought, forgetful (or rather perhaps unconscious, for she had not yet learned the facts of life) that time and the tide of years submerge the loftiest youthful sorrow. To a warm and stedfast heart like hers, and a nature strong but self-controlled, no casual change, or light diversion, or sudden interest in other matters, could take the place of the motive lost. Therefore, being of a deep true faith, and staunch in the belief of a great God, good to all who seek His goodness, she never went away from what she meant, that faith and hope should feed each other.

This saved her from being a trouble to any one, or damping anybody's cheerfulness, or diminishing the gaiety around her. She took a lively interest in the affairs of other people, which a "blighted being" declines to do; and their pleasures ministered to her own good cheer without, or at any rate beyond, her knowledge. Therefore she was liked by everybody, and beloved by all who had any heart for a brave and pitiful story. Thus a sweet flower, half closed by the storm, continues to breathe forth its sweetness.

However, there were times when even Faith was lost in sad remembrance, and her bright young spirit became depressed by the hope deferred that maketh sick the heart. As time grew longer, hope grew less; and even the cheerful Admiral, well versed in perils of the deep, and acquainted with many a wandering story, had made up his mind that Erle Twemlow was dead, and would never more be heard of. The rector also, the young man's father, could hold out no longer against that conclusion; and even the mother, disdaining the mention, yet understood the meaning, of despair. And so among those to whom the subject was the most interesting in the world, it was now the strict rule to avoid it with the lips, though the eyes were often filled with it.

Faith Darling at first scorned this hard law. "It does seem so unkind," she used to say, "that even his name should be interdicted, as if he had disgraced himself. If he is dead, he has died with honour. None who ever saw him can doubt that. But he is not dead. He will come back to us, perhaps next week, perhaps to-morrow, perhaps even while we are afraid to speak of him. If it is for my sake that you behave thus, I am not quite so weak as to require it."

The peculiar circumstances of the case had not only baffled enquiry, but from the very beginning precluded it. The man with the keenest eyes, sharpest nose, biggest ears, and longest head, of all the many sneaks who now conduct what they call "special enquiries," could have done nothing with a case like this, because there was no beginning it. Even now, in fair peace, and with large knowledge added, the matter would not have been easy; but in war universal, and blank ignorance, there was nothing to be done but to sit down and think. And the story invited a good deal of thinking, because of its disappointing turn.

During the negotiations for peace in 1801, and before any articles were signed, orders were sent to the Cape of Good Hope for the return of a regiment of the line, which had not been more than three months there. But the Cape was likely to be restored to Holland, and two empty transports returning from India were to call under convoy, and bring home these troops. One of the officers was Captain Erle Twemlow, then about twenty-five years of age, and under probation, by the Admiral's decree, for the hand of the maiden whose heart had been his from a time to itself immemorial. After tiresome days of impatience, the transports arrived under conduct of a frigate; and after another week, the soldiers embarked with fine readiness for their native land.

But before they had cleared the Bay, they met a brig-of-war direct from Portsmouth, carrying despatches for the officer in command of the troops, as well as for the captain of the frigate. Some barbarous tribes on the coast of Guinea, the part that is called the Ivory Coast, had plundered and burnt a British trading station within a few miles of Cape Palmas, and had killed and devoured the traders. These natives must be punished, and a stern example made, and a negro monarch of the name of Hunko Jum must have his palace burned, if he possessed one; while his rival, the king of the Crumbo tribe, whose name was Bandeliah, who had striven to protect the traders, must be rewarded, and have a treaty made with him, if he could be brought to understand it. Both sailors and soldiers were ready enough to undertake this little spree, as they called it, expecting to have a pleasant run ashore, a fine bit of sport with the negroes, and perhaps a few noserings of gold to take home to their wives and sweethearts.

But, alas! the reality was not so fine. The negroes who had done all the mischief made off, carrying most of their houses with them; and the palace of Hunko Jum, if he possessed one, was always a little way further on. The Colonel was a stubborn man, and so was the sea-captain—good Tories both, and not desirous to skulk out of scrapes, and leave better men to pick up their clumsy breakages. Blue and red vied with one another to scour the country, and punish the natives—if only they could catch them—and to vindicate, with much strong language, the dignity of Great Britain, and to make an eternal example.

But white bones are what the white man makes, under that slimy sunshine and putrefying moon. Weary, slack-jointed, low-hearted as they were, the deadly coast-fever fell upon them, and they shivered, and burned, and groaned, and raved, and leaped into holes, or rolled into camp fires. The Colonel died early, and the Naval Captain followed him; none stood upon the order of their going; but man followed man, as in a funeral, to the grave, until there was no grave to go to. The hand of the Lord was stretched out against them; and never would one have come back to England, out of more than five hundred who landed, except for the manhood and vigour of a seaman, Captain Southcombe, of the transport Gwalior.

This brave and sensible man had been left with his ship lying off to be signalled for, in case of mishap, while his consort and the frigate were despatched in advance to a creek, about twenty leagues westward, where the land-force triumphant was to join them. Captain Southcombe, with every hand he could muster, traced the unfortunate party inland, and found them led many leagues in the wrong direction, lost among quagmires breathing death, worn out with vermin, venom, and despair, and hemmed in by savages lurking for the night, to rush in upon and make an end of them. What need of many words? This man, and his comrades, did more than any other men on the face of this earth could have done without British blood in them. They buried the many who had died without hope of the decent concealment which our life has had, and therefore our death longs for; they took on their shoulders, or on cane wattles, the many who had made up their minds to die, and were in much doubt about having done it, and they roused up and worked up by the scruff of their loose places the few who could get along on their own legs. And so, with great spirit, and still greater patience, they managed to save quite as many as deserved it.

Because, when they came within signal of the Gwalior, Captain Southcombe, marching slowly with his long limp burdens, found ready on the sand the little barrel, about as big as a kilderkin, of true and unsullied Stockholm pitch, which he had taken, as his brother took Madeira, for ripeness and for betterance, by right of change of climate. With a little of this given choicely and carefully at the back of every sick man's tongue, and a little more spread across the hollow of his stomach, he found them so enabled in the afternoon that they were glad to sit up in the bottom of a boat, and resign themselves to an All-wise Providence.

Many survived, and blessed Captain Southcombe, not at first cordially—for the man yet remains to be discovered who is grateful to his doctor—but gradually more and more, and with that healthy action of the human bosom which is called expectoration, whenever grateful memories were rekindled by the smell of tar. But this is a trifle; many useful lives were saved, and the Nation should have thanked Captain Southcombe, but did not.

After these sad incidents, when sorrow for old friends was tempered by the friendly warmth afforded by their shoes, a muster was held by the Major in command, and there was only one officer who could neither assert himself alive, nor be certified as dead. That one was Erle Twemlow, and the regiment would rather have lost any other two officers. Urgent as it was, for the safety of the rest, to fly with every feather from this pestilential coast, sails were handed, boats despatched, and dealings tried with Hunko Jum, who had reappeared with promptitude, the moment he was not wanted. From this noble monarch, and his chiefs, and all his nation, it was hard to get any clear intelligence, because their own was absorbed in absorbing. They had found upon the sands a cask of Admiralty rum, as well as a stout residue of unadulterated pitch. Noses, and tongues, and historical romance—for a cask had been washed ashore five generations since, and set up for a god, when the last drop was licked—induced this brave nation to begin upon the rum; and fashion (as powerful with them as with us) compelled them to drink the tar likewise, because they had seen the white men doing it. This would have made it hard to understand them, even if they had been English scholars, which their ignorance of rum proved them not to be; and our sailors very nearly went their way, after sadly ascertaining nothing, except that the cask was empty.

But luckily, just as they were pushing off, a very large, black head appeared from behind a vegetable-ivory tree, less than a quarter of a mile away, and they knew that this belonged to Bandeliah, the revered king of the Crumbos, who had evidently smelled rum far inland. With him they were enabled to hold discourse, partly by signs, and partly by means of an old and highly polished negro, who had been the rat-catcher at the factory now consumed; and the conclusion, or perhaps the confusion, arrived at from signs, grunts, grins, nods, waggings of fingers and twistings of toes, translated grandiloquently into broken English, was not far from being to the following effect:

To wit, that two great kings reigned inland, either of them able to eat up Hunko Jum and Bandeliah at a mouthful, but both of them too proud to set foot upon land that was flat, or in water that was salt. They ruled over two great nations called the Houlas, and the Quackwas, going out of sight among great rivers and lands with clear water standing over them. And if the white men could not understand this, it was because they drank salt-water.

Moreover, they said that of these two kings, the king of the Houlas was a woman, the most beautiful ever seen in all the world, and able to jump over any man's head. But the king of the Quackwas was a man, and although he had more than two thousand wives, and was taller by a joint of a bamboo than Bandeliah—whose stature was at least six feet four—yet nothing would be of any use to him, unless he could come to an agreement with Mabonga, the queen of the Houlas, to split a durra straw with him. But Mabonga was coy, and understanding men, as well as jumping over them, would grant them no other favour than the acceptance of their presents. However, the other great king was determined to have her for his wife, if he abolished all the rest, and for this reason he had caught and kept the lost Englishman as a medicine-man; and it was not likely that he would kill him, until he failed or succeeded.

To further enquiries Bandeliah answered that to rescue the prisoner was impossible. If it had been his own newest wife, he would not push out a toe for her. The great king Golo lived up in high places that overlooked the ground, as he would these white men, and his armies went like wind and spread like fire. None of his warriors ate white man's flesh; they were afraid it would make them cowardly.

A brave heart is generally tender in the middle, to make up for being so firm outside, even as the Durian fruit is. Captain Southcombe had walked the poop-deck of the Gwalior many a time, in the cool of the night, with Erle Twemlow for his companion, and had taken a very warm liking to him. So that when the survivors of the regiment were landed at Portsmouth, this brave sailor travelled at his own cost to Springhaven, and told the Rector the whole sad story, making it clear to him beyond all doubt, that nothing whatever could be done to rescue the poor young man from those savages, or even to ascertain his fate. For the Quackwas were an inland tribe, inhabiting vast regions wholly unknown to any European, and believed to extend to some mighty rivers, and lakes resembling inland seas.

Therefore Mr. Twemlow, in a deep quiet voice, asked Captain Southcombe one question only—whether he might keep any hope of ever having, by the mercy of the Lord, his only son restored to him. And the sailor said—yes; the mistake would be ever to abandon such a hope, for at the moment he least expected it, his son might stand before him. He pretended to no experience of the western coast of Africa, and niggers he knew were a very queer lot, acting according to their own lights, which differed according to their natures. But he was free to say, that in such a condition he never would think of despairing, though it might become very hard not to do so, as time went on without bringing any news. He himself had been in sad peril more than once, and once it appeared quite hopeless; but he thought of his wife and his children at home, and the Lord had been pleased to deliver him.

The parson was rebuked by this brave man's faith, who made no pretence whatever to piety; and when they said Goodbye, their eyes were bright with the goodwill and pity of the human race, who know trouble not inflicted as yet upon monkeys. Mr. Twemlow's heart fell when the sailor was gone, quite as if he had lost his own mainstay; but he braced himself up to the heavy duty of imparting sad news to his wife and daughter, and worst of all to Faith Darling. But the latter surprised him by the way in which she bore it; for while she made no pretence to hide her tears, she was speaking as if they were needless. And the strangest thing of all, in Mr. Twemlow's opinion, was her curious persistence about Queen Mabonga. Could any black woman—and she supposed she must be that—be considered by white people to be beautiful? Had Captain Southcombe ever even seen her; and if not, how could he be in such raptures about her attractions? She did not like to say a word, because he had been so kind and so faithful to those poor soldiers, whom it was his duty to bring home safe; but if it had not been for that, she might have thought that with so many children and a wife at Limehouse, he should not have allowed his mind to dwell so fondly on the personal appearance of a negress!

The Rector was astonished at this injustice, and began to revise his opinion about Faith as the fairest and sweetest girl in all the world; but Mrs. Twemlow smiled, when she had left off crying, and said that she liked the dear child all the better for concluding that Ponga—or whatever her name was—must of necessity and at the first glance fall desperately in love with her own Erle. Then the Rector cried, "Oh, to be sure, that explained it! But he never could have thought of that, without his wife's assistance."

Two years now, two years of quiet patience, of busy cheerfulness now and then, and of kindness to others always, had made of Faith Darling a lady to be loved for a hundred years, and for ever. The sense of her sorrow was never far from her, yet never brought near to any other by herself; and her smile was as warm, and her eyes as bright, as if there had never been a shadow on her youth. To be greeted by her, and to receive her hand, and one sweet glance of her large goodwill, was enough to make an old man feel that he must have been good at some time, and a young man hope that he should be so by-and-by; though the tendency was generally contented with the hope.

CHAPTER XXXIII

FAREWELL, DANIEL

Thoughtful for others as she always was, this lovely and loveable young woman went alone, on the morning of the day that was so sorrowful for her, to bear a little share of an elder lady's sorrow, and comfort her with hopes, or at any rate with kindness. They had shed tears together when the bad news arrived, and again when a twelvemonth had weakened feeble hope; and now that another year had well-nigh killed it in old hearts too conversant with the cruelties of the world, a little talk, a tender look, a gentle repetition of things that had been said at least a hundred times before, might enter by some subtle passage to the cells of comfort. Who knows how the welted vine leaf, when we give it shade and moisture, crisps its curves again, and breathes new bloom upon its veinage? And who can tell how the flagging heart, beneath the cool mantle of time, revives, shapes itself into keen sympathies again, and spreads itself congenially to the altered light?

Without thinking about it, but only desiring to do a little good, if possible, Faith took the private way through her father's grounds leading to the rectory, eastward of the village. It was scarcely two o'clock, and the sun was shining, and the air clear and happy, as it can be in October. She was walking rather fast, for fear of dropping into the brooding vein, when in the little fir plantation a man came forth on her path, and stood within a few yards in front of her. She was startled for an instant, because the place was lonely, and Captain Stubbard's battery crew had established their power to repulse the French by pounding their fellow-countrymen. But presently she saw that it was Dan Tugwell, looking as unlike himself as any man can do (without the aid of an artist), and with some surprise she went on to meet him.

Instead of looking bright, and bold, and fearless, with the freedom of the sea in his open face, and that of the sun in his clustering curls, young Daniel appeared careworn and battered, not only unlike his proper self, but afraid of and ashamed of it. He stood not firmly on the ground, nor lightly poised like a gallant sailor, but loosely and clumsily like a ploughman who leaves off at the end of his furrow to ease the cramp. His hat looked as if he had slept in it, and his eyes as if he had not slept with them.

Miss Darling had always been fond of Dan, from the days when they played on the beach together, in childhood's contempt of social law. Her old nurse used to shut her eyes, after looking round to make sure that there was "nobody coming to tell on them," while as pretty a pair of children as the benevolent sea ever prattled with were making mirth and music and romance along its margin. And though in ripe boyhood the unfaithful Daniel transferred the hot part of his homage to the more coquettish Dolly, Faith had not made any grievance of that, but rather thought all the more of him, especially when he saved her sister's life in a very rash boating adventure.

So now she went up to him with a friendly mind, and asked him softly and pitifully what trouble had fallen upon him. At the sweet sound of her voice, and the bright encouragement of her eyes, he felt as if he was getting better.

"If you please, miss," he said, with a meek salutation, which proved his panisic ideas to be not properly wrought into his system as yet—"if you please, miss, things are very hard upon me."

"Is it money?" she asked, with the true British instinct that all common woes have their origin there; "if it is, I shall be so glad that I happen to have a good bit put by just now."

But Dan shook his head with such dignified sadness that Faith was quite afraid of having hurt his feelings. "Oh, I might have known," she said, "that it was nothing of that kind. You are always so industrious and steady. But what can it be? Is it anything about Captain Stubbard and his men, because I know you do not like them, and none of the old Springhaven people seem to do so? Have you been obliged to fight with any of them, Daniel?"

"No, miss, no. I would not soil my hand by laying it on any of such chaps as those. Unless they should go for to insult me, I mean, or any one belonging to me. No, miss, no. It is ten times worse than money, or assault and battery."

"Well, Daniel, I would not on any account," said Faith, with her desire of knowledge growing hotter by delay, as a kettle boils by waiting—"on no account would I desire to know anything that you do not seem to think my advice might help you to get out of. I am not in a hurry, but still my time is getting rather late for what I have to do. By the time I come back from the rectory, perhaps you will have made up your mind about it. Till then, good-bye to you, Daniel."

He stepped out of the path, that she might go by, and only said, "Then goodbye, miss; I shall be far away when you come back."

This was more than the best-regulated, or largest—which generally is the worst-regulated—feminine mind could put up with. Miss Darling came back, with her mind made up to learn all, or to know the reason why.

"Dan, this is unworthy of you," she said, with her sweet voice full of sorrow. "Have I ever been hard or unkind to you, Dan, that you should be so afraid of me?"

"No, miss, never. But too much the other way. That makes it so bad for me to say good-bye. I am going away, miss. I must be off this evening. I never shall see Springhaven no more, nor you, miss—nor nobody else."

"It is quite impossible, Dan. You must be dreaming. You don't look at all like yourself to-day. You have been doing too much over-time. I have heard all about it, and how very hard you work. I have been quite sorry for you on Sundays, to see you in the gallery, without a bit of rest, still obliged to give the time with your elbow. I have often been astonished that your mother could allow it. Why, Dan, if you go away, you will break her heart, and I don't know how many more in Springhaven."

"No, miss, no. They very soon mends them. It is the one as goes away that gets a deal the worst of it. I am sure I don't know whatever I shall do, without the old work to attend to. But it will get on just as well without me."

"No, it won't," replied Faith, looking at him very sadly, and shaking her head at such cynical views; "nothing will be the same, when you are gone, Daniel; and you ought to have more consideration."

"I am going with a good man, at any rate," he answered, "the freest-minded gentleman that ever came to these parts. Squire Carne, of Carne Castle, if you please, miss."

"Mr. Caryl Carne!" cried Faith, in a tone which made Daniel look at her with some surprise. "Is he going away? Oh, I am so glad!"

"No, miss; not Squire Carne himself. Only to provide for me work far away, and not to be beholden any more to my own people. And work where a man may earn and keep his own money, and hold up his head while adoing of it."

"Oh, Dan, you know more of such things than I do. And every man has a right to be independent, and ought to be so, and I should despise him otherwise. But don't be driven by it into the opposite extreme of disliking the people in a different rank—"

"No, miss, there is no fear of that—the only fear is liking some of them too much."

"And then," continued Faith, who was now upon one of her favourite subjects past interruption, "you must try to remember that if you work hard, so do we, or nearly all of us. From the time my father gets up in the morning, to the time when he goes to bed at night, he has not got five minutes—as he tells us every day—for attending to anything but business. Even at dinner, when you get a good hour, and won't be disturbed—now will you?"

"No, miss; not if all the work was tumbling down. No workman as respects himself would take fifty-nine minutes for sixty."

"Exactly so; and you are right. You stand up for your rights. Your dinner you have earned, and you will have it. And the same with your breakfast, and your supper too, and a good long night to get over it. Do you jump up in bed, before you have shut both eyes, hearing or fancying you have heard the bell, that calls you out into the cold, and the dark, and a wet saddle, from a warm pillow? And putting that by, as a trouble of the war, and the chance of being shot at by dark tall men"—here Faith shuddered at her own presentment, as the image of Caryl Carne passed before her—"have you to consider, at every turn, that whatever you do—though you mean it for the best—will be twisted and turned against you by some one, and made into wickedness that you never dreamed of, by envious people, whose grudge against you is that they fancy you look down on them? Though I am sure of one thing, and that is that my father, instead of looking down upon any honest man because he is poor, looks up to him; and so do I; and so does every gentleman or lady. And any one who goes about to persuade the working-people—as they are called, because they have to use their hands more—that people like my father look down upon them, and treat them like dogs, and all those wicked stories—all I can say is, any man who does it deserves to be put in the stocks, or the pillory, or even to be transported as an enemy to his country."

Dan looked at the lady with great surprise. He had always known her to be kind and gentle, and what the old people called "mannersome," to every living body that came near her. But to hear her put, better than he could put them, his own budding sentiments (which he thought to be new, with the timeworn illusion of young Liberals), and to know from her bright cheeks, and brighter eyes, that her heart was in every word of it, and to feel himself rebuked for the evil he had thought, and the mischief he had given ear to—all this was enough to make him angry with himself, and uncertain how to answer.

"I am certain that you never thought of such things," Miss Darling continued, with her gentle smile returning; "you are much too industrious and sensible for that. But I hear that some persons are now in our parish who make it their business, for some reason of their own, to spread ill-will and jealousy and hatred everywhere, to make us all strangers and foes to one another, and foreigners to our own country. We have enemies enough, by the will of the Lord (as Mr. Twemlow says), for a sharp trial to us, and a lesson to our pride, and a deep source of gratitude, and charity, and good-will—though I scarcely understand how they come in—and, above all, a warning to us to stick together, and not exactly hate, but still abhor, everybody who has a word to say against his own country at a time like this. And ten thousand times as much, if he is afraid to say it, but crawls with crafty poison into simple English bosoms."

"There is nothing of that, miss, to my knowledge, here," the young fisherman answered, simply; "Springhaven would never stand none of that; and the club drinks the health of King George every night of their meeting, and stamps on the floor for him. But I never shall help to do that any more. I must be going, miss—and thank you."

"Then you will not tell me why you go? You speak of it as if it was against your will, and yet refuse to say what drives you. Have you been poaching, Dan? Ah, that is it! But I can beg you off immediately. My father is very good even to strangers, and as for his doing anything to you—have no fear, Dan; you shall not be charged with it, even if you have been in Brown Bushes."

Brown Bushes, a copse about a mile inland, was the Admiral's most sacred spot, when peace allowed him to go shooting, because it was beloved by woodcocks, his favourite birds both for trigger and for fork. But Daniel only shook his head; he had not been near Brown Bushes. Few things perhaps will endure more wear than feminine curiosity. But when a trap has been set too long, it gets tongue-bound, and grows content without contents.

"Daniel Tugwell," said Miss Darling, severely, "if you have not been fighting, or conspiring against society, or even poaching, I can well understand that you may have reasons for not desiring my assistance or advice. And I only wonder that under such circumstances you took the trouble to wait for me here, as you appear to have done. Good-bye."

"Oh, don't be cross, miss! please not to be cross," cried Daniel, running after her; "I would tell you all about it this very instant moment, if it were behoving to me. You will hear all about it when you get to Parson Twemlow's, for I saw mother going there, afore she had her breakfast, though I was not concernable to let her see me. If the Squire had been home, she would have gone up to Hall first. No, miss, no. I done nothing to be ashamed of; and if you turn back on me, you'll be sorry afterwards."

Faith was more apt to think that she had been too sharp than to be so in behaviour to any one. She began at once, with a blush for her bad ideas, to beg Dan's pardon, and he saw his way to say what he was come to say.

"You always were too good, Miss Faith, too good to be hard upon any one, and I am sure you have not been hard upon me; for I know that I look disrespectable. But I couldn't find words to say what I wanted, until you spoke so soft and kind. And perhaps, when I say it, you'll be angry with me, and think that I trespass upon you."

"No, I won't, Dan; I will promise you that. You may tell me, as if I were Mr. Swipes, who says that he never lost his temper in his life, because he is always right, and other people wrong."

"Well, miss, I'm afraid that I am not like that, and that makes me feel so uncomfortable with the difference between us. Because it is all about Miss Dolly, and I might seem so impudent. But you know that I would go through fire and water to serve Miss Dolly, and I durstn't go away forever without one message to her. If I was in her own rank of life, God Almighty alone should part us, whether I was rich or whether I was poor, and I'd like to see any one come near her! But being only an ignorant fellow without any birth or book-learning, I am not such a fool as to forget that the breadth of the world lies between us. Only I may wish her well, all the same—I may wish her well and happy, miss?"

"Certainly you may." Faith blushed at the passion of his words, and sighed at their despair. "You have saved her life. She respects and likes you, the same as my father and I do. You may trust me with your message, Dan."

"I suppose it would not be the proper thing for me to see her once before I go; just for one minute, with you standing by her, that I might—that she might —"

"No," answered Faith, though it grieved her to say it; "we must not think of that, Dan. It could do you no good, and it might do her harm. But if you have any message, to be useful to her—"

"The useful part of it must be through you, miss, and not sent to her at all, I think, or it would be very impertinent. The kind part is to give her my good-bye, and say that I would die to help her. And the useful part is for yourself. For God's sake, miss, do keep Miss Dolly out of the way of Squire Carne! He hath a tongue equal to any woman, with the mind of a man beneath it. He hath gotten me body and soul; because I care not the skin of a dab what befalls me. But oh, miss, he never must get Miss Dolly. He may be a very good man in some ways, and he is wonderful free-minded; but any young lady as marries him had better have leaped into the Culver Hole. Farewell, miss, now that I have told you." He was gone before Faith could even offer him her hand, but he took off his hat and put one finger to his curls, as he looked back from the clearing; and her eyes filled with tears, as she waved her hand and answered, "Farewell, Daniel!"

CHAPTER XXXIV

CAULIFLOWERS

"They cocks and hens," Mr. Swipes used to say in the earlier days of his empire—"bless you, my lord, they cocks and hens knows a good bit of gardening as well as I do. They calls one another, and they comes to see it, and they puts their heads to one side and talks about it, and they say to one another, 'Must be something good there, or he wouldn't have made it so bootiful'; and then up go their combs, and they tear away into it, like a passel of Scotchmen at a scratching-match. If your lordship won't put a lock on the door, you will never taste a bit of good vegetable."

Admiral Darling was at length persuaded to allow Mr. Swipes the privilege of locking himself in the kitchen-garden; and then, for the purpose of getting at him, a bell was put in the gable of the tool-house, with a long handle hanging outside the door in the courtyard towards the kitchen. Thus he was able to rest from his labours, without incurring unjust reproach; and gradually as he declined, with increasing decision, to answer the bell when it rang, according to the highest laws of nature it left off ringing altogether. So Mr. Swipes in the walled kitchen-garden sought peace and ensued it.

One quiet November afternoon, when the disappearance of Dan Tugwell had been talked out and done with, a sad mishap befell this gardener, during the performance, or, to speak more correctly, the contemplation of his work. A yawn of such length and breadth and height and profundity took possession of him that the space it had so well occupied still retained the tender memory. In plainer words, he had ricked his jaw, not from general want of usage, but from the momentary excess.

"Sarves me right," he muttered, "for carrying on so, without nothing inside of 'un. Must go to doctor, quick step, and no mistake."

In this strait he set off for John Prater's (for it was a matter of luck to get ale at the Hall, and in such emergency he must not trust to fortune), and passing hastily through the door, left it unlocked behind him. Going down the hill he remembered this, and had a great mind to go back again, but the unanimous demand of his system for beer impelled him downwards. He never could get up that hill again without hydraulic pressure.

All might have gone well, and all would have gone well, except for the grievous mistake of Nature in furnishing women with eyes whose keenness is only exceeded by that of their tongues. The cook at the Hall, a superior person

—though lightly esteemed by Mrs. Cloam—had long been ambitious to have a voice in the selection of her raw material. If anything was good, who got the credit? Mr. Swipes, immediately. But if everything was bad, as more often happened, who received the blame? Mary Knuckledown. Her lawful name was "Knuckleup," but early misfortunes had reduced her to such mildness that her name became converted—as she expressed it—in harmony with her nature. Facts having generally been adverse to her, she found some comfort in warm affection for their natural enemies and ever-victorious rivals—words. Any words coming with a brave rush are able to scatter to the winds the strongest facts; but big words—as all our great orators know—knock them at once on the head and cremate them. But the cook was a kind-hearted woman, and liked both little and big words, without thinking of them.

She had put down her joint, a good aitch-bone, for roasting—than which, if well treated, are few better treats—to revolve in the distant salute of the fire (until it should ripen for the close embrace, where the tints of gold and chestnut vie), when it came into her provident mind with a flash that neither horse-radish nor cauliflower had yet been delivered by Mr. Swipes. She must run out and pull the long handle in the yard, and remind him gently of her needs, for she stood in some awe of his character, as a great annalist of little people's lives.

Leaving the small dog Dandolo with stern orders to keep the jack steadily going, with a stick on the dresser to intimidate one eye, and a sop in the dripping-pan to encourage the other, Mrs. Knuckledown ran into the court-yard, just in time to see the last swing of the skirt of that noble gardener's coat, as he turned the wall corner on his march towards the tap. She longed to call him back, but remembered just in time how fearfully cross that had made him once before, and she was yielding with a sigh to her usual bad luck, when an eager and triumphant cluck made her look about. The monarch and patriarch of cocks, a magnificent old Dorking, not idly endowed with five claws for the scratch, had discovered something great, and was calling all his wives, and even his sons, as many as yet crowed not against him, to share this special luck of fortune, or kind mood of Providence. In a minute or two he had levied an army, some half-hundred strong, and all spurring the land, to practise their liberal claws betimes for the gorgeous joy of scattering it. Then the grand old cock, whose name was "Bill," made them all fall in behind him, and strutting till he almost tumbled on his head, led the march of destruction to the garden door.

But, alas, he had waited for his followers too long, eager as they were for rapine. When he came to his portal of delight, there stood, stout as Britannia herself, and sweeping a long knife for her trident, the valiant cook, to protect her cauliflowers. "You be off, Bill," she cried. "I don't want to hurt you, because you have been a good bird in your time, but now you be growing outrageous." Bill made a rush for it, but losing a slice of his top-heavy comb, retired.

"Now's my opportunity," said Mary to herself, "for to cut my own cabbage for once in my life, and to see what that old beast does in here. Oh my! The old villain, and robber that he is! Bamboozlement is the language for it." Embezzlement she should have said, and to one who knew as she did how badly the table of the master was supplied, the suspicion was almost unavoidable. For here she saw in plenteous show, and appetising excellence, a many many of the very things she had vainly craved from Mr. Swipes. And if it was so now in November, what must it have been two months ago? Why, poor Miss Faith—Mary Knuckledown's idol, because of her kindness and sad disappointment—had asked a little while ago for a bit of salsify, not for herself—she never thought of herself—but for a guest who was fond of it; also the Admiral himself had called out for a good dish of skirrets. But no; Mr. Swipes said the weather and the black blight had destroyed them. Yet here they were; Mary could swear to them both, with their necks above-ground, as if waiting for the washing! Cauliflowers also (as the cooks call broccoli of every kind), here they were in abundance, ten long rows all across the middle square, very beautiful to behold. Some were just curling in their crinkled coronets, to conceal the young heart that was forming, as Miss in her teens draws her tresses around the first peep of her own palpitation; others were showing their broad candid bosoms, with bold sprigs of nature's green lace crisping round; while others had their ripe breasts shielded from the air by the breakage of their own broad fringe upon them.

Mary knew that this was done by Mr. Swipes himself, because he had brought her some in that condition; but the unsuspicious master had accepted his assurance that "they was only fit for pigs as soon as the break-stalk blight come on 'em"; and then the next day he had bought the very same, perhaps at ninepence apiece, from Mr. Cheeseman's window, trimmed and shorn close, like the head of a monk. "I'll see every bit of 'un, now that I be here." Mrs. Knuckledown spoke aloud, to keep up her courage. "Too bad for that old beast to keep us locked out from the very place us ought to have for pommylarding, because he saith all the fruit would go into our pockets. And what goes into his'en, I should like to know? Suppose I lock him out, as he hath locked us out. He won't be back yet for half an hour, anyway. Wish I could write—what a list I would make, if it was only of the things he denieth he hath got!"

Strong in her own honesty and loyalty to her master, the cook turned the key in the lock, and left Swipes to ring himself into his own garden, as he always called it. That is to say, if he should return, which was not very likely, before she had time for a good look round. But she saw such a sight of things she had longed for, to redeem her repute in the vegetable way, as well as such herbs for dainty stuffing, of which she knew more than cooks generally do, that her cap nearly came off her head with amazement, and time flew by unheeded. Until she was startled and terrified sadly by the loud, angry clang of the bell in the gable. Not only was Mr. Swipes come back, but he was in a furious rage outside, though his fury was chilled with some shivers of fear. At first, when he found the door locked against him, he thought that the Admiral must have come home unexpected, and failing to find him at work, had turned the key against him, while himself inside. If so, his situation would be in sad peril, and many acres of lies would be required to redeem it. For trusting in his master's long times of absence, and full times of public duty when at home, Mr. Swipes had grown more private stock, as he called it, and denied the kitchen more, than he had ever done before, in special preparation for some public dinners about to be given at the Darling Arms, by military officers to naval, and in turn by the latter to the former; for those were hospitable days, when all true Britons stuck their country's enemy with knife and fork, as well as sword.

But learning, as he soon did at the stables, that the Admiral was still away, and both the young ladies were gone for a ride with Miss Twemlow, the gardener came back in a rage, and rang the bell. "Oh, whatever shall I do?" the trembling Mary asked herself. "Best take the upper hand if I can. He's a thief, and a rogue, and he ought to be frighted. Does he know I can't write? No, for certain he dothn't. One of his big lies about me was a letter I wrote to poor Jonadab."

With her courage renewed by the sense of that wrong, she opened the door, and stood facing Mr. Swipes, with a piece of paper in her hand, which a woman's quick wit bade her fetch from her pocket.

"Halloa, madam!" the gardener exclaimed, with a sweep of his hat and a low salute, which he meant to be vastly satirical; "so your ladyship have come to take the air in my poor garden, instead of tending the spit. And what do your ladyship think of it, so please you? Sorry as I had any dung about, but hadn't no warning of this royal honour."

"Sir," said Mrs. Knuckledown, pretending to be frightened a great deal more than she was—"oh, sir, forgive me! I am sure I meant no harm. But the fowls was running in, and I ran up to stop them."

"Oh, that was how your ladyship condescended; and to keep out the fowls, you locked out me! Allow me the royal and unapparelled honour of showing your ladyship to her carriage; and if I ever catch her in here again, I'll pitch you down the court-yard pretty quick. Be off, you dirty baggage, or I won't answer for it now!"

"Oh, you are too kind, Mr. Swipes; I am sure you are too gentle, to forgive me, like of that! And the little list I made of the flowers in your garden, I shall put it in a teapot till the Quality wants something."

Mr. Swipes gave a start, and his over-watered eyes could not meet those of Mary, which were mildly set upon them. "List!" he muttered—"little list! What do you please to mean, Miss?"

"Well, the 'dirty baggage' means nothing unparalleled, sir, but just the same as anybody else might do. Some people calls it a Inventionary, and some an Emmarandum, and some a Catalogue. It don't interfere with you, Mr. Swipes; only the next time as Miss Dolly asks, the same as she was doing the other day—"

"Oh, she was, was she? The little ——!" Mr. Swipes used a word concerning that young lady which would have insured his immediate discharge, together with one from the Admiral's best toe. "And pray, what was her observations, ma'am?"

"It was Charles told me, for he was waiting at dinner. Seems that the turnip was not to her liking, though I picked out the very best of what few you sent in, so she looks up from her plate, and she says: 'Well, I cannot understand it! To me it is the greatest mistress in the world,' she says, 'that we never can get a bit of vegetable fit for eating. We've got,' she says, 'a kitchen-garden close upon two acres, and a man who calls himself head gardener, by the name of Swipes'—my pardoning to you, Mr. Swipes, for the young lady's way of saying it—'and his two sons, and his nephew, and I dare say soon his grandsons. Well, and what comes of it?' says she. 'Why, that we never has a bit of any kind of vegetable, much less of fruit, fit to lay a fork to!' Charles was a-pricking up his ears at this, because of his own grumbles, and the master saw it, and he says, 'Hush, Dolly!' But she up and answers spiritly: 'No, I won't hush, papa, because it is too bad. Only you leave it to me,' she says, 'and if I don't keep the key from that old thief—excoose me, Mr. Swipes, for her shocking language—'and find out what he locks up in there, my name's not Horatia Dorothy Darling.' Oh, don't let it dwell so on your mind, Mr. Swipes! You know what young ladies be. They says things random, and then goes away and never thinks no more about it. Oh, don't be upset so —or I shall have to call Charles!"

Mr. Swipes took his hat off to ease his poor mind, which had lost its way altogether in other people's wickedness. "May I never set eyes on that young man no more!" he exclaimed, with more pathetic force than reasoning power. "Either him or me quits this establishment to-morrow. Ah, I know well why he left his last place, and somebody else shall know to-morrow!"

"What harm have poor Charles done?" the cook asked sharply; "it wasn't him that said it; it was Miss Dolly. Charley only told me conferentially."

"Oh, I know what 'conferentially' means, when anything once gets among the womenkind! But I know a thing or two about Miss Dolly, as will give her enough to do at home, I'll warrant, without coming spying after me and my affairs. Don't you be surprised, cook, whatever you may hear, as soon as ever the Admiral returneth. He's a soft man enough in a number of ways, but he won't put up with everything. The nasty little vixen, if she don't smart for this!"

"Oh, don't 'e, now don't 'e, Mr. Swipes, that's a dear!" cried the soft-hearted Mrs. Knuckledown; "don't 'e tell on her, the poor young thing. If her hath been carrying on a bit with some of them young hofficers, why, it's only natteral, and her such a young booty. Don't 'e be Dick-tell-tale, with a name to it, or without. And perhaps her never said half the things that Charles hath contributed to her." The truth was that poor Dolly had said scarcely one of them.

"Bain't no young hofficer," Mr. Swipes replied, contemptuously; "ten times wuss than that, and madder for the Admiral. Give me that paper, Miss, and then, perhaps, I'll tell 'e. Be no good to you, and might be useful to me."

Mary could not give up the paper, because it was a letter from one of her adorers, which, with the aid of Jenny Shanks, she had interpreted. "No, no," she said, with a coaxing look; "by-and-by, Mr. Swipes, when you have told me who it is, and when you have promised not to tell on poor Miss Dolly. But nobody sha'n't see it, without your permission. We'll have another talk about that to-morrow. But, oh my! look at the time you have kept me, with all the good things to make a hangel's mouth water! Bring me two cauliflowers in two seconds. My beef will want basting long ago; and if Dandy hathn't left his job, he'll be pretty well roasted hisself by now."

Mr. Swipes went muttering up the walk, and was forced to cut two of the finest cauliflowers intended for Cheeseman's adornment to-morrow. This turned his heart very sour again, and he shook his head, growling in self-commune: "You see if I don't do it, my young lady. You speaks again me, behind my back, and I writes again you, before your face; though, in course, I need not put my name to it."

CHAPTER XXXV

LOYAL, AYE LOYAL

One of the dinners at the Darling Arms, and perhaps the most brilliant and exciting of the whole, because even the waiters understood the subject, was the entertainment given in the month of December, A.D. 1803, not only by the officers of two regiments quartered for the time near Stonnington, but also by all the leading people round about those parts, in celebration of the great work done by His Majesty's 38-gun frigate Leda. Several smaller dinners had been consumed already, by way of practice, both for the cooks and the waiters and the chairman, and Mr. John Prater, who always stood behind him, with a napkin in one hand and a corkscrew in the other, and his heart in the middle, ready either to assuage or stimulate. As for the guests, it was always found that no practice had been required.

"But now, but now"—as Mr. Prater said, when his wife pretended to make nothing of it, for no other purpose than to aggravate him, because she thought that he was making too much money, in proportion to what he was giving her —"now we shall see what Springhaven can do for the good of the Country and the glory of herself. Two bottles and a half a head is the lowest that can be charged for, with the treble X outside, and the punch to follow after. His lordship is the gentleman to keep the bottle going."

For the Lord-Lieutenant of the county, the popular Marquis of Southdown, had promised to preside at this grand dinner; and everybody knew what that meant. "Short tongue and long throat," was his lordship's motto in the discharge of all public business, and "Bottle to the gentleman on my left!" was the practical form of his eulogies. In a small space like this, there would be no chance for a sober-minded guest to escape his searching eye, and Blyth Scudamore (appointed to represent the officers of the Leda, and therefore the hero of the evening) felt as happy as a dog being led to be drowned, in view of this liquid ordeal. For Blyth was a temperate and moderate young man, neither such a savage as to turn his wine to poison, nor yet so Anti-Christian as to turn it into water.

Many finer places had been offered for the feast, and foremost amongst them the Admiral's house; but the committee with sound judgment had declined them all. The great point was to have a place within easy reach of boats, and where gallant naval officers could be recalled at once, if the French should do anything outrageous, which they are apt to do at the most outrageous time. But when a partition had been knocked down, and the breach tacked over with festoons of laurel, Mr. Prater was quite justified in rubbing his red hands and declaring it as snug a box as could be for the business. There was even a dark elbow where the staircase jutted out, below the big bressemer of the partition, and made a little gallery for ladies to hear speeches, and behold the festive heroes while still fit to be beholden. And Admiral Darling, as vice-chairman, entering into facts masculine and feminine, had promised his daughters and Miss Twemlow, under charge of the rector's wife and Mrs. Stubbard, a peep at this heroic scene, before it should become too convivial. The rescuers also of the Blonde, the flesh and bone, without which the master brain must still have lain stranded, were to have a grand supper in the covered skittle-alley, as the joints came away from their betters, this lower deck being in command of Captain Tugwell, who could rouse up his crew as fast as his lordship roused his officers.

Admiral Darling had been engaged of late in the service of his Country so continually, and kept up and down the great roads so much, or in and out of any little port where sailors grew, that his own door had nearly forgotten his shadow, and his dining-room table the reflection of his face. For, in those days, to keep a good table implied that the table must be good, as well as what was put upon it; and calico spread upon turpentine was not yet considered the proper footing for the hospitable and social glass.

"When shall Twemlow and I have a hobnob again?" the Admiral asked himself many a time. "How the dear old fellow loves to see the image of his glass upon the table, and the ruby of his port reflected! Heigho! I am getting very stiff in the back, and never a decent bit of dinner for'ard. And as for a glass of good wine—oh Lord! my timbers will be broken up, before it comes to mend them. And when I come home for even half an hour, there is all this small rubbish to attend to. I must have Frank home, to take this stuff off my hands, or else keep what I abominate, a private secretary."

Among the pile of letters that had lain unopened was one which he left to the last, because he disliked both the look and the smell of it. A dirty, ugly scrawl it was, bulged out with clumsy folding, and dabbed with wax in the creases. With some dislike he tore it open; and the dislike became loathing, as he read:

"Hon'd Sir. These foo lines comes from a umble but arty frend to command. Rekwesting of your pardon sir, i have kep a hi same been father of good dawters on the goings on of your fammeley. Miss Faith she is a hangel sir but Miss Dolly I fere no better than she ort to be, and wonderful fond of been noticed. I see her keeping company and carryin on dreadful with a tall dark young man as meens no good and lives to Widow Shankses. Too nites running when the days was short she been up to the cornder of your grounds to meat he there ever so long. Only you hask her if you don't believe me and wash her fase same time sir. Too other peple besides me nose it. Excoose hon'd sir this trubble from your obejiant servant

"FAX AND NO MISSTAKE."

The Admiral's healthy face turned blue with rage and contempt, and he stamped with his heel, as if he had the writer under it. To write a stabbing letter, and to dare to deal the stab, and yet fear to show the hand that deals it, was at that time considered a low thing to do. Even now there are people who so regard it, though a still better tool for a blackguard—the anonymous postcard—is now superseding it.

All the old man's pleasure, and cheer, and comfort, and joy in having one day at home at last, were dashed and shattered and turned into wretched anxiety by this vile scrawl. He meant to have gone down, light of heart, with a smiling daughter upon either arm, to the gallant little festival where everybody knew him, and every one admired and loved him. His two pretty daughters would sit upstairs, watching from a bow-window (though themselves unseen) all the dashing arrivals and the grand apparel. Then when the Marquis made his speech, and the King and Queen and Royal Family rode upon the clouds, and the grandeur of Great Britain was above the stars of heaven, the ladies in the gallery would venture just to show themselves, not for one moment with a dream of being looked at, but from romantic loyalty, and the fervour of great sentiments. People pretending not to know would ask, "Who are those very lovely ladies?" And he would make believe to know nothing at all about it, but his heart would know whether he knew it or not.

On the very eve of all this well-earned bliss, when it would have refreshed his fagged body and soul—which were now not so young as they used to be —to hear from some scoundrel without a name, that his pet child, the life of his life, was no better than she ought to be, which being said of a woman means that she is as bad as she can be! This fine old gentleman had never received such a cowardly back-handed blow till now, and for a moment he bent under it.

Then, greatly ashamed of himself, he arose, and with one strong word, which even Mr. Twemlow might have used under such provocation, he trod the vile stuff under foot, and pitched it with the fire-tongs into the fire. After this he felt better, and resolving most stoutly that he never would let it cross his mind again, made a light and cheerful answer to the profligate one—his young girl who came seeking him.

"Oh, father, and you ought to be dressed!" she cried. "Shall we keep His Majesty the Lord-Lieutenant waiting? Don't let us go at all. Let us stop at home, papa. We never see you now, more than once in a month; and we don't want to see you from a staircase hole, where we mustn't even blow a kiss to you. I have got such a lot of things to tell you, dear father; and I could make you laugh much more than they will."

"But, my darling—all these grand things?" said the father, gently fingering but half afraid to look at her, because of what had been in his own mind; "the sweetest Navy blue, and the brightest Army red, and little bits of silver lace so quiet in between them! I am sure I don't know what to call a quarter of it; but the finest ship ever seen under full sail, with the sun coming through her from her royals to her courses—"

"Now, papa, don't be so ridiculous. You know that I am not a fine ship at all, but only a small frigate, about eighteen guns at the outside, I should say—though she would be a sloop of war, wouldn't she?—and come here at any rate for you to command her, if you are not far too lofty an Admiral."

"Do you love your old father, my dear?" said he, being carried beyond his usual state by the joy in her eyes as she touched him.

"What a shame to ask me such a question? Oh, papa, I ought to say, 'Do you love me?' when you go away weeks and months almost together! Take that, papa; and be quite ashamed of yourself."

She swept all her breast-knots away anyhow—that had taken an hour to arbitrate—and flung back her hair that would never be coiled, and with a flash of tears leaping into laughing eyes, threw both arms round her father's neck, and pressed her cool sweet lips to his, which were not at all in the same condition.

"There, see what you've done for me now!" she cried. "It will take three-quarters of an hour, papa, to make me look fit to be looked at again. The fashions are growing so ridiculous now—it is a happy thing for us that we are a hundred years behind them, as Eliza Twemlow had the impudence to say; and really, for the daughter of a clergyman—"

"I don't care that for Eliza Twemlow," the Admiral exclaimed, with a snap of his thumb. "Let her show herself as much as there is demand for. Or rather, what I mean to say is, let Miss Twemlow be as beautiful as nature has made her, my dear; and no doubt that is very considerable. But I like you to be different; and you are. I like you to be simple, and shy, and retiring, and not to care twopence what any one thinks of you, so long as your father is contented."

Dolly looked at her father, as if there were no other man in the world for the moment. Then her conscience made her bright eyes fall, as she whispered:

"To be sure, papa. I only put these things on to please you; and if you don't like them, away they go. Perhaps I should look nicer in my great-aunt's shawl. And my feet would be warmer, oh ever so much! I know where it is, and if you prefer the look of it—"

"No, no!" cried the simple old father, as the girl tripped away in hot haste to seek for it; "I forbid you to make such a guy of yourself. You must not take my little banter, darling, in such a matter-of-fact way, or I must hold my tongue."

"Thank God," he continued to himself, as Miss Dolly ran away, to repair her damages; "the simple little soul thinks of nobody but me! How could I be such a fool as to imagine harm of her? Why, she is quite a child, a bigger child than I am. I shall enjoy my evening all the more for this."

And truly there seemed to be no reason why all the guests at that great festival, save those who had speeches to make, should not enjoy their evening thoroughly. Great preparations had been made, and goodly presents contributed; plenty of serving-men would be there, and John Prater (now growing white-headed and portly) was becoming so skilful a caterer that if anything was suggested to him, he had always thought of it long ago. The only grief was that the hour should be so late—five o'clock, an unchristian time, as they said, for who could have manners after starving so long?

There was some sense in this; but the unreasonable lateness of the hour could not be helped, because the Lord-Lieutenant had to wait upon the King at eight o'clock that morning. That he could do so, and yet be in Springhaven by five, seemed almost impossible; for only ten years ago the journey took two days. But the war seemed to make everything go quicker, and it was no use to wonder at anything. Only if everything else went quicker, why should dinner (the most important of them all) come slower? And as yet there was nobody to answer this; though perhaps there is no one to ask it now.

All things began very beautifully. The young ladies slipped in unobserved, and the elder blessings of mankind came after, escorting themselves with dignity. Then the heroes who had fought, and the gallants who had not had the luck yet, but were eager for it, came pleasantly clanking in, well girt to demolish ox and sheep, like Ajax, in lack of loftier carnage. The rector said grace, and the Marquis amen, and in less than two minutes every elbow was up, and every mouth at business. There was very little talking for the first half hour. In those days emptiness was not allowed to make the process of filling a misery.

While these fine fellows were still in the prime of their feeding, bent over and upon it, two men with empty stomachs, and a long way between them and their victuals, stood afar regarding them. That is to say, just far enough to be quite out of sight from the windows, in the gloom of the December evening; but at the same time near enough, to their own unhappiness, to see and even smell the choice affairs across the road.

"For what, then, hast thou brought me here?" the shorter man sharply asked the tall one, both being in an uncomfortable place in a hedge, and with briars that scratched them. "Is it to see other people eat, when to eat myself is impossible? You have promised to show me a very fine thing, and leagues have I traversed to please you. Fie, then, what is it? To see eat, eat, eat, and drink, drink, drink, and have nothing for myself!"

"My friend," said the tall man, "I have not brought you here with any desire to improve your appetite, which is always abundant, and cannot be gratified for several hours, and with poor stuff then, compared to what you are beholding. Those men are feeding well. You can see how they enjoy it. There is not a morsel in their mouths that has not a very choice flavour of its own distinguished relish. See, there is the venison just waiting to be carved, and a pheasant between every two of them. If only the wind was a little more that way, and the covers taken off the sauce-boats, and the gravy—ah, do I perceive a fine fragrance, or is it a desirous imagination?"

"Bah! you are of the cold-blood, the wicked self-command. For me it is either to rush in, or rush away. No longer can I hold my nose and mouth. And behold they have wine—grand wine—the wine of Sillery, of Medoc, of Barsac, and of Burgundy! By the bottles I can tell them, and by all the Saints —"

"Be not so excited, for you cannot smack the lips. It is too late now to envy them their solids, because they have made such speed with them. But listen, my dear friend"—and here the tall man whispered into the ear of his brisk companion, who danced with delight in the ungenial hedge, till his face was scarred with brambles.

"It is magnificent, it is droll, it is what you call in England one grand spree, though of that you understand not the signification. But, my faith, it is at the same time barbarous, and almost too malignant."

"Too benevolent Charron," said the tall stern man, "that shall rest upon my conscience, not on yours. The object is not to spoil their noisy revel, but to gain instruction of importance. To obtain a clear idea of the measures they adopt—ah, you see, you are as quick as lightning. This urgent message is upon official paper, which I have taken from the desk of that very stupid Stubbard. Take the horse Jerry holds at the corner, and the officer's hat and cape provided are ample disguise for so dark a night. Take the lane behind the hills, and gallop two miles eastward, till you come to the shore again, then turn back towards the village by way of the beach, and you will meet the Coast-guard on duty, a stupid fellow called Vickers. Your horse by that time will be piping and roaring: he can go like the wind, but his own is broken. The moment you see Vickers, begin to swear at your horse. I have practised you in d—ns, for an emergency."

"Ten thousand thunders, I can say d—n now to equal and surpass the purest born of all Britons."

"Not so loud, my friend, until by-and-by. The Coast-guard will come to you, and you pull up with your horse hanging down his head, as if dead-beaten. Using your accomplishment again, you say: 'Here, take this on to Admiral Darling. My nag is quite done, and I must get to Stonnington to call Colonel James. For your life, run, run. You'll get a guinea, if you look sharp.' Before he can think of it, turn your horse, and make back to the lane, as if for Stonnington. But instead of that, gallop back to our ruins; and we'll go up the hill, and see what comes of it."

"It is very good, it is magnificent. But will not the sentinel perceive my voice and accent?"

"Not he; he is a very honest and therefore stupid fellow. Give him no time, answer no questions. Be all in a rush, as you so generally are. I would do it myself, but I am too well known. Say, will you undertake it? It will be a fine joke for you."

About half an hour after this, the Lord-Lieutenant having hammered on the table with an empty bottle, stood up to propose the chief toast of the evening —the gallant crew of the Leda, and the bold sailors of Springhaven. His lordship had scarcely had a bottle and a half, and was now in the prime of his intellect. A very large man, with a long brocaded coat of ruby-coloured cloth, and white satin breeches, a waistcoat of primrose plush emblazoned with the Union-jack (then the popular device) in gorgeous silks with a margin of bright gold, and a neckcloth pointed and plaited in with the rarest lace, worth all the rest put together—what a pity it seemed that such a man should get drunk, or at any rate try so hard to do it. There was not a pimple on his face, his cheeks were rosy and glistening, but not flushed; and his eyes were as bright and clear and deep as a couple of large sapphires.

This nobleman said a few words, without any excitement, or desire to create it, every word to the point, and the best that could be chosen not to go beyond the point. There was no attempt at eloquence, and yet the speech was eloquent, because it suggested so much more than was said. More excitable natures, overcome by half a bottle, resolved to have the other half, in honour of that toast.

Then the Marquis did a very kind and thoughtful thing, for which he deserved a bottle of the Royal Tokay, such as even Napoleon could not obtain. When the cheering was done, and every eye was fixed upon the blushing Scudamore—who felt himself, under that fixture, like an insect under a lens which the sun is turning into a burning-glass—the Chairman perceived his sad plight, and to give him more time and more spirit, rose again.

"Gentlemen," he said, "or I would rather call you brother Englishmen at this moment, I have forgotten one thing. Before our young hero replies to his health, let us give him that spirited song 'Billy Blue,' which is well known to every man here, I'll be bound. Tell the drummer down there to be ready for chorus." Billy Blue, though almost forgotten now (because the enemy would not fight him), the blockader of Brest, the hardy, skilful, and ever watchful Admiral Cornwallis, would be known to us nearly as well as Nelson, if fame were not a lottery.

As the Lord-Lieutenant waved his hand, the company rose with one accord, and followed the lead of his strong clear voice in the popular song, called

"BILLY BLUE"

1

"'Tis a terrible time for Englishmen;
All tyrants do abhor them;
Every one of them hath to fight with ten,
And the Lord alone is for them.
But the Lord hath given the strong right hand,
And the courage to face the thunder;
If a Frenchman treads this English land,
He shall find his grave thereunder.

CHORUS

Britannia is the Ocean-Queen, and she standeth staunch and
  true,
With Nelson for her faulchion keen, and her buckler Billy Blue.

2

"They are mustering on yon Gallic coasts,
You can see them from this high land,
The biggest of all the outlandish hosts
That ever devoured an island.
There are steeds that have scoured the Continent,
Ere ever one might say, 'Whoa, there!'
And ships that would fill the Thames and Trent,
If we would let them go there.

CHORUS

But England is the Ocean-Queen, and it shall be hard to do;
Not a Frenchman shall skulk in between herself and her Billy
  Blue.

3

"From the smiling bays of Devonshire
To the frowning cliffs of Filey,
Leaps forth every son of an English sire,
To fight for his native isley.
He hath drawn the sword of his father now
From the rusty sheath it rattled in;
And Dobbin, who dragged the peaceful plough,
Is neighing for the battle-din.

CHORUS

For Albion still is Ocean-Queen, and though her sons be few,
They challenge the world with a dauntless mien, and the flag
  of Billy Blue.

4

"Then pledge me your English palm, my lad;
Keep the knuckles for Sir Frenchman;
No slave can you be till you change your dad,
And no son of yours a henchman.
The fight is to come; and we will not brag,
Nor expect whatever we sigh for,
But stand as the rock that bears the flag
Our duty is to die for.

CHORUS

For Englishmen confront serene whatever them betideth;
And England shall be Ocean's Queen as long as the world
  abideth."

What with the drum and the fifes of one of the regiments now at Stonnington, and the mighty bass of some sea-captains vehement in chorus, these rough and rolling lines were enough to frighten a thousand Frenchmen, while proving the vigour of British nerve, and fortitude both of heart and ear. When people have done a thing well, they know it, and applaud one another to include themselves; and even the ladies, who were meant to be unseen, forgot that and waved their handkerchiefs. Then up and spoke Blyth Scudamore, in the spirit of the moment; and all that he said was good and true, well-balanced and well-condensed, like himself. His quiet melodious voice went further than the Lord-Lieutenant's, because it was new to the air of noise, and that fickle element loves novelty. All was silence while he spoke, and when he ceased—great uproar.

"That lad will do," said the Marquis to his supporter on the right hand; "I was just like him at that age myself. Let me draw this cork—it is the bottle of the evening. None but my own fellows understand a cork, and they seem to have got away somewhere. What the doose are they about—why, halloa, Darling! What's the meaning of all this, at such a time?"

"Well, my lord, you must judge for yourself," said the Admiral, who had made his way quietly from the bottom of the table. "We know that false alarms are plentiful. But this looks like business, from the paper it is written on; and I know that old Dudgeon is as solid as myself. Vickers the Coast-guard brought it in, from an officer whose horse was blown, who had orders to get somehow to Stonnington."

"Is Vickers a knave, or a fool who is likely to be made the victim of a very low joke? There are hundreds of jealous scoundrels eager to spoil every patriotic gathering. Ah, this looks rather serious, though, if you can vouch for the paper."

"I can vouch for the paper, my lord, and for Vickers; but not for Dudgeon's signature. Of that I have no knowledge—though it looks right enough, so far as I know. Shall I read it aloud, and let officers who are not under my command judge for themselves, as I shall judge for those I have the honour to command?"

The Lord-Lieutenant, with his cork just squeaking in the neck of the bottle, nodded; and the Admiral, with officers crowding round, read aloud as follows, part being in type, and part in manuscript:

"Commander of Coast-defence at Hythe, to Vice-Admiral Darling, Springhaven.

"French fleet standing in, must have slipped Cornwallis. Do all you can.

Not a moment to lose.

(Signed) "BELLAMY DUDGEON."

"Well, it may be true, or it may be a lie," said the Marquis, pouring carefully; "my opinion is the latter; but I have nothing to do with it officially, according to the new arrangements. Every gentleman must judge for himself. And I mean to abide by my own judgment, which strongly recommends me to finish this bottle."

"Probably you are right enough; and in your place perhaps I should do the same," the Admiral answered, quietly; "but be the alarm either true or false, I am bound to act otherwise. All Naval Officers present will be good enough to follow me, and prepare to rejoin if ordered. We shall very soon know from the signal-point, unless fog has set in suddenly, whether we are bound to beat a general alarm."

All the sons of the sea arose quietly, and were despatched with brief orders to the right and left, to communicate with their signal stations, while Stubbard hurried back to his battery.

"What cold blood they do display!" whispered the Frenchman, who had returned with the author of the plot to watch the issue from a point of vantage. "My faith, they march slowly for their native land! Not less than six bottles of great French wine did I anticipate to steal through the window, while they fell out precipitous. But there sits a man big enough to leave me nothing—not even a remainder of my own body. Soul of St. Denis, can it be that they question the word of a gentleman?"

"Not they!" replied Carne, who was vexed, however; "they are taking things easily, according to the custom of the nation. But two good things we have done, friend Charron; we have learned their proceedings, and we have spoiled their feasting."

"But not at all; they are all coming back to enjoy it all the more!" cried the Frenchman. "Oh that I were an Englishman, to get such a dinner, and to be so loyal to it!"

CHAPTER XXXVI

FAIR CRITICISM

Few things can be worse for a very young woman than to want to be led by somebody, and yet find nobody fit to do it. Or at any rate, through superior quickness and the knowledge of it, to regard old friends and relatives of experience as very slow coaches, and prigs or prudes, who cannot enter into quick young feelings, but deal in old saws which grate upon them.

Not to moralise about it—for if young ladies hate anything, it is such moralising—Miss Dolly Darling was now in that uncomfortable frame of mind when advice is most needed, yet most certain to be spurned. She looked upon her loving and sensible sister as one who was fated to be an old maid, and was meant perhaps by nature for that condition, which appeared to herself the most abject in the world. And even without that conclusion about Faith she would have been loth to seek counsel from her, having always resented most unduly what she called her "superior air of wisdom." Dolly knew that she was quicker of wit than her sister—as shallow waters run more rapidly— and she fancied that she possessed a world of lively feelings into which the slower intellect could not enter. For instance, their elder brother Frank had just published a volume of poems, very noble in their way, and glowing with ardour for freedom, democracy, and the like, as well as exhibiting fine perception of sound, and great boldness in matters beyond sounding, yet largely ungifted with knowledge of nature, whether human or superior.

"Better stick to his law-books," the Admiral had said, after singing out some of the rhyme of it to the tune of "Billy Benbow"; "never sit on the wool-sack by spewing oakum this way."

Faith had tried, as a matter of duty, to peruse this book to its cover; but she found it beyond even her good-will, and mild sympathy with everything, to do so. There was not the touch of nature in it which makes humble people feel, and tickles even the very highest with desire to enter into it. So Faith declared that it must be very clever, and no doubt very beautiful, but she herself was so stupid that she could not make out very clearly what it was all about.

"Well, I understand every word of it," Miss Dolly cried, with a literary look. "I don't see how you can help doing that, when you know all about Frank, who wrote it. Whenever it is not quite clear, it is because he wants us to think that he knows too much, or else because he is not quite certain what he wants to mean himself. And as for his talk about freedom, and all that, I don't see why you should object to it. It is quite the fashion with all clever people now, and it stops them from doing any mischief. And nobody pays much attention to them, after the cruel things done in France when I was seven or eight years old. If I see Frank, I shall tell him that I like it."

"And I shall tell him that I don't," said Faith. "It cannot do anybody any good. And what they call 'freedom' seems to mean making free with other people's property."

These poems were issued in one volume, and under one title—The Harmodiad—although there must have been some half-hundred of them, and not more than nine odes to freedom in the lot. Some were almost tolerable, and others lofty rubbish, and the critics (not knowing the author) spoke their bright opinions freely. The poet, though shy as a mouse in his preface, expected a mountain of inquiry as to the identity of this new bard, and modestly signed himself "Asteroid," which made his own father stare and swear. Growing sore prematurely from much keelhauling—for the reviewers of the period were patriotic, and the English public anti-Gallic—Frank quitted his chambers at Lincoln's Inn, and came home to be comforted for Christmas. This was the wisest thing that he could do, though he felt that it was not Harmodian. In spite of all crotchets, he was not a bad fellow, and not likely to make a good lawyer.

As the fates would have it (being naturally hostile to poets who defy them), by the same coach to Stonnington came Master Johnny, in high feather for his Christmas holidays. Now these two brothers were as different of nature as their sisters were, or more so; and unlike the gentler pair, each of these cherished lofty disdain for the other. Frank looked down upon the school-boy as an unlicked cub without two ideas; the bodily defect he endeavoured to cure by frequent outward applications, but the mental shortcoming was beneath his efforts. Johnny meanwhile, who was as hard as nails, no sooner recovered from a thumping than he renewed and redoubled his loud contempt for a great lout over six feet high, who had never drawn a sword or pulled a trigger. And now for the winter this book would be a perpetual snowball for him to pelt his big brother with, and yet (like a critic) be scarcely fair object for a hiding. In season out of season, upstairs down-stairs, even in the breakfast and the dinner chambers, this young imp poked clumsy splinters— worse than thorns, because so dull—into the tender poetic side; and people, who laugh at the less wit the better, laughed very kindly, to please the boy, without asking whether they vexed the man. And the worst of it was that the author too must laugh.

All this might be looked down at by a soul well hoisted upon the guy-ropes of contempt; and now and then a very solid drubbing given handsomely (upon other grounds) to the chief tormentor solaced the mind of unacknowledged merit. But as the most vindictive measure to the man who has written an abusive letter is to vouchsafe him no reply, so to the poet who rebukes the age the bitterest answer it can give is none. Frank Darling could retaliate upon his brother Johnny, and did so whenever he could lay hold of him alone; but the stedfast silence of his sister Faith (to whom one of his loftiest odes was addressed), and of his lively father, irked him far more than a thousand low parodies. Dolly alone was some comfort to him, some little vindication of true insight; and he was surprised to find how quickly her intelligence (which until now he had despised) had strengthened, deepened, and enlarged itself. Still he wanted some one older, bigger, more capable of shutting up the mouth, and nodding (instead of showing such a lot of red tongue and white teeth), before he could be half as snug as a true poet should be, upon the hobs of his own fire. And happily he found his Anti-Zoilus ere long.

One day he was walking in a melancholy mood along the beach towards Pebbleridge, doubting deeply in his honest mind whether he ever should do any good, in versification, or anything else. He said to himself that he had been too sanguine, eager, self-confident, ardent, impetuous, and, if the nasty word must be faced, even too self-conceited. Only yesterday he had tried, by delicate setting of little word-traps, to lead Mr. Twemlow towards the subject, and obtain that kind-hearted man's comforting opinion. But no; the gentle Rector would not be brought to book, or at any rate not to that book; and the author had sense enough to know without a wink that his volume had won volumes of dislike.

Parnassus could never have lived till now without two heads—one to carry on with, while the other is being thumped to pieces. While the critics demolish one peak, the poet withdraws to the other, and assures himself that the general public, the larger voice of the nation, will salute him there. But alas, Frank Darling had just discovered that even that eminence was not his, except as a desert out of human sight. For he had in his pocket a letter from his publishers, received that dreary morning, announcing a great many copies gone gratis, six sold to the trade at a frightful discount, and six to the enterprising public. All these facts combined to make him feel uncommonly sad and sore to-day.

A man of experience could have told him that this disappointment was for his good; but he failed to see it in that light, and did not bless the blessing. Slowly and heavily he went on, without much heed of anything, swinging his clouded cane now and then, as some slashing reviews occurred to him, yet becoming more peaceful and impartial of mind under the long monotonous cadence and quiet repetitions of the soothing sea. For now he was beyond the Haven head—the bulwark that makes the bay a pond in all common westerly weather—and waves that were worthy of the name flowed towards him, with a gentle breeze stepping over them.

The brisk air was like a fresh beverage to him, and the fall of the waves sweet music. He took off his hat, and stopped, and listened, and his eyes grew brighter. Although the waves had nothing very distinct to say in dying, yet no two (if you hearkened well), or at any rate no two in succession, died with exactly the same expression, or vanished with precisely the same farewell. Continual shifts went on among them, and momentary changes; each in proper sequence marching, and allowed its proper time, yet at any angle traversed, even in its crowning curl, not only by the wind its father, but by the penitent return and white contrition of its shattered elder brother. And if this were not enough to make a samely man take interest in perpetually flowing changes, the sun and clouds, at every look and breath, varied variety.

Frank Darling thought how small his griefs were, and how vain his vanity. Of all the bubbly clots of froth, or frayed and shattered dabs of drift, flying beside him or falling at his feet, every one was as good as his ideas, and as valuable as his labours. And of all the unreckoned waves advancing, lifting their fugitive crests, and roaring, there certainly was not one that fell with weight so futile as his own. Who cared even to hear his sound? What ear was soothed by his long rhythm, or what mind solaced by the magnitude of his rolling?

Suddenly he found that some mind was so. For when he had been standing a long while thus, chewing the salt cud of marine reflections, he seemed to hear something more intelligible than the sea. With more surprise than interest he walked towards the sound, and stood behind the corner of a jutting rock to listen. In another second his interest overpowered his surprise, for he knew every word of the lines brought to his ears, for the very simple reason that they were his own. Round the corner of that rock, so absorbed in admiration that he could hear no footstep, a very fine young man of the highest order was reading aloud in a powerful voice, and with extremely ardent gesticulation, a fine passage from that greatly undervalued poem, the Harmodiad, of and concerning the beauties of Freedom—

```
"No crown upon her comely head she bore,
    No wreath her affluent tresses to restrain;
    A smile the only ornament she wore,
    Her only gem a tear for others' pain.
    Herself did not her own mishaps deplore,
    Because she lives immortal as the dew,
    Which falling from the stars soon mounts again;
    And in this wise all space she travels through,
    Beneficent as heaven, and to the earth more true.
```

> "Her blessings all may win who seek the prize,
> If only they be faithful, meek, and strong,
> And crave not that which others' right denies,
> But march against the citadel of wrong.
> A glorious army this, that finds allies
> Wherever God hath built the heart of man
> With attributes that to Himself belong;
> By Him ordained to crown what He began,
> And shatter despotism, which is the foul fiend's ban."

Frank thought that he had never heard nobler reading, sonorous, clear, well timed, well poised, and of harmonious cadence. The curved rock gave a melodious ring, and the husky waves a fine contrast to it, while the reader was so engrossed with grandeur—the grandeur of Frank's own mind!—that his hat could evidently not contain his head, but was flung at the mercy of his feet. What a fine, expressive, and commanding face!

If Frank Darling had been a Frenchman—which he sometimes longed to be, for the sake of that fair Liberty—the scene, instead of being awkward, would have been elegant, rapturous, ennobling. But being of the clumsy English race, he was quite at a loss what to do with himself. On paper he could be effusive, ardent, eloquent, sentimental; but not a bit of that to meet the world in his own waistcoat. He gave a swing to his stick, and walked across the opening as if he were looking at sea-gulls. And on he would have walked without further notice, except a big gulp in his throat, if it had not been for a trifling accident.

Somehow or other the recitative gentleman's hat turned over to the wind, and that active body (which never neglects any sportive opportunity) got into the crown, with the speed of an upstart, and made off with it along the stones. A costly hat it was, and comely with rich braid and satin loops, becoming also to a well-shaped head, unlike the chimney-pot of the present day, which any man must thank God for losing. However, the owner was so wrapped up in poetry that his breeches might have gone without his being any wiser.

"Sir," said Frank Darling, after chasing the hat (which could not trundle as our pots do, combining every possible absurdity), "excuse me for interrupting you, but this appears to be your hat, and it was on its way to a pool of salt-water."

"Hat!—my hat?" replied the other gentleman. "Oh, to be sure! I had quite forgotten. Sir, I am very much obliged to you. My hat might have gone to the devil, I believe, I was so delightfully occupied. Such a thing never happened to me before, for I am very hard indeed to please; but I was reading, sir; I was reading. Accept my thanks, sir; and I suppose I must leave off."

"I thought that I heard a voice," said Frank, growing bold with fear that he should know no more, for the other was closing his book with great care, and committing it to a pouch buckled over his shoulder; "and I fear that I broke in upon a pleasant moment. Perhaps I should have pleased you better if I had left this hat to drown."

"I seem ungrateful," the stranger answered, with a sweet but melancholy smile, as he donned his hat and then lifted it gracefully to salute its rescuer; "but it is only because I have been carried far away from all thoughts of self, by the power of a much larger mind. Such a thing may have occurred to you, sir, though it happens very seldom in one life. If so, you will know how to forgive me."

"I scarcely dare ask—or rather I would say"—stammered the anxious poet —"that I cannot expect you to tell me the name of the fortunate writer who has moved you so."

"Would to Heaven that I could!" exclaimed the other. "But this great poet has withheld his name—all great poets are always modest—but it cannot long remain unknown. Such grandeur of conception and force of language, combined with such gifts of melody, must produce universal demand to know the name of this benefactor. I cannot express myself as I would desire, because I have been brought up in France, where literature is so different, and people judge a work more liberally, without recourse to politics. This is a new work, only out last week; and a friend of mine, a very fine judge of literature, was so enchanted with it that he bought a score of copies at once, and as my good stars prevailed, he sent me one. You are welcome to see it, sir. It is unknown in these parts; but will soon be known all over Europe, unless these cruel wars retard it."

With a face of deep gravity, Caryl Carne put into Frank Darling's hand a copy of his own book, quite young, but already scored with many loving marks of admiration and keen sympathy. Frank took it, and reddened with warm delight.

"You may not understand it at first," said the other; "though I beg your pardon for saying that. What I mean is, that I can well suppose that an Englishman, though a good judge in general, would probably have his judgment darkened by insular prejudices, and the petty feeling which calls itself patriotism, and condemns whatever is nobler and larger than itself. My friend tells me that the critics have begun to vent their little spite already. The author would treat them with calm disdain!"

"Horribly nasty fellows!" cried Frank. "They ought to be kicked; but they are below contempt. But if I could only catch them here—"

"I am delighted to find," replied Carne, looking at him with kind surprise, "that you agree with me about that, sir. Read a few lines, and your indignation against that low lot will grow hotter."

"It cannot grow hotter," cried the author; "I know every word that the villains have said. Why, in that first line that I heard you reading, the wretches actually asked me whether I expected my beautiful goddess to wear her crown upon her comely tail!"

"I am quite at a loss to understand you, sir. Why, you speak as if this great work were your own!"

"So it is, every word of it," cried Frank, hurried out of all reserve by excitement. "At least, I don't mean that it is a great work—though others, besides your good self, have said—Are you sure that your friend bought twenty copies? My publishers will have to clear up that. Why, they say, under date of yesterday, that they have only sold six copies altogether. And it was out on Guy Fawkes' Day, two months ago!"

Caryl Carne's face was full of wonder. And the greatest wonder of all was its gravity. He drew back a little, in this vast surprise, and shaded his forehead with one hand, that he might think.

"I can hardly help laughing at myself," he said, "for being so stupid and so slow of mind. But a coincidence like this is enough to excuse anything. If I could be sure that you are not jesting with me, seeing how my whole mind is taken up with this book—"

"Sir, I can feel for your surprise," answered Frank, handing back the book, for which the other had made a sign, "because my own is even greater; for I never have been read aloud before—by anybody else I mean, of course; and the sound is very strange, and highly gratifying—at least, when done as you do it. But to prove my claim to the authorship of the little work which you so kindly esteem, I will show you the letter I spoke of."

The single-minded poet produced from near his heart a very large letter with much sealing-wax endorsed, and the fervent admirer of his genius read:

"DEAR SIR,—In answer to your favour to hand, we beg to state that your poetical work the Harmodiad, published by our firm, begins to move. Following the instructions in your last, we have already disposed of more than fifty copies. Forty-two of these have been distributed to those who will forward the interests of the book, by commending it to the Public; six have been sold to the trade at a discount of 75 per cent.; and six have been taken by private purchasers, at the full price of ten shillings. We have reason to anticipate a more rapid sale hereafter. But the political views expressed in the poems—as we frankly stated to you at first—are not likely to be popular just now, when the Country is in peril, and the Book trade incommoded, by the immediate prospect of a French invasion. We are, dear sir, your obedient servants, TICKLEBOIS, LATHERUP, BLINKERS, & Co.—To Mr. FRANK DARLING, Springhaven Hall."

"You cannot call that much encouragement," said Frank; "and it is a most trusty and honourable house. I cannot do what a friend of mine has done, who went to inferior publishers—denounce them as rogues, and call myself a martyr. If the book had been good, it would have sold; especially as all the poets now are writing vague national songs, full of slaughter and brag, like that 'Billy Blue' thing all our fishermen are humming."

"You have nothing to do but to bide your time. In the long-run, fine work is sure to make its way. Meanwhile I must apologise for praising you to your face, in utter ignorance, of course. But it must have made you feel uncomfortable."

"Not at all; far otherwise," said the truthful Frank. "It has been the very greatest comfort to me. And strange to say, it came just when I wanted it most sadly. I shall never forget your most kind approval."

"In that case I may take the liberty of introducing myself, I trust. You have told me who you are, in the most delightful way. I have no such claim upon your attention, or upon that of the world at large. I am only the last of an ill-fated race, famous for nothing except ruining themselves. I am Caryl Carne, of yonder ruin, which you, must have known from childhood."

Frank Darling lifted his hat in reply to the other's more graceful salutation, and then shook hands with him heartily. "I ought to have known who you are," he said; "for I have heard of you often at Springhaven. But you have not been there since I came down, and we thought that you had left the neighbourhood. Our little village is like the ear of the tyrant, except that it carries more false than true sound. I hope you are come to remain among us, and I hope that we shall see you at my father's house. Years ago I have heard that there used to be no especial good-will between your family and mine— petty disputes about boundaries, no doubt. How narrow and ridiculous such things are! We live in a better age than that, at any rate, although we are small enough still in many ways."

"You are not; and you will enlarge many others," Carne answered, as if the matter were beyond debate. "As for boundaries now, I have none, because the estates are gone, and I am all the richer. That is the surest way to liberate the mind."

"Will you oblige me," said Frank, to change the subject, for his mind did not seek to be liberated so, and yet wished its new admirer to remain in admiration, "by looking along the shore towards Springhaven as far as you can see, and telling me whether any one is coming? My sisters were to follow me, if the weather kept fine, as soon as they had paid a little visit at the rectory. And my sight is not good for long distances."

"I think I can see two ladies coming, or at any rate two figures moving, about a mile or more away, where the sands are shining in a gleam of sunlight. Yes, they are ladies. I know by their walk. Good-bye. I have a way up the cliff from here. You must not be surprised if you do not see me again. I may have to be off for France. I have business there, of which I should like to talk to you. You are so far above mean prejudice. If I go, I shall carry this precious volume with me. Farewell, my friend, if I may call you so."

"Do wait a minute," cried the much admiring Frank; "or walk a few yards with me towards Springhaven. It would give me such pleasure to introduce you to my sisters. And I am sure they will be so glad to know you, when I tell them what I think. I very seldom get such a chance as this."

"There is no resisting that!" replied the graceful Carne; "I have not the honour of knowing a lady in England, except my aunt Mrs. Twemlow, and my cousin Eliza—both very good, but to the last degree insular."

"It is very hard to help being that, when people have never been out of an island. But I fear that I am taking you out of your way."

In a few minutes these two young men drew near to the two young women, whose manners were hard put to hide surprise. When their brother introduced Mr. Carne to them, Faith bowed rather stiffly, for she had formed without reason a dark and obstinate dislike to him. But the impetuous Dolly ran up and offered him both her hands, and said, "Why, Mr. Carne saved both our lives only a few days ago."

CHAPTER XXXVII

NEITHER AT HOME

Though Admiral Darling had not deigned to speak to his younger daughter about that vile anonymous charge, he was not always quite comfortable in his inner mind concerning it. More than once he thought of asking Faith's opinion, for he knew her good sense and discretion; but even this was repugnant to him, and might give her the idea that he cherished low suspicions. And then he was called from home again, being occupied among other things with a vain enquiry about the recent false alarm. For Carne and Charron had managed too well, and judged too correctly the character of Vickers, to afford any chance of discovery. So that, when the Admiral came home again, his calm and—in its fair state—gentle nature was ruffled by the prosperity of the wicked.

"Oh, he is a fine judge of poetry, is he?" he said, more sarcastically than his wont; "that means, I suppose, that he admires yours, Frank. Remember what Nelson said about you. The longer I live, the more I find his views confirmed."

"Papa, you are too bad! You are come home cross!" cried Dolly, who always took Frank's part now. "What does my godfather know of poetry, indeed? If he ever had any ear for it, the guns would have ruined it long ago."

"No mostacchio in my house!" said the master, without heeding her. "I believe that is the correct way to pronounce the filthy thing—a foreign abomination altogether. Who could keep his lips clean, with that dirt over them? A more tolerant man than myself never lived—a great deal too tolerant, as everybody knows. But I'll never tolerate a son of mine in disgusting French hairiness of that sort."

"Papa, you are come home as cross as a bear!" cried Dolly, presuming on her favour. "Lord Dashville was here the other day with a very nice one, and I hear that all Cavalry Officers mean to have one, when they can. And Mr. Carne, Frank's friend, encourages it."

"The less you have to say about that young man, the better. And the less he has to say to any child of mine, the better, both for him and her, I say. I know that the age is turned upside down. But I'll not have that sort of thing at my table."

When a kind and indulgent father breaks forth thus, the result is consternation, followed by anxiety about his health. Faith glanced at Dolly, who was looking quite bewildered, and the two girls withdrew without a word. Johnny was already gone to visit Captain Stubbard, with whose eldest daughter Maggie and the cannons of the battery he was by this time desperately in love; and poor Frank was left to have it out with the angry father.

"I very seldom speak harshly, my boy," said the Admiral, drawing near his son gradually, for his wrath (like good vegetables) was very short of staple; "and when I do so you may feel quite certain that there is sound reason at the bottom of it"—here he looked as if his depth was unfathomable. "It is not only that I am not myself, because of the many hours spent upon hard leather, and vile chalks of flint that go by me half asleep, when I ought to be snoring in the feathers; neither has it anything to do with my consuming the hide of some quadruped for dinner, instead of meat. And the bread is made of rye, if of any grain at all; I rather think of spent tan, kneaded up with tallow ends, such as I have seen cast by in bushels, when the times were good. And every loaf of that costs two shillings—one for me, and one for Government. They all seem to acknowledge that I can put up with that; and I make a strict point of mild language, which enables them to do it again with me. And all up and down the roads, everybody likes me. But if I was shot to-morrow, would they care twopence?"

"I am sure they would, sir; and a good deal more than that," answered Frank, who perceived that his father was out of his usual lines of thinking, perhaps because he had just had a good dinner—so ill do we digest our mercies. "I am sure that there is nobody in Sussex, Kent, or Hampshire who does not admire and respect and trust you."

"I dare say, and rejoice to see me do the work they ought to do. They have long nights in bed, every one of them, and they get their meals when they want them. I am not at all astonished at what Nelson said. He is younger than I am by a good many years, but he seems to have picked up more than I have, in the way of common sentiments, and such like. 'You may do everybody's work, if you are fool enough,' he said to me the last time I saw him; 'and ease them of their souls as well, if you are rogue enough, as they do in the Popish countries. I am nearly sick of doing it,' he said, and he looked it. 'If you once begin with it, you must go on.' I find it more true every day of my life. Don't interrupt me; don't go on with comfortable stuff about doing good, and one's duty towards one's Country—though I fear that you think very little of that. If I thought I had done good enough to make up for my back-aches, and three fine stumps lost through chewing patriotic sentiments, why, of course I should be thankful, and make the best of my reward. But charity begins at home, my boy, and one's shirt should be considered before one's cloak. A man's family is the nearest piece of his country, and the dearest one."

"I am sure, sir, I hope," replied Frank, who had never heard his father talk like this before, "that nothing is going on amiss with us here. When you are away, I keep a sharp lookout. And if I saw anything going wrong, I should let you know of it immediately."

"No doubt you would; but you are much too soft. You are quite as easygoing as I used to be at your age"—here the Admiral looked as if he felt himself to be uncommonly hard-going now—"and that sort of thing will not do in these days. For my own discomforts I care nothing. I could live on lobscouse, or soap and bully, for a year, and thank God for getting more than I deserved. But my children, Frank, are very different. From me you would never hear a grumble, or a syllable of anything but perfect satisfaction, so long as I felt that I was doing good work, and having it appreciated. And all my old comrades have just the same feeling. But you, who come after us, are not like that. You must have everything made to fit you, instead of making yourselves fit them. The result will be, I have very little doubt, the downfall of England in the scale of nations. I was talking to my old friend St. Vincent last week, and he most heartily agreed with me. However, I don't mean to blame you, Frank. You cannot help your unfortunate nature for stringing ends of words together that happen to sound alike. Johnny will make a fine Officer, not in the Navy, but of Artillery—Stubbard says that he has the rarest eyes he ever came across in one so young, and he wishes he could put them into his Bob's head. He shall not go back to Harrow; he can spell his own name, which seems to be all they teach them there, instead of fine scholarship, such as I obtained at Winton. But to spell his own name is quite enough for a soldier. In the Navy we always were better educated. Johnny shall go to Chatham, when his togs are ready. I settled all about it in London, last week. Nothing hurts him. He is water-proof and thunder-proof. Toss him up anyhow, he falls upon his feet. But that sort of nature very seldom goes up high. But you, Frank, you might have done some good, without that nasty twist of yours for writing and for rhyming, which is a sure indication of spinal complaint. Don't interrupt me; I speak from long experience. Things might be worse, and I ought to be thankful. None of my children will ever disgrace me. At the same time, things would go on better if I were able to be more at home. That Caryl Carne, for instance, what does he come here for?"

"Well, sir, he has only been here twice. And it took a long time to persuade him at all. He said that as you had not called upon him, he felt that he might be intruding here. And Faith, who is sometimes very spiteful, bowed, as much as to say that he had better wait. But Dolly, who is very kind-hearted, assured him that she had heard you say at least a dozen times: 'Be sure that I call upon Mr. Carne to-day. What will he think of my neglect? But I hope that he will set it down to the right cause—the perpetual demands upon my time.' And when she told him that, he said that he would call the next day, and so he did."

"Ah!" cried the old man, not well pleased; "it was Dolly who took that little business off my shoulders! She might have been content with her elder sister's judgment, in a family question of that sort. But I dare say she thought it right to make my excuses. Very well, I'll do that for myself. To-morrow I shall call upon that young man, unless I get another despatch to-night. But I hear he wants nobody at his ruins. I suppose he has not asked even you to go there?"

"No, sir; I think he took his little place here, because it would be so painful for him to receive any friends at that tumble-down castle. He has not yet been able to do any repairs."

"I respect him for that," said the Admiral, with his generous sympathies aroused; "they have been a grand old family, though I can't say much for those I knew—except, of course, Mrs. Twemlow. But he may be a very fine young fellow, though a great deal too Frenchified, from all I hear. And why my friend Twemlow cold-shoulders him so, is something of a mystery to me. Twemlow is generally a judicious man in things that have nothing to do with the Church. When it comes to that, he is very stiff-backed, as I have often had to tell him. Perhaps this young man is a Papist. His mother was, and she brought him up."

"I am sure I don't know, sir," answered Frank. "I should think none the worse of him if he were, unless he allowed it to interfere with his proper respect for liberty."

"Liberty be hanged!" cried the Admiral; "and that's the proper end for most of those who prate about it, when they ought to be fighting for their Country. I shall sound him about that stuff to-morrow. If he is one of that lot, he won't come here with my good-will, I can assure him. What time is he generally to be found down there? He is right over Stubbard's head, I believe, and yet friend Adam knows nothing about him. Nor even Mrs. Adam! I should have thought that worthy pair would have drawn any badger in the kingdom. I suppose the youth will see me, if I call. I don't want to go round that way for nothing. I did want to have a quiet day at home, and saunter in the garden, as the weather is so mild, and consult poor Swipes about Spring crops, and then have a pipe or two, and take my gun to Brown Bushes for a woodcock, or a hare, and come home with a fine appetite to a good dinner. But I never must hope for a bit of pleasure now."

"You may depend upon it, sir," said Frank, "that Caryl Carne will be greatly pleased to see you. And I think you will agree with me that a more straightforward and simple-minded man is not to be found in this country. He combines what we are pleased to call our national dignity and self-respect with the elegant manners, and fraternal warmth, and bonhomie—as they themselves express it—of our friends across the water."

"You be off! I don't want to be cross any more. Two hundred thousand friends there at this moment eager to burn down our homes and cut our throats! Tired as I am, I ought to take a stick to you, as friend Tugwell did to his son for much less. I have the greatest mind not to go near that young man. I wish I had Twemlow here to talk it over. Pay your fine for a French word, and be off!"

Frank Darling gravely laid down five shillings on his dessert plate, and walked off. The fine for a French word in that house, and in hundreds of other English houses at this patriotic period, was a crown for a gentleman, and a shilling for a lady, the latter not being liable except when gentlemen were present. The poet knew well that another word on his part would irritate his father to such a degree that no visit would be paid to-morrow to the admirer of the Harmodiad, whose admiration he was longing to reward with a series of good dinners. And so he did his utmost to ensure his father's visit.

But when the Admiral, going warily—because he was so stiff from saddle-work—made his way down to the house of Widow Shanks, and winking at the Royal Arms in the lower front window, where Stubbard kept Office and convenience, knocked with the knocker at the private door, there seemed to be a great deal of thought required before anybody came to answer.

"Susie," said the visitor, who had an especial knack of remembering Christian names, which endeared him to the bearers, "I am come to see Mr. Carne, and I hope he is at home."

"No, that 'a bain't, sir," the little girl made answer, after looking at the Admiral as if he was an elephant, and wiping her nose with unwonted diligence; "he be gone away, sir; and please, sir, mother said so."

"Well, here's a penny for you, my dear, because you are the best little needle-woman in the school, they tell me. Run and tell your mother to come and see me.—Oh, Mrs. Shanks, I am very glad to see you, and so blooming in spite of all your hard work. Ah, it is no easy thing in these hard times to maintain a large family and keep the pot boiling. And everything clean as a quarter-deck! My certy, you are a woman in a thousand!"

"No, sir, no. It is all the Lord's doing. And you to the back of Him, as I alway say. Not a penny can they make out as I owes justly, bad as I be at the

257

figures, Squire. Do 'e come in, and sit down, there's a dear. Ah, I mind the time when you was like a dart, Squire!"

"Well, and now I am like a cannon-ball," said the Admiral, who understood and liked this unflattering talk; "only I don't travel quite so fast as that. I scarcely get time to see any old friends. But I came to look out for a young friend now, the gentleman you make so comfortable upstairs. Don't I wish I was a young man without incumbrance, to come and lodge with such a wonderful landlady!"

"Ah, if there was more of your sort, sir, there'd be a deal less trouble in the world, there would. Not that my young gentleman is troublesome, mind you, only so full of them outlandish furrin ways—abideth all day long without ating ort, so different from a honest Englishman. First I used to think as he couldn't afford it, and long to send him up a bit of my own dinner, but dursn't for the life of me—too grand for that, by ever so—till one day little Susie there comes a-running down the stairs, and she sings out, with her face as red as ever a boiled lobster: 'Looky see, mother! Oh, do 'e come and looky see! Pollyon hath got a heap of guineas on his table; wouldn't go into the big yellow pudding-basin!' And sure enough he had, your Honour, in piles, as if he was telling of them. He had slipped out suddenly, and thought the passage door was bolted. What a comfort it was to me, I can't configurate. Because I could eat my dinner comfortable now, for such a big heap of money never I did see."

"I am very glad—heartily glad," exclaimed the smiling Admiral. "I hope he may get cash enough to buy back all the great Carne property, and kick out those rascally Jews and lawyers. But what makes Susie call him that?"

"Well, sir, the young ones must have a nickname for anything beyond them; and because he never takes any notice of them—so different from your handsome Master Frank—and some simility of his black horse, or his proud walk, to the pictur', 'Pollyon' is the name they give him, out of Pilgrim's Progress. Though not a bit like him, for such a gentleman to pay his rent and keep his place untroublesome I never had before. And a fortnight he paid me last night, afore going, and took away the keys of all three doors."

"He is gone, then, is he? To London, I dare say. It would be useless to look for him at the castle. My son will be disappointed more than I am. To tell you the truth, Mrs. Shanks, in these days the great thing is to stick to the people that we know. The world is so full, not of rogues, but of people who are always wanting something out of one, that to talk with a thoroughly kind, honest person, like yourself, is a real luxury. When the gentleman comes back, let him know that I have called."

"And my Jenny, sir?" cried the anxious mother, running after him into the passage; "not a word have you said about my Jenny. I hope she show no sign of flightiness?"

"Jenny is as steady as the church," replied the Admiral. "We are going to put her on a pound a year from next quarter-day, by Mrs. Cloam's advice. She'll have a good stocking by the time she gets married."

"There never was such a pleasant gentleman, nor such a kind-hearted one, I do believe," said Widow Shanks, as she came in with bright eyes. "What are they Carnes to the Darlings, after all? As different as night and day."

But the Admiral's next visit was not quite so pleasant; for when he got back into the village road, expecting a nice walk to his luncheon and his pipe, a man running furiously almost knocked him down, and had no time to beg his pardon. The runner's hat was off his head, and his hair blowing out, but luckily for itself his tongue was not between his teeth.

"Has the devil got hold of you at last, Jem Prater?" the Admiral asked, not profanely; for he had seen a good deal of mankind, and believed in diabolical possession.

"For Parson! for Parson!" cried Jem, starting off again as hard as he could go. "Butter Cheeseman hath hanged his self in his own scales. And nobody is any good but Parson."

Admiral Darling was much disturbed. "What will the world come to? I never knew such times," he exclaimed to himself, with some solemnity; and then set off, as fast as his overridden state permitted, for the house of Mr. Cheeseman. Passing through the shop, which had nobody in it, he was led by the sound of voices into a little room beyond it—the room in which Mr. Cheeseman had first received Caryl Carne. Here he beheld an extraordinary scene, of which he often had to dream thereafter.

From a beam in the roof (which had nothing to do with his scales, as Jem Prater had imagined), by a long but not well-plaited cord, was dangling the respected Church-warden Cheeseman. Happily for him, he had relied on his own goods; and the rope being therefore of very bad hemp, had failed in this sad and too practical proof. The weight of its vendor had added to its length some fifteen inches—as he loved to pull out things—and his toes touched the floor, which relieved him now and then.

"Why don't you cut him down, you old fools?" cried the Admiral to three gaffers, who stood moralising, while Mrs. Cheeseman sat upon a barrel, sobbing heavily, with both hands spread to conceal the sad sight.

"We was afraid of hurting of him," said the quickest-witted of the gaffers;

"Us wanted to know why 'a doed it," said the deepest; and, "The will of the Lord must be done," said the wisest.

After fumbling in vain for his knife, and looking round, the Admiral ran back into the shop, and caught up the sharp steel blade with which the victim of a troubled mind had often unsold a sold ounce in the days of happy commerce. In a moment the Admiral had the poor Church-warden in his sturdy arms, and with a sailor's skill had unknotted the choking noose, and was shouting for brandy, as he kept the blue head from falling back.

When a little of the finest eau de vie that ever was smuggled had been administered, the patient rallied, and becoming comparatively cheerful, was enabled to explain that "it was all a mistake altogether." This removed all misunderstanding; but Rector Twemlow, arriving too late for anything but exhortation, asked a little too sternly—as everybody felt—under what influence of the Evil One Cheeseman had committed that mistake. The reply was worthy of an enterprising tradesman, and brought him such orders from a score of miles around that the resources of the establishment could only book them.

"Sir," he said, looking at the parson sadly, with his right hand laid upon his heart, which was feeble, and his left hand intimating that his neck was sore, "if anything has happened that had better not have been, it must have been by reason of the weight I give, and the value such a deal above the prices."

CHAPTER XXXVIII

EVERYBODY'S MASTER

The peril of England was now growing fast; all the faster from being in the dark. The real design of the enemy escaped the penetration even of Nelson, and our Government showed more anxiety about their great adversary landing on the coast of Egypt than on that of England. Naval men laughed at his flat-bottomed boats, and declared that one frigate could sink a hundred of them; whereas it is probable that two of them, with their powerful guns and level fire, would have sunk any frigate we then possessed. But the crafty and far-seeing foe did not mean to allow any frigate, or line-of-battle ship, the chance of enquiring how that might be.

His true scheme, as everybody now knows well, was to send the English fleet upon a wild-goose chase, whether to Egypt, the west coast of Ireland, or the West Indies, as the case might be; and then, by a rapid concentration of his ships, to obtain command of the English Channel, if only for twenty-four hours at a time. Twenty-four hours of clearance from our cruisers would have seen a hundred thousand men landed on our coast, throwing up entrenchments, and covering the landing of another hundred thousand, coming close upon their heels. Who would have faced them? A few good regiments, badly found, and perhaps worse led, and a mob of militia and raw volunteers, the reward of whose courage would be carnage.

But as a chip smells like the tree, and a hair like the dog it belongs to, so Springhaven was a very fair sample of the England whereof (in its own opinion) it formed a most important part. Contempt for the body of a man leads rashly to an under-estimate of his mind; and one of the greatest men that ever grew on earth—if greatness can be without goodness—was held in low account because not of high inches, and laughed at as "little Boney."

However, there were, as there always are, thousands of sensible Englishmen then; and rogues had not yet made a wreck of grand Institutions to scramble for what should wash up. Abuses existed, as they always must; but the greatest abuse of all (the destruction of every good usage) was undreamed of yet. And the right man was even now approaching to the rescue, the greatest Prime-Minister of any age or country.

Unwitting perhaps of the fine time afforded by the feeble delays of Mr. Addington, and absorbed in the tissue of plot and counterplot now thickening fast in Paris—the arch-plotter in all of them being himself—the First Consul had slackened awhile his hot haste to set foot upon the shore of England. His bottomless ambition for the moment had a top, and that top was the crown of France; and as soon as he had got that on his head, the head would have no rest until the crown was that of Europe.

But before any crown could be put on at all, the tender hearts of Frenchmen must be touched by the appearance of great danger—the danger which is of all the greatest, that to their nearest and dearest selves. A bloody farce was in preparation, noble lives were to be perjured away, and above all, the only great rival in the hearts of soldiers must be turned out of France. This foul job worked—as foul Radical jobs do now—for the good of England. If the French invasion had come to pass, as it was fully meant to do, in the month of February, 1804, perhaps its history must have been written in French, for us to understand it.

So, at any rate, thought Caryl Carne, who knew the resources of either side, and the difference between a fine army and a mob. He felt quite sure that his mother's country would conquer his father's without much trouble, and he knew that his horn would be exalted in the land, when he had guided the conqueror into it. Sure enough then he would recover his ancestral property with interest and be able to punish his enemies well, and reward his friends if they deserved it. Thinking of these things, and believing that his own preparations would soon be finished, he left Widow Shanks to proclaim his merits, while under the bold and able conduct of Captain Renaud Charron he ran the gauntlet of the English fleet, and was put ashore southward of Cape Grisnez. Here is a long reach of dreary exposure, facing the west unprofitably, with a shallow slope of brown sand, and a scour of tide, and no pleasant moorings. Jotted as the coast was all along (whereon dry batteries grinned defiance, or sands just awash smiled treachery) with shallow transports, gun-boats, prames, scows, bilanders, brigs, and schooners, row-galleys, luggers, and every sort of craft that has a mast, or gets on without one, and even a few good ships of war pondering malice in the safer roadsteads, yet here the sweep of the west wind, and the long roll from the ocean following, kept a league or two, northward of the mighty defences of Boulogne, inviolate by the petty enmities of man. Along the slight curve of the coast might be seen, beyond Ambleteuse and Wimereux, the vast extent of the French flotilla, ranged in three divisions, before the great lunette of the central camp, and hills jotted with tents thick as limpets on a rock.

Carne (whose dealings were quite unknown to all of the French authorities save one, and that the supreme one) was come by appointment to meet his commander in a quiet and secluded spot. It was early February now, and although the day was waning, and the wind, which was drawing to the north of west, delivered a cold blow from the sea, yet the breath of Spring was in the air already, and the beat of her pulse came through the ground. Almost any man, except those two concerting to shed blood and spread fire, would have looked about a little at the pleasure of the earth, and felt a touch of happiness in the goodness of the sky.

Caryl Carne waited in the shelter of a tree, scarcely deserving to be called a tree, except for its stiff tenacity. All the branches were driven by the western gales, and scourged flat in one direction—that in which they best could hold together, and try to believe that their life was their own. Like the wings of a sea bird striving with a tempest, all the sprays were frayed alike, and all the twigs hackled with the self-same pile. Whoever observes a tree like this should stop to wonder how ever it managed to make itself any sort of trunk at all, and how it was persuaded to go up just high enough to lose the chance of ever coming down again. But Carne cared for nothing of this sort, and heeded very little that did not concern himself. All he thought of was how he might persuade his master to try the great issue at once.

While he leaned heavily against the tree, with his long sea-cloak flapping round his legs, two horsemen struck out of the Ambleteuse road, and came at hand-gallop towards him. The foremost, who rode with short stirrups, and sat his horse as if he despised him, was the foremost man of the world just now, and for ten years yet to come.

Carne ran forward to show himself, and the master of France dismounted. He always looked best upon horseback, as short men generally do, if they ride well; and his face (which helped to make his fortune) appeared even more commanding at a little distance. An astonishing face, in its sculptured beauty, set aspect, and stern haughtiness, calm with the power of transcendant mind, and a will that never met its equal. Even Carne, void of much imagination, and contemptuous of all the human character he shared, was the slave of that face when in its presence, and could never meet steadily those piercing eyes. And yet, to the study of a neutral dog, or a man of abstract science, the face was as bad as it was beautiful.

Napoleon—as he was soon to be called by a cringing world—smiled affably, and offered his firm white hand, which Carne barely touched, and bent over with deference. Then the foaming horse was sent away in charge of the attendant trooper, and the master began to take short quick steps, to and fro, in front of the weather-beaten tree; for to stand still was not in his nature. Carne, being beckoned to keep at his side, lost a good deal of what he had meant to say, from the trouble he found in timing his wonted stride to the brisk pace of the other.

"You have done well—on the whole very well," said Napoleon, whose voice was deep, yet clear and distinct as the sound of a bell. "You have kept me well informed; you are not suspected; you are enlarging your knowledge of the enemy and of his resources; every day you become more capable of conducting us to the safe landing. For what, then, this hurry, this demand to see me, this exposing of yourself to the risk of capture?"

Carne was about to answer; but the speaker, who undershot the thoughts of others before they were shaped—as the shuttle of the lightning underweaves a cloud—raised his hand to stop him, and went on:

"Because you suppose that all is ripe. Because you believe that the slow beasts of islanders will strengthen their defences more by delay than we shall strengthen our attack. Because you are afraid of incurring suspicion, if you continue to prepare. And most of all, my friend, because you are impatient to secure the end of a long enterprise. But, Captain, it must be longer yet. It is not for you, but for me, to fix the time. Behold me! I am come from a grand review. We have again rehearsed the embarkation. We have again put two thousand horses on board. The horses did it well; but not the men. They are as brave as eagles, but as clumsy as the ostrich, and as fond of the sand without water. They will all be sea-sick. It is in their countenances, though many have been practised in the mouths of rivers. Those infamous English will not permit us to proceed far enough from our native land to acquire what they call the legs of the sea. If our braves are sea-sick, how can they work the cannon, or even navigate well for the accursed island? They must have time. They must undergo more waves, and a system of diet before embarkation. Return, my trusted Captain, and continue your most esteemed services for three months. I have written these new instructions for you. You may trust me to remember this addition to your good works."

Carne's heart fell, and his face was gloomy, though he did his best to hide it. So well he knew the arrogance and fierce self-will of his commanding officer that he durst not put his own opposite view of the case directly before him. This arrogance grew with the growth of his power; so that in many important matters Napoleon lost the true state of the case through the terror felt by his subordinates. So great was the mastery of his presence that Carne felt himself guilty of impertinence in carrying his head above the level of the General's plume, and stooped unconsciously—as hundreds of tall men are said to have done—to lessen this anomaly of Nature.

"All shall be done to your orders, my General," he replied, submissively. "For my own position I have no fear. I might remain there from year to year without any suspicion arising, so stupid are the people all around, and so well is my name known among them. The only peril is in the landing of stores, and I think we should desist from that. A few people have been wondering about that, though hitherto we have been most fortunate. They have set it down so far to smuggling operations, with which in that tyrannical land all the lower orders sympathise. But it would be wiser to desist awhile, unless you, my General, have anything of moment which you still desire to send in."

"What sort of fellow is that Sheeseman?" asked Napoleon, with his wonderful memory of details. "Is he more to be confided in as a rogue or as a fool?"

"As both, sir; but more especially as a rogue, though he has the compunctions of a fool sometimes. But he is as entirely under my thumb, as I am under that of my Commander."

"That is very good," answered the First Consul, smiling with the sense of his own power; "and at an hour's notice, with fifty chosen men landed from the London Trader—ah, I love that name; it is appropriate—you could spike all the guns of that pretentious little battery, and lock the Commander of the Coast-Defence in one of his own cellars. Is it not so, my good Captain? Answer me not. That is enough. One question more, and you may return. Are you certain of the pilotage of the proud young fisherman who knows every grain of sand along his native shore? Surely you can bribe him, if he hesitates at all, or hold a pistol at his ear as he steers the leading prame into the bay! Charron would be the man for that. Between you and Charron, there should be no mistake."

"He requires to be handled with much delicacy. He has no idea yet what he is meant to do. And if I understand his nature, neither bribes nor fear would move him. He is stubborn as a Breton, and of that simple character."

"One can always befool a Breton; but I hate that race," said Napoleon. "If he cannot be made useful, tie a round shot to him, throw him overheard, and get a gentler native."

"Alas, I fear that we cannot indulge in that pleasure," said Carne, with a smile of regret. "It cost me a large outlay of skill to catch him, and the natives of that place are all equally stubborn. But I have a plan for making him do our work without being at all aware of it. Is it your wish, my General, that I should now describe that plan?"

"Not now," replied Napoleon, pulling out a watch of English make, "but in your next letter. I start for Paris in an hour's time. You will hear of things soon which will add very greatly to the weight and success of this grand enterprise. We shall have perfidious Albion caught in her own noose, as you shall see. You have not heard of one Captain Wright, and the landing-place at Biville. We will have our little Biville at Springhaven. There will be too many of us to swing up by a rope. Courage, my friend! The future is with you. Our regiments are casting dice for the fairest English counties. But your native county is reserved for you. You shall possess the whole of it—I swear it by the god of war—and command the Southern army. Be brave, be wise, be vigilant, and above all things be patient."

The great man held up his hand, as a sign that he wanted his horse, and then offered it to Caryl Carne, who touched it lightly with his lips, and bent one knee. "My Emperor!" he said, "my Emperor!"

"Wait until the proper time," said Napoleon, gravely, and yet well pleased. "You are not the first, and you will not be the last. Observe discretion. Farewell, my friend!"

In another minute he was gone, and the place looked empty without him. Carne stood gloomily watching the horsemen as their figures grew small in the distance, the large man behind pounding heavily away, like an English dragoon, on the scanty sod, of no importance to anybody—unless he had a wife or children—the little man in front (with the white plume waving, and the well-bred horse going easily), the one whose body would affect more bodies, and certainly send more souls out of them, than any other born upon this earth as yet, and—we hope—as long as ever it endureth.

Caryl Carne cared not a jot about that. He was anything but a philanthropist; his weaknesses, if he had any, were not dispersive, but thoroughly concentric. He gathered his long cloak round his body, and went to the highest spot within his reach, about a mile from the watch-tower at Cape Grisnez, and thence he had a fine view of the vast invasive fleet and the vaster host behind it.

An Englishman who loved his Country would have turned sick at heart and faint of spirit at the sight before him. The foe was gathered together there to eat us up on every side, to get us into his net and rend us, to tear us asunder as a lamb is torn when its mother has dropped it in flight from the wolves. For forty square miles there was not an acre without a score of tents upon it, or else of huts thrown up with slabs of wood to keep the powder dry, and the steel and iron bright and sharp to go into the vitals of England. Mighty docks had been scooped out by warlike hands, and shone with ships crowded with guns and alive with men. And all along the shore for leagues, wherever any shelter lay, and great batteries protected them, hundreds of other ships tore at their moorings, to dash across the smooth narrow line, and blacken with fire and redden with blood the white cliffs of the land they loathed.

And what was there to stop them? The steam of the multitude rose in the air, and the clang of armour filled it. Numbers irresistible, and relentless power urged them. At the beck of the hand that had called the horse, the grey sea would have been black with ships, and the pale waves would have been red with fire. Carne looked at the water way touched with silver by the soft descent of the winter sun, and upon it, so far as his gaze could reach, there were but a dozen little objects moving, puny creatures in the distance—mice in front of a lion's den. And much as he hated with his tainted heart the land of his father, the land of his birth, some reluctant pride arose that he was by right an Englishman.

"It is the dread of the English seaman, it is the fame of Nelson, it is the habit of being beaten when England meets them upon the sea—nothing else keeps this mighty host like a set of trembling captives here, when they might launch forth irresistibly. And what is a great deal worse, it will keep me still in my ruined dungeons, a spy, an intriguer, an understrapper, when I am fit to be one of the foremost. What a fool I am so to be cowed and enslaved, by a man no better endowed than myself with anything, except self-confidence! I should have looked over his head, and told him that I had had enough of it, and if he would not take advantage of my toils, I would toil for him no longer. Why, he never even thanked me, that I can remember, and my pay is no more than Charron's! And a pretty strict account I have to render of every Republican coin he sends. He will have his own head on them within six months, unless he is assassinated. His manners are not those of a gentleman. While I was speaking to him, he actually turned his back upon me, and cleared his throat! Every one hates him as much as fears him, of all who are in the rank of gentlemen. How would it pay me to throw him over, denounce my own doings, excuse them as those of a Frenchman and a French officer, and bow the knee to Farmer George? Truly if it were not for my mother, who has sacrificed her life for me, I would take that course, and have done with it. Such all-important news would compel them to replace me in the property of my forefathers; and if neighbours looked coldly on me at first, I could very soon conquer that nonsense. I should marry little Dolly, of course, and that would go half-way towards doing it. I hate that country, but I might come to like it, if enough of it belonged to me. Aha! What would my mother say, if she dreamed that I could have such ideas? And the whole of my life belongs to her. Well, let me get back to my ruins first. It would never do to be captured by a British frigate. We had a narrow shave of it last time. And there will be a vile great moon to-night."

With these reflections—which were upon the whole more to his credit than the wonted web of thought—Carne with his long stride struck into a path towards the beach where his boat was waiting. Although he knew where to find several officers who had once been his comrades, he kept himself gladly to his loneliness; less perhaps by reason of Napoleon's orders than from the growing charm which Solitude has for all who begin to understand her.

CHAPTER XXXIX

RUNNING THE GAUNTLET

Though Carne had made light, in his impatient mood, of the power of the blockading fleet, he felt in his heart a sincere respect for its vigilance and activity. La Liberte (as the unhappy Cheeseman's schooner was called within gunshot of France) was glad enough to drop that pretentious name, and become again the peaceful London Trader, when she found herself beyond the reach of French batteries. The practice of her captain, the lively Charron, was to give a wide berth to any British cruiser appearing singly; but whenever more than one hove in sight, to run into the midst of them and dip his flag. From the speed of his schooner he could always, in a light wind, show a clean pair of heels to any single heavy ship, and he had not yet come across any cutter, brig of war, or light corvette that could collar the Liberte in any sort of weather. Renaud Charron was a brave young Frenchman, as fair a specimen as could be found, of a truly engaging but not overpowering type, kindly, warm-hearted, full of enterprise, lax of morals (unless honour—their veneer —was touched), loving excitement, and capable of anything, except skulking, or sulking, or running away slowly.

"None of your risky tricks to-night!" said Carne, as he stood on the schooner's deck, in the dusk of the February evening, himself in a dark mood growing darker—for his English blood supplied the elements of gloom, and he felt a dull pleasure in goading a Frenchman, after being trampled on by one of French position. "You will just make straight, as the tide and shoals allow, for our usual landing-place, set me ashore, and follow me to the old quarters. I have orders to give you, which can be given only there."

"My commanding officer shall be obeyed," the Frenchman answered, with a light salute and smile, for he was not endowed with the power of hating, or he might have indulged that bad power towards Carne; "but I fear that he has not found things to his liking."

"What concern is that of yours? Your duty is to carry out my orders, to the utmost of your ability, and offer opinion when asked for."

The light-hearted Frenchman shrugged his shoulders. "My commanding officer is right," he said; "but the sea is getting up, and there will be wind, unless I mistake the arising of the moon. My commanding officer had better retire, until his commands are needed. He has been known to feel the effects of high tossing, in spite of his unequalled constitution. Is it not so, my

271

commander? I ask with deference, and anxiety."

Carne, who liked to have the joke on his side only, swore at the moon and the wind, in clear English, which was shorter and more efficacious than French. He longed to say, "Try to keep me out of rough water," but his pride, and the fear of suggesting the opposite to this sailor who loved a joke, kept him silent, and he withdrew to his little cuddy, chewing a biscuit, to feed, if it must be so, the approaching malady.

"We shall have some game, and a fine game too," said Renaud Charron to himself, as he ordered more sail to be made. "Milord gives himself such mighty airs! We will take him to the cross-run off the Middle Bank, and offer him a basin through the key-hole. To make sea-sick an Englishman—for, after all, what other is he?—will be a fine piece of revenge for fair France."

Widow Shanks had remarked with tender sorrow—more perhaps because she admired the young man, and was herself a hearty soul, than from any loss of profit in victualling him—that "he was one of they folk as seems to go about their business, and do their jobs, and keep their skins as full as other people, without putting nort inside of them." She knew one of that kind before, and he was shot by the Coast-guard, and when they postmartyred him, an eel twenty foot long was found inside him, doubled up for all the world like a love-knot. Squire Carne was of too high a family for that; but she would give a week's rent to know what was inside him.

There was no little justice in these remarks, as is pretty sure to be the case with all good-natured criticism. The best cook that ever was roasted cannot get out of a pot more than was put in it; and the weight of a cask, as a general rule, diminishes if the tap is turned, without any redress at the bung-hole. Carne ran off his contents too fast, before he had arranged for fresh receipts; and all who have felt what comes of that will be able to feel for him in the result.

But a further decrease was in store for him now. As the moon arose, the wind got higher, and chopped round to one point north of west, raising a perkish head-sea, and grinning with white teeth against any flapping of sails. The schooner was put upon the starboard tack as near to the wind as she would lie, bearing so for the French coast more than the English, and making for the Vergoyers, instead of the Varne, as intended. This carried them into wider water, and a long roll from the southwest crossing the pointed squabble of the strong new wind.

"General," cried Charron, now as merry as a grig, and skipping to the door of Carne's close little cabin, about an hour before midnight, "it would afford us pleasure if you would kindly come on deck and give us the benefit of your advice. I fear that you are a little confined down here, and in need of more solid sustenance. My General, arise; there is much briskness upon deck, and the waves are dancing beautifully in the full moon. Two sail are in sight, one upon the weather bow, and the other on the weather quarter. Ah, how superior your sea-words are to ours! If I were born an Englishman, you need not seek far for a successor to Nelson, when he gets shot, as he is sure to be before very long."

"Get out!" muttered Carne, whose troubles were faintly illuminated by a sputtering wick. "Get out, you scoundrel, as you love plain English. Go direct to the devil—only let me die in peace."

"All language is excusable in those affected with the malady of the sea," replied the Frenchman, dancing a little to encourage his friend. "Behold, if you would get up and do this, you would be as happy inside as I am. But stay —I know what will ease you in an instant, and enable you to order us right and left. The indefatigable Sherray put a fine piece of fat pork in store before we sailed; I have just had it cooked, for I was almost starving. It floats in brown liquor of the richest order, such as no Englishman can refuse. Take a sip of pure rum, and you will enjoy it surely. Say, my brave General, will you come and join me? It will cure any little disquietude down here."

With a pleasant smile Charron laid his hand on the part of his commander which he supposed to be blameable. Carne made an effort to get up and kick him, but fell back with everything whirling around, and all human standards inverted. Then the kindly Frenchman tucked him up, for his face was blue and the chill of exhaustion striking into him. "I wish you could eat a little bit," said Charron, gently; but Carne gave a push with his elbow. "Well, you'll be worse before you are better, as the old women say in your country. But what am I to do about the two British ships—for they are sure to be British—now in sight?" But Carne turned his back, and his black boots dangled from the rim of his bunk as if there was nothing in them.

"This is going a little too far," cried Charron; "I must have some orders, my commander. You understand that two English ships are manifestly bearing down upon us—"

"Let them come and send us to the bottom—the sooner the better," his commander groaned, and then raised his limp knuckles with a final effort to stop his poor ears forever.

"But I am not ready to go to the bottom, nor all the other people of our fourteen hands"—the Frenchman spoke now to himself alone—"neither will I even go to prison. I will do as they do at Springhaven, and doubtless at every other place in England. I will have my dish of pork, which is now just crackling—I am capable of smelling it even here—and I will give some to Sam Polwhele, and we will put heads together over it. To outsail friend Englishman is a great delight, and to out-gun him would be still greater; but if we cannot accomplish those, there will be some pleasure of outwitting him."

Renaud Charron was never disposed to make the worst of anything. When he went upon deck again, to look out while his supper was waiting, he found no change, except that the wind was freshening and the sea increasing, and the strangers whose company he did not covet seemed waiting for no invitation. With a light wind he would have had little fear of giving them the go-by, or on a dark night he might have contrived to slip between or away from them. But everything was against him now. The wind was so strong, blowing nearly half a gale, and threatening to blow a whole one, that he durst not carry much canvas, and the full moon, approaching the meridian now, spread the white sea with a broad flood of light. He could see that both enemies had descried him, and were acting in concert to cut him off. The ship on his weather bow was a frigate, riding the waves in gallant style, with the wind upon her beam, and travelling two feet for every one the close-hauled schooner could accomplish. If the latter continued her present course, in another half-league she would be under the port-holes of the frigate.

The other enemy, though further off, was far more difficult to escape. This was a gun-brig, not so very much bigger than La Liberte herself—for gun-brigs in those days were very small craft—and for that very reason more dangerous. She bore about two points east of north from the greatly persecuted Charron, and was holding on steadily under easy sail, neither gaining much upon the chase nor losing.

"Carry on as we are for about ten minutes," said Charron to his mate, Sam Polwhele; "that will give us period to eat our pork. Come, then, my good friend, let us do it."

Polwhele—as he was called to make believe that he and other hands were Cornishmen, whereas they were Yankees of the sharpest order, owing no allegiance and unhappily no good-will to their grandmother—this man, whose true name was Perkins, gave the needful orders, and followed down. Charron could talk, like many Frenchmen, quite as fast with his mouth full as empty, and he had a man to talk to who did not require anything to be said twice to him.

"No fear of me!" was all he said. "You keep out of sight, because of your twang. I'll teach them a little good English—better than ever came out of Cornwall. The best of all English is not to say too much."

The captain and his mate enjoyed their supper, while Carne in the distance bore the pangs of a malady called bulimus, that is to say, a giant's ravening for victuals, without a babe's power of receiving them. For he was turning the corner of his sickness now, but prostrate and cold as a fallen stalactite.

"Aha! We have done well. We have warmed our wits up. One glass of what you call the grog; and then we will play a pleasant game with those Englishmen!" Carne heard him say it, and in his heart hoped that the English would pitch him overboard.

It was high time for those two to finish their supper. The schooner had no wheel, but steered—as light craft did then, and long afterwards—with a bulky ash tiller, having iron eyes for lashing it in heavy weather. Three strong men stood by it now, obedient, yet muttering to one another, for another cable's length would bring them into danger of being run down by the frigate.

"All clear for stays!" cried Polwhele, under orders from Charron. "Down helm! Helm's alee! Steady so. Let draw! Easy! easy! There she fills!" And after a few more rapid orders the handy little craft was dashing away, with the wind abaft the beam, and her head about two points north of east. "Uncommon quick in stays!" cried Polwhele, who had taken to the helm, and now stood there. "Wonder what Britishers will think of that?"

The British ship soon let him know her opinion, by a roar and a long streak of smoke blown toward him, as she put up her helm to consider the case. It was below the dignity of a fine frigate to run after little smuggling craft, such as she voted this to be, and a large ship had been sighted from her tops down channel, which might afford her nobler sport. She contented herself with a harmless shot, and leaving the gun-brig to pursue the chase, bore away for more important business.

"Nonplussed the big 'un; shall have trouble with the little 'un," said Master Polwhele to his captain. "She don't draw half a fathom more than we do. No good running inside the shoals. And with this wind, she has the foot of us."

"Bear straight for her, and let her board us," Charron answered, pleasantly. "Down with all French hands into the forepart of the hold, and stow the spare foresail over them. Show our last bills of lading, and ask them to trade. You know all about Cheeseman; double his prices. If we make any cash, we'll divide it. Say we are out of our course, through supplying a cruiser that wanted our goods for nothing. I shall keep out of sight on account of my twang, as you politely call it. The rest I may safely leave to your invention. But if you can get any ready rhino, Sam Polwhele is not the man to neglect it."

"Bully for you!" cried the Yankee, looking at him with more admiration than he expected ever to entertain for a Frenchman. "There's five ton of cheeses that have been seven voyages, and a hundred firkins of Irish butter, and five-and-thirty cases of Russian tongues, as old as old Nick, and ne'er a sign of weevil! Lor' no, never a tail of weevil! Skipper, you deserve to go to heaven out of West Street. But how about him, down yonder?"

"Captain Carne? Leave him to me to arrange. I shall be ready, if they intrude. Announce that you have a sick gentleman on board, a passenger afflicted with a foreign illness, and having a foreign physician. Mon Dieu! It is good. Every Englishman believes that anything foreign will kill him with a vault. Arrange you the trading, and I will be the doctor—a German; I can do the German."

"And I can do the trading," the American replied, without any rash self-confidence; "any fool can sell good stuff; but it requireth a good man to sell bad goods."

The gun-brig bore down on them at a great pace, feeling happy certitude that she had got a prize—not a very big one, but still worth catching. She saw that the frigate had fired a shot, and believed that it was done to call her own attention to a matter below that of the frigate. On she came, heeling to the lively wind, very beautiful in the moonlight, tossing the dark sea in white showers, and with all her taut canvas arched and gleaming, hovered with the shades of one another.

"Heave to, or we sink you!" cried a mighty voice through a speaking trumpet, as she luffed a little, bringing her port broadside to bear; and the schooner, which had hoisted British colours, obeyed the command immediately. In a very few seconds a boat was manned, and dancing on the hillocks of the sea; and soon, with some danger and much care, the visitors stood upon the London Trader's deck, and Sam Polwhele came to meet them.

"We have no wish to put you to any trouble," said the officer in command, very quietly, "if you can show that you are what you profess to be. You sail under British colours; and the name on your stern is London Trader. We will soon dismiss you, if you prove that. But appearances are strongly against you. What has brought you here? And why did you run the risk of being fired at, instead of submitting to his Majesty's ship Minerva?"

"Because she haven't got any ready money, skipper, and we don't like three months' bills," said the tall Bostonian, looking loftily at the British officer. "Such things is nothing but piracy, and we had better be shot at than lose such goods as we carry fresh shipped, and in prime condition. Come and see them, all with Cheeseman's brand, the celebrated Cheeseman of Springhaven— name guarantees the quality. But one thing, mind you—no use to hanker after them unless you come provided with the ready."

"We don't want your goods; we want you," answered Scudamore, now first luff of the brig of war Delia, and staring a little with his mild blue eyes at this man's effrontery. "That is to say, our duty is to know all about you. Produce your papers. Prove where you cleared from last, and what you are doing here, some thirty miles south of your course, if you are a genuine British trader."

"Papers all in order, sir. First-chop wafers, as they puts on now, to save sealing-wax. Charter-party, and all the rest. Last bills of lading from Gravesend, but you mustn't judge our goods by that. Bulk of them from St. Mary Axe, where Cheeseman hath freighted from these thirty years. If ever you have been at Springhaven, Captain, you'd jump at anything with Cheeseman's brand. But have you brought that little bag of guineas with you?"

"Once more, we want none of your goods. You might praise them as much as you liked, if time permitted. Show me to the cabin, and produce your papers. After that we shall see what is in the hold."

"Supercargo very ill in best cabin. Plague, or black fever, the German doctor says. None of our hands will go near him but myself. But you won't be like that, will you?"

Less for his own sake than his mother's—who had none but him to help her—Scudamore dreaded especially that class of disease which is now called "zymotic." His father, an eminent physician, had observed and had written a short work to establish that certain families and types of constitution lie almost at the mercy of such contagion, and find no mercy from it. And among those families was his own. "Fly, my boy, fly," he had often said to Blyth, "if you ever come near such subjects."

"Captain, I will fetch them," continued Mr. Polwhele, looking grave at his hesitation. "By good rights they ought to be smoked, I dare say, though I don't hold much with such stuff myself. And the doctor keeps doing a heap of herbs hot. You can see him, if you just come down these few steps. Perhaps you wouldn't mind looking into the hold, to find something to suit your judgment—quality combined with low figures there—while I go into the infected den, as the cleverest of my chaps calls it. Why, it makes me laugh! I've been in and out, with this stand-up coat on, fifty times, and you can't smell a fluc of it, though wonderful strong down there."

Scudamore shuddered, and drew back a little, and then stole a glance round the corner. He saw a thick smoke, and a figure prostrate, and another tied up in a long white robe, waving a pan of burning stuff in one hand and a bottle in the other, and plainly conjuring Polwhele to keep off. Then the latter returned, quite complacently.

"Can't find all of them," he said, presenting a pile of papers big enough to taint Sahara. "That doctor goes on as bad as opening a coffin. Says he understands it, and I don't. The old figure-head! What does he know about it?"

"Much more than you do, perhaps," replied Blyth, standing up for the profession, as he was bound to do. "Perhaps we had better look at these on deck, if you will bring up your lantern."

"But, Captain, you will have a look at our hold, and make us a bid—we need not take it, any more than you need to double it—for as prime a lot of cheese, and sides of bacon—"

"If your papers are correct, it will not be my duty to meddle with your cargo. But what are you doing the wrong side of our fleet?"

"Why, that was a bad job. There's no fair trade now, no sort of dealing on the square nohow. We run all this risk of being caught by Crappos on purpose to supply British ship Gorgeous, soweastern station; and blow me tight if I couldn't swear she had been supplied chock-full by a Crappo! Only took ten cheeses and fifteen sides of bacon, though she never knew nought of our black fever case! But, Captain, sit down here, and overhaul our flimsies. Not like rags, you know; don't hold plague much."

The young lieutenant compelled himself to discharge his duty of inspection behind a combing, where the wind was broken; but even so he took good care to keep on the weather side of the documents; and the dates perhaps flew away to leeward. "They seem all right," he said, "but one thing will save any further trouble to both of us. You belong to Springhaven. I know most people there. Have you any Springhaven hands on board?"

"I should think so. Send Tugwell aft; pass the word for Dan Tugwell. Captain, there's a family of that name there—settled as long as we have been at Mevagissey. Ah, that sort of thing is a credit to the place, and the people too, in my opinion."

Dan Tugwell came slowly, and with a heavy step, looking quite unlike the spruce young fisherman whom Scudamore had noticed as first and smartest in the rescue of the stranded Blonde. But he could not doubt that this was Dan, the Dan of happier times and thoughts; in whom, without using his mind about it, he had felt some likeness to himself. It was not in his power to glance sharply, because his eyes were kindly open to all the little incidents of mankind, but he managed to let Dan know that duty compelled him to be particular. Dan Tugwell touched the slouched hat upon his head, and stood waiting to know what he was wanted for.

"Daniel," said Scudamore, who could not speak condescendingly to any one, even from the official point of view, because he felt that every honest man was his equal, "are you here of your own accord, as one of the crew of this schooner?"

Dan Tugwell had a hazy sense of being put upon an untrue balance. Not by this kind gentleman's words, but through his own proceedings. In his honest mind he longed to say: "I fear I have been bamboozled. I have cast my lot in with these fellows through passion, and in hasty ignorance. How I should like to go with you, and fight the French, instead of getting mixed up with a lot of things I can't make out!"

But his equally honest heart said to him: "You have been well treated. You are well paid. You shipped of your own accord. You have no right to peach, even if you had anything to peach of; and all you have seen is some queer trading. None but a sneak would turn against his shipmates and his ship, when overhauled by the Royal Navy."

Betwixt the two voices, Dan said nothing, but looked at the lieutenant with that gaze which the receiver takes to mean doubt of his meaning, while the doubt more often is—what to do with it.

"Are you here of your own accord? Do you belong to this schooner of your own accord? Are you one of this crew, of your own free-will?"

Scudamore rang the changes on his simple question, as he had often been obliged to do in the Grammar-school at Stonnington, with the slow-witted boys, who could not, or would not, know the top from the bottom of a sign-post. "Do you eat with your eyes?" he had asked them sometimes; and they had put their thumbs into their mouths to enquire.

"S'pose I am," said Dan at last, assuming stupidity, to cover hesitation; "yes, sir, I come aboard of my own free-will."

"Very well. Then I am glad to find you comfortable. I shall see your father next week, perhaps. Shall I give him any message for you?"

"No, sir! For God's sake, don't let him know a word about where you have seen me. I came away all of a heap, and I don't want one of them to bother about me."

"As you wish, Dan. I shall not say a word about you, until you return with your earnings. But if you found the fishing business dull, surely you might have come to us, Dan. Any volunteers here for His Majesty's service?" Scudamore raised his voice, with the usual question. "Good pay, good victuals, fine promotion, and prize-money, with the glory of fighting for their native country, and provision for life if disabled!"

Not a man came forward, though one man longed to do so; but his sense of honour, whether true or false, forbade him. Dan Tugwell went heavily back to his work, trying to be certain that it was his duty. But sad doubts arose as he watched the brave boat, lifting over the waves in the moonlight, with loyal arms tugging towards a loyal British ship; and he felt that he had thrown away his last chance.

CHAPTER XL

SHELFING THE QUESTION

There is a time of day (as everybody must have noticed who is kind enough to attend to things) not to be told by the clock, nor measured to a nicety by the position of the sun, even when he has the manners to say where he is—a time of day dependent on a multiplicity of things unknown to us (who have made our own brains, by perceiving that we had none, and working away till we got them), yet palpable to all those less self-exalted beings, who, or which, are of infinitely nobler origin than we, and have shown it, by humility. At this time of day every decent and good animal feels an unthought-of and untraced desire to shift its position, to come out and see its fellows, to learn what is happening in the humble grateful world—out of which man has hoisted himself long ago, and is therefore a spectre to them—to breathe a little sample of the turn the world is taking, and sue their share of pleasure in the quiet earth and air.

This time is more observable because it follows a period of the opposite tendency, a period of heaviness, and rest, and silence, when no bird sings and no quadruped plays, for about half an hour of the afternoon. Then suddenly, without any alteration of the light, or weather, or even temperature, or anything else that we know of, a change of mood flashes into every living creature, a spirit of life, and activity, and stir, and desire to use their own voice and hear their neighbour's. The usual beginning is to come out first into a place that cannot knock their heads, and there to run a little way, and after that to hop, and take a peep for any people around, and espying none—or only one of the very few admitted to be friends—speedily to dismiss all misgivings, take a very little bit of food, if handy (more as a duty to one's family than oneself, for the all-important supper-time is not come yet), and then, if gifted by the Lord with wings—for what bird can stoop at such a moment to believe that his own grandfather made them?—up to the topmost spray that feathers in the breeze, and pour upon the grateful air the voice of free thanksgiving. But an if the blade behind the heart is still unplumed for flying, and only gentle flax or fur blows out on the wind, instead of beating it, does the owner of four legs sit and sulk, like a man defrauded of his merits? He answers the question with a skip and jump; ere a man can look twice at him he has cut a caper, frolicked an intricate dance upon the grass, and brightened his eyes for another round of joy.

At any time of year almost, the time of day commands these deeds, unless the weather is outrageous; but never more undeniably than in the month of April. The growth of the year is well established, and its manner beginning to be schooled by then; childish petulance may still survive, and the tears of penitence be frequent; yet upon the whole there is—or used to be—a sense of responsibility forming, and an elemental inkling of true duty towards the earth. Even man (the least observant of the powers that walk the ground, going for the signs of weather to the cows, or crows, or pigs, swallows, spiders, gnats, and leeches, or the final assertion of his own corns) sometimes is moved a little, and enlarged by influence of life beyond his own, and tickled by a pen above his thoughts, and touched for one second by the hand that made him. Then he sees a brother man who owes him a shilling, and his soul is swallowed up in the resolve to get it.

But well in the sky-like period of youth, when the wind sits lightly, and the clouds go by in puffs, these little jumps of inspiration take the most respectable young man sometimes off his legs, and the young maid likewise —if she continues in these fine days to possess such continuation. Blyth Scudamore had been appointed now, partly through his own good deserts, and wholly through good influence—for Lord St. Vincent was an ancient friend of the excellent Admiral Darling—to the command of the Blonde, refitted, thoroughly overhauled at Portsmouth, and pronounced by the dock-yard people to be the fastest and soundest corvette afloat, and in every way a credit to the British navy. "The man that floated her shall float in her," said the Earl, when somebody, who wanted the appointment, suggested that the young man was too young. "He has seen sharp service, and done sharp work. It is waste of time to talk of it; the job is done." "Job is the word for it," thought the other, but wisely reserved that great truth for his wife. However, it was not at all a bad job for England. And Scudamore had now seen four years of active service, counting the former years of volunteering, and was more than twenty-five years old.

None of these things exalted him at all in his own opinion, or, at any rate, not very much. Because he had always regarded himself with a proper amount of self-respect, as modest men are almost sure to do, desiring less to know what the world thinks of them than to try to think rightly of it for themselves. His opinion of it seemed to be that it was very good just now, very kind, and fair, and gentle, and a thing for the heart of man to enter into.

For Dolly Darling was close beside him, sitting on a very pretty bench, made of twisted oak, and turned up at the back and both ends, so that a gentleman could not get very far away from a lady without frightening her. Not only in this way was the spot well adapted for tender feelings, but itself truly ready to suggest them, with nature and the time of year to help. There was no stream issuing here, to puzzle and perpetually divert the human mind (whose origin clearly was spring-water poured into the frame of the jelly-fish), neither was there any big rock, like an obstinate barrier rising; but gentle slopes of daisied pasture led the eye complacently, sleek cows sniffed the herbage here and there, and brushed it with the underlip to fetch up the blades for supper-time, and placable trees, forgetting all the rudeness of the winter winds, began to disclose to the fond deceiving breeze, with many a glimpse to attract a glance, all the cream of their summer intentions. And in full enjoyment of all these doings, the poet of the whole stood singing—the simple-minded thrush, proclaiming that the world was good and kind, but himself perhaps the kindest, and his nest, beyond doubt, the best of it.

"How lovely everything is to-day!" Blyth Scudamore spoke slowly, and gazing shyly at the loveliest thing of all, in his opinion—the face of Dolly Darling. "No wonder that your brother is a poet!"

"But he never writes about this sort of thing," said Dolly, smiling pleasantly. "His poems are all about liberty, and the rights of men, and the wrongs of war. And if he ever mentions cows or sheep, it is generally to say what a shame it is to kill them."

"But surely it is much worse to kill men. And who is to be blamed for that, Miss Darling? The Power that wants to overrun all the rest, or the Country that only defends itself? I hope he has not converted you to the worship of the new Emperor; for the army and all the great cities of France have begged him to condescend to be that; and the King of Prussia will add his entreaties, according to what we have heard."

"I think anything of him!" cried Dolly, as if her opinion would settle the point. "After all his horrible murders—worst of all of that very handsome and brave young man shot with a lantern, and buried in a ditch! I was told that he had to hold the lantern above his poor head, and his hand never shook! It makes me cry every time I think of it. Only let Frank come back, and he won't find me admire his book so very much! They did the same sort of thing when I was a little girl, and could scarcely sleep at night on account of it. And then they seemed to get a little better, for a time, and fought with their enemies, instead of one another, and made everybody wild about liberty, and citizens, and the noble march of intellect, and the dignity of mankind, and the rights of labour—when they wouldn't work a stroke themselves—and the black superstition of believing anything, except what they chose to make a fuss about themselves. And thousands of people, even in this country, who have been brought up so much better, were foolish enough to think it very grand indeed, especially the poets, and the ones that are too young. But they ought to begin to get wiser now; even Frank will find it hard to make another poem on them."

"How glad I am to hear you speak like that! I had no idea—at least I did not understand—"

"That I had so much common-sense?" enquired Dolly, with a glance of subtle yet humble reproach. "Oh yes, I have a great deal sometimes, I can assure you. But I suppose one never does get credit for anything, without claiming it."

"I am sure that you deserve credit for everything that can possibly be imagined," Scudamore answered, scarcely knowing, with all his own common-sense to help him, that he was talking nonsense. "Every time I see you I find something I had never found before to—to wonder at—if you can understand—and to admire, and to think about, and to—to be astonished at."

Dolly knew as well as he did the word he longed to use, but feared. She liked this state of mind in him, and she liked him too for all his kindness, and his humble worship; and she could not help admiring him for his bravery and simplicity. But she did not know the value yet of a steadfast and unselfish heart, and her own was not quite of that order. So many gallant officers were now to be seen at her father's house, half a cubit taller than poor Blyth, and a hundred cubits higher in rank, and wealth, and knowledge of the world, and the power of making their wives great ladies. Moreover, she liked a dark man, and Scudamore was fair and fresh as a rose called Hebe's Cup in June. Another thing against him was that she knew how much her father liked him; and though she loved her father well, she was not bound to follow his leadings. And yet she did not wish to lose this useful and pleasant admirer.

"I am not at all ambitious," she replied, without a moment's hesitation, for the above reflections had long been dealt with, "but how I wish I could do something to deserve even half that you say of me! But I fear that you find the air getting rather cold. The weather is so changeable."

"Are you sure that you are not ambitious?" Scudamore was too deeply plunged to get out of it now upon her last hint; and to-morrow he must be far away. "You have every right to be ambitious, if such a word can be used of you, who are yourself the height of so many ambitions. It was the only fault I could imagine you to have, and it seems too bad that you should have none at all."

"You don't know anything about it," said Dolly, with a lovely expression in her face of candour, penitence, and pleasantry combined; "I am not only full of faults, but entirely made up of them. I am told of them too often not to know."

"By miserably jealous and false people." It was impossible to look at her and not think that. "By people who cannot have a single atom of perception, or judgment, or even proper feeling. I should like to hear one of them, if you would even condescend to mention it. Tell me one—only one—if you can think of it. I am not at all a judge of character, but—but I have often had to study it a good deal among the boys."

This made Miss Dolly laugh, and drop her eyes, and smoothe her dress, as if to be sure that his penetration had not been brought to bear on her. And the gentle Scuddy blushed at his clumsiness, and hoped that she would understand the difference.

"You do say such things!" She also was blushing beautifully as she spoke, and took a long time before she looked at him again. "Things that nobody else ever says. And that is one reason why I like you so."

"Oh, do you like me—do you like me in earnest? I can hardly dare to dream even for one moment—"

"I am not going to talk about that any more. I like Mr. Twemlow, I like Captain Stubbard, I like old Tugwell—though I should have liked him better if he had not been so abominably cruel to his son. Now I am sure it is time to go and get ready for dinner."

"Ah, when shall I dine with you again? Perhaps never," said the young man, endeavouring to look very miserable and to inspire sadness. "But I ought to be very happy, on the whole, to think of all the pleasures I have enjoyed, and how much better I have got on than I had any right in the world to hope for."

"Yes, to be the Commander of a beautiful ship, little more than a year from the date of your commission. Captain Stubbard is in such a rage about it!"

"I don't mean about that—though that of course is rare luck—I mean a much more important thing; I mean about getting on well with you. The first time I saw you in that fine old school, you did not even want to shake hands with me, and you thought what a queer kind of animal I was; and then the first time or two I dined at the Hall, nothing but fine hospitality stopped you from laughing at my want of practice. But gradually, through your own kind nature, and my humble endeavours to be of use, I began to get on with you better and better; and now you are beginning almost to like me."

"Not almost, but altogether," she answered, with quite an affectionate glance. "I can tell you there are very few, outside of my own family, that I like half so well as I like you. But how can it matter to you so much?"

She looked at him so that he was afraid to speak, for fear of spoiling everything; and being a very good-natured girl, and pleased with his deep admiration, she sighed—just enough to make him think that he might hope.

"We are all so sorry to lose you." she said; "and no one will miss you so much as I shall, because we have had such pleasant times together. But if we can carry out our little plot, we shall hear of you very often, and I dare say not very unfavourably. Faith and I have been putting our heads together, and for our own benefit, and that of all the house, if we can get you to second it. My father jumped at the idea, and said how stupid we were not to think of it before. You know how very little he can be at home this summer, and he says he has to sacrifice his children to his country. So we suggested that he should invite Lady Scudamore to spend the summer with us, if she can be persuaded to leave home so long. We will do our very utmost to make her comfortable, and she will be a tower of strength to us; for you know sometimes it is very awkward to have only two young ladies. But we dare not do anything until we asked you. Do you think she would take compassion upon us? A word from you perhaps would decide her; and Faith would write a letter for you to send."

Scudamore reddened with delight, and took her hand. "How can I thank you? I had better not try," he answered, with some very tender play of thumb and fore-finger, and a strong impulse to bring lips too into action. "You are almost as clever as you are good; you will know what I mean without my telling you. My mother will be only too glad to come. She knows what you are, she has heard so much from me. And the reality will put to shame all my descriptions."

"Tell me what you told her I was like. The truth, now, and not a word of afterthought or flattery. I am always so irritated by any sort of flattery."

"Then you must let me hold your hands, to subdue your irritation; for you are sure to think that it was flattery—you are so entirely ignorant of yourself, because you never think of it. I told my dear mother that you were the best, and sweetest, and wisest, and loveliest, and most perfect, and exquisite, and innocent, and unselfish of all the human beings she had ever seen, or heard, or read of. And I said it was quite impossible for any one after one look at you to think of himself any more in this world."

"Well done!" exclaimed Dolly, showing no irritation, unless a gleam of pearls inside an arch of coral showed it. "It is as well to do things thoroughly, while one is about it. I can understand now how you get on so fast. But, alas, your dear mother will only laugh at all that. Ladies are so different from gentlemen. Perhaps that is why gentlemen never understand them. And I would always a great deal rather be judged by a gentleman than a lady. Ladies pick such a lot of holes in one another, whereas gentlemen are too large-minded. And I am very glad upon the whole that you are not a lady, though you are much more gentle than they make believe to be. Oh dear! We must run; or the ladies will never forgive us for keeping them starving all this time."

CHAPTER XLI

LISTENERS HEAR NO GOOD

"Not that there is anything to make one so very uneasy," said Mr. Twemlow, "only that one has a right to know the meaning of what we are expected to put up with. Nothing is clear, except that we have not one man in the Government who knows his own mind, or at any rate dares to pronounce it. Addington is an old woman, and the rest—oh, when shall we have Pitt back again? People talk of it, and long for it; but the Country is so slow. We put up with everything, instead of demanding that the right thing shall be done at once. Here is Boney, a fellow raised up by Satan as the scourge of this island for its manifold sins; and now he is to be the Emperor forsooth—not of France, but of Europe, continental Europe. We have only one man fit to cope with him at all, and the voice of the nation has been shouting for him; but who pays any attention to it? This state of things is childish—simply childish; or perhaps I ought to say babyish. Why, even the children on the sea-shore know, when they make their little sand walls against the tide, how soon they must be swept away. But the difference is this, that they don't live inside them, and they haven't got all that belongs to them inside them. Nobody must suppose for a moment that a clergyman's family would fail to know where to look for help and strength and support against all visitations; but, in common with the laity, we ask for Billy Pitt."

"And in another fortnight you will have him," replied Captain Stubbard, who was dining there that day. "Allow me to tell you a little thing that happened to my very own self only yesterday. You know that I am one of the last people in the world to be accused of any—what's the proper word for it? Mrs. Stubbard, you know what I mean—Jemima, why the deuce don't you tell them?"

"Captain Stubbard always has more meaning than he can well put into words," said his wife; "his mind is too strong for any dictionary. Hallucination is the word he means."

"Exactly!" cried the Captain. "That expresses the whole of what I wanted to say, but went aside of it. I am one of the last men in the world to become the victim of any—there, I've lost it again! But never mind. You understand now; or if you don't, Mrs. Stubbard will repeat it. What I mean is that I see all things square, and straight, and with their own corners to them. Well, I know London pretty well; not, of course, as I know Portsmouth. Still, nobody need come along with me to go from Charing Cross to St. Paul's Church-yard; and pretty tight I keep all my hatches battened down, and a sharp pair of eyes in the crow's-nest—for to have them in the foretop won't do there. It was strictly on duty that I went up—the duty of getting a fresh stock of powder, for guns are not much good without it; and I had written three times, without answer or powder. But it seems that my letters were going the rounds, and would turn up somewhere, when our guns were stormed, without a bit of stuff to make answer."

"Ah, that's the way they do everything now!" interrupted Mr. Twemlow. "I thought you had been very quiet lately; but I did not know what a good reason you had. We might all have been shot, and you could not have fired a salute, to inform the neighbourhood!"

"Well, never mind," replied the Captain, calmly; "I am not complaining, for I never do so. Young men might; but not old hands, whose duty it is to keep their situation in life. Well, you must understand that the air of London always makes me hungry. There are so many thousands of people there that you can't name a time when there is nobody eating, and this makes a man from the country long to help them. Anyhow, I smelled roast mutton at a place where a little side street comes up into the Strand; and although it was scarcely half past twelve, it reminded me of Mrs. Stubbard. So I called a halt, and stood to think upon a grating, and the scent became flavoured with baked potatoes. This is always more than I can resist, after all the heavy trials of a chequered life. So I pushed the door open, and saw a lot of little cabins, right and left of a fore and aft gangway, all rigged up alike for victualling. Jemima, I told you all about it. You describe it to the Rector and Mrs. Twemlow."

"Don't let us trouble Mrs. Stubbard," said the host; "I know the sort of thing exactly, though I don't go to that sort of place myself."

"No, of course you don't. And I was a little scared at first, for there was sawdust enough to soak up every drop of my blood, if they had pistolled me. Mrs. Twemlow, I beg you not to be alarmed. My wife has such nerves that I often forget that all ladies are not like her. Now don't contradict me, Mrs. Stubbard. Well, sir, I went to the end of this cockpit—if you like to call it so —and got into the starboard berth, and shouted for a ration of what I had smelled outside. And although it was far from being equal to its smell—as the character is of everything—you might have thought it uncommon good, if you had never tasted Mrs. Stubbard's cooking, after she had been to the butcher herself. Very well. I don't care for kickshaws, even if I could afford them, which has never yet been my destiny. So I called for another ration of hot sheep—beg your pardon, ladies, what I mean is mutton—and half a dozen more of baked potatoes; and they reminded me of being at home so much that I called for a pint of best pine-apple rum and a brace of lemons, to know where I was—to remind me that I wasn't where I couldn't get them."

"Oh, Adam!" cried Mrs. Stubbard, "what will you say next? Not on weekdays, of course, but nearly every Sunday—and the samples of his powder in his pocket, Mr. Twemlow!"

"Jemima, you are spoiling my story altogether. Well, you must understand that this room was low, scarcely higher than the cabin of a fore-and-after, with no skylights to it, or wind-sail, or port-hole that would open. And so, with the summer coming on, as it is now—though a precious long time about it—and the smell of the meat, and the thoughts of the grog, and the feeling of being at home again, what did I do but fall as fast asleep as the captain of the watch in a heavy gale of wind! My back was to the light, so far as there was any, and to make sure of the top of my head, I fetched down my hat—the soft-edged one, the same as you see me wear on fine Sundays.

"Well, I may have gone on in that way for an hour, not snoring, as Mrs. Stubbard calls it, but breathing to myself a little in my sleep, when I seemed to hear somebody calling me, not properly, but as people do in a dream —'Stoobar—Stoobar—Stoobar,' was the sound in my ears, like my conscience hauling me over the coals in bad English. This made me wake up, for I always have it out with that part of me when it mutinies; but I did not move more than to feel for my glass. And then I perceived that it was nothing more or less than a pair of Frenchmen talking about me in the berth next to mine, within the length of a marlin-spike from my blessed surviving ear.

"Some wiseacre says that listeners never hear good of themselves, and upon my word he was right enough this time, so far as I made out. The French language is beyond me, so far as speaking goes, for I never can lay hold of the word I want; but I can make out most of what those queer people say, from being a prisoner among them once, and twice in command of a prize crew over them. And the sound of my own name pricked me up to listen sharply with my one good ear. You must bear in mind, Rector, that I could not see them, and durst not get up to peep over the quarter-rail, for fear of scaring them. But I was wearing a short hanger, like a middy's dirk—the one I always carry in the battery."

"I made Adam promise, before he went to London," Mrs. Stubbard explained to Mrs. Twemlow, "that he would never walk the streets without steel or firearms. Portsmouth is a very wicked place indeed, but a garden of Eden compared with London."

"Well, sir," continued Captain Stubbard, "the first thing I heard those Frenchmen say was: 'Stoobar is a stupid beast, like the ox that takes the prize up here, except that he has no claim to good looks, but the contrary—wholly the contrary.' Mrs. Stubbard, I beg you to preserve your temper; you have heard others say it, and you should now despise such falsehoods. 'But the ox has his horns, and Stoobar has none. For all his great guns there is not one little cup of powder.' The villains laughed at this, as a very fine joke, and you may well suppose that I almost boiled over. 'You have then the command of this beast Stoobar?' the other fellow asked him, as if I were a jackass. 'How then have you so very well obtained it?' 'In a manner the most simple. Our chief has him by the head and heels: by the head, by being over him; and by the heels, because nothing can come in the rear without his knowledge. Behold! you have all.' 'It is very good,' the other villain answered; 'but when is it to be, my most admirable Charron?—how much longer?—how many months?' 'Behold my fingers,' said the one who had abused me; 'I put these into those, and then you know. It would have been already, except for the business that you have been employed upon in this black hole. Hippolyte, you have done well, though crookedly; but all is straight for the native land. You have made this Government appear more treacherous in the eyes of France and Europe than our own is, and you have given a good jump to his instep for the saddle. But all this throws us back. I am tired of tricks; I want fighting; though I find them quite a jolly people.' 'I don't,' said the other, who was clearly a low scoundrel, for his voice was enough to settle that; 'I hate them; they are of thick head and thick hand, and would come in sabots to catch their enemy asleep. And now there is no chance to entangle any more. Their Government will be of the old brutal kind, hard knocks, and no stratagems. In less than a fortnight Pitt will be master again. I know it from the very best authority. You know what access I have.' 'Then that is past,' the other fellow answered, who seemed to speak more like a gentleman, although he was the one that ran down me; 'that is the Devil. They will have their wits again, and that very fat Stoobar will be supplied with powder. Hippolyte, it is a very grand joke. Within three miles of his head (which is empty, like his guns) we have nearly two hundred barrels of powder, which we fear to bring over in those flat-bottoms for fear of a volley among them. Ha! ha! Stoobar is one fine fat ox!'

"This was all I heard, for they began to move, having had enough sugar and water, I suppose; and they sauntered away to pay their bill at the hatch put up at the doorway. It was hopeless to attempt to follow them; but although I am not so quick in stays as I was, I slewed myself round to have a squint at them. One was a slight little active chap, with dapper legs, and jerks like a Frenchman all over. I could pardon him for calling me a great fat ox, for want of a bit of flesh upon his own bones. But he knows more about me than I do of him, for I never clapped eyes on him before, to my knowledge. The other was better built, and of some substance, but a nasty, slouchy-looking sort of cur, with high fur collars and a long grey cloak. And that was the one called Hippolyte, who knows all about our Government. And just the sort of fellow who would do so in these days, when no honest man knows what they are up to."

"That is true," said the Rector—"too true by half. But honest men soon will have their turn, if that vile spy was well informed. The astonishing thing is that England ever puts up with such shameful anarchy. What has been done to defend us? Nothing, except your battery, without a pinch of powder! With Pitt at the helm, would that have happened? How could we have slept in our beds, if we had known it? Fourteen guns, and not a pinch of powder!"

"But you used to sleep well enough before a gun was put there." Mrs. Stubbard's right to spare nobody was well established by this time. "Better have the guns, though they could not be fired, than no guns at all, if they would frighten the enemy."

"That is true, ma'am," replied Mr. Twemlow; "but until the guns came, we had no sense of our danger. Having taught us that, they were bound to act up to their teaching. It is not for ourselves that I have any fear. We have long since learned to rest with perfect faith in the Hand that overruleth all. And more than that—if there should be a disturbance, my nephew and my godson Joshua has a house of fourteen rooms in a Wiltshire valley, quite out of the track of invaders. He would have to fight, for he is Captain in the Yeomanry; and we would keep house for him till all was over. So that it is for my parish I fear, for my people, my schools, and my church, ma'am."

"Needn't be afraid, sir; no call to run away," cried the Captain of the battery, having now well manned his own portholes with the Rector's sound wine; "we shall have our powder in to-morrow, and the French can't come to-night; there is too much moon. They never dare show their noses nor'ard of their sands, with the man in the moon—the John Bull in the moon—looking at them. And more than that, why, that cursed Boney—"

"Adam, in Mr. Twemlow's house! You must please to excuse him, all good people. He has sate such a long time, without saying what he likes."

"Jemima, I have used the right word. The parson will back me up in every letter of it, having said the same thing of him, last Sunday week. But I beg Mrs. Twemlow's pardon, if I said it loud enough to disturb her. Well, then, this blessed Boney, if you prefer it, is a deal too full of his own dirty tricks for mounting the throne of the King they murdered, to get into a flat-bottomed boat at Boulogne, and a long sight too jealous a villain he is, to let any one command instead of him. Why, the man who set foot upon our shore, and beat us—if such a thing can be supposed—would be ten times bigger than Boney in a month, and would sit upon his crown, if he gets one."

"Well, I don't believe they will ever come at all," the solid Mrs. Stubbard pronounced, with decision. "I believe it is all a sham, and what they want is to keep us from attacking them in France. However, it is a good thing on the whole, and enables poor Officers, who have fought well for their country, to keep out of the Workhouse with their families."

"Hearken, hearken to Mrs. Stubbard!" the veteran cried, as he patted his waistcoat—a better one than he could have worn, and a larger one than he could have wanted, except for the promised invasion. "I will back my wife against any lady in the land for common-sense, and for putting it plainly. I am not ashamed to say thank God for the existence of that blessed Boney. All I hope is that he will only try to land at Springhaven—I mean, of course, when I've got my powder."

"Keep it dry, Captain," said the Rector, in good spirits. "Your confidence makes us comfortable; and of course you would draw all their fire from the village, and the houses standing near it, as this does. However, I pray earnestly every night that they may attempt it in some other parish. But what was it you heard that Frenchman say about two or three hundred barrels of powder almost within three miles of us? Suppose it was to blow up, where should we be?"

"Oh, I don't believe a word of that. It must be brag and nonsense. To begin with, there is no place where they could store it. I know all the neighbourhood, and every house in it. And there are no caves on this coast in the cliff, or holes of that kind such as smugglers use. However, I shall think it my duty to get a search-order from Admiral Darling, and inspect large farm-buildings, such as Farmer Graves has got, and another man the other side of Pebbleridge. Those are the only places that could accommodate large stores of ammunition. Why, we can take only forty barrels in the fire-proof magazine we have built. We all know what liars those Frenchmen are. I have no more faith in the 200 barrels of powder than I have in the 2000 ships prepared on the opposite coast to demolish us."

"Well, I hope you are right," Mr. Twemlow answered. "It does seem a very unlikely tale. But the ladies are gone. Let us have a quiet pipe. A man who works as hard as you and I do is entitled to a little repose now and then."

CHAPTER XLII

ANSWERING THE QUESTION

If Scudamore had not seen Dan Tugwell on board of the London Trader, and heard from his own lips that he was one of her crew, it is certain that he would have made a strict search of her hold, according to his orders in suspicious cases. And if he had done this, it is probable that he never would have set his nimble feet on deck again, for Perkins (the American who passed as Sam Polwhele) had a heavy ship-pistol in his great rough pocket, ready for the back of the young officer's head if he had probed below the cheeses and firkins of butter. Only two men had followed the lieutenant from their boat, the rest being needed for her safety in the strong sea running, and those two at the signal would have been flung overboard, and the schooner (put about for the mouth of the Canche, where heavy batteries were mounted) would have had a fair chance of escape, with a good start, while the gun-brig was picking up her boat. Unless, indeed, a shot from the Delia should carry away an important spar, which was not very likely at night, and with a quick surf to baffle gunnery. However, none of these things came to pass, and so the chances require no measurement.

Carne landed his freight with his usual luck, and resolved very wisely to leave off that dangerous work until further urgency. He had now a very fine stock of military stores for the ruin of his native land, and especially of gunpowder, which the gallant Frenchmen were afraid of stowing largely in their flat-bottomed craft. And knowing that he owed his success to moderation, and the good-will of his neighbours towards evasion of the Revenue, he thought it much better to arrange his magazine than to add to it for a month or two.

Moreover, he was vexed at the neglect of his advice, on the part of his arrogant Commander, a man who was never known to take advice from any mind external to his own body, and not even from that clear power sometimes, when his passionate heart got the uppermost. Carne, though of infinitely smaller mind, had one great advantage—he seldom allowed it to be curdled or crossed in its clear operations by turbulent bodily elements. And now, when he heard from the light-hearted Charron, who had lately been at work in London, that the only man they feared was about to take the lead once more against the enemies of Great Britain, Caryl Carne grew bitter against his Chief, and began for the first time to doubt his success.

"I have a great mind to go to Mr. Pitt myself, tell him everything, and throw myself upon his generosity," he thought, as he sate among his ruins sadly. "I could not be brought to trial as a common traitor. Although by accident of birth I am an Englishman, I am a French officer, and within my duty in acting as a pioneer for the French army. But then, again, they would call me at the best a spy, and in that capacity outside the rules of war. It is a toss-up how they might take it, and the result would depend perhaps on popular clamour. The mighty Emperor has snubbed me. He is not a gentleman. He has not even invited me to Paris, to share in the festivities and honours he proclaims. I would risk it, for I believe it is the safer game, except for two obstacles, and both of those are women. Matters are growing very ticklish now. That old bat of a Stubbard has got scent of a rat, and is hunting about the farm-houses. It would be bad for him if he came prowling here; that step for inspectors is well contrived. Twenty feet fall on his head for my friend; even his bull-neck would get the worst of that. And then, again, there is that wretch of a Cheeseman, who could not even hang himself effectually. If it were not for Polly, we would pretty soon enable him, as the Emperor enabled poor Pichegru. And after his own bona fide effort, who would be surprised to find him sus. per coll.? But Polly is a nice girl, though becoming too affectionate. And jealous—good lack! a grocer's daughter jealous, and a Carne compelled to humour her! What idiots women are in the hands of a strong man! Only my mother—my mother was not; or else my father was a weak one; which I can well believe from my own remembrance of him. Well, one point at least shall be settled to-morrow."

It was early in May, 1804, and Napoleon having made away to the best of his ability—which in that way was pre-eminent—with all possible rivals and probable foes, was receiving addresses, and appointing dummies, and establishing foolscap guarantees against his poor fallible and flexible self—as he had the effrontery to call it—with all the gravity, grand benevolence, confidence in mankind (as fools), immensity of yearning for universal good, and intensity of planning for his own, which have hoodwinked the zanies in every age, and never more than in the present age and country. And if France licked the dust, she could plead more than we can—it had not been cast off from her enemy's shoes.

Carne's love of liberty, like that of most people who talk very largely about it, was about as deep as beauty is declared to be; or even less than that, for he would not have imperilled the gloss of his epiderm for the fair goddess. So that it irked him very little that his Chief had smashed up the Republic, but very greatly that his own hand should be out in the cold, and have nothing put inside it to restore its circulation. "If I had stuck to my proper line of work, in the Artillery, which has made his fortune"—he could not help saying to himself sometimes—"instead of losing more than a year over here, and perhaps another year to follow, and all for the sake of these dirty old ruins, and my mother's revenge upon this country, I might have been a General by this time almost—for nothing depends upon age in France—and worthy to claim something lofty and grand, or else to be bought off at a truly high figure. The little gunner has made a great mistake if he thinks that his flat thumb of low breed can press me down shuddering, and starving, and crouching, just until it suits him to hold up a finger for me. My true course is now to consider myself, to watch events, and act accordingly. My honour is free to go either way, because he has not kept his word with me; he promised to act upon my advice, and to land within a twelvemonth."

There was some truth in this, for Napoleon had promised that his agent's perilous commission in England should be discharged within a twelvemonth, and that time had elapsed without any renewal. But Carne was clear-minded enough to know that he was bound in honour to give fair notice, before throwing up the engagement; and that even then it would be darkest dishonour to betray his confidence. He had his own sense of honour still, though warped by the underhand work he had stooped to; and even while he reasoned with himself so basely, he felt that he could not do the things he threatened.

To a resolute man it is a misery to waver, as even the most resolute must do sometimes; for instance, the mighty Napoleon himself. That great man felt the misery so keenly, and grew so angry with himself for letting in the mental pain, that he walked about vehemently, as a horse is walked when cold water upon a hot stomach has made colic—only there was nobody to hit him in the ribs, as the groom serves the nobler animal. Carne did not stride about in that style, to cast his wrath out of his toes, because his body never tingled with the sting-nettling of his mind—as it is bound to do with all correct Frenchmen— and his legs being long, he might have fallen down a hole into ancestral vaults before he knew what he was up to. Being as he was, he sate still, and thought it out, and resolved to play his own game for a while, as his master was playing for himself in Paris.

The next day he reappeared at his seaside lodgings, looking as comely and stately as of old; and the kind Widow Shanks was so glad to see him that he felt a rare emotion—good-will towards her; as the hardest man must do sometimes, especially if others have been hard upon him. He even chucked little Susy under the chin, which amazed her so much that she stroked her face, to make sure of its being her own, and ran away to tell her mother that the gentleman was come home so nice. Then he ordered a special repast from John Prater's—for John, on the strength of all his winter dinners, had now painted on his sign-board "Universal Victualler," caring not a fig for the offence to Cheeseman, who never came now to have a glass with him, and had spoiled all the appetite inspired by his windows through the dismal suggestions of his rash act on the premises. Instead of flattening their noses and opening their mouths, and exclaiming, "Oh, shouldn't I like a bit of that?" the children, if they ventured to peep in at all, now did it with an anxious hope of horrors, and a stealthy glance between the hams and bacon for something that might be hanging up among the candles. And the worst of it was that the wisest man in the village had failed to ascertain as yet "the reason why 'a doed it." Until that was known, the most charitable neighbours could have no hope of forgiving him.

Miss Dolly Darling had not seen her hero of romance for a long time; but something told her—or perhaps somebody—that he was now at hand; and to make sure about it, she resolved to have a walk. Faith was very busy, as the lady of the house, in preparing for a visitor, the mother of Blyth Scudamore, whom she, with her usual kindness, intended to meet and bring back from the coach-road that evening; for no less than three coaches a day passed now within eight miles of Springhaven, and several of the natives had seen them. Dolly was not to go in the carriage, because nobody knew how many boxes the visitor might bring, inasmuch as she was to stop ever so long. "I am tired of all this fuss," cried Dolly; "one would think Queen Charlotte was coming, at the least; and I dare say nearly all her luggage would go into the door-pocket. They are dreadfully poor; and it serves them right, for being so dreadfully honest."

"If you ever fall into poverty," said Faith, "it will not be from that cause. When you get your money, you don't pay your debts. You think that people should be proud to work for you for nothing. There is one house I am quite ashamed to pass by with you. How long have you owed poor Shoemaker Stickfast fifteen shillings and sixpence? And you take advantage of him, because he dare not send it in to father."

"Fashionable ladies never pay their debts," Dolly answered, as she spun round on one light heel, to float out a new petticoat that she was very proud of; "this isn't paid for, nor this, nor this; and you with your slow head have no idea how it adds to the interest they possess. If I am not allowed to have a bit of fashion in my dress, I can be in the fashion by not paying for it."

"It is a most happy thing for you, dear child, that you are kept under some little control. What you would do, I have not the least idea, if you were not afraid of dear father, as you are. The worst of it is that he is never here now for as much as two days together. And then he is so glad to see us that he cannot attend to our discipline or take notice of our dresses."

"Ha! you have inspired me!" exclaimed Dolly, who rejoiced in teasing

Faith. "The suggestion is yours, and I will act upon it. From the village of Brighthelmstone, which is growing very fine, I will procure upon the strictest credit a new Classic dress, with all tackle complete—as dear father so well expresses it—and then I will promenade me on the beach, with Charles in best livery and a big stick behind me. How then will Springhaven rejoice, and every one that hath eyes clap a spy-glass to them! And what will old Twemlow say, and that frump of an Eliza, who condescends to give me little hints sometimes about tightening up SO, perhaps, and letting out so, and permitting a little air to come in HERE—"

"Do be off, you wicked little animal!" cried Faith, who in spite of herself could not help laughing, so well was Dolly mimicking Eliza Twemlow's voice, and manner, and attitude, and even her figure, less fitted by nature for the Classic attire; "you are wasting all my time, and doing worse with your own. Be off, or I'll take a stick to 'e, as old Daddy Stakes says to the boys."

Taking advantage of this state of things, the younger Miss Darling set forth by herself to dwell upon the beauty of the calm May sea, and her own pretty figure glassed in tidal pools. She knew that she would show to the utmost of her gifts, with her bright complexion softly gleaming in the sun, and dark gray eyes through their deep fringe receiving and returning tenfold the limpid glimmer of the shore. And she felt that the spring of the year was with her, the bound of old Time that renews his youth and powers of going at any pace; when the desire of the young is to ride him at full gallop, and the pleasure of the old is to stroke his nose and think.

Dolly, with everything in her favour, youth and beauty, the time of year, the time of day, and the power of the place, as well as her own wish to look lovely, and to be loved beyond reason, nevertheless came along very strictly, and kept herself most careful not to look about at all. At any rate, not towards the houses, where people live, and therefore must look out. At the breadth of sea, with distant ships jotted against the sky like chips, or dotted with boats like bits of stick; also at the playing of the little waves that ran at the bottom of the sands, just now, after one another with a lively turn, and then jostled into white confusion, like a flock of sheep huddled up and hurrying from a dog—at these and at the warm clouds loitering in the sun she might use her bright eyes without prejudice. But soon she had to turn them upon a nearer object.

"How absorbed we are in distant contemplation! A happy sign, I hope, in these turbulent times. Miss Darling, will you condescend to include me in your view?"

"I only understand simple English," answered Dolly. "Most of the other comes from France, perhaps. We believed that you were gone abroad again."

"I wish that the subject had more interest for you," Carne answered, with his keen eyes fixed on hers, in the manner that half angered and half conquered her. "My time is not like that of happy young ladies, with the world at their feet, and their chief business in it, to discover some new amusement."

"You are not at all polite. But you never were that, in spite of your French education."

"Ah, there it is again! You are so accustomed to the flattery of great people that a simple-minded person like myself has not the smallest chance of pleasing you. Ah, well! It is my fate, and I must yield to it."

"Not at all," replied Dolly, who could never see the beauty of that kind of resignation, even in the case of Dan Tugwell. "There is no such thing as fate for a strong-willed man, though there may be for poor women."

"May I tell you my ideas about that matter? If so, come and rest for a moment in a quiet little shelter where the wind is not so cold. For there is no such thing as Spring in England."

Dolly hesitated, and with the proverbial result. To prove himself more polite than she supposed, Caryl Carne, hat in hand and with low bows preserving a respectful distance, conducted her to a little place of shelter, so pretty and humble and secluded by its own want of art, and simplicity of skill, that she was equally pleased and surprised with it.

"Why, it is quite a little bower!" she exclaimed; "as pretty a little nest as any bird could wish for. And what a lovely view towards the west and beyond Pebbleridge! One could sit here forever and see the sun set. But I must have passed it fifty times without the least suspicion of it. How on earth have you managed to conceal it so? That is to say, if it is your doing. Surely the children must have found it out, because they go everywhere."

"One brat did. But I gave him such a scare that he never stopped roaring till next Sunday, and it frightened all the rest from looking round that corner. If any other comes, I shall pitch-plaster him, for I could not endure that noise again. But you see, at a glance, why you have failed to see it, as we always do with our little oversights, when humbly pointed out to us. It is the colour of the ground and the background too, and the grayness of the scanty growth that hides it. Nobody finds it out by walking across it, because of this swampy place on your side, and the shoot of flints down from the cliff on the other, all sharp as a knife, and as rough as a saw. And nobody comes down to this end of the warren, neither is it seen from the battery on the hill. Only from the back is it likely to be invaded, and there is nothing to make people look, or come, up here. So you have me altogether at your mercy, Miss Darling."

Dolly thought within herself that it was much the other way, but could not well express her thoughts to that effect. And being of a brisk and versatile— not to say volatile—order, she went astray into a course of wonder concerning the pretty little structure she beheld. Structure was not the proper word for it at all; for it seemed to have grown from the nature around, with a little aid of human hands to guide it. Branches of sea-willow radiant with spring, and supple sprays of tamarisk recovering from the winter, were lightly inwoven and arched together, with the soft compliance of reed and rush from the marsh close by, and the stout assistance of hazel rods from the westward cliff. The back was afforded by a grassy hillock, with a tuft or two of brake-fern throwing up their bronzy crockets among the sprayed russet of last year's pride. And beneath them a ledge of firm turf afforded as fair a seat as even two sweet lovers need desire.

"How clever he is, and how full of fine taste!" thought the simple-minded Dolly; "and all this time I have been taking him for a gloomy, hard-hearted, unnatural man. Blyth Scudamore never could have made this lovely bower."

In this conclusion she was altogether wrong. Scudamore could have made it, and would have made it gladly, with bright love to help him. But Carne never could, and would have scorned the pleasant task. It was Charron, the lively Frenchman, who, with the aid of old Jerry, had achieved this pretty feat, working to relieve his dull detention, with a Frenchman's playful industry and tasteful joy in nature. But Carne was not likely to forego this credit.

"I think I have done it pretty well," he said, in reply to her smile of admiration; "with such scanty materials, I mean, of course. And I shall think I have done it very well indeed, if you say that you like it, and crown it with new glory by sitting for a moment in its unpretentious shade. If your brother comes down, as I hope he will, next week, I shall beg him to come and write a poem here. The place is fitter for a poet than a prosy vagabond like me."

"It is very hard that you should be a—a wanderer, I mean," Dolly answered, looking at him with a sweet thrill of pity; "you have done nothing to deserve it. How unfairly fortune has always treated you!"

"Fortune could make me a thousand times more than the just compensation even now, if she would. Such a glorious return for all my bitter losses and outcast condition, that I should—but it is useless to think of such things, in my low state. The fates have been hard with me, but never shall they boast that they drove me from my pure sense of honour. Oh yes, it is damp. But let me cure it thus."

For Dolly, growing anxious about his meaning, yet ready to think about another proposal, was desirous to sit down on the sweet ledge of grass, yet uneasy about her pale blue sarsenet, and uncertain that she had not seen something of a little sea-snail (living in a yellow house, dadoed with red), whom to crush would be a cruel act to her dainty fabric. But if he was there, he was sat upon unavenged; for Carne, pulling off his light buff cloak, flung it on the seat; after which the young lady could scarcely be rude enough not to sit.

"Oh, I am so sorry now! Perhaps it will be spoiled," she said; "for you say that the fates are against you always. And I am sure that they always combine against me, when I wear anything of that colour."

"I am going the wrong way to work," thought Carne. "What a little vixen it is; but what a beauty!" For his love for her was chiefly a man's admiration. And bodily she looked worthy now of all that could be done in that way, with the light flowing in through the budded arch and flashing upon the sweet flush of her cheeks. Carne gazed at her without a word or thought, simply admiring, as he never had admired anything, except himself, till now. Then she felt all the meaning of his gaze, and turned away.

"But you must look at me and tell me something," he said, in a low voice, and taking both her hands; "you shall tell me what my fate must be. Whether you can ever come to love me, as I have loved you, long and long."

"You have no right to speak to me like that," she answered, still avoiding his eyes, and striving to show proper anger; "no gentleman would think of taking advantage of a lady so."

"I care not what is right or wrong. Look up, and tell me that you hate me. Dolly, I suppose you do."

"Then you are quite wrong"—she gave him one bright glance of contradiction; "no. I have always been so sorry for you, and for all your troubles. You must not ask me to say more."

"But I must; I must. That is the very thing that I must do. Only say that you love me, Dolly. Dolly darling, tell me that. Or let your lovely eyes say it for you."

"My lovely eyes must not tell stories"—they were gazing softly at him now —"and I don't think I can say it—yet."

"But you will—you shall!" he exclaimed, with passion growing as he drew her near; "you shall not slip from me, you shall not stir, until you have answered me one question—is there anybody else, my Dolly?"

"You frighten me. You forget who I am. Of course there are a great many else, as you call it; and I am not to be called, for a moment, YOUR DOLLY."

"No, not for a moment, but forever." Carne was accustomed to the ways of girls, and read all their words by the light of their eyes. "Your little heart begins to know who loves it better than all the world put together. And for that reason I will leave you now. Farewell, my darling; I conquer myself, for the sake of what is worth a thousand of it."

Dolly was in very sad confusion, and scarcely knew what she might do next—that is to say, if he still went on. Pleasant conceit and bright coquetry ill supply the place of honest pride and gentle self-respect, such as Faith was blest with. Carne might have kissed Dolly a hundred times, without much resistance, for his stronger will had mastered hers; but she would have hated him afterwards. He did not kiss her once; and she almost wished that he had offered one—one little tribute of affection (as the Valentines express it)—as soon as he was gone, and the crisis of not knowing what to do was past. "I should have let him—I believe I should," she reflected, sagely recovering herself; "but how glad I ought to be that he didn't! And I do hope he won't come back again. The next time I meet him, I shall sink into the earth."

For her hat had fallen off, and her hair was out of order, and she saw two crinkles near the buckle of her waist; and she had not so much as a looking-glass to be sure that she looked nice again. With a heavy sigh for all these woes, she gathered a flossy bud of willow, and fixed it on her breast-knot, to defy the world; and then, without heed of the sea, sun, or sands, went home with short breath, and quick blushes, and some wonder; for no man's arm, except her father's, had ever been round her waist till now.

CHAPTER XLIII

LITTLE AND GREAT PEOPLE

If ever a wise man departed from wisdom, or a sober place from sobriety, the man was John Prater, and the place Springhaven, towards the middle of June, 1804. There had been some sharp rumours of great things before; but the best people, having been misled so often, shook their heads without produce of their contents; until Captain Stubbard came out in his shirt sleeves one bright summer morning at half past nine, with a large printed paper in one hand and a slop basin full of hot paste in the other. His second boy, George, in the absence of Bob (who was now drawing rations at Woolwich), followed, with a green baize apron on, and carrying a hearth-brush tied round with a string to keep the hair stiff.

"Lay it on thick on the shutter, my son. Never mind about any other notices, except the one about young men wanted. No hurry; keep your elbow up; only don't dab my breeches, nor the shirt you had on Sunday."

By this time there were half a dozen people waiting; for this shutter of Widow Shanks was now accepted as the central board and official panel of all public business and authorised intelligence. Not only because all Royal Proclamations, Offers of reward, and Issues of menace were posted on that shutter and the one beyond the window (which served as a postscript and glossary to it), but also inasmuch as the kind-hearted Captain, beginning now to understand the natives—which was not to be done pugnaciously, as he had first attempted it, neither by any show of interest in them (than which they detested nothing more), but by taking them coolly, as they took themselves, and gradually sliding, without any thought about it, into the wholesome contagion of their minds, and the divine gift of taking things easily—our Captain Stubbard may be fairly now declared to have made himself almost as good as a native, by the way in which he ministered to their content.

For nothing delighted them more than to hear of great wonders going on in other places—of battles, plague, pestilence, famine, and fire; of people whose wives ran away with other people, or highwaymen stopping the coach of a bishop. Being full of good-nature, they enjoyed these things, because of the fine sympathies called out to their own credit, and the sense of pious gratitude aroused towards Heaven, that they never permitted such things among them. Perceiving this genial desire of theirs, the stout Captain of the Foxhill battery was kind enough to meet it with worthy subjects. Receiving officially a London newspaper almost every other day, as soon as it had trodden the round of his friends, his regular practice was to cut out all the pieces of lofty public interest—the first-rate murders, the exploits of highwaymen, the episodes of high life, the gallant executions, the embezzlements of demagogues, in a word, whatever quiet people find a fond delight in ruminating—and these he pasted (sometimes upside down) upon his shutter. Springhaven had a good deal of education, and enjoyed most of all what was hardest to read.

But this great piece of news, that should smother all the rest, seemed now to take a terrible time in coming. All the gaffers were waiting who had waited to see the result of Mr. Cheeseman's suicide, and their patience was less on this occasion. At length the great Captain unfolded his broad sheet, but even then held it upside down for a minute. It was below their dignity to do anything but grunt, put their specs on their noses, and lean chin upon staff. They deserved to be rewarded, and so they were.

For this grand poster, which overlapped the shutters, was a Royal Proclamation, all printed in red ink, announcing that His Majesty King George the 3rd would on the 25th of June then ensuing hold a grand review upon Shotbury Down of all the Volunteer forces and Reserve, mounted, footmen, or artillery, of the four counties forming the Southeast Division, to wit, Surrey, Kent, Sussex, and Hants. Certain regiments of the line would be appointed to act with them; and officers in command were ordered to report at once, &c., &c. God save the King.

If Shotbury Down had been ten miles off, Springhaven would have thought very little of the matter; for no one would walk ten miles inland to see all the sojers that ever were shot, or even the "King and Queen, and their fifteen little ones." Most of the little ones were very large now; but the village had seen them in a travelling show, and expected them to continue like it. But Shotbury Down was only three miles inland; and the people (who thought nothing of twenty miles along the coast) resolved to face a league of perils of the solid earth, because if they only turned round upon their trudge, they could see where they lived from every corner of the road. They always did all things with one accord; the fishing fleet all should stand still on the sand, and the houses should have to keep house for themselves. That is to say, perhaps, all except one.

"Do as you like," said Mrs. Tugwell to her husband; "nothing as you do makes much differ to me now. If you feel you can be happy with them thousands of young men, and me without one left fit to lift a big crock, go your way, Zeb; but you don't catch me going, with the tears coming into my eyes every time I see a young man to remind me of Dan—though there won't be one there fit to stand at his side. And him perhaps fighting against his own

King now!"

"Whatever hath coom to Dannel is all along of your own fault, I tell 'e." Captain Tugwell had scarcely enjoyed a long pipe since the night when he discharged his paternal duty, with so much vigour, and such sad results. Not that he felt any qualms of conscience, though his heart was sometimes heavy, but because his good wife was a good wife no longer, in the important sphere of the pan, pot, and kettle, or even in listening to his adventures with the proper exclamations in the proper places. And not only she, but all his children, from Timothy down to Solomon, instead of a pleasant chatter around him, and little attentions, and a smile to catch a smile, seemed now to shrink from him, and hold whispers in a corner, and watch him with timid eyes, and wonder how soon their own time would come to be lashed and turned away. And as for the women, whether up or down the road—but as he would not admit, even to himself, that he cared twopence what they thought, it is useless to give voice to their opinions, which they did quite sufficiently. Zebedee Tugwell felt sure that he had done the right thing, and therefore admired himself, but would have enjoyed himself more if he had done the wrong one.

"What fault of mine, or of his, poor lamb?" Mrs. Tugwell asked, with some irony. She knew that her husband could never dare to go to see the King without her—for no married man in the place would venture to look at him twice if he did such a thing—and she had made up her own mind to go from the first; but still, he should humble himself before she did it. "Was it I as colted him? Or was it him as gashed himself, like the prophets of Baal, when 'a was gone hunting?"

"No; but you cockered him up, the same as was done to they, by the wicked king, and his wife—the worst woman as ever lived. If they hadn't gashed theirselves, I reckon, the true man of God would 'a done it for them, the same as he cut their throats into the brook Kishon. Solomon was the wisest man as ever lived, and Job the most patient—the same as I be—and Elijah, the Tishbite, the most justest."

"You better finish up with all the Psalms of David, and the Holy Children, and the Burial Service. No more call for Parson Twemlow, or the new Churchwarden come in place of Cheeseman, because 'a tried to hang his self. Zebedee Tugwell in the pulpit! Zebedee, come round with the plate! Parson Tugwell, if you please, a-reading out the ten commandments! But 'un ought to leave out the sixth, for fear of spoiling 's own dinner afterwards; and the seventh, if 'a hopes to go to see King George the third, with another man's woman to his elbow!"

"When you begins to go on like that," Captain Tugwell replied, with some dignity, "the only thing as a quiet man can do is to go out of houze, and have a half-pint of small ale." He put his hat on his head and went to do it.

Notwithstanding all this and much more, when the great day came for the Grand Review, very few people saw more of the King, or entered more kindly into all his thoughts—or rather the thoughts that they made him think—than Zebedee Tugwell and his wife Kezia. The place being so near home, and the smoke of their own chimneys and masts of their smack as good as in sight—if you knew where to look—it was natural for them to regard the King as a stranger requiring to be taught about their place. This sense of proprietary right is strong in dogs and birds and cows and rabbits, and everything that acts by nature's laws. When a dog sits in front of his kennel, fast chained, every stranger dog that comes in at the gate confesses that the premises are his, and all the treasures they contain; and if he hunts about—which he is like enough to do, unless full of self-respect and fresh victuals—for any bones invested in the earth to ripen, by the vested owner, he does it with a low tail and many pricks of conscience, perhaps hoping in his heart that he may discover nothing to tempt him into breach of self-respect. But now men are ordered, in this matter, to be of lower principle than their dogs.

King George the third, who hated pomp and show, and had in his blood the old German sense of patriarchal kingship, would have enjoyed a good talk with Zebedee and his wife Kezia, if he had met them on the downs alone; but, alas, he was surrounded with great people, and obliged to restrict himself to the upper order, with whom he had less sympathy. Zebedee, perceiving this, made all allowance for him, and bought a new Sunday hat the very next day, for fear of wearing out the one he had taken off to His Majesty, when His Majesty looked at him, and Her Majesty as well, and they manifestly said to one another, what a very fine subject they had found. Such was loyalty—aye, and royalty—in those times that we despise.

But larger events demand our heed. There were forty thousand gallant fellows, from the age of fifteen upwards, doing their best to look like soldiers, and some almost succeeding. True it is that their legs and arms were not all of one pattern, nor their hats put on their heads alike—any more than the heads on their shoulders were—neither did they swing together, as they would have done to a good swathe of grass; but for all that, and making due allowance for the necessity they were under of staring incessantly at the King, any man who understood them would have praised them wonderfully. And they went about in such wide formation, and occupied so much of their native land, that the best-drilled regiment Napoleon possessed would have looked quite small among them.

"They understand furze," said a fine young officer of the staff, who had ridden up to Admiral Darling's carriage and saluted three ladies who kept watch there. "I doubt whether many of the Regular forces would have got through that brake half so well; certainly not without double gaiters. If the French ever land, we must endeavour to draw them into furzy ground, and then set the Volunteers at them. No Frenchman can do much with prickles in his legs."

Lady Scudamore smiled, for she was thinking of her son, who would have jumped over any furze-bush there—and the fir-trees too, according to her conviction; Dolly also showed her very beautiful teeth; but Faith looked at him gratefully.

"It is very kind of you, Lord Dashville, to say the best of us that you can find to say. But I fear that you are laughing to yourself. You know how well they mean; but you think they cannot do much."

"No, that is not what I think at all. So far as I can judge, which is not much, I believe that they would be of the greatest service, if the Country should unfortunately need them. Man for man, they are as brave as trained troops, and many of them can shoot better. I don't mean to say that they are fit to meet a French army in the open; but for acting on their flanks, or rear, or in a wooded country—However, I have no right to venture an opinion, having never seen active service."

Miss Darling looked at him with some surprise, and much approval of his modesty. So strongly did most of the young officers who came to her father's house lay down the law, and criticise even Napoleon's tactics.

"How beautiful Springhaven must be looking now!" he said, after Dolly had offered her opinion, which she seldom long withheld. "The cottages must be quite covered with roses, whenever they are not too near the sea; and the trees at their best, full of leaves and blossoms, by the side of the brook that feeds them. All the rest of the coast is so hard and barren, and covered with chalk instead of grass, and the shore so straight and staring. But I have never been there at this time of year. How much you must enjoy it! Surely we ought to be able to see it, from this high ground somewhere."

"Yes, if you will ride to that shattered tree," said Faith, "you will have a very fine view of all the valley. You can see round the corner of Foxhill there, which shuts out most of it just here. I think you have met our Captain Stubbard."

"Ah, I must not go now; I may be wanted at any moment"—Lord Dashville had very fine taste, but it was not the inanimate beauties of Springhaven that he cared a dash for—"and I fear that I could never see the roses there. I think there is nothing in all nature to compare with a rose—except one thing."

Faith had a lovely moss-rose in her hat—a rose just peeping through its lattice at mankind, before it should open and blush at them—and she knew what it was that he admired more than the sweetest rose that ever gemmed itself with dew. Lord Dashville had loved her, as she was frightened to remember, for more than a year, because he could not help it, being a young man of great common-sense, as well as fine taste, and some knowledge of the world. "He knows to which side his bread will be buttered," Mr. Swipes had remarked, as a keen observer. "If 'a can only get Miss Faith, his bread 'll be buttered to both sides for life—his self to one side, and her to do the tother. The same as I told Mother Cloam—a man that knoweth his duty to head gardeners, as his noble lordship doth, the same know the differ atwixt Miss Faith—as fine a young 'ooman as ever looked into a pink—and that blow-away froth of a thing, Miss Dolly."

This fine young woman, to use the words of Mr. Swipes, coloured softly, at his noble lordship's gaze, to the tint of the rose-bud in her hat; and then spoke coldly to countervail her blush.

"There is evidently something to be done directly. All the people are moving towards the middle of the down. We must not be so selfish as to keep you here, Lord Dashville."

"Why, don't you see what it is?" exclaimed Miss Dolly, hotly resenting the part of second fiddle; "they are going to have the grand march-past. These affairs always conclude with that. And we are in the worst part of the whole down for seeing it. Lord Dashville will tell us where we ought to go."

"You had better not attempt to move now," he answered, smiling as he always smiled at Dolly, as if she were a charming but impatient child; "you might cause some confusion, and perhaps see nothing. And now I must discharge my commission, which I am quite ashamed of having left so long. His Majesty hopes, when the march-past is over, to receive a march-up of fair ladies. He has a most wonderful memory, as you know, and his nature is the kindest of the kind. As soon as he heard that Lady Scudamore was here, and Admiral Darling's daughters with her, he said: 'Bring them all to me, every one of them; young Scudamore has done good work, good work. And I want to congratulate his mother about him. And Darling's daughters, I must see them. Why, we owe the security of the coast to him.' And so, if you please, ladies, be quite ready, and allow me the honour of conducting you."

With a low bow, he set off about his business, leaving the ladies in a state of sweet disturbance. Blyth Scudamore's mother wept a little, for ancient troubles and present pleasure. Lord Dashville could not repeat before her all that the blunt old King had said: "Monstrous ill-treated woman, shameful, left without a penny, after all her poor husband did for me and the children! Not my fault a bit—fault of the Whigs—always stingy—said he made away with himself—bad example—don't believe a word of it; very cheerful man. Blown by now, at any rate—must see what can be done for her—obliged to go for governess—disgrace to the Crown!"

Faith, with her quiet self-respect, and the largeness learned from sorrow, was almost capable of not weeping that she had left at home her apple-green Poland mantlet and jockey bonnet of lilac satin checked with maroon. But Dolly had no such weight of by-gone sorrow to balance her present woe, and the things she had left at home were infinitely brighter than that dowdy Faith's.

"Is there time to drive back? Is there time to drive home? The King knows father, and he will be astonished to see a pair of frumps, and he won't understand one bit about the dust, or the sun that takes the colour out. He will think we have got all our best things on. Oh, Lady Scudamore, how could you do it? You told us to put on quite plain things, because of the dust, and the sun, and all that; and it might come to rain, you said—as if it was likely, when the King was on the hill! And with all your experience of the King and Queen, that you told us about last evening, you must have known that they would send for us. Gregory, how long would it take you to go home, at full gallop, allow us half an hour in the house, and be back here again, when all these people are gone by?"

"Well, miss, there be a steepish bit of road, and a many ockard cornders; I should say 'a might do it in two hours and a half, with a fresh pair of nags put in while you ladies be a-cleaning of yourselves, miss. Leastways, if Hadmiral not object."

"Hadmiral, as you call him, would have nothing to do with it"—Dolly was always free-spoken with the servants, which made her very popular with some of them—"he has heavier duty than he can discharge. But two hours and a half is hopeless; we must even go as we are."

Coachman Gregory smiled in his sleeve. He knew that the Admiral had that day a duty far beyond his powers—to bring up his Sea-Fencibles to see the King—upon which they had insisted—and then to fetch them all back again, and send them on board of their several craft in a state of strict sobriety. And Gregory meant to bear a hand, and lift it pretty frequently towards the most loyal part of man, in the large festivities of that night. He smacked his lips at the thought of this, and gave a little flick to his horses.

After a long time, long enough for two fair drives to Springhaven and back, and when even the youngest were growing weary of glare, and dust, and clank, and din, and blare, and roar, and screeching music, Lord Dashville rode up through a cloud of roving chalk, and after a little talk with the ladies, ordered the coachman to follow him. Then stopping the carriage at a proper distance, he led the three ladies towards the King, who was thoroughly tired, and had forgotten all about them. His Majesty's sole desire was to get into his carriage and go to sleep; for he was threescore years and six of age, and his health not such as it used to be. Ever since twelve o'clock he had been sitting in a box made of feather-edged boards, which the newspapers called a pavilion, having two little curtains (both of which stuck fast) for his only defence against sun, noise, and dust. Moreover, his seat was a board full of knots, with a strip of thin velvet thrown over it; and Her Majesty sitting towards the other end (that the public might see between them), and weighing more than he did, every time she jumped up, he went down, and every time she plumped down, he went up. But he never complained, and only slowly got tired. "Thank God!" he said, gently, "it's all over now. My dear, you must be monstrous tired; and scarcely a bit to eat all day. But I locked some in the seat-box this morning—no trusting anybody but oneself. Let us get into the coach and have at them." "Ja, ja, meinherr," said the Queen.

"If it please your Majesties"—a clear voice entered between the bonnet-hoods of the curtains—"here are the ladies whose attendance I was ordered to require."

"Ladies!—what ladies?" asked King George, rubbing his eyes, and yawning. "Oh yes, to be sure! I mustn't get up so early to-morrow. Won't take a minute, my dear. Let them come. Not much time to spare."

But as soon as he saw Lady Scudamore, the King's good-nature overcame the weariness of the moment. He took her kindly by the hand, and looked at her face, which bore the mark of many heavy trials; and she, who had often seen him when the world was bright before her, could not smother one low sob, as she thought of all that had been since.

"Don't cry, don't cry, my dear," said the King, with his kind heart showing in his eyes; "we must bow to the will of the Lord, who gives sad trials to every one of us. We must think of the good, and not the evil. Bless me, keep your spirits up. Your son is doing very well indeed, very well indeed, from all I hear. Good chip of the old block, very good chip. Will cure my grandchildren, as soon as they want it; and nobody is ever in good health now."

"No, your Majesty, if you please, my son is in the Royal Navy, fighting for his Country and his King. And he has already captured—"

"Three French frigates. To be sure, I know. Better than curing three hundred people. Fine young officer—very fine young officer. Must come to

314

see me when he gets older. There, you are laughing! That's as it should be. Goodbye, young ladies. Forty miles to go tonight, and very rough roads— very rough indeed. Monstrous pretty girls! Uncommon glad that George wasn't here to see them. Better stay in the country—too good for London. Must be off; sha'n't have a bit o' sleep to-night, because of sleeping the whole way there, and then sure to be late in the morning, not a bit of breakfast till eight o'clock, and all the day thrown upside down! Darlings, Darlings—the right name for them! But they mustn't come to London. No, no, no. Too much wickedness there already. Very glad George wasn't here to-day!"

His Majesty was talking, as he always did, with the firm conviction that his words intended for the public ear would reach it, while those addressed, without change of tone, to himself, would be strictly private. But instead of offending any one, this on the whole gave great satisfaction, and impressed nine people out of ten with a strong and special regard for him, because almost every one supposed himself to be admitted at first sight to the inner confidence of the King. And to what could he attribute this? He would do his own merits great demerit unless he attributed it to them, and to the King an unusual share of sagacity in perceiving them.

CHAPTER XLIV

DOWN AMONG THE DEAD MEN

That grand review at Shotbury was declared by all who took part in it, or at all understood the subject, to have been a most remarkable and quite unparalleled success. Not only did it show what noble stuff there is in Englishmen, and how naturally they take to arms, but also it inspired with martial feeling and happy faith the wives and mothers of all the gallant warriors there. It would make the blood-stained despot cower upon his throne of murder, and teach him the madness of invading any land so fortified.

However, Napoleon failed to see the matter in that wholesome light, and smiled a grim and unkind smile as he read Caryl Carne's report of those "left-handed and uncouth manoeuvres." "One of your Majesty's feeblest regiments would send the whole of those louts to the devil; and I am bound to impress once more, with all deference to your infallible judgment, the vast importance of carrying out your grand designs at the first moment. All is prepared on my part. One day's notice is all I need."

So wrote Carne; and perhaps the truth, as usual, lay about half-way between the two opinions. Even Carne was not admitted to a perfect knowledge of his master's schemes. But to keep things moving and men alert, the Emperor came to the coast at once, busy as he was in Paris, and occupied for several weeks, with short intervals of absence, the house prepared for him near Boulogne, whence he watched and quickened the ripening of his mighty plans against us.

Now Carne himself, while working with new vigour and fresh enterprise, had a narrow escape from invasion. Captain Stubbard, stirred up now and again by Mr. Twemlow, had thoroughly searched all covered places, likely to harbour gunpowder, within at least six miles of his fort, that is to say, all likely places, save and except the right one. By doing this he had done for himself—as regards sweet hospitality—among all the leading farmers, maltsters, tanners, and millers for miles around. Even those whose premises were not entered, as if they had been Frenchmen, had a brother-in-law, or at least a cousin, whose wooden bars had been knocked up. And the most atrocious thing of all, if there could be anything worse than worst, was that the Captain dined one day, at a market-ordinary, with Farmer, or you might say Squire Hanger—for the best part of his land followed to him from his father—and had rum and water with him, and spoke his health, and tucked Mrs. Hanger up into the shay, and rode alongside to guarantee them; and then the next day, on the very same horse, up he comes at Hanger-dene, and overhauls every tub on the premises, with a parchment as big as a malt-shovel! Such a man was not fit to lay a knife and fork by.

Some sense of the harm he had done to himself, without a bit of good to any one, dwelt heavily in the Captain's mind, as he rode up slowly upon the most amiable of the battery-horses—for all sailors can ride, from long practice on the waves—and struck a stern stroke, with a stick like a linstock, upon the old shutter that served for a door and the front entrance to Carne Castle. There used to be a fine old piece of workmanship in solid and bold oak here, a door divided in the middle—else no man might swing it back—and even so pierced with a wicket, for small people to get through. That mighty door was not worn out, for it was not three hundred years old yet, and therefore scarcely in middle life; but the mortgagees who had sacked the place of all that was worth a sack to hold it, these had a very fine offer for that door, from a rich man come out of a dust-bin. And this was one of the many little things that made Caryl Carne unpleasant.

"I do not require production of your warrant. The whole place is open to your inspection," said Carne, who had long been prepared for this visit; "open to all the winds and rains, and the lower part sometimes filled with water. The upper rooms, or rather the few that remain of them, are scarcely safe for a person of any weight to walk in, but you are most welcome to try them, if you like; and this gentleman, I think, might not fall through. Here are my quarters; not quite so snug as my little room at the widow's; but I can offer you some bread and cheese, and a glass of country cider. The vaults or cellars have held good wine in their time, but only empty casks and broken bottles now."

Captain Stubbard had known for many years the silent woes of poverty, and now he observed with some good-will the young man's sad but haughty smile. Then he ordered his young subaltern, his battery-mate, as he called him, to ascend the broad crumbling staircase, and glance into the dismantled chambers, while himself with the third of the party—a trusty old gunner—should inspect the cellarage.

"We will not keep you long, sir," he said to Carne; "and if you are kind enough to show us the way, which is easily lost in a place of this kind, we shall be all the quicker. Wilkins, when you have done up there, wait here for us. Shall we want a light, sir?"

"In the winter, you could hardly do without one, but at this time of year, I think you may. At any rate I will bring a lantern, and we can light it if wanted. But the truth is that I know next to nothing of those sepulchral places. They would not be very tempting, even without a ghost, which they are said to have."

"A ghost!" cried the Captain; "I don't like that. Not that I have much faith in them; although one never can be sure. But at this time of day—What is it like?"

"I have never seen her, and am quite content without it. It is said to be an ancestress of mine, a Lady Cordelia Carne, who was murdered, when her husband was away, and buried down there, after being thrown into the moat. The old people say that whenever her ghost is walking, the water of the moat bursts in and covers the floor of the vaults, that she may flit along it, as she used to do. But of course one must not listen to that sort of fable."

"Perhaps you will go in front, sir, because you know the way. It is my duty to inspect these places; and I am devilish sorry for it; but my duty must be done."

"You shall see every hole and corner, including the stone that was put up to commemorate her murder and keep her quiet. But I should explain that these vaults extend for the entire length of the building, except just in the middle, where we now stand. For a few yards the centre of the building seems to have never been excavated, as to which you will convince yourself. You may call the cellars east and west, or right and left, or north and south, or uphill and downhill, or anything else, for really they are so much alike, and partitioned into cells so much alike, that I scarcely know which is which myself, coming suddenly from the daylight. But you understand those things much better. A sailor always knows his bearings. This leads to the entrance of one set."

Carne led the Captain and old Gunner Bob—as he was called in the battery —along a dark and narrow passage, whose mouth was browed with ivy. Half-way through, they found an archway on the right-hand side, opening at right angles into long and badly lighted vaults. In this arch there was no door; but a black step-ladder (made of oak, no doubt), very steep and rather rickety, was planted to tempt any venturesome foot.

"Are you sure this ladder is safe?"—the Captain was by no means in love with the look of it. "My weight has increased remarkably in the fine air of Springhaven. If the bottom is rotten, the top won't help us."

"Let me go first. It is my duty, as the owner; and I have no family dependent on me. My neck is of no value, compared to yours, Captain."

"How I have mistaken this young man!" thought the brave yet prudent Stubbard. "I called him a Frenchified fool, whereas he is a downright Englishman! I shall ask him to dinner next week, if Jemima can get a new leg for the dripping-pan."

Following warily, with Gunner Bob behind him, and not disdaining the strong arm of the owner, the Captain of Foxhill was landed in the vault, and being there, made a strict examination. He even poked his short sword into the bung-holes of three or four empty barrels, that Bob might be satisfied also in his conscience. "Matter of form," he said, "matter of form, sir, when we know who people are; but you might have to do it yourself, sir, if you were in the service of your King. You ought to be that, Mr. Carne; and it is not too late, in such days as these are, to begin. Take my advice—such a fine young man!"

"Alas, my dear sir, I cannot afford it. What officer can live upon his pay for a generation?"

"Gospel truth!" cried the Captain, warmly; "Gospel truth! and more than that—he must be the last of his generation, or else send his young 'uns to the workhouse. What things I could tell you, Mr. Carne! But here we are at the end of the vaults; all empty, as I can certify; and I hope, my dear sir, that you may live to see them filled with good wine, as they used to be."

"Thank you, but there is no hope of that. Shall we take the vaults of the other end next, or examine the chapel, and the outer buildings—outer ruins, I should say?"

"Oh, a little open air first, for goodness sake!" said the Captain, going heavily up the old steps; "I am pretty nearly choked with all this mildew. A little fresh air, before we undertake the other lot."

As soon as the echo of their steps was dead, Charron, old Jerry, and another man jumped down from a loop-hole into the vault they had left, piled up a hoarding at the entrance, and with a crowbar swung back a heavy oak hatch in the footings of the outer wall. A volume of water poured in from the moat, or rather from the stream which had once supplied it. Seeing this, they disappeared with a soft and pleasant chuckle.

The owner kept Stubbard such a time among the ruins, telling him some fine old legends, and otherwise leading him in and out, that when a bit of food and a glass of old Cognac was proposed by way of interlude, the Captain heartily embraced the offer. Then Carne conducted his three visitors, for Wilkins had now rejoined them, into a low room poorly furnished, and regaled them beyond his promise. "Rare stuff!" exclaimed Stubbard, with a wink at Carne. "Ah, I see that free-trade still exists. No concern of mine, except to enjoy its benefits. Here's to your very good health, sir, and I am proud to have made your acquaintance."

"Have another drop; it can hurt no one," Carne declared, and the Captain acquiesced.

"Well, I suppose we must finish our job," the official visitor at length pronounced; "a matter of form, sir, and no offence; but we are bound to carry out our duty. There is nothing left, except the other lot of vaults; but the light begins to fail us, for underground work. I hope they are not so dark as those we have been through."

"Just about the same. You would hardly know one set from the other, as I told you, except for the stone that records the murder. Perhaps we had better light the lantern now?"

"By all means. I don't half like that story of the lady that walks on the water. It does seem so gashly and unchristian altogether. Not that I have any fear of ghosts—not likely, for I have never even seen one."

"I have," said Gunner Bob, in a deep voice, which made them all glance through the ivy. "I have, and a fearful one it were."

"Don't be a fool, Bob," the Captain whispered; "we don't want to hear about that now. Allow me to carry the lantern, Mr. Carne; it throws such shadows from the way you hold it. Why, surely, this is where we were before!"

"You might easily fancy so," Carne answered, smiling, "especially with a mind at all excited—"

"My mind is not excited, sir; not at all excited; but as calm as it ever was in all its life."

"Then two things will show you that these are the other vaults. The arch is on your left hand, instead of on your right"—he had brought them in now from the other end of the passage—"and this entrance, as you see, has a door in it, which the other had not. Perhaps the door is to keep the ghost in"—his laugh sounded hollow, and like a mocking challenge along the dark roof —"for this is the part she is supposed to walk in. But so much for the door! The money-lenders have not left us a door that will stand a good kick. You may find our old doors in Wardour Street."

As he spoke, he set foot against the makeshift door, and away it went, as he had predicted. Crashing on the steps as it fell, it turned over, and a great splash arose at the bottom.

"Why, bless my heart, there is a flood of water there!" cried Stubbard, peeping timidly down the steps, on which (if the light had been clear, and that of his mind in the same condition) he might have seen the marks of his own boots. "A flood of water, perhaps six feet deep! I could scarcely have believed, but for that and the door, that these were not the very vaults that we have examined. But what business has the water there?"

"No business at all, any more than we have," Carne answered, with some rudeness, for it did not suit him to encourage too warmly the friendship of Captain Stubbard; "but I told you that the place becomes covered with water whenever the ghost intends to walk. Probably there is not more than a foot of water"—there was in fact about three inches—"and as you are bound to carry out your duty—"

"My dear sir, I am satisfied, perfectly satisfied. Who could keep gunpowder under water, or even in a flooded cellar? I shall have the greatest pleasure in reporting that I searched Carne Castle—not of course suspiciously, but narrowly, as we are bound to do, in execution of our warrant—"

"If you would not mind looking in this direction," whispered Carne, who could never be contented, "I think I could show you, just beyond the murder-stone—yes, and it seems to be coming towards us, as white as a winding-sheet; do come and look."

"No, sir, no; it is not my duty"—the Captain turned away, with his hair upon the rise. "I was sent here to look for saltpetre, not spectres. No officer in His Majesty's service can be expected—Bob, and Wilkins, are you there?"

"Yes, sir, yes—we have had quite enough of this; and unless you give the orders—"

"Here she comes, I do declare!" whispered Carne, with extraordinary calmness.

"Bob, and Wilkins, give me one arm each. Make for daylight in close order. You may be glad to see your grandmother, young man; but I decline to have anything to say to her. Bob, and Wilkins, bear a hand; I feel a little shaky in my lower timbers. Run for your lives, but don't leave me behind. Run, lads, like the very devil!" For a groan of sepulchral depth, and big enough to lift a granite tombstone, issued from the vault, and wailed along the sombre archway. All the Artillerymen fled, as if the muzzle of their biggest gun was slewed upon them, and very soon the sound of horses' heels, urged at a perilous pace down the hill, rang back as the echo of that grand groan.

"I think I did that pretty well, my Captain," cried Charron, ascending from the vault with dripping boots; "I deserve a glass of Cognac, if they have left me any. Happy is Stoobar that he was contented, without breaking his neck at the inspector's step."

"He has satisfied his conscience," Carne answered, grimly; "yet it cannot be blameless, to make him run so fast. I am glad we have been saved from killing them. It would have been hard to know what to do next. But he will never trouble us here again."

CHAPTER XLV

FATHER, AND CHILD

"Tell Miss Faith, when she comes in, that I shall be glad to see her," said Admiral Darling to his trusty butler, one hot afternoon in August. He had just come home from a long rough ride, to spend at least one day in his own house, and after overhauling his correspondence, went into the dining-room, as the coolest in the house, to refresh himself a little with a glass of light wine before going up to dress for dinner. There he sat in an arm-chair, and looked at his hands, which were browned by the sun, and trembling from a long period of heavy work and light sleep. He was getting too old to endure it with impunity, yet angry with himself for showing it. But he was not thinking of himself alone.

"I hope she will be sensible"—he was talking to himself, as elderly people are apt to do, especially after being left to themselves; "I hope she will see the folly of it—of living all her life as the bride of a ghost; and herself such a beautiful, cheerful darling! Loving, warm-hearted, sweet-tempered, adoring children, and adored by them; obedient, gentle—I can't think of anything good that she hasn't got, except common-sense. And even for that, I like her all the more; because it is so different from all the other girls. They have got too much—one lover out of sight, even for a month or two, gone fighting for his Country, what do they do but take up with another, as I very greatly fear our Dolly would? But Faith—Why, my darling, how well you look!"

"How I wish that I could say the same of you, dear father!" said the lovely young woman, while kissing him, and smoothing with her soft hand his wrinkled forehead; "you never used to have these little tucks and gathers here. I would rather almost that the French should come and devour us all, than see my father, whenever we do see him, once in a month, say, gauffred like this— as their laundresses do it—and getting reduced to the Classical shape, so that I can put one arm round him."

"My darling," said the Admiral, though proud at heart of the considerable reduction of his stomach, "you should not say such things to me, to remind me how very old I am!"

Fathers are crafty, and daughters childish, as behoves the both of them. The Admiral knew, as well as if he had ordered it, what Faith would do. And she must have perceived his depth, if only she had taken a moment to think of it. Because when she plumped, like a child, into his arms, how came his arms to be so wide open? and when two great tears rolled down her cheeks, how sprang his handkerchief so impromptu out from beneath his braided lappet?

"Tell me what harm I have done," she asked, with a bright smile dawning through the dew of her dark eyes; "what have I done to vex you, father, that you say things fit to make me cry? And yet I ought to laugh, because I know so well that you are only fishing for compliments. You are getting so active that I shall be frightened to go for a walk or a ride with you. Only I do love to see you look fat, and your darling forehead smooth and white."

"My dear child, I must get up my substance. This very day I begin in earnest. Because I am to be a great man, Faith. How would you like to have to call me 'Sir Charles'?"

"Not at all, darling; except when you deserve it, by being cross to me; and that never, never happens. I wish there was more chance of it."

"Well, dear, if you won't, the other people must; for His Majesty has been graciously pleased to turn me into a Baronet. He says that I have earned it; and perhaps I have; at any rate, he put it so nicely that without being churlish I could not refuse. And it will be a good thing for Frank, I hope, by bringing him back from his democratic stuff. To myself it is useless; but my children ought to like it."

"And so they will, father, for your own dear sake. Let me be the first to salute you, father. Oh, Dolly will be in such a rage because you told me, without telling her!"

"I never thought of that," said the Admiral, simply; "I am afraid that I shall get in for it. However, I have a right to please myself, and you need not tell her until I do. But that is not all my news, and not by any means the best of it. The King was reminded, the other day, of all that he and his family owe to the late Sir Edmond Scudamore, and better late than never, he has ordered your governess, as he called her, to be put on the list for a pension of 300 pounds a year. Nothing that once gets into his head can ever be got out of it, and he was shocked at seeing his old physician's widow 'gone out as a governess—gone out as a governess—great disgrace to the royal family!' I am very glad that it happened so."

"And so am I. She ought to have had it long and long ago, especially after the sad misfortune of her husband. You will let me tell her? It will be such a pleasure."

"Certainly, my dear; you are the very one to do it. Tell her that her eldest pupil is come with a little piece of news for her; it will make her smile—she has a very pretty smile, which reminds me of the gallant Blyth. And now, my child, the third piece of news concerns yourself—your good, and dutiful, and exceedingly sensible self. Ahem!" cried the Admiral, as he always did, when he feared that he might have overstepped the truth.

"I know what it is; you need not tell me," Faith answered, confirming her fear at once. "It is no use, father; it is no good at all—unless you intend to forget your own promise."

"That I shall never do," he replied, while looking at her sadly; "no, my dear child, I shall never attempt to drive instead of lead you. But you have not heard me out as yet. You don't even know who it is I mean."

"Oh yes, I do; I know well enough, father. I am not like Dolly, universally admired. Because I do not want to be. You mean Lord Dashville—can you tell me that you don't?"

"No, my dear"—Sir Charles was a little surprised that Faith should be so quick, for (like most people of gentle nature) she was taken to be slow, because she never snapped—"I cannot deny that it is Lord Dashville, because that is the man, and no other. But how you could tell surpasses me, and it shows that he must be very often in your mind:" the Admiral thought he had caught her there. "Now can you say anything against him? Is he not honest, manly, single-minded, faithful as yourself, I do believe, good-looking, well-bred, a Tory, and a gentleman, certain to make any woman happy whom he loves? Can you say a syllable against all that?"

"No," replied Faith—a very long, slow "no," as if she only wished she could say something hard about him.

"Very well," her father went on, with triumph, "and can you deny that he is just the person you might have taken a great liking to—fallen in love with, as they call it—if only he had come before your mind was full of somebody else —a very fine young fellow, no doubt; but—my darling, I won't say a word against him, only you know what I mean too well. And are you forever to be like a nun because it has pleased the Lord to take him from you?"

"Lord Dashville has not advanced himself in my good opinion, if he cares for that," said Faith, starting sideways, as a woman always does, from the direct issue, "by going to you, when I declined to have anything more to say to him."

"My dear, you are unjust," replied Sir Charles; "not purposely, I know, for you are the most upright darling that can be, in general. But you accuse young Dashville of what he never did. It was his good mother, the Countess of Blankton, a most kind-hearted and lady-like person, without any nonsense about her, who gave me the best cup of tea I ever tasted, and spoke with the very best feeling possible. She put it so sweetly that I only wish you could have been there to hear her."

"Father, what is the good of it all? You hate turncoats even worse than traitors. Would you like your daughter to be one? And when she would seem to have turned her coat—for the ladies wear coats now, the horrid ugly things! —for the sake of position, and title, and all that. If Lord Dashville had been a poor man, with his own way to make in the world, a plain Mister, there might have been more to be said for it. But to think that I should throw over my poor darling because he will come home without a penny, and perhaps tattoed, but at any rate turned black, for the sake of a coronet, and a heap of gold—oh, father, I shall break down, if you go on so!"

"My dear girl, I will not say a word to vex you. But you are famous for common-sense, as well as every other good quality, and I would ask you to employ just a little of it. Can you bear me to speak of your trouble, darling?"

"Oh yes, I am so well accustomed to it now; and I know that it is nothing compared to what thousands of people have to bear. Sometimes I am quite ashamed of giving way to it."

"You do not give way to it, Faith. No person can possibly say that of you. You are my brave, unselfish, cheerful, sweet-natured, upright, and loving child. Nobody knows, but you and I—and perhaps I know it even more than you do—the greatness of the self-command you use, to be pleasant and gay and agreeable, simply for the sake of those around you."

"Then, father," cried Faith, who was surprised at this, for the Admiral had never said a word about such matters, "you think, after all, that I am—that I am almost as good as Dolly!"

"You jealous little vixen, I shall recall every word I have said in your favour! My child, and my pride, you are not only as good as Dolly, but my best hope is that when Dolly grows older she may be like you. Don't cry, darling; I can't stand crying, when it comes from eyes that so seldom do it. And now that you know what I think of you, allow me to think a little for you. I have some right to interfere in your life; you will allow that—won't you?"

"Father, you have all right, and a thousand times as much, because you are so gentle about using it."

"I calls that bad English, as Zeb Tugwell says when he doesn't want to understand a thing. But, my pretty dear, you must remember that you will not have a father always. Who will look after you, when I am gone, except the Almighty?—and He does not do it, except for the few who look after themselves. It is my duty to consider these points, and they override sentimentality. To me it is nothing that Dashville will be an Earl, and a man of great influence, if he keeps up his present high character; but it is something to me that I find him modest, truthful, not led away by phantoms, a gentleman —which is more than a nobleman—and with his whole heart given to my dear child Faith."

Faith sighed heavily, partly for herself, but mainly, perhaps, for the sake of a fine heart sadly thrown away on her. "I believe he is all that," she said.

"In that case, what more can you have?" pursued the triumphant Admiral. "It is one of the clearest things I ever knew, and one of the most consistent"— consistent was a great word in those days—"as well as in every way desirable. Consider, not yourself—which you never do—but the state of the Country, and of Dolly. They have made me a baronet, for being away from home nearly every night of my life; and if I had Dashville to see to things here, I might stay away long enough to be a lord myself, like my late middy the present Duke of Bronte."

Faith laughed heartily. "You call me jealous! My dear father, I know that you could have done a great deal more than Lord Nelson has, because he learned all that he knows from you. And now who is it that really defends the whole south coast of England against the French? Is it Lord Nelson? He has as much as he can do to look after their fleet in the Mediterranean. Admiral Cornwallis and Sir Charles Darling are the real defenders of England."

"No, my dear, you must never say that, except of course in private. There may be some truth in it, but it would be laughed at in the present condition of the public mind. History may do me justice; but after all it is immaterial. A man who does his duty should be indifferent to the opinion of the public, which begins more and more to be formed less by fact than by the newspapers of the day. But let us return to more important matters. You are now in a very sensible frame of mind. You see what my wishes are about you, and how reasonable they are. I should be so happy, my darling child, if you would consider them sensibly, and yield some little of your romantic views. I would not ask you unless I were sure that this man loves you as you deserve, and in his own character deserves your love."

"Then, father, will this content you, dear? Unless I hear something of Erle Twemlow, to show that he is living, and still holds to me, in the course of another twelvemonth, Lord Dashville, or anybody else, may try—may try to take his place with me. Only I must not be worried—I mean, I must not hear another word about it, until the time has quite expired."

"It is a very poor concession, Faith. Surely you might say half a year. Consider, it is nearly three years now—"

"No, papa, I should despise myself if I were so unjust to one so unlucky. And I only go so much from my own wishes because you are such a dear and good father. Not a bit of it for Lord Dashville's sake."

"Well, my poor darling," the Admiral replied, for he saw that she was upon the brink of tears, and might hate Lord Dashville if further urged, "half a loaf is better than no bread. If Dashville is worthy of your constant heart, he will stand this long trial of his constancy. This is the tenth day of August, 1804. I hope that the Lord may be pleased to spare me till the 10th of August, 1805. High time for them to come and lay the cloth. I am as hungry as a hunter."

CHAPTER XLVI

CATAMARANS

Napoleon had shown no proper dread of the valiant British volunteers, but kept his festival in August, and carried on his sea-side plans, as if there were no such fellows. Not content with that, he even flouted our blockading fleet by coming out to look at them. And if one of our frigates had shot straight, she might have saved millions of lives and billions of money, at the cost of one greatly bad life. But the poor ship knew not her opportunity, or she would rather have gone to the bottom than waste it.

Now the French made much of this affair, according to their nature; and histories of it, full of life and growth, ran swiftly along the shallow shore, and even to Paris, the navel of the earth. Frenchmen of letters—or rather of papers —declared that all England was smitten with dismay; and so she might have been, if she had heard of it. But as our neighbours went home again, as soon as the water was six fathoms deep, few Englishmen knew that they had tried to smell a little of the sea-breeze, outside the smell of their inshore powder. They were pleased to get ashore again, and talk it over, with vivid description of the things that did not happen.

"Such scenes as these tended much to agitate England," writes a great French historian. "The British Press, arrogant and calumnious, as the Press always is in a free country, railed much at Napoleon and his preparations; but railed as one who trembles at that which he would fain exhibit as the object of his laughter." It may have been so, but it is not to be seen in any serious journal of that time. He seems to have confounded coarse caricaturists with refined and thoughtful journalists, even as, in the account of that inshore skirmish, he turns a gun-brig into a British frigate. However, such matters are too large for us.

It was resolved at any rate to try some sort of a hit at all these very gallant Frenchmen, moored under their own batteries, and making horse-marines of themselves, whenever Neptune, the father of the horse, permitted. The jolly English tars, riding well upon the waves, sent many a broad grin through a spy-glass at Muncher Crappo tugging hard to get his nag into his gun-boat and then to get him out again, because his present set of shoes would not be worn out in England. Every sailor loves a horse, regarding him as a boat on legs, and therefore knowing more about him than any landlubber may feign to know.

But although they would have been loth to train a gun on the noble animal, who was duly kept beyond their range, all the British sailors longed to have a bout with the double tier of hostile craft moored off the shore within shelter of French batteries. Every day they could reckon at least two hundred sail of every kind of rig invented since the time of Noah, but all prepared to destroy instead of succouring the godly. It was truly grievous to see them there and not be able to get at them, for no ship of the line or even frigate could get near enough to tackle them. Then the British Admiral, Lord Keith, resolved after much consultation to try what could be done with fire-ships.

Blyth Scudamore, now in command of the Blonde, had done much excellent service, in cutting off stragglers from the French flotilla, and driving ashore near Vimereux some prames and luggers coming from Ostend. He began to know the French coast and the run of the shoals like a native pilot; for the post of the Blonde, and some other light ships, was between the blockading fleet and the blockaded, where perpetual vigilance was needed. This sharp service was the very thing required to improve his character, to stamp it with decision and self-reliance, and to burnish his quiet, contemplative vein with the very frequent friction of the tricks of mankind. These he now was strictly bound not to study, but anticipate, taking it as first postulate that every one would cheat him, if permitted. To a scrimpy and screwy man, of the type most abundant, such a position would have done a deal of harm, shutting him up into his own shell harder, and flinting its muricated horns against the world. But with the gentle Scuddy, as the boys at school had called him, the process of hardening was beneficial, as it is with pure gold, which cannot stand the wear and tear of the human race until it has been reduced by them at least to the mark of their twenty carats.

And now it was a fine thing for Scudamore—even as a man too philanthropic was strengthened in his moral tone (as his wife found out) by being compelled to discharge the least pleasant of the duties of a county sheriff—or if not a fine thing, at least it was a wholesome and durable corrective to all excess of lenience, that duty to his country and mankind compelled the gentle Scuddy to conduct the western division of this night-attack.

At this time there was in the public mind, which is quite of full feminine agility, a strong prejudice against the use of fire-ships. Red-hot cannon-balls, and shrapnel, langrage, chain-shot, and Greek-fire—these and the like were all fair warfare, and France might use them freely. But England (which never is allowed to do, without hooting and execration, what every other country does with loud applause)—England must rather burn off her right hand than send a fire-ship against the ships full of fire for her houses, her cottages, and churches. Lord Keith had the sense to laugh at all that stuff, but he had not the grand mechanical powers which have now enabled the human race, not to go, but to send one another to the stars. A clumsy affair called a catamaran, the acephalous ancestor of the torpedo, was expected to relieve the sea of some thousands of people who had no business there. This catamaran was a water-proof box about twenty feet long, and four feet wide, narrowed at the ends, like a coffin for a giant. It was filled with gunpowder, and ballasted so that its lid, or deck, was almost awash; and near its stern was a box containing clock movements that would go for about ten minutes, upon the withdrawal of a peg outside, and then would draw a trigger and explode the charge. This wondrous creature had neither oar nor sail, but demanded to be towed to the tideward of the enemy, then have the death-watch set going, and be cast adrift within hail of the enemy's line. Then as soon as it came across their mooring cables, its duty was to slide for a little way along them in a friendly manner, lay hold of them kindly with its long tail, which consisted of a series of grappling-hooks buoyed with cork, and then bringing up smartly alongside of the gun-boats, blow itself up, and carry them up with it. How many there were of these catamarans is not quite certain, but perhaps about a score, the intention being to have ten times as many, on the next occasion, if these did well. And no doubt they would have done well, if permitted; but they failed of their purpose, like the great Guy Fawkes, because they were prevented.

For the French, by means of treacherous agents—of whom perhaps Caryl Carne was one, though his name does not appear in the despatches—knew all about this neat little scheme beforehand, and set their wits at work to defeat it. Moreover, they knew that there were four fire-ships, one of which was the Peggy of Springhaven, intended to add to the consternation and destruction wrought by the catamarans. But they did not know that, by some irony of fate, the least destructive and most gentle of mankind was ordered to take a leading part in shattering man, and horse, and even good dogs, into vapours.

Many quiet horses, and sweet-natured dogs, whose want of breeding had improved their manners, lived in this part of the great flotilla, and were satisfied to have their home where it pleased the Lord to feed them. The horses were led to feed out of the guns, that they might not be afraid of them; and they struggled against early prejudice, to like wood as well as grass, and to get sea-legs. Man put them here to suit his own ideas; of that they were quite aware, and took it kindly, accepting superior powers, and inferior use of them, without a shade of question in their eyes. To their innocent minds it was never brought home that they were tethered here, and cropping clots instead of clover, for the purpose of inspiring in their timid friends ashore the confidence a horse reposes in a brother horse, but very wisely doubts about investing in mankind. For instance, whenever a wild young animal, a new recruit for the cavalry, was haled against his judgment by a man on either side to the hollow-sounding gangway over dancing depth of peril, these veteran salts of horses would assure him, with a neigh from the billowy distance, that they were not drowned yet, but were walking on a sort of gate, and got their victuals regular. On the other hand, as to the presence of the dogs, that requires no explanation. Was there ever a time or place in which a dog grudged his sprightly and disinterested service, or failed to do his best when called upon? These French dogs, whom the mildest English mastiff would have looked upon, or rather would have shut his eyes at, as a lot of curs below contempt, were as full of fine ardour for their cause and country as any noble hound that ever sate like a statue on a marble terrace.

On the first of October all was ready for this audacious squibbing of the hornet's nest, and the fleet of investment (which kept its distance according to the weather and the tides) stood in, not bodily so as to arouse excitement, but a ship at a time sidling in towards the coast, and traversing one another's track, as if they were simply exchanging stations. The French pretended to take no heed, and did not call in a single scouting craft, but showed every sign of having all eyes shut. Nothing, however, was done that night, by reason perhaps of the weather; but the following night being favourable, and the British fleet brought as nigh as it durst come, the four fire-ships were despatched after dark, when the enemy was likely to be engaged with supper. The sky was conveniently overcast, with a faint light wandering here and there, from the lift of the horizon, just enough to show the rig of a vessel and her length, at a distance of about a hundred yards. Nothing could be better—thought the Englishmen; and the French were of that opinion too, especially as Nelson was not there.

Scudamore had nothing to do with the loose adventure of the fire-ships, the object of which was to huddle together this advanced part of the flotilla, so that the catamarans might sweep unseen into a goodly thicket of vessels, and shatter at least half a dozen at once.

But somehow the scheme was not well carried out, though it looked very nice upon paper. One very great drawback, to begin with, was that the enemy were quite aware of all our kind intentions; and another scarcely less fatal was the want of punctuality on our part. All the floating coffins should have come together, like a funeral of fifty from a colliery; but instead of that they dribbled in one by one, and were cast off by their tow-boats promiscuously. Scudamore did his part well enough, though the whole thing went against his grain, and the four catamarans under his direction were the only ones that did their duty. The boats of the Blonde had these in tow, and cast them off handsomely at the proper distance, and drew the plugs which set their clock-springs going. But even of these four only two exploded, although the clocks were not American, and those two made a tremendous noise, but only singed a few French beards off. Except, indeed, that a fine old horse, with a white Roman nose and a bright chestnut mane, who was living in a flat-bottomed boat, broke his halter, and rushed up to the bows, and gave vent to his amazement, as if he had been gifted with a trumpet.

Hereupon a dog, loth to be behind the times, scampered up to his side, and with his forefeet on the gunwale, contributed a howl of incalculable length and unfathomable sadness.

In the hurly of the combat and confusion of the night, with the dimness streaked with tumult, and the water gashed with fire, that horse and this dog might have gone on for ever, bewailing the nature of the sons of men, unless a special fortune had put power into their mouths. One of the fire-ships, as scandal did declare, was that very ancient tub indeed—that could not float on its bottom—the Peggy of Springhaven, bought at thrice her value, through the influence of Admiral Darling. If one has to meet every calumny that arises, and deal with it before going further, the battle that lasted for a fortnight and then turned into an earthquake would be a quick affair compared with the one now in progress. Enough that the Peggy proved by the light she gave, and her grand style of burning to the water's edge before she blew up, that she was worth at least the hundred pounds Widow Shanks received for her. She startled the French more than any of the others, and the strong light she afforded in her last moments shone redly on the anguish of that poor horse and dog. There was no sign of any one to help them, and the flames in the background redoubled their woe.

Now this apparently deserted prame, near the centre of the line, was the Ville de Mayence; and the flag of Rear-Admiral Lacrosse was even now flying at her peak. "We must have her, my lads," cried Scudamore, who was wondering what to do next, until he descried the horse and dog and that fine flag; "let us board her, and make off with all of them."

The crew of his launch were delighted with that. To destroy is very good; but to capture is still better; and a dash into the midst of the enemy was the very thing they longed for. "Ay, ay, sir," they cried, set their backs to their oars, and through the broad light that still shone upon the waves, and among the thick crowd of weltering shadows, the launch shot like a dart to the side of the foe.

"Easy all! Throw a grapple on board," cried the young commander; and as the stern swung round he leaped from it, and over the shallow bulwarks, and stood all alone on the enemy's fore-deck. And alone he remained, for at that moment a loud crash was heard, and the launch filled and sank, with her crew of sixteen plunging wildly in the waves.

This came to pass through no fault of their own, but a clever device of the enemy. Admiral Lacrosse, being called away, had left his first officer to see to the safety of the flag-ship and her immediate neighbours, and this brave man had obtained permission to try a little plan of his own, if assailed by any adventurous British boats in charge of the vessels explosive. In the bows of some stout but handy boats he had rigged up a mast with a long spar attached, and by means of a guy at the end of that spar, a brace of heavy chain-shot could be swung up and pitched headlong into any boat alongside. While the crew of Scudamore's launch were intent upon boarding the prame, one of these boats came swiftly from under her stern, and with one fling swamped the enemy. Then the Frenchmen laughed heartily, and offered oars and buoys for the poor British seamen to come up as prisoners.

Scudamore saw that he was trapped beyond escape, for no other British boat was anywhere in hail. His first impulse was to jump overboard and help his own drowning men, but before he could do so an officer stood before him, and said, "Monsieur is my prisoner. His men will be safe, and I cannot permit him to risk his own life. Mon Dieu, it is my dear friend Captain Scudamore!"

"And you, my old friend, Captain Desportes! I see it is hopeless to resist"—for by this time a score of Frenchmen were round him—"I can only congratulate myself that if I must fall, it is into such good hands."

"My dear friend, how glad I am to see you!" replied the French captain, embracing him warmly; "to you I owe more than to any man of your nation. I will not take your sword. No, no, my friend. You shall not be a prisoner, except in word. And how much you have advanced in the knowledge of our language, chiefly, I fear, at the expense of France. And now you will grow perfect, at the expense of England."

CHAPTER XLVII

ENTER AND EXIT

The summer having been fine upon the whole, and a very fair quantity of fish brought in, Miss Twemlow had picked up a sweetheart, as the unromantic mothers of the place expressed it. And the circumstances were of such a nature that very large interest was aroused at once, and not only so, but was fed well and grew fast.

The most complete of chronicles is no better than a sponge of inferior texture and with many mouths shut. Parts that are full of suctive power get no chance of sucking; other parts have a flood of juice bubbling at them, but are waterproof. This is the only excuse—except one—for the shameful neglect of the family of Blocks, in any little treatise pretending to give the dullest of glimpses at Springhaven.

The other excuse—if self-accusation does not poke a finger through it—is that the Blockses were mainly of the dry land, and never went to sea when they could help it. If they had lived beyond the two trees and the stile that marked the parish boundary upon the hill towards London, they might have been spotless, and grand, and even honest, yet must have been the depth of the hills below contempt. But they dwelt in the village for more generations than would go upon any woman's fingers, and they did a little business with the fish caught by the others, which enabled it to look after three days' journey as if it swam into town upon its own fins. The inventions for wronging mankind pay a great deal better than those for righting them.

Now the news came from John Prater's first, that a gentleman of great renown was coming down from London city to live on fish fresh out of the sea. His doctors had ordered him to leave off butcher's meat, and baker's bread, and tea-grocer's tea, and almost every kind of inland victuals, because of the state of his—something big, which even Springhaven could not pronounce. He must keep himself up, for at least three months, upon nothing but breezes of the sea, and malt-liquor, and farm-house bread and milk and new-laid eggs, and anything he fancied that came out of the sea, shelly, or scaly, or jellified, or weedy. News from a public-house grows fast—as seeds come up quicker for soaking—and a strong competition for this gentleman arose; but he knew what he was doing, and brought down his cook and house-maid, and disliking the noise at the Darling Arms, took no less than five rooms at the house of Matthew Blocks, on the rise of the hill, where he could see the fish come in.

He was called at once Sir Parsley Sugarloaf, for his name was Percival Shargeloes; and his cook rebuked his housemaid sternly, for meddling with matters beyond her sphere, when she told Mrs. Blocks that he was not Sir Percival, but only Percival Shargeloes, Esquire, very high up in the Corporation, but too young to be Lord Mayor of London for some years. He appeared to be well on the right side of forty; and every young lady on the wrong side of thirty possessing a pony, or even a donkey, with legs enough to come down the hill, immediately began to take a rose-coloured view of the many beauties of Springhaven.

If Mr. Shargeloes had any ambition for title, it lay rather in a military direction. He had joined a regiment of City Volunteers, and must have been a Captain, if he could have stood the drill. But this, though not arduous, had outgone his ambition, nature having gifted him with a remarkable power of extracting nourishment from food, which is now called assimilation. He was not a great feeder—people so blessed seldom are—but nothing short of painful starvation would keep him lean. He had consulted all the foremost physicians about this, and one said, "take acids," another said, "walk twenty miles every day with two Witney blankets on," a third said, "thank God for it, and drink before you eat," and a fourth (a man of wide experience) bade him marry the worst-tempered woman he knew. Then they all gave him pills to upset his stomach; but such was its power that it assimilated them. Despairing of these, he consulted a Quack, and received the directions which brought him to Springhaven. And a lucky day for him it was, as he confessed for the rest of his life, whenever any ladies asked him.

Because Miss Twemlow was intended for him by the nicest adjustment of nature. How can two round things fit together, except superficially? And in that case one must be upper and the other under; which is not the proper thing in matrimony, though generally the prevailing one. But take a full-moon and a half-moon, or even a square and a tidy triangle—with manners enough to have one right angle—and when you have put them into one another's arms, there they stick, all the firmer for friction. Jack Spratt and his wife are a case in point; and how much more pointed the case becomes when the question is not about what is on the plate, but the gentleman is in his own body fat, and the lady in her elegant person lean!

Mr. Sugarloaf—which he could not bear to be called—being an ardent admirer of the Church, and aware that her ministers know what is good, returned with great speed the Rector's call, having earnest hopes of some heart-felt words upon the difference between a right and left handed sole. One of these is ever so much better than the other—according to our evolutionists, because when he was a cod, a few milliards of years back, he chose the right side to begin lying down on, that his descendants in the thirty-millionth generation might get flat. His wife, from sheer perversity, lay down upon the other side, and this explains how some of their descendants pulled their eyes through their heads to one side, and some (though comparatively few) to the other. And the worst of it is that the fittest for the frying-pan did not survive this well-intended involution, except at a very long figure in the market.

As it fell out upon that day, Miss Twemlow was sitting in the drawing-room alone, waiting till her mother's hair was quite done up, her own abundant locks being not done up at all, for she had lately taken to set her face against all foreign fashions. "I have not been introduced to the King," she said, "nor even to the Queen, like those forward Darlings, and I shall do my hair to please myself." When her father objected, she quenched him with St. Paul; and even her mother, though shocked, began to think that Eliza knew what she was about. The release of her fine hair, which fell in natural waves about her stately neck, made her look nearly ten years younger than she was, for by this time she must have been eight-and-twenty. The ladies of the Carne race, as their pictures showed (until they were sold to be the grandmothers of dry-salters), had always been endowed with shapely necks, fit columns for their small round heads. And this young lady's hair, with no constraint but that of a narrow band across the forehead, clustered and gleamed like a bower of acanthus round that Parian column.

Mr. Shargeloes, having obeyed his orders always to dine early, was thrilled with a vision of poetry and romance, as he crossed the first square of the carpet. The lady sat just where the light fell best from a filtered sunbeam to illumine her, without entering into the shady parts; and the poetry of her attitude was inspired by some very fine poetry upon her lap. "I don't care what the doctors say, I shall marry that girl," said Mr. Shargeloes to himself.

He was a man who knew his own mind, and a man with that gift makes others know it. Miss Twemlow clenched in the coat upon his back the nail she had driven through his heart, by calling him, at every other breath, "Colonel Shargeloes." He said he was not that; but she felt that he was, as indeed every patriotic man must be. Her contempt for every man who forsook his country in this bitter, bitter strait was at once so ruthless and so bewitching that he was quite surprised into confessing that he had given 10,000 pounds, all in solid gold, for the comfort of the Royal Volunteers, as soon as the autumnal damps came on. He could not tell such an elegant creature that what he had paid for was flannel drawers, though she had so much strength of mind that he was enabled to tell her before very long.

A great deal of nonsense is talked about ladies who are getting the better of their first youth, as if they then hung themselves out as old slates for any man to write his name on. The truth is that they have better judgment then, less trouble in their hearts about a gentleman's appearance, and more enquiry in their minds as to his temper, tastes, and principles, not to mention his prospects of supporting them. And even as concerns appearance, Mr. Shargeloes was very good. Nature had given him a fine stout frame, and a very pleasant countenance; and his life in the busy world had added that quickness of decision and immediate sense of right which a clever woman knows to be the very things she wants. Moreover, his dress, which goes a very long way into the heart of a lady, was most correct and particular. For his coat was of the latest Bond Street fashion, the "Jean de Brie," improved and beautified by suggestions from the Prince of Wales himself. Bright claret was the colour, and the buttons were of gold, bright enough to show the road before him as he walked. The shoulders were padded, as if a jam pot stood there, and the waist buttoned tight, too tight for any happiness, to show the bright laticlave of brocaded waistcoat. Then followed breeches of rich purple padusoy, having white satin bows at the knee, among which the little silver bells of the Hessian boots jingled.

Miss Twemlow was superior to all small feeling, but had great breadth of sympathy with the sterling truth in fashion. The volume of love, like a pattern-book, fell open, and this well-dressed gentleman was engraved upon her heart. The most captious young chit, such as Dolly herself, could scarcely have called him either corpulent or old. Every day he could be seen to be growing younger, with the aid of fresh fish as a totally novel ingredient in his system; his muscle increased with the growth of brain-power, and the shoemaker was punching a fresh hole in his belt, an inch further back, every week he stopped there. After buckling up three holes, he proposed. Miss Twemlow referred him to her dear papa; and the Rector took a week to enquire and meditate. "Take a month, if you like," said Mr. Shargeloes.

This reply increased the speed. Mr. Twemlow had the deepest respect for the Corporation, and to live to be the father of a Lord Mayor of London became a new ambition to lead on his waning years. "Come and dine with us on Saturday, and we will tell you all about it," he said, with a pleasant smile, and warm shake of the hand; and Shargeloes knew that the neck and the curls would bend over the broad gold chain some day.

How grievous it is to throw a big stone into a pool which has plenty of depth and length and width for the rings to travel pleasantly, yet not to make one ring, because of wind upon the water! In the days that were not more than two years old, Springhaven could have taken all this news, with a swiftly expanding and smoothly fluent circle, with a lift of self-importance at the centre of the movement, and a heave of gentle interest in the far reflective corners. Even now, with a tumult of things to consider, and a tempest of judgment to do it in, people contrived to be positive about a quantity of things still pending. Sir Parsley Sugarloaf had bought Miss Twemlow for 50,000 pounds, they said, and he made her let her curls down so outrageous, because she was to be married at Guildhall, with a guinea at the end of every hair. Miss Faith would be dirt-cheap at all that money; but as for Miss Eliza, they wished him better knowledge, which was sure to come, when it was no good to him.

"What a corner of the world this is for gossip!" Mr. Shargeloes said, pleasantly, to his Eliza, having heard from his cook, who desired no new mistress, some few of the things said about him. "I am not such a fool as to care what they say. But I am greatly surprised at one thing. You know that I am a thorough Englishman; may I tell you what I think, without offending you? It is a delicate matter, because it concerns a relative of your own, my dear."

"I know what you mean. You will not offend me. Percival, I know how straightforward you are, and how keen of perception. I have expected this."

"And yet it seems presumptuous of me to say that you are all blind here, from the highest to the lowest. Except indeed yourself, as I now perceive. I will tell you my suspicions, or more than suspicions—my firm belief—about your cousin, Mr. Carne. I can trust you to keep this even from your father. Caryl Carne is a spy, in the pay of the French."

"I have long thought something, though not quite so bad as that," Miss Twemlow answered, calmly; "because he has behaved to us so very strangely. My mother is his own father's sister, as you know, and yet he has never dined with us more than once, and then he scarcely said a word to any one. And he never yet has asked us to visit him at the castle; though for that we can make all allowance, of course, because of its sad condition. Then everybody thought he had taken to smuggling, and after all his losses, no one blamed him, especially as all the Carnes had done it, even when they were the owners of the land. But ever since poor Mr. Cheeseman, our church-warden, tried to destroy himself with his own rope, all the parish began to doubt about the smuggling, because it pays so well and makes the people very cheerful. But from something he had seen, my father felt quite certain that the true explanation was smuggling."

"Indeed! Do you know at all what it was he saw, and when, and under what circumstances?" Mr. Shargeloes put these questions with more urgency than Miss Twemlow liked.

"Really I cannot tell you all those things; they are scarcely of general interest. My dear father said little about it: all knowledge is denied in this good world to women. But no doubt he would tell you, if you asked him, when there were no ladies present."

"I will," said Mr. Shargeloes. "He is most judicious; he knows when to speak, and when to hold his tongue. And I think that you combine with beauty one of those two gifts—which is the utmost to be expected."

"Percival, you put things very nicely, which is all that could be expected of a man. But do take my advice in this matter, and say no more about it."

Mr. Shargeloes feigned to comply, and perhaps at the moment meant to do so. But unluckily he was in an enterprising temper, proud of recovered activity, and determined to act up to the phosphate supplied by fish diet. Therefore when the Rector, rejoicing in an outlet for his long pent-up discoveries, and regarding this sage man as one of his family, repeated the whole of his adventure at Carne Castle, Mr. Shargeloes said, briefly, "It must be seen to."

"Stubbard has been there," replied Mr. Twemlow, repenting perhaps of his confidence; "Stubbard has made an official inspection, which relieves us of all concern with it."

"Captain Stubbard is an ass. It is a burning shame that important affairs should be entrusted to such fellows. The country is in peril, deadly peril; and every Englishman is bound to act as if he were an officer."

That very same evening Carne rode back to his ruins in a very grim state of mind. He had received from the Emperor a curt and haughty answer to his last appeal for immediate action, and the prospect of another gloomy winter here, with dangers thickening round him, and no motion to enliven them, was almost more than he could endure. The nights were drawing in, and a damp fog from the sea had drizzled the trees, and the ivy, and even his own moustache with cold misery.

"Bring me a lantern," he said to old Jerry, as he swung his stiff legs from the back of the jaded horse, "and the little flask of oil with the feather in it. It is high time to put the Inspector's step in order."

Jerry Bowles, whose back and knees were bent with rheumatism and dull service, trotted (like a horse who has become too stiff to walk) for the things commanded, and came back with them. Then his master, without a word, strode towards the passage giving entry to the vaults which Stubbard had not seen—the vaults containing all the powder, and the weapons for arming the peasantry of England, whom Napoleon fondly expected to rise in his favour at the sight of his eagles.

"How does it work? Quite stiff with rust. I thought so. Nothing is ever in order, unless I see to it myself. Give me the lantern. Now oil the bearings thoroughly. Put the feather into the socket, and work the pin in and out, that the oil may go all round. Now pour in some oil from the lip of the flask; but not upon the treadle, you old blockhead. Now do the other end the same. Ah, now it would go with the weight of a mouse! I have a great mind to make you try it."

"What would you do, sir, if my neck was broken? Who would do your work, as I do?"

They were under an arch of mouldy stone, opening into the deep dark vaults, where the faint light of the lantern glanced on burnished leather, brass, and steel, or fell without flash upon dull round bulk. The old man, kneeling on the round chalk-flints set in lime for the flooring of the passage, was handling the first step of narrow step-ladder leading to the cellar-depth. This top step had been taken out of the old oak mortice, and cut shorter, and then replaced in the frame, with an iron pin working in an iron collar, just as the gudgeon of a wheelbarrow revolves. Any one stepping upon it unawares would go down without the aid of any other step.

"Goes like spittle now, sir," said old Jerry; "but I don't want no more harm in this crick of life. The Lord be pleased to keep all them Examiners at home. Might have none to find their corpusses until next leap-year. I hope with all my heart they won't come poking their long noses here."

"Well, I rather hope they will. They want a lesson in this neighbourhood," muttered Carne, who was shivering, and hungry, and unsweetened.

CHAPTER XLVIII

MOTHER SCUDAMORE

If we want to know how a tree or flower has borne the gale that flogged last night, or the frost that stung the morning, the only sure plan is to go and see. And the only way to understand how a friend has taken affliction is to go—if it may be done without intrusion—and let him tell you, if he likes.

Admiral Darling was so much vexed when he heard of Blyth Scudamore's capture by the French, and duty compelled him to inform the mother, that he would rather have ridden a thousand miles upon barley-bread than face her. He knew how the whole of her life was now bound up with the fortunes of her son, and he longed to send Faith with the bad news, as he had sent her with the good before; but he feared that it might seem unkind. So he went himself, with the hope of putting the best complexion upon it, yet fully expecting sad distress, and perhaps a burst of weeping. But the lady received his tidings in a manner that surprised him. At first she indulged in a tear or two, but they only introduced a smile.

"In some ways it is a sad thing," she said, "and will be a terrible blow to him, just when he was rising so fast in the service. But we must not rebel more than we can help, against the will of the Lord, Sir Charles."

"How philosophical, and how commonplace!" thought the Admiral; but he only bowed, and paid her some compliment upon her common-sense.

"Perhaps you scarcely understand my views, and perhaps I am wrong in having them," Lady Scudamore continued, quietly. "My son's advancement is very dear to me, and this will of course retard it. But I care most of all for his life, and now that will be safe for a long while. They never kill their prisoners, do they?"

"No, ma'am, no. They behave very well to them; better, I'm afraid, than we do to ours. They treat them quite as guests, when they fall into good hands. Though Napoleon himself is not too mild in that way."

"My son has fallen into very good hands, as you yourself assure me—that Captain Desportes, a gallant officer and kind gentleman, as I know from your daughter's description. Blyth is quite equal to Lord Nelson in personal daring, and possibly not behind him in abilities. Consider how shockingly poor Nelson has been injured, and he feels convinced himself that they will have his life at last. No officer can be a hero without getting very sad wounds, and perhaps losing his life. Every one who does his duty must at least be wounded."

The Admiral, who had never received a scratch, was not at all charmed with this view of naval duty; but he was too polite to enter protest, and only made one of his old-fashioned scrapes.

"I am sure every time I have heard a gun coming from the sea, and especially after dark," the lady resumed, without thinking of him, "it has made me miserable to know that probably Blyth was rushing into some deadly conflict. But now I shall feel that he cannot do that; and I hope they will keep him until the fighting grows milder. He used to send me all his money, poor dear boy! And now I shall try to send him some of mine, if it can be arranged about bank-notes. And now I can do it very easily, thanks to your kindness, Sir Charles, his father's best friend, and his own, and mine."

Lady Scudamore shed another tear or two, not of sorrow, but of pride, while she put her hand into her pocket, as if to begin the remittance at once. "You owe me no thanks, ma'am," said the Admiral, smiling; "if any thanks are due, they are due to the King, for remembering at last what he should have done before."

"Would he ever have thought of me, but for you? It is useless to talk in that way, Sir Charles; it only increases the obligation, which I must entreat you not to do. How I wish I could help you in anything!"

"Every day you are helping me," he replied, with truth; "although I am away too often to know all about it, or even to thank you. I hope my dear Faith has persuaded you not to leave us for the winter, as you threatened."

"Faith can persuade me to anything she pleases. She possesses the power of her name," replied the lady; "but the power is not called for, when the persuasion is so pleasant. For a month, I must be away to visit my dear mother, as I always have done at this time of year; and then, but for one thing, I would return most gladly. For I am very selfish, you must know, Sir Charles —I have a better chance of hearing of my dear son at these head-quarters of the defence of England, than I should have even in London."

"Certainly," cried the Admiral, who magnified his office; "such a number of despatches pass through my hands; and if I can't make them out, why, my daughter Dolly can. I don't suppose, Lady Scudamore, that even when you lived in the midst of the world you ever saw any girl half so clever as my Dolly. I don't let her know it—that would never do, of course—but she always gets the best of me, upon almost any question."

Sir Charles, for the moment, forgot his best manners, and spread his coat so that one might see between his legs. "I stand like this," he said, "and she stands there; and I take her to task for not paying her bills—for some of those fellows have had to come to me, which is not as it should be in a country place, where people don't understand the fashionable system. She stands there, ma'am, and I feel as sure as if I were an English twenty-four bearing down upon a Frenchman of fifty guns, that she can only haul her colours down and rig out gangway ladders—when, bless me and keep me! I am carried by surprise, and driven under hatchways, and if there is a guinea in my hold, it flies into the enemy's locker! If it happened only once, I should think nothing of it. But when I know exactly what is coming, and have double-shotted every gun, and set up hammock-nettings, and taken uncommon care to have the weather-gage, 'tis the Devil, Lady Scudamore—excuse me, madam—'tis the Devil to a ditty-bag that I have her at my mercy. And yet it always comes to money out of pocket, madam!"

"She certainly has a great power over gentlemen"—Blyth's mother smiled demurely, as if she were sorry to confess it; "but she is exceedingly young, Sir Charles, and every allowance must be made for her."

"And by the Lord Harry, she gets it, madam. She takes uncommonly good care of that. But what is the one thing you mentioned that would prevent you from coming back to us with pleasure?"

"I scarcely like to speak of it. But it is about that self-same Dolly. She is not fond of advice, and she knows how quick she is, and that makes her resent a word from slower people. She has taken it into her head, I fear, that I am here as a restraint upon her; a sort of lady spy, a duenna, a dictatress, all combined in one, and all unpleasant. This often makes me fancy that I have no right to be here. And then your sweet Faith comes, and all is smooth again."

"Dolly has the least little possible touch of the vixen about her. I have found it out lately," said the Admiral, as if he were half doubtful still; "Nelson told me so, and I was angry with him. But I believe he was right, as he generally is. His one eye sees more than a score of mine would. But, my dear madam, if that is your only objection to coming back to us, or rather to my daughters, I beg you not to let it weigh a feather's weight with you. Or, at any rate, enhance the obligation to us, by putting it entirely on one side. Dolly has the very finest heart in all the world; not so steady perhaps as Faith's, nor quite so fair to other people, but wonderfully warm, ma'am, and as sound as —as a roach."

Lady Scudamore could not help laughing a little, and she hoped for her son's sake that this account was true. Her gratitude and good-will to the Admiral, as well as her duty to her son, made her give the promise sought for;

and she began to prepare for her journey at once, that she might be back in good time for the winter. But she felt very doubtful, at leaving the Hall, whether she had done quite right in keeping her suspicions of Dolly from Dolly's father. For with eyes which were sharpened by jealousy for the interests, or at least the affections, of her son, she had long perceived that his lady-love was playing a dangerous game with Caryl Carne. Sometimes she believed that she ought to speak of this, for the good of the family; because she felt the deepest mistrust and dislike of Carne, who strictly avoided her whenever he could; but on the other hand she found the subject most delicate and difficult to handle. For she had taken good care at the outset not to be here upon any false pretences. At the very first interview with her host she had spoken of Blyth's attachment to his younger daughter, of which the Admiral had heard already from that youthful sailor. And the Admiral had simply said, as in Captain Twemlow's case: "Let us leave them to themselves. I admire the young man. If she likes him, I shall make no objection, when they are old enough, and things are favourable." And now if she told him of the other love-affair, it would look like jealousy of a rival. Perhaps a hundred times a day, as her love for gentle Faith grew faster than her liking for the sprightly Dolly, she would sigh that her son did not see things like herself; but bitter affliction had taught her that the course of this life follows our own wishes about as much as another man's dog heeds our whistle. But, for all that, this good lady hoped some day to see things come round as she would like to bring them.

"No wonder that we like her son so much," said Faith when they had done waving handkerchiefs at the great yellow coach going slowly up the hill, with its vast wicker basket behind, and the guard perched over it with his blunderbus; "he takes after his mother in so many ways. They are both so simple and unsuspicious, and they make the best of every one."

"Including themselves, I suppose," answered Dolly. "Well I like people who have something on their minds, and make the worst of everybody. They have so much more to talk about."

"You should never try to be sarcastic, dear. And you know that you don't mean it. I am sure you don't like to have the worst made of yourself."

"Oh, I have long been used to that. And I never care about it, when I know it is not true. I am sure that Mother Scudamore runs me down, when I am out of hearing. I never did like those perfect people."

"Mother Scudamore, indeed! You are getting into a low way of talking, which is not at all pretty in a girl. And I never heard her say an unkind word about you. Though she may not have found you quite so perfect as she hoped."

"I tell you, Miss Darling," cried Dolly, with her bright colour deepened, and her grey eyes flashing, "that I don't care a—something that papa often says—what she thinks about me, or you either. I know that she has come here to spy out all my ways."

"You should not have any to be spied out, Dolly," Faith answered, with some sternness, and a keen look at her sister, whose eyes fell beneath her gaze. "You will be sorry, when you think of what you said to me, who have done nothing whatever to offend you. But that is a trifle compared with acting unfairly to our father. Father is the kindest man that ever lived; but he can be stern in great matters, I warn you. If he ever believes that you have deceived him, you will never be again to him what you have always been."

They had sent the carriage home that they might walk across the fields, and this little scene between the sisters took place upon a foot-path which led back to their grounds. Dolly knew that she was in the wrong, and that increased her anger.

"So you are another spy upon me, I suppose. 'Tis a pretty thing to have one's sister for an old duenna. Pray who gave you authority to lord it over me?"

"You know as well as I do"—Faith spoke with a smile of superior calmness, as Dolly tossed her head—"that I am about the last person in the world to be a spy. Neither do I ever lord it over you. If anything, that matter is very much the other way. But being so much older, and your principal companion, it would be very odd of me, and as I think most unkind, if I did not take an interest in all your goings on."

"My goings on! What a lady-like expression! Who has got into a low way of talking now? Well, if you please, madam, what have you found out?"

"I have found out nothing, and made no attempt to do so. But I see that you are altered very much from what you used to be; and I am sure that there is something on your mind. Why not tell me all about it? I would promise to let it go no further, and I would not pretend to advise, unless you wished. I am your only sister, and we have always been together. It would make you so much more comfortable, I am certain of that, in your own mind, darling. And you know when we were little girls, dear mother on her death-bed put her hands upon our heads and said, 'Be loving sisters always, and never let anything come between you.' And for father's sake, too, you should try to do it. Put aside all nonsense about spies and domineering, and trust me as your sister, that's my own darling Dolly."

"How can I resist you? I will make a clean breast of it;" Dolly sighed deeply, but a wicked smile lay ambushed in her bright eyes and upon her rosy lips. "The sad truth is that my heart has been quite sore since I heard the shocking tidings about poor old Daddy Stokes. He went to bed the other night with his best hat on, both his arms in an old muff he found in the ditch, and his leathern breeches turned inside out."

"Then the poor old man had a cleaner breast than yours," cried Faith, who had prepared her heart and eyes for tears of sympathy; "he goes upon his knees every night, stiff as they are, and his granddaughter has to help him up. But as for you, you are the most unfeeling, mocking, godless, unnatural creature that ever never cared what became of anybody. Here we are at the corner where the path divides. You go home that way, and I'll go home by this."

"Well, I'm so glad! I really did believe that it was quite impossible to put you in a rage. Now don't be in a hurry, dear, to beg my pardon."

"Of that you may be quite sure," cried Faith across the corner of the meadow where the paths diverged; "I never was less in a passion in my life; and it will be your place to apologise."

Dolly sent a merry laugh across the widening interval; and Faith, who was just beginning to fear that she had been in a passion, was convinced by that laugh that she had not. But the weight lifted from her conscience fell more heavily upon her heart.

CHAPTER XLIX

EVIL COMMUNICATIONS

Although she pretended to be so merry, and really was so self-confident (whenever anybody wanted to help her), Miss Dolly Darling, when left to herself, was not like herself, as it used to be. Her nature was lively, and her spirit very high; every one had petted her, before she could have earned it by aught except childish beauty; and no one had left off doing it, when she was bound to show better claim to it. All this made doubt, and darkness, and the sense of not being her own mistress, very snappish things to her, and she gained relief—sweet-tempered as she was when pleased—by a snap at others. For although she was not given, any more than other young people are, to plaguesome self-inspection, she could not help feeling that she was no longer the playful young Dolly that she loved so well. A stronger, and clearer, yet more mysterious will than her own had conquered hers; but she would not confess it, and yield entire obedience; neither could she cast it off. Her pride still existed, as strong as ever, whenever temper roused it; but there was too much of vanity in its composition, and too little of firm self-respect. Contempt from a woman she could not endure; neither from a man, if made manifest; but Carne so calmly took the upper hand, without any show of having it, that she fell more and more beneath his influence.

He, knowing thoroughly what he was about, did nothing to arouse resistance. So far as he was capable of loving any one, he was now in love with Dolly. He admired her quickness, and pretty girlish ways, and gaiety of nature (so unlike his own), and most of all her beauty. He had made up his mind that she should be his wife when fitted for that dignity; but he meant to make her useful first, and he saw his way to do so. He knew that she acted more and more as her father's secretary, for she wrote much faster than her sister Faith, and was quicker in catching up a meaning. Only it was needful to sap her little prejudices—candour, to wit, and the sense of trust, and above all, patriotic feeling. He rejoiced when he heard that Lady Scudamore was gone, and the Rector had taken his wife and daughter for change of air to Tunbridge Wells, Miss Twemlow being seriously out of health through anxiety about Mr. Shargeloes. For that gentleman had disappeared, without a line or message, just when Mr. Furkettle, the chief lawyer in the neighbourhood, was beginning to prepare the marriage-settlement; and although his cook and house-maid were furious at the story, Mrs. Blocks had said, and all the parish now believed, that Sir Parsley Sugarloaf had flown away to Scotland rather than be brought to book—that fatal part of the Prayer-book—by the Rector and three or four brother clergymen.

This being so, and Frank Darling absorbed in London with the publication of another batch of poems, dedicated to Napoleon, while Faith stood aloof with her feelings hurt, and the Admiral stood off and on in the wearisome cruise of duty, Carne had the coast unusually clear for the entry and arrangement of his contraband ideas. He met the fair Dolly almost every day, and their interviews did not grow shorter, although the days were doing so.

"You should have been born in France," he said, one bright November morning, when they sat more comfortable than they had any right to be, upon the very same seat where the honest but hapless Captain Scuddy had tried to venture to lisp his love; "that is the land you belong to, darling, by beauty and manners and mind and taste, and most of all by your freedom from prejudice, and great liberality of sentiment."

"But I thought we were quite as good-looking in England;" Dolly lifted her long black lashes, with a flash which might challenge the brilliance of any French eyes; "but of course you know best. I know nothing of French ladies."

"Don't be a fool, Dolly;" Carne spoke rudely, but made up for it in another way. "There never was a French girl to equal you in loveliness; but you must not suppose that you beat them all round. One point particularly you are far behind in. A French woman leaves all political questions, and national matters, and public affairs, entirely to her husband, or her lover, as the case may be. Whatever he wishes is the law for her. Thy gods shall be my gods."

"But you said they had great liberality of sentiment, and now you say they have no opinions of their own! How can the two things go together?"

"Very easily," said Carne, who was accustomed to be baffled by such little sallies; "they take their opinions from their husbands, who are always liberal. This produces happiness on both sides—a state of things unknown in England. Let me tell you of something important, mainly as it concerns yourself, sweet Dolly. The French are certain to unite with England, and then we shall be the grandest nation in the world. No power in Europe can stand before us. All will be freedom, and civilization, and great ideas, and fine taste in dress. I shall recover the large estates, that would now be mine, but for usury and fraud. And you will be one of the first ladies in the world, as nature has always intended you to be."

"That sounds very well; but how is it to be done? How can France unite with England, when they are bitter enemies? Is France to conquer England first? Or are we to conquer France, as we always used to do?"

"That would be a hard job now, when France is the mistress of the Continent. No, there need be no conquering, sweet Dolly, but only a little removal. The true interest of this country is—as that mighty party, the Whigs, perceive—to get rid of all the paltry forms and dry bones of a dynasty which is no more English than Napoleon is, and to join that great man in his warfare against all oppression. Your brother Frank is a leading spirit; he has long cast off that wretched insular prejudice which defeats all good. In the grand new scheme of universal right, which must prevail very shortly, Frank Darling will obtain that foremost place to which his noble views entitle him. You, as his sister, and my wife, will be adored almost as much as you could wish."

"It sounds very grand," answered Dolly, with a smile, though a little alarmed at this turn of it; "but what is to become of the King, and Queen, and all the royal family? And what is my father to do, and Faith? Although she has not behaved well to me."

"Those details will be arranged to everybody's satisfaction. Little prejudices will subside, when it is seen that they are useless. Every possible care will be taken not to injure any one."

"But how is it all to be done?" asked Dolly, whose mind was practical, though romantic. "Are the French to land, and overrun the country? I am sure I never should agree to that. Are all our defenders to be thrown into prison?"

"Certainly not. There will be no prisons. The French might have to land, as a matter of form; but not to overrun the country, only to secure British liberties and justice. All sensible people would hasten to join them, and any opposition would be quenched at once. Then such a glorious condition of mankind would ensue as has never been known in this world—peace, wealth, universal happiness, gaiety, dancing everywhere, no more shabby clothes, no more dreary Sundays. How do you like the thought of it?"

"Well, some of it sounds very nice; but I don't see the use of universal justice. Justice means having one's own rights; and it is impossible for everybody to do that, because of other people. And as for the French coming to put things right, they had better attend to their own affairs first. And as if any Englishman would permit it! Why, even Frank would mount his wig and gown (for he is a full-fledged barrister now, you know), and come and help to push them back into the sea. And I hope that you would do so too. I am not going to marry a Frenchman. You belong to an old English family, and you were born in England, and your name is English, and the property that ought to belong to you. I hope you don't consider yourself a Frenchman because your mother is a great French lady, after so many generations of Carnes, all English, every bit of them. I am an English girl, and I care very little for things that I don't see—such as justice, liberty, rights of people, and all that.

But I do care about my relations, and our friends, and the people that live here, and the boats, and all the trees, and the land that belongs to my father. Very likely you would want to take that away, and give it to some miserable Frenchman."

"Dolly, my dear, you must not be excited," Carne answered, in the manner of a father; "powerful as your comprehension is, for the moment these things are beyond it. Your meaning is excellent, very good, very great; but to bring it to bear requires further information. We will sit by the side of the sea to-morrow, darling, if you grant me a view of your loveliness again; and there you will see things in a larger light than upon this narrow bench, with your father's trees around us, and your father's cows enquiring whether I am good to eat. Get away, cow! Do you take me for a calf?"

One of the cows best loved by Dolly, who was very fond of good animals, had come up to ask who this man was that had been sitting here so long with her. She was gifted with a white face and large soft eyes—even beyond the common measure of a cow—short little horns, that she would scarcely think of pushing even at a dog (unless he made mouths at her infant), a flat broad nose ever genial to be rubbed, and a delicate fringe of finely pointed yellow hairs around her pleasant nostrils and above her clovery lips. With single-hearted charity and enviable faith she was able to combine the hope that Dolly had obtained a lover as good as could be found upon a single pair of legs. Carne was attired with some bravery, of the French manner rather than the English, and he wanted no butter on his velvet and fine lace. So he swung round his cane of heavy snakewood at the cow, and struck her poor horns so sharply that her head went round.

"Is that universal peace, and gentleness, and justice?" cried Dolly, springing up and hastening to console her cow. "Is this the way the lofty French redress the wrongs of England? What had poor Dewlips done, I should like to know? Kiss me, my pretty, and tell me how you would like the French army to land, as a matter of form? The form you would take would be beef, I'm afraid; not even good roast beef, but bouillon, potage, fricandeau, friture —anything one cannot taste any meat in; and that is how your wrongs would be redressed, after having had both your horns knocked off. And about the same fate for John Bull, your master, unless he keeps his horns well sharpened. Do I not speak the truth, monsieur?"

When Carne did anything to vex Miss Dolly—which happened pretty often, for he could not stop to study much her little prejudices—she addressed him as if he were a Frenchman, never doubting that this must reduce him sadly in his self-esteem.

"Never mind matters political," he said, perceiving that his power must not be pressed until he had deepened its foundations; "what are all the politics in the world compared with your good opinion, Beauty?" Dolly liked to be called "Beauty," and the name always made her try to deserve it by looking sweet. "You must be quite certain that I would do nothing to injure a country which contains my Dolly. And as for Madam Cow, I will beg her pardon, though my cane is hurt a great deal more than her precious horns are. Behold me snap it in twain, although it is the only handsome one I possess, because it has offended you!"

"Oh, what a pity! What a lovely piece of wood!" cried Dolly; and they parted on the best of terms, after a warm vow upon either side that no nasty politics should ever come between them.

But Carne was annoyed and discontented. He came to the edge of the cliff that evening below his ruined castle; for there are no cliffs at Springhaven, unless the headland deserves that name; and there he sat gloomily for some hours, revolving the chances of his enterprise. The weather had changed since the morning, and a chill November wind began to urge the waves ashore. The sky was not very dark, but shredded with loose grey vapours from the west, where a heavy bank of clouds lay under the pale crescent of a watery moon. In the distance two British cruisers shone, light ships of outlook, under easy sail, prepared to send the signal for a hundred leagues, from ship to ship and cliff to cliff, if any of England's foes appeared. They shone upon the dark sea, with canvas touched by moonlight, and seemed ready to spring against the lowering sky, if it held any menace to the land they watched, or the long reach of water they had made their own.

"A pest upon those watch-dogs!" muttered Carne. "They are always wide-awake, and forever at their stations. Instead of growing tired, they get sharper every day. Even Charron can scarcely run through them now. But I know who could do it, if he could only be trusted. With a pilot-boat—it is a fine idea—a pilot-boat entered as of Pebbleridge. The Pebbleridge people hate Springhaven, through a feud of centuries, and Springhaven despises Pebbleridge. It would answer well, although the landing is so bad, and no anchorage possible in rough weather. I must try if Dan Tugwell will undertake it. None of the rest know the coast as he does, and few of them have the bravery. But Dan is a very sulky fellow, very difficult to manage. He will never betray us; he is wonderfully grateful; and after that battle with the press-gang, when he knocked down the officer and broke his arm, he will keep pretty clear of the Union-jack. But he goes about moping, and wondering, and mooning, as if he were wretched about what he has to do. Bless my soul, where is my invention? I see the way to have him under my thumb. Reason is an old coat hanging on a peg; passion is the fool who puts it on and runs away with it. Halloa! Who are you? And what do you want at such a time as this? Surely you can see that I am not at leisure now. Why, Tugwell, I thought that you were far away at sea!"

"So I was, sir; but she travels fast. I never would believe the old London Trader could be driven through the water so. Sam Polwhele knows how to pile it on a craft, as well as he do upon a man, sir. I won't serve under him no more, nor Captain Charcoal either. I have done my duty by you. Squire Carne, the same as you did by me, sir; and thanking you for finding me work so long, my meaning is to go upon the search to-morrow."

"What fools they must have been to let this fellow come ashore!" thought Carne, while he failed to see the wisest way to take it. "Tugwell, you cannot do this with any honour, after we have shown you all the secrets of our enterprise. You know that what we do is of the very highest honour, kind and humane and charitable, though strictly forbidden by a most inhuman government. How would you like, if you were a prisoner in France, to be debarred from all chance of getting any message from your family, your wife, your sweetheart, or your children, from year's end to year's end, and perhaps be dead for months without their knowing anything about it?"

"Well, sir, I should think it very hard indeed; though, if I was dead, I shouldn't know much more about it. But, without reproach to you, I cannot make out altogether that our only business is to carry letters for the prisoners, as now may be in England, from their loving friends to command in their native country. I won't say against you, sir, if you say it is—that is, to the outside of all your knowledge. And twenty thousand of them may need letters by the sack. But what use they could make, sir, of cannon as big as I be, and muskets that would kill a man a hundred yards of distance, and bayonets more larger and more sharper than ever I see before, even with the Royal Volunteers—this goes out of all my calculation."

"Daniel, you have expressed your views, which are remarkable—as indeed they always are—with your usual precision. But you have not observed things with equal accuracy. Do you know when a gun is past service?"

"No, sir; I never was a poacher, no-how. Squire Darling, that is to say, Sir Charles Darling now, according to a chap on board, he was always so good upon his land that nobody durst go a-poaching."

"I mean a cannon, Dan. They don't poach with cannon yet, though they may come to do it, as the game-laws increase. Do you know when a cannon is unsafe to fire, though it may look as bright as ever, like a worn-out poker? All those things that have frightened you are only meant for ornament. You know that every ancient building ought to have its armoury, as this castle always had, until they were taken away and sold. My intention is to restore it, when I can afford to do so. And having a lot of worn-out weapons offered me for next to nothing, I seized the chance of bringing them. When times are better, and the war is over, I may find time to arrange them. But that is not of much importance. The great point is to secure the delivery of letters from their native land to the brave men here as prisoners. I cannot afford to do that for nothing, though I make no profit out of it. I have so many things to think about that I scarcely know which to consider first. And after all, what matters to us whether those poor men are allowed to die, and be buried like dogs, without knowledge of their friends? Why should we run the risk of being punished for them?"

"Well, sir, that seems hard doctrine, if I may be allowed to say so, and not like your kind-heartedness. Our Government have no right to stop them of their letters."

"It is a cruel thing. But how are we to help it? The London Trader is too large for the purpose, and she is under suspicion now. I tell you everything, Daniel, because I know that you are a true-hearted fellow, and far above all blabbing. I have thought once or twice of obtaining leave to purchase a stout and handy pilot-boat, with her licence and all that transferred to us, and so running to and fro when needful. The only risk then would be from perils of the sea; and even the pressmen dare not meddle with a pilot-boat. By-the-by, I have heard that you knocked some of them about. Tugwell, you might have got us all into sad trouble."

"Was I to think of what I was doing, Squire Carne, when they wanted to make a slave of me? I would serve King George with a good heart, in spite of all that father has said against it. But it must be with a free will, Squire Carne, and not to be tied hand and foot to it. How would you like that yourself, sir?"

"Well, I think I should have done as you did, Dan, if I had been a British sailor. But as to this pilot-boat, I must have a bold and good seaman to command it. A man who knows the coast, and is not afraid of weather. Of course we should expect to pay good wages; 3 pounds a week, perhaps, and a guinea for every bag of letters landed safe. There are plenty of men who would jump at such a chance, Dan."

"I'll be bound there are, sir. And it is more than I am worth, if you mean offering the place to me. It would suit me wonderful, if I was certain that the job was honest."

"Daniel Tugwell"—Carne spoke with great severity—"I will not lose my temper, for I am sure you mean no insult. But you must be of a very low, suspicious nature, and quite unfit for any work of a lofty and unselfish order, if you can imagine that a man in my position, a man of my large sentiments —"

"Oh, no, sir, no; it was not at all that"—Dan scarcely knew how to tell what it was—"it was nothing at all of that manner of thinking. I heartily ask your pardon, sir, if it seemed to go in that way."

"Don't do that," replied Carne, "because I can make allowances. I know what a fine nature is, and how it takes alarm at shadows. I am always tender with honest scruples, because I find so many of them in myself. I should not have been pleased with you, if you had accepted my offer—although so advantageous, and full of romantic interest—until you were convinced of its honourable nature. I have no time for argument, and I am sorry that you must not come up to the castle for supper, because we have an old Springhaven man there, who would tell your father all about you, which you especially wish to avoid. But if you feel inclined for this berth—as you sailors seem to call it—and hesitate through some patriotic doubts, though I cannot understand what they are, I will bring you a document (if you meet me here to-morrow night) from Admiral Sir Charles Darling, which I think will satisfy you."

"And shall I be allowed to keep it, sir, to show, in case of trouble?"

"Very likely. But I cannot say for certain. Some of those official forms must be returned, others not; all depends upon their rules. Now go and make yourself comfortable. How are you off for money?"

"Plenty, sir, plenty. I must not go where anybody knows me, or to-morrow half the talk at old Springhaven would be about me. Good-night, sir, and God bless you."

CHAPTER L

HIS SAVAGE SPIRIT

At this time letters came very badly, not only to French prisoners in England, but even to the highest authorities, who had the very best means of getting them. Admiral Darling had often written to his old friend Nelson, but had long been without any tidings from him, through no default on the hero's part. Lord Nelson was almost as prompt with the pen as he was with the sword, but despatches were most irregular and uncertain.

"Here at last we have him!" cried Sir Charles one morning early in December; "and not more than five weeks old, I declare! Dolly, be ready, and call Faith down. Now read it, my dear, for our benefit. Your godfather writes a most excellent hand, considering that it is his left hand; but my eyes are sore from so much night-work. Put on my specs, Dolly; I should like to see you in them."

"Am I to read every word, papa, just as it comes? You know that he generally puts in words that are rather strong for me."

"Nelson never thought or wrote a single word unfit for the nicest young lady. But you may hold up your hand if you come to any strong expressions, and we shall understand them."

"Then I shall want both hands as soon as ever we come to the very first Frenchman. But this is what my godfather says:

"'VICTORY, OFF TOULON, October 31st, 1804.

"'MY DEAR LINGO,—It was only yesterday that I received your letter of July 21st; it went in a Spanish smuggling boat to the coast of Italy and returned again to Spain, not having met any of our ships. And now I hope that you will see me before you see this letter. We are certain to be at war with Spain before another month is out, and I am heartily sorry for it, for I like those fellows better than the French, because they are not such liars. My successor has been appointed, I have reason to hope, and must be far on his way by this time; probably Keith, but I cannot say. Ministers cannot suppose that I want to fly the service; my whole life has proved the contrary; if they refuse, I shall most certainly leave in March or April, for a few months' rest I must have, or else die. My cough is very bad, and my side where I was struck off Cape St. Vincent is very much swelled, at times a lump as large as my fist is brought on by violent coughing, but I hope and believe my lungs are sound.

I hope to do good service yet, or else I should not care so much. But if I am in my grave, how can I serve the Country?

"'You will say, this is not at all like Nelson, to write about nothing but his own poor self; and thank God, Lingo, I can say that you are right; for if ever a man lived for the good of England and the destruction of those'"—here Dolly held a hand up—"'Frenchmen, it is the man in front of this ink-bottle. The Lord has appointed me to that duty, and I shall carry out my orders. Mons. La Touche, who was preached about in France as the man that was to extinguish me, and even in the scurvy English newspapers, but never dared to show his snivelly countenance outside of the inner buoys, is dead of his debosheries, for which I am deeply grieved, as I fully intended to send him to the devil.

"'I have been most unlucky for some time now, and to tell the truth I may say always. But I am the last man in the world to grumble—as you, my dear Lingo, can testify. I always do the utmost, with a single mind, and leave the thought of miserable pelf to others, men perhaps who never saw a shotted cannon fired. You know who made eighty thousand pounds, without having to wipe his pigtail—dirty things, I am glad they are gone out—but my business is to pay other people's debts, and receive all my credits in the shape of cannon-balls. This is always so, and I should let it pass as usual, except for a blacker trick than I have ever known before. For fear of giving me a single chance of earning twopence, they knew that there was a million and a half of money coming into Cadiz from South America in four Spanish frigates, and instead of leaving me to catch them, they sent out Graham Moore—you know him very well—with orders to pocket everything. This will create a war with Spain, a war begun with robbery on our part, though it must have come soon in any case. For everywhere now, except where I am, that fiend of a Corsican is supreme.

"'There is not a sick man in this fleet, unless it is the one inside my coat. That liar La Touche said HE CHASED ME AND I RAN. I keep a copy of his letter, which it would have been my duty to make him eat, if he had ventured out again. But he is gone to the lake of brimstone now, and I have the good feeling to forgive him. If my character is not fixed by this time, it is not worth my trouble to put the world right. Yesterday I took a look into the port within easy reach of their batteries. They lay like a lot of mice holed in a trap, but the weather was too thick to count them. They are certainly nearly twice our number; and if any one was here except poor little Nelson, I believe they would venture out. But my reputation deprives me always of any fair chance to increase it.

"'And now, my dear Lingo, allow me to enquire how you are getting on with your Coast-defence. I never did attach much importance to their senseless invasion scheme. The only thing to make it formidable would be some infernal traitor on the coast, some devilish spy who would keep them well informed, and enable them to land where least expected. If there is such a scoundrel, may the Lord Almighty'"—here both Dolly's hands went up, with the letter in them, and her face turned as white as the paper.

"'I have often told you, as you may remember, that Springhaven is the very place I should choose, if I were commander of the French flotilla. It would turn the flank of all the inland defences, and no British ship could attack their intrenchments, if once they were snug below the windows of the Hall. But they are not likely to know this, thank God; and if they did, they would have a job to get there. However, it is wise to keep a sharp lookout, for they know very well that I am far away.

"'And now that I have got to your own doors, which I heartily hope to do, perhaps before you see this, let me ask for yourself and all your dear family. Lingo, the longer I live the more I feel that all the true happiness of life is found at home. My glory is very great, and satisfies me, except when it scares the enemy; but I very often feel that I would give it all away for a quiet life among those who love me. Your daughter Faith is a sweet young woman, just what I should wish for a child of mine to be. And Horatia, my godchild, will turn out very well, if a sharp hand is kept over her. But she takes after me, she is daring and ambitious, and requires a firm hand at the helm. Read this to her, with my love, and I dare say she will only laugh at it. If she marries to my liking, she will be down for a good thing in my will, some day. God bless us all. Amen. Amen.

"'Yours affectionately,

"'NELSON AND BRONTE.'"

"Take it to heart, my dear; and so must I," said the Admiral, laughing at the face his daughter made; "your godfather is a most excellent judge of everybody's character except his own. But, bless me, my dear, why, you are crying! You silly little thing! I was only in fun. You shall marry to his liking, and be down for the good thing. Look up, and laugh at everybody, my darling. No one laughs so merrily as my pretty Dolly. Why, Faith, what does she mean by this?"

To the coaxing voice of her father, and the playful glance that she used to play with, Dolly had not rushed up at all, either with mind, or, if that failed, with body, as she always used to do. She hurried towards the door, as if she longed to be away from them; and then, as if she would rather not make any stir about it, sat down and pretended to have caught her dress in something.

"The only thing is to let her go on as she likes," Faith said aloud, so that

Dolly might hear all of it; "I have done all I can, but she believes herself superior. She cannot bear any sort of contradiction, and she expects one to know what she says, without her saying it. There is nothing to be done but to treat her the same way. If she is left to herself, she may come back to it."

"Well, my dear children," said the Admiral, much alarmed at the prospect of a broil between them, such as he remembered about three years back, "I make no pretence to understand your ways. If you were boys, it would be different altogether. But the Almighty has been pleased to make you girls, and very good ones too; in fact, there are none to be found better. You have always been bound up with one another and with me; and every one admires all the three of us. So that we must be content if a little thing arises, not to make too much of it, but bear with one another, and defy anybody to come in between us. Kiss one another, my dears, and be off; for I have much correspondence to attend to, besides the great Nelson's, though I took him first, hoping for something sensible. But I have not much to learn about Springhaven, even from his lordship. However, he is a man in ten thousand, and we must not be vexed about any of his crotchets, because he has never had children to talk about; and he gets out of soundings when he talks about mine. I wish Lady Scudamore was come back. She always agrees with me, and she takes a great load off my shoulders."

The girls laughed at this, as they were meant to do. And they hurried off together, to compare opinions. After all these years of independence, no one should be set up over them. Upon that point Faith was quite as resolute as Dolly; and her ladyship would have refused to come back, if she had overheard their council. For even in the loftiest feminine nature lurks a small tincture of jealousy.

But Dolly was now in an evil frame of mind about many things which she could not explain even to herself, with any satisfaction. Even that harmless and pleasant letter from her great godfather went amiss with her; and instead of laughing at the words about herself, as with a sound conscience she must have done, she brooded over them, and turned them bitter. No man could have mixed up things as she did, but her mind was nimble. For the moment, she hated patriotism, because Nelson represented it; and feeling how wrong he had been about herself, she felt that he was wrong in everything. The French were fine fellows, and had quite as much right to come here as we had to go and harass them, and a little abatement of English conceit might be a good thing in the long-run. Not that she would let them stay here long; that was not to be thought of, and they would not wish it. But a little excitement would be delightful, and a great many things might be changed for the better, such as the treatment of women in this country, which was barbarous, compared to what it was in France. Caryl had told her a great deal about that; and the longer she knew him the more she was convinced of his wisdom and the largeness of his views, so different from the savage spirit of Lord Nelson.

CHAPTER LI

STRANGE CRAFT

While his love was lapsing from him thus, and from her own true self yet more, the gallant young sailor, whose last prize had been that useful one misfortune, was dwelling continually upon her image, because he had very little else to do. English prisoners in France were treated sometimes very badly, which they took good care to proclaim to Europe; but more often with pity, and good-will, and a pleasant study of their modes of thought. For an Englishman then was a strange and ever fresh curiosity to a Frenchman, a specimen of another race of bipeds, with doubts whether marriage could make parentage between them. And a century of intercourse, good-will, and admiration has left us still inquisitive about each other.

Napoleon felt such confidence in his plans for the conquest of England that if any British officer belonging to the fleet in the narrow seas was taken (which did not happen largely), he sent for him, upon his arrival at Boulogne, and held a little talk with any one who could understand and answer. He was especially pleased at hearing of the capture of Blyth Scudamore (who had robbed him of his beloved Blonde), and at once restored Desportes to favour, which he had begun to do before, knowing as well as any man on earth the value of good officers. "Bring your prisoner here to-morrow at twelve o'clock," was his order; "you have turned the tables upon him well."

Scudamore felt a little nervous tingling as he passed through the sentries, with his friend before him, into the pavilion of the greatest man in Europe. But the Emperor, being in high good-humour, and pleased with the young man's modest face and gentle demeanour, soon set him at his ease, and spoke to him as affably as if he had been his equal. For this man of almost universal mind could win every heart, when he set himself to do it. Scudamore rubbed his eyes, which was a trick of his, as if he could scarcely believe them. Napoleon looked—not insignificant (that was impossible for a man with such a countenance), but mild, and pleasing, and benevolent, as he walked to and fro, for he never could stay still, in the place which was neither a tent nor a room, but a mixture of the two, and not a happy one. His hat, looped up with a diamond and quivering with an ostrich feather, was flung anyhow upon the table. But his wonderful eyes were the brightest thing there.

"Ha! ha!" said the Emperor, a very keen judge of faces; "you expected to find me a monster, as I am portrayed by your caricaturists. Your countrymen are not kind to me, except the foremost of them—the great poets. But they will understand me better by-and-by, when justice prevails, and the blessings of peace, for which I am striving perpetually. But the English nation, if it were allowed a voice, would proclaim me its only true friend and ally. You know that, if you are one of the people, and not of the hateful House of Lords, which engrosses all the army and the navy. Are you in connection with the House of Lords?"

Scudamore shook his head and smiled. He was anxious to say that he had a cousin, not more than twice removed, now an entire viscount; but Napoleon never encouraged conversation, unless it was his own, or in answer to his questions.

"Very well. Then you can speak the truth. What do they think of all this grand army? Are they aware that, for their own good, it will very soon occupy London? Are they forming themselves to act as my allies, when I have reduced them to reason? Is it now made entirely familiar to their minds that resistance to me is as hopeless as it has been from the first unwise? If they would submit, without my crossing, it would save them some disturbance, and me a great expense. I have often hoped to hear of it."

"You will never do that, sire," Scudamore answered, looking calmly and firmly at the deep gray eyes, whose gaze could be met by none of the millions who dread passion; "England will not submit, even if you conquer her."

"It is well said, and doubtless you believe it," Napoleon continued, with a smile so slight that to smile in reply to it would have been impertinent; "but England is the same as other nations, although the most obstinate among them. When her capital is occupied, her credit ruined, her great lords unable to obtain a dinner, the government (which is not the country) will yield, and the country must follow it. I have heard that the King, and the Court, and the Parliament, talk of flying to the north, and there remaining, while the navy cuts off our communications, and the inferior classes starve us. Have you heard of any such romance as that?"

"No, sire:" Scudamore scarcely knew what to call him, but adopted this vocative for want of any better. "I have never heard of any such plan, and no one would think of packing up, until our fleet has been demolished."

"Your fleet? Yes, yes. How many ships are now parading to and fro, and getting very tired of it?"

"Your Majesty's officers know that best," Scudamore answered, with his pleasant open smile. "I have been a prisoner for a month and more, and kept ten miles inland, out of sight of the sea."

"But you have been well treated, I hope. You have no complaint to make,

Monsieur Scutamour? Your name is French, and you speak the language well. We set the fair example in the treatment of brave men."

"Sire, I have been treated," the young officer replied, with a low bow, and eyes full of gratitude, "as a gentleman amongst gentlemen. I might say as a friend among kind friends."

"That is as it should be. It is my wish always. Few of your English fabrications annoy me more than the falsehoods about that. It is most ungenerous, when I do my best, to charge me with strangling brave English captains. But Desportes fought well, before you took his vessel. Is it not so? Speak exactly as you think. I like to hear the enemy's account of every action."

"Captain Desportes, sire, fought like a hero, and so did all his crew. It was only his mishap in sticking fast upon a sand-bank that enabled us to overpower him."

"And now he has done the like to you. You speak with a brave man's candour. You shall be at liberty to see the sea, monsieur; for a sailor always pines for that. I will give full instructions to your friend Desportes about you. But one more question before you go—is there much anxiety in England?"

"Yes, sire, a great deal. But we hope not to allow your Majesty's armament to enter and increase it."

"Ah, we shall see, we shall see how that will be. Now farewell, Captain. Tell Desportes to come to me."

"Well, my dear friend, you have made a good impression," said the French sailor, when he rejoined Scudamore, after a few words with the Master of the State; "all you have to do is to give your word of honour to avoid our lines, and keep away from the beach, and of course to have no communication with your friends upon military subjects. I am allowed to place you for the present at Beutin, a pleasant little hamlet on the Canche, where lives an old relative of mine, a Monsieur Jalais, an ancient widower, with a large house and one servant. I shall be afloat, and shall see but little of you, which is the only sad part of the business. You will have to report yourself to your landlord at eight every morning and at eight o'clock at night, and only to leave the house between those hours, and not to wander more than six miles from home. How do these conditions approve themselves to you?"

"I call them very liberal, and very handsome," Scudamore answered, as he well might do. "Two miles' range is all that we allow in England to French officers upon parole. These generous terms are due to your kind friendship."

Before very long the gentle Scuddy was as happy as a prisoner can expect to be, in his comfortable quarters at Beutin. Through friendly exchanges he had received a loving letter from his mother, with an amiable enclosure, and M. Jalais being far from wealthy, a pleasant arrangement was made between them. Scudamore took all his meals with his host, who could manage sound victuals like an Englishman, and the house-keeper, house-cleaner, and house-feeder (misdescribed by Desportes as a servant, according to our distinctions), being a widow of mark, sat down to consider her cookery upon choice occasions. Then for a long time would prevail a conscientious gravity, and reserve of judgment inwardly, everybody waiting for some other body's sentiments; until the author of the work, as a female, might no more abide the malignant silence of male reviewers.

Scudamore, being very easily amused, as any good-natured young man is, entered with zest into all these doings, and became an authority upon appeal; and being gifted with depth of simplicity as well as high courtesy of taste, was never known to pronounce a wrong decision. That is to say, he decided always in favour of the lady, which has been the majestic course of Justice for centuries, till the appearance of Mrs. ——, the lady who should have married the great Home-Ruler.

Thus the wily Scudamore obtained a sitting-room, with the prettiest outlook in the house, or indeed in any house in that part of the world for many leagues of seeking. For the mansion of M. Jalais stood in an elbow of the little river, and one window of this room showed the curve of tidal water widening towards the sea, while the other pleasantly gave eye to the upper reaches of the stream, where an angler of rose-coloured mind might almost hope to hook a trout. The sun glanced down the stream in the morning, and up it to see what he had done before he set; and although M. Jalais' trees were leafless now, they had sleeved their bent arms with green velvetry of moss.

Scudamore brought his comfortable chair to the nook between these windows, and there, with a book or two belonging to his host, and the pipe whose silver clouds enthrone the gods of contemplation, many a pleasant hour was passed, seldom invaded by the sounds of war. For the course of the roads, and sands of the river, kept this happy spot aloof from bad communications. Like many other streams in northern France, the Canche had been deepened and its mouth improved, not for uses of commerce, but of warfare. Veteran soldier and raw recruit, bugler, baker, and farrier, man who came to fight and man who came to write about it, all had been turned into navvies, diggers, drivers of piles, or of horses, or wheelbarrows, by the man who turned everybody into his own teetotum. The Providence that guides the world showed mercy in sending that engine of destruction before there was a Railway for him to run upon.

Now Scudamore being of a different sort, and therefore having pleased Napoleon (who detested any one at all of his own pattern), might have been very well contented here, and certainly must have been so, if he had been without those two windows. Many a bird has lost his nest, and his eggs, and his mate, and even his own tail, by cocking his eyes to the right and left, when he should have drawn their shutters up. And why? Because the brilliance of his too projecting eyes has twinkled through the leaves upon the narrow oblong of the pupils of a spotty-eyed cat going stealthily under the comb of the hedge, with her stomach wired in, and her spinal column fluted, to look like a wrinkled blackthorn snag. But still worse is it for that poor thrush, or lintie, or robin, or warbler-wren, if he flutters in his bosom when he spies that cat, and sets up his feathers, and begins to hop about, making a sad little chirp to his mate, and appealing to the sky to protect him and his family.

Blyth Scudamore's case was a mixture of those two. It would have been better for his comfort if he had shut his eyes; but having opened them, he should have stayed where he was, without any fluttering. However, he acted for the best; and when a man does that, can those who never do so find a word to say against him?

According to the best of his recollection, which was generally near the mark, it was upon Christmas Eve, A.D. 1804, that his curiosity was first aroused. He had made up his room to look a little bit like home, with a few sprigs of holly, and a sheaf of laurel, not placed daintily as a lady dresses them, but as sprightly as a man can make them look, and as bright as a captive Christmas could expect. The decorator shed a little sigh—if that expression may be pardoned by analogy, for he certainly neither fetched nor heaved it— and then he lit his pipe to reflect upon home blessings, and consider the free world outside, in which he had very little share at present.

Mild blue eyes, such as this young man possessed, are often short-sighted at a moderate range, and would be fitted up with glasses in these artificial times, and yet at long distance they are most efficient, and can make out objects that would puzzle keener organs. And so it was that Scudamore, with the sinking sun to help him, descried at a long distance down the tidal reach a peaceful-looking boat, which made his heart beat faster. For a sailor's glance assured him that she was English—English in her rig and the stiff cut of her canvas, and in all those points of character to a seaman so distinctive, which apprise him of his kindred through the length of air and water, as clearly as we landsmen know a man from a woman at the measure of a furlong, or a quarter of a mile. He perceived that it was an English pilot-boat, and that she was standing towards him. At first his heart fluttered with a warm idea, that there must be good news for him on board that boat. Perhaps, without his knowledge, an exchange of prisoners might have been agreed upon; and what a grand Christmas-box for him, if the order for his release was there! But another thought showed him the absurdity of this hope, for orders of release do not come so. Nevertheless, he watched that boat with interest and wonder.

Presently, just as the sun was setting, and shadows crossed the water, the sail (which had been gleaming like a candle-flame against the haze and upon the glaze) flickered and fell, and the bows swung round, and her figure was drawn upon the tideway. She was now within half a mile of M. Jalais' house, and Scudamore, though longing for a spy-glass, was able to make out a good deal without one. He saw that she was an English pilot-boat, undecked, but fitted with a cuddy forward, rigged luggerwise, and built for speed, yet fit to encounter almost any Channel surges. She was light in the water, and bore little except ballast. He could not be sure at that distance, but he thought that the sailors must be Englishmen, especially the man at the helm, who was beyond reasonable doubt the captain.

Then two long sweeps were manned amidship, with two sturdy fellows to tug at each; and the quiet evening air led through the soft rehearsal of the water to its banks the creak of tough ash thole-pins, and the groan of gunwale, and the splash of oars, and even a sound of human staple, such as is accepted by the civilized world as our national diapason.

The captive Scuddy, who observed all this, was thoroughly puzzled at that last turn. Though the craft was visibly English, the crew might still have been doubtful, if they had held their tongues, or kept them in submission. But that word stamped them, or at any rate the one who had been struck in the breast by the heavy timber, as of genuine British birth. Yet there was no sign that these men were prisoners, or acting by compulsion. No French boat was near them, no batteries there commanded their course, and the pilot-boat carried no prize-crew to direct reluctant labours. At the mouth of the river was a floating bridge, for the use of the forces on either side, and no boat could have passed it without permission. Therefore these could be no venturesome Britons, spying out the quarters of the enemy; either they must have been allowed to pass for some special purpose, under flag of truce, or else they were traitors, in league with the French, and despatched upon some dark errand.

In a few minutes, as the evening dusk began to deepen round her, the mysterious little craft disappeared in a hollow of the uplands on the other side of the water, where a narrow creek or inlet—such as is called a "pill" in some parts of England—formed a sheltered landing-place, overhung with clustering trees. Then Scudamore rose, and filled another pipe, to meditate upon this strange affair. "I am justly forbidden," he thought, as it grew dark, "to visit the camp, or endeavour to learn anything done by the army of invasion. And I have pledged myself to that effect. But this is a different case altogether. When Englishmen come here as traitors to their country, and in a place well within my range, my duty is to learn the meaning of it; and if I find treachery of importance working, then I must consider about my parole, and probably withdraw it. That would be a terrible blow to me, because I should certainly be sent far inland, and kept in a French prison perhaps for years, with little chance of hearing from my friends again. And then she would give me up as lost, that faithful darling, who has put aside all her bright prospects for my sake. How I wish I had never seen that boat! and I thought it was coming to bring me such good news! I am bound to give them one day's grace, for they might not know where to find me at once, and to-night I could not get near them, without overstaying my time to be in-doors. But if I hear nothing to-morrow, and see nothing, I must go round, so as not to be seen, and learn something about her the very next morning."

Hearing nothing and seeing no more, he spent an uncomfortable Christmas Day, disappointing his host and kind Madame Fropot, who had done all they knew to enliven him with a genuine English plum-pudding. And the next day, with a light foot but rather heavy heart, he made the long round by the bridge up-stream, and examined the creek which the English boat had entered. He approached the place very cautiously, knowing that if his suspicions were correct, they might be confirmed too decisively, and his countrymen, if they had fire-arms, would give him a warm reception. However, there was no living creature to be seen, except a poor terrified ox, who had escaped from the slaughter-houses of the distant camp, and hoped for a little rest in this dark thicket. He was worn out with his long flight and sadly wounded, for many men had shot at him, when he desired to save his life; and although his mouth was little more than the length of his tail from water, there he lay gasping with his lips stretched out, and his dry tongue quivering between his yellow teeth, and the only moisture he could get was running out instead of into his mouth.

Scudamore, seeing that the coast was clear, and no enemy in chase of this poor creature, immediately filled his hat with fresh water—for the tide was out now, and the residue was sweet—and speaking very gently in the English language, for he saw that he must have been hard-shouted at in French, was allowed without any more disturbance of the system to supply a little glad refreshment. The sorely afflicted animal licked his lips, and looked up for another hatful.

Captain Scuddy deserved a new hat for this—though very few Englishmen would not have done the like—and in the end he got it, though he must have caught a bad cold if he had gone without a hat till then.

Pursuing his search, with grateful eyes pursuing him, he soon discovered where the boat had grounded, by the impress of her keel and forefoot on the stiff retentive mud. He could even see where a hawser had been made fast to a staunch old trunk, and where the soil had been prodded with a pole in pushing her off at the turn of tide. Also deep tracks of some very large hound, or wolf, or unknown quadruped, in various places, scarred the bank. And these marks were so fresh and bright that they must have been made within the last few hours, probably when the last ebb began. If so, the mysterious craft had spent the whole of Christmas Day in that snug berth; and he blamed himself for permitting his host's festivities to detain him. Then he took a few bearings to mark the spot, and fed the poor crippled ox with all the herbage he could gather, resolving to come with a rope to-morrow, and lead him home, if possible, as a Christmas present to M. Jalais.

CHAPTER LII

KIND ENQUIRIES

That notable year, and signal mark in all the great annals of England, the year 1805, began with gloom and great depression. Food was scarce, and so was money; wars, and rumours of worse than war; discontent of men who owed it to their birth and country to stand fast, and trust in God, and vigorously defy the devil; sinkings even of strong hearts, and quailing of spirits that had never quailed before; passionate outcry for peace without honour, and even without safety; savage murmurings at wise measures and at the burdens that must be borne—none but those who lived through all these troubles could count half of them. If such came now, would the body of the nation strive to stand against them, or fall in the dust, and be kicked and trampled, sputtering namby-pamby? Britannia now is always wrong, in the opinion of her wisest sons, if she dares to defend herself even against weak enemies; what then would her crime be if she buckled her corselet against the world! To prostitute their mother is the philanthropy of Communists.

But while the anxious people who had no belief in foreigners were watching by the dark waves, or at the twilight window trembling (if ever a shooting-star drew train, like a distant rocket-signal), or in their sleepy beds scared, and jumping up if a bladder burst upon a jam-pot, no one attempted to ridicule them, and no public journal pronounced that the true British flag was the white feather. It has been left for times when the power of England is tenfold what it was then, and her duties a hundredfold, to tell us that sooner than use the one for the proper discharge of the other, we must break it up and let them go to pot upon it, for fear of hurting somebody that stuck us in the back.

But who of a right mind knows not this, and who with a wrong one will heed it? The only point is that the commonest truisms come upon utterance sometimes, and take didactic form too late; even as we shout to our comrade prone, and beginning to rub his poor nose, "Look out!" And this is what everybody did with one accord, when he was down upon his luck—which is far more momentous than his nose to any man—in the case of Rector Twemlow.

That gentleman now had good reason for being in less than his usual cheer and comfort. Everything around him was uneasy, and everybody seemed to look at him, instead of looking up to him, as the manner used to be. This was enough to make him feel unlike himself; for although he was resolute in his way, and could manage to have it with most people, he was not of that iron style which takes the world as wax to write upon. Mr. Twemlow liked to heave his text at the people of his parish on Sunday, and to have his joke with them on Monday; as the fire that has burned a man makes the kettle sing to comfort him. And all who met him throughout the week were pleased with him doubly, when they remembered his faithfulness in the pulpit.

But now he did his duty softly, as if some of it had been done to him; and if anybody thanked him for a fine discourse, he never endeavoured to let him have it all again. So far was he gone from his natural state that he would rather hear nothing about himself than be praised enough to demand reply; and this shows a world-wide depression to have arrived in the latitude of a British waistcoat. However, he went through his work, as a Briton always does, until he hangs himself; and he tried to try some of the higher consolation, which he knew so well how to administer to others.

Those who do not understand the difference of this might have been inclined to blame him; but all who have seen a clever dentist with the toothache are aware that his knowledge adds acuteness to the pain. Mr. Twemlow had borne great troubles well, and been cheerful even under long suspense; but now a disappointment close at home, and the grief of beholding his last hopes fade, were embittered by mystery and dark suspicions. In despair at last of recovering his son, he had fastened upon his only daughter the interest of his declining life; and now he was vexed with misgivings about her, which varied as frequently as she did. It was very unpleasant to lose the chance of having a grandchild capable of rocking in a silver cradle; but that was a trifle compared with the prospect of having no grandchild at all, and perhaps not even a child to close his eyes. And even his wife, of long habit and fair harmony, from whom he had never kept any secret—frightful as might be the cost to his honour—even Mrs. Twemlow shook her head sometimes, when the arrangement of her hair permitted it, and doubted whether any of the Carne Castle Carnes would have borne with such indignity.

"Prosecute him, prosecute him," this good lady always said. "You ought to have been a magistrate, Joshua—the first magistrate in the Bible was that— and then you would have known how to do things. But because you would have to go to Sir Charles Darling—whose Sir can never put him on the level of the Carnes—you have some right feeling against taking out a summons. In that I agree with you; it would be very dreadful here. But in London he might be punished, I am sure; and I know a great deal about the law, for I never had any one connected with me who was not a magistrate; the Lord Mayor has a Court of his own for trying the corporation under the chair; and if this was put properly before him by a man like Mr. Furkettle, upon the understanding that he should not be paid unless he won his case, I am sure the result would be three years' imprisonment. By that time he would have worn out his coat with jailer's keys upon it, which first attracted our poor Eliza; or if he was not allowed to wear it, it would go out of fashion, and be harmless. No one need know a word about it here, for Captain Stubbard would oblige us gladly by cutting it out of the London papers. My dear, you have nobody ill in the parish; I will put up your things, and see you off to-morrow. We will dine late on Friday, to suit the coach; and you will be quite fit for Sunday work again, if you keep up your legs on a chair all Saturday."

"If ever I saw a straightforward man," Mr. Twemlow used to answer, "it was poor Percival Shargeloes. He is gone to a better world, my dear. And if he continued to be amenable to law, this is not a criminal, but a civil case."

"A nice case of civility, Joshua! But you always stand up for your sex. Does the coach take people to a better world? A stout gentleman, like him, was seen inside the coach, muffled up in a cravat of three colours, and eating at frequent intervals."

"The very thing poor Percival never did. That disposes to my mind of that foolish story. My dear, when all truth comes to light, you will do justice to his memory."

"Yes, I dare say. But I should like to do it now. If you entertain any dark ideas, it is your duty to investigate them. Also to let me share them, Joshua, as I have every right to do."

This was just what the Rector could not do; otherwise he might have been far more happy. Remembering that last conversation with his prospective son-in-law, and the poor man's declaration that the suspicious matter at the castle ought to be thoroughly searched out at once, he nourished a dark suspicion, which he feared to impart to his better half, the aunt of the person suspected. But the longer he concealed it, the more unbearable grew this misery to a candid nature, until he was compelled, in self-defence, to allow it some sort of outlet. "I will speak to the fellow myself," he said, heartily disliking the young man now, "and judge from his manner what next I ought to do."

This resolution gave him comfort, much as he hated any interview with Carne, who treated him generally with cold contempt. And, like most people who have formed a decision for the easing of the conscience, he accepted very patiently the obstacles encountered. In the first place, Carne was away upon business; then he was laid up with a heavy cold; then he was much too hard at work (after losing so much time) to be able to visit Springhaven; and to seek him in his ruins was most unsafe, even if one liked to do it. For now it was said that two gigantic dogs, as big as a bull and as fierce as a tiger, roved among the ruins all day, and being always famished, would devour in two minutes any tempting stranger with a bit of flesh or fat on him. The Rector, patting his gaiters, felt that instead of a pastor he might become a very sweet repast to them, and his delicacy was renewed and deepened. He was bound to wait until his nephew appeared at least inside his parish.

Therefore the time of year was come almost to the middle of February when Mr. Twemlow at last obtained the chance he required and dreaded. He heard that his nephew had been seen that day to put up his horse in the village, and would probably take the homeward road as soon as it grew too dark to read. So he got through his own work (consisting chiefly of newspaper, dinner, and a cool clay pipe, to equalise mind with matter), and having thus escaped the ladies, off he set by the lobby door, carrying a good thick stick. As the tide would be up, and only deep sand left for the heavy track of the traveller, he chose the inland way across the lower part of the Admiral's grounds, leading to the village by a narrow plank bridge across the little stream among some trees. Here were banks of earth and thicket, shadowy dells where the primrose grew, and the cuckoo-pint, and wood-sorrel, and perhaps in summer the glowworm breathed her mossy gleam under the blackberries.

And here Parson Twemlow was astonished, though he had promised himself to be surprised no more, after all he had been through lately. As he turned a sharp corner by an ivied tree, a breathless young woman ran into his arms.

"Oh!" cried the Rector, for he was walking briskly, with a well-nourished part of his system forward—"oh, I hope you have not hurt yourself. No doubt it was my fault. Why, Dolly! What a hurry you are in! And all alone—all alone, almost after dark!"

"To be sure; and that makes me in such a hurry;" Miss Dolly was in sad confusion. "But I suppose I am safe in my father's own grounds."

"From everybody, except yourself, my dear," Mr. Twemlow replied, severely. "Is your father aware, does your sister know, that you are at this distance from the house after dark, and wholly without a companion?"

"It is not after dark, Mr. Twemlow; although it is getting darker than I meant it to be. I beg your pardon for terrifying you. I hope you will meet with no other perils! Good-night! Or at least I mean, good-afternoon!"

"The brazen creature!" thought Mr. Twemlow, as the girl without another word disappeared. "Not even to offer me any excuse! But I suppose she had no fib handy. She will come to no good, I am very much afraid. Maria told me that she was getting very wilful; but I had no idea that it was quite so bad as this. I am sorry for poor Scudamore, who thinks her such an angel. I wonder if Carne is at the bottom of this? There is nothing too bad for that dark young man. I shall ascertain at any rate whether he is in the village. But unless I look sharp I shall be too late to meet him. Oh, I can't walk so fast as I did ten years ago."

Impelled by duty to put best leg foremost, and taking a short-cut above the village, he came out upon the lane leading towards the castle, some half-mile or so beyond the last house of Springhaven. Here he waited to recover breath, and prepare for what he meant to say, and he was sorry to perceive that light would fail him for strict observation of his nephew's face. But he chose the most open spot he could find, where the hedges were low, and nothing overhung the road.

Presently he heard the sound of hoofs approaching leisurely up the hill, and could see from his resting-place that Carne was coming, sitting loosely and wearily on his high black horse. Then the Rector, to cut short an unpleasant business, stood boldly forth and hailed him.

"No time for anything now," shouted Carne; "too late already. Do you want my money? You are come to the wrong man for that; but the right one, I can tell you, for a bullet."

"Caryl, it is I, your uncle Twemlow, or at any rate the husband of your aunt. Put up your pistol, and speak to me a minute. I have something important to say to you. And I never can find you at the castle."

"Then be quick, sir, if you please;" Carne had never condescended to call this gentleman his uncle. "I have little time to spare. Out with it."

"You were riding very slowly for a man in a hurry," said the Rector, annoyed at his roughness. "But I will not keep you long, young man. For some good reasons of your own you have made a point of avoiding us, your nearest relatives in this country, and to whom you addressed yourself before you landed in a manner far more becoming. Have I ever pressed my attentions upon you?"

"No, I confess that you have not done that. You perceived as a gentleman how little there was in common between the son of a devoted Catholic and a heretic clergyman."

"That is one way to put it," Mr. Twemlow answered, smiling in spite of his anger at being called a heretic; "but I was not aware that you had strong religious views. However that may be, we should have many things in common, as Englishmen, at a time like this. But what I came to speak of is not that. We can still continue to get on without you, although we would rather have met with friendly feeling and candour, as becomes relatives. But little as you know of us, you must be well aware that your cousin Eliza was engaged to be married to a gentleman from London, Mr. Percival Shargeloes, and that he—"

"I am sure I wish her all happiness, and congratulate you, my dear sir, as well as my aunt Maria. I shall call, as soon as possible, to offer my best wishes. It was very kind of you to tell me. Goodnight, sir, good-night! There is a shower coming."

"But," exclaimed the Rector, nonplussed for the moment by this view of the subject, yet standing square before the horse, "Shargeloes has disappeared. What have you done with him?"

Carne looked at his excellent uncle as if he had much doubt about his sanity. "Try to explain yourself, my dear sir. Try to connect your ideas," he said, "and offer me the benefit another time. My horse is impatient; he may strike you with his foot."

"If he does, I shall strike him upon the head," Mr. Twemlow replied, with his heavy stick ready. "It will be better for you to hear me out. Otherwise I shall procure a search-warrant, and myself examine your ruins, of which I know every crick and cranny. And your aunt Maria shall come with me, who knows every stone even better than you do. That would be a very different thing from an overhauling by Captain Stubbard. I think we should find a good many barrels and bales that had paid no duty."

"My dear uncle," cried Carne, with more affection than he ever yet had shown, "that is no concern of yours; you have no connection with the Revenue; and I am sure that Aunt Maria would be loth to help in pulling down the family once more. But do as you please. I am accustomed to ill fortune. Only I should like to know what this is about poor Cousin Eliza. If any man has wronged her, leave the case to me. You have no son now, and the honour of the family shall not suffer in my hands. I will throw up everything, busy as I am, to make such a rascal bite the dust. And Eliza so proud, and so upright herself!"

"Caryl," said his uncle, moved more than he liked to show by this fine feeling, "you know more, I see, than you liked to show at first, doubtless through goodwill to us. Your dear aunt wished to keep the matter quiet, for the sake of poor Eliza, and her future chances. But I said—No. Let us have it all out. If there is wrong, we have suffered, not done it. Concealment is odious to every honest mind."

"Deeply, deeply odious. Upon that point there can be no two opinions"—he forgets his barrels, thought the Rector—"but surely this man, whatever his name is—Charleygoes—must have been hiding from you something in his own history. Probably he had a wife already. City men often do that when young, and then put their wives somewhere when they get rich, and pay visits, and even give dinners, as if they were bachelors to be sought after. Was Charleygoes that sort of a man?"

"His name is 'Shargeloes,' a name well known, as I am assured, in the highest quarters. And he certainly was not sought after by us, but came to me with an important question bearing on ichthyology. He may be a wanderer, as you suggest, and as all the ladies seem to think. But my firm belief is to the contrary. And my reason for asking you about him is a very clear one. He had met you twice, and felt interest in you as a future member of our family. You had never invited him to the castle; and the last intention he expressed in my hearing was to call upon you without one. Has he met with an accident in your cellars? Or have your dogs devoured him? He carried a good deal of flesh, in spite of all he could do to the contrary; and any man naturally might endeavour to hush up such an incident. Tell me the truth, Caryl. And we will try to meet it."

"My two dogs (who would never eat any one, though they might pull down a stranger, and perhaps pretend to bite him) arrived here the first week in January. When did Charleygoes disappear? I am not up in dates, but it must have been weeks and weeks before that time. And I must have heard of it, if it had happened. I may give you my honour that Orso and Leo have not eaten Charleygoes."

"You speak too lightly of a man in high position, who would have been Lord Mayor of London, if he had never come to Springhaven. But living or dead, he shall never be that now. Can you answer me, in the same straightforward manner, as to an accident in your cellars; which, as a gentleman upon a private tour, he had clearly no right to intrude upon?"

"I can answer you quite as clearly. Nothing accidental has happened in my cellars. You may come and see them, if you have any doubt about it. And you need not apply for a search-warrant."

"God forbid, my dear fellow," cried the uncle, "that I should intrude upon any little matters of delicacy, such as are apt to arise between artificial laws and gentlemen who happen to live near the sea, and to have large places that require restoring! I shall go home with a lighter heart. There is nothing in this world that brings the comfort of straightforwardness."

CHAPTER LIII

TIME AND PLACE

In a matter like that French invasion, which had been threatened for such a time, and kept so long impending, "the cry of wolf" grows stale at last, and then the real danger comes. Napoleon had reckoned upon this, as he always did upon everything, and for that good reason he had not grudged the time devoted to his home affairs. These being settled according to his will, and mob turned into pomp as gaily as grub turns into butterfly, a strong desire for a little more glory arose in his mighty but ill-regulated mind. If he could only conquer England, or even without that fetch her down on her knees and make her lick her own dust off the feet of Frenchmen, from that day forth all the nations of the earth must bow down before him. Russia, Prussia, Austria, Spain, though they might have had the power, never would have plucked the spirit up, to resist him hand in hand, any more than skittle-pins can back one another up against the well-aimed ball.

The balance of to-be or not-to-be, as concerned our country (which many now despise, as the mother of such disloyal children), after all that long suspension, hung in the clouds of that great year; and a very cloudy year it was, and thick with storms on land and sea. Storm was what the Frenchmen longed for, to disperse the British ships; though storm made many an Englishman, pulling up the counterpane as the window rattled, thank the Father of the weather for keeping the enemy ashore and in a fright. But the greatest peril of all would be in the case of fog succeeding storm, when the mighty flotilla might sweep across before our ships could resume blockade, or even a frigate intercept.

One of the strangest points in all this period of wonders, to us who after the event are wise, is that even far-sighted Nelson and his watchful colleagues seem to have had no inkling of the enemy's main project. Nelson believed Napoleon to be especially intent on Egypt; Collingwood expected a sudden dash on Ireland; others were sure that his object was Jamaica; and many maintained that he would step ashore in India. And these last came nearest to the mark upon the whole, for a great historian (who declares, like Caryl Carne, that a French invasion is a blessing to any country) shows that, for at least a month in the spring of 1805, his hero was revolving a mighty scheme for robbing poor England of blissful ravage, and transferring it to India.

However, the master of the world—as he was called already, and meant soon to be—suddenly returned to his earlier design, and fixed the vast power of his mind upon it. He pushed with new vigour his preparations, which had been slackened awhile, he added 30,000 well-trained soldiers to his force already so enormous, and he breathed the quick spirit of enterprise into the mighty mass he moved. Then, to clear off all obstacles, and ensure clear speed of passage, he sent sharp orders to his Admirals to elude and delude the British fleets, and resolved to enhance that delusion by his own brief absence from the scene.

Meanwhile a man of no importance to the world, and of very moderate ambition, was passing a pleasant time in a quiet spot, content to be scarcely a spectator even of the drama in rehearsal around him. Scudamore still abode with M. Jalais, and had won his hearty friendship, as well as the warm good-will of that important personage Madame Fropot. Neither of these could believe at first that any Englishman was kind and gentle, playful in manner, and light-hearted, easily pleased, and therefore truly pleasing. But as soon as they saw the poor wounded ox brought home by a ford, and settled happily in the orchard, and received him as a free gift from their guest, national prejudices dwindled very fast, and domestic good feeling grew faster. M. Jalais, although a sound Frenchman, hated the Empire and all that led up to it; and as for Madame Fropot, her choicest piece of cookery might turn into cinders, if anybody mentioned conscription in her presence. For she had lost her only son, the entire hope of her old days, as well as her only daughter's lover, in that lottery of murder.

Nine out of ten of the people in the village were of the same way of thinking. A great army cannot be quartered anywhere, even for a week, without scattering brands of ill-will all around it. The swagger of the troops, their warlike airs, and loud contempt of the undrilled swain, the dash of a coin on the counter when they deign to pay for anything, the insolent wink at every modest girl, and the coarse joke running along apish mouths—even before dark crime begins, native antipathy is sown and thrives. And now for nearly four years this coast had never been free from the arrogant strut, the clanking spur, and the loud guffaw, which in every age and every clime have been considered the stamp of valour by plough-boys at the paps of Bellona. So weary was the neighbourhood of this race, new conscripts always keeping up the pest, that even the good M. Jalais longed to hear that the armament lay at the bottom of the Channel. And Scudamore would have been followed by the good wishes of every house in the village, if he had lifted his hat and said, "Good-bye, my dear friends; I am breaking my parole."

For this, though encouraged by the popular voice, he was not sufficiently liberal, but stayed within bounds of space and time more carefully than if he had been watched. Captain Desportes, who had been in every way a true friend to him, came to see him now and then, being now in command of a division of the prames, and naturally anxious for the signal to unmoor. Much discourse was held, without brag on either side, but with equal certainty on both sides of success. And in one of these talks the Englishman in the simplest manner told the Frenchman all that he had seen on Christmas Eve, and his own suspicions about it.

"Understand this well," continued Scudamore; "if I discover any treachery on the part of my own countrymen, I shall not be able to stop here on the terms that have been allowed me. Whatever the plan may be, I shall feel as if I were a party to it, if I accepted my free range and swallowed my suspicions. With your proceedings I do not meddle, according to fair compact, and the liberal conditions offered. But to see my own countrymen playing my country false is more than I could stand. You know more of such things than I do. But if you were an Englishman, could you endure to stand by and hide treachery, for the sake of your own comfort?"

"Beyond a doubt, no," Captain Desportes answered, spreading his hand with decision: "in such a case I should throw up my parole. But a mere suspicion does not justify an act so ungracious to the commander, and personally so unkind to me. I hoped that bright eyes might persuade you to forego hard knocks, and wear none but gentle chains among us. Nature intended you for a Frenchman. You have the gay heart, and the easy manner, and the grand philosophy of our great nation. Your name is Blyth, and I know what that intends."

Scudamore blushed, for he knew that Madame Fropot was doing her best to commit him with a lovely young lady not far off, who had felt a tender interest in the cheerful English captive. But after trying to express once more the deep gratitude he felt towards those who had been so wonderfully kind and friendly, he asked with a smile, and a little sigh behind it, what he must do, if compelled by duty to resign his present privileges.

"My faith! I scarcely know," replied Desportes; "I have never had such a case before. But I think you must give me a written notice, signed by yourself and by M. Jalais, and allow a week to pass, and then, unless you have heard from me, present yourself to the commandant of the nearest post, which must be, I suppose, at Etaples. Rather a rough man he is; and I fear you will have reason for regret. The duty will then remain with him. But I beg you, my dear friend, to continue as you are. Tush, it is nothing but some smuggler's work."

Scudamore hoped that he might be right, and for some little time was not disturbed by any appearance to the contrary. But early in the afternoon one day, when the month of March was near its close, he left his books for a little fresh air, and strolled into the orchard, where his friend the ox was dwelling.

This worthy animal, endowed with a virtue denied to none except the human race, approached him lovingly, and begged to draw attention to the gratifying difference betwixt wounds and scars. He offered his broad brow to the hand, and his charitable ears to be tickled, and breathed a quick issue of good feeling and fine feeding, from the sensitive tucks of his nostrils, as a large-hearted smoker makes the air go up with gratitude.

But as a burnt child dreads the fire, the seriously perforated animal kept one eye vigilant of the northern aspect, and the other studious of the south. And the gentle Scuddy (who was finding all things happy, which is the only way to make them so) was startled by a sharp jerk of his dear friend's head. Following the clue of gaze, there he saw, coming up the river with a rollicking self-trust, a craft uncommonly like that craft which had mounted every sort of rig and flag, and carried every kind of crew, in his many dreams about her. This made him run back to his room at once, not only in fear of being seen upon the bank, but also that he might command a better view, with the help of his landlord's old spy-glass.

Using this, which he had cleaned from the dust of ages, he could clearly see the faces of the men on board. Of these there were six, of whom five at least were Englishmen, or of English breed. As the pilot-boat drew nearer, and the sunlight fell upon her, to his great surprise he became convinced that the young man at the tiller was Dan Tugwell, the son of the captain of Springhaven. Four of the others were unknown to him, though he fancied that he had seen two of them before, but could not remember when or where. But he watched with special interest the tall man lounging against the little door of the cuddy in the bows, whose profile only was presented to him. Then the boat canted round towards the entrance of the creek, and having his glass upon the full face of the man, he recognised him as Caryl Carne, whom he had met more than once at Springhaven.

His darkest suspicions were at once redoubled, and a gush of latent jealousy was added to them. In happier days, when he was near his lady-love, some whispers had reached him about this fellow, whose countenance had always been repulsive to him, arrogant, moody, and mysterious. His good mother also, though most careful not to harass him, had mentioned that Carne in her latest letter, and by no means in a manner to remove his old misgivings. As a matter now of duty to his country and himself, the young sailor resolved to discover, at any risk, what traitorous scheme had brought this dark man over here.

To escape the long circuit by the upper bridge, he had obtained leave, through M. Jalais, to use an old boat which was kept in a bend of the river about a mile above the house. And now, after seeing that English boat make for the creek where she had been berthed on Christmas Eve, he begged Madame Fropot to tell his host not to be uneasy about him, and taking no weapon but a ground-ash stick, set forth to play spy upon traitors. As surely as one foot came after the other, he knew that every step was towards his grave, if he made a mistake, or even met bad luck; but he twirled his light stick in his broad brown hand, and gently invaded the French trees around with an old English song of the days when still an Englishman could compose a song. But this made him think of that old-fashioned place Springhaven; and sadness fell upon him, that the son of its captain should be a traitor.

Instead of pulling across the river, to avoid the splash of oars he sculled with a single oar astern, not standing up and wallowing in the boat, but sitting and cutting the figure of 8 with less noise than a skater makes. The tide being just at slack-water, this gave him quite as much way as he wanted, and he steered into a little bight of the southern bank, and made fast to a stump, and looked about; for he durst not approach the creek until the light should fade and the men have stowed tackle and begun to feed. The vale of the stream afforded shelter to a very decent company of trees, which could not have put up with the tyranny of the west wind upon the bare brow of the coast. Most of these trees stood back a little from the margin of high tide, reluctant to see themselves in the water, for fear of the fate of Narcissus. But where that clandestine boat had glided into gloom and greyness, a fosse of Nature's digging, deeply lined with wood and thicket, offered snug harbourage to craft and fraud.

Scudamore had taken care to learn the ups and downs of the riverside ere this, and knew them now as well as a native, for he had paid many visits to the wounded ox, whom he could not lead home quite as soon as he had hoped, and he had found a firm place of the little river, easy to cross when the tide was out. With the help of this knowledge he made his way to the creek, without much risk of being observed, and then, as he came to the crest of the thicket, he lay down and watched the interlopers.

There was the boat, now imbedded in the mud, for the little creek was nearly dry by this time. Her crew had all landed, and kindled a fire, over which hung a kettle full of something good, which they seemed to regard with tender interest; while upon a grassy slope some few yards to the right a trooper's horse was tethered. Carne was not with them, but had crossed the creek, as the marks of his boots in the mud declared; and creeping some little way along the thicket, Scudamore descried him walking to and fro impatiently in a little hollow place, where the sailors could not see him. This was on Scudamore's side of the creek, and scarcely fifty yards below him. "He is waiting for an interview with somebody," thought Scuddy: "if I could only get down to that little shanty, perhaps I should hear some fine treason. The wind is the right way to bring me every word he says."

Keeping in shelter when the traitor walked towards him, and stealing on silently when his back was turned, the young sailor managed to ensconce himself unseen in the rough little wattle shed made by his own hands for the shelter of his patient, when a snow-storm had visited the valley of the Canche last winter. Nothing could be better fitted for his present purpose, inasmuch as his lurking-place could scarcely be descried from below, being sheltered by two large trees and a screen of drooping ivy, betwixt and below which it looked no more than a casual meeting of bushes; while on the other hand the open space beneath it was curved like a human ear, to catch the voice and forward it.

While Scudamore was waiting here and keenly watching everything, the light began to falter, and the latest gleam of sunset trembled with the breath of Spring among the buds and catkins. But the tall man continued his long, firm stride, as if the watch in his pocket were the only thing worth heeding. Until, as the shadows lost their lines and flowed into the general depth, Carne sprang forward, and a horse and rider burst into the silence of the grass and moss and trees.

Carne made a low obeisance, retired a little, and stood hat in hand, until it should please the other man to speak. And Scudamore saw, with a start of surprise, that the other man was Napoleon.

This great man appeared, to the mild English eyes that were watching him so intently, of a very different mood and visage from those of their last view of him. Then the face, which combined the beauty of Athens with the strength of Rome, was calm, and gentle, and even sweet, with the rare indulgence of a kindly turn. But now, though not disturbed with wrath, nor troubled by disappointment, that face (which had helped to make his fortune, more than any woman's had ever done for her) was cast, even if the mould could be the same, in a very different metal. Stern force and triumphant vigour shone in every lineament, and the hard bright eyes were intent with purpose that would have no denial.

Refusing Carne's aid, he remained on his horse, and stroked his mane for a moment, for he loved any creature that served him well, and was tender of heart when he could afford it; which added to his power with mankind.

"Are all your men well out of earshot?" he asked; and receiving assurance from Carne, went on. "Now you will be satisfied at length. You have long been impatient. It is useless to deny it. All is arranged, and all comes to a head within three months, and perhaps within two. Only four men will know it besides yourself, and three of those four are commanders of my fleet. A short time will be occupied in misleading those British ships that beleaguer us; then we concentrate ours, and command the Channel; if only for three days, that will be enough. I depart for Italy in three days or in four, to increase the security of the enemy. But I shall return, without a word to any one, and as fast as horses can lay belly to the ground, when I hear that our ships have broken out. I shall command the invasion, and it will be for England to find a man to set against me."

"England will have difficulty, sire, in doing that," Carne answered, with a grim smile, for he shared the contempt of English Generals then prevalent. "If the Continent cannot do it, how can the poor England? Once let your Majesty land, and all is over. But what are your Majesty's orders for me? And where do you propose to make the landing?"

"Never ask more than one question at a time," Napoleon answered, with his usual curtness; "my orders to you are to return at once. Prepare your supplies for a moment's notice. Through private influence of some fair lady, you have command of the despatches of that officer at Springport, who has the control of the naval forces there. Ha! what was that? I heard a sound up yonder. Hasten up, and see if there is any listener. It seemed to be there, where the wood grows thick."

Blyth Scudamore, forgetful of himself, had moved, and a dry stick cracked beneath his foot. Carne, at the Emperor's glance and signal, sprang up the bank, with the help of some bushes, drew his sword and passed it between the wattles, then parted them and rushed through, but saw no sign of any one. For Scuddy had slipped away, as lightly as a shadow, and keeping in a mossy trough, had gained another shelter. Here he was obliged to slink in the smallest possible compass, kneeling upon both knees, and shrugging in both shoulders. Peering very sharply through an intertwist of suckers (for his shelter was a stool of hazel, thrown up to repair the loss of stem), he perceived that the Emperor had moved his horse a little when Carne rejoined and reassured him. And this prevented Scudamore from being half so certain as he would have liked to be, about further particulars of this fine arrangement.

"No," was the next thing he heard Napoleon say whose power of saying "no" had made his "yes" invincible; "no, it is not to be done like that. You will await your instructions, and not move until you receive them from my own hand. Make no attempt to surprise anybody or anything, until I have ten thousand men ashore. Ten thousand will in six hours attain to fifty thousand, if the shore proves to be as you describe; so great is the merit of flat-bottomed boats. Your duty will be to leave the right surprise to us, and create a false one among the enemy. This you must do in the distance of the West, as if my Brest fleet were ravaging there, and perhaps destroying Plymouth. You are sure that you can command the signals for this?"

"Sire, I know everything as if I sat among it. I can do as I please with the fair secretary; and her father is an ancient fool."

"Then success is more easy than I wish to have it, because it will not make good esteem. If Nelson comes at all, he will be too late, as he generally is too early. London will be in our hands by the middle of July at the latest, probably much earlier, and then Captain Carne shall name his own reward. Meanwhile forget not any word of what I said. Make the passage no more. You will not be wanted here. Your services are far more important where you are. You may risk the brave Charron, but not yourself. Send over by the 20th of May a letter to me, under care of Decres, to be opened by no hand but mine, upon my return from Italy, and let the messengers wait for my reply. Among them must be the young man who knows the coast, and we will detain him for pilot. My reply will fix the exact date of our landing, and then you will despatch, through the means at your command, any English force that might oppose our landing, to the West, where we shall create a false alarm. Is all this clear to you? You are not stupid. The great point is to do all at the right time, having consideration of the weather."

"All is clear, and shall be carried out clearly, to the best of your Majesty's humble servant's power."

Napoleon offered his beautiful white hand, which Carne raised to his lips, and then the Emperor was gone. Carne returned slowly to the boat, with triumph written prematurely on his dark stern face; while Scudamore's brisk and ruddy features were drawn out to a wholly unwonted length, as he quietly made his way out of the covert.

CHAPTER LIV

IN A SAD PLIGHT

"How shall I get out of this parole? Or shall I break it, instead of getting out? Which shall I think of first, my honour, or my country? The safety of millions, or the pride of one? An old Roman would have settled it very simply. But a Christian cannot do things so. Thank God there is no hurry, for a few days yet! But I must send a letter to Desportes this very night. Then I must consider about waiting for a week."

Scudamore, unable to think out his case as yet—especially after running as if his wind could turn a vane—was sitting on the bank, to let the river-bed get darker, before he put his legs into the mud to get across. For the tide was out, and the old boat high and dry, and a very weak water remained to be crossed (though, like nearly all things that are weak, it was muddy), but the channel had a moist gleam in the dry spring air, and anybody moving would be magnified afar. He felt that it would never do for him, with such a secret, to be caught, and brought to book, or even to awake suspicion of his having it. The ancient Roman of whom he had thought would have broken parole for his country's sake, and then fallen on his sword for his own sake; but although such behaviour should be much admired, it is nicer to read of such things than to do them. Captain Scuddy was of large and steady nature, and nothing came to him with a jerk or jump—perhaps because he was such a jumper—and he wore his hat well on the back of his head, because he had no fear of losing it. But for all that he found himself in a sad quandary now.

To begin with, his parole was not an ordinary leave, afforded by his captors to save themselves trouble; but a special grace, issuing from friendship, and therefore requiring to be treated in a friendly vein. The liberality of these terms had enabled him to dwell as a friend among friends, and to overhear all that he had heard. In the balance of perplexities, this weighed heavily against his first impulse to cast away all except paramount duty to his country. In the next place, he knew that private feeling urged him as hotly as public duty to cast away all thought of honour, and make off. For what he had heard about the "fair secretary" was rankling bitterly in his deep heart. He recalled at this moment the admirable precept of an ancient sage, that in such a conflict of duties the doubter should incline to the course least agreeable to himself, inasmuch as the reasons against it are sure to be urged the most feebly in self-council. Upon the whole, the question was a nice one for a casuist; and if there had not been a day to spare, duty to his country must have overridden private faith.

However, as there was time to spare, he resolved to reconcile private honour with the sense of public duty; and returning to his room, wrote a careful letter (of which he kept a copy) to his friend Desportes, now on board, and commanding the flagship of one division of the flotilla. He simply said, without giving his reason, that his parole must expire in eight days after date, allowing one day for delivery of his letter. Then he told M. Jalais what he had done, and much sorrow was felt in the household. When the time had expired without any answer from Captain Desportes, who meant to come and see him but was unable to do so, Scudamore packed up a few things needful, expecting to be placed in custody, and resolved to escape from it, at any risk of life. Then he walked to Etaples, a few miles down the river, and surrendered himself to the commandant there. This was a rough man—as Desportes had said—and with more work to do than he could manage. With very little ceremony he placed the English prisoner in charge of a veteran corporal, with orders to take him to the lock-up in the barracks, and there await further instructions. And then the commandant, in the hurry of his duties, forgot all about him.

Captain Scuddy now found himself in quarters and under treatment very trying to his philosophy. Not that the men who had him in charge were purposely unkind to him, only they were careless about his comfort, and having more important work to see to, fed him at their leisure, which did not always coincide with his appetite. Much of his food was watery and dirty, and seemed to be growing its own vegetables, and sometimes to have overripened them. Therefore he began to lose substance, and his cheeks became strangers to the buxom gloss which had been the delight of Madame Fropot. But although they did not feed him well, they took good care of him in other ways, affording no chance of exit.

But sour fruit often contains good pips. Scudamore's food was not worth saying grace for, and yet a true blessing attended it: forasmuch as the Frenchmen diminished the width of their prisoner, but not of the window. Falling away very rapidly, for his mind was faring as badly as his body (having nothing but regrets to feed upon, which are no better diet than daisy soup), the gentle Scuddy, who must have become a good wrangler if he had stopped at Cambridge, began to frame a table of cubic measure, and consider the ratio of his body to that window, or rather the aperture thereof. One night, when his supper had been quite forgotten by everybody except himself, he lay awake thinking for hours and hours about his fair Dolly and the wicked Carne, and all the lies he must have told about her—for not a single syllable would Scudamore believe—and the next day he found himself become so soft and limp, as well as reduced to his lowest dimension, that he knew, by that just measure which a man takes of himself when he has but a shred of it left, that now he was small enough to go between the bars. And now it was high time to feel that assurance, for the morning brought news that the order for his removal to a great prison far inland was come, and would be carried out the next day. "Now or never" was the only chance before him.

Having made up his mind, he felt refreshed, and took his food with gratitude. Then, as soon as the night was dark and quiet, and the mighty host for leagues and leagues launched into the realms of slumber, springing with both feet well together, as he sprang from the tub at Stonnington, Scuddy laid hold of the iron bars which spanned the window vertically, opened the lattice softly, and peeped out in quest of sentinels. There were none on duty very near him, though he heard one pacing in the distance. Then flinging himself on his side, he managed, with some pain to his well-rounded chest, to squeeze it through the narrow slit, and hanging from the bar, dropped gently. The drop was deep, and in spite of all precautions he rolled to the bottom of a grassy ditch. There he lay quiet to rest his bruises, and watch whether any alarm was raised. Luckily for him, the moon was down, and no one had observed his venture. Crawling on all fours along a hollow place, he passed the outposts, and was free.

Free in mind as well as body, acquitted from all claims of honour, and able without a taint upon his name to bear most important news to England, if he could only get away from France. This would be difficult, as he was well aware; but his plan had been thoroughly considered in his prison, and he set forth to make the best of it. Before his escape had been discovered, he was under M. Jalais' roof once more, and found his good friends resolved never to betray him. "But I must not expose you to the risk," said he, "of heavy fine and imprisonment. I shall have to say good-bye to all your goodness in an hour. And I shall not even allow you to know what road I take, lest you should be blamed for sending my pursuers on the wrong one. But search my room in three days' time, and you will find a packet to pay for something which I must steal for the present. I pray you, ask nothing, for your own sake."

They fed him well, and he took three loaves, and a little keg of cider, as well as the bag he had packed before he surrendered himself at Etaples. Madame Fropot wept and kissed him, because he reminded her of her lost son; and M. Jalais embraced him, because he was not at all like any son of his. With hearty good wishes, and sweet regret, and promises never to forget them, the Englishman quitted this kind French house, and became at once a lawful and a likely mark for bullets.

The year was now filled with the flurry of Spring, the quick nick of time when a man is astonished at the power of Nature's memory. A great many things had been left behind, mainly for their own good, no doubt—some of the animal, some of the vegetable, some of the mineral kingdom even—yet none of them started for anarchy. All were content to be picked up and brought on according to the power of the world, making allowance for the pinches of hard times, and the blows of east winds that had blown themselves out. Even the prime grumbler of the earth—a biped, who looks up to heaven for that purpose mainly—was as nearly content with the present state of things as he can be with anything, until it is the past. Scudamore only met one man, but that one declared it was a lovely night; and perhaps he was easier to please because he had only one leg left.

The stars had appeared, and the young leaves turned the freshness of their freedom towards them, whether from the crisp impulse of night, or the buoyant influence of kindness in the air. There was very little wind, and it was laden with no sound, except the distant voice of an indefatigable dog; but Scudamore perceived that when the tide set downwards, a gentle breeze would follow down the funnel of the river. Then he drew the ancient boat which he had used before to the mossy bank, and having placed his goods on board, fetched a pair of oars and the short mast and brown sail from the shed where they were kept, and at the top of a full tide launched forth alone upon his desperate enterprise.

There was faint light in the channel, but the banks looked very dark; and just as he cast loose he heard the big clock at Montreuil, a great way up the valley, slowly striking midnight. And he took it for good omen, as he swiftly passed the orchard, that his old friend the ox trotted down to the corner, and showed his white forehead under a sprawling apple-tree, and gave him a salute, though he scarcely could have known him. By this time the breeze was freshening nicely, and Scudamore, ceasing to row, stepped the mast, and hoisting the brown sail, glided along at a merry pace and with a hopeful heart. Passing the mouth of the creek, he saw no sign of the traitorous pilot-boat, neither did he meet any other craft in channel, although he saw many moored at either bank. But nobody challenged him, as he kept in mid-stream, and braced up his courage for the two great perils still before him ere he gained the open sea. The first of these would be the outposts on either side at Etaples, not far from the barracks where he had been jailed, and here no doubt the sentinels would call him to account. But a far greater danger would be near the river's mouth, where a bridge of boats, with a broad gangway for troops, spanned the tidal opening.

There was no bridge across the river yet near the town itself, but, upon challenge from a sentry, Scudamore stood up and waved his hat, and shouted in fine nasal and provincial French, "The fisherman, Auguste Baudry, of Montreuil!" and the man withdrew his musket, and wished him good success. Then he passed a sandy island with some men asleep upon it, and began to fear the daybreak as he neared the bridge of boats. This crossed the estuary at a narrow part, and having to bear much heavy traffic, was as solid as a floating bridge can be. A double row of barges was lashed and chained together, between piles driven deep into the river's bed; along them a road of heavy planks was laid, rising and falling as they rose and fell with tide, and a drawbridge near the middle of about eight yards' span must suffice for the traffic of the little river. This fabric was protected from the heavy western surges by the shoals of the bar, and from any English dash by a strong shore battery at either end. At first sight it looked like a black wall across the river.

The darkness of night is supposed to be deepest just before dawn—but that depends upon the weather—and the sleep of weary men is often in its prime at that time. Scudamore (although his life, and all that life hangs on from heaven, were quivering at the puff of every breeze) was enabled to derive some satisfaction from a yawn, such as goes the round of a good company sometimes, like the smell of the supper of sleep that is to come. Then he saw the dark line of the military bridge, and lowered his sail, and unstepped his little mast. The strength of the tide was almost spent, so that he could deal with this barrier at his leisure, instead of being hurled against it.

Unshipping the rudder and laying one oar astern, Scudamore fetched along the inner row of piles, for he durst not pass under the drawbridge, steering his boat to an inch while he sat with his face to the oar, working noiselessly. Then he spied a narrow opening between two barges, and drove his boat under the chain that joined them, and after some fending and groping with his hands in the darkness under the planks of the bridge, contrived to get out, when he almost despaired of it, through the lower tier of the supporters. He was quit of that formidable barrier now, but a faint flush of dawn and of reflection from the sea compelled him to be very crafty. Instead of pushing straightway for the bar and hoisting sail—which might have brought a charge of grape-shot after him—he kept in the gloom of the piles nearly into the left bank, and then hugged the shadow it afforded. Nothing but the desolate sands surveyed him, and the piles of wrack cast up by gales from the west. Then with a stout heart he stepped his little mast, and the breeze, which freshened towards the rising of the sun, carried him briskly through the tumble of the bar.

The young man knelt and said his morning prayer, with one hand still upon the tiller; for, like most men who have fought well for England, he had staunch faith in the Power that has made and guides the nations, until they rebel against it. So far his success had been more than his own unaided hand might work, or his brain with the utmost of its labours second. Of himself he cast all thoughts away, for his love seemed lost, and his delight was gone; the shores of his country, if he ever reached them, would contain no pleasure for him; but the happiness of millions might depend upon his life, and first of all that of his mother.

All by himself in this frail old tub, he could scarcely hope to cross the Channel, even in the best of weather, and if he should escape the enemy, while his scanty supplies held out. He had nothing to subsist on but three small loaves, and a little keg of cider, and an old tar tub which he had filled with brackish water, upon which the oily curdle of the tar was floating. But, for all that, he trusted that he might hold out, and retain his wits long enough to do good service.

The French coast, trending here for leagues and leagues nearly due north and south, is exposed to the long accumulating power of a western gale, and the mountain roll of billows that have known no check. If even a smart breeze from the west sprang up, his rickety little craft, intended only for inland navigation, would have small chance of living through the tumult. But his first care was to give a wide berth to the land and the many French vessels that were moored or moving, whether belonging to the great flotilla, or hastening to supply its wants. Many a time he would have stood forth boldly, as fast as the breeze and tide permitted; but no sooner had he shaped a course for the open sea than some hostile sail appeared ahead and forced him to bear away until she was far onward. Thus, after a long day of vigilance and care, he was not more than five miles from land when the sun set, and probably further from the English coast than when he set forth in the morning; because he had stood towards the south of west all day, to keep out of sight of the left wing of the enemy; and as the straight outline of the coast began to fade, he supposed himself to be about half-way between the mouth of the Canche and that of the little Authie.

Watching with the eyes of one accustomed to the air the last communication of the sun, and his postscript (which, like a lady's, is the gist of what he means), Scudamore perceived that a change of weather might come shortly, and must come ere long. There was nothing very angry in the sky, nor even threatening; only a general uncertainty and wavering; "I wish you well all round," instead of "Here's a guinea apiece for you." Scuddy understood it, and resolved to carry on.

Having no compass, and small knowledge of the coast—which lay out of range of the British investment—he had made up his mind to lie by for the night, or at any rate to move no more than he could help, for fear of going altogether in the wrong direction. He could steer by the stars—as great mariners did, when the world was all discovery—so long as the stars held their skirts up; but, on the other hand, those stars might lead him into the thick of the enemy. Of this, however, he must now take his chance, rather than wait and let the wind turn against him. For his main hope was to get into the track where British frigates, and ships of light draught like his own dear Blonde, were upon patrol, inside of the course of the great war chariots, the ships of the line, that drave heavily. Revolving much grist in the mill of his mind, as the sage Ulysses used to do, he found it essential to supply the motive power bodily. One of Madame Fropot's loaves was very soon disposed of, and a good draught of sound cider helped to renew his flagging energy.

Throughout that night he kept wide-awake, and managed to make fair progress, steering, as well as he could judge, a little to the west of north. But before sunrise the arrears of sleep increased at compound interest, and he lowered his sail, and discharged a part of the heavy sum scored against him. But when he awoke, and glanced around him with eyes that resented scanty measure, even a sleepy glance sufficed to show much more than he wished to see. Both sky and sea were overcast with doubt, and alarm, and evil foreboding. A dim streak lay where the land had been, and a white gleam quivered from the sunrise on the waves, as if he were spreading water-lilies instead of scattering roses. As the earth has its dew that foretells a bright day —whenever the dew is of the proper sort, for three kinds are established now —so the sea has a flit of bloom in the early morning (neither a colour, nor a sparkle, nor a vapour) which indicates peace and content for the day. But now there was no such fair token upon it, but a heavy and surly and treacherous look, with lumps here and there; as a man who intends to abuse us thrusts his tongue to get sharp in his cheek.

Scudamore saw that his poor old boat, scarcely sound enough for the men of Gotham, was already complaining of the uncouth manners of the strange place to which she had been carried in the dark. That is to say, she was beginning to groan, at a very quiet slap in the cheeks, or even a thoroughly well-meaning push in the rear.

"You are welcome to groan, if you don't strain," exclaimed the heartless Captain Scuddy.

Even as he spoke he beheld a trickle of water glistening down the forward bends, and then a little rill, and then a spurt, as if a serious leak was sprung. He found the source of this, and contrived to caulk it with a strand of tarred rope for the present; but the sinking of his knife into the forward timber showed him that a great part of the bows was rotten. If a head-sea arose, the crazy old frame would be prone to break in bodily, whereas if he attempted to run before the sea, already beginning to rise heavily from the west, there was nothing to save the frail craft from being pooped. On every side it was a bad lookout, there was every sign of a gale impending, which he could not even hope to weather, and the only chance of rescue lay in the prompt appearance of some British ship.

Even in this sad plight his courage and love of native land prevailed against the acceptance of aid from Frenchmen, if any should approach to offer it. Rather would he lie at the bottom of the Channel, or drift about among contending fishes, than become again a prisoner with his secret in his mind, and no chance of sending it to save his country. As a forlorn hope, he pulled out a stump of pencil, and wrote on the back of a letter from his mother a brief memorandum of what he had heard, and of the urgency of the matter. Then taking a last draught of his tarry water, he emptied the little tub, and fixed the head in, after he had enclosed his letter. Then he fastened the tub to an oar, to improve the chance of its being observed, and laid the oar so that it would float off, in case of the frail boat foundering. The other oar he kept at hand to steer with, as long as the boat should live, and to help him to float, when she should have disappeared.

This being done, he felt easier in his mind, as a man who has prepared for the worst should do. He renewed his vigour, which had begun to flag under constant labour and long solitude, by consuming another of his loaves, and taking almost the last draught of his cider, and after that he battled throughout the dreary day against the increase of bad weather. Towards the afternoon he saw several ships, one of which he took to be a British frigate; but none of them espied his poor labouring craft, or at any rate showed signs of doing so. Then a pilot-boat ran by him, standing probably for Boulogne, and at one time less than a league away. She appeared to be English, and he was just about to make signal for aid, when a patch in her foresail almost convinced him that she was the traitor of the Canche returning. She was probably out of her proper course in order to avoid the investing fleet, and she would run inside it when the darkness fell. Better to go to the bottom than invoke such aid; and he dropped the oar with his neckerchief upon it, and faced the angry sea again and the lonely despair of impending night.

What followed was wiped from his memory for years, and the loss was not much to be regretted. When he tried to think about it, he found nothing but a roaring of wind and of waves in his ears, a numbness of arms as he laboured with the oar tholed abaft to keep her heavy head up, a prickly chill in his legs as the brine in the wallowing boat ran up them, and then a great wallop and gollop of the element too abundant round him.

But at last, when long years should have brought more wisdom, he went poaching for supper upon Welsh rabbits. That night all the ghastly time came back, and stood minute by minute before him. Every swing of his body, and sway of his head, and swell of his heart, was repeated, the buffet of the billows when the planks were gone, the numb grasp of the slippery oar, the sucking down of legs which seemed turning into sea-weed, the dashing of dollops of surf into mouth and nose closed ever so carefully, and then the last sense of having fought a good fight, but fallen away from human arms, into "Oh Lord, receive my spirit!"

CHAPTER LV

IN SAVAGE GUISE

"A man came out of the sea to-day, and made me believe we were all found out," said the gay Charron to the gloomy Carne, a day or two after poor Scudamore's wreck. "I never beheld a more strange-looking creature as the owner of our human face divine, as some of your poets have found to say. He has hair from his head all down to here"—the little Captain pointed to a part of his system which would have been larger in more tranquil times—"and his clothes were so thin that one was able to see through them, and the tint of his face was of roasted sugar, such as it is not to obtain in England. A fine place for fat things, but not for thin ones."

"My friend, you arouse my curiosity," the master of the feast, which was not a very fat one, answered, as he lazily crossed his long legs; "you are always apprehensive about detection, of which I have ceased to entertain all fear, during the short time that remains. This stranger of yours must have been very wet, if he had just appeared out of the sea. Was it that which made his clothes transparent, like those of the higher class of ladies?"

"You have not the right understanding of words. He was appeared out of the sea, but the wood of a boat was spread between them. He was as dry as I am; and that is saying much, with nothing but this squeezing of bad apples for to drink."

"Ah, we shall have better soon. What an impatient throat it is! Well, what became of this transparent man, made of burnt sugar, and with hair below his belt?"

"I tell you that you take it in a very different way. But he was a long man, as long almost as you are, and with much less of indolence in the moving of his legs. It was not sincerely wise for me to exhibit myself, in the land. I was watching for a signal from the sea, and a large ship, not of the navy but of merchants, was hanging off about a league and delaying for her boat. For this reason I prevented him from seeing me, and that created difficulty of my beholding him. But he was going along the basin of the sea towards Springhaven—'Springport' it is designated by the Little Corporal; ah ha, how the language of the English comes left to him!"

"And how right it comes to you, my friend, through your fine self-denial in speaking it with me! It is well for our cause that it is not sincerely wise for you to exhibit yourself in the land, or we should have you making sweet eyes at English young ladies, and settling down to roast beef and nut-brown ale. Fie, then, my friend! where is your patriotism?"

"These English young ladies," said the Frenchman, unabashed, "are very fine, in my opinion—very fine indeed; and they could be made to dress, which is sincerely an external thing. By occasion, I have seen the very most belle, and charming and adorable of all the creatures ever made by the good God. And if she was to say to me, 'Abandon France, my Captain, and become my good husband'—and she has the money also—the fair France would go to the bottom, and the good ship Charron hoist the Union-jack."

"This becomes serious:" Carne had long learned to treat his French colleague with a large contempt: "I shall have to confine you in the Yellow Jar, my friend. But what young lady has bewitched you so, and led your most powerful mind astray?"

"I will tell you. I will make no secret of it. You have none of those lofty feelings, but you will be able in another to comprehend them. It is the daughter of the Coast-Defender—Admiral Charles Sir Darling."

"Admiral Darling has two daughters. Which of them has the distinguished honour of winning the regard of Captain Charron?"

"If there are two, it is so much more better. If I succeed not with one, I will try with the other. But the one who has made me captive for the present is the lady with the dark hair done up like this."

In a moment Charron had put up his hair, which was thick but short, into a double sheaf; and Carne knew at once that it was Faith whose charms had made havoc of the patriotism of his colleague. Then he smiled and said, "My friend, that is the elder daughter."

"I have some knowledge of the laws of England," the Frenchman continued, complacently; "the elder will have the most money, and I am not rich, though I am courageous. In the confusion that ensues I shall have the very best chance of commending myself; and I confide in your honourable feeling to give me the push forward by occasion. Say, is it well conceived, my friend? We never shall conquer these Englishmen, but we may be triumphant with their ladies."

"It is a most excellent scheme of invasion," Carne answered, with his slow sarcastic smile, "and you may rely on me for what you call the push forward, if a Frenchman ever needs it with a lady. But I wish to hear more about that brown man."

"I can tell you no more. But the matter is strange. Perhaps he was visiting the fat Captain Stoobar. I feel no solicitude concerning him with my angel.

She would never look twice at such a savage."

But the gallant French Captain missed the mark this time. The strange-looking man with the long brown beard quitted the shore before he reached the stepping-stones, and making a short-cut across the rabbit-warren, entered the cottage of Zebedee Tugwell, without even stopping to knock at the door. The master was away, and so were all the children; but stout Mrs. Tugwell, with her back to the door, was tending the pot that hung over the fire. At the sound of a footstep she turned round, and her red face grew whiter than the ashes she was stirring.

"Oh, Mr. Erle, is it you, or your ghostie?" she cried, as she fell against the door of the brick oven. "Do 'e speak, for God's sake, if He have given the power to 'e."

"He has almost taken it away again, so far as the English language goes," Erle Twemlow answered, with a smile which was visible only in his eyes, through long want of a razor; "but I am picking up a little. Shake hands, Kezia, and then you will know me. Though I have not quite recovered that art as yet."

"Oh, Mr. Erle!" exclaimed Zebedee's wife, with tears ready to start for his sake and her own, "how many a time I've had you on my knees, afore I was blessed with any of my own, and a bad sort of blessing the best of 'em proves. Not that I would listen to a word again' him. I suppose you never did happen to run again' my Dan'el, in any of they furrin parts, from the way they makes the hair grow. I did hear tell of him over to Pebbleridge; but not likely, so nigh to his own mother, and never come no nigher. And if they furrin parts puts on the hair so heavily, who could 'a known him to Pebbleridge? They never was like we be. They'd as lief tell a lie as look at you, over there."

In spite of his own long years of trouble, or perhaps by reason of them, Erle Twemlow, eager as he was to get on, listened to the sad tale that sought for his advice, and departed from wisdom—as good-nature always does—by offering useless counsel—counsel that could not be taken, and yet was far from being worthless, because it stirred anew the fount of hope, towards which the parched affections creep.

"But Lor bless me, sir, I never thought of you!" Mrs. Tugwell exclaimed, having thought out her self. "What did Parson say, and your mother, and Miss Faith? It must 'a been better than a play to see them."

"Not one of them knows a word about it yet; nor anybody in Springhaven, except you, Kezia. You were as good as my nurse, you know; I have never had a chance of writing to them, and I want you to help me to let them know it slowly."

"Oh, Mr. Erle, what a lovely young woman your Miss Faith is grown up by now! Some thinks more of Miss Dolly, but, to my mind, you may as well put a mackerel before a salmon, for the sake of the stripes and the glittering. Now what can I do to make you decent, sir, for them duds and that hair is barbarious? My Tabby and Debby will be back in half an hour, and them growing up into young maidens now."

Twemlow explained that after living so long among savages in a burning clime, he had found it impossible to wear thick clothes, and had been rigged up in some Indian stuff by the tailor of the ship which had rescued him. But now he supposed he must reconcile himself by degrees to the old imprisonment. But as for his hair, that should never be touched, unless he was restored to the British Army, and obliged to do as the others did. With many little jokes of a homely order, Mrs. Tugwell, regarding him still as a child, supplied him with her husband's summer suit of thin duck, which was ample enough not to gall him; and then she sent her daughters with a note to the Rector, begging him to come at seven o'clock to meet a gentleman who wished to see him upon important business, near the plank bridge across the little river. Erle wrote that note, but did not sign it; and after many years of happy freedom from the pen, his handwriting was so changed that his own father would not know it. What he feared was the sudden shock to his good mother; his father's nerves were strong, and must be used as buffers.

"Another trouble, probably; there is nothing now but trouble," Mr. Twemlow was thinking, as he walked unwillingly towards the place appointed. "I wish I could only guess what I can have done to deserve all these trials, as I become less fit to bear them. I would never have come to this lonely spot, except that it may be about Shargeloes. Everything now is turned upside down; but the Lord knows best, and I must bear it. Sir, who are you? And what do you want me for?"

At the corner where Miss Dolly had rushed into the Rector's open arms so fast, a tall man, clad in white, was standing, with a staff about eight feet long in his hand. Having carried a spear for four years now, Captain Twemlow found no comfort in his native land until he had cut the tallest growth in Admiral Darling's osier bed, and peeled it, and shaved it to a seven-sided taper. He rested this point in a socket of moss, that it might not be blunted, and then replied:

"Father, you ought to know me, although you have grown much stouter in my absence; and perhaps I am thinner than I used to be. But the climate disagreed with me, until I got to like it."

"Erle! Do you mean to say you are my boy Erle?" The Rector was particular about his clothes. "Don't think of touching me. You are hair all over, and I dare say never had a comb. I won't believe a word of it until you prove it."

"Well, mother will know me, if you don't." The young man answered calmly, having been tossed upon so many horns of adventure that none could make a hole in him. "I thought that you would have been glad to see me; and I managed to bring a good many presents; only they are gone on to London. They could not be got at, to land them with me; but Captain Southcombe will be sure to send them. You must not suppose, because I am empty-handed now —"

"My dear son," cried the father, deeply hurt, "do you think that your welcome depends upon presents? You have indeed fallen into savage ways. Come, and let me examine you through your hair; though the light is scarcely strong enough now to go through it. To think that you should be my own Erle, alive after such a time, and with such a lot of hair! Only, if there is any palm-oil on it—this is my last new coat but one."

"No, father, nothing that you ever can have dreamed of. Something that will make you a bishop, if you like, and me a member of the House of Lords. But I did not find it out myself—which makes success more certain."

"They have taught you some great truths, my dear boy. The man who begins a thing never gets on. But I am so astonished that I know not what I say. I ought to have thanked the Lord long ago. Have you got a place without any hair upon it large enough for me to kiss you?"

Erle Twemlow, whose hand in spite of all adventures trembled a little upon his spear, lifted his hat and found a smooth front, sure to be all the smoother for a father's kiss.

"Let us go home," said the old man, trying to exclude all excitement from his throat and heart; "but you must stay outside until I come to fetch you. I feel a little anxious, my dear boy, as to how your dear mother will get over it. She has never been strong since the bad news came about you. And somebody else has to be considered. But that must stand over till to-morrow."

CHAPTER LVI

THE SILVER VOICE

Many shrewd writers have observed that Britannia has a special luck—which the more devout call Providence—in holding her own, against not only her true and lawful enemies, but even those of her own bosom who labour most to ruin her. And truly she had need of all her fortune now, to save her from the skulking traitor, as well as the raging adversary.

"Now I will have my revenge," said Carne, "on all who have outraged and plundered me. Crows—carrion-crows—I will turn them into owls without a nest. Prowling owls, to come blinking even now at the last of my poor relics! Charron, what did that fellow say to old Jerry, the day I tied the dogs up?"

"He said, my dear friend, that he missed from the paintings which he had taken to his house the most precious of them all—the picture of your dear grandmother, by a man whose name it is hard to pronounce, but a Captain in the British Army, very much fond of beloving and painting all the most beautiful ladies; and since he had painted the mother of Vash—Vash—the man that conquered England in America—all his work was gone up to a wonderful price, and old Sheray should have one guinea if he would exhibit to him where to find it. Meedle or Beedle—he had set his heart on getting it. He declared by the good God that he would have it, and that you had got it under a tombstone."

"A sample of their persecutions! You know that I have never seen it, nor even heard of the Captain Middleton who went on his rovings from Springhaven. And, again, about my own front-door, or rather the door of my family for some four centuries, because it was carved as they cannot carve now, it was put into that vile Indenture. I care very little for my ancestors—benighted Britons of the county type—but these things are personal insults to me. I seldom talk about them, and I will not do so now."

"My Captain, you should talk much about it. That would be the good relief to your extensive mind. Revenge is not of the bright French nature; but the sky of this island procreates it. My faith! how I would rage at England, if it were not for the people, and their daughters! We shall see; in a few days more we shall astonish the fat John Bull; and then his little kittens—what do you call them?—calves of an ox, will come running to us."

"Enough of your foolish talk," said Carne. "The women are as resolute as the men. Even when we have taken London, not an English woman will come near us, until all the men have yielded. Go down to your station and watch for the boat. I expect an important despatch to-night. But I cannot stay here for the chance of it. I have business in Springhaven."

His business in Springhaven was to turn young love to the basest use, to make a maiden (rash and flighty, but not as yet dishonourable) a traitor to her friends and father-land, and most of all to her own father. He had tried to poison Dolly's mind with doses of social nonsense—in which he believed about as much as a quack believes in his own pills—but his main reliance now was placed in his hold upon her romantic heart, and in her vague ambitions. Pure and faithful love was not to be expected from his nature; but he had invested in Dolly all the affection he could spare from self. He had laboured long, and suffered much, and the red crown of his work was nigh.

Riding slowly down the hill about half a mile from the village, Carne saw a tall man coming towards him with a firm, deliberate walk. The stranger was dressed very lightly, and wore a hat that looked like a tobacco leaf, and carried a long wand in his hand, as if he were going to keep order in church. These things took the eye afar, but at shorter range became as nothing, compared with the aspect of the man himself. This was grand, with its steadfast gaze—no stare, but a calm and kind regard—its large tranquillity and power of receiving without believing the words of men; and most of all in the depth of expression reserved by experience in the forest of its hair.

Carne was about to pass in silent wonder and uneasiness, but the other gently laid the rod across his breast and stopped him, and then waited for him to ask the reason why.

"Have you any business with me, good sir?" Carne would have spoken rudely, but saw that rudeness would leave no mark upon a man like this. "If so, I must ask you to be quick. And perhaps you will tell me who you are."

"I think that you are Caryl Carne," said the stranger, not unpleasantly, but as if it mattered very little who was Caryl Carne, or whether there was any such existence.

Carne stared fiercely, for he was of touchy temper; but he might as well have stared at a bucket of water in the hope of deranging its tranquillity. "You know me. But I don't know you," he answered at last, with a jerk of his reins.

"Be in no hurry," said the other, mildly; "the weather is fine, and time plentiful. I hope to have much pleasant knowledge of you. I have the honour to be your first cousin, Erle Twemlow. Shake hands with your kinsman."

Carne offered his hand, but without his usual grace and self-possession. Twemlow took it in his broad brown palm, in which it seemed to melt away, firm though it was and muscular.

"I was going up to call on you," said Twemlow, who had acquired a habit of speaking as if he meant all the world to hear. "I feel a deep interest in your fortunes, and hope to improve them enormously. You shall hear all about it when I come up. I have passed four years in the wilds of Africa, where no white man ever trod before, and I have found out things no white man knows. We call those people savages, but they know a great deal more than we do. Shall I call to-morrow, and have a long talk?"

"I fear," replied Carne, who was cursing his luck for bringing this fellow home just now, "that I shall have no time for a week or two. I am engaged upon important business now, which will occupy my whole attention. Let me see! You are staying at the rectory, I suppose. The best plan will be for me to let you know when I can afford the pleasure of receiving you. In a fortnight, or three weeks at the latest—"

"Very well. I am never in a hurry. And I want to go to London to see about my things. But I dare say you will not object to my roving about the old castle now and then. I loved the old place as a boy, and I know every crick and cranny and snake-hole in it."

"How glad they must have been to see you—restored from the dead, and with such rich discoveries! But you must be more careful, my good cousin, and create no more anxiety. Glad as I shall be to see you, when time allows that indulgence, I must not encourage you to further rovings, which might end in your final disappearance. Two boar-hounds, exceedingly fierce and strong, and compelled by my straitened circumstances to pick up their own living, are at large on my premises night and day, to remonstrate with my creditors. We fear that they ate a man last night, who had stolen a valuable picture, and was eager for another by the same distinguished artist. His boots and hat were found unhurt; but of his clothes not a shred remained, to afford any pattern for enquiry. What would my feelings be if Aunt Maria arrived hysterically in the pony-carriage, and at great personal risk enquired—"

"I fear no dogs," said Erle Twemlow, without any flash of anger in his steadfast eyes. "I can bring any dog to lick my feet. But I fear any man who sinks lower than a dog, by obtaining a voice and speaking lies with it. If you wish, for some reason of your own, to have nought to do with me, you should have said so; and I might have respected you afterwards. But flimsy excuses and trumpery lies belong to the lowest race of savages, who live near the coast, and have been taught by Frenchmen."

Erle Twemlow stood, as he left off speaking, just before the shoulder of Carne's horse, ready to receive a blow, if offered, but without preparation for returning it. But Carne, for many good reasons—which occurred to his mind long afterwards—controlled his fury, and consoled his self-respect by repaying in kind the contempt he received.

"Well done, Mr. Savage!" he said, with a violent effort to look amiable. "You and I are accustomed to the opposite extremes of society, and the less we meet, the better. When a barbarian insults me, I take it as a foul word from a clodhopper, which does not hurt me, but may damage his own self-respect, if he cherishes such an illusion. Perhaps you will allow me to ride on, while you curb your very natural curiosity about a civilized gentleman."

Twemlow made no answer, but looked at him with a gentle pity, which infuriated Carne more than the keenest insult. He lashed his horse, and galloped down the hill, while his cousin stroked his beard, and looked after him with sorrow.

"Everything goes against me now," thought Caryl Carne, while he put up his horse and set off for the Admiral's Roundhouse. "I want to be cool as a cucumber, and that insolent villain has made pepper of me. What devil sent him here at such a time?"

For the moment it did not cross his mind that this man of lofty rudeness was the long-expected lover of Faith Darling, and therefore in some sort entitled to a voice about the doings of the younger sister. By many quiet sneers, and much expressive silence, he had set the brisk Dolly up against the quiet Faith, as a man who understands fowl nature can set even two young pullets pulling each other's hackles out.

"So you are come at last!" said Dolly. "No one who knows me keeps me waiting, because I am not accustomed to it. I expect to be called for at any moment, by matters of real importance—not like this."

"Your mind is a little disturbed," replied Carne, as he took her hand and kissed it, with less than the proper rapture; "is it because of the brown and hairy man just returned from Africa?"

"Not altogether. But that may be something. He is not a man to be laughed at. I wish you could have seen my sister."

"I would rather see you; and I have no love of savages. He is my first cousin, and that affords me a domestic right to object to him. As a brother-in-law I will have none of him."

"You forget," answered Dolly, with a flash of her old spirit, which he was subduing too heavily, "that a matter of that sort depends upon us, and our father, and not upon the gentlemen. If the gentlemen don't like it, they can always go away."

"How can they go, when they are chained up like a dog? Women may wander from this one to that, because they have nothing to bind them; but a man is of steadfast material."

"Erle Twemlow is, at any rate—though it is hard to see his material through his hair; but that must come off, and I mean to do it. He is the best-natured man I have ever yet known, except one; and that one had got nothing to shave. Men never seem to understand about their hair, and the interest we feel concerning it. But it does not matter very much, compared to their higher principles."

"That is where I carry every vote, of whatever sex you please"—Carne saw that this girl must be humoured for the moment. "Anybody can see what I am. Straightforward, and ready to show my teeth. Why should an honest man live in a bush?"

"Faith likes it very much; though she always used to say that it did seem so unchristian. Could you manage to come and meet him, Caryl? We shall have a little dinner on Saturday, I believe, that every one may see Erle Twemlow. His beloved parents will be there, who are gone quite wild about him. Father will be at home for once; and the Marquis of Southdown, and some officers, and Captain Stubbard and his wife will come, and perhaps my brother Frank, who admires you so much. You shall have an invitation in the morning."

"Such delights are not for me," Carne answered, with a superior smile; "unhappily my time is too important. But perhaps these festivities will favour me with the chance of a few words with my darling. How I long to see her, and how little chance I get!"

"Because, when you get it, you spend three-quarters of the time in arguing, and the rest in finding fault. I am sure I go as far as anybody can; and I won't take you into my father's Roundhouse, because I don't think it would be proper."

"Ladies alone understand such subjects; and a gentleman is thankful that they do. I am quite content to be outside the Roundhouse—so called because it is square, perhaps—though the wind is gone back to the east again, as it always does now in an English summer, according to a man who has studied the subject—Zebedee Tugwell, the captain of the fleet. Dolly, beloved, and most worthy to be more so, clear your bright mind from all false impressions, whose only merit is that they are yours, and allow it to look clearly at a matter of plain sense."

She was pleased to have compliments paid to her mind, even more than to her body—because there was no doubt about the merits of the latter—and she said: "That is very nice. Go on."

"Well, beauty, you know that I trust you in everything, because of your very keen discretion, and freedom from stupid little prejudice. I have been surprised at times, when I thought of it in your absence, that any one so young, who has never been through any course of political economy, should be able to take such a clear view of subjects which are far beyond the intellect of even the oldest ladies. But it must be your brother; no doubt he has helped you to—"

"Not he!" cried the innocent Dolly, with fine pride; "I rather look down upon his reasoning powers; though I never could make such a pretty tink of rhymes—like the bells of the sheep when the ground is full of turnips."

"He approves of your elevated views," said Carne, looking as grave as a crow at a church clock; "they may not have come from him, because they are your own, quite as much as his poetry is his. But he perceives their truth, and he knows that they must prevail. In a year or two we shall be wondering, sweet Dolly, when you and I sit side by side, as the stupid old King and Queen do now, that it ever has been possible for narrow-minded nonsense to prevail as it did until we rose above it. We shall be admired as the benefactors, not of this country only, but of the whole world."

Miss Dolly was fairly endowed with common-sense, but often failed to use it. She would fain have said now, "That sounds wonderfully fine; but what does it mean, and how are we to work it?" But unluckily she could not bring herself to say it. And when millions are fooled by the glibness of one man— even in these days of wisdom—who can be surprised at a young maid's weakness?

"You wish me to help you in some way," she said; "your object is sure to be good; and you trust me in everything, because of my discretion. Then why not tell me everything?"

"You know everything," Carne replied, with a smile of affection and sweet reproach. "My object is the largest that a man can have; and until I saw you, there was not the least taint of self-interest in my proceedings. But now it is not for the universe alone, for the grandeur of humanity, and the triumph of peace, that I have to strive, but also for another little somebody, who has come—I am ashamed to say—to outweigh all the rest in the balance of my too tender heart."

This was so good, and so well delivered, that the lady of such love could do no less than vouchsafe a soft hand and a softer glance, instead of pursuing hard reason.

"Beauty, it is plain enough to you, though it might not be so to stupid people," Carne continued, as he pressed her hand, and vanquished the doubt

416

of her enquiring eyes with the strength of his resolute gaze, "that bold measures are sometimes the only wise ones. Many English girls would stand aghast to hear that it was needful for the good of England that a certain number, a strictly limited number, of Frenchmen should land upon this coast."

"I should rather think they would!" cried Dolly; "and I would be one of them—you may be quite sure of that."

"For a moment you might, until you came to understand." Carne's voice always took a silver tone when his words were big with roguery; as the man who is touting for his neighbour's bees strikes the frying-pan softly at first, to tone the pulsations of the murmuring mob. "But every safeguard and every guarantee that can be demanded by the wildest prudence will be afforded before a step is taken. In plain truth, a large mind is almost shocked at such deference to antique prejudice. But the feelings of old women must be considered; and our measures are fenced with such securities that even the most timid must be satisfied. There must be a nominal landing, of course, of a strictly limited number, and they must be secured for a measurable period from any ill-judged interruption. But the great point of all is to have no blood-guiltiness, no outbreak of fanatic natives against benefactors coming in the garb of peace. A truly noble offer of the olive-branch must not be misinterpreted. It is the finest idea that has ever been conceived; and no one possessing a liberal mind can help admiring the perfection of this plan. For the sake of this country, and the world, and ourselves, we must contribute our little share, darling."

Carne, with the grace of a lofty protector, as well as the face of an ardent lover, drew the bewildered maiden towards him, and tenderly kissed her pretty forehead, holding up his hand against all protest.

"It is useless to dream of drawing back," he continued; "my beauty, and my poor outcast self, are in the same boat, and must sail on to success—such success as there never has been before, because it will bless the whole world, as well as secure our own perfect happiness. You will be more than the Queen of England. Statues of you will be set up everywhere; and where could the sculptors find such another model? I may count upon your steadfast heart, I know, and your wonderful quickness of perception."

"Yes, if I could only see that everything was right. But I feel that I ought to consult somebody of more experience in such things. My father, for instance, or my brother Frank, or even Mr. Twemlow, or perhaps Captain Stubbard."

"If you had thought of it a little sooner, and allowed me time to reason with them," Carne replied, with a candid smile, "that would have been the very thing I should have wished, as taking a great responsibility from me. But alas, it would be fatal now. The main object now is to remove all chance of an ill-judged conflict, which would ruin all good feeling, and cost many valuable lives, perhaps even that of your truly gallant father. No, my Dolly, you must not open your beautiful lips to any one. The peace and happiness of the world depend entirely upon your discretion. All will be arranged to a nicety, and a happy result is certain. Only I must see you, about some small points, as well as to satisfy my own craving. On Saturday you have that dinner party, when somebody will sit by your side instead of me. How miserably jealous I shall be! When the gentlemen are at their wine, you must console me by slipping away from the ladies, and coming to the window of the little room where your father keeps his papers. I shall quit everything and watch there for you among the shrubs, when it grows dark enough."

CHAPTER LVII

BELOW THE LINE

Of the British Admirals then on duty, Collingwood alone, so far as now appears, had any suspicion of Napoleon's real plan.

"I have always had an idea that Ireland alone was the object they have in view," he wrote in July, 1805, "and still believe that to be their ultimate destination—that they [i. e., the Toulon fleet] will now liberate the Ferrol squadron from Calder, make the round of the bay, and taking the Rochefort people with them, appear off Ushant, perhaps with 34 sail, there to be joined by 20 more. Cornwallis collecting his out-squadrons may have 30 and upwards. This appears to be a probable plan; for unless it is to bring their great fleets and armies to some point of service—some rash attempt at conquest—they have been only subjecting them to chance of loss; which I do not believe the Corsican would do, without the hope of an adequate reward. This summer is big with events."

This was written to Lord Nelson upon his return to Europe, after chasing that Toulon fleet to the West Indies and back again. And a day or two later, the same Vice-Admiral wrote to his friend very clearly, as before:

"Truly glad will I be to see you, and to give you my best opinion on the present state of affairs, which are in the highest degree intricate. But reasoning on the policy of the present French government, who never aim at little things while great objects are in view, I have considered the invasion of Ireland as the real mark and butt of all their operations. The flight to the West Indies was to take off the naval force, which is the great impediment to their undertaking. The Rochefort squadron's return confirmed me. I think they will now collect their force at Ferrol—which Calder tells me are in motion—pick up those at Rochefort, who, I am told, are equally ready, and will make them above thirty sail; and then, without going near Ushant or the Channel fleet, proceed to Ireland. Detachments must go from the Channel fleet to succour Ireland, when the Brest fleet—21 I believe of them—will sail, either to another part of Ireland, or up the Channel—a sort of force that has not been seen in those seas, perhaps ever."

Lord Nelson just lately had suffered so much from the disadvantage of not "following his own head, and so being much more correct in judgment than following the opinion of others," that his head was not at all in a receptive state; and like all who have doubted about being right, and found the doubt wrong, he was hardened into the merits of his own conclusion. "Why have I gone on a goose-chase?" he asked; "because I have twice as many ears as eyes."

This being so, he stuck fast to the conviction which he had nourished all along, that the scheme of invasion was a sham, intended to keep the British fleet at home, while the enemy ravaged our commerce and colonies afar. And by this time the country, grown heartily tired of groundless alarms and suspended menace, was beginning to view with contempt a camp that was wearing out its own encampment. Little was it dreamed in the sweet rose gardens of England, or the fragrant hay-fields, that the curl of blue smoke while the dinner was cooking, the call of milkmaids, the haymaker's laugh, or the whinny of Dobbin between his mouthfuls, might be turned (ere a man of good appetite was full) into foreign shouts, and shriek of English maiden, crackling homestead, and blazing stack-yard, blare of trumpets, and roar of artillery, cold flash of steel, and the soft warm trickle of a father's or a husband's blood.

But the chance of this hung upon a hair just now. One hundred and sixty thousand soldiers—the finest sons of Mars that demon has ever yet begotten —fifteen thousand warlike horses, ready to devour all the oats of England, cannons that never could be counted (because it was not always safe to go near them), and ships that no reckoner could get to the end of, because he was always beginning again.

Who was there now to meet all these? Admiral Darling, and Captain Stubbard, and Zebedee Tugwell (if he found them intrusive), and Erle Twemlow, as soon as he got his things from London. There might be a few more to come forward, as soon as they saw the necessity; but Mr. John Prater could not be relied on—because of the trade he might expect to drive; Mr. Shargeloes had never turned up again; and as for poor Cheeseman, he had lost himself so entirely now that he made up the weight of a pound of sausages, in the broad summer light, with a tallow candle. Like others concerned in this history, he had jumped at the stars, and cracked his head against a beam, in manner to be recorded.

The country being destitute thus of defenders—for even Stubbard's battery was not half manned, because it had never been wanted—the plan of invasion was thriving well, in all but one particular. The fleet under Villeneuve was at large, so was that under Lallemand, who had superseded Missiessy, so was the force of Gravina and another Spanish admiral; but Ganteaume had failed to elude the vigilance of that hero of storms, Cornwallis. Napoleon arrived at Boulogne on the 3rd of August, and reviewed his troops, in a line on the beach some eight miles long. A finer sight he had never seen, and he wrote in his pride: "The English know not what is hanging over their ears. If we are masters of the passage for twelve hours, England is conquered." But all depended on Villeneuve, and happily he could not depend upon his nerves.

Meanwhile the young man who was charged with a message which he would gladly have died to discharge was far away, eating out his heart in silence, or vainly relieving it with unknown words. At the last gasp, or after he ceased to gasp for the time, and was drifting insensible, but happily with his honest face still upward, a Dutchman, keeping a sharp lookout for English cruisers, espied him. He was taken on board of a fine bark bound from Rotterdam for Java, with orders to choose the track least infested by that ravenous shark Britannia. Scudamore was treated with the warmest kindness and the most gentle attention, for the captain's wife was on board, and her tender heart was moved with compassion. Yet even so, three days passed by with no more knowledge of time on his part than the face of a clock has of its hands; and more than a week was gone before both body and mind were in tone and tune again. By that time the stout Dutch bark, having given a wide berth to the wakes of war, was forty leagues west of Cape Finisterre, under orders to touch no land short of the Cape, except for fresh water at St. Jago.

Blyth Scudamore was blest with that natural feeling of preference for one's own kin and country which the much larger minds of the present period flout, and scout as barbarous. Happily our periodical blight is expiring, like cuckoo-spit, in its own bubbles; and the time is returning when the bottle-blister will not be accepted as the good ripe peach. Scudamore was of the times that have been (and perhaps may be coming again, in the teeth and the jaw of universal suffrage), of resolute, vigorous, loyal people, holding fast all that God gives them, and declining to be led by the tail, by a gentleman who tacked their tail on as his handle.

This certainty of belonging still to a firm and substantial race of men (whose extinction would leave the world nothing to breed from) made the gallant Scudamore so anxious to do his duty, that he could not do it. Why do we whistle to a horse overburdened with a heavy load uphill? That his mind may grow tranquil, and his ears train forward, his eyes lose their nervous contraction, and a fine sense of leisure pervade him. But if he has a long hill to surmount, with none to restrain his ardour, the sense of duty grows stronger than any consideration of his own good, and the best man has not the conscience needful to understand half his emotions.

Thus the sense of duty kept Blyth Scudamore full of misery. Every day carried him further from the all-important issues; and the chance of returning in time grew faint, and fainter at every sunset. The kindly Dutchman and his wife were aware of some burden on his mind, because of its many groaning sallies while astray from judgment. But as soon as his wits were clear again, and his body fit to second them, Blyth saw that he could not crave their help, against the present interests of their own land. Holland was at enmity with England, not of its own accord, but under the pressure of the man who worked so hard the great European mangle. Captain Van Oort had picked up some English, and his wife could use tongue and ears in French, while Scudamore afforded himself and them some little diversion by attempts in Dutch. Being of a wonderfully happy nature—for happiness is the greatest wonder in this world—he could not help many a wholesome laugh, in spite of all the projects of Napoleon.

Little things seldom jump into bigness, till a man sets his microscope at them. According to the everlasting harmonies, Blyth had not got a penny, because he had not got a pocket to put it in. A pocketful of money would have sent him to the bottom of the sea, that breezy April night, when he drifted for hours, with eyes full of salt, twinkling feeble answer to the twinkle of the stars. But he had made himself light of his little cash left, in his preparation for a slow decease, and perhaps the fish had paid tribute with it to the Caesar of this Millennium. Captain Van Oort was a man of his inches in length, but in breadth about one-third more, being thickened and spread by the years that do this to a body containing a Christian mind. "You will never get out of them," said Mrs. Van Oort, when he got into her husband's large smallclothes; but he who had often jumped out of a tub felt no despair about jumping out of two. In every way Scudamore hoped for the best—which is the only right course for a man who has done his own best, and is helpless.

Keeping out of the usual track of commerce, because of the privateers and other pests of war waylaying it, they met no sail of either friend or foe until they cast anchor at St. Jago. Here there was no ship bound for England, and little chance of finding one, for weeks or perhaps for months to come. The best chance of getting home lay clearly in going yet further away from home, and so he stuck to the good ship still, and they weighed for the Cape on the 12th of May. Everything set against poor Scuddy—wind, and wave, and the power of man. It had been the 16th of April when he was rescued from the devouring sea; some days had been spent by the leisurely Dutchman in providing fresh supplies, and the stout bark's favourite maxim seemed to be, "the more haste the less speed." Baffling winds and a dead calm helped to second this philosophy, and the first week of June was past before they swung to their moorings in Table Bay.

"What chance is there now of my doing any good?" the young Englishman asked himself, bitterly. "This place is again in the hands of the Dutch, and the English ships stand clear of it, or only receive supplies by stealth. I am friendless here, I am penniless; and worst of all, if I even get a passage home, there will be no home left. Too late! too late! What use is there in striving?"

Tears stood in his blue eyes, which were gentle as a lady's; and his forehead (usually calm and smooth and ready for the flicker of a very pleasant smile) was as grave and determined as the brow of Caryl Carne. Captain Van Oort would have lent him 500 guilders with the greatest pleasure, but Scudamore would not take more than fifty, to support him until he could obtain a ship. Then with hearty good-will, and life-long faith in each other, the two men parted, and Scudamore's heart was uncommonly low—for a substance that was not a "Jack-in-the-box"—as he watched from the shore the slow fading into dream-land of the Katterina.

Nothing except patriotic feeling may justify a man, who has done no harm, in long-continued misery. The sense of violent bodily pain, or of perpetual misfortune, or of the baseness of all in whom he trusted, and other steady influx of many-fountained sorrow, may wear him for a time, and even fetch his spirit lower than the more vicarious woe can do. But the firm conviction that the family of man to which one belongs, and is proud of belonging, has fallen into the hands of traitors, eloquent liars, and vile hypocrites, and cannot escape without crawling in the dust—this produces a large deep gloom, and a crushing sense of doom beyond philosophy. Scudamore could have endured the loss and the disillusion of his love—pure and strong as that power had been—but the ruin of his native land would turn his lively heart into a lump of stone.

For two or three days he roved about among the people of the water-side— boatmen, pilots, shipping agents, store-keepers, stevedores, crimps, or any others likely to know anything to help him. Some of these could speak a little English, and many had some knowledge of French; but all shook their heads at his eagerness to get to England. "You may wait weeks, or you may wait months," said the one who knew most of the subject; "we are very jealous of the English ships. That country swallows up the sea so. It has been forbidden to supply the English ships; but for plenty money it is done sometimes; but the finger must be placed upon the nose, and upon the two eyes what you call the guinea; and in six hours where are they? Swallowed up by the mist from the mountain. No, sir! If you have the great money, it is very difficult. But if you have not that, it is impossible."

"I have not the great money; and the little money also has escaped from a quicksand in the bottom of my pocket."

"Then you will never get to England, sir," this gentleman answered, pleasantly; "and unless I have been told things too severely, the best man that lives had better not go there, without a rock of gold in his pocket grand enough to fill a thousand quicksands."

Scudamore lifted the relics of his hat, and went in search of some other Job's comforter. Instead of a passage to England, he saw in a straight line before him the only journey which a mortal may take without paying his fare.

To save himself from this gratuitous tour, he earned a little money in a porter's gang, till his quick step roused the indignation of the rest. With the loftiest perception of the rights of man, they turned him out of that employment (for the one "sacred principle of labour" is to play), and he, understanding now the nature, of democracy, perceived that of all the many short-cuts to starvation, the one with the fewest elbows to it is—to work.

While he was meditating upon these points—which persons of big words love to call "questions of political economy"—his hat, now become a patent ventilator, sat according to custom on the back of his head, exposing his large calm forehead, and the kind honesty of his countenance. Then he started a little, for his nerves were not quite as strong as when they had good feeding, at the sudden sense of being scrutinized by the most piercing gaze he had ever encountered.

The stranger was an old man of tall spare frame, wearing a shovel-hat and long black gown drawn in with a belt, and around his bare neck was a steel chain supporting an ebony cross. With a smile, which displayed the firm angles of his face, he addressed the young man in a language which Scudamore could not understand, but believed to be Portuguese.

"Thy words I am not able to understand. But the Latin tongue, as it is pronounced in England, I am able to interpret, and to speak, not too abundantly." Scudamore spoke the best Latin he could muster at a moment's notice, for he saw that this gentleman was a Catholic priest, and probably therefore of good education.

"Art thou, then, an Englishman, my son?" the stranger replied, in the same good tongue. "From thy countenance and walk, that opinion stood fast in my mind at first sight of thee. Every Englishman is to me beloved, and every Frenchman unfriendly—as many, at least, as now govern the state. Father Bartholomew is my name, and though most men here are heretical, among the faithful I avail sufficiently. What saith the great Venusian? 'In straitened fortunes quit thyself as a man of spirit and of mettle.' I find thee in straitened fortunes, and would gladly enlarge thee, if that which thou art doing is pleasing to the God omnipotent."

After a few more words, he led the hapless and hungry Englishman to a quiet little cot which overlooked the noble bay, and itself was overlooked by a tall flag-staff bearing the colours of Portugal. Here in the first place he regaled his guest with the flank of a kid served with cucumber, and fruit gathered early, and some native wine, scarcely good enough for the Venusian bard, but as rich as ambrosia to Scudamore. Then he supplied him with the finest tobacco that ever ascended in spiral incense to the cloud-compelling Jove. At every soft puff, away flew the blue-devils, pagan, or Christian, or even scientific; and the brightness of the sleep-forbidden eyes returned, and the sweetness of the smile so long gone hence in dread of trespass. Father Bartholomew, neither eating, drinking, nor smoking, till the sun should set— for this was one of his fast-days—was heartily pleased with his guest's good cheer, and smiled with the large benevolence which a lean face expresses with more decision than a plump and jolly one. "And now, my son," he began again, in Latin more fluent and classical than the sailor could compass after Cicero thrown by, "thou hast returned thanks to Almighty God, for which I the more esteem thee. Oblige me, therefore, if it irk thee not, among smoke of the genial Nicotium, by telling thy tale, and explaining what hard necessity hath driven thee to these distant shores. Fear not, for thou seest a lover of England, and hater of France the infidel."

Then Scudamore, sometimes hesitating and laughing at his own bad Latin, told as much of his story as was needful, striving especially to make clear the importance of his swift return, and his fear that even so it would be too late.

"Man may believe himself too late, but the Lord ariseth early," the good priest answered, with a smile of courage refreshing the heart of the Englishman. "Behold how the hand of the Lord is steadfast over those who serve him! To-morrow I might have been far away; to-day I am in time to help thee. Whilst thou wert feeding, I received the signal of a swift ship for Lisbon, whose captain is my friend, and would neglect nothing to serve me. This night he will arrive, and with favourable breezes, which have set in this morning, he shall spread his sails again to-morrow, though he meant to linger perhaps for three days. Be of good cheer, my son; thou shalt sail to-morrow. I will supply thee with all that is needful, and thank God for a privilege so great. Thou shalt have money as well for the passage from Lisbon to England, which is not long. Remember in thy prayers—for thou art devout—that old man, Father Bartholomew."

CHAPTER LVIII

IN EARLY MORN

One Saturday morning in the month of August, an hour and a half before sunrise, Carne walked down to the big yew-tree, which stood far enough from the brink of the cliff to escape the salt, and yet near enough to command an extensive sea-view. This was the place where the young shoemaker, belonging to the race of Shanks, had been scared so sadly that he lost his sweetheart, some two years and a half ago; and this was the tree that had been loved by painters, especially the conscientious Sharples, a pupil of Romney, who studied the nicks and the tricks of the bole, and the many fantastic frets of time, with all the loving care which ensured the truth of his simple and powerful portraits. But Sharples had long been away in the West; and Carne, having taste for no art except his own, had despatched his dog Orso, the fiercer of the pair, at the only son of a brush who had lately made ready to encamp against that tree; upon which he decamped, and went over the cliff, with a loss of much personal property.

The tree looked ghostly in the shady light, and gaunt armstretch of departing darkness, going as if it had not slept its sleep out. Now was the time when the day is afraid of coming, and the night unsure of going, and a large reluctance to acknowledge any change keeps everything waiting for another thing to move. What is the use of light and shadow, the fuss of the morning, and struggle for the sun? Fair darkness has filled all the gaps between them, and why should they be sever'd into single life again? For the gladness of daybreak is not come yet, nor the pleasure of seeing the way again, the lifting of the darkness leaves heaviness beneath it, and if a rashly early bird flops down upon the grass, he cannot count his distance, but quivers like a moth.

"Pest on this abominable early work!" muttered Carne with a yawn, as he groped his way through the deep gloom of black foliage, and entered the hollow of the ancient trunk; "it is all very well for sailors, but too hard upon a quiet gentleman. Very likely that fellow won't come for two hours. What a cursed uncomfortable maggoty place! But I'll have put the sleep he has robbed me of." He stretched his long form on the rough bench inside, gathered his cloak around him, and roused the dull echo of the honey-combed hollow with long loud snores.

"Awake, my vigilant commander, and behold me! Happy are the landsmen, to whom the stars bring sleep. I have not slept for three nights, and the fruits are here for you."

It was the lively voice of Renaud Charron; and the rosy fan of the dawn, unfolded over the sea and the gray rocks, glanced with a flutter of shade into the deep-ribbed tree. Affecting a lofty indifference, Carne, who had a large sense of his own dignity, rose slowly and came out into the better light. "Sit down, my dear friend," he said, taking the sealed packet; "there is bread and meat here, and a bottle of good Macon. You are nearly always hungry, and you must be starved now."

Charron perceived that his mouth was offered employment at the expense of his eyes; but the kernel of the matter was his own already, and he smiled to himself at the mystery of his chief. "In this matter, I should implore the tree to crush me, if my father were an Englishman," he thought; "but every one to his taste; it is no affair of mine." Just as he was getting on good terms with his refreshment, Carne came back, and watched him with a patronising smile.

"You are the brother of my toil," he said, "and I will tell you as much as it is good for you to know. A few hours now will complete our enterprise. Napoleon is at Boulogne again, and even he can scarcely restrain the rush of the spirits he has provoked. The first Division is on board already, with a week's supplies, and a thousand horses, ready to sail when a hand is held up. The hand will be held up at my signal, and that I shall trust you to convey to-night, as soon as I have settled certain matters. Where is that sullen young Tugwell? What have you done with him?"

"Wonderfully clever is your new device, my friend," Charron replied, after a long pull at the bottle. "To vanquish the mind by a mind superior is a glory of high reason; but to let it remain in itself and compel it to perform what is desired by the other, is a stroke of genius. And under your pharmacy he must do it—that has been proved already. The idea was grand, very noble, magnificent. It never would have shown itself to my mind."

"Probably not. When that has been accomplished, we will hang him for a traitor. But, my dear friend, I have sad news for you, even in this hour of triumph. The lady of your adoration, the Admiral's eldest daughter, Faith, has recovered the man for whom she has waited four years, and she means to marry him. The father has given his consent, and her pride is beyond description. She has long loved a mystery—what woman can help it? And now she has one for life, a husband eclipsed in his own hair. My Renaud, all rivalry is futile. Your hair, alas, is quite short and scanty. But this man has discovered in Africa a nut which turns a man into the husk of himself. No wonder that he came out of the sea all dry!"

"Tush! he is a pig. It is a pig that finds the nuts. I will be the butcher for that long pig, and the lady will rush into the arms of conquest. Then will I possess all the Admiral's lands, and pursue the fine chase of the rabbits. And I will give dinners, such dinners, my faith! Ha! that is excellent said—embrace me—my Faith will sit at the right side of the table, and explain to the English company that such dinners could proceed from nobody except a French gentleman commingling all the knowledge of the joint with the loftier conception of the hash, the mince—the what you call? Ah, you have no name for it, because you do not know the proper thing. Then, in the presence of admiring Englishmen, I will lean back in my chair, the most comfortable chair that can be found—"

"Stop. You have got to get into it yet," Carne interrupted, rudely; "and the way to do that is not to lean back in it. The fault of your system has always been that you want to enjoy everything before you get it."

"And of yours," retorted Charron, beginning to imbibe the pugnacity of an English landlord, "that when you have got everything, you will enjoy what? Nothing!"

"Even a man of your levity hits the nail on the head sometimes," said Carne, "though the blow cannot be a very heavy one. Nature has not fashioned me for enjoyment, and therefore affords me very little. But some little I do expect in the great inversion coming, in the upset of the scoundrels who have fattened on my flesh, and stolen my land, to make country gentlemen—if it were possible—of themselves. It will take a large chimney to burn their title-deeds, for the robbery has lasted for a century. But I hold the great Emperor's process signed for that; and if you come to my cookery, you will say that I am capable of enjoyment. Fighting I enjoy not, as hot men do, nor guzzling, nor swigging, nor singing of songs; for all of which you have a talent, my friend. But the triumph of quiet skill I like; and I love to turn the balance on my enemies. Of these there are plenty, and among them all who live in that fishy little hole down there."

Carne pointed contemptuously at Springhaven, that poor little village in the valley. But the sun had just lifted his impartial face above the last highland that baulked his contemplation of the home of so many and great virtues; and in the brisk moisture of his early salute the village in the vale looked lovely. For a silvery mist was flushed with rose, like a bridal veil warmed by the blushes of the bride, and the curves of the land, like a dewy palm leaf, shone and sank alternate.

"What a rare blaze they will make!" continued Carne, as the sunlight glanced along the russet thatch, and the blue smoke arose from the earliest chimney. "Every cottage there shall be a bonfire, because it has cast off allegiance to me. The whole race of Darling will be at my mercy—the pompous old Admiral, who refused to call on me till his idiot of a son persuaded him—that wretched poetaster, who reduced me to the ignominy of reading his own rubbish to him—and the haughty young woman that worships a savage who has treated me with insult. I have them all now in the hollow of my hand, and a thorough good crumpling is prepared for them. The first house to burn shall be Zebedee Tugwell's, that conceited old dolt of a fishing fellow, who gives me a nod of suspicion, instead of pulling off his dirty hat to me. Then we blow up the church, and old Twemlow's house, and the Admiral's, when we have done with it. The fishing-fleet, as they call their wretched tubs, will come home, with the usual fuss, to-night, and on Monday it shall be ashes. How like you my programme? Is it complete?"

"Too much, too much complete; too barbarous," answered the kindly hearted Frenchman. "What harm have all the poor men done to you? And what insanity to provoke enemies of the people all around who would bring us things to eat! And worse—if the houses are consumed with fire, where will be the revenue that is designed for me, as the fair son of the Admiral? No, no; I will allow none of that. When the landing is made, you will not be my master. Soult will have charge of the subjects inferior, and he is not a man of rapine. To him will I address myself in favour of the village. Thus shall I ascend in the favour of my charming, and secure my property."

"Captain, I am your master yet, and I will have no interference. No more talk; but obey me to the letter. There is no sign of any rough weather, I suppose? You sailors see things which we do not observe."

"This summer has not been of fine weather, and the sky is always changing here. But there is not any token of a tempest now. Though there is a little prospect of rain always."

"If it rains, all the better, for it obscures the sea. You have fed enough now to last even you till the evening; or if not, you can take some with you. Remain to the westward, where the cliffs are higher, and look out especially for British ships of war that may be appearing up Channel. Take this second spy-glass; it is quite strong enough. But first of all tell Perkins to stand off again with the pilot-boat, as if he was looking out for a job, and if he sees even a frigate coming eastward, to run back and let you know by a signal arranged between you. Dan Tugwell, I see, was shipped yesterday on board of Prame No. 801, a very handy vessel, which will lead the van, and five hundred will follow in her track on Sunday evening. My excellent uncle will be at the height of his eloquence just when his favourite Sunday-school boy is bringing an addition to his congregation. But the church shall not be blown up until Monday, for fear of premature excitement. By Monday night about two hundred thousand such soldiers as Britain could never produce will be able to quell any childish excitement such as Great Britain is apt to give way to."

"But what is for me, this same Saturday night? I like very much to make polite the people, and to marry the most beautiful and the richest; but not to kill more than there is to be helped."

"The breaking of the egg may cut the fingers that have been sucked till their skin is gone. You have plagued me all along with your English hankerings, which in your post of trust are traitorous."

Charron was accustomed to submit to the infinitely stronger will of Carne. Moreover, his sense of discipline often checked the speed of his temper. But he had never been able to get rid of a secret contempt for his superior, as a traitor to the race to which he really belonged, at least in the Frenchman's opinion. And that such a man should charge him with treachery was more than his honest soul could quite endure, and his quick face flushed with indignation as he spoke:

"Your position, my commander, does not excuse such words. You shall answer for them, when I am discharged from your command; which, I hope, will be the case next week. To be spoken of as a traitor by you is very grand."

"Take it as you please," Carne replied, with that cold contemptuous smile which the other detested. "For the present, however, you will not be grand, but carry out the orders which I give you. As soon as it is dark, you will return, keep the pilot-boat in readiness for my last despatch, with which you will meet the frigate Torche about midnight, as arranged on Thursday. All that and the signals you already understand. Wait for me by this tree, and I may go with you; but that will depend upon circumstances. I will take good care that you shall not be kept starving; for you may have to wait here three or four hours for me. But be sure that you do not go until I come."

"But what am I to do if I have seen some British ships, or Perkins has given me token of them?"

"Observe their course, and learn where they are likely to be at nightfall. There will probably be none. All I fear is that they may intercept the Torche. Farewell, my friend, and let your sense of duty subdue the small sufferings of temper."

CHAPTER LIX

NEAR OUR SHORES

"This is how it is," said Captain Tugwell, that same day, to Erle Twemlow: "the folk they goes on with a thing, till a man as has any head left twists it round on his neck, with his chin looking down his starn-post. Then the enemy cometh, with his spy-glass and his guns, and afore he can look round, he hath nothing left to look for."

"Then you think, Tugwell, that the danger is not over?—that the French mean business even now, when every one is tired of hearing of it? I have been away so long that I know nothing. But the universal opinion is—"

"Opinion of the universe be dashed!" Master Zebedee answered, with a puff of smoke. "We calls ourselves the universe, when we be the rope that drags astern of it. Cappen, to my mind there is mischief in the wind, more than there hath been for these three years; and that's why you see me here, instead of going with the smacks. Holy Scripture saith a dream cometh from the Lord; leastways, to a man of sense, as hardly ever dreameth. The wind was so bad again us, Monday afternoon, that we put off sailing till the Tuesday, and Monday night I lay on my own bed, without a thought of nothing but to sleep till five o'clock. I hadn't taken nothing but a quart of John Prater's ale—and you know what his measures is—not a single sip of grog; but the Hangel of the Lord he come and stand by me in the middle of the night. And he took me by the hand, or if he didn't it come to the same thing of my getting there, and he set me up in a dark high place, the like of the yew-tree near Carne Castle. And then he saith, 'Look back, Zeb'; and I looked, and behold Springhaven was all afire, like the bottomless pit, or the thunder-storm of Egypt, or the cities of Sodom and Gomorrah. And two figures was jumping about in the flames, like the furnace in the plain of Dura, and one of them was young Squire Carne, and the other was my son Daniel, as behaveth below his name. And I called out, 'Daniel, thou son of Zebedee and Kezia Tugwell, come forth from the burning fiery furnace'; but he answered not, neither heeded me. And then Squire Darling, Sir Charles is now the name of him, out he come from his Round-house, and by the white gate above high-water mark, to order out the fire, because they was all his own cottages. But while he was going about, as he doth for fear of being hard upon any one, out jumps Squire Carne, from the thickest of the blazes, and takes the poor Squire by the forepart of his neck, which he liketh to keep open when he getteth off of duty, and away with him into the burning fiery furnace made of his own houses! That was more than I could put up with, even under the Hangel, and I give such a kick that Kezia, though she saith she is the most quietest of women, felt herself a forced to bounce me up."

"A dream of that sort deserves notice," answered Erle, who had passed many months among sailors; "and over and above that, I see proofs of a foolish security in England, and of sharp activity in France. Last Monday I was only five miles from Boulogne, on board of our frigate the Melpomene, for I wanted the captain's evidence to help me in my own affairs; and upon my word I was quite amazed at the massing of the French forces there, and the evident readiness of their hundreds of troop-ships. Scores of them even had horses on board, for I saw them quite clearly with a spy-glass. But the officers only laughed at me, and said they were tired of seeing that. And another thing I don't like at all is the landing of a French boat this side of Pebbleridge. I was coming home after dark one night, and as soon as they saw me they pushed off, and pretended to be English fishermen; but if ever I saw Frenchmen, these were French; and I believe they had a ship not far away, for I saw a light shown and then turned off. I examined the place in the morning, and saw the footprints of men on a path up the cliff, as if they had gone inland towards Carne Castle. When the Admiral came home, I told him of it; but he seemed to think it was only some smuggling."

"Ah, there's smooglin' of a bad kind over there, to my belief. I wouldn't tell your honour not a quarter what I thinks, because of the young gentleman being near akin to you. But a thing or two have come to my ears, very much again a young squire over that way. A man as will do what he have done is a black one in some ways; and if some, why not in all?"

"Tell me what you mean," said Twemlow, sternly. "After saying so much, you are bound to say more. Caryl Carne is no friend of mine, although he is my cousin. I dislike the man, though I know but little of him."

"For sartin then a kind gentleman like you won't like him none the better for betraying of a nice young maid as put her trust in him, as lively and pretty a young maid as ever stepped, and might have had the pick of all the young men in the parish."

"What!" exclaimed Erle, with a sudden chill of heart, for Faith had not concealed from him her anxiety about Dolly. "Tugwell, do you mean to say —"

"Yes, sir; only you must keep it to yourself, for the sake of the poor young thing; though too many knows it already, I'm afeared. And that was how poor Jem Cheeseman changed from a dapper money-turning man, as pleasant as could be, to a down-hearted, stick-in-doors, honest-weighted fellow. Poor little Polly was as simple as a dove, and her meant to break none of the Lord's commandments, unless it was a sin to look so much above her. He took her aboard her father's trading-craft, and made pretence to marry her across the water, her knowing nothing of the lingo, to be sure; and then when there come a thumping boy, and her demanded for the sake of the young 'un that her marriage should be sartified in the face of all the world, what does he do but turn round and ask her if she was fool enough to suppose that a Carne had married a butter-man's daughter? With a few words more, she went off of her head, and have never been right again, they say; and her father, who was mighty proud to have a grandson heir to an old ancient castle, he was so took aback with this disappointment that he puzzled all the village, including of me, as I am free to own, by jumping into his own rope. 'Twas only now just that I heard all this; and as the captain of this here place, I shall ask leave of Cheeseman to have it out with Master Carne, as soon as may be done without hurting the poor thing. If she had been my child, the rope should have gone round his neck first, if it come to mine there-arter!"

"The —— villain!" Twemlow used a strong short word, without adding heavily, it may be hoped, to the score against him. "And to think that all this time he has been daring to address himself—But never mind that now. It will be a bad time for him when I catch him by himself, though I must not speak of Polly. Poor little Polly! what a pretty child she was! I used to carry sugar-plums on purpose for her. Good-bye, Tugwell; I must think about all this."

"And so must I, sir. What a strapping chap 'a be!" Captain Zebedee continued to himself, as Twemlow strode away with the light step of a mountain savage, carrying a long staff from force of habit, and looking even larger than himself from the flow of chestnut hair and beard around him. "Never did see such a hairy chap. Never showed no signs of it when 'a was a lad, and Miss 'Liza quite smooth in the front of her neck. Must come of Hottentot climate, I reckon. They calls it the bush, from the folk been so bushy. I used to think as my beard was a pretty good example; but, Lord bless me and keep me, it would all go on his nose! If 'a spreadeth that over the face of Squire Carne, 'a will ravish him, as the wicked doth ravish the poor."

Twemlow had many sad things to consider, and among them the impending loss of this grand mane. After divers delays, and infinitude of forms, and much evidence of things self-evident—in the spirit which drove Sir Horatio Nelson to pin a certificate of amputation to the sleeve of his lost arm—this Twemlow had established that he was the Twemlow left behind upon the coast of Africa, and having been captured in the service of his country, was entitled at least to restoration. In such a case small liberality was shown in those days, even as now prevaileth, the object of all in authority being to be hard upon those who are out of it. At last, when he was becoming well weary, and nothing but an Englishman's love of his country and desire to help in her dangers prevented him from turning to private pursuits—wherein he held a key to fortune—he found himself restored to his rank in the Army, and appointed to another regiment, which happened to be short of officers. Then he flung to the winds, until peace should return, his prospect of wealth beyond reckoning, and locked in a black leather trunk materials worth their weight in diamonds. But, as life is uncertain, he told his beloved one the secret of his great discovery, which she, in sweet ignorance of mankind, regarded as of no importance.

But as wars appear and disappear, nations wax and wane, and the holiest principles of one age become the scoff of the next, yet human nature is the same throughout, it would be wrong to cast no glance—even with the French so near our shores—at the remarkable discovery of this young man, and the circumstances leading up to it. For with keen insight into civilized thought, which yearns with the deepest remorse for those blessings which itself has banished, he knew that he held a master-key to the treasuries of Croesus, Mycerinus, Attalus, and every other King who has dazzled the world with his talents. The man who can minister to human needs may, when he is lucky, earn a little towards his own; the man who contributes to the pleasure of his fellows must find reward in his own; but he who can gratify the vanity of his race is the master of their pockets.

Twemlow had been carried from the deadly coast (as before related by Captain Southcombe) to the mountainous district far inland, by the great King Golo of the Quackwas nation, mighty warriors of lofty stature. Here he was treated well, and soon learned enough of their simple language to understand and be understood; while the King, who considered all white men as of canine origin, was pleased with him, and prepared to make him useful. Then Twemlow was sent, with an escort of chiefs, to the land of the Houlas, as a medicine-man, to win Queen Mabonga for the great King Golo. But she—so strange is the perversity of women—beholding this man of a pearly tint, as fair as the moon, and as soft as a river—for he took many months to get properly tanned—with one long gaze of amazement yielded to him what he sought for another. A dwarf and a whipster he might be among the great darkies around her—for he had only six feet and one inch of stature, and forty-two inches round the chest—but, to her fine taste, tone and quality more than covered defect of quantity. The sight of male members of her race had never moved her, because she had heard of their wickedness; but the gaze of this white man, so tender and so innocent, set her on a long course of wondering about herself. Then she drew back, and passed into the private hut behind, where no one was allowed to disturb her. For she never had felt like this before, and she wanted nobody to notice it.

But the Houla maidens, with the deepest interest in matters that came home to them outside their understanding, held council with their mothers, and these imparted to the angelic stranger, as plainly as modesty permitted, the distressing results of his whiteness, and implored him to depart, before further harm was done. Twemlow perceived that he had tumbled into a difficult position, and the only way out of it was to make off. Giving pledges to return in two moons at the latest, he made his salaam to the sensitive young Queen, whose dignity was only surpassed by her grace, and expecting to be shortened by the head, returned with all speed to the great King Golo. Honesty is the best policy—as we all know so well that we forbear to prove it—and the Englishman saw that the tale would be darker from the lips of his black attendants. The negro monarch was of much-enduring mind, but these tidings outwent his philosophy. He ordered Twemlow's head to come off by dinner-time, and, alas, that royal household kept very early hours; and the poor captain, corded to a tree, sniffed sadly the growth of good roast, which he never should taste, and could only succeed in succession of fare. For although that enlightened King had discarded the taste of the nations around him, it was not half so certain as the prisoner could have wished that his prejudice would resist the relish of a candid rival in prime condition.

While Twemlow was dwelling upon this nice question, and sympathising deeply with the animal on the spit, Tuloo, the head councillor of the realm, appeared, an ancient negro full of wisdom and resource. Discovering that the white man set more value on his head than is usual with these philosophers, he proposed conditions which were eagerly accepted, and releasing the captive, led him into his own hut. Here the man of wisdom spat three times into his very ample bosom, to exorcise evil spells, and took from a hole in the corner something which he handled very carefully, and with a touch as light as possible. Following everything with his best eyes, Twemlow perceived in the hand of Tuloo a spongy-looking substance of conical form, and in colour and size very like a morel, but possessing a peculiar golden glow. "Kneel here, my son, and move not until I tell you," the old man whispered, and was obeyed. Then he stripped off all covering from the white neck and shoulders, and beginning immediately below the eyes, brushed all the cheeks and the chin, throat and neck and upper part of the bosom, with the substance in his hand, from which a yellow powder passed, moist rather than dusty, into the open pores. "In one moon you will be a beast of the woods, and in two you shall return to the Queen that loves you," said Councillor Tuloo, with a sly little grin.

But Twemlow was robbed of no self-respect by the growth of a forest about

438

him; and when he was sent again to Queen Mabonga, and the dewy glance of love died at the very first wink into a stony glare—because of his face being covered with hair—he said to himself that he knew where he could inflict a very different impression upon ladies. For these cannot have too much hair in England, at the back of their own heads, and front of their admirers'.

Councillor Tuloo was gifted with a deep understanding of a thing which looks shallow to a man who has never yet heard of false bottoms. He said to King Golo: "I know what women are. As long as she never had thought about men, you might crawl, and be only a hog to her. But her eyes have been opened to this white man, and there is room for a black one to go into them. And unless you are at hand, it will be done by some one else."

In short, all was managed so beautifully that in six more moons the coy Mabonga split the Durra straw with King Golo, amid vast rejoicings and in din almost equal to that which a wedding in Wales arouses. But from time to time it was considered needful to keep up her Majesty's repulsion by serving Erle Twemlow with another dose of that which would have created for the English fair capillary attraction. Thus he became a great favourite with the King, who listened with deep interest to his descriptions of the houseful of beads and buttons to be earned in England by a little proper management of Tuloo's magic dust. Before very long it was arranged that as soon as a good supply of Pong could be collected, Twemlow should be sent back to the coast and placed under the charge of Bandeliah, who was now a tributary of this great King. And here he might have waited years and years—for the trading station was abandoned now—but for the benevolence of Captain Southcombe, who, being driven to the eastward of his course upon one of his returns from India, stood in a little further to enquire about his friend, and with no small pleasure conveyed him home.

CHAPTER LX

NO DANGER, GENTLEMEN

The little dinner at Springhaven Hall, appointed for that same Saturday, had now grown into a large one. Carne had refused Dolly's offer to get him an invitation, and for many reasons he was not invited. He ought to have been glad of this, because he did not want to be there; but his nature, like a saw's, was full of teeth, and however he was used, he grated. But without any aid of his teeth, a good dinner, well planned and well served, bade fair in due course to be well digested also by forty at least of the forty-two people who sat down to consider it. For as yet the use of tongue was understood, and it was not allowed to obstruct by perpetual motion the duties of the palate. And now every person in the parish of high culture—which seems to be akin to the Latin for a knife, though a fork expels nature more forcibly—as well as many others of locality less favoured, joined in this muster of good people and good things. At the outset, the Admiral had intended nothing more than a quiet recognition of the goodness of the Lord in bringing home a husband for the daughter of the house; but what Englishman can forbear the pleasure of killing two birds with one stone?

It was Stubbard who first suggested this, and Sir Charles at once saw the force of it, especially with the Marquis of Southdown coming. Captain Stubbard had never admired anybody, not even himself—without which there is no happiness—much less Mr. Pitt, or Lord Nelson, or the King, until justice was done to the race of Stubbard, and their hands were plunged into the Revenue. But now, ever since the return of the war to its proper home in England, this Captain had been paid well for doing the very best thing that a man can do, i. e., nothing. He could not help desiring to celebrate this, and as soon as he received his invitation, he went to the host and put it clearly. The Admiral soon entered into his views, and as guests were not farmed by the head as yet at tables entertaining self-respect, he perceived the advantage of a good dinner scored to his credit with forty at the cost of twenty; and Stubbard's proposal seemed thoroughly well timed, so long was it now since the leaders of Defence had celebrated their own vigilance. Twenty-two, allowing for the ladies needful, were thus added to the score of chairs intended, and the founder of the feast could scarcely tell whether the toast of the evening was to be the return of the traveller, or the discomfiture of Boney. That would mainly depend upon the wishes of the Marquis, and these again were likely to be guided by the treatment he had met with from the government lately and the commanders of his Division.

This nobleman was of a character not uncommon eighty years ago, but now very rare among public men, because a more flexible fibre has choked it. Steadfast, honourable, simple, and straightforward, able to laugh without bitterness at the arrogant ignorance of mobs, but never to smile at the rogues who led them, scorning all shuffle of words, foul haze, and snaky maze of evasion, and refusing to believe at first sight that his country must be in the wrong and her enemies in the right, he added to all these exterminated foibles a leisurely dignity now equally extinct. Trimmers, time-servers, and hypocrites feared him, as thieves fear an honourable dog; and none could quote his words against one another. This would have made him unpopular now, when perjury means popularity. For the present, however, self-respect existed, and no one thought any the worse of his lordship for not having found him a liar. Especially with ladies, who insist on truth in men as a pleasant proof of their sex, Lord Southdown had always been a prime favourite, and an authority largely misquoted. And to add to his influence, he possessed a quick turn of temper, which rendered it very agreeable to agree with him.

Lord Southdown was thinking, as he led Miss Darling to her chair at the head of the table, that he never had seen a more pleasing young woman, though he grieved at her taste in preferring the brown young man on her left to his elegant friend Lord Dashville. Also he marvelled at hearing so much, among the young officers of his acquaintance, concerning the beauty of the younger sister, and so little about this far sweeter young person—at least in his opinion. For verily Dolly was not at her best; her beautiful colour was gone, her neck had lost its sprightly turn, and her gray eyes moved heavily instead of sparkling. "That girl has some burden upon her mind," he thought as he watched her with interest and pity; "she has put on her dress anyhow, and she does not even look to see who is looking at her!"

For the "Belle of all Sussex," as the young sparks entitled her, was ill at ease with herself, and ready to quarrel with every one except herself. She had conscience enough to confess, whenever she could not get away from it, that for weeks and months she had been slipping far and further from the true and honest course. Sometimes, with a pain like a stitch in the side, the truth would spring upon her; and perhaps for a moment she would wonder at herself, and hate the man misleading her. But this happened chiefly when he was present, and said or did something to vex her; and then he soon set it to rights again, and made everything feel delightful. And this way of having her misgivings eased made them easier when they came again with no one to appease them. For she began to think of what he had done, and how kind and considerate his mind must be, and how hard it must seem to mistrust him.

Another thing that urged her to keep on now, without making any fuss about it, was the wonderful style her sister Faith had shown since that hairy monster came back again. It was manifest that the world contained only one man of any high qualities, and nobody must dare to think even twice about any conclusion he laid down. He had said to her, with a penetrating glance—and it must have been that to get through such a thicket—that dangerous people were about, and no girl possessing any self-respect must think of wandering on the shore alone. The more she was spied upon and admonished, the more she would do what she thought right; and a man who had lived among savages for years must be a queer judge of propriety. But, in spite of all these defiant thoughts, her heart was very low, and her mind in a sad flutter, and she could not even smile as she met her father's gaze. Supposing that she was frightened at the number of the guests, and the noise of many tongues, and the grandeur of the people, the gentle old man made a little signal to her to come and have a whisper with him, as a child might do, under courtesy of the good company. But Dolly feigned not to understand, at the penalty of many a heart-pang.

The dinner went on with a very merry sound, and a genuine strength of enjoyment, such as hearty folk have who know one another, and are met together not to cut capers of wit, but refresh their goodwill and fine principles. And if any dinner party can be so arranged that only five per cent. has any trouble on its mind, the gentleman who whips away the plates, at a guinea a mouth, will have to go home with a face of willow pattern.

The other whose mind was away from her food, and reckless of its own nourishment, was Blyth Scudamore's mother, as gentle a lady as ever tried never to think of herself. In spite of all goodness, and faith in the like, she had enough to make her very miserable now, whenever she allowed herself to think about it, and that was fifty-nine minutes out of sixty. For a brief account of her son's escape from Etaples had reached her, through the kindness of Captain Desportes, who found means to get a letter delivered to the Admiral. That brave French officer spoke most highly of the honourable conduct of his English friend, but had very small hope of his safety. For he added the result of his own inquiries to the statement of M. Jalais, and from these it was clear that poor Scuddy had set forth alone in a rickety boat, ill found and ill fitted to meet even moderate weather in the open Channel. Another young Englishman had done the like, after lurking in the forest of Hardelot, but he had been recaptured by the French at the outset of his hopeless voyage. Scudamore had not been so retaken; and the Captain (who had not received his letter until it was too late to interfere, by reason of his own despatch to Dieppe) had encountered a sharp summer gale just then, which must have proved fatal to the poor old boat. The only chance was that some English ship might have picked up the wanderer, and if so the highly respected Admiral would have heard of it before he received this letter. As no such tidings had been received, there could be little doubt about the issue in any reasonable mind. But the heart of a woman is not a mind, or the man that is born of her might as well forego the honour.

However, as forty people were quite happy, the wisest course is to rejoin them. The ladies were resolved upon this occasion to storm the laws of usage which required their withdrawal before the toasts began; and so many gentle voices challenged the garrison of men behind their bottles that terms of unusual scope were arranged. It was known that the Marquis would make a fine speech—short, and therefore all the finer—in proposing the toast of the evening, to wit, "Our King, and our Country." Under the vigorous lead of Mrs. Stubbard, the ladies demanded to hear every word; after which they would go, and discuss their own affairs, or possibly those of their neighbours. But the gentlemen must endure their presence till his lordship had spoken, and the Admiral replied. Faith was against this arrangement, because she foresaw that it would make them very late; but she yielded to the wishes of so many of her guests, consoled with the thought that she would be supported by some one on her left hand, who would be her support for life.

When all had done well, except the two aforesaid, and good-will born of good deeds was crowning comfort with jocund pleasure, and the long oak table, rich of grain and dark with the friction of a hundred years, shone in the wavering flow of dusk with the gleam of purple and golden fruit, the glance of brilliant glass that puzzles the light with its claim to shadow, and the glow of amber and amethyst wine decanted to settle that question—then the bold Admiral, standing up, said, "Bring in the lights, that we may see his lordship."

"I like to speak to some intelligence," said the guest, who was shrewd at an answer. And Dolly, being quick at occasion, seized it, and in the shifting of chairs left her own for some one else.

The curtains were drawn across the western window, to close the conflict between God's light and man's, and then this well-known gentleman, having placed his bottle handily—for he never "put wine into two whites," to use his own expression—arose with his solid frame as tranquil as a rock, and his full-fronted head like a piece of it. Every gentleman bowed to his bow, and waited with silent respect for his words, because they would be true and simple.

"My friends, I will take it for granted that we all love our country, and hate its enemies. We may like and respect them personally, for they are as good as we are; but we are bound to hate them collectively, as men who would ruin all we love. For the stuff that is talked about freedom, democracy, march of intellect, and so forth, I have nothing to say, except to bid you look at the

444

result among themselves. Is there a man in France whose body is his own if he can carry arms, or his soul if it ventures to seek its own good? As for mind —there is only the mind of one man; a large one in many ways; in others a small one, because it considers its owner alone.

"But we of England have refused to be stripped of all that we hold dear, at the will of a foreign upstart. We have fought for years, and we still are fighting, without any brag or dream of glory, for the rights of ourselves and of all mankind. There have been among us weak-minded fellows, babblers of abstract nonsense, and even, I grieve to say—traitors. But, on the whole, we have stood together, and therefore have not been trodden on. How it may end is within the knowledge of the Almighty only; but already there are signs that we shall be helped, if we continue to help ourselves.

"And now for the occasion of our meeting here. We rejoice most heartily with our good host, the vigilant Defender of these shores, at the restoration to his arms—or rather, to a still more delightful embrace—of a British officer, who has proved a truth we knew already, that nothing stops a British officer. I see a gentleman struck so keenly with the force of that remark, because he himself has proved it, that I must beg his next neighbour to fill up his glass, and allow nothing to stop him from tossing it off. And as I am getting astray from my text, I will clear my poor head with what you can see through."

The Marquis of Southdown filled his glass from a bottle of grand old Chambertin—six of which had been laid most softly in a cupboard of the wainscote for his use—and then he had it filled again, and saw his meaning brilliantly.

"Our second point is the defeat of the French, and of this we may now assure ourselves. They have not been defeated, for the very good reason that they never would come out to fight; but it comes to the same thing, because they are giving it over as a hopeless job. I have seen too many ups and downs to say that we are out of danger yet; but when our fleets have been chasing theirs all over the world, are they likely to come and meet us in our own waters? Nelson has anchored at Spithead, and is rushing up to London, as our host has heard to-day, with his usual impetuosity. Every man must stick to his own business, even the mighty Nelson; and he might not meddle with Billy Blue, or anybody else up Channel. Still, Nelson is not the sort of man to jump into a chaise at Portsmouth if there was the very smallest chance of the French coming over to devour us.

"Well, my friends, we have done our best, and have some right to be proud of it; but we should depart from our nature if we even exercised that right. The nature of an Englishman is this—to be afraid of nothing but his own renown. Feeling this great truth, I will avoid offence by hiding as a crime my admiration of the glorious soldiers and sailors here, yet beg them for once to remember themselves, as having enabled me to propose, and all present to pledge, the welfare of our King and Country."

The Marquis waved his glass above his head, without spilling a single drop, although it was a bumper, then drained it at a draught, inverted it, and cleverly snapped it in twain upon the table, with his other hand laid on his heart, and a long low reverence to the company. Thereupon up stood squires and dames, and repeating the good toast, pledged it, with a deep bow to the proposer; and as many of the gentlemen as understood the art, without peril to fair neighbours, snapped the glass.

His lordship was delighted, and in the spirit of the moment held up his hand, which meant, "Silence, silence, till we all sing the National Anthem!" In a clear loud voice he led off the strain, Erle Twemlow from his hairy depths struck in, then every man, following as he might, and with all his might, sustained it, and the ladies, according to their wont, gave proof of the heights they can scale upon rapture.

The Admiral, standing, and beating time now and then with his heel— though all the time deserved incessant beating—enjoyed the performance a great deal more than if it had been much better, and joined in the main roar as loudly as he thought his position as host permitted. For although he was nearing the haven now of threescore years and ten, his throat and heart were so sea-worthy that he could very sweetly have outroared them all. But while he was preparing just to prove this, if encouraged, and smiling very pleasantly at a friend who said, "Strike up, Admiral," he was called from the room, and in the climax of the roar slipped away for a moment, unheeded, and meaning to make due apology to his guests as soon as he came back.

CHAPTER LXI

DISCHARGED FROM DUTY

While loyalty thus rejoiced and throve in the warmth of its own geniality, a man who was loyal to himself alone, and had no geniality about him, was watching with contempt these British doings. Carne had tethered his stout black horse, who deserved a better master, in a dusky dell of dark-winged trees at the back of the eastern shrubbery. Here the good horse might rest unseen, and consider the mysterious ways of men; for the main approach was by the western road, and the shades of evening stretched their arms to the peaceful yawn of sunset. And here he found good stuff spread by nature, more worthy of his attention, and tucking back his forelegs, fared as well as the iron between his teeth permitted.

Then the master drew his green riding-coat of thin velvet closer round him, and buttoned the lappet in front, because he had heavy weight in the pockets. Keeping warily along the lines of shadow, he gained a place of vantage in the shrubbery, a spot of thick shelter having loops of outlook. Above and around him hung a curtain of many-pointed ilex, and before him a barberry bush, whose coral clusters caught the waning light. In this snug nook he rested calmly, leaning against the ilex trunk, and finished his little preparations for anything adverse to his plans. In a belt which was hidden by his velvet coat he wore a short dagger in a sheath of shagreen, and he fixed it so that he could draw it in a moment, without unfastening the riding-coat. Then from the pockets on either side he drew a pair of pistols, primed them well from a little flask, and replaced them with the butts beneath the lappets. "Death for at least three men," he muttered, "if they are fools enough to meddle with me. My faith, these Darlings are grown very grand, on the strength of the land that belongs to us!"

For he heard the popping of champagne corks, and the clink of abundant silver, and tuning of instruments by the band, and he saw the flash of lights, and the dash of serving-men, and the rush of hot hospitality; and although he had not enough true fibre in his stomach to yearn for a taste of the good things going round, there can be little doubt, from what he did thereafter, that his gastric juices must have turned to gall.

With all these sounds and sights and scents of things that he had no right to despise, his patience was tried for an hour and a half, or at any rate he believed so. The beautiful glow in the west died out, where the sun had been ripening his harvest-field of sheafy gold and awny cloud; and the pulse of quivering dusk beat slowly, so that a man might seem to count it, or rather a child, who sees such things, which later men lose sight of. The forms of the deepening distances against the departure of light grew faint, and prominent points became obscure, and lines retired into masses, while Carne maintained his dreary watch, with his mood becoming darker. As the sound of joyful voices, and of good-will doubled by good fare, came to his unfed vigil from the open windows of the dining-room, his heart was not enlarged at all, and the only solace for his lips was to swear at British revelry. For the dining-room was at the western end, some fifty yards away from him, and its principal window faced the sunset, but his lurking-place afforded a view of the southern casements obliquely. Through these he had seen that the lamps were brought, and heard the increase of merry noise, the clapping of hands, and the jovial cheers at the rising of the popular Marquis.

At last he saw a white kerchief waved at the window nearest to him, the window of the Admiral's little study, which opened like a double door upon the eastern grass-plat. With an ill-conditioned mind, and body stiff and lacking nourishment, he crossed the grass in a few long strides, and was admitted without a word.

"What a time you have been! I was giving it up," he whispered to the trembling Dolly. "Where are the candles? I must strike a light. Surely you might have brought one. Bolt the door, while I make a light, and close the curtains quietly, but leave the window open. Don't shake, like a child that is going to be whipped. Too late now for nonsense. What are you afraid of? Silly child!"

As he spoke he was striking a light in a little French box containing a cube of jade, and with very little noise he lit two candles standing on the high oak desk. Dolly drew a curtain across the window, and then went softly to the door, which opened opposite the corner of a narrow passage, and made pretence to bolt it, but shot the bolt outside the socket.

"Come and let me look at you," said Carne, for he knew that he had been rough with her, and she was not of the kind that submits to that. "Beauty, how pale you look, and yet how perfectly lovely in this evening gown! I should like to kill the two gentlemen who sat next to you at dinner. Darling, you know that whatever I do is only for your own sweet sake."

"If you please not to touch me, it will be better," said the lady, not in a whisper, but a firm and quiet voice, although her hands were trembling; "you are come upon business, and you should do it."

If Carne had but caught her in his arms, and held her to his heart, and vowed that all business might go to the devil while he held his angel so, possibly the glow of nobler feelings might have been lost in the fire of passion. But he kept his selfish end alone in view, and neglected the womanly road to it.

"A despatch from London arrived today; I must see it," he said, shortly; "as well as the copy of the answer sent. And then my beauty must insert a NOT in the order to be issued in the morning, or otherwise invert its meaning, simply to save useless bloodshed. The key for a moment, the key, my darling, of this fine old piece of furniture!"

"Is it likely that I would give you the key? My father always keeps it. What right have you with his private desk? I never promised anything so bad as that."

"I am not to be trifled with," he whispered, sternly. "Do you think that I came here for kissing? The key I must have, or break it open; and how will you explain that away?"

His rudeness settled her growing purpose. The misery of indecision vanished; she would do what was right, if it cost her life. Her face was as white as her satin dress, but her dark eyes flashed with menace.

"There is a key that opens it," she said, as she pointed to the bookcase; "but I forbid you to touch it, sir."

Carne's only reply was to snatch the key from the upper glass door of the book-shelves, which fitted the lock of the Admiral's desk, though the owner was not aware of it. In a moment the intruder had unlocked the high and massive standing-desk, thrown back the cover, and placed one candlestick among the documents. Many of them he brushed aside, as useless for his purpose, and became bewildered among the rest, for the Commander of the Coast-defence was not a man of order. He never knew where to put a thing, nor even where it might have put itself, but found a casual home for any paper that deserved it. This lack of method has one compensation, like other human defects, to wit, that it puzzles a clandestine searcher more deeply than cypher or cryptogram. Carne had the Admiral's desk as wide as an oyster thrown back on his valve, and just being undertucked with the knife, to make him go down easily. Yet so great was the power of disorder that nothing could be made out of anything. "Watch at the door," he had said to Dolly; and this suited her intention.

For while he was thus absorbed, with his back towards her, she opened the door a little, and presently saw the trusty Charles come hurrying by, as if England hung upon his labours. "Tell my father to come here this moment; go softly, and say that I sent you." As she finished her whisper she closed the door, without any sound, and stood patiently.

"Show me where it is; come and find it for me. Everything here is in the vilest mess," cried Carne, growing reckless with wrath and hurry. "I want the despatch of this morning, and I find tailors' bills, way to make water-proof blacking, a list of old women, and a stump of old pipe! Come here, this instant, and show me where it is."

"If you forget your good manners," answered Dolly, still keeping in the dark near the door, "I shall have to leave you. Surely you have practice enough in spying, to find what you want, with two candles."

Carne turned for a moment, and stared at her. Her attitude surprised him, but he could not believe in her courage to rebel. She stood with her back to the door, and met his gaze without a sign of fear.

"There are no official papers here," he said, after another short ransack; "there must have been some, if this desk is the one. Have you dared to delude me by showing the wrong desk?"

Dolly met his gaze still, and then walked towards him. The band had struck up, and the company were singing with a fine patriotic roar, which rang very nobly in the distance—"Britannia, rule the waves!" Dolly felt like a Briton as the words rolled through her, and the melody lifted her proud heart.

"You have deluded yourself," she said, standing proudly before the baffled spy; "you have ransacked my father's private desk, which I allowed you to do, because my father has no secrets. He leaves it open half the time, because he is a man of honour. He is not a man of plots, and wiles, and trickery upon women. And you have deluded yourself, in dreaming that a daughter of his would betray her Country."

"By the God that made me, I will have your life!" cried Carne in French, as he dashed his hand under his coat to draw his dagger; but the pressure of the desk had displaced that, so that he could not find it. She thought that her time was come, and shrieked—for she was not at all heroic, and loved life very dearly—but she could not take her eyes from his, nor turn to fly from the spell of them; all she could do was to step back; and she did so into her father's arms.

"Ho!" cried the Admiral, who had entered with the smile of good cheer and good company glowing on his fine old countenance; "my Dolly and a stranger at my private desk! Mr. Carne! I have had a glass or two of wine, but my eyes must be playing me extraordinary tricks. A gentleman searching my desk, and apparently threatening my dear daughter! Have the kindness to explain, before you attempt to leave us."

If the curtain had not been drawn across the window, Carne would have made his escape, and left the situation to explain itself. But the stuff was thick, and it got between his legs; and before he could slip away, the stout old Admiral had him by the collar with a sturdy grasp, attesting the substance of the passing generation. And a twinkle of good-humour was in the old eyes still—such a wonder was his Dolly that he might be doing wrong in laying hands of force upon a visitor of hers. Things as strange as this had been within his knowledge, and proved to be of little harm—with forbearance. But his eyes grew stern, as Carne tried to dash his hand off.

"If you value your life, you will let me go," said the young man to the old one.

"I will not let you go, sir, till you clear up this. A gentleman must see that he is bound to do so. If I prove to be wrong, I will apologise. What! Are you going to fire at me? You would never be such a coward!"

He dropped upon the floor, with a bullet in his brain, and his course of duty ended. Carne dashed aside the curtain, and was nearly through the window, when two white arms were cast round his waist. He threw himself forward with all his might, and wrenched at the little hands clasped around him, but they held together like clenched iron. "Will you force me to kill you?" "You may, if you like"—was the dialogue of these lovers.

The strength of a fit was in her despair. She set her bent knees against the window-frame, and a shower of glass fell between them; but she flinched not from her convulsive grasp. "Let me come back, that I may shoot myself," Carne panted, for his breath was straitened; "what is life to me after losing you?" She made no answer, but took good care not to release so fond a lover. Then he threw himself back with all his weight, and she fell on the floor beneath him. Her clasp relaxed, and he was free; for her eyes had encountered her father's blood, and she swooned away, and lay as dead.

Carne arose quickly, and bolted the door. His breath was short, and his body trembling, but the wits of the traitor were active still. "I must have something to show for all this," he thought as he glanced at the bodies on the floor. "Those revellers may not have heard this noise. I know where it is now, and I will get it."

But the sound of the pistol, and shriek of the girl, had rung through the guests, when the wine was at their lips, and all were nodding to one another. Faith sprang up, and then fell back trembling, and several men ran towards the door. Charles, the footman, met them there, with his face whiter than his napkin, and held up his hands, but could not speak. Erle Twemlow dashed past him and down the passage; and Lord Southdown said: "Gentlemen, see to the ladies. There has been some little mishap, I fear. Bob, and Arthur, come with me."

Twemlow was first at the study door, and finding it fastened, struck with all his force, and shouted, at the very moment when Carne stood before the true desk of office. "Good door, and good bolt," muttered Carne; "my rule is never to be hurried by noises. Dolly will be quiet for a quarter of an hour, and the old gentleman forever. All I want is about two minutes."

Twemlow stepped back a few yards, and then with a good start delivered a rushing kick; but the only result was a jar of his leg through the sole of his thin dress sandal.

"The window!" cried the Marquis. "We'll stop here; you know the house; take the shortest cut to the window. Whoever is there, we shall have him so. I am too slow. Boy Bob, go with him."

"What a fool I was not to think of that!" shouted Twemlow, as he set off for the nearest house door, and unluckily Carne heard him. He had struck up the ledge of the desk with the butt of the pistol he had fired, and pocketing a roll of fresh despatches, he strode across the body of the Admiral, and with a glance at Dolly—whose eyes were wide open, but her face drawn aside, like a peach with a split stone—out he went. He smiled as he heard the thundering of full-bodied gentlemen against the study door, and their oaths, as they damaged their knuckles and knee-caps. Then he set off hot-foot, but was stopped by a figure advancing from the corner of the house.

This was not a graceful figure, as of gentle maiden, nor venerable and slow of foot, as that of an ancient mariner, but a man in the prime of strength, and largely endowed with that blessing—the mate of truth. Carne perceived that he had met his equal, and perhaps his better, in a bout of muscle, and he tried to escape by superior mind.

"Twemlow, how glad I am that I have met you! You are the very man I wanted. There has been a sad accident in there with one of the Admiral's pistols, and the dear old man is badly wounded. I am off for a doctor, for my horse is at hand. For God's sake run in, and hold his head up, and try to staunch the bleeding. I shall be back in half an hour with the man that lives at Pebbleridge. Don't lose a moment. Particulars hereafter."

"Particulars now!" replied Twemlow, sternly, as he planted himself before his cousin. "For years I have lived among liars, and they called a lie Crom, and worshipped it. If this is not Crom, why did you bolt the door?"

"You shall answer for this, when time allows. If the door was bolted, he must have done it. Let me pass; the last chance depends on my speed."

Carne made a rush to pass, but Twemlow caught him by the breast, and held him. "Come back," he said, fiercely, "and prove your words. Without that, you go no further."

Carne seized him by the throat, but his mighty beard, like a collar of hemp, protected him, and he brought his big brown fist like a hammer upon the traitor's forehead. Carne wrenched at his dagger, but failed to draw it, and the two strong men rolled on the grass, fighting like two bull-dogs. Reason, and thought, and even sense of pain were lost in brutal fury, as they writhed, and clutched, and dug at one another, gashing their knuckles, and gnashing their teeth, frothing with one another's blood, for Carne bit like a tiger. At length tough condition and power of endurance got the mastery, and Twemlow planted his knee upon the gasping breast of Carne.

"Surrend," he said, for his short breath could not fetch up the third syllable; and Carne with a sign of surrender lay on his back, and put his chin up, and shut his eyes as if he had fainted. Twemlow with self-congratulation waited a little to recover breath, still keeping his knee in the post of triumph, and pinning the foe's right arm to his side. But the foe's left hand was free, and with the eyes still shut, and a continuance of gasping, that left hand stole its way to the left pocket, quietly drew forth the second pistol, pressed back the hammer on the grass, and with a flash (both of eyes and of flint) fired into the victor's forehead. The triumphant knee rolled off the chest, the body swung over, as a log is rolled by the woodman's crowbar, and Twemlow's back was on the grass, and his eyes were closed to the moonlight.

Carne scrambled up and shook himself, to be sure that all his limbs were sound. "Ho, ho, ho!" he chuckled; "it is not so easy to beat me. Why, who are you? Down with you, then!"

Lord Robert Chancton, a lad of about sixteen, the eldest son of the Marquis, had lost his way inside the house, in trying to find a short-cut to the door, and coming up after the pistol was fired, made a very gallant rush at the enemy. With a blow of the butt Carne sent him sprawling; then dashing among the shrubs and trees, in another minute was in the saddle, and galloping towards the ancestral ruins.

As he struck into the main road through the grounds, Carne passed and just missed by a turn of the bridle another horseman ascending the hill, and urging a weary animal. The faces of the men shot past each other within a short yard, and gaze met gaze; but neither in the dark flash knew the other, for a big tree barred the moonlight. But Carne, in another moment, thought that the man who had passed must be Scudamore, probably fraught with hot tidings. And the thought was confirmed, as he met two troopers riding as hard as ride they might; and then saw the beacon on the headland flare. From point to point, and from height to height, like a sprinkle of blood, the red lights ran; and the roar of guns from the moon-lit sea made echo that they were ready. Then the rub-a-dub-dub of the drum arose, and the thrilling blare of trumpet; the great deep of the night was heaved and broken with the stir of human storm; and the staunchest and strongest piece of earth—our England—was ready to defend herself.

CHAPTER LXII

THE WAY OUT OF IT

"My father! my father! I must see my father. Who are you, that dare to keep me out? Let me know the worst, and try to bear it. What are any of you to him?"

"But, my dear child," Lord Southdown answered, holding the door against poor Faith, as she strove to enter the room of death, "wait just one minute, until we have lifted him to the sofa, and let us bring your poor sister out."

"I have no sister. She has killed my father, and the best thing she can do is to die. I feel that I could shoot her, if I had a pistol. Let me see him, where he lies."

"But, my poor dear, you must think of others. Your dear father is beyond all help. Your gallant lover lies on the grass. They hope to bring him round, God willing! Go where you can be of use."

"How cruel you are! You must want to drive me mad. Let his father and mother see to him, while I see to my own father. If you had a daughter, you would understand. Am I crying? Do I even tremble?"

The Marquis offered his arm, and she took it in fear of falling, though she did not tremble; so he led her to her father's last repose. The poor Admiral lay by the open window, with his head upon a stool which Faith had worked. The ghastly wound was in his broad smooth forehead, and his fair round cheeks were white with death. But the heart had not quite ceased to beat, and some remnant of the mind still hovered somewhere in the lacerated brain. Stubbard, sobbing like a child, was lifting and clumsily chafing one numb hand; while his wife, who had sponged the wound, was making the white curls wave with a fan she had shaped from a long official paper found upon the floor.

Dolly was recovering from her swoon, and sat upon a stool by the bookcase, faintly wondering what had happened, but afraid to ask or think. The corner of the bookcase, and the burly form of Stubbard, concealed the window from her, and the torpid oppression which ensues upon a fit lay between her and her agony. Faith, as she passed, darted one glance at her, not of pity, not of love, but of cold contempt and satisfaction at her misery.

Then Faith, the quiet and gentle maid, the tranquil and the self-controlled (whom every one had charged with want of heart, because she had borne her own grief so well), stood with the body of her father at her feet, and uttered an exceeding bitter cry. The others had seen enough of grief, as every human being must, but nothing half so sad as this. They feared to look at her face, and durst not open lips to comfort her.

"Don't speak. Don't look at him. You have no right here. When he comes to himself, he will want none but me. I have always done everything for him since dear mother died; and I shall get him to sit up. He will be so much better when he sits up. I can get him to do it, if you will only go. Oh, father, father, it is your own Faith come to make you well, dear, if you will only look at me!"

As she took his cold limp hand and kissed it, and wiped a red splash from his soft white hair, the dying man felt, by nature's feeling, that he was being touched by a child of his. A faint gleam flitted through the dimness of his eyes, which he had not the power to close, and the longing to say "farewell" contended with the drooping of the underlip. She was sure that he whispered, "Bless you, darling!" though nobody else could have made it out; but a sudden rush of tears improved her hearing, as rain brings higher voices down.

"Dolly too!" he seemed to whisper next; and Faith made a sign to Mrs. Stubbard. Then Dolly was brought, and fell upon her knees, at the other side of her father, and did not know how to lament as yet, and was scarcely sure of having anything to mourn. But she spread out her hands, as if for somebody to take them, and bowed her pale face, and closed her lips, that she might be rebuked without answering.

Her father knew her; and his yearning was not to rebuke, but to bless and comfort her. He had forgotten everything, except that he was dying, with a daughter at each side of him. This appeared to make him very happy, about everything, except those two. He could not be expected to have much mind left; but the last of it was busy for his children's good. Once more he tried to see them both, and whispered his last message to them—"Forgive and love each other."

Faith bowed her head, as his fell back, and silently offered to kiss her sister; but Dolly neither moved nor looked at her. "As you please," said Faith; "and perhaps you would like to see a little more of your handiwork."

For even as she spoke, her lover's body was carried past the window, with his father and mother on either side, supporting his limp arms and sobbing. Then Dolly arose, and with one hand grasping the selvage of the curtain, fixed one long gaze upon her father's corpse. There were no tears in her eyes, no sign of anguish in her face, no proof that she knew or felt what she had done. And without a word she left the room.

"Hard to the last, even hard to you!" cried Faith, as her tears fell upon the cold forehead. "Oh, darling, how could you have loved her so?"

"It is not hardness; it is madness. Follow your sister," Lord Southdown said. "We have had calamities enough."

But Faith was fighting with all her strength against an attack of hysterics, and fetching long gasps to control herself. "I will go," replied Mrs. Stubbard; "this poor child is quite unfit. What on earth is become of Lady Scudamore? A doctor's widow might have done some good."

The doctor's widow was doing good elsewhere. In the first rush from the dining-room, Lady Scudamore had been pushed back by no less a person than Mrs. Stubbard; when at last she reached the study door she found it closed against her, and entering the next room, saw the flash of the pistol fired at Twemlow. Bravely hurrying to the spot by the nearest outlet she could find, she became at once entirely occupied with this new disaster. For two men who ran up with a carriage lamp declared that the gentleman was as dead as a door-nail, and hastened to make good their words by swinging him up heels over head. But the lady made them set him down and support his head, while she bathed the wound, and sent to the house for his father and mother, and when he could be safely brought in-doors, helped with her soft hands beneath his hair, and then became so engrossed with him that the arrival of her long-lost son was for several hours unknown to her.

For so many things coming all at once were enough to upset any one. Urgent despatches came hot for the hand that now was cold for ever; not a moment to lose, when time had ceased for the man who was to urge it. There were plenty of officers there, but no one clearly entitled to take command. Moreover, the public service clashed with the personal rage of the moment. Some were for rushing to the stables, mounting every horse that could be found, and scouring the country, sword in hand, for that infernal murderer. Some, having just descried the flash of beacon from the headland, and heard the alarm-guns from shore and sea, were for hurrying to their regiments, or ships, or homes and families (according to the head-quarters of their life), while others put their coats on to ride for all the doctors in the county, who should fetch back the Admiral to this world, that he might tell everybody what to do. Scudamore stood with his urgent despatches in the large well-candled hall, and vainly desired to deliver them. "Send for the Marquis," suggested some one.

Lord Southdown came, without being sent for. "I shall take this duty upon myself," he said, "as Lord-Lieutenant of the county. Captain Stubbard, as commander of the nearest post, will come with me and read these orders. Gentlemen, see that your horses are ready, and have all of the Admiral's saddled. Captain Scudamore, you have discharged your trust, and doubtless ridden far and hard. My orders to you are a bottle of wine and a sirloin of roast beef at once."

For the sailor was now in very low condition, weary, and worried, and in want of food. Riding express, and changing horses twice, not once had he recruited the inner man, who was therefore quite unfit to wrestle with the power of sudden grief. When he heard of the Admiral's death, he staggered as if a horse had stumbled under him, and his legs being stiff from hard sticking to saddle, had as much as they could do to hold him up. Yet he felt that he could not do the right thing now, he could not go and deal with the expedient victuals, neither might he dare intrude upon the ladies now; so he went out to comfort himself by attending to the troubles of his foundered horse, and by shedding unseen among the trees the tears which had gathered in his gentle eyes.

According to the surest law of nature, that broken-down animal had been forgotten as soon as he was done with. He would have given his four legs—if he could legally dispose of them—for a single draught of sweet delicious rapturous ecstatic water; but his bloodshot eyes sought vainly, and his welted tongue found nothing wet, except the flakes of his own salt foam. Until, with the help of the moon, a sparkle (worth more to his mind than all the diamonds he could draw)—a sparkle of the purest water gleamed into his dim eyes from the distance. Recalling to his mind's eyes the grand date of his existence when he was a colt, and had a meadow to himself, with a sparkling river at the end of it, he set forth in good faith, and, although his legs were weary, "negotiated"—as the sporting writers say—the distance between him and the object of his desire. He had not the least idea that this had cost ten guineas—as much as his own good self was worth; for it happened to be the first dahlia seen in that part of the country. That gaudy flower at its first appearance made such a stir among gardeners that Mr. Swipes gave the Admiral no peace until he allowed him to order one. And so great was this gardener's pride in his profession that he would not take an order for a rooted slip or cutting, from the richest man in the neighbourhood, for less than half a guinea. Therefore Mr. Swipes was attending to the plant with the diligence of a wet-nurse, and the weather being dry, he had soaked it overhead, even before he did that duty to himself.

A man of no teeth can take his nourishment in soup; and nature, inverting her manifold devices—which she would much rather do than be beaten—has provided that a horse can chew his solids into liquids, if there is a drop of juice in their composition, when his artificial life has failed to supply him with the bucket. This horse, being very dry, laid his tongue to the water-drops that sparkled on the foliage. He found them delicious, and he longed for more, and very soon his ready mind suggested that the wet must have come out of the leaves, and there must be more there. Proceeding on this argument, he found it quite correct, and ten guineas' worth of dahlia was gone into his stomach by the time that Captain Scudamore came courteously to look after him.

Blyth, in equal ignorance of his sumptuous repast, gave him a pat of approval, and was turning his head towards the stable yard, when he saw a white figure gliding swiftly through the trees beyond the belt of shrubbery. Weary and melancholy as he was, and bewildered with the tumult of disasters, his heart bounded hotly as he perceived that the figure was that of his Dolly— Dolly, the one love of his life, stealing forth, probably to mourn alone the loss of her beloved father. As yet he knew nothing of her share in that sad tale, and therefore felt no anxiety at first about her purpose. He would not intrude upon her grief; he had no right to be her comforter; but still she should have some one to look after her, at that time of night, and with so much excitement and danger in the air. So the poor horse was again abandoned to his own resources, and being well used to such treatment, gazed as wistfully and delicately after the young man Scudamore as that young man gazed after his lady-love.

To follow a person stealthily is not conducive to one's self-respect, but something in the lady's walk and gesture impelled the young sailor to follow her. She appeared to be hastening, with some set purpose, and without any heed of circumstance, towards a part of the grounds where no house was, no living creature for company, nor even a bench to rest upon. There was no foot-path in that direction, nor anything to go to, but the inland cliff that screened the Hall from northeastern winds, and at its foot a dark pool having no good name in the legends of the neighbourhood. Even Parson Twemlow would not go near it later than the afternoon milking of the cows, and Captain Zeb would much rather face a whole gale of wind in a twelve-foot boat than give one glance at its dead calm face when the moon like a ghost stood over it.

"She is going towards Corpse-walk pit," thought Scuddy—"a cheerful place at this time of night! She might even fall into it unawares, in her present state of distraction. I am absolutely bound to follow her."

Duty fell in with his wishes, as it has a knack of doing. Forgetting his weariness, he followed, and became more anxious at every step. For the maiden walked as in a dream, without regard of anything, herself more like a vision than a good substantial being. To escape Mrs. Stubbard she had gone upstairs and locked herself in her bedroom, and then slipped out without changing dress, but throwing a dark mantle over it. This had fallen off, and she had not cared to stop or think about it, but went on to her death exactly as she went in to dinner. Her dress of white silk took the moonlight with a soft gleam like itself, and her clustering curls (released from fashion by the power of passion) fell, like the shadows, on her sweet white neck. But she never even asked herself how she looked; she never turned round to admire her shadow: tomorrow she would throw no shade, but be one; and how she looked, or what she was, would matter, to the world she used to think so much of, never more.

Suddenly she passed from the moonlight into the blackness of a lonely thicket, and forced her way through it, without heed of bruise or rent. At the bottom of the steep lay the long dark pit, and she stood upon the brink and gazed into it. To a sane mind nothing could look less inviting. All above was air and light, freedom of the wind and play of moon with summer foliage; all below was gloom and horror, cold eternal stillness, and oblivion everlasting. Even the new white frock awoke no flutter upon that sullen breast.

Dolly heaved a sigh and shuddered, but she did not hesitate. Her mind was wandering, but her heart was fixed to make atonement, to give its life for the life destroyed, and to lie too deep for shame or sorrow. Suddenly a faint gleam caught her eyes. The sob of self-pity from her fair young breast had brought into view her cherished treasures, bright keepsakes of the girlish days when many a lover worshipped her. Taking from her neck the silken braid, she kissed them, and laid them on the bank. "They were all too good for me," she thought; "they shall not perish with me."

Then, with one long sigh, she called up all her fleeting courage, and sprang upon a fallen trunk which overhung the water. "There will be no Dan to save me now," she said as she reached the end of it. "Poor Dan! He will be sorry for me. This is the way out of it."

Her white satin shoes for a moment shone upon the black bark of the tree, and, with one despairing prayer to Heaven, she leaped into the liquid grave.

Dan was afar, but another was near, who loved her even more than Dan. Blyth Scudamore heard the plunge, and rushed to the brink of the pit, and tore his coat off. For a moment he saw nothing but black water heaving silently; then something white appeared, and moved, and a faint cry arose, and a hopeless struggle with engulfing death began.

"Keep still, don't struggle, only spread your arms, and throw your head back as far as you can," he cried, as he swam with long strokes towards her. But if she heard, she could not heed, as the lights of the deep sky came and went, and the choking water flashed between, and gurgled into her ears and mouth, and smothered her face with her own long hair. She dashed her poor helpless form about, and flung out her feet for something solid, and grasped in dim agony at the waves herself had made. Then her dress became heavily bagged with water, and the love of life was quenched, and the night of death enveloped her. Without a murmur, down she went, and the bubbles of her breath came up.

Scudamore uttered a bitter cry, for his heart was almost broken—within an arm's-length of his love, and she was gone for ever! For the moment he did not perceive that the clasp of despair must have drowned them both. Pointing his hands and throwing up his heels, he made one vain dive after her, then he knew that the pit was too deep for the bottom to be reached in that way. He swam to the trunk from which Dolly had leaped, and judging the distance by the sullen ripple, dashed in with a dive like a terrified frog. Like a bullet he sank to the bottom, and groped with three fathoms of water above him. Just as his lungs were giving out, he felt something soft and limp and round. Grasping this by the trailing hair, he struck mightily up for the surface, and drew a long breath, and sustained above water the head that fell back upon his panting breast.

Some three hours later, Dolly Darling lay in her own little bed, as pale as death, but sleeping the sleep of the world that sees the sun; while her only sister knelt by her side, weeping the tears of a higher world than that. "How could I be so brutal, and so hard?" sobbed Faith. "If father has seen it, will he ever forgive me? His last words were—'forgive, and love.'"

CHAPTER LXIII

THE FATAL STEP

As Carne rode up the hill that night towards his ruined castle, the flush of fierce excitement and triumphant struggle died away, and self-reproach and miserable doubt struck into him like ague. For the death of Twemlow—as he supposed—he felt no remorse whatever. Him he had shot in furious combat, and as a last necessity; the fellow had twice insulted him, and then insolently collared him. And Faith, who had thwarted him with Dolly, and been from the first his enemy, now would have to weep and wail, and waste her youth in constancy. All that was good; but he could not regard with equal satisfaction the death of the ancient Admiral. The old man had brought it upon himself by his stupid stubbornness; and looking fairly upon that matter, Carne scarcely saw how to blame himself. Still, it was a most unlucky thing, and must lead to a quantity of mischief. To-morrow, or at the latest Monday, was to have crowned with grand success his years of toil and danger. There still might be the landing, and he would sail that night to hasten it, instead of arranging all ashore; but it could no longer be a triumph of crafty management. The country was up, the Admiral's death would spread the alarm and treble it; and worst of all, in the hot pursuit of himself, which was sure to follow when people's wits came back to them, all the stores and ammunition, brought together by so much skill and patience and hardihood, must of necessity be discovered and fall into the hands of the enemy. Farewell to his long-cherished hope of specially neat retribution, to wit, that the ruins of his family should be the ruin of the land which had rejected him! Then a fierce thought crossed his mind, and became at once a stern resolve. If he could never restore Carne Castle, and dwell there in prosperity, neither should any of his oppressors. The only trace of his ancestral home should be a vast black hole in earth.

For even if the landing still succeeded, and the country were subdued, he could never make his home there, after what he had done to-night. Dolly was lost to him for ever; and although he had loved her with all the ardor he could spare from his higher purposes, he must make up his mind to do without her, and perhaps it was all the better for him. If he had married her, no doubt he could soon have taught her her proper place; but no one could tell how she might fly out, through her self-will and long indulgence. He would marry a French woman; that would be the best; perhaps one connected with the Empress Josephine. As soon as he had made up his mind to this, his conscience ceased to trouble him.

From the crest of the hill at the eastern gate many a bend of shore was clear, and many a league of summer sea lay wavering in the moonlight. Along the beach red torches flared, as men of the Coast-Defence pushed forth, and yellow flash of cannon inland signalled for the Volunteers, while the lights gleamed (like windows opened from the depth) where sloop and gun-boat, frigate and ship of the line, were crowding sail to rescue England. For the semaphore, and when day was out the beacon-lights, had glowed along the backbone of the English hills, and England called every Englishman to show what he was made of.

"That will do. Enough of that, John Bull!" Defying his native land, Carne shook his fist in the native manner. "Stupid old savage, I shall live to make you howl. This country has become too hot to hold me, and I'll make it hotter before I have done. Here, Orso and Leo, good dogs, good dogs! You can kill a hundred British bull-dogs. Mount guard for an hour, till I call you down the hill. You can pull down a score of Volunteers apiece, if they dare to come after me. I have an hour to spare, and I know how to employ it. Jerry, old Jerry Bowles, stir your crooked shanks. What are you rubbing your blear eyes at?"

The huge boar-hounds, who obeyed no voice but his, took post upon the rugged road (which had never been repaired since the Carnes were a power in the land), and sat side by side beneath the crumbling arch, with their long fangs glistening and red eyes rolling in the silver moonlight, while their deep chests panted for the chance of good fresh human victuals. Then Carne gave his horse to ancient Jerry, saying, "Feed him, and take him with his saddle on to the old yew-tree in half an hour. Wait there for Captain Charron, and for me. You are not to go away till I come to you. Who is in the old place now? Think well before you answer me."

"No one now in the place but her"—the old man lifted his elbow, as a coachman does in passing—"and him down in the yellow jug. All the French sailors are at sea. Only she won't go away; and she moaneth worse than all the owls and ghosts. Ah, your honour should never 'a done that—respectable folk to Springhaven too!"

"It was a slight error of judgment, Jerry. What a mealy lot these English are, to make such a fuss about a trifle! But I am too soft-hearted to blow her up. Tell her to meet me in half an hour by the broken dial, and to bring the brat, and all her affairs in a bundle such as she can carry, or kick down the hill before her. In half an hour, do you understand? And if you care for your stiff old bones, get out of the way by that time."

In that half-hour Carne gathered in small compass, and strapped up in a little "mail"—as such light baggage then was called—all his important documents, despatches, letters, and papers of every kind, and the cash he was entrusted with, which he used to think safer at Springhaven. Then he took from a desk which was fixed to the wall a locket bright with diamonds, and kissed it, and fastened it beneath his neck-cloth. The wisp of hair inside it came not from any young or lovely head, but from the resolute brow of his mother, the woman who hated England. He should have put something better to his mouth; for instance, a good beef sandwich. But one great token of his perversion was that he never did feed well—a sure proof of the unrighteous man, as suggested by the holy Psalmist, and more distinctly put by Livy in the character he gives Hannibal.

Regarding as a light thing his poor unfurnished stomach, Carne mounted the broken staircase, in a style which might else have been difficult. He had made up his mind to have one last look at the broad lands of his ancestors, from the last that ever should be seen of the walls they had reared and ruined. He stood upon the highest vantage-point that he could attain with safety, where a shaggy gnarl of the all-pervading ivy served as a friendly stay. To the right and left and far behind him all had once been their domain—every tree, and meadow, and rock that faced the moon, had belonged to his ancestors. "Is it a wonder that I am fierce?" he cried, with unwonted self-inspection; "who, that has been robbed as I have, would not try to rob in turn? The only thing amazing is my patience and my justice. But I will come back yet, and have my revenge."

Descending to his hyena den—as Charron always called it—he caught up his packet, and took a lantern, and a coil of tow which had been prepared, and strode forth for the last time into the sloping court behind the walls. Passing towards the eastern vaults, he saw the form of some one by the broken dial, above the hedge of brambles, which had once been of roses and sweetbriar. "Oh, that woman! I had forgotten that affair!" he muttered, with annoyance, as he pushed through the thorns to meet her.

Polly Cheeseman, the former belle of Springhaven, was leaning against the wrecked dial, with a child in her arms and a bundle at her feet. Her pride and gaiety had left her now, and she looked very wan through frequent weeping, and very thin from nursing. Her beauty (like her friends) had proved unfaithful under shame and sorrow, and little of it now remained except the long brown tresses and the large blue eyes. Those eyes she fixed upon Carne with more of terror than of love in them; although the fear was such as turns with a very little kindness to adoring love.

Carne left her to begin, for he really was not without shame in this matter;

and Polly was far better suited than Dolly for a scornful and arrogant will like his. Deeply despising all the female race—as the Greek tragedian calls them —save only the one who had given him to the world, he might have been a God to Polly if he had but behaved as a man to her. She looked at him now with an imploring gaze, from the gentleness of her ill-used heart.

Their child, a fine boy about ten months old, broke the silence by saying "booh, booh," very well, and holding out little hands to his father, who had often been scornfully kind to him.

"Oh, Caryl, Caryl, you will never forsake him!" cried the young mother, holding him up with rapture, and supporting his fat arms in that position; "he is the very image of you, and he seems to know it. Baby, say 'Da-da.' There, he has put his mouth up, and his memory is so wonderful! Oh, Caryl, what do you think of that—and the first time of trying it by moonlight?"

"There is no time for this nonsense, Polly. He is a wonderful baby, I dare say; and so is every baby, till he gets too old. You must obey orders, and be off with him."

"Oh no! You are come to take us with you. There, I have covered his face up, that he may not suppose you look cross at me. Oh, Caryl, you would never leave him behind, even if you could do that to me. We are not grand people, and you can put us anywhere, and now I am nearly as well as ever. I have put up all his little things; it does not matter about my own. I was never brought up to be idle, and I can earn my own living anywhere; and it might be a real comfort for you, with the great people going against you, to have somebody, not very grand, of course, but as true to you as yourself, and belonging altogether to you. I know many people who would give their eyes for such a baby."

"There is no time for this," Carne answered, sternly; "my arrangements are made, and I cannot take you. I have no fault to find with you, but argument is useless."

"Yes, I know that, Caryl; and I am sure that I never would attempt to argue with you. You should have everything your own way, and I could attend to so many things that no man ever does properly. I will be a slave to you, and this little darling love you, and then you will feel that you have two to love you, wherever you go, and whatever you do. And if I spoke crossly when first I found out that—that I went away for nothing with you, you must have forgiven me by this time, and I never will remind you again of it; if I do, send me back to the place I belong to. I belong to you now, Caryl, and so does he; and when we are away from the people who know me, I shall be pleasant and cheerful again. I was only two-and-twenty the day the boats came home last week, and they used to say the young men jumped into the water as soon as they caught sight of me. Try to be kind to me, and I shall be so happy that I shall look almost as I used to do, when you said that the great ladies might be grander, but none of them fit to look into my looking-glass. Dear Caryl, I am ready; I don't care where it is, or what I may have to put up with, so long as you will make room for your Polly, and your baby."

"I am not at all a hard man," said Carne, retreating as the impulsive Polly offered him the baby, "but once for all, no more of this. I have quite forgiven any strong expressions you may have made use of when your head was light; and if all goes well, I shall provide for you and the child, according to your rank in life. But now you must run down the hill, if you wish to save your life and his."

"I have run down the hill already. I care not a pin for my own life; and hard as you are you would never have the heart to destroy your own little Caryl. He may be called Caryl—you will not deny him that, although he has no right to be called Carne. Oh, Caryl, Caryl, you can be so good, when you think there is something to gain by it. Only be good to us now, and God will bless you for it, darling. I have given up all the world for you, and you cannot have the heart to cast me off."

"What a fool the woman is! Have you ever known me change my mind? If you scorn your own life, through your own folly, you must care for the brat's. If you stop here ten minutes, you will both be blown to pieces."

"Through my own folly! Oh, God in heaven, that you should speak so of my love for you! Squire Carne, you are the worst man that ever lived; and it serves me right for trusting you. But where am I to go? Who will take me and support me, and my poor abandoned child?"

"Your parents, of course, are your natural supporters. You are hurting your child by this low abuse of me. Now put aside excitement, and run home, like a sensible woman, before your good father goes to bed."

She had watched his face all the time, as if she could scarcely believe that he was in earnest, but he proved it by leaving her with a wave of his hat, and hastening back to his lantern. Then taking up that, and the coil of tow, but leaving his package against the wall, he disappeared in the narrow passage leading to the powder vaults. Polly stood still by the broken dial, with her eyes upon the moon, and her arms around the baby, and a pang in her heart which prevented her from speaking, or moving, or even knowing where she was.

Then Carne, stepping warily, unlocked the heavy oak door at the entrance of the cellarage, held down his lantern, and fixed with a wedge the top step of the ladder, which had been made to revolve with a pin and collar at either end, as before described. After trying the step with his hand, to be sure that it was now wedged safely, he flung his coil into the vault and followed. Some recollection made him smile as he was going down the steps: it was that of a stout man lying at the bottom, shaken in every bone, yet sound as a grape ensconced in jelly. As he touched the bottom he heard a little noise as of some small substance falling, but seeing a piece of old mortar dislodged, he did not turn round to examine the place. If he had done so he would have found behind the ladder the wedge he had just inserted to secure the level of the "Inspector's step."

Unwinding his coil of tow, which had been steeped in saltpetre to make a long fuse, with a toss of his long legs he crossed the barricade of solid oak rails about six feet high securely fastened across the vault, for the enclosure of the dangerous storage. Inside it was a passage, between chests of arms, dismounted cannon, and cases from every department of supply, to the explosive part of the magazine, the devourer of the human race, the pulp of the marrow of the Furies—gunpowder.

Of this there was now collected here, and stored in tiers that reached the roof, enough to blow up half the people of England, or lay them all low with a bullet before it; yet not enough, not a millionth part enough, to move for the breadth of a hair the barrier betwixt right and wrong, which a very few barrels are enough to do with a man who has sapped the foundations. Treading softly for fear of a spark from his boots, and guarding the lantern well, Carne approached one of the casks in the lower tier, and lifted the tarpaulin. Then he slipped the wooden slide in the groove, and allowed some five or six pounds to run out upon the floor, from which the cask was raised by timber baulks. Leaving the slide partly open, he spread one end of his coil like a broad lamp-wick in the pile of powder which had run out, and put a brick upon the tow to keep it from shifting. Then he paid out the rest of the coil on the floor like a snake some thirty feet long, with the tail about a yard inside the barricade. With a very steady hand he took the candle from inside the horn, and kindled that tail of the fuse; and then replacing his light, he recrossed the open timber-work, and swiftly remounted the ladder of escape. "Twenty minutes' or half an hour's grace," he thought, "and long before that I shall be at the yew-tree."

But, as he planted his right foot sharply upon the top step of the ladder, that step swung back, and cast him heavily backwards to the bottom. The wedge had dropped out, and the step revolved like the treadle of a fox-trap.

For a minute or two he lay stunned and senseless, with the lantern before him on its side, and the candle burning a hole in the bubbly horn. Slowly recovering his wits, he strove to rise, as the deadly peril was borne in upon him. But instead of rising, he fell back again with a curse, and then a long-drawn groan; for pain (like the thrills of a man on the rack) had got hold of him and meant to keep him. His right arm was snapped at the elbow, and his left leg just above the knee, and the jar of his spine made him feel as if his core had been split out of him. He had no fat, like Shargeloes, to protect him, and no sheath of hair like Twemlow's.

Writhing with anguish, he heard a sound which did not improve his condition. It was the spluttering of the fuse, eating its merry way towards the five hundred casks of gunpowder. In the fury of peril he contrived to rise, and stood on his right foot with the other hanging limp, while he stayed himself with his left hand upon the ladder. Even if he could crawl up this, it would benefit him nothing. Before he could drag himself ten yards, the explosion would overtake him. His only chance was to quench the fuse, or draw it away from the priming. With a hobble of agony he reached the barricade, and strove to lift his crippled frame over it. It was hopeless; the power of his back was gone, and his limbs were unable to obey his brain. Then he tried to crawl through at the bottom, but the opening of the rails would not admit his body, and the train of ductile fire had left only ash for him to grasp at.

Quivering with terror, and mad with pain, he returned to the foot of the steps, and clung till a gasp of breath came back. Then he shouted, with all his remaining power, "Polly, oh, Polly, my own Polly!"

Polly had been standing, like a statue of despair, beside the broken dial. To her it mattered little whether earth should open and swallow her, or fire cast her up to heaven. But his shout aroused her from this trance, and her heart leaped up with the fond belief that he had relented, and was calling her and the child to share his fortunes. There she stood in the archway and looked down, and the terror of the scene overwhelmed her. Through a broken arch beyond the barricade pale moonbeams crossed the darkness, like the bars of some soft melody; in the middle the serpent coil was hissing with the deadly nitre; at the foot of the steps was her false lover—husband he had called himself—with his hat off, and his white face turned in the last supplication towards her, as hers had been turned towards him just now. Should a woman be as pitiless as a man?

"Come down, for God's sake, and climb that cursed wood, and pull back the fuse, pull it back from the powder. Oh, Polly! and then we will go away together."

"It is too late. I will not risk my baby. You have made me so weak that I could never climb that fence. You are blowing up the castle which you promised to my baby; but you shall not blow up him. You told me to run away, and run I must. Good-bye; I am going to my natural supporters."

Carne heard her steps as she fled, and he fancied that he heard therewith a mocking laugh, but it was a sob, a hysterical sob. She would have helped him, if she dared; but her wits were gone in panic. She knew not of his shattered limbs and horrible plight; and it flashed across her that this was another trick of his—to destroy her and the baby, while he fled. She had proved that all his vows were lies.

Then Carne made his mind up to die like a man, for he saw that escape was impossible. Limping back to the fatal barrier, he raised himself to his full height, and stood proudly to see, as he put it, the last of himself. Not a quiver of his haughty features showed the bodily pain that racked him, nor a flinch of his deep eyes confessed the tumult moving in his mind and soul. He pulled out his watch and laid it on the top rail of the old oak fence: there was not enough light to read the time, but he could count the ticks he had to live. Suddenly hope flashed through his heart, like the crack of a gun, like a lightning fork—a big rat was biting an elbow of the yarn where some tallow had fallen upon it. Would he cut it, would he drag it away to his hole? would he pull it a little from its fatal end? He was strong enough to do it, if he only understood. The fizz of saltpetre disturbed the rat, and he hoisted his tail and skipped back to his home.

The last thoughts of this unhappy man went back upon his early days; and things, which he had passed without thinking of, stood before him like his tombstone. None of his recent crimes came now to his memory to disturb it— there was time enough after the body for them—but trifles which had first depraved the mind, and slips whose repetition had made slippery the soul, like the alphabet of death, grew plain to him. Then he thought of his mother, and crossed himself, and said a little prayer to the Virgin.

Charron was waiting by the old yew-tree, and Jerry sat trembling, with his eyes upon the castle, while the black horse, roped to a branch, was mourning the scarcity of oats and the abundance of gnats.

"Pest and the devil, but the coast is all alive!" cried the Frenchman, soothing anxiety with solid and liquid comforts. "Something has gone wrong behind the tail of everything. And there goes that big Stoobar, blazing with his sordid battery! Arouse thee, old Cheray! The time too late is over. Those lights thrice accursed will display our little boat, and John Bull is rushing with a thousand sails. The Commander is mad. They will have him, and us too. Shall I dance by a rope? It is the only dancing probable for me in England."

"I have never expected any good to come," the old man answered, without moving. "The curse of the house is upon the young Squire. I saw it in his eyes this morning, the same as I saw in his father's eyes, when the sun was going down the very night he died. I shall never see him more, sir, nor you either, nor any other man that bides to the right side of his coffin."

"Bah! what a set you are of funerals, you Englishmen! But if I thought he was in risk, I would stay to see the end of it."

"Here comes the end of it!" the old man cried, leaping up and catching at a rugged cord of trunk, with his other hand pointing up the hill. From the base of the castle a broad blaze rushed, showing window and battlement, arch and tower, as in a flicker of the Northern lights. Then up went all the length of fabric, as a wanton child tosses his Noah's ark. Keep and buttress, tower and arch, mullioned window and battlement, in a fiery furnace leaped on high, like the outburst of a volcano. Then, with a roar that rocked the earth, they broke into a storm of ruin, sweeping the heavens with a flood of fire, and spreading the sea with a mantle of blood. Following slowly in stately spires, and calmly swallowing everything, a fountain of dun smoke arose, and solemn silence filled the night.

"All over now, thank the angels and the saints! My faith, but I made up my mind to join them," cried Charron, who had fallen, or been felled by the concussion. "Cheray, art thou still alive? The smoke is in my neck. I cannot liberate my words, but the lumps must be all come down by this time, without adding to the weight of our poor brains. Something fell in this old tree, a long way up, as high as where the crows build. It was like a long body, with one leg and one arm. I hope it was not the Commander; but one thing is certain— he is gone to heaven. Let us pray that he may stop there, if St. Peter admits a man who was selling the keys of his country to the enemy. But we must do duty to ourselves, my Cheray. Let us hasten to the sea, and give the signal for the boat. La Torche will be a weak light after this."

"I will not go. I will abide my time." The old man staggered to a broken column of the ancient gateway which had fallen near them, and flung his arms around it. "I remember this since I first could toddle. The ways of the Lord are wonderful."

"Come away, you old fool," cried the Frenchman; "I hear the tramp of soldiers in the valley. If they catch you here, it will be drum-head work, and you will swing before morning in the ruins."

"I am very old. My time is short. I would liefer hang from an English beam than deal any more with your outlandish lot."

"Farewell to thee, then! Thou art a faithful clod. Here are five guineas for thee, of English stamp. I doubt if napoleons shall ever be coined in England."

He was off while he might—a gallant Frenchman, and an honest enemy;

such as our country has respected always, and often endeavoured to turn into fast friends. But the old man stood and watched the long gap, where for centuries the castle of the Carnes had towered. And his sturdy faith was rewarded.

"I am starving"—these words came feebly from a gaunt, ragged figure that approached him. "For three days my food has been forgotten; and bad as it was, I missed it. There came a great rumble, and my walls fell down. Ancient Jerry, I can go no further. I am empty as a shank bone when the marrow-toast is serving. Your duty was to feed me, with inferior stuff at any rate."

"No, sir, no;" the old servitor was roused by the charge of neglected duty. "Sir Parsley, it was no fault of mine whatever. Squire undertook to see to all of it himself. Don't blame me, sir; don't blame me."

"Never mind the blame, but make it good," Mr. Shargeloes answered, meagrely, for he felt as if he could never be fat again. "What do I see there? It is like a crust of bread, but I am too weak to stoop for it."

"Come inside the tree, sir." The old man led him, as a grandsire leads a famished child. "What a shame to starve you, and you so hearty! But the Squire clean forgotten it, I doubt, with his foreign tricks coming to this great blow-up. Here, sir, here; please to sit down a moment, while I light a candle. They French chaps are so wasteful always, and always grumbling at good English victual. Here's enough to feed a family Captain Charron has throwed by—bread, and good mutton, and pretty near half a ham, and a bottle or so of thin nasty foreign wine. Eat away, Sir Parsley; why, it does me good to see you. You feeds something like an Englishman. But you know, sir, it were all your own fault at bottom, for coming among them foreigners a-meddling."

"You are a fine fellow. You shall be my head butler," Percival Shargeloes replied, while he made such a meal as he never made before, and never should make again, even when he came to be the Right Honourable the Lord Mayor of London.

CHAPTER LXIV

WRATH AND SORROW

The two most conspicuous men of the age were saddened and cast down just now—one by the natural kindly sorrow into which all men live for others, till others live into it for them; and one by the petulant turns of fortune, twisting and breaking his best-woven web. Lord Nelson arrived at Springhaven on Monday, to show his affection for his dear old friend; and the Emperor Napoleon, at the same time, was pacing the opposite cliffs in grief and dudgeon.

He had taken his post on some high white land, about a league southward of Boulogne, and with strong field-glasses, which he pettishly exchanged in doubt of their power and truth, he was scanning all the roadways of the shore and the trackless breadths of sea. His quick brain was burning for despatches overland—whether from the coast road past Etaples, or further inland by the great route from Paris, or away to the southeast by special courier from the Austrian frontier—as well as for signals out at sea, and the movements of the British ships, to show that his own were coming. He had treated with disdain the suggestions of his faithful Admiral Decres, who had feared to put the truth too plainly, that the fleet ordered up from the west had failed, and with it the Master's mighty scheme. Having yet to learn the lesson that his best plans might be foiled, he was furious when doubt was cast upon this pet design. Like a giant of a spider at the nucleus of his web, he watched the broad fan of radiant threads, and the hovering of filmy woof, but without the mild philosophy of that spider, who is versed in the very sad capriciousness of flies.

Just within hearing (and fain to be further, in his present state of mind) were several young officers of the staff, making little mouths at one another, for want of better pastime, but looking as grave, when the mighty man glanced round, as schoolboys do under the master's eye. "Send Admiral Decres to me," the Emperor shouted, as he laid down his telescope and returned to his petulant to-and-fro.

In a few minutes Admiral Decres arrived, and after a salute which was not acknowledged, walked in silence at his master's side. The great man, talking to himself aloud, and reviling almost every one except himself, took no more notice of his comrade for some minutes than if he had been a poodle keeping pace with him. Then he turned upon him fiercely, with one hand thrown out, as if he would have liked to strike him.

"What then is the meaning of all this?" He spoke too fast for the other to catch all his words. "You have lost me three days of it. How much longer will you conceal your knowledge? Carne's scheme has failed, through treachery— probably his own. I never liked the man. He wanted to be the master of me— of me! I can do without him; it is all the better, if my fleet will come. I have three fleets, besides these. Any one of them would do. They would do, if even half their crews were dead, so long as they disturbed the enemy. You know where Villeneuve is, but you will not tell me."

"I told your Majesty what I thought," M. Decres replied, with dignity, "but it did not please you to listen to me. Shall I now tell your Majesty what I know?"

"Ha! You have dared to have secret despatches! You know more of the movements of my fleets than I do! You have been screening him all along. Which of you is the worse traitor?"

"Your Majesty will regret these words. Villeneuve and myself are devoted to you. I have not heard from him. I have received no despatches. But in a private letter just received, which is here at your Majesty's service, I find these words, which your Majesty can see. 'From my brother on the Spanish coast I have just heard. Admiral Villeneuve has sailed for Cadiz, believing Nelson to be in chase of him. My brother saw the whole fleet crowding sail southward. No doubt it is the best thing they could do. If they came across Nelson, they would be knocked to pieces.' Your Majesty, that is an opinion only; but it seems to be shared by M. Villeneuve."

Napoleon's wrath was never speechless—except upon one great occasion —and its outburst put every other in the wrong, even while he knew that he was in the right. Regarding Decres with a glare of fury, such as no other eyes could pour, or meet—a glare as of burnished steel fired from a cannon—he drove him out of every self-defence or shelter, and shattered him in the dust of his own principles. It was not the difference of rank between them, but the difference in the power of their minds, that chased like a straw before the wind the very stable senses of the man who understood things. He knew that he was right, but the right was routed, and away with it flew all capacity of reason in the pitiless torrent of passion, like a man in a barrel, and the barrel in Niagara.

M. Decres knew not head from tail, in the rush of invective poured upon him; but he took off his hat in soft search for his head, and to let in the compliments rained upon it.

"It is good," replied the Emperor, replying to himself, as the foam of his fury began to pass; "you will understand, Decres, that I am not angry, but only lament that I have such a set of fools. You are not the worst. I have bigger fools than you. Alas that I should confess it!"

Admiral Decres put his hat upon his head, for the purpose of taking it off, to acknowledge the kindness of this compliment. It was the first polite expression he had received for half an hour. And it would have been the last, if he had dared to answer.

"Villeneuve cannot help it that he is a fool," continued Napoleon, in a milder strain; "but he owes it to his rank that he should not be a coward. Nelson is his black beast. Nelson has reduced him to a condition of wet pulp. I shall send a braver man to supersede him. Are French fleets forever to turn tail to an inferior force of stupid English? If I were on the seas, I would sweep Nelson from them. Our men are far braver, when they learn to spread their legs. As soon as I have finished with those filthy Germans, I will take the command of the fleets myself. It will be a bad day for that bragging Nelson. Give me pen and paper, and send Daru to me. I must conquer the Continent once more, I suppose; and then I will return and deal with England."

In a couple of hours he had shaped and finished the plan of a campaign the most triumphant that even he ever planned and accomplished. Then his mind became satisfied with good work, and he mounted his horse, and for the last time rode through the grandest encampment the sun has ever seen, distributing his calm smile, as if his nature were too large for tempests.

On the sacred white coast, which the greatest of Frenchmen should only approach as a prisoner, stood a man of less imperious mould, and of sweet and gentle presence—a man who was able to command himself in the keenest disappointment, because he combined a quick sense of humour with the power of prompt action, and was able to appreciate his own great qualities without concluding that there were no other. His face, at all times except those of hot battle, was filled with quiet sadness, as if he were sent into the world for some great purpose beyond his knowledge, yet surely not above his aim. Years of deep anxiety and ever urgent duty had made him look old before his time, but in no wise abated his natural force. He knew that he had duty before him still, and he felt that the only discharge was death.

But now, in the tenderness of his heart, he had forgotten all about himself, and even for the moment about his country. Nelson had taken the last fond look at the dear old friend of many changeful years, so true and so pleasant throughout every change. Though one eye had failed for the work of the brain, it still was in sympathy with his heart; and a tear shone upon either wrinkled cheek, as the uses of sadness outlast the brighter view. He held Faith by the hand, or she held by his, as they came forth, without knowing it, through nature's demand for an open space, when the air is choked with sorrow.

"My dear, you must check it; you must leave off," said Nelson, although he was going on himself. "It is useless for me to say a word to you, because I am almost as bad myself. But still I am older, and I feel that I ought to be able to comfort you, if I only knew the way."

"You do comfort me, more than I can tell, although you don't say anything. For any one to sit here, and be sorry with me, makes it come a little lighter. And when it is a man like you, Lord Nelson, I feel a sort of love that makes me feel less bitter. Mr. Twemlow drove me wild with a quantity of texts, and a great amount of talk about a better land. How would he like to go to it himself, I wonder? There is a great hole in my heart, and nothing that anybody says can fill it."

"And nothing that any one can do, my dear," her father's friend answered, softly, "unless it is your own good self, with the kindness of the Lord to help you. One of the best things to begin with is to help somebody else, if you can, and lead yourself away into another person's troubles. Is there any one here very miserable?"

"None that I can think of half so miserable as I am. There is great excitement, but no misery. Miss Twemlow has recovered her Lord Mayor— the gentleman that wore that extraordinary coat—oh, I forgot, you were not here then. And although he has had a very sad time of it, every one says that the total want of diet will be much better for him than any mere change. I am ashamed to be talking of such trifles now; but I respect that man, he was so straightforward. If my brother Frank had been at all like him, we should never have been as we are this day."

"My dear, you must not blame poor Frank. He would not come down to the dinner because he hated warlike speeches. But he has seen the error of his ways. No more treasonable stuff for him. He thought it was large, and poetic, and all that, like giving one's shirt to an impostor. All of us make mistakes sometimes. I have made a great many myself, and have always been the foremost to perceive them. But your own brave lover—have you forgotten him? He fought like a hero, I am told; and nothing could save his life except that he wore a new-fashioned periwig."

"I would rather not talk of him now, Lord Nelson, although he had no periwig. I am deeply thankful that he escaped; and no doubt did his best, as he was bound to do. I try to be fair to everybody, but I cannot help blaming every one, when I come to remember how blind we have been. Captain Stubbard must have been so blind, and Mrs. Stubbard a great deal worse, and worst of all his own aunt, Mrs. Twemlow. Oh, Lord Nelson, if you had only stopped here, instead of hurrying away for more glory! You saw the whole of it; you predicted everything; you even warned us again in your last letter! And yet you must go away, and leave us to ourselves; and this is how the whole of it has ended."

"My dear child, I will not deny that the eye of Nelson has a special gift for piercing the wiles of the scoundrelly foe. But I was under orders, and must go. The nation believed that it could not do without me, although there are other men every bit as good, and in their own opinion superior. But the enemy has never been of that opinion; and a great deal depends upon what they think. And the rule has been always to send me where there are many kicks but few coppers. I have never been known to repine. We all err; but if we do our duty as your dear father did his, the Lord will forgive us, when our enemies escape. When my time comes, as it must do soon, there will be plenty to carp at me; but I shall not care, if I have done my best. Your father did his best, and is happy."

Faith Darling took his hand again, and her tears were for him quite as much as for herself. "Give me one of the buttons of your coat," she said; "here is one that cannot last till you get home."

It was hanging by a thread, and yet the hero was very loth to part with it, though if it had parted with him, the chances were ten to one against his missing it. However, he conquered himself, but not so entirely as to let her cut it off. If it must go, it should be by his own hand. He pulled out a knife and cut it off, and she kissed it when he gave it to her.

"I should like to do more than that," he said, though he would sooner have parted with many guineas. "Is there nobody here that I can help, from my long good-will to Springhaven?"

"Oh, yes! How stupid I am!" cried Faith. "I forget everybody in my own trouble. There is a poor young man with a broken heart, who came to me this morning. He has done no harm that I know of, but he fell into the power of that wicked—but I will use no harsh words, because he is gone most dreadfully to his last account. This poor youth said that he only cared to die, after all the things that had happened here, for he has always been fond of my father. At first I refused to see him, but they told me such things that I could not help it. He is the son of our chief man here, and you said what a fine British seaman he would make."

"I remember two or three of that description, especially young Dan Tugwell." Nelson had an amazing memory of all who had served under him, or even had wished to do so. "I see by your eyes that it is young Tugwell. If it will be any pleasure to you, I will see him, and do what I can for him. What has he done, my dear, and what can I do for him?"

"He has fallen into black disgrace, and his only desire is to redeem it by dying for his country. His own father has refused to see him, although he was mainly the cause of it; and his mother, who was Erle Twemlow's nurse, is almost out of her mind with grief. A braver young man never lived, and he was once the pride of Springhaven. He saved poor Dolly from drowning, when she was very young, and the boat upset. His father chastised him cruelly for falling under bad influence. Then he ran away from the village, and seems to have been in French employment. But he was kept in the dark, and had no idea that he was acting against his own country."

"He has been a traitor," said Lord Nelson, sternly. "I cannot help such a man, even for your sake."

"He has not been a traitor, but betrayed," cried Faith; "he believed that his only employment was to convey private letters for the poor French prisoners, of whom we have so many hundreds. I will not contend that he was right in that; but still it was no very great offence. Even you must have often longed to send letters to those you loved in England; and you know how hard it is in war time. But what they really wanted him for was to serve as their pilot upon this coast. And the moment he discovered that, though they offered him bags of gold to do it, he faced his death like an Englishman. They attempted to keep him in a stupid state with drugs, so that he might work like a mere machine. But he found out that, and would eat nothing but hard biscuit. They had him in one of their shallow boats, or prames, as they call them, which was to lead them in upon signal from the arch-traitor. This was on Saturday, Saturday night—that dreadful time when we were all so gay. They held a pair of pistols at poor Dan's head, or at least a man was holding one to each of his ears, and they corded his arms, because he ventured to remonstrate. That was before they had even started, so you may suppose what they would have done to us. Poor Daniel made up his mind to die, and it would have eased his mind, he says now, if he had done so. But while they were waiting for the signal, which through dear father's vigilance they never did receive, Dan managed to free both his hands in the dark, and as soon as he saw the men getting sleepy, he knocked them both down, and jumped overboard; for he can swim like a fish, or even better. He had very little hopes of escaping, as he says, and the French fired fifty shots after him. With great presence of mind, he gave a dreadful scream, as if he was shot through the head at least, then he flung up his legs, as if he was gone down; but he swam under water for perhaps a hundred yards, and luckily the moon went behind a black cloud. Then he came to a boat, which had broken adrift, and although he did not dare to climb into her, he held on by her, on the further side from them. She was drifting away with the tide, and at last he ventured to get on board of her, and found a pair of oars, and was picked up at daylight by a smuggling boat running for Newhaven. He was landed last night, and he heard the dreadful news, and having plenty of money, he hired a post-chaise, and never stopped until he reached Springhaven. He looks worn out now; but if his mind was easier, he would soon be as strong as ever."

"It is a strange story, my dear," said Nelson; "but I see that it has done you good to tell it, and I have known many still stranger. But how could he have money, after such a hard escape?"

"That shows as much as anything how brave he is. He had made up his mind that if he succeeded in knocking down both those sentinels, he would have the bag of gold which was put for his reward in case of his steering them successfully. And before he jumped overboard he snatched it up, and it helped him to dive and to swim under water. He put it in his flannel shirt by way of ballast, and he sticks to it up to the present moment."

"My dear," replied Lord Nelson, much impressed, "such a man deserves to be in my own crew. If he can show me that bag, and stand questions, I will send him to Portsmouth at my own expense, with a letter to my dear friend Captain Hardy."

CHAPTER LXV

TRAFALGAR

Lord Nelson sailed from Portsmouth on the 15th of September, in his favourite ship the Victory, to take his last command. He knew that he never should come home, except as a corpse for burial, but he fastened his mind on the work before him, and neglected nothing. "A fair fight, and no favour," was the only thing he longed for.

And this he did obtain at last. The French commander-in-chief came forth, with all his mighty armament, not of his own desire, but goaded by imperious sneers, and stings that made his manhood tingle. He spread the sea-power of two nations in a stately crescent, double-lined (as the moon is doubled when beheld through fine plate-glass)—a noble sight, a paramount temptation for the British tow-rope.

"What a lot for we to take to Spithead!" was the British tar's remark, as forty ships of the line and frigates showed their glossy sides, and canvas bosomed with the gentle air and veined with gliding sunlight. A grander spectacle never was of laborious man's creation; and the work of the Lord combined to show it to the best advantage—dark headlands in the distance standing as a massive background, long pellucid billows lifting bulk Titanic, and lace-like maze, sweet air wandering from heaven, early sun come fresh from dew, all the good-will of the world inspiring men to merriness.

Nelson was not fierce of nature, but as gentle as a lamb. His great desire, as he always proved, was never to destroy his enemies by the number of one man spareable. He had always been led by the force of education, confirmed by that of experience, to know that the duty of an Englishman is to lessen the stock of Frenchmen; yet he never was free from regret when compelled to act up to his conscience, upon a large scale.

It is an old saying that nature has provided for every disease its remedy, and challenges men to find it out, which they are clever enough not to do. For that deadly disease Napoleon, the remedy was Nelson; and as soon as he should be consumed, another would appear in Wellington. Such is the fortune of Britannia, because she never boasts, but grumbles always. The boaster soon exhausts his subject; the grumbler has matter that lasts for ever.

Nelson had much of this national virtue. "Half of them will get away," he said to Captain Blackwood, of the Euryalus, who was come for his latest orders, "because of that rascally port to leeward. If the wind had held as it was last night, we should have had every one of them. It does seem hard, after waiting so long. And the sky looks like a gale of wind. It will blow to-night, though I shall not hear it. A gale of wind with disabled ships means terrible destruction. Do all you can to save those poor fellows. When they are beaten, we must consider their lives even more than our own, you know, because we have been the cause of it. You know my wishes as well as I do. Remember this one especially."

"Good-bye, my lord, till the fight is over." Captain Blackwood loved his chief with even more than the warm affection felt by all the fleet for him. "When we have got them, I shall come back, and find you safe and glorious."

"God bless you, Blackwood!" Lord Nelson answered, looking at him with a cheerful smile. "But you will never see me alive again."

The hero of a hundred fights, who knew that this would be his last, put on his favourite ancient coat, threadbare through many a conflict with hard time and harder enemies. Its beauty, like his own, had suffered in the cause of duty; the gold embroidery had taken leave of absence in some places, and in others showed more fray of silk than gleam of yellow glory; and the four stars fastened on the left breast wanted a little plate-powder sadly. But Nelson was quite contented with them, and like a child—for he always kept in his heart the childhood's freshness—he gazed at the star he was proudest of, the Star of the Bath, and through a fond smile sighed. Through the rays of that star his death was coming, ere a quarter of a day should be added to his life.

With less pretension and air of greatness than the captain of a penny steamer now displays, Nelson went from deck to deck, and visited every man at quarters, as if the battle hung on every one. There was scarcely a man whom he did not know, as well as a farmer knows his winter hands; and loud cheers rang from gun to gun when his order had been answered. His order was, "Reserve your fire until you are sure of every shot." Then he took his stand upon the quarter-deck, assured of victory, and assured that his last bequest to the British nation would be honoured sacredly—about which the less we say the better.

In this great battle, which crushed the naval power of France, and saved our land from further threat of inroad, Blyth Scudamore was not engaged, being still attached to the Channel fleet; but young Dan Tugwell bore a share, and no small share by his own account and that of his native village, which received him proudly when he came home. Placed at a gun on the upper deck, on the starboard side near the mizzen-mast, he fought like a Briton, though dazed at first by the roar, and the smoke, and the crash of timber. Lord Nelson had noticed him more than once, as one of the smartest of his crew, and had said to him that very morning, "For the honour of Springhaven, Dan, behave well in your first action." And the youth had never forgotten that, when the sulphurous fog enveloped him, and the rush of death lifted his curly hair, and his feet were sodden and his stockings hot with the blood of shattered messmates.

In the wildest of the wild pell-mell, as the Victory lay like a pelted log, rolling to the storm of shot, with three ships at close quarters hurling all their metal at her, and a fourth alongside clutched so close that muzzle was tompion for muzzle, while the cannon-balls so thickly flew that many sailors with good eyes saw them meet in the air and shatter one another, an order was issued for the starboard guns on the upper deck to cease firing. An eager-minded Frenchman, adapting his desires as a spring-board to his conclusions, was actually able to believe that Nelson's own ship had surrendered! He must have been off his head; and his inductive process was soon amended by the logic of facts, for his head was off him. The reason for silencing those guns was good—they were likely to do more damage to an English ship which lay beyond than to the foe at the portholes. The men who had served those guns were ordered below, to take the place of men who never should fire a gun again. Dan Tugwell, as he turned to obey the order, cast a glance at the Admiral, who gave him a little nod, meaning, "Well done, Dan."

Lord Nelson had just made a little joke, such as he often indulged in, not from any carelessness about the scene around him—which was truly awful—but simply to keep up his spirits, and those of his brave and beloved companion. Captain Hardy, a tall and portly man, clad in bright uniform, and advancing with a martial stride, cast into shade the mighty hero quietly walking at his left side. And Nelson was covered with dust from the quarter-gallery of a pounded ship, which he had not stopped to brush away.

"Thank God," thought Dan, "if those fellows in the tops, who are picking us off so, shoot at either of them, they will be sure to hit the big man first."

In the very instant of his thought, he saw Lord Nelson give a sudden start, and then reel, and fall upon both knees, striving for a moment to support himself with his one hand on the deck. Then his hand gave way, and he fell on his left side, while Hardy, who was just before him, turned at the cabin ladderway, and stooped with a loud cry over him. Dan ran up, and placed his bare arms under the wounded shoulder, and helped to raise and set him on his staggering legs.

"I hope you are not much hurt, my lord?" said the Captain, doing his best to smile.

"They have done for me at last," the hero gasped. "Hardy, my backbone is shot through."

Through the roar of battle, sobs of dear love sounded along the blood-stained deck, as Dan and another seaman took the pride of our nation tenderly, and carried him down to the orlop-deck. Yet even so, in the deadly pang and draining of the life-blood, the sense of duty never failed, and the love of country conquered death. With his feeble hand he contrived to reach the handkerchief in his pocket, and spread it over his face and breast, lest the crew should be disheartened.

"I know who fired that shot," cried Dan, when he saw that he could help no more. "He never shall live to boast of it, if I have to board the French ship to fetch him."

He ran back quickly to the quarterdeck, and there found three or four others eager to give their lives for Nelson's death. The mizzen-top of the Redoutable, whence the fatal shot had come, was scarcely so much as fifty feet from the starboard rail of the Victory. The men who were stationed in that top, although they had no brass cohorn there, such as those in the main and fore tops plied, had taken many English lives, while the thick smoke surged around them.

For some time they had worked unheeded in the louder roar of cannon, and when at last they were observed, it was hard to get a fair shot at them, not only from the rolling of the entangled ships, and clouds of blinding vapour, but because they retired out of sight to load, and only came forward to catch their aim. However, by the exertions of our marines—who should have been at them long ago—these sharp-shooters from the coign of vantage were now reduced to three brave fellows. They had only done their duty, and perhaps had no idea how completely they had done it; but naturally enough our men looked at them as if they were "too bad for hanging." Smoky as the air was, the three men saw that a very strong feeling was aroused against them, and that none of their own side was at hand to back them up. And the language of the English—though they could not understand it—was clearly that of bitter condemnation.

The least resolute of them became depressed by this, being doubtless a Radical who had been taught that Vox populi is Vox Dei. He endeavoured, therefore, to slide down the rigging, but was shot through the heart, and dead before he had time to know it. At the very same moment the most desperate villain of the three—as we should call him—or the most heroic of these patriots (as the French historians describe him) popped forward and shot a worthy Englishman, who was shaking his fist instead of pointing his gun.

Then an old quartermaster, who was standing on the poop, with his legs spread out as comfortably as if he had his Sunday dinner on the spit before him, shouted—"That's him, boys—that glazed hat beggar! Have at him all together, next time he comes forrard." As he spoke, he fell dead, with his teeth in his throat, from the fire of the other Frenchman. But the carbine dropped from the man who had fired, and his body fell dead as the one he had destroyed, for a sharp little Middy, behind the quartermaster, sent a bullet through the head, as the hand drew trigger. The slayer of Nelson remained alone, and he kept back warily, where none could see him.

"All of you fire, quick one after other," cried Dan, who had picked up a loaded musket, and was kneeling in the embrasure of a gun; "fire so that he may tell the shots; that will fetch him out again. Sing out first, 'There he is!' as if you saw him."

The men on the quarter-deck and poop did so, and the Frenchman, who was watching through a hole, came forward for a safe shot while they were loading. He pointed the long gun which had killed Nelson at the smart young officer on the poop, but the muzzle flew up ere he pulled the trigger, and leaning forward he fell dead, with his legs and arms spread, like a jack for oiling axles. Dan had gone through some small-arm drill in the fortnight he spent at Portsmouth, and his eyes were too keen for the bull's-eye. With a rest for his muzzle he laid it truly for the spot where the Frenchman would reappear; with extreme punctuality he shot him in the throat; and the gallant man who deprived the world of Nelson was thus despatched to a better one, three hours in front of his victim.

CHAPTER LXVI

THE LAST BULLETIN

To Britannia this was but feeble comfort, even if she heard of it. She had lost her pet hero, the simplest and dearest of all the thousands she has borne and nursed, and for every penny she had grudged him in the flesh, she would lay a thousand pounds upon his bones. To put it more poetically, her smiles were turned to tears—which cost her something—and the laurel drooped in the cypress shade. The hostile fleet was destroyed; brave France would never more come out of harbour to contend with England; the foggy fear of invasion was like a morning fog dispersed; and yet the funds (the pulse of England) fell at the loss of that one defender.

It was a gloomy evening, and come time for good people to be in-doors, when the big news reached Springhaven. Since the Admiral slept in the green churchyard, with no despatch to receive or send, the importance of Springhaven had declined in all opinion except its own, and even Captain Stubbard could not keep it up. When the Squire was shot, and Master Erle as well, and Carne Castle went higher than a lark could soar, and folk were fools enough to believe that Boney would dare put his foot down there, John Prater had done a most wonderful trade, and never a man who could lay his tongue justly with the pens that came spluttering from London had any call for a fortnight together to go to bed sober at his own expense. But this bright season ended quite as suddenly as it had begun; and when these great "hungers"—as those veterans were entitled who dealt most freely with the marvellous—had laid their heads together to produce and confirm another guinea's worth of fiction, the London press would have none of it. Public interest had rushed into another channel; and the men who had thriven for a fortnight on their tongues were driven to employ them on their hands again.

But now, on the sixth of November, a new excitement was in store for them. The calm obscurity of night flowed in, through the trees that belonged to Sir Francis now, and along his misty meadows; and the only sound in the village lane was the murmur of the brook beside it, or the gentle sigh of the retiring seas. Boys of age enough to make much noise, or at least to prolong it after nightfall, were away in the fishing-boats, receiving whacks almost as often as they needed them; for those times (unlike these) were equal to their fundamental duties. In the winding lane outside the grounds of the Hall, and shaping its convenience naturally by that of the more urgent brook, a man—to show what the times were come to—had lately set up a shoeing forge. He had done it on the strength of the troopers' horses coming down the hill so fast, and often with their cogs worn out, yet going as hard as if they had no knees, or at least none belonging to their riders. And although he was not a Springhaven man, he had been allowed to marry a Springhaven woman, one of the Capers up the hill; and John Prater (who was akin to him by marriage, and perhaps had an eye to the inevitable ailment of a man whose horse is ailing) backed up his daring scheme so strongly that the Admiral, anxious for the public good, had allowed this smithy to be set up here.

John Keatch was the man who established this, of the very same family (still thriving in West Middlesex) which for the service of the state supplied an official whose mantle it is now found hard to fill; and the blacksmith was known as "Jack Ketch" in the village, while his forge was becoming the centre of news. Captain Stubbard employed him for battery uses, and finding his swing-shutters larger than those of Widow Shanks, and more cheaply lit up by the glow of the forge, was now beginning, in spite of her remonstrance, to post all his very big proclamations there.

"Rouse up your fire, Ketch," he said that evening, as he stood at the door of the smithy, with half a dozen of his children at his heels. "Bring a dozen clout-nails; here's a tremendous piece of news!"

The blacksmith made a blaze with a few strokes of his bellows, and swung his shutter forward, so that all might read.

"GREAT AND GLORIOUS VICTORY. Twenty line-of-battle ships destroyed or captured. Lord Nelson shot dead. God save the King!"

"Keep your fire up. I'll pay a shilling for the coal," cried the Captain, in the flush of excitement. "Bring out your cow's horn, and go and blow it at the corner. And that drum you had to mend, my boy and girl will beat it. Jack, run up to the battery, and tell them to blaze away for their very lives."

In less than five minutes all the village was there, with the readers put foremost, all reading together at the top of their voices, for the benefit of the rest. Behind them stood Polly Cheeseman, peeping, with the glare of the fire on her sad pale face and the ruddy cheeks of her infant. "Make way for Widow Carne, and the young Squire Carne," the loud voice of Captain Zeb commanded; "any man as stands afront of her will have me upon him. Now, ma'am, stand forth, and let them look at you."

This was a sudden thought of Captain Tugwell's; but it fixed her rank among them, as the order of the King might. The strong sense of justice, always ready in Springhaven, backed up her right to be what she had believed herself, and would have been, but for foul deceit and falsehood. And if the proud spirit of Carne ever wandered around the ancestral property, it would have received in the next generation a righteous shock at descrying in large letters, well picked out with shade: "Caryl Carne, Grocer and Butterman, Cheese-monger, Dealer in Bacon and Sausages. Licensed to sell Tea, Coffee, Snuff, Pepper, and Tobacco."

For Cheeseman raised his head again, with the spirit of a true British tradesman, as soon as the nightmare of traitorous plots and contraband imports was over. Captain Tugwell on his behalf led the fishing fleet against that renegade La Liberte, and casting the foreigners overboard, they restored her integrity as the London Trader. Mr. Cheeseman shed a tear, and put on a new apron, and entirely reformed his political views, which had been loose and Whiggish. Uprightness of the most sensitive order—that which has slipped and strained its tendons—stamped all his dealings, even in the butter line; and facts having furnished a creditable motive for his rash reliance upon his own cord, he turned amid applause to the pleasant pastimes of a smug church-warden. And when he was wafted to a still sublimer sphere, his grandson carried on the business well.

Having spread the great news in this striking manner, Captain Stubbard—though growing very bulky now with good living, ever since his pay was doubled—set off at a conscientious pace against the stomach of the hill, lest haply the Hall should feel aggrieved at hearing all this noise and having to wonder what the reason was. He knew, and was grateful at knowing, that Carne's black crime and devilish plot had wrought an entire revulsion in the candid but naturally too soft mind of the author of the Harmodiad. Sir Francis was still of a liberal mind, and still admired his own works. But forgetting that nobody read them, he feared the extensive harm they might produce, although he was now resolved to write even better in the opposite direction. On the impulse of literary conscience, he held a council with the gardener Swipes, as to the best composition of bonfire for the consumption of poetry. Mr. Swipes recommended dead pea-haulm, with the sticks left in it to ensure a draught. Then the poet in the garden with a long bean-stick administered fire to the whole edition, not only of the Harmodiad, but also of the Theiodemos, his later and even grander work. Persons incapable of lofty thought attributed this—the most sage and practical of all forms of palinode—to no higher source than the pretty face and figure, and sweet patriotism, of Lady Alice, the youngest sister of Lord Dashville. And subsequent facts, to some extent, confirmed this interpretation.

The old house looked gloomy and dull of brow, with only three windows showing light, as stout Captain Stubbard, with his short sword swinging from the bulky position where his waist had been, strode along the winding of the hill towards the door. At a sharp corner, under some trees, he came almost shoulder to shoulder with a tall man striking into the road from a foot-path. The Captain drew his sword, for his nerves had been flurried ever since the great explosion, which laid him on his back among his own cannon.

"A friend," cried the other, "and a great admirer of your valour, Captain, but not a worthy object for its display."

"My dear friend Shargeloes!" replied the Captain, a little ashamed of his own vigilance. "How are you, my dear sir? and how is the system?"

"The system will never recover from the tricks that infernal Carne has played with it. But never mind that, if the intellect survives; we all owe a debt to our country. I have met you in the very nick of time. Yesterday was Guy Fawkes' Day, and I wanted to be married then; but the people were not ready. I intend to have it now on New-Year's Day, because then I shall always remember the date. I am going up here to make a strange request, and I want you to say that it is right and proper. An opinion from a distinguished sailor will go a long way with the daughters of an Admiral. I want the young ladies to be my bridesmaids—and then for the little ones, your Maggy and your Kitty. I am bound to go to London for a month to-morrow, and then I could order all the bracelets and the brooches, if I were only certain who the blessed four would be."

"I never had any bridesmaids myself, and I don't know anything about them. I thought that the ladies were the people to settle that."

"The ladies are glad to be relieved of the expense, and I wish to start well," replied Shargeloes. "Why are ninety-nine men out of a hundred henpecked?"

"I am sure I don't know, except that they can't help it. But have you heard the great news of this evening?"

"The reason is," continued the member of the Corporation, "that they begin with being nobodies. They leave the whole management of their weddings to the women, and they never recover the reins. Miss Twemlow is one of the most charming of her sex; but she has a decided character, which properly guided will be admirable. But to give it the lead at the outset would be fatal to future happiness. Therefore I take this affair upon myself. I pay for it all, and I mean to do it all."

"What things you do learn in London!" the Captain answered, with a sigh. "Oh, if I had only had the money—but it is too late to talk of that. Once more, have you heard the news?"

"About the great battle, and the death of Nelson? Yes, I heard of all that this morning. But I left it to come in proper course from you. Now here we are; mind you back me up. The Lord Mayor is coming to be my bestman."

The two sisters, dressed in the deepest mourning, and pale with long sorrow and loneliness, looked wholly unfit for festive scenes; and as soon as they heard of this new distress—the loss of their father's dearest friend, and their own beloved hero—they left the room, to have a good cry together, while their brother entertained the visitors. "It can't be done now," Mr. Shargeloes confessed; "and after all, Eliza is the proper person. I must leave that to her, but nothing else that I can think of. There can't be much harm in my letting her do that."

It was done by a gentleman after all, for the worthy Rector did it. The bride would liefer have dispensed with bridesmaids so much fairer than herself, and although unable to advance that reason, found fifty others against asking them. But her father had set his mind upon it, and together with his wife so pressed the matter that Faith and Dolly, much against their will, consented to come out of mourning for a day, but not into gay habiliments.

The bride was attired wonderfully, stunningly, carnageously—as Johnny, just gifted with his commission, and thereby with much slang, described her; and in truth she carried her bunting well, as Captain Stubbard told his wife, and Captain Tugwell confirmed it. But the eyes of everybody with half an eye followed the two forms in silver-grey. That was the nearest approach to brightness those lovers of their father allowed themselves, within five months of his tragic death; though if the old Admiral could have looked down from the main-top, probably he would have shouted, "No flags at half-mast for me, my pets!"

Two young men with melancholy glances followed these fair bridesmaids, being tantalized by these nuptial rites, because they knew no better. One of them hoped that his time would come, when he had pushed his great discovery; and if the art of photography had been known, his face would have been his fortune. For he bore at the very top of it the seal and stamp of his patent—the manifest impact of a bullet, diffracted by the power of Pong. The roots of his hair—the terminus of blushes, according to all good novelists—had served an even more useful purpose, by enabling him to blush again. Strengthened by Pong, they had defied the lead, and deflected it into a shallow channel, already beginning to be overgrown by the aid of that same potent drug. Erle Twemlow looked little the worse for his wound; to a lady perhaps, to a man of science certainly, more interesting than he had been before. As he gazed at the bride all bespangled with gold, he felt that he had in his trunk the means of bespangling his bride with diamonds. But the worst of it was that he must wait, and fight, and perhaps get killed, before he could settle in life and make his fortune. As an officer of a marching regiment, ordered to rejoin immediately, he must flesh his sword in lather first—for he had found no razor strong enough—and postpone the day of riches till the golden date of peace.

The other young man had no solace of wealth, even in the blue distance, to whisper to his troubled heart. Although he was a real "Captain Scuddy" now, being posted to the Danae, 42-gun frigate, the capacity of his cocked hat would be tried by no shower of gold impending. For mighty dread of the Union-jack had fallen upon the tricolor; that gallant flag perceived at last that its proper flight was upon dry land, where as yet there was none to flout it. Trafalgar had reduced by 50 per cent. the British sailor's chance of prize-money.

Such computations were not, however, the chief distress of Scudamore. The happiness of his fair round face was less pronounced than usual, because he had vainly striven for an interview with his loved one. With all her faults he loved her still, and longed to make them all his own. He could not help being sadly shocked by her fatal coquetry with the traitor Carne, and slippery conduct to his own poor self. But love in his faithful heart maintained that she had already atoned for that too bitterly and too deeply; and the settled sorrow of her face, and listless submission of her movements, showed that she was now a very different Dolly. Faith, who had always been grave enough, seemed gaiety itself in comparison with her younger sister, once so gay. In their simple dresses—grey jaconet muslin, sparely trimmed with lavender—and wearing no jewel or ornament, but a single snow-drop in the breast, the lovely bridesmaids looked as if they defied all the world to make them brides.

But the Rector would not let them off from coming to the breakfast party, and with the well-bred sense of fitness they obeyed his bidding. Captain Stubbard (whose jokes had missed fire too often to be satisfied with a small touch-hole now) was broadly facetious at their expense; and Johnny, returning thanks for them, surprised the good company by his manly tone, and contempt of life before beginning it. This invigorated Scudamore, by renewing his faith in human nature as a thing beyond calculation. He whispered a word or so to his friend Johnny while Mr. and Mrs. Shargeloes were bowing farewell from the windows of a great family coach from London, which the Lord Mayor had lent them, to make up for not coming. For come he could not—though he longed to do so, and all Springhaven expected him—on account of the great preparations in hand for the funeral of Lord Nelson.

"Thy servant will see to it," the boy replied, with a wink at his sisters, whom he was to lead home; for Sir Francis had made his way down to the beach, to meditate his new poem, Theriodemos.

"His behaviour," thought Dolly, as she put on her cloak, "has been perfect.

495

How thankful I feel for it! He never cast one glance at me. He quite enters into my feelings towards him. But how much more credit to his mind than to his heart!"

Scudamore, at a wary distance, kept his eyes upon her, as if she had been a French frigate gliding under strong land batteries, from which he must try to cut her out. Presently he saw that his good friend Johnny had done him the service requested. At a fork of the path leading to the Hall, Miss Dolly departed towards the left upon some errand among the trees, while her brother and sister went on towards the house. Forgetting the dignity of a Post-Captain, the gallant Scuddy made a cut across the grass, as if he were playing prisoner's base with the boys at Stonnington, and intercepted the fair prize in a bend of the brook, where the winter sun was nursing the first primrose.

"You, Captain Scudamore!" said the bridesmaid, turning as if she could never trust her eyes again. "You must have lost your way. This path leads nowhere."

"If it only leads to you, that is all that I could wish for. I am content to go to nothing, if I may only go with you."

"My brother sent me," said Dolly, looking down, with more colour on her cheeks than they had owned for months, and the snow-drop quivering on her breast, "to search for a primrose or two for him to wear when he dines at the rectory this evening. We shall not go, of course. We have done enough. But Frank and Johnny think they ought to go."

"May I help you to look? I am lucky in that way. I used to find so many things with you, in the happy times that used to be." Blyth saw that her eyelids were quivering with tears. "I will go away, if you would rather have it so. But you used to be so good-natured to me."

"So I am still. Or at least I mean that people should now be good-natured to me. Oh, Captain Scudamore, how foolish I have been!"

"Don't say so, don't think it, don't believe it for a moment," said Scudamore, scarcely knowing what he said, as she burst into a storm of sobbing. "Oh, Dolly, Dolly, you know you meant no harm. You are breaking your darling heart, when you don't deserve it. I could not bear to look at you, and think of it, this morning. Everybody loves you still, as much and more than ever. Oh, Dolly, I would rather die than see you cry so terribly."

"Nobody loves me, and I hate myself. I could never have believed I should ever hate myself. Go away, you are too good to be near me. Go away, or I shall think you want to kill me. And I wish you would do it, Captain Scudamore."

"Then let me stop," said the Captain, very softly. She smiled at the turn of his logic, through her tears. Then she wept with new anguish, that she had no right to smile.

"Only tell me one thing—may I hold you? Not of course from any right to do it, but because you are so overcome, my own, own Dolly." The Captain very cleverly put one arm round her, at first with a very light touch, and then with a firmer clasp, as she did not draw away. Her cloak was not very cumbrous, and her tumultuous heart was but a little way from his.

"You know that I never could help loving you," he whispered, as she seemed to wonder what the meaning was. "May I ever hope that you will like me?"

"Me! How can it matter now to anybody? I used to think it did; but I was very foolish then. I know my own value. It is less than this. This little flower has been a good creature. It has been true to its place, and hurt nobody."

Instead of seeking for any more flowers, she was taking from her breast the one she had—the snow-drop, and threatening to tear it in pieces.

"If you give it to me, I shall have some hope." As he spoke, he looked at her steadfastly, without any shyness or fear in his eyes, but as one who knows his own good heart, and has a right to be answered clearly. The maiden in one glance understood all the tales of his wonderful daring, which she never used to believe, because he seemed afraid to look at her.

"You may have it, if you like," she said; "but, Blyth, I shall never deserve you. I have behaved to you shamefully. And I feel as if I could never bear to be forgiven for it."

For the sake of peace and happiness, it must be hoped that she conquered this feminine feeling, which springs from an equity of nature—the desire that none should do to us more than we ever could do to them. Certain it is that when the Rector held his dinner party, two gallant bosoms throbbed beneath the emblem of purity and content. The military Captain's snow-drop hung where every one might observe it, and some gentle-witted jokes were made about its whereabouts that morning. By-and-by it grew weary on its stalk and fell, and Erle Twemlow never missed it. But the other snow-drop was not seen, except by the wearer with a stolen glance, when people were making a loyal noise—a little glance stolen at his own heart. He had made a little cuddy there inside his inner sarcenet, and down his plaited neck-cloth ran a sly companionway to it, so that his eyes might steal a visit to the joy that was over his heart and in it. Thus are women adored by men, especially those who deserve it least.

"Attention, my dear friends, attention, if you please," cried the Rector, rising, with a keen glance at Scuddy. "I will crave your attention before the ladies go, and theirs, for it concerns them equally. We have passed through a period of dark peril, a long time of trouble and anxiety and doubt. By the mercy of the Lord, we have escaped; but with losses that have emptied our poor hearts. England has lost her two foremost defenders, Lord Nelson, and Admiral Darling. To them we owe it that we are now beginning the New Year happily, with the blessing of Heaven, and my dear daughter married. Next week we shall attend the grand funeral of the hero, and obtain good places by due influence. My son-in-law, Percival Shargeloes, can do just as he pleases at St. Paul's. Therefore let us now, with deep thanksgiving, and one hand upon our hearts, lift up our glasses, and in silence pledge the memory of our greatest men. With the spirit of Britons we echo the last words that fell from the lips of our dying hero—'Thank God, I have done my duty!' His memory shall abide for ever, because he loved his country."

The company rose, laid hand on heart, and deeply bowing, said—"Amen!"

THE END.

CPSIA information can be obtained
at www.ICGtesting.com
Printed in the USA
LVHW090450171019
634226LV00008BC/352/P